READER'S DIGEST CONDENSED BOOKS

EX LIBRIS

READER'S DIGEST
CONDENSED BOOKS

Volume 5 • 1975

THE READER'S DIGEST ASSOCIATION

Pleasantville, New York

READER'S DIGEST CONDENSED BOOKS

Editor: John T. Beaudouin

Executive Editor: Joseph W. Hotchkiss

Managing Editor: Anthony Wethered

Senior Editors: Ann Berryman, Doris E. Dewey (Copy Desk), Marcia Drennen, Noel Rae, Robert L. Reynolds, Jane Siepmann, Jean N. Willcox, John S. Zinsser, Jr.

Associate Editors: Istar H. Dole, Barbara J. Morgan, Marjorie Palmer, Frances Travis, Patricia Nell Warren, Angela Weldon, Angela C. Woods

Art Editor: William Gregory

Associate Art Editors: Marion Davis, Soren Noring, Angelo Perrone, Thomas Von Der Linn

Art Research: George Calas, Jr., Katherine Kelleher

Senior Copy Editor: Olive Farmer

Associate Copy Editors: Jean E. Aptakin, Catherine T. Brown, Estelle T. Dashman, Alice Murtha

Assistant Copy Editors: Dorothy G. Flynn, Jean S. Friedman, Enid P. Leahy, Marian I. Murphy

Research Editor: Linn Carl

SPECIAL PROJECTS

Executive Editor: Stanley E. Chambers

Senior Editors: Marion C. Conger, Sherwood Harris, Herbert H. Lieberman

Associate Editors: Elizabeth Stille, John Walsh

Rights and Permissions: Elizabeth Thole

Reader's Digest Condensed Books are published every two to three months at Pleasantville, N.Y.

The original editions of the books in this volume are published and copyrighted as follows:

Lord of the Far Island, published at $7.95 by Doubleday & Company, Inc., © 1975 by Victoria Holt

Alexander Dolgun's Story: An American in the Gulag, published at $10.00 by Alfred A. Knopf, Inc., © 1975 by Alexander Dolgun

Minnie Santangelo's Mortal Sin, published at $7.95 by Coward, McCann & Geoghegan, Inc., © 1975 by Anthony Mancini

A Sporting Proposition, published at $6.95 by Little, Brown and Company, © 1973 by James Aldridge

Power, published at $9.95 by David McKay Company, Inc., © 1975 by Richard Martin Stern

CONTENTS

Ellen,
apparently
doomed to a drab
life of service
as a governess,
receives an
enigmatic invitation . . .

Lord of the Far Island

A CONDENSATION OF THE NOVEL BY

Victoria Holt

ILLUSTRATED BY
Ron Lessor

Living "between stairs" in her
cousin's London town house,
Ellen Kellaway's life as a Poor
Relation seemed about to take
a dramatic turn for the better
when handsome Philip
Carrington singled her out
and proposed marriage.
But fate was to
intervene—twice—first
tragically, then with an
intriguing invitation that
drew Ellen to a remote island
off the coast of Cornwall and
into the orbit of her
newfound cousin, Jago.

A recurrent nightmare of
Ellen's since childhood is
finally put to rest as the
discovery of past secrets and
the dawn of love come
together in Victoria Holt's
new romantic mystery.

A Proposal of Marriage

THE dream disturbed my sleep on the eve of Esmeralda's coming-out ball. It was not the first time I had had that same dream. It had come to me periodically over my nineteen years. There is something vaguely alarming about these recurring dreams because it seems certain that they have a significance which one must discover.

When I awoke from it I would be trembling with terror and I could never be entirely sure why. It was not exactly the dream itself, but the impression it brought of impending doom.

I would be in a room. I knew that room very well by now, for it was always the same each time I dreamed. There was a brick fireplace with chimney seats, a red carpet, and heavy red curtains tied back with thick cords. Over the fireplace was a picture of a storm at sea. There were a few chairs and a gateleg table, and in one corner was a rocking chair. Voices came and went in the dream. I would have a feeling that something was being hidden from me; and suddenly there would come this overpowering sense of doom from which I would awake in horror.

9

Afterward, lying in my bed, I would ask myself why my imagination had conjured up that room and why I should have dreamed of the same room over the years. I had talked to no one of this, though, for the whole matter seemed so foolish in the daytime. Yet somewhere deep in my thoughts was the conviction that a strange and as yet incomprehensible force was warning me of impending danger, and that perhaps someday I should discover what.

I was not given to wild fancies. Life had been too grim and earnest for that. Ever since I had been cast on the mercy of Cousin Agatha I had been encouraged to remember I was that most despised of creatures: a Poor Relation. Even the claim that I was a member of the family was frail, for Cousin Agatha was in fact merely my mother's second cousin, a very slender bond indeed.

Everything about Cousin Agatha was outsize—her body, her voice, her personality. She dominated the household, which consisted of her small husband—perhaps he only seemed small compared with his wife—and her daughter, Esmeralda.

Cousin William Loring was a wealthy man, a power outside his home, though inside it he was completely subservient to his forceful wife. He was quiet, and always gave me a weak smile when he saw me; I think he would have been a kind man if he had had the strength of will to oppose Cousin Agatha.

Poor Esmeralda, with the splendid name which didn't fit her one little bit! She had pale blue eyes which watered frequently, as she was often on the verge of tears, and wispy hair. I did her sums for her and helped her with her essays. She was quite fond of me.

Cousin Agatha would be very annoyed when people mistook Esmeralda for the Poor Relation and me for the daughter of the house. Actually, Esmeralda's lot wasn't much better than mine. It would be: "Don't slouch so, Esmeralda." Or "Don't mumble."

It was one of Cousin Agatha's regrets that she had only one daughter. She had wanted many offspring whom she could have moved about like pieces on a chessboard. That she had only one rather fragile daughter she blamed entirely on her husband. The rule of the household was that good flowed from Cousin Agatha's actions and anything that was not desirable from other people's.

Cousin Agatha was noted for her good works. She surrounded herself with a perpetual haze of virtue. Small wonder that both her husband and daughter felt at a disadvantage. Oddly enough, I did not. I had long made up my mind that her good works were done for the satisfaction they brought to herself as much as to anyone else. She often must have noticed the smile which I could not keep from my lips when she was talking of her newest schemes for someone's good. She deplored this lack of appreciation in me. No doubt she sensed in me a reluctance to conform. She would convince herself, of course, that it was due to the bad blood I had inherited from my father's side, though she protested she knew nothing else of that family connection.

Her attitude was apparent when she first sent for me.

There I was, a sturdy ten-year-old with a mass of almost black hair, dark blue eyes, a short nose and a rather long stubborn chin. I was made to stand before her on the great Persian rug in the room she called her study, where her social secretary wrote her letters and did most of the committee work for which she took the credit.

"Now, Ellen," she said to me, "we want to make clear your position in the household. I am sure you are grateful to me and to Cousin William Loring for taking you in. We could, of course, on the death of your mother have put you into an orphanage, but because you are of the family—though scarcely a close relation— we have decided that you must be given our protection. Your mother, as you know, married a Charles Kellaway. You are a result of this marriage." Her large nose twitched a little, which showed the contempt in which she held both my parents and their offspring. "A rather unfortunate marriage."

"It must have been a love match," I said, for I had heard about it from Nanny Grange, whose aunt had been Cousin Agatha's nanny and was therefore knowledgeable about family affairs.

"Pray," went on Cousin Agatha, "do not interrupt me. Your mother, against her family's wishes, went off and married this man from some outlandish place. In something less than a year you were born. When you were three years old your mother left her new home irresponsibly and came back to her family, bringing you.

11

She had simply nothing. You and she became a burden to your grandmother. Your mother died two years later."

I had been five years old at the time. All I remembered about my mother were the embraces which I loved and the feeling of security which I did not recognize until she was gone. There was also a vague memory of sitting on cool grass, with her beside me, a sketchbook in her hand. I often wondered about my father, but he was never mentioned and I could discover nothing about him. As for my grandmother, she was a formidable old lady. Fortunately I was resilient and had managed a stoical indifference to all her reproaches and appeals to God as to what would become of me.

"Just before your grandmother died," added Cousin Agatha, "she asked me to care for you, so I took you into my house as a member of my family. I do not ask for gratitude, but I expect it. Do not think that you will have the same advantages as my own daughter. That would not be good for your character. When you are of age it well may be that you will have to earn a living, either as a maid in some household or perhaps, if you show an aptitude for learning, as a governess. You will share Esmeralda's nanny and her governess, so that by the time you reach your eighteenth birthday you will be an educated young woman. Learn all you can and always remember that these opportunities are due to my bounty."

I was meant to go away and marvel at my good fortune and to cultivate humility, in which, alas, I seemed sadly lacking.

At first the threat of the orphanage hung over me, but I quickly learned that Cousin Agatha could never allow her friends to know that she had disposed of me in such a way. I came to understand that the more of a burden I was, the greater her virtue in keeping me. And I did grow shrewd and naughty, "artful as a wagonload of monkeys," as Nanny Grange put it. If there was mischief about, I'd lead Cousin Esmeralda to it.

IN THE winter we lived in London in a tall house opposite Hyde Park. Esmeralda and I used to sit at one of the topmost windows and watch the hansom cabs clopping by. We both shed tears when we saw a man running behind a cab on its way to Paddington

Station, where he hoped to earn a few pence by carrying the luggage. I made up a story of heartrending squalor which had Esmeralda weeping bitterly. She was so kindhearted and so easily swayed. It was a pity that she was so ineffectual; it gave me an exaggerated idea of my own cleverness.

In the summer we went to Cousin William Loring's country estate in Sussex. There Esmeralda and I learned to ride, visit the poor, help at the church fete and indulge in the usual activities of the gentry. And it was there that I became aware of the great importance of the Carringtons. They owned most of the Sussex hamlet and the surrounding farms, and they lived in Trentham Towers, a very grand mansion on a hill. Like Cousin William, Mr. Josiah Carrington had big interests in the City and an elegant London residence in Park Lane.

Mr. Carrington's wife, Lady Emily, was the daughter of an earl. One of Cousin Agatha's great ambitions was to live on terms of familiarity with the Carringtons, and she would be most disconsolate if they were not present at her dinner parties and balls.

Philip Carrington was about a year older than I and some two years older than Esmeralda; Cousin Agatha was very anxious that he and Esmeralda be good friends. I remember meeting Philip for the first time. It was early summer and Esmeralda had been formally introduced to him in the drawing room; I had been excluded. Then Cousin Agatha had instructed Esmeralda to take Philip to the stables and show him her pony. I waylaid them and joined them.

Philip was fair, with freckles across his nose, and light blue eyes.

"I suppose you ride ponies," he said rather scornfully.

"Well, what do you ride?" I asked.

"A horse, of course."

"We shall have horses later on," said Esmeralda.

He ignored her. Obviously he had already decided to despise her, this puny girl he'd been sent off with.

I said, "We could ride horses just as well as ponies."

He looked interested in me. But we bickered all the way to the stables. He sneered at our ponies, and I was angry, because I loved my Brownie passionately. Then he showed us his horse.

"A very small one," I pointed out.

"I bet you couldn't ride it."

That was a challenge. Esmeralda trembled with fear and kept murmuring, "No, Ellen, don't," as I mounted his horse bareback and rode it recklessly around the paddock. I must admit I was a bit scared, but I wasn't going to let him score over me.

Then Philip mounted and did some tricks, showing off blatantly.

Despite our not getting along in the beginning, we saw a great deal of Philip that summer. And this was when I first heard of Rollo, his elder brother. Philip was about twelve then and Rollo was twenty-two. He was a student at Oxford and according to Philip could do everything.

"What a silly name," I said just to plague Philip.

"It's a great name, you silly thing. It's a Viking name."

"They were pirates," I said disdainfully.

"They ruled the seas. Everywhere they went they conquered."

And that was how it was, Philip and I sparring all the time. It used to upset Esmeralda because she thought we hated each other.

Once she said to me, "Mama would be cross if she knew you quarreled with Philip. You ought to remember he's a Carrington."

I first saw Rollo as he was riding in the lanes with Philip. His horse was white, and if he had had one of those helmets with wings at the side, he would have looked just like a Viking. Philip called a greeting as he passed; Rollo scarcely looked at us.

When we returned to London that year I saw more of Rollo. Once, while he was on vacation from Oxford, he even called on us with his parents. Cousin Agatha fawned on him, and Nanny Grange said that Madam had her claws out to pick him up for Miss Esmeralda. The idea made me want to laugh and I debated whether to tell Esmeralda. But there was no point in scaring her *completely* out of her wits.

Those were enjoyable days. Life was full of interest, especially that part I spent belowstairs in the servants' quarters. If Esmeralda were with me, the servants would be self-conscious; but they talked quite freely in front of me, perhaps because my fate would one day be not dissimilar to theirs.

I was particularly enthralled when the servants talked about the market. Once I prevailed on Rose, one of the parlormaids, to take me there. She was a flighty girl who had at last found a lover who wanted to marry her. He was Harry, the Carringtons' coachman, and she was going to live in a mews cottage with him.

I shall never forget that expedition to the market with Rose. It was November, and already holly and mistletoe were being displayed among the goods. The naphtha flares were like erupting volcanoes, and people bargained at the stalls where raucous cockney voices called their goods. I admired the crockery, the ironmongery, the secondhand clothes, the mounds of polished fruit, the stewed and jellied eels to be eaten on the spot or taken home; and I sniffed ecstatically at the cloud of appetizing steam which came from the fish-and-chips shop. Most of all I liked the people, who bargained and jostled and laughed their way through the market. I thought it was one of the most exciting places I had visited.

I returned starry-eyed, and my outrageous stories about the market had Esmeralda breathless with excitement. I promised that I would take her there, and soon the perfect opportunity came along. It was about a week before Christmas—a dark misty day— and there was to be a dinner party that night. The household could think of nothing else. Nanny Grange and our governess had been pressed into service to help. It was the very day when we could get away and be back before they noticed.

I told Nanny Grange that Esmeralda and I would look out for ourselves, and soon after tea, taken at half past three that afternoon to get it over quickly, we set off. I had carefully noted the number of the omnibus and the stop where Rose and I had gotten off, and we reached the market at about five.

I dragged Esmeralda through stalls piled with fruit and nuts; then we watched the organ-grinder with his little monkey, into whose cap people dropped money. Esmeralda loved it. As we stood there listening, a cart brimming with rattling ironmongery came pushing its way through the crowds.

"Make way for Rag and Bone 'Arry," cried a cheerful voice. "Stand aside, please."

I leaped out of the way and was caught up in the press of people. Suddenly I realized that Esmeralda was not beside me. I looked around; I fought my way through the crowd; I called her name, but there was no sign of her.

I didn't panic immediately. I had told her to keep close to me and she was not adventurous. But after half an hour of frantic searching I began to be very frightened.

Esmeralda was clearly lost. I must go back to the house and confess what I had done, so that search parties could be sent out. And I knew it might even result in my being sent to an orphanage.

I finally left the market and braved the journey back, to discover that the striped awning—for important receptions only—was up and the red carpet down and that guests had begun to arrive. I ran around to the servants' entrance and made my way up the stairs to the hall, and then I heard voices.

A policeman stood there, and beside him, looking very small, was a pale-faced Esmeralda, who immediately began to cry.

"Lost," the policeman was saying. "We brought her home as soon as she told us where, ma'am."

It was a tableau I believed I should never forget. Cousin Agatha, very stately in a low-cut gown twinkling with emeralds and diamonds, and Cousin William Loring, immaculate in his evening clothes, had been summoned to the hall from the top of the staircase, where they had been receiving their guests, to receive instead their truant daughter, brought home by a policeman. Several guests stood on the stairs, including the Carringtons.

Cousin Agatha's emerald earrings quivered with passionate indignation. When Esmeralda saw me through her tears and called my name, Cousin Agatha turned and directed her basilisk gaze straight at me. "Ellen!" she said in a voice full of evil omen.

"We only went to the market—" I began.

"Wilton!" There he was, in all his butlerian dignity.

"Yes, madam," he said. "I will have the young ladies taken to the nursery."

Then Nanny Grange appeared. "This could very well cost me my job," she muttered venomously as she hustled us up the stairs.

We were packed off to bed without supper, and I lay there wondering what life was like in orphanages.

Cousin Agatha sent for me the first thing next morning. She looked as though she had had a sleepless night.

"Such conduct, such deceit," she began. "Do you know I despair of you. I know that these inclinations come to you. It's in the blood. Most people would send a wicked child like you away. After all, we have our own daughter to consider. But blood is thicker than water and you are of the family. Nevertheless, I must warn you, Ellen, that you will have to mend your ways if you wish to stay under our roof. What the Carringtons thought of you I can't imagine. I shan't be surprised if you are not allowed to be with Philip again."

However, by Christmas the affair of the market began to be forgotten. Philip appeared during school holidays and was allowed to play with us in the park. I told him how Esmeralda had gotten lost in the market and in an excess of contempt he pushed her into the Serpentine. He laughed as I waded in and dragged her out. Then Nanny Grange came along and rushed us back to the house to get our wet things off before we caught our deaths.

Poor Esmeralda! I'm afraid we were very careless with her. It was not exactly that Philip and I banded together against her, but simply that she lacked our adventurous spirit.

THE years sped away. My eighteenth birthday came and went. The time when I must earn my own living was coming nearer and nearer. Esmeralda used to comfort me. "When I'm married, Ellen," she would say, "you'll always have a home with me."

I didn't envy Esmeralda; she was so mild. It was true she had grown a little pretty, but I couldn't help noticing that when we were out together it was at me that people glanced. But at least *her* future was secure. Soon she would be coming out into society and we were beginning to be segregated. Esmeralda was taken visiting and to the theater with her parents, and I was left behind. Tilly Parsons, the dressmaker, settled in for a spell and worked on lovely clothes for Esmeralda. There was nothing special for me.

I could feel that vague doom. It was as in the dream.

The Carringtons were now Cousin Agatha's closest friends. Lady Emily's name was mentioned twenty times a day. Philip was often a member of a family party and he, with Esmeralda, visited the theater with Cousin Agatha and Cousin William. I longed to go to see a witty comedy and laugh with Philip.

The day after they had attended an unusually sparkling comedy, Esmeralda and I walked in the park with Nanny Grange, who was still with us. However, now that we were older she walked a few paces behind us like a watchdog. We met Philip and he said accusingly to me, "Why didn't you come to the play?"

"Nobody asked me," I replied. "Didn't you know I was the Poor Relation?"

"Oh, Ellen," wailed Esmeralda. "I can't bear you to talk like that."

"Whether you can bear it or not," I said, "it's true."

"When my parents return the visit to the theater I shall insist that you are included," Philip assured me.

"That's nice of you, Philip," I said. I felt very pleased because at least he didn't see me as the Poor Relation. Before we parted he gave me a playful push, just as he had when we were children.

THERE was going to be a grand dance, Esmeralda's coming-out ball, and I was to be allowed to go. For this I was to have a new gown. I dreamed of deep blue chiffon which would heighten the color of my eyes.

Cousin Agatha sent for me. "Ah, Ellen. You may sit down."

I sat nervously.

"You realize, of course, that you are now of an age to go out into the world. My efforts to place you have been rewarded."

My heart started beating fast with apprehension.

"Mrs. Oman Lemming—the *Honorable* Mrs. Oman Lemming—is losing her governess in six months' time. She is willing to see you with the possibility of giving you the post. I have known her well all my life. I had thought it would not be good for you to be in a house which we might visit, but these are special circumstances.

You will have to be discreet and keep out of the way if we should be there. Mrs. Oman Lemming will understand the delicacy of the situation. She is taking tea with me next week. While she is here she will look you over, and I trust you will be mindful of your duty to please her. Such posts do not grow on trees."

I was dumbfounded. My absurd optimism had let me believe it would never come to this. But now my approaching doom was but six months away.

Cousin Agatha, who had clearly expected me to express my gratitude, sighed and lifted her shoulders. "I should not wish you to go ill equipped to your post, and that brings me to the matter of your ball dress. I have chosen the material for you and I am asking Tilly Parsons to make it in a style which will not date."

The dress would be expected to last a long time. My heart sank.

Then, to make matters worse, when I met the Honorable Mrs. Oman Lemming I could see a kindred spirit to Cousin Agatha. She was a large woman with sweeping feathers in her hat; a heavy gold chain descended the mountain of her bosom; a large brooch sparkled on her blouse. Her eyes were too closely set together, and her mouth when she studied me was thin and cold.

"This is Ellen Kellaway," said Cousin Agatha.

Mrs. Oman Lemming raised her lorgnette and studied me. "She is very young," she commented.

"It is so much easier to mold the young to our ways, Letty," said Cousin Agatha, and I thought how incongruous the name sounded for such a militant-looking female.

And so it was arranged that in five months' time I should enter the Oman Lemming household and be instructed by the departing governess as to my duties.

When Esmeralda and I walked in the park the next morning Philip joined us.

"You look like thunder today," he said to me.

"It's this wretched governessing," put in Esmeralda. "Mama found a place for Ellen with Mrs. Oman Lemming."

"You . . . a governess!" Philip burst out laughing at the idea.

"If you find it amusing, I don't," I snapped. "Cousin Agatha says it's time I earned a living, that I've lived on charity too long."

"Never mind," said Philip, slipping his arm through mine, "I'll come and see you at the Honorable Lemmings'."

"You'll forget all about me," I said angrily.

He didn't answer, but he continued to hold my arm.

It was through my parlormaid friend Rose that I heard the gossip. She got it from her fiancé, the Carringtons' coachman.

"Oh, there's been some conferences going on, at Park Lane as well as here. My word, they're planning an early wedding! Young people are impatient, they say. 'Impatient!' I said. 'Why, Miss Esmeralda don't know what she's got to be impatient about!'"

"You mean they're planning Esmeralda's wedding?"

"To Philip," whispered Rose. "Of course your Cousin Agatha would have liked the elder brother, Rollo, for a son-in-law."

"Why don't they try for him?"

Rose pressed her lips together to indicate that she was about to divulge a secret. "Well, about a year ago Mr. Rollo got married . . . runaway match. Eloped and all that, and the family wasn't too pleased. Then Mr. Rollo persuaded them that it was all right and they all got reconciled. But no one ever saw *her* at the house. That was what was so odd. It was just said that Mr. Rollo was abroad with his wife. . . . Then we found out why. It seems there was something wrong with the marriage. She's somewhere, but she don't come to the house."

"Then he's still married to her?"

"Of course he's still married to her and that's why your family has got to have Mr. Philip for Miss Esmeralda."

I had always thought there was something so unusual about Rollo that nothing ordinary could happen to him. I had been right.

A week or so passed. There was a visit to the theater with the Carringtons and to my delight I was a member of the party. Cousin Agatha was most put out. "I cannot think why Lady Emily should have included Ellen," I heard her comment. "It's really quite unsuitable, considering that she will soon be working more or less in our own circle." My habit of thrusting aside the unpleasant was not quite so successful as usual. But my spirits rose that night of the performance at the Haymarket Theatre. I was greatly excited by the play and between the acts I discussed it animatedly with Philip and Mr. Carrington.

The next day Cousin Agatha took me to task. "You talk far too much, Ellen. I think Mr. Carrington was a little put out."

"He didn't seem to be," I couldn't help retorting.

"My dear Ellen," said Cousin Agatha in a tone implying that I was anything but dear, "he is a gentleman, and therefore would not dream of expressing his disapproval. I really must ask you to assume a more modest role in future."

The night of the dance was fast approaching. The folding doors of the three large drawing rooms had been thrown open to make a magnificent ballroom. There were balconies in all three rooms, and these gave a view of Hyde Park and of gardens and some rather fine buildings. Evergreen plants ornamented the balconies, and the rooms were decorated with flowers.

There was to be a buffet supper in the dining room, and musicians for the dancing. No expense was to be spared; Cousin Agatha wanted all to know, particularly the Carringtons, that from Esmeralda's parents a very good dowry could be expected.

I was caught up in the excitement although I was not at all pleased with my dress. It was black, heavy velvet, and only just managed to creep into the ball-gown category. When I saw Esmeralda's beautiful concoction of sea-blue silk and lace I knew it was just the dress I should have loved. But it wasn't serviceable, whereas mine would never date.

The night before the ball I had dreamed once more of the room with the red carpet. I was standing near the fireplace and I heard the whispering voices. Then suddenly that feeling of doom overtook me. I was staring at the door and—this was new—it started to open. A creeping fear possessed me then, for I knew that whatever it was I dreaded was behind that door.

I woke up trembling. It had been a very vivid dream, as always, but on this occasion the doom had come a little nearer.

I tried, but without success, to shake off the feeling of approaching disaster. And I kept reminding myself that this coming night would be that of the dance.

The next morning Rose brought up a little box. "My word, Miss Ellen," she said. "It's for you. Admirers, is it!"

And there, nestling in the box, was a delicate pinkish-mauve orchid—just the decoration I needed to liven up my dress.

I thought, It's from Esmeralda, and hurried to thank her. But she looked blank. "I wish I'd sent it, Ellen. I assumed there'd be flowers provided for anyone who wanted them."

I enjoyed trying to think who had sent it to me. I decided it must be Cousin William, because I fancied he was a little disturbed at my going to work for Mrs. Oman Lemming.

The orchid transformed my dress and, piling hair high on my head, I actually thought I looked quite elegant.

Esmeralda looked pretty in her magnificent gown, but she was very conscious that she was the reason for the ball and she was apprehensive at the notion of receiving a proposal. The prospect of a grand marriage appalled her. "They all think I'm going to marry Philip, but I know he doesn't like me very much."

I tried to comfort her. There was no reason, I told her, why she should marry anyone she didn't want to marry.

Cousin Agatha had given me my instructions. "Make yourself useful, Ellen. At supper, be sure that people are well served, especially Lady Emily. I shall introduce you to one or two gentlemen, and perhaps they may even ask you to dance." I could visualize it all: Ellen in somber black to distinguish her from the real guests; "Ellen, do tell Wilton we need more salmon"; "Ellen, old Mr. Something is alone. I'll introduce you." And there would be Ellen stumbling around with old Mr. Something, longing to be gliding over the floor with a kindred spirit.

How different it was. Right from the first, Philip was beside me.

"So you received my orchid," he said.

"Yours!"

"No one else would send you flowers, I hope."

We danced the first waltz and our steps fitted perfectly. After all, we had gone to dancing classes together.

"Do you know I am here with the chores of the Poor Relation?" I asked. "I have to keep my eyes open for neglected guests."

"That's all right. You keep your eyes on me, for if you don't I shall feel neglected. Now listen," he went on, "I must talk to you. It's deadly serious. Where can we get away to be quiet?"

"There are one or two smaller rooms on this floor."

"Let's go then."

We sat on a settee in a room filled with potted plants.

"Ellen," he said, "we've got to put a stop to this governessing thing. We're not having you sent away to that poisonous woman and her dreadful brood."

I turned to him and my fear of the future suddenly enveloped me in earnest. "What authority have you to stop them?" I asked.

He took me by the shoulders and held me against him. "The best of all authority. You and I are going to get married. I always meant we should."

"But . . . but you're going to marry Esmeralda. That's what this dance is for."

"What nonsense!"

"That's where you're wrong. During this dance or after it, they are hoping to announce your engagement to Esmeralda."

"But 'they,' by whom I presume you mean the Lorings, are going to find they have made a mistake. Engagement yes, but to Ellen, not Esmeralda."

"You mean you'd announce your engagement to *me* tonight? At *her* coming-out ball?"

"Of course. I have a sense of the dramatic. You know that."

"What will your parents say?"

"They'll be delighted."

"To accept *me!* You're joking."

"I am *not*." He looked very serious. "My father likes you. And my mother will too. She wants me to be happy above all else."

"Perhaps, but they can't possibly want me as your wife."

"I've already hinted to them and they're full of approval. They've been at me to marry soon."

Cousin Agatha had so impressed on me my inferior status and

the glory of the Carringtons that I could never imagine myself marrying into that family. Now the prospect excited me, not, alas, so much because of Philip—whom I liked very much, of course—but because marrying him would mean that I did not have to take up the post of governess with Mrs. Oman Lemming. Chiefly, perhaps, I was savoring the triumph of being the chosen one. The sight of Cousin Agatha's face if our engagement were announced would compensate me for all the years of humiliation.

"You seem at a loss for words. I've never known you to be so."

"It's the first time I have ever had a proposal of marriage. And I hadn't thought of you as a husband," I said.

"Whyever not? I thought it was obvious." He took my hands in his and kissed me. "Well?" he said.

"What about Cousin Agatha? She has set her heart on a Carrington son-in-law. And what she wants she usually gets."

"Well, who cares about her anyway?"

"I'm liking you more every minute."

He put his arm about me. "We'll have fun together, Ellen."

He went on to talk of what our life would be like. We would travel a great deal—to places like India and Hong Kong. It would be necessary, for he was learning all about his father's business. We would have an establishment of our own in London where we would entertain frequently. And Philip would see that I was introduced to the most exclusive dressmakers. "You'll be stunning in the right clothes, Ellen," he said. "You're a beauty, only it's never shown to advantage."

"You know I have no dowry. Esmeralda has a good one."

"I'm not tempted. It has to be Ellen or no one."

I put my arms about his neck and kissed him heartily; at just that moment Cousin Agatha appeared.

"Ellen!" Her voice was shrill with disbelief and anger.

I broke away from Philip and stood up uneasily.

"This is disgraceful. I shall talk to you later. In the meantime, guests are being neglected."

"Not all of them," said Philip cheekily. He had always liked to disconcert Cousin Agatha.

I said, "I'll go and see what I can do."

I wanted to get away because I still could not entirely believe that Philip was serious. But I was in a whirl. I caught a glimpse of myself in one of the mirrors. My cheeks were flushed, my eyes brilliant. The black gown was not so unbecoming after all.

Then Mr. Carrington asked me to dance with him. He was courteous and charming, and I sat out with him afterward. Soon Philip joined us. "She's said yes, Father."

Mr. Carrington nodded, smiling. "I am very happy. Ellen is a remarkable young woman."

"Your Cousin Agatha is glaring like a gorgon," Philip informed me as we started to dance.

"Let her," I answered. "I think I know just how Cinderella felt when she went to the ball."

"I must make a delightful Prince Charming," Philip said.

When the waltz was over he escorted me in to supper. Mr. Carrington made the announcement. He said that this was a very special occasion for his family because his son Philip had confided to him that he had asked for the hand of a young lady who had promised to be his wife. He wanted everyone to drink to the health and future happiness of Miss Ellen Kellaway and his son Philip.

What a hush there was in the dining room, where the great table, so expertly dressed, was laden with cold salmon, meats of all descriptions, salads and desserts; and where the black-gowned, white-capped staff stood like sentries waiting to serve.

All eyes were on me. Philip gripped my hand firmly and I sensed that he was proud of me. Yes, I was happy as I had rarely been. For there was Philip beside me, and in my mind he *was* Prince Charming, fitting the glass slipper on my foot.

Lady Emily wafted up and kissed me. Then Esmeralda threw her arms about me. Dear Esmeralda! Even though she had not wanted to marry Philip, she might have felt a little piqued. Not she! She could see that I was happy, and she was contented too. Cousin Agatha tried bravely to hide the fury in her heart, but when I met her gaze it was quite venomous.

Mr. Carrington said he thought there should be no unnecessary delay in the marriage. Once two people had made up their minds, why should they hesitate?

Philip said good night and told me he would call the next day. We had so many plans to make, and he agreed with his father that there should be no delay.

I went to my room. I took off my serviceable ball gown and was in my petticoats when Cousin Agatha burst in. She was breathing deeply. "Well, you have made a fine fool of us all."

"I?" I cried. I could not resist adding, "Why, I thought you would be pleased. It gets me off your hands!"

"My, but you have suddenly grown innocent. You must have known all this time, and poor Esmeralda has been thinking it would be her wedding that would be announced. You are wicked and I'm sorry for the Carringtons."

"You have always led me to believe that the Carringtons are one of the most important families," I said. "I scarcely think they will want your pity." I was thoroughly intoxicated with my success. "I know such a marriage was not what you intended for me," I went on. "To be governess for the Oman Lemming children was not what I wanted for myself. But fate has raised me from the status of Poor Relation, which I can assure you, Cousin Agatha, has sometimes been hard to bear."

"When I think of all I did for you . . . I took you into my home, because you were of the family. . . ."

"Though the connection was not strong," I added.

And with that she turned and went out.

How life had changed for me! Josiah Carrington was not only a financier of great standing in the City, he was also an adviser to the government and a power in diplomatic circles. Cousin William, although comfortably off, was small fry in comparison.

Philip said we would set about choosing a house right away. I had to keep assuring myself I hadn't imagined the whole thing. There I would be, the Poor Relation who had never been sure of her room, with a house all my own!

I had taken on new status. Esmeralda was delighted. She said how happy she was for me. "You two always went so well together. It's right, Ellen. You'll be ever so content."

I kissed her. "You are a dear, Esmeralda. Are you sure you really don't love Philip?"

"*Quite* sure," she answered emphatically.

Soon Cousin Agatha had gotten over the first shock and was now swallowing her disappointment. I wondered whether she was consoling herself that even a Poor Relation's link was better than none. "Of course," she said, "you will have to have some clothes. We can't have people saying that we kept you short. After all, it will reflect on us, and we have Esmeralda's future to think of."

I'm gloriously happy, I thought. I suppose this is being in love.

Philip was always calling at the house, and because he was a Carrington we were constantly being photographed for the society papers. We rode together in the Row in Hyde Park. I had a new riding habit—a present from Cousin William, prodded no doubt by Cousin Agatha, for riding in the Row made one suitably prominent.

Philip was very happy and it was wonderful to know that he was so much in love with me. I was nineteen; he was nearly twenty-one, and there was not a cloud in my sky during those first weeks of our engagement. I believed it would go on like that forever.

We went down to Sussex for a week as the Carringtons wanted to celebrate our engagement among their friends in the country. I had always been attracted by the house, but now that it would occasionally be my home too, I was more than ever excited by it.

Trentham Towers was an old Tudor mansion. It was built on a hill and looked imperiously down on the countryside in what I had thought of as a true Carrington manner. But it was Cousin Agatha who had given me my opinion of them. No family could have welcomed me more warmly, which was really very remarkable considering the circles in which they moved.

Philip was delighted to show me the house. We explored the first floor, stopping in the dining room, where the portraits of his mother's family were displayed. Then he led me down a stone staircase and, throwing open an oak door, said, "This is the old armory. It's now our gun room."

"What a lot of weapons!" I cried. "Just ornaments, I hope?"

He laughed. "They're used during the season."

"I hate shooting things," I said vehemently.

"I don't suppose you mind partaking of a succulent pheasant now and then," he said. He had opened a case lined with red satin, in which was a silver-gray pistol and a place for another. "Isn't that a beauty?" he demanded.

"I'd scarcely call it that. And where's the other one?"

"It's in a safe place. What if I'm alone in a wing of the house? In comes a man in a mask. He's going to steal the family treasure. I feel under my pillow and draw out my pistol. 'Hands up,' I cry. And the family treasure is saved." He touched the pistol lovingly before he closed the case.

"You don't really keep a pistol under your pillow, do you?"

"Yes. But after we are married I'll have you to protect me."

"You are an idiot," I said. "Let's continue exploring."

I was enchanted by the old butteries and storing houses, but most delightful was the room in which Queen Elizabeth was reputed to have slept; it was here that I turned to Philip and said, "When shall I meet Rollo's wife?"

Philip looked at me tensely. "We don't see her. We don't even talk about her. One couldn't imagine Rollo involved in anything like that. He's always been so wrapped up in the business . . . every bit as much as my father . . . perhaps more. They're always dashing about the world. And then for Rollo to marry so hastily! A common enough story of infatuation, I suppose. Then after the honeymoon he found that he'd made a terrible mistake."

"What kind of mistake?"

"I never heard the details. I just knew she wasn't the sort who could mix in society. . . . Though beautiful, she would be a hindrance to his career. There was also a rumor that she drank too much. In any case, Rollo's marriage was a ghastly error and he keeps her out of the way. She lived here at one time, with a good woman who looked after her. But it was difficult when the family came. So now his wife and her companion are elsewhere."

"Where?"

"I don't know. It's Rollo's affair. He wants it that way."

"He must be very unhappy."

"You never know with Rollo. He doesn't show his feelings."

"I'd like to see the rooms she occupied when she was here."

"Whatever for? They're right at the top."

"I've just a feeling I'd like to. Come on."

We mounted the oak staircase almost to the top of the house. From there a spiral staircase took us right to her rooms. There were four of them together—a sort of small apartment. Two were bedrooms. One for Rollo's wife, I thought. One for her companion.

I am sensitive about dwellings and I fancied I could detect suffering here. I shivered, and Philip said, "Let's go down. I can't tell you anything more about her."

We don't even talk about her, Philip had said. That was the Carrington way of life. When something was unpleasant you pretended it didn't exist. I could never be like that and I couldn't stop thinking about Rollo's wife. I wanted to know about her. Perhaps I could talk to her, help her in some way.

BACK in London, Philip and I liked to walk in the park and talk about our plans. It was during one of our strolls that I became aware of a man watching us. There was nothing remarkable about him except his unusually bushy eyebrows. He was seated not far from us. He gave me an uneasy feeling.

"Philip," I said, "do you see that man on the bench over there? He seems to be watching us."

"Yes, he must be thinking how pretty you look." Philip squeezed my arm and we forgot about the man. Soon he got up and left.

The House in Finlay Square

WE WENT to see a house in Knightsbridge. I was so excited when Philip produced the key and we went in. It was a tall white Queen Anne house with a small garden in front.

There is something about empty houses; they can be welcoming or forbidding. I don't think I have any special perception, perhaps merely an overcharged imagination, but this house affected me as the top rooms of Trentham Towers had done, and for the second time in my newfound happiness a coldness touched me.

Philip was saying eagerly, "Do you like it?"

"I haven't seen it yet. You can't judge a house by the hall."

We went through the lower rooms; they were far too intimate— their walls closing in around me. No, I thought. No!

We rushed up the stairs—there were five stories—and the rooms on the second floor were light and airy. I liked them better.

"We'll give our parties here," he said. "Elegant, isn't it?"

We climbed higher. There were more big rooms and on the top floor more, and above that attics.

"It's too big," I said, finding an excuse.

He looked startled. By Carrington standards it was quite small. "We shall need these rooms. There are the servants to be accommodated, and guests. . . . And you want a nursery, don't you?"

"Yes, very much. But I feel there is something . . . not quite right about this house. It looks so"—I floundered—"empty!"

He laughed. "What do you expect it to be, you goose? Besides, the sooner we get a place, the sooner we can get married."

He took my hands and kissed me. Then we raced downstairs.

I couldn't shake off my uneasiness about the house in Finlay Square. It was to be Mr. Carrington's wedding present. Philip was eager to acquire it and I hated to curb his enthusiasm. I couldn't find anything specific to dislike about the place; yet when I imagined myself alone there I had the same feeling as in the dream.

It was very disturbing. Even though I knew this could never be the house for me, I became so obsessed by it that one day I went to the agent and asked if I could look it over alone. So I got a key.

It was afternoon, about three o'clock, when I arrived at Finlay Square, determined not to give way to my odd misgivings.

I let myself in and stood in the hall. Then I mounted the stairs slowly, and on the second floor I studied the elegant drawing room. I furnished it in my mind and imagined myself as the hostess—a graceful Carrington hostess, I thought with a curl of the lips.

Then I felt my heart leap in terror, for I had the uncanny feeling that there was someone else in the house. I stood very still in the center of the room; I heard a sound. Someone *was* in the house.

My heart began to hammer painfully. Who? It couldn't be Philip. He was at his father's London office.

I listened. There it was again. A muffled sound, then the creak of an opening door, and footsteps on the stairs.

I found it difficult to move. I was petrified. The footsteps were coming nearer. Someone was immediately outside the room.

The door slowly opened. I gasped. Rollo Carrington stood there. "I'm afraid I startled you," he said. "I thought no one was here."

Although I had glimpsed him before, I felt I was seeing him for the first time. He looked so tall, and he exuded a sort of magnetism. I said, "You are Mr. Carrington, Philip's brother. I am Ellen Kellaway, his fiancée."

"Yes, I know. My best wishes for your happiness."

"Thank you. I didn't know you were in London."

"I arrived from Rome last night. Philip told me about the house and I said I'd check it over, so he gave me the key."

"I wanted to see it on my own," I explained. "Shall you advise your father to buy it?"

"It's very likely a sound proposition."

He kept his eyes on me and I felt uncomfortable because he seemed to be assessing me, and I was not at all sure what he was thinking. He appeared so cool, so much in command of himself, that it was impossible to imagine him caught up in a love affair passionate enough to make him marry so hastily. I thought I detected a certain bitterness about his mouth. He was no doubt reviling fate for making his beautiful wife a secret drinker and allowing him to discover this after he had married her.

"Shall we look around together?" he asked.

"Yes, of course."

"Come then, we'll start from the top."

He talked about the snares to watch for. He'd had some experience in buying property, he said. But I was hardly paying attention. I just wanted to hear his voice, which was deep and authoritative; he was so mature compared with Philip and me.

We went through all the rooms, then out into the garden. I looked back at the house. It seemed more menacing than ever, even though Rollo was there to protect me.

He stared at me intently. "I'll call a cab and take you home."

A great relief swept over me.

THERE was something enigmatic—completely baffling—about Rollo, and I could not get him out of my mind. He certainly was a man who could conceal his true feelings.

When I saw Philip that evening I told him about my meeting with Rollo. He was amused.

"He came home only last night," he said. "Quite unexpectedly. Mother had written to him about our engagement. He thinks the house is quite a good bargain. He suggests we make an offer for it."

"He doesn't object to our marriage?"

"Object! Why on earth should he?"

"Well, you're so rich and I have no money at all."

Philip burst out laughing. "What notions you get! As if they would care about that. Mother was poor when she married my father and he was already a rich man then."

"She had a title."

"Well, you're beautiful and kind, and kind hearts are more than coronets. You should know that."

Philip was so jaunty, so sure that life was going to be good. How different he was from his brother.

I said, "It's marvelous the way your family has accepted me. Cousin Agatha is truly amazed at it."

"Why, they're delighted. They think it will be good for me. And they'd like some little Carringtons. As for Rollo, he's as pleased as he could be."

And so we talked. He was kind. He was affectionate. I was fond of him. But I was suddenly afraid of the future, for I wasn't quite in love with him.

I wanted to hear more about Rollo. Rose was a good informant by way of Harry, her coachman. "What about the Carrington son?" I asked her.

"Why, miss, you know more about Mr. Philip than anyone."

"I mean Mr. Rollo."

"Oh, him. He's another like his father. All business. Very cool and aloof, and since that mysterious marriage, very touchy."

"Rose, did you ever see *her?*"

"Harry did. He drove them once or twice. But he never heard her speak—never heard him, either. She was just in the carriage with him. Like two deaf-mutes they were. Then she went away."

"What did she look like?"

"I've asked Harry that, Miss Ellen, but men never seem to notice. Just that there was something sad about her. That she was like a gray ghost. She was always dressed in gray."

"A sad gray ghost," I echoed. Then I excused myself. I knew I shouldn't be gossiping with one of the servants in my old manner. I must mend my ways, now that I was to be a Carrington.

STRANGELY enough Lady Emily liked me, which was very comforting since she could hardly have been delighted by my poverty. She encouraged me to visit her frequently. She liked to talk a great deal in a rambling fashion, and from her conversation I learned more about the Carringtons. She confided in me once that it was a Carrington tradition to have boys, and in view of Rollo's misfortune in marriage, Philip and I were to produce the male heirs.

"I do hope I'm going to have these babies," I said.

"You will, because you're in love. Tell me, have the two of you decided on a date yet?"

"Philip thinks the end of June."

"That's a lovely month for a marriage."

One day Philip took me down to the mews to show me a new horse he had acquired. I immediately noticed one of the grooms because I had seen him somewhere before. Philip introduced me.

"This is Hawley," he said. "He hasn't been with us very long."

Hawley said, "Good afternoon, Miss Kellaway," and I continued to be puzzled.

When we left the mews Philip said, "I think we'll have the house in Finlay Square."

"I'd like to look at it again, Philip."

"Oh, come, Ellen, where are we going to live when we're married if we haven't a house? We'll have to be in my father's house for a while as it is—I doubt everything will be ready by June."

I felt a shiver of apprehension then. June. It was so near and I was very uneasy.

When I went to bed that night I remembered where I had seen the new groom before: he was the man I had thought was watching us in the park.

THERE was to be a musical evening at the Carringtons'. Lady Emily had engaged a famous Italian pianist. Cousin Agatha was delighted to be going. "Half London will be there," she said. "At least anybody who *is* anybody will be."

"I suppose," I retorted, "everybody is somebody, and I doubt whether even Lady Emily's drawing room would accommodate more than seventy people in comfort."

I could never resist the temptation to be what in the old days she would have called pert. I shouldn't have been human if I had been able to resist exploiting my situation a little.

It was amusing how my stature grew daily. Tilly was sewing for me all day and into the night, and I was making frequent informal visits to the house in Park Lane. However, deep down I knew that I was trying to reassure myself. This sudden turnabout provided by the Carringtons was too good to be true.

A few days later, as I stood with Philip at the Carringtons' musical soiree, people came up to congratulate us.

"We'll go on the Continent," Philip was saying. "Venice. Rome perhaps." He turned to me. "Will you like that, Ellen?"

I said it would be lovely.

"Perhaps the house will be ready by the time we come back. Rollo's taking over arrangements for it now that he's in London for a spell. He likes doing that sort of thing and my father hasn't the time. Rollo's most anxious to conclude it all as soon as possible."

I nodded. "It's good of Rollo."

The recital was over and there was a buffet supper to follow.

Everyone was discussing the romantic Chopin preludes, and Philip, having caught sight of an old friend, went over to have a word with him, leaving me temporarily alone.

A voice behind me said, "I've wanted to meet you all evening."

I turned sharply and looked up at one of the tallest men I have ever seen. I knew at once that I had not met him before, because if I had, I could not have forgotten him. There was something un-usual about him—an aura of power. His eyes were dark, deep-set, heavy-lidded, but very bright and expressive. His nose was high-bridged and arrogant-looking; his mouth could be either cruel or gentle. I guessed his age to be about thirty. "I have seen your pictures in the papers," he went on. "May I say that none of them does you justice."

"That's kind of you," I replied. "Are you a friend of the family?"

"A connection."

"I hope you enjoyed the recital."

"Very much, thank you. Have you set a date for the wedding?"

"It's to be in June, but the actual day is not decided."

"I shall be there. I'm determined to be at your wedding."

"Lady Emily is giving my cousin her guest list." Then our con-versation ended rather abruptly, for Philip was looking across the room at me.

My companion bowed and turned away, and I went over to Philip. "Who was the tall fellow you were talking to?" he asked.

"I don't know. He said he was a connection of yours."

Philip shrugged his shoulders. "He's probably one of my father's or Rollo's business friends."

"Do you think so? I thought he looked the outdoor type."

We went over to greet old Sir Bevis, one of the most peevish of the family's friends. He congratulated Philip, but I could see that I was the one he was really congratulating. Like many people, he could not understand why the Carringtons were accepting a girl without money. And yet a logical explanation was that they were so rich that another fortune wouldn't make much difference.

When we had left Sir Bevis I noticed the new groom we'd seen in the Carrington stables. I told Philip I thought he was the man

we'd seen in the park, but Philip laughed at my being concerned. "Oh, Hawley. He has many talents. He's butler for us now."

During the rest of the evening I looked for the tall stranger who had spoken to me at the buffet supper. But it was in vain. I wished I had had the presence of mind to ask his name when he'd simply said he was "a connection."

"It seems," said Esmeralda a few days later, "that one of the Carrington servants is courting our maid Bessie. So there's Rose and her coachman and now Bessie and Hawley."

"Did you say Hawley?"

"Yes, I'm sure that was the name. There seem to be several bonds between us and the Carringtons."

"Isn't that what your mother always wanted?" I asked, and I was thinking: Hawley! The man in the park. Philip might laugh at my concern, but ever since I had first noticed him watching us, I'd been in some uneasy way aware of him.

The time was passing and we were halfway through May. The horse chestnuts were ready to bloom and I should have been joyous, but I would often wake with a vague presentiment of doom.

The contracts for the house in Finlay Square were being drawn up. Philip and I still had a key apiece, and I didn't want to return mine because I continued to go there now and then, trying to get used to the place, trying to reconcile myself to it. Was it really misgivings about the place, or was it apprehension for the future and the life Philip and I would lead there?

Did I want to marry Philip? Certainly, when I thought of the alternative. The past few weeks had made me forget how humiliating my position had been before Philip proposed. And the reason I had forgotten my gratitude to him was that I had seen his brother and realized suddenly that one does not necessarily want an old playmate—whatever affection one has for him—for a husband.

I was marrying Philip to escape. I knew that was not really a good reason for marriage, but how could I possibly back out now? Then it came to me, almost as though the house was telling me: It's not too late. You could escape the marriage.

Escape? Where to? To Mrs. Oman Lemming and the dreary life which I knew I was going to hate? Maybe. But to escape from her is no reason for marriage.

Then, I reproached myself, why was it only at this, the eleventh hour, that I realized I was plunging into marriage without enough experience of life?

And the uneasiness crept over me again. The house was rejecting me. These rooms are not for you, it seemed to be saying.

I clenched my fists. If I want to live here, I will. It's my life. How could I possibly be a governess to that old tyrant and her loathsome offspring now?

Suddenly I sensed that I was not alone in the house. Then sounds were distinct. The creak of feet on wood. Footsteps coming up the stairs. It's Rollo again, I reassured myself, thinking of the other time he had startled me in the house.

The door opened slowly. I almost cried out, "Rollo!" Then my flesh started to creep, for it was not Rollo. It was the tall dark man who had spoken to me at the Chopin recital.

I stammered, "How . . . how did you get in?"

He held up a door key.

"Where did you get it?" I demanded.

He laughed and answered, "The house is for sale, the agent led me to believe."

"No, it's sold . . . or all but sold."

"That's a pity because I quite like it. But you never know. . . . The sale could fall through and then I could jump into the breach. So while I'm here I shall look it over."

As he spoke his hooded eyes regarded me intently. I was sure there was something more in this than he would have me believe.

He advanced. The fact that I was alone in the house with this man struck me forcibly. I desperately wanted to get out.

"I'll leave you to look around," I said hurriedly.

"Couldn't we do so together? I'd welcome your comments."

I thought cunningly that I would pretend to go around with him and when we reached the ground floor I would walk out the front door before he had time to stop me. "I must remind you that this house is definitely off the market. All the same, if you want to look around, do. Let's start at the bottom."

"You are kind." He stood aside for me to pass, and as I started to walk downstairs I was aware of his being very close behind me. He seemed so powerful that he made me feel helpless. Moreover, somehow I didn't quite believe he had come to see the house, or that the agent had given him the key when the Carringtons had all but bought the place. I had rarely been so frightened in my life. Is he mad? I asked myself. He had a motive for coming, and it was not to see the house. But I could not think what it might be.

I prayed, O God, let me get away. I'll never want to come to this house again. Please let me get away from this man.

He sensed my fear, I was sure. It amused him. Out of the corner of my eye I could see the curl of his lips, the glint in his eyes.

And then my prayer was answered. We were on the stairs, looking down into the hall, when I saw a shadow behind the glass panel of the door. He saw it too. I heard his quick intake of breath as the door opened and Rollo entered.

He seemed as surprised to see us as we were to see him.

As I stood rooted to the stair, I heard myself explaining, "There's been a misunderstanding. This gentleman didn't know the house was sold. He came to look it over."

Rollo frowned. "Didn't the agent explain? He had no right to give you a false impression."

The dark man smiled. "I shall have a word with him. I didn't realize negotiations had gone so far." He bowed to me and went to the door. Then, just before the door shut, he turned and looked straight at me.

"How extraordinary!" cried Rollo. "I can't understand the agent's giving him a key with the deal so near completion."

"Who is he?" I asked. "He was at the recital. He said he was a connection of yours."

"A connection? I've no notion who he is. What's his name?"

"I don't know. We weren't introduced. He addressed a few words to me. The next time I saw him was here."

"How very strange, and you seem so upset. We'll certainly have to find out who he is. Well, I've come to look at the dining-room ceiling. There's a certain amount of damp there. The surveyor pointed it out."

I was still feeling dazed as I followed Rollo through the house. "It's good of you to take so much trouble," I told him.

"For my own brother and his future wife!" He looked at me, his eyes appraising but warm. "I want you to know, Ellen, how very much we welcome you into the family."

Despite his words, I still felt deeply troubled. Nothing could induce me to come to this house again.

We went out and Rollo called a cab. He sat beside me looking satisfied, as though something he had undertaken had succeeded very well. As we turned into the square my heart gave a leap of terror, for standing on the pavement looking into the cab was the dark man. He lifted his hat and bowed to me. I glanced at Rollo, but he had not noticed.

THE wedding was three weeks away. My dress was being made by Lady Emily's own dressmaker. It was going to be one of *the* weddings of the year and even Cousin Agatha was excited, bustling about as if she had arranged it all. Her great sorrow was that all this fuss was for me, but when she convinced herself that it was a rehearsal for Esmeralda's wedding she was somewhat reconciled.

I should have been congratulating myself on my good fortune and at times I did, but into my thoughts would creep an insidious notion that I was making a mistake, a mistake fraught with danger. It's marriage, I thought. I'm not ready for it. What I wanted more than anything was time. I would lie awake at night and my problem would niggle away at me. And adding to my disturbance was that I fancied Rollo had been avoiding me.

It was the Sunday before the wedding. There were six more days to go. We were to be married in London at St. George's Hanover Square and then go back to the Lorings' house for the reception. In the late afternoon we should leave for Venice.

Philip and I walked through the park to Kensington Gardens. We skirted the palace and then we walked back across the grass and sat by the Serpentine. He took my hand and held it firmly. "Six whole days," he was saying. "It seems a lifetime. I'll be glad when all the fuss is over."

Philip was exuberant. At least *he* had no doubts, capable as he was of complete enthusiasm for whatever obsessed him at the moment. I have never known anyone who had such a capacity for living in each moment and enjoying it. What a wonderful gift! Darling Philip. I was to be grateful later that he had possessed it.

There was never any entertaining on Sundays, so I retired early. I sat by my window, looking out on the gardens. This time next week Philip and I would be on our way to Italy.

The next morning Rose, her face chalky, came into my bedroom, where I was sorting my clothes. "What's wrong?" I asked.

"There's been an accident. Mr. Rollo's here, asking to see you."

I went down to the drawing room. Rollo was standing by the fireplace, his face drawn and anxious. "Something terrible has happened," he began. "You must try to be calm. It's Philip. . . . He was found dead in his room this morning."

"Philip . . . *dead!* No. How could that be? He wasn't ill."

"He was found shot."

"Shot! But who . . . ?"

Rollo shook his head. "It seems the wound was self-inflicted."

I felt myself growing dizzy. "There's a mistake," I said shrilly. "I don't believe it."

"Alas. There is no mistake."

Everything was collapsing about me. The world had become a strange place full of distorted nightmares. And the greatest of these was Rollo, standing before me, saying in a low tragic voice, "Philip is dead. He took his own life."

I couldn't believe it. Philip dead! Only the day before he had talked exuberantly of our future. What could have happened so suddenly to make him take his own life?

That very day a newspaper ran the story with the headline SUICIDE OF BRIDEGROOM-TO-BE. "Six days before he was to have married Miss Ellen Kellaway, Philip, son of Josiah Carrington, took his own life. What is the story behind the tragedy?"

Everyone believed that there was a story and that I was the one who held the vital clue. Why should a young man who had every blessing shoot himself a few days before his wedding? That he would rather die than marry me was the implication.

Esmeralda told me what had happened. "He was shot with one of the guns from Trentham Towers. He must have brought it with him from the country."

"It's not possible. That would mean that he had planned it."

My mind raced back to that day when we had been in the gun room at Trentham Towers. I remembered the silver-gray pistol he had touched so lovingly. There had been an empty compartment in the case, and he had talked, jokingly I had thought, about keeping a pistol under his pillow. Even if he had been serious, what could have possessed him to turn the pistol on himself?

"Imagine, Esmeralda, the despair a man must be in to take his own life!" I cried out. "Can you imagine Philip in despair? I never saw him so. Nobody knew Philip better than I, and I say it's *impossible*. I shall never believe it."

Esmeralda said, "There'll be an inquest. You'll have to go."

"I want to go," I said. "I want to discover the reason for this."

The inquest was like a dream. . . . Mr. Josiah Carrington, his face distorted with grief; Lady Emily more bewildered than ever, with a tragic look in her eyes. And Rollo grown stern, his eyes like ice. They all looked searchingly at me, making me shiver.

There could be only one conclusion. Suicide. I wanted to cry out my protest. But that was the court's verdict.

I begged not to go to the funeral. I just lay on my bed in shocked stillness, weak from despair and lack of sleep.

"The press keep calling," Esmeralda said. "Mother thinks you should go to the country for a while. I'm to go with you."

So we went, and what a comfort Esmeralda was! I felt a little better there, but I could not sleep well. I had nightmares of Philip, the pistol in his hand and the blood on his bed.

I had been in the country for about two weeks when Rollo came to see me. He insisted that we be alone. And as he stood before me in the small sitting room and bowed stiffly, I thought how he had changed. He was not the godlike creature I had seen when we were young.

He came straight to the point. "I want you to tell me why Philip killed himself," he said harshly.

"If only I knew. If I had known what he was going to do, I would have found some way of stopping him."

Rollo kept his eyes on me. "Are you absolutely sure that there were no differences between you? Perhaps you had deceived him."

I cried out, "You can't believe such nonsense!"

"Who was the man with you in the house in Finlay Square?"

"I told you. I don't know who he is. He was at the recital at your home . . . and then he came to the house. That's all I know."

Rollo looked skeptical. "How did he get in?"

"He told you. He got the key from the agent."

"No, Ellen. He met you by appointment and I surprised you."

"That's monstrous."

"I can only draw the obvious conclusions. You had one key, Philip had the other, which I used. There was no third key. I have spoken to the agent and he swears he gave no one else a key. So there was only one way that man could have entered the house. You let him in. Don't lie to me anymore."

"This is absurd. How dare you! I was as surprised to see that man as you were. He did have a key and the agent is lying."

"I would have respected you more had you confessed the truth. I wish to God Philip had never seen you."

I was desolate. I had lost Philip and with him everything. And now Rollo despised me and suspected me so cruelly and unfairly.

I went for long walks, but there was hardly any spot in the neighborhood where I had not been with Philip. In the village where they had known us as children, people looked at me covertly and I knew the thought that was in all their minds: Philip's death had something to do with me.

WE COULD not stay in the country forever, and after three weeks Cousin Agatha recalled us to London.

I felt a quiver of alarm when I entered the house and was

confronted by her. Her expression was one of exasperation and veiled triumph: exasperation because I had managed to get myself "talked about," as she put it; veiled triumph because I had had to come back to be victimized at her will. My brief glory was over.

It was not long before I was summoned to Cousin Agatha's sitting room. "I suppose," she said with distaste, "it will take us a long time to live down this very unfortunate affair. Of course I never really believed that marriage would take place." She sighed.

I no longer felt the irresistible desire to defy her. In fact, I had lost my spirit and made no comment.

"However, every cloud has a silver lining, they say, and it seems that in your case this may be so. Mrs. Oman Lemming has not yet completed her search for the right governess. She has decided in her kindness to ignore convention and give you another chance."

I looked at Cousin Agatha in astonishment and she gave me a wintry smile. I might have known her pleasure would be my pain. "Oh no," I protested.

"Yes. I know it is unbelievably generous of her. She is of the opinion that in due course this scandal will be forgotten and that it may have a salutary effect upon you. I had to be honest and inform her that you could at times be pert. After all, one in your present position should be especially contrite."

"Why? What have I done?"

"My dear Ellen," she said in a voice that showed I continued to be far from dear to her, "when a man commits suicide rather than marry, people will always look askance at the woman who was to have been his wife."

"Philip wanted our marriage more than anything. And he did not kill himself. I am sure of it."

"No hysterics, please. Remember your place. You are distraught, and the best thing for you is to begin your new life as quickly as possible. Work will help you over an unfortunate spell. I have told Mrs. Oman Lemming to expect you the end of the month."

I felt as though I were drowning in my misery. With Philip's death I had lost my champion. But what saddened me most was that I had not appreciated him when he lived.

I set about preparing my trunk. According to Cousin Agatha, I would need good serviceable clothes. What I did have was a wardrobe of beautiful garments which were to have been my trousseau. Ironically, now that I was about to leave London society, I was better equipped for it than ever before. But what comfort were clothes when one was lost in a cruel world!

I awoke the next day to find a letter waiting. I did not know the bold writing on the envelope.

The letter was headed the Far Island, Polcrag, Cornwall, and ran:

Dear Miss Kellaway,

When you read this letter you will be wondering why I have not written before. The truth is that I only recently discovered your whereabouts. I live in this remote spot which was your father's home. When he died, about a year ago, he appointed me your guardian until your next birthday, when you reach the age of twenty-one. I believe you have been kept in ignorance of your father's family and I am sure would like to know more. It would give me great pleasure if you would come and visit us here.

                                                            Jago Kellaway

The Far Island. My father's home! I knew nothing of all this and my first impulse was to ask Cousin Agatha. But I hesitated. She was so set on my becoming governess in the Oman Lemming household that she might do anything to prevent my escaping it.

There was something fateful—and exciting—about receiving a letter so fortuitously. The Far Island sounded romantic.

I said nothing about the letter, not even to Esmeralda, until by good luck I found an opportunity to show it to Cousin William.

"Why, yes," he said, "your mother did marry and go off to that island. Something went wrong and she left, taking you with her."

"Who is this Jago Kellaway?"

"He must be some sort of relation." He looked at me quizzically and I saw the compassion in his eyes. "Unfortunately I can tell you no more, but if your father is now dead and these people are asking you to visit them, perhaps they will make amends for his not bothering with you all these years." He laid a hand on my arm. "It

46

is not my wish that you should take this post as a governess, Ellen."

"Thank you, Cousin William. And you think that I ought to go and see my father's family?"

He nodded and I could see that he thought it might be a fortunate way out of my present difficulties.

That afternoon from my window I saw Mrs. Oman Lemming arrive. Soon I should be sent for, to stand before them, eyes downcast, the Poor Relation to whom they were being so generous.

And so without further delay I wrote to Jago Kellaway, telling him that I should be delighted to come to the Far Island. I had just completed the letter when Bessie came to summon me.

Defiantly I went downstairs, my old spirit briefly reviving. I was not going to Mrs. Oman Lemming's to be bullied and treated with disdain. I was going to join members of my family at the Far Island off the coast of Cornwall.

Hydrock Manor and the Castle

IT WAS late afternoon when I arrived at Polcrag with three moderate-sized bags and a purse of sovereigns slipped to me by Cousin William. There was a carriage waiting at the railway station, and I asked the driver to take me to the Polcrag Inn. Jago Kellaway had suggested this procedure when he had written to say he was delighted that I was accepting his invitation.

As we clopped along I took stock of the little town which nestled below the surrounding cliffs. The houses were of gray Cornish stone and many had glassed-in porches, undoubtedly for the dual purpose of catching the sun and keeping out the strong sea winds. The Polcrag Inn, a building of three stories with an archway at the side, stood in the main street, and we drove under this arch to the stables. Just as I was about to alight, a man whom I guessed rightly to be the host came into the yard.

"You'm Miss Kellaway if I be not mistook," he said.

I said that I was indeed Miss Kellaway.

"I've been warned of your coming. Orders is you'm to be well looked after till the boat do come for 'ee."

"I thought I should cross to the island today," I said.

"Lord love you, no, miss. The sea be proper treacherous. Did you notice the white horses out there on the water? When you see them you know 'tis no time to take the boat for the island."

I followed him across the courtyard, through a door and into a hall, where I was greeted by his wife.

"This be Miss Kellaway," said the innkeeper.

The woman's eyes opened wide as she looked at me wonderingly. "Be it so then?" she said, and dropped a curtsy. "I'd best be taking her to her room."

As we ascended the stairs she said, " 'Tis a fine room I have for 'ee, Miss Kellaway. 'Twouldn't do to give you aught but the best."

We reached the landing and she opened the door. All this time she had scarcely taken her eyes off me, and after a second's hesitation she burst out, "I knew your mother. You'm like her. I were maid to her . . . until she left."

"I'm so glad to meet someone who knew her," I said. "I was five when she died and one doesn't remember much at that age."

"Time passes," she mused. "It seems only yesterday, though much have happened since, I reckon. Tom Pengelly and I were married soon after your mother went off, and I had Augustus. There be nothing wrong with the lad. 'Twere just that he were born two months too soon. When he were little he showed himself not quite like other children, and I used to say 'twere because he came before he was quite done. I said he was slack-baked and then people started to call him Slack. He'm a good boy at heart. He's over there." She nodded toward the window. "He works for Mr. Jago. I'd take it kindly if you'd look out for him over there."

"I will," I promised.

There was a knock on the door and a maid appeared with hot

water. She was followed by a boy with my bags. Mrs. Pengelly went out and I crossed to the window. I strained my eyes for a glimpse of the island, but all I could see were ominous dark clouds.

As I washed and changed I became more and more excited, for now I should learn something about my parents. All I knew was that they had been unhappy together, and because my mother had left my father, I was sure he had been an ogre. I also wondered about Jago Kellaway. His letter of welcome had been so warm.

As I descended the stairs the savory smell of roast pork made me feel hungry for the first time since Philip's death. It was early yet and there were no other guests in the dining room. I was glad because it gave me an opportunity to talk with Mrs. Pengelly.

"You must have known my mother very well," I began.

"Oh yes, Miss Kellaway. You too, when you was a little un."

"Why did my mother leave the island?"

Mrs. Pengelly looked taken aback. "Well, my dear, that were for reasons best known to herself."

The innkeeper came into the room to ask how I was enjoying the meal, and when I told him it was excellent, he looked pleased; but before he left I intercepted a look he gave his wife and I wondered whether he had come in to warn her against indiscreet talk.

I finished my coffee and went up to bed. I fancied the sea was calmer and the wind less persistent. It was inevitable that I should have the dream.

When I awoke, my feelings were not so much of apprehension but of excitement, as though I were at last on the verge of learning the meaning behind the mists of my dream. However, I was dismayed to discover that the wind had risen again and the waves were pounding on the shore. Yesterday's white horses had not returned to the stable; in fact, more had come out to join them.

I knew there would be no boat that morning, so after breakfast I decided to stroll out to look at the town.

There was not a great deal to Polcrag when one left the main street, just a few shops and houses. The post office was the general store, and I decided to buy some stamps, for I had promised to let Esmeralda know how I had fared on my journey.

The postmistress looked up when I walked in and, recognizing me as a stranger, asked if I was visiting.

"Yes," I replied. "I'm waiting for the sea to grow calm so I can cross to the island. My family have asked me to stay with them."

"And have you never been there before?"

"Actually I was born on the island but I haven't been back since I was three."

"You can't be . . ."

"I'm Ellen Kellaway."

She stared at me in astonishment. "Well now," she said at length, "that be something!"

"You know my family?"

"Everyone do know the Kellaways. There's been Kellaways on the Far Island for hundreds of years, 'tis said."

"Mr. Jago Kellaway has invited me to stay."

"Well, he be the lord of the island, as they do say."

I was aware that everyone in the shop was interested in me, so I hastily bought the stamps and returned to the inn, where I ate a cold luncheon of ham, cheese and fruit.

The long afternoon stretched before me. The clouds were as lowering as they had been the day before, and the waves, edged with white froth, were thundering on the sands.

I decided to walk again, and took a winding path through some woods, thinking of all I was trying to forget. I saw Philip's face creased in laughter, gently mocking, but he was always ready to protect me; and as frequently I felt Rollo's accusing eyes on me.

I must not get lost, I thought, so I turned and, I assumed, went back the way I had come. But after I had walked for half an hour I was still deep in the woods, and I very soon realized with dismay that I *was* lost. I continued walking, trying to retrace my steps, and eventually I came to a gate. I opened it, passed through and all at once I found myself in a clearing. Suddenly a man on a gray horse rode into sight and pulled up beside me.

"Can you help me?" I asked. "I'm lost. I was trying to find my way back to the Polcrag Inn."

"You are a long way off course," he said. "The easiest way now is past the house. Actually these woods are private because of the pheasants, but it's a shortcut."

"Oh dear, do you think the owner would mind?"

"I'm sure he wouldn't," he said with a smile. "As a matter of fact, it's my house and these are my woods. I'm Michael Hydrock."

"I *am* sorry. I must apologize."

"Oh, strangers often stray in. We should post more notices."

Just then I took a step forward and, as I did so, tripped over an old beech trunk and fell sprawling onto the grass.

The man sprang from his horse and helped me up. I noticed what a pleasant face he had. "Are you hurt?" he asked.

"I don't think so." I stood up, then touched my ankle.

"You certainly can't walk all the way back. I tell you what we'll do. I'll help you onto my horse and I'll lead it back to the house. We'll go in and see how badly hurt you are. Then I could take you to the inn in a carriage."

"This is too kind."

"Not at all," he said as he helped me onto the saddle.

I shall never forget my first glimpse of Hydrock Manor. We had come out of the woods and there it stood—a gray stone dwelling with a gatehouse and a Gothic arch at the entrance.

The place affected me with a profound sense of peace. We followed a gravel path across a brilliant green lawn, then went through the archway into a cobbled courtyard. Michael Hydrock helped me dismount as a groom came hurrying to take the horse.

"Come this way," said my host, and he led me through a doorway and into a hall—not large but beautifully proportioned, with a hammer-beam roof. "I think," he said, "that I'd better call my housekeeper. She would know whether the ankle is badly hurt or not. But first, do sit down."

He pulled a bell rope and a manservant quickly appeared. "Tell Mrs. Hocking to come here, please," Michael Hydrock said.

Within minutes Mrs. Hocking had joined us. She was in her late sixties, I imagined, and there was about her the air of the servant who has been with the family for so many years that she regards herself as privileged.

Michael Hydrock explained what had happened, and she knelt and gently prodded my ankle. "Does that hurt?" she asked.

"A little."

"Now stand up and step on it," she commanded. I did that. "All right?" she asked, and I said I thought it was.

" 'Tis only a slight sprain," she announced. "Like as not it will be fine by tomorrow. But you oughtn't do any walking today."

"I don't know how to thank you both," I said.

"We're only too pleased to help, Miss . . . er . . ."

"Kellaway," I said. "I'm Ellen Kellaway."

The silence was immediate. Then Michael Hydrock said, "You must be related to the Kellaways of the island."

"Yes. I'm on my way to them. I'm only staying at the Polcrag Inn until the weather permits me to cross."

Mrs. Hocking seemed to be directing a look of cold disapproval at me, and I fancied that the fact that I was Ellen Kellaway had not exactly endeared me to her. I wondered why.

Michael Hydrock said, "I daresay you would like some tea. Mrs. Hocking, would you have it sent to the winter parlor, please."

The winter parlor was an intimate room nearby with an oval table in the center. We sat down on tapestry-covered chairs and I said I thought the house was delightful, which pleased him. He said, "It has been my family's home for about four hundred years."

Tea was brought by a young girl, and the tray, with its Georgian silver teapot and kettle on a spirit lamp, was set on the table.

I offered to pour, and as I did so, felt completely at ease. I was liking my rescuer more every moment. Suddenly I was talking of my life in London, and before I realized it I was explaining that I had been on the point of marriage when my fiancé died in a tragic accident. I wondered whether he had heard the story. Heaven knew it had been publicized enough. But I realized that Michael Hydrock was the sort of man whose good manners would not allow him to mention that he knew it already.

"As a matter of fact," I went on, "I didn't know I had this family until a few weeks ago, and I'm longing to meet them. What sort of a man is Jago Kellaway?"

Michael Hydrock smiled. "It's hard to describe him. There can't be another person in the world like him."

"Do you often go to the island and do they come here?"

"I do know some members of the household," he said gravely, but there was a hint in his manner which meant that he hoped I would not carry that inquiry further.

He told me about the countryside then, of the places to visit, the customs of the people and how the old superstitions about witchcraft still prevail here. His company was delightful, but I was staying too long. So I thanked him for his hospitality and said I must be on my way.

A groom helped me into the pony trap. Michael Hydrock sat beside me and took the reins. I studied his clean-cut profile and thought what a kindly face his was. Here was a man who, I felt, could be relied on to act in a predictable manner.

He said, "I fancy the wind is softening a little. The sea may well be calm enough for you to go out to the island tomorrow."

"I had no idea that I should be delayed so long."

"It's the geographical location of the island actually. You see this coast is extremely treacherous. There's a mass of rock which has to be carefully skirted, and there are quicksands about a mile or so east of Polcrag beach. It has been said that was why it was called the Far Island, not that it is so very far from the mainland—only three miles—just that conditions so often put it out of reach."

We were entering the inn yard and I was sorry, for I wanted to go on riding with Michael Hydrock.

Mrs. Pengelly looked at us in blank amazement.

Michael Hydrock said, "Miss Kellaway hurt her ankle and I've brought her back." Michael had leaped down and was helping me out. He then took my hand and smiled at me gently. "Be careful of the ankle. And when you come to the mainland . . . or if you feel at any time you need . . . do call. I should be delighted."

"You have been most good to me," I said earnestly.

"It was nothing and has been my pleasure." Then he was back in the trap and turning the horse out of the courtyard.

Mrs. Pengelly and I stood together watching him.

53

Then I went into the inn and up to my room. I had not been there five minutes when there was a tap on the door and Mrs. Pengelly came in, her eyes alight with curiosity. "I wondered if there was anything I could get you, Miss Kellaway?"

I assured her there was not, but I could see she wanted to talk.

"It was strange that you should meet Sir Michael," she began.

"I had no idea that he was *Sir* Michael."

"Oh yes, one of the Hydrocks was knighted years ago. The Hydrocks have been the squires of these lands ever since—and that's going back a few years—just as the Kellaways have owned the Far Island for about as many years."

"They own the island?"

"Why yes, 'tis often known as Kellaway's Isle."

"There are surely not just Kellaways there."

"Bless you, no. It's a thriving community."

"Mrs. Pengelly, what do you know about my parents?"

She gazed down at her hands as though looking for inspiration. "Your mother just couldn't abide the place. She came from London. She hated the sound of the waves pounding on the shores. She said the cries of the gulls were like voices jeering at her because she was a prisoner."

"A prisoner!"

"That was how she felt. She was always saying she would leave. There were quarrels. Your father was not easy to live with. Then she went away and took you with her."

"She must have been very unhappy."

Mrs. Pengelly raised her eyes and looked at me. "She was so bright and lively when she came here; then she changed. Kellaway's Isle wouldn't suit some people and she was one of them."

"Didn't my father try to bring her back?"

"No, he just let her go."

"So he didn't care very much about either of us."

"He wasn't the sort of man to be very interested in children. And then of course . . ."

She trailed off and I said eagerly, "Yes, what?"

"Nothing. I left and came back here. My father had this inn. I married Pengelly and when my father died the inn passed to us."

"Who is Jago Kellaway . . . what relation to me?"

"Now that's something he'll tell you. He wouldn't want me to be talking too much."

"You seem afraid of him."

"He's not the type a body would want to offend."

"There seems to be a sort of mystery about the island or the Kellaways. I notice a change in people when they learn who I am."

"They'd be surprised, I reckon. Hereabouts people know something about others' business. They're just interested to see what you've grown up like. Oh my dear life, I be forgetting I have work to do. I'd best be off."

The evening passed quickly. I admitted to myself that I should not be completely sorry if the sea prevented my crossing to the island for another day, for I might see Michael Hydrock again.

Next morning I awoke to a calm sea, glittering in the sunshine, and at ten o'clock the boat arrived.

FROM my window I saw a man alight. Two oarsmen remained in the boat. I went downstairs. Then one of the stable hands took my bags, and by that time the man had come into the inn.

Mrs. Pengelly bustled around, very eager to please. "Oh, Mr. Tregardier, Miss Kellaway will be glad to see 'ee."

The man held out his hand and shook mine. "I am so pleased to meet you at last," he said. "I'm William Tregardier, Mr. Kellaway's estate manager. He wants me to tell you how eagerly he is awaiting your arrival. Alas, we have been at the mercy of the sea. But you can be sure we crossed as soon as was possible."

Mrs. Pengelly brought us some of her special bees wine and saffron cakes, and half an hour later we set out.

There was a light breeze blowing—just enough to ruffle the water—and I felt my excitement rising. It was not long before the island came into sight.

"There it is!" said William Tregardier.

A sudden pride took possession of me. It was thrilling to have my name associated with such a splendid place.

"It's beautiful," I cried. "And there's another island!"

"That's the nearest. It's not cultivated like the main island. It's more rocky, and there's some sort of deposit on the rocks which in some lights gives them a bluish tinge. That's why it's known as Blue Rock Island. And now you can see yet another, Sanctuary Island. It's a refuge for birds. It's uninhabited but for the choughs and sea gulls that congregate there."

I turned my gaze back to the main island. The rock on one side rose in a stark cliff face beneath which was a sandy cove where several boats were moored.

"Are we going in there?" I asked.

"No," answered William Tregardier. "We land on the other side. There are dangerous rocks and currents here."

The island was now showing a different aspect. I could see picturesque little houses with whitewashed walls and orange roofs. There was a ridge of low hills running down to the sea—all green and beautiful, brightened by purple heather and yellow gorse.

We ran onto a beach where two men were waiting with horses.

"I trust you ride," said my companion. "Jago was sure you did."

"I wonder how he knew. Yes, I've always been keen on riding."

"That's excellent. It's the best way of getting around the island. We have a docile little mare for you now, Miss Kellaway. Later you can select your own horse. Jago keeps a very good stable."

As we rode up from the beach he said, "The castle is close by."

"The castle?" I asked.

"We always call it that. Kellaway Castle. It's very ancient."

The castle—and it was indeed a castle—was a massive quadrangular edifice with thick stone walls flanked by four circular towers rising above the crenellated parapets of the roof. We passed through a stone gatehouse topped by yet another tower and were in a cobbled courtyard; from there we went under a Norman arch into another courtyard, where a groom was waiting for us.

"Take our horses, Albert. This is Miss Kellaway, who has come to stay with us."

Albert touched his forelock to me. He took the horses and William Tregardier led the way toward a heavy iron-studded door. "I daresay you will wish to change before meeting Jago. I'll get one of the maids to show you to your room."

I was bemused. I had certainly been unprepared for such a castle. It was grander in its way than Hydrock Manor and clearly of an earlier period. We had entered a reception room; there was a suit of armor in one corner and shields and weapons on the walls, and I imagined it had once been a guardroom.

It seemed as though everyone in the house was awaiting my arrival, for no sooner had we stepped into this room than a maid came in from another door.

"Ah, Janet," said William Tregardier, "here is Miss Kellaway. Take her to her room and see that she has everything she needs."

I followed Janet, marveling. We went through several stone-floored passages and mounted a stone staircase. Then we came to a gallery and were clearly in the residential part of the castle, for the medieval aspect gave way to a more modern air of comfort.

Janet threw open a door and we entered a luxurious room hung with ancient tapestries in shades of red and gray. There was a red carpet on the floor and the curtains were of red velvet trimmed with gold fringe. The four-poster had red velvet curtains about it. I looked round the room at the dressing table and mirror, the big cupboard, the fireplace, and a mantel on which stood large candlesticks. The ceiling was lofty and ornately carved.

The window—semicircular and cut out of an amazingly thick wall—had a stone window seat reached by three steps. I climbed them and looked out. Although the castle was a little isolated, standing on its incline, I could see that the island was well populated. I made out what must have been a main street with shops. I could see farmhouses surrounded by fields, and there were orchards and even a small forest. It was like a miniature town. I even caught a glimpse of Blue Rock—just a small channel of sea separated us. Then I gazed at the mainland and wondered what Michael Hydrock was doing and whether he had given me another thought.

"It's magnificent," I said, turning to survey the room.

" 'Tis one of the best rooms in the castle," said Janet. Then she gave a little giggle. "We've all been warned, miss. We got to take very special care of 'ee. If there's anything you do want"—she walked to the bell rope—"you just pull this and I'll be with 'ee."

At that moment a boy arrived with my baggage.

"I'll bring 'ee hot water, miss," said Janet.

"Thank you," I said.

When she had left, I opened a valise and took out some of the dresses which had been made for my honeymoon. Suddenly I felt quite wretched, and I could not stop thinking of our honeymoon plans. "Venice," Philip had said. "Gondoliers. Serenades on the Grand Canal. Very romantic."

While I was standing there, lost in my painful reverie, Janet came back with the hot water. "Mr. Jago has just come in, miss," she said. "He says I'm to take you to him in his parlor. I reckon you'll want to hurry, miss. Mr. Jago isn't one to be kept waiting."

I washed while Janet hung up my dresses. I realized that my hands were trembling, for I was about to see this man of whom I had begun to build a formidable picture in my mind.

And so I went down to my first meeting with Jago Kellaway. That parlor was a gracious, dignified room, with a deep bow window overlooking the sea. There was a big open fireplace with andirons, and a long stool in front. Tapestries covered the walls, and the ceiling was decorated in a pattern that incorporated the arms of the family. But all this I noticed much later.

Janet had knocked at the door and when it opened, as if by magic, I advanced into the room. At first I thought there was no one there and then I heard a laugh behind me. The door was shut and he was leaning against it, studying me with amusement.

"You!" I cried. "You . . . Jago Kellaway!"

For the man who faced me was the mysterious dark stranger who had been at the recital and later in the house in Finlay Square.

My spine tingled in horror and amazement. "But I don't understand," I stammered.

"I thought you'd be surprised." There was laughter in his voice as he took my arm and led me to the window. There he put his hands on my shoulders and looked into my face. "Ellen. At last!"

"I should like to know what you were doing at the recital and at the house in Finlay Square? Why didn't you tell me who you were? And who *are* you anyway?"

"You ask too many questions to answer all at once. First, I want to tell you how very happy I am to welcome you to Kellaway's Isle. You are indeed a Kellaway. You take after your father. He was a very impatient man. But come sit down, my dear, and I will answer every question."

He led me to a chair with carved arms and a petit point seat, and almost pushed me into it. Then very deliberately, as though he enjoyed my impatience, he drew up a chair for himself. It was like a throne, that chair—large, ornately carved, and inlaid with lapis.

Jago was even more impressive than he had been in London. His hair was thick and dark. I noticed again those heavy-lidded eyes which could hide so much; they were surveying me with obvious pleasure. He wore a midnight-blue velvet smoking jacket and a white cravat. His hands were well shaped and slightly bronzed, and he wore a signet ring on the little finger of his right hand.

"Now," he said, "you ask who I am and you wonder just what my connection with you is. Well, dear Ellen, it is a complicated but rather common story. Perhaps it is a little indelicate for your ears. But no. You come from the sophisticated London world and will know that matters of this nature arise now and then even in the most sedate families. Am I right?"

"I can't say until I hear it," I replied sharply. Something about him irritated me and made me want to do battle with him. I was eager to understand the mystery which surrounded him, and yet he deliberately took his time explaining it. He had already acted in a strange manner, and it was clear he thought it all a great joke.

"The mark of illegitimacy comes into this," he said. "One of our ancestors—your great-grandfather—had a sister named Gwennol. Gwennol was beautiful and wild. There is a picture of her in the gallery which I must show you. The Kellaways were a great family. They owned the islands and they lived here in some state. A grand marriage would have been arranged for Gwennol, but one day she proudly announced that she was going to have a child. She would not name the father nor had she any intention of marrying. Her own father, furious with her, threatened to turn her out of the castle unless she told him who her lover was. She refused and left the castle, taking several of the servants with her; whether they went through love or fear I don't know, for by some she was reputed to be a witch, and it was even said that the devil was the father of her child." Again Jago Kellaway's eyes showed that flicker of amusement. "Well, Gwennol went to Blue Rock Island, which is only a short distance from here. You have seen it perhaps?"

"I have. Mr. Tregardier pointed it out, and I can see it from my window."

"The house Gwennol had built for herself still stands there. In it her son was born. He was my father."

Jago paused. "So, Ellen, you and I are cousins. Several times removed, but we are both Kellaways. My father died when I was quite young and I came to live at the castle. Your father and I grew up together, and later we shared the management of the island estate for some years. When he became too ill to do much I took over completely. Then last year he died."

"And my father never wanted to know where I was?"

Jago looked at me steadily and shook his head. "But before he died he asked me to find you and to be your guardian until you reached the age of twenty-one. It was not easy to find you. Your mother had determined to lose herself when she left the island. But when I saw the papers and learned that you were about to be married, I came to London."

"Why didn't you tell me then who you were?"

"Ah, a quirk in my nature—to surprise, to be dramatic. I wanted to know you before you knew me. So I came to the recital."

"How? The Carringtons didn't know you."

"Shall we say I gate-crashed."

"What . . . impudence! And the house in Finlay Square. The agent denied having given you a key."

"Well, you know how these agents are. They want to make sure of a sale and apparently there was some hesitation about this one, so the agent gave me a key. Then I waited until I saw you enter the house. Let me tell you this: I had a duty. I wanted to make sure about the family you were marrying into."

"You quickly found out who the Carringtons were, I'm sure."

"Yes, I discovered a good deal about them. Then the tragedy happened and I asked you to come here. Is it clear now?"

"Yes," I answered.

"I hope, Ellen," he said earnestly, "that you will stay with us for a very long time."

"You are kind," I replied with a touch of asperity, for I didn't believe he was telling me the whole truth.

"I want you to like this place," he went on. "You have had a bitter experience, and I hope we'll help you grow away from it."

He looked sincere now. His eyes seemed serene and friendly. His was the most expressive face I had ever seen. A few moments before, he had looked mischievous, almost satanic; now he had become the kindly, protective guardian.

"What shall I call you?" I asked.

"Jago, of course. That is my name. Don't let the fact that I'm your guardian overawe you."

"Indeed I shall not. I have stood on my own feet most of my life. I certainly don't need a guardian at this stage."

"But you have one, Ellen; and as he is a man blessed—or cursed—with a very strong sense of duty, he will feel obliged to honor his promises, however much you object to his guardianship. Now, let me tell you something of the family. There's Jenifry, my older sister. She's a widow who lost her husband some years ago during a typhoid epidemic. You might say that she is the chatelaine of the castle. Her daughter, Gwennol, will be company for you. She's about your age.

"You must," he went on, "discover something of your Kellaway heritage while you're here, Ellen. As to the island, which has been in our possession for centuries, it is wonderfully fertile, for the climate is conducive to growing things. The rock formations on the east protect us from the colder winds, and those on the west from the southwest gales, while the Gulf Stream keeps us warm—I even have palms in my sheltered gardens. We have our township, our church, our cemetery, our inn. We are independent—almost—of the mainland."

As he was speaking his manner changed again. Now he was glowing with pride of possession, and I warmed to his fierce enthusiasm. I waited to hear more. My interest clearly pleased him.

"I shall enjoy showing you everything, Ellen," he continued. "But for now, let us talk about your life in your cousin's house. It wasn't very comfortable, was it? She had a daughter who wasn't half as attractive as you. I saw that much. And she made you feel as if you were living on her bounty."

I was surprised that he had been so perceptive.

"And then," he went on, "this rich young man came forward. They wanted him for their daughter and he chose you, the wise fellow. But then he killed himself."

"He didn't. If you had known him, you would realize he would never do anything like that."

"It's all over." Jago's voice had become soft and soothing. "We will not speak of it again. But tell me, what were your plans before you received my letter?"

"I was going to be a governess."

"You . . . a governess! My dear Ellen, you're too proud for such a menial position. You should be engaging governesses for your own children. An attractive girl such as you are will not remain single long, and as your guardian I should like to see you happily married. Well now, I daresay you would like to go to your room and rest awhile before dinner. If there is anything you need, just ring."

I rose and he did the same. Then he laid his hand on my shoulder, and as we walked to the door I could feel the strength of his fingers.

I went to my room in a strange mood. My guardian-cousin, Jago, was the most unusual man I had ever met. His moods and personality seemed to change so quickly.

I was much too excited to rest. Everything was so different from what I had imagined. A grand castle and a guardian who was not middle-aged, but a gentleman of about thirty—a sort of joker in an unconventional way—a man who liked dramatic happenings. The prospect of living here dominated by such a man stimulated me; I felt more alive than I had since Philip's death. I was also determined to find out why my mother had left so mysteriously.

I had been told that I was to make myself at home. Well, I would begin by taking stock of my surroundings. So I descended the staircase and came to the guardroom. As I stood there the room seemed to take on a menacing aspect. Perhaps I was just feeling uneasy because of the shock of finding that Jago Kellaway was the man who had frightened me in the house in Finlay Square. But then, hadn't I always been susceptible to atmosphere in unfamiliar houses? I shuddered now to recall the repulsion I had felt when I had first entered that house in London.

This room, medieval in aspect, with the weapons on its walls— two crossed swords, an axe, a halberd—reminded me of the gun room at Trentham Towers. This shadowy memory was conjuring up hidden dangers, and I fancied that just as I had sensed a warning in the house in Finlay Square, so I did now in Kellaway Castle. Stupid imaginings, but I was in an uncertain state.

I moved toward the door, and my footsteps ringing on the marble paving stones filled the guardroom with an eerie sound. Then I stepped out into a courtyard and saw an archway which appeared to be cut into the wall. It led to several other courtyards and then to a winding pathway with stone walls on either side.

Suddenly I heard the flutter of wings and the cooing of birds. I had come into another courtyard. Little dovecotes were attached to the walls, and several pigeons were pecking at maize that had been scattered over the cobblestones. Most of the pigeons were bluish gray, but some were brown. I had never seen pigeons that color before. As I stood there looking at the birds I was aware of a shadow at a lower window. Someone was watching me.

I called, "Are these your birds?"

There was no answer. I went closer to the window, but the shadow had disappeared. There was a little door in the wall and I tapped on it. I realized that it had been slightly ajar, and as I stood there it was quietly shut. Someone on the other side of the door was clearly determined to keep me out.

63

How unfriendly! I shrugged, left the birds' courtyard and found my way back to my room in time to dress for dinner.

I put on my sapphire-blue silk, and just as I had finished dressing a servant came to conduct me down to an anteroom where the family was waiting for me. Jago was standing in front of the fireplace, his hands clasped behind his back, dominating the room. On either side of him was a woman—the older one about forty years of age, whom I guessed to be his sister, Jenifry, the younger his niece, Gwennol, who he had said was about my age.

"Ellen," said Jago. "This is Jenifry, my sister."

My heart sank a little as she stepped forward to take my hand. She was almost as dark as Jago and had the same high-bridged nose, which gave her the arrogant look I had noticed in him. But her voice was soft and warm. "We are delighted to have you at last, Ellen," she said. However, there was something coolly appraising about her eyes which was in contrast to her words. I felt the same uncertainty about her as I did about her brother.

Gwennol was dark too. Her hair was almost black, her eyes dark brown, her nose a trifle retroussé, her mouth wide. Her face was made striking by her soulful dreamy eyes and the alertness her nose and mouth seemed to betray. "Hello, Ellen," she said. "Welcome to Kellaway Island."

Almost immediately a servant announced dinner, and Jago put his arm through mine and led the way. "We are dining in the hall," he said. "It is a custom reserved for feast days and special occasions, and what occasion could be more special than this?"

There was something royal about the vast hall with its lofty roof, and its thick stone walls partially covered with fine tapestries. At one end was a door leading to the kitchens, through which servants hurried back and forth; above the door was the minstrels' gallery, its balustrade decorated with antlers. Places had been laid at the long oak table and on the dais and already the benches on either side of the table were occupied. These people, Jago told me later, were employed on the estate—those who farmed the land, managers of the various concerns, his clerks, and—I could scarcely believe this—there below the salt, those who worked in a more menial capacity. This was the manner in which kings had feasted in medieval times.

When the minstrels began to play softly I was touched by Jago's determination to create an atmosphere of bygone days, because I knew it had been done to honor me.

All those at the long table rose as we entered. Jago led the way to the dais, his arm still through mine, and he stood at the table with me beside him. "I have great pleasure," he announced, "in introducing you all to Miss Ellen Kellaway, my ward and cousin, who has come to stay with us, I hope, for a very long time. I know that you are as delighted to see her here as I am."

There was a murmur of assent. I smiled and, as Jago held my chair out for me, I sat down. There was a shuffling of chairs and benches, and everyone did the same.

"What do you think of it?" Jago whispered to me.

"It's incredible. I have never had such a welcome in my life."

"Then our purpose is served," he said, patting my hand.

We had excellent soup, followed by venison. Jenifry sat on Jago's left and Gwennol was beside me.

"Christmas is the time when we really go back to the old ways," explained Jago. "Then the hall is decorated with holly and ivy, and the carol singers and mummers perform here. It's been a custom of the family for centuries."

"We are trying to discover the exact age of the castle," put in Jenifry. "It was originally merely a fortress to protect the island."

"I want to show you around myself," Jago said to me. "We'll begin tomorrow. You ride, I know."

"Oh yes. We used to ride in London. And in the country I rode a good deal. But tell me more about the island," I said.

"There are times," interjected Gwennol, "when it's impossible to get to the mainland. And that can last for days."

Jago cut her short. "Ellen knows that. But people here don't feel they're missing anything by not being able to reach the mainland. People come and stay at our local inn to get away from the mainland. It has only four bedrooms, however, for we don't want the island spoiled with too many visitors."

I was learning how obsessed he was with the island. It was his and he was proud of it. To him it was perfect.

"Do you ever have any criminals here?" I asked.

"Hardly ever," he assured me. "I know how to keep the people lawful, but there are dungeons in the castle which serve on the rare occasions they are necessary."

"And the law allows this?"

"I'm a justice of the peace. Of course, in the case of a major crime—murder for instance—the criminal would be taken to the mainland. But we deal with petty matters here."

"Is there anyone in the dungeons now?"

Jago laughed. "No, Ellen, there very rarely is."

Gwennol said, "They're horrible. Dank, dark, and said to be haunted by the ghosts of those who didn't obey Kellaway law. In the past, Kellaways put their enemies there and left them to die."

"I'd like to see the dungeons," I said.

"So you shall," Jago promised me. "The whole place is yours to explore."

"As a matter of fact I did explore a little before dinner, and was surprised to see some brown pigeons. I'd never seen pigeons that color before."

"We've always kept a few brown pigeons at Kellaway," said Jago. "You tell her the story, Jenifry."

"It's simply that one of our ancestors was saved by a brown pigeon," his sister said. "I think they originated in Italy. He was imprisoned there after being captured in some battle, and a little brown pigeon and his mate perched on his windowsill. He tamed them and used to attach messages to their legs, hoping that some of his friends would see them. When, after a long long time, the message actually did reach his friends, it was regarded as a miracle. He was rescued and he brought the two brown pigeons back to the island with him. And then it was said that as long as there are brown pigeons at the castle there will be Kellaways on the island."

"What a charming story," I commented.

When the meal was over, Jago, Jenifry, Gwennol and I went to his parlor, where coffee was served. The atmosphere there was decidedly more intimate. We talked more about the island, then about my life in London, which now seemed remote.

It was half past ten when Jago remarked that I must be tired.

"Jenifry will take you to your room," he said.

She took a candle from a table. We left them and made our way back through the hall, then up the stone staircase into the long gallery, which, with candles burning in wall sconces, looked more medieval than ever.

I opened the door to my room, but it appeared different and alien now. There were too many dark shadows. The curtains had been drawn, and the four-poster, from which the curtains had been looped back, seemed to dominate the room.

Jenifry lit the candles from the one she carried. There were two on the dressing table and the ones on the mantel. She was smiling at me, her expression benign. "I'll say good night," she said. "If you need anything, ring."

I glanced in the mirror and caught a glimpse of Jenifry's face. Her expression had changed; her eyes had narrowed; her mouth had hardened; it was as though a mask had slipped to reveal a different woman. I turned sharply and looked at her. But her face had changed and now she was smiling again.

"Good night," I said, "and thank you for everything."

"Sleep well," she said, closing the door behind her. I stared at it blankly for a moment. My heart was beating unnaturally fast. Then I looked back at the mirror and saw that it was a very old one—a little mottled perhaps—and it had probably stood there for two hundred years. It would distort, but had she really looked at me like that? Speculatively, as though she hated me?

I sat down and took the pins out of my hair. It fell to my waist.

The trouble is, I told myself, I'm so used to being unwanted that I can't really believe in all this friendship. That was why I imagined she looked at me as she did.

The flickering candlelight threw long, eerie shadows about the room. I looked in the mirror again, and as I did so I seemed to see Jenifry's face suddenly distorted into an evil smile. It was all fancy, of course. I was overwrought. But as I looked in the mirror I heard

a sudden sound behind me. Startled, I grabbed a candle and swung around. No one was there.

I went to the door and turned the key, locking myself in. Then I heard the sound again. I looked around the room and laughed aloud when I realized that the sound had come from the cupboard door, which was not securely fastened.

I opened it. My clothes were hanging neatly, and as I stood there a dress slid slowly from its hanger and fell in a heap on the floor. I picked it up and, in doing so, saw some writing that had been scratched on the cupboard wall.

I pushed aside the clothes and held the candle closer. I read, "I am a prisoner here. S.K."

I wondered what S.K. meant. I guessed that this had been written by a child, because the lettering was childish.

Although the incident had made me feel not at all sleepy, I blew out the candles and got into the bed, which seemed very large. I lay there for some time while scenes from the day's events kept flashing in and out of my mind. I thought of all the people who had slept in this bed over the past hundred years. S.K. had probably been one of them. Finally I was so tired, I suppose, that I slept.

It was inevitable that the dream should come.

The room was as vivid as ever. The wind was blowing the red curtains and the door was moving. Slowly it opened. Now . . . that awful fear, the certainty that I was in great danger.

I was awake. My heart was racing and I was trembling.

It's only the dream, I soothed myself, but the doom seemed to have come nearer.

Discovery in a Sketchbook

SUNSHINE filled my room and the terrors of the night had completely disappeared with the coming of daylight.

When I went down to breakfast I found Gwennol, Jenifry and Jago at the table. "Help yourself from the sideboard," said Jenifry. "There's ham, eggs and deviled kidneys."

I took some and sat down. Jago inquired solicitously if I had slept well, and said that in an hour or so he would be ready to show me the island.

"Which mount will you give her?" asked Gwennol.

"I was thinking of Daveth for a start."

"Isn't she a bit spirited?"

"Perhaps they'll be well matched." Jago was eyeing me with an expression I couldn't quite understand, but it made me determined to ride the spirited Daveth.

After breakfast I changed into my pale gray riding habit—part of my trousseau. I also had a gray riding hat—tall-crowned like a man's top hat—which suited me well.

Jago looked at me with approval when I met him in the stable yard. "You are so elegant," he said. "The people of the island will be enchanted with you."

He was riding a white horse with a black mane, and I had to admit that horse and rider looked magnificent; they suited each other. I did find Daveth somewhat sprightly, but I was able to manage her. Jago glanced sideways at me, and I was delighted because I believed I had his approval.

We rode first to the highest peak on the island. What a sight lay before us! There was the castle with its gray stone walls and battlemented towers. It seemed impregnable, and in the past it would have been a perfect fortification against marauders. I could also see Blue Rock Island.

Jago followed my gaze. "Blue Rock," he said. "It's a pity we allowed it to pass out of our hands. It belonged to the Kellaways at one time, but your grandfather sold it. He was in financial difficulties; he was a bit of a gambler. And that's Blue Rock House. The one built by the Gwennol I told you about. An artist lives there now. He inherited it from the man your grandfather sold it to. I think he's that man's great-nephew."

"Does he live there alone?"

"Quite alone. But he travels around a bit, I believe. His name is James Manton. Have you ever heard of him?"

"I can't say I have, although I don't know very much about painters. Perhaps I shall meet him one day."

"He doesn't visit the island. He and your father didn't like each other. We're polite when we meet, but we don't visit. Look! You can see the mainland."

"It's a comforting sight," I commented.

"Comforting?" A faint frown appeared between his eyes.

"One doesn't feel so cut off from the world," I explained.

He nodded, and we cantered off across a green stretch and came to the shore.

"I will show you our community," he said. "It is complete in itself. We are a little kingdom, you might say. There is much of long-ago times left on the island and I intend to keep it that way."

We had come to a group of houses surrounded by fields. In the center was a shop which seemed to be that of a linen draper, hosier, tallow chandler, ironmonger, grocer and baker all combined. I decided to visit that shop as soon as possible.

From one house came the cheerful sound of merrymaking.

"It must be a christening party," said Jago. "There's a new baby in the house. We'll join them for a moment. They wouldn't like it if I passed by and didn't well-wish the baby." He shouted, "Boy!" And as if by magic a boy appeared.

"Take my horse and the lady's," said Jago. We dismounted and entered a small cottage, where several people were gathered.

"Why, 'tis the master," said a woman, dropping a curtsy.

" 'Tis honored we be," said her husband.

"Where's the baby?" asked Jago.

"She be in her cradle, Mr. Jago. 'Twould be an honor if you'd bless the child and take a piece of the cheeld's fuggan."

He would, he said, and I should too.

The cake was cut, and both Jago and I had a piece and also a glass of sloe gin, which burned my throat a little.

"Good luck to the child," said Jago.

"May she grow up to be a good servant to her master," said the baby's mother.

"Aye," said Jago, "so be it."

We came out into the street, where the boy was patiently waiting with our horses. We mounted and continued our ride.

"All these people are our tenants," Jago told me. "And every bit of the land is Kellaway land, owned by the family for six hundred years. You'd find most of the houses similar. They're what are known as Lives Cottages. A man who builds one has to start construction after dark and be finished before the next dawn. He thereby has a right to occupy it for his own lifetime, as will his son and his grandson."

"Can people really build a cottage in one night?"

"If they have their materials ready, they can have the four walls standing and the roof on. That is all that's necessary. How did you like the cheeld's fuggan?"

"A little too yellow."

"Oh, that's the saffron—a great delicacy here."

I had learned much about the island that morning. It was a community of about one hundred people, fishermen mainly, although there was some agriculture. There were many little coves where boats were moored, and we passed fishermen mending their nets as they sat among the lobster pots. They all greeted Jago, and I felt a certain pleasure in their respect for him.

He told me of their customs and superstitions. "Fishermen don't like to land with their catch before daybreak. They think the little people might carry them off if they did. And when they are at sea it's unlucky to mention rabbits or any wild animals. Once a superstition is born it seems to live forever.

"In the old days," he continued, "these islands were a sanctuary for people who wanted to evade the law. Many outlaws found asylum here and became subjects of the ruling Kellaway."

"And the Kellaway line is unbroken through the ages?" I asked.

"Yes. If a female inherited, she was duty-bound to marry and her husband would then take the name of Kellaway."

"It's been a wonderful morning," I said, "edifying too."

He turned to me and laid his hand on my arm. "I can't tell you how much I want you to stay here, Ellen," he said. "When I saw you in London it was the devil's own job to restrain myself from snatching you up and insisting that you come down and get to know your family before you rushed into marriage."

"I still can't understand why you didn't tell me who you were."

"It was the whim of a moment. You were so immersed in the prospect of marriage . . . and then, when it fell through, I felt my chance had come. I wanted you to come here freely. . . ."

I was touched by the tenderness in his voice. I was finding his company stimulating. He had intrigued me at the recital; he had frightened me in the house in Finlay Square. But now I decided he was the most fascinating man I had ever met.

He seemed to make a great effort to curb his emotions. "Alas," he said, "we must return to the castle. There is so much more I want to show you, but another day."

"I look forward to that. You must be rather proud when the people show you such obvious respect, as they did this morning."

"They daren't do aught else." He laughed. "I will say, though, that since I've been in control we've prospered. Crops have been good; I've introduced modern farming and marketing methods. Your father and I didn't always see eye to eye, Ellen."

"Oh?" I said, wanting him to go on about my father.

"He was ill for a long time. That left the reins in my hands."

"And it was then that things began to improve?"

"People on the island will tell you so. But let's not talk about the past, Ellen. You're here. Let's go on from there."

He smiled at me, and I fancied I saw in his eyes that which faintly alarmed me. But it had been such a good morning that I was in a happy mood as we rode into the stables.

THAT afternoon Gwennol went to the mainland. "She often gets one of the men to row her over on calm days like this," Jenifry explained. Jago was off on some estate business and Jenifry wanted to rest. So I decided to stroll around the castle by myself.

It was about half past two when I set out—a beautiful September day with the sun picking out pearly tints in the water. Soon I found myself in a familiar-looking courtyard. I heard the cooing of the pigeons and recognized this as the spot I had visited on the previous evening.

Then I saw him. He was very small, with a thatch of almost

white hair; his eyes were pale and his fair eyebrows and lashes gave him a look of surprise. I judged him to be about fourteen.

He carried a bowl of maize, and a look of fear came over his face when he saw me. He started to walk toward the outbuilding.

"Don't go, please. The pigeons must be fed," I reminded him. "Do let me watch; I love the way they flutter around you."

While he considered his next move, I had an inspiration. "I think you must be Slack," I said. "I met your mother at the inn."

He paused. Then a smile appeared on his face and he nodded.

"I'm Ellen Kellaway. I'm staying here for a while. I heard the wonderful story of the brown pigeons taking the messages."

"These take messages," he said proudly. "I train them." He then took a handful of maize from the bowl and threw it onto the cobbles. Several of the birds flew down and pecked at it.

"I saw you in there last night," I said, pointing to the outbuilding. "I called you, but you didn't hear."

"I saw you," he replied with a sly smile.

"May I look in your pigeon house now? I am very interested."

He opened the door and we stepped into a small room where sacks of maize and drinking troughs were stored.

"I've been looking after the pigeons ever since I came here," he said. "Now I've got to finish feeding them."

We went back into the courtyard. He held out his arm and two birds immediately alighted on it. "There, my pretties," he murmured. "Be 'ee come to see Slacky, then? You like pigeons, miss. Her liked 'em too. Her'd help me feed 'em. Then her went away."

"Her? Who was that, Slack?" I asked.

"Her," he said, looking bewildered. "Her just went away."

He was so disturbed by the memory that he had almost forgotten my existence, and because I could see that to question him further would only make him less inclined to talk, I strolled off.

THE next day Gwennol gave me a tour of the castle.

"Let's begin with the dungeons," she said.

Clinging to a rope banister, we descended a treacherous spiral staircase. At the bottom was an enclosure with a cobbled floor. It was surrounded by doors, about eighteen in all. I pushed one open and saw a cavelike cell in which it would have been difficult for a man of normal height to stand upright. Fixed to the wall on a chain was a heavy iron ring. I shuddered, realizing that this had been used to prevent the cell's inmate from escaping. The walls were seeping with moisture and there was a damp, noisome odor about the place. I explored other cells, some lofty but all equally dark and dismal. On one wall the sketch of a gallows was cut into the stone; on another an evil grinning face had been drawn.

"It's gruesome," I said. "Imagine yourself a prisoner. You'd call and no one would hear, or even care."

Gwennol nodded. "Ugh! Morbid," she commented. "I can see you've had enough of the dungeons, but you had to have a look at them, of course. They're an important part of the castle."

We climbed the stairs to the upper regions and she took me through so many rooms, towers and galleries that I lost count. She showed me the kitchens, the bakery, the buttery, the winery and the slaughterhouse; she introduced me to the servants, who watched me guardedly and with obvious curiosity.

One room which led off the hall interested me particularly because as we entered, Gwennol said, "I heard this was your mother's favorite room. I don't think anyone has used it since she went."

There was a step leading down to the room, which was furnished as a sitting room with a table and a few chairs. There was also a wooden settle that fitted into an alcove.

I looked around eagerly, trying to picture my mother there. It was certainly not a bright room. The window was small and its panes leaded. I said, "I wonder if any of her things are still here."

"Why don't you look in the cupboard?" suggested Gwennol.

I opened the door and immediately spotted an easel and some rolls of paper. "These must have been hers," I cried in triumph. Then I saw a sketchbook lying on the floor. Written across it was her name: Frances Kellaway. I was so excited by this discovery that my hand shook as I turned the pages. There were paintings and sketches; some were of the castle from various angles. She had been quite an artist.

"I want to take this to study at my leisure. You're probably amused by my excitement, but I knew so little of my mother, and my father I can't remember at all. You must have known him."

"Nobody knew him well. But I don't think he liked young people. He was ill for a long time and mostly kept to his own rooms. I'd see him now and then in a wheelchair. Fenwick, his secretary-valet, looked after him, and he could tell you more about him than anyone else, I daresay. But he left when your father died."

"Do you know where he went?"

"I think he lives on the mainland, but I'm not sure where."

Then, seeming to find the conversation about my father boring, she changed the subject. "Let's go and see Slack," she said. "I want him to row me over to the mainland tomorrow. Would you care to come? I always like to take advantage of calm seas. I shall be visiting friends, so perhaps you'd enjoy exploring a bit. We could go to the inn and get horses there. It's what I often do."

I said I would go along.

"Good. Slack always loves to take me. It gives him an opportunity to see his mother."

"He's a strange boy. I discovered him feeding the pigeons."

"Oh, so you've already met him. They say he's 'lacking,' but in some things he's quite bright. It's just that he's different. I think people underestimate him. He came to us when he was about eleven. He had found a baby robin and was looking after it. Jago noticed him and thought he'd be useful to look after the pigeons, which at that time were being attacked by some disease—and you remember the legend about when the pigeons go, the Kellaways will lose the island. Not that Jago would believe it, but he says he respects superstitions because other people believe in them. Well, the pigeons thrived immediately under Slack's care. There's no doubt he's got a way with birds. Come. Let's find him now."

Slack was nursing a pigeon. "She have hurt her leg," he murmured. "But I can heal it. You see, there be this power in me."

Gwennol smiled. "I want you to row Miss Ellen and me over to the mainland tomorrow, Slack. That's if the sea's like it is today."

"I'll have the boat for 'ee, Miss Gwennol."

Gwennol and I went back through the courtyards.

When I retired that night I felt drowsy. But as I was about to get ready for bed, I noticed my mother's sketchbook. So I set the candle down on a little table that stood beside the bed and started to look through it.

She had had considerable talent. One could feel the antiquity of those gray stone castle walls which she had painted so realistically. There was a lovely picture of Blue Rock Island, and there were some portraits too. One depicted a plump child with large inquiring eyes. The caption read: "E. Aged Two." Why yes, I recognized myself. I turned the pages. There was Jago—two portraits of him, facing each other. How she had caught the resemblance! They were like two different people. Strangely enough, he was smiling in both of them, but in one the smile was benign and in the other the eyes had a veiled, almost sinister look; and there was a certain twist about the mouth, as though he were plotting something evil.

Could my mother have been saying, "Beware, there are two Jagos"? I felt uneasy, because I was beginning to enjoy his company more than I cared to admit to myself.

I turned the pages and came to another double portrait. In one of these I saw a rather demure girl, her hair in braids. She was looking up as though in prayer and she held a Bible in her hands. In the picture on the opposite page, her face peeped out from a curtain of unbound hair; the eyes were wild, yet pleading, and the expression was tortured; she looked as though she were trying to tell some secret and did not know how. It was a horrible picture.

Under it was the initial S.

I was quite shaken. I knew this was the S.K. who had written her message on the cupboard wall. Who, I asked myself, was she?

Sleep had completely deserted me. I turned over the pages and studied the peaceful landscapes, hoping they would soothe me. But instead an even greater shock came from that sketchbook.

I gasped in amazement when I first saw it, for there on a page was the room of my dream! The fireplace, the chimney seats, the rocking chair, the painting of the storm at sea . . . everything!

One thought kept hammering on my brain: The phantom room

really existed; my mother had seen it. What did this mean? What *could* it mean? I felt that my mother's spirit was trying to get in touch with me through her sketchbook.

She had seen Jago as two different people; the sinister portrait had taken me right back to those awful moments in the house in Finlay Square. What did she know of Jago? And who was S., who could look so demure and so wild?

But it was the picture of the room which haunted me. One thing I could now be sure of: The dream room existed. But where?

I SLEPT fitfully that night and oddly enough I did not have the dream. The first thing I did the next morning was to pick up the sketchbook. Yes. It was really there—the room I knew so well.

After breakfast Gwennol came to my room to see if I was ready.

"I've been looking through my mother's sketchbook," I said. "Look at this picture. Do you know the room?"

She was puzzled. "Should I? It's just an ordinary room."

An ordinary room! How odd to hear the room that has been haunting me so described! I wanted to say: That room haunts me. If I could only find it, I might understand why I dream about it and always feel such an overwhelming dread. But I found it difficult to talk about, so I merely said, "I wondered if it might be in the castle."

She shook her head as though vaguely surprised that I should make so much of such an insignificant matter.

At that moment there was a knock on the door. I called, "Come in," and Slack entered.

"What's wrong?" asked Gwennol, surprised to see him upstairs.

" 'Tis just I thought we'd best get an early start because of the tide," he said.

"You're right. We're almost ready," Gwennol replied.

On impulse I showed the sketch to Slack and asked, "Have you ever seen that room?"

He stared tensely at the page and did not look at me. It seemed as though a shutter had dropped over his eyes. "I can't tell 'ee about a picture room, miss," he said slowly.

"My dear Ellen." Gwennol laughed. "You're becoming obsessed. Your mother sketched a cozy room and that's all there is to it."

Slack nodded. I thought, He is stupid after all.

"Let's be going," said Gwennol. "Is everything ready, Slack?" They exchanged a glance that seemed to have a meaning from which I was excluded.

"Everything be done and we'm ready to go," said Slack.

We left the castle and went to the shore where the boats were moored. The sea was calm and the boat skimmed lightly over the water. There was a seraphic smile on Slack's face, for he clearly loved the task. He looked different from the way he had when I asked him about the room. I watched him—slack-baked—not finished off, his mother had said. It was an apt description of him in a way. His hands were strong, yet like a child's; his eyes were child-like too, except when the shutter came down.

In due course we ran ashore on a beach, and then made our way to the inn. Mrs. Pengelly came out, beaming with delight. "Welcome to 'ee, Miss Gwennol, Miss Ellen. You'll be wanting horses?"

"I shall," said Gwennol. "And you, Ellen?"

I said I would, for I thought it would be pleasant to call at Hydrock Manor.

"Well, you go to the stables then, Augustus, and tell your father the ladies be here and what they do want. Then come to the kitchen, where I'll have a tidbit for 'ee. And what refreshment would the ladies be looking for? A glass of wine while you'm waiting?"

Gwennol asked, "Has anyone arrived at the inn yet?"

"No, Miss Gwennol. No one be here yet."

"We'll drink a glass of wine then, please," she said.

We went inside to the parlor, and Mrs. Pengelly brought out her blackberry wine and some saffron cakes. We had not been there long when we heard the sound of a horse's hoofs.

Gwennol sat very still in her seat and a smile touched her face, making it not only striking but beautiful.

"In the parlor?" asked a voice which I recognized with pleasure as that of Sir Michael Hydrock.

As he entered, Gwennol rose and went to him, holding out both her hands, which he took and covered with both of his. Then he saw me and a smile of delighted recognition lit up his face.

"Miss Kellaway," he cried.

Gwennol looked astonished. "You . . . you know each other?"

"Yes," said Michael, advancing toward me. "How are you enjoying the island?" he asked.

"I'm finding it enormously interesting," I told him.

"I don't understand," said Gwennol rather impatiently.

"It's easily explained," Michael told her.

And I added, "When I was waiting to come to the island I got lost in Hydrock Manor's woods. Sir Michael rescued me."

"I see," said Gwennol coolly.

"You must come to the manor with us," said Michael warmly.

"Thank you. I should love that."

"Are the Pengellys' horses ready for you?" he asked.

"I've already ordered them," said Gwennol, "but Ellen may have other plans."

"As a matter of fact," I answered, "it had occurred to me that I might call at the manor."

"And I," he said, "should have been very hurt if you hadn't. But now you've lived in the castle. We're not as grand as that."

"The manor is enchanting," I said.

"It's the most beautiful house I've ever seen," added Gwennol fervently.

We went into the yard, where the horses were ready for us. Off we rode, and in a short time we were at the manor.

"By the way, Miss Kellaway," asked Michael, "how's the ankle?"

"Fine, thank you. By the next morning I wouldn't have known anything had happened to it."

"You hurt your ankle, then?" asked Gwennol.

I told her about it; she listened intently, but her expression was less pleasant.

We went into the hall, and I felt the same peace I had experienced when I was there last. "There's something so friendly about this house," I commented.

81

"We all feel it," said Gwennol shortly.

"Yes," added Michael. "There's a saying in the family that Hydrock Manor will either welcome or reject you. It certainly seems to welcome you, Miss Kellaway. I should like to show it to you. You don't mind, Gwennol? Gwennol is a very old friend," he told me. "She knows the manor as well as I do."

"I'd love to see it," I assured him.

And Gwennol put in, "I can't see enough of the place."

"Look at that armor on the walls," he said. "Those breastplates were worn by ancestors of mine during Cromwell's time. These pewter vessels have been used by the family for hundreds of years. I like to keep everything as it was as far as possible."

"Jago is like that too, isn't he, Gwennol?" I said, for I was anxious that she should join the conversation. I realized by this time that her feelings toward Michael were warmer than those of friendship. The softness of her eyes and mouth was rare with her.

"Jago would like to go back to feudal days," she said sharply. "He'd like to be not only the lord of the manor but of us all."

"He's proud of the island," I said. "He's done so much for the people."

"My dear, they're afraid to say a word against him. He could turn them out of their homes tomorrow if they offended him."

In his easy manner Michael diverted the subject from Jago by saying, "Come and look at the chapel."

We crossed the hall and ascended a spiral staircase.

"There are lots of documents in the vaults under the chapel," said Michael. "Someday I intend to compile a history of the family. And Gwennol has promised to help me."

"There's nothing I should like more," she said, becoming animated. She almost looked as though she would like to get down to the task immediately.

There were about twelve pews in the chapel, and on the altar was a very fine cloth, worked, he told me, by his mother. He spoke then of his mother's illness and her untimely death when he was just ten years old.

I was deeply moved by the story, as was Gwennol. Her eyes

never left Michael as he talked. I thought, Yes, she is in love with him. I'm in the way. I ought to have gone off on my own exploring the countryside. Just because he's too polite to show he doesn't really want me, I had imagined he was eager for me to come.

"Now," he said, "we'll go to luncheon."

"How kind of you," I said. "Gwennol was expected, but I . . ."

"We're delighted to have you," said Michael warmly. "Yes, Gwennol was expected. I had the message," he told her. Then turning back to me, he explained, "We've an excellent method of communication. Slack sends messages over by carrier pigeon. We have trained pigeons here too."

I enjoyed the view from the dining room, with its window looking out over smooth lawns. It seemed to me that Michael Hydrock was completely contented. I could not help comparing him with Jago—that restless spirit—whose changing moods and unpredictability were half attractive, half repelling, but always intriguing.

After luncheon Michael accompanied us to the inn, where Slack was waiting. "Come again soon," said Michael, and there was no doubt that I was included in that invitation.

Gwennol was silent as we were rowed back, and I sensed that she was suspicious of me.

When we reached the island we left Slack to tie up the boat and made our way to the castle. Gwennol said, "How strange that you should have met Michael and not mentioned it." Then she gave a little laugh. "You apparently didn't hurt your ankle badly. It must have been one of those convenient little twists." And before I could express my indignation she had turned and run into the castle.

Jago looked at me reproachfully. We were at dinner that night and he had asked how I had been spending the day.

"What, Ellen, deserting us for the mainland already? And where did you go?"

"To Hydrock Manor. I'd met Sir Michael before."

Jago put down his knife and fork and gazed at me. I was aware of Jenifry's eyes on me too.

I explained how I had hurt my ankle.

83

"It was one of those temporary twists," said Gwennol.

I detected a note of sarcasm in her voice. And I realized that this information had disturbed both Jago and Jenifry.

Jago said, "Tomorrow I will show you more of the island. I've been thinking, by the way, that you should practice rowing. You have done it before?"

"Yes, but not at sea; on a river, which I suppose was different."

"It's the same really," said Gwennol, "only you have to be more careful at sea—mostly because of the weather."

"I'll take you out tomorrow," said Jago. "Until you've practiced enough, always have someone with you. Slack will take you where you want to go. But just don't go alone at first."

I was exhausted when I went to my room that night. I had enjoyed visiting Hydrock Manor even though the day had been spoiled by Gwennol's jealousy. I should have to stay away from the manor from now on, which was a pity because it had been rather comforting to have such a pleasant friend on the mainland.

I was sitting at my dressing table plaiting my hair by candlelight when there was a knock on the door. I started up in dismay. I wasn't sure why, but always when the candles were lighted in this room I felt uneasy. There was a further knock and the door was quietly opened. Jenifry stood there holding a candle.

"I want to have a word with you," she said. She set down the candle and drew up a chair, so that we were both sitting at the dressing table. "It's about Gwennol and Michael Hydrock. He's one of the most eligible bachelors in the neighborhood. He and Gwennol have always been good friends. In fact, general opinion has been that they will make a match of it. But then Gwennol came back today more than a little upset.

"His is a great family," she went on. "There are some who wouldn't think Gwennol quite suitable. The Hydrocks are so proud of their ancestry." Her lips curled in contempt. "That woman Mrs. Hocking, for one. She was his nurse, and still clucks over him, pampers him. Nobody but the daughter of a duke or an earl is good enough for her dear Michael."

"I would think the Kellaways are good enough for anybody."

"Yes, but there's the story of our illegitimate branch, of our having something of the devil in us, and although Michael Hydrock might not believe it, he'd be aware of what people were thinking."

She moved closer to me, but I could not look at her face. If I did, I knew I should see the evil expression which I had caught in the mirror on my first night.

"He was very taken with you, wasn't he?" she said. "I daresay he found you more sophisticated than most of the country girls he meets. And although you're a Kellaway too, yours is the pure strain, isn't it?"

I felt exasperated. "Listen," I said almost fiercely. "I was lost in his woods and he took me back to the inn. I met him again with Gwennol and lunched at his house. I like him. I like his house. There's nothing more in it than that. I am not trying to snatch him from under the nose of an ambitious mother with a marriageable daughter. And I can assure you I am not desperate for a husband."

She rose, and as she stood there I shivered. She was holding the candle in front of her, and it had the effect of lighting up her face while the rest of her was shadowy; the image in the mirror was like a disembodied face. She looked malevolent.

"From what I know of Michael Hydrock," I told Jenifry, "he is a man who will make his own choice."

At that she said good night, and when the door had shut on her, I was certain that there was something more than her fear for her daughter's happiness that had filled me with apprehension. It was as though she were warning me.

That was the night I found the first of the notebooks.

I was so disturbed by Jenifry's visit that I knew it would be foolish to try to sleep, so I decided I would write a letter to Esmeralda. There was a charming desk in my room, with a sloping top covered with leather and inlaid with ivory. I had already put my writing materials inside it. Now I tried to open it but it had jammed, and so I forced it open. As I did so a flap, which I had not noticed in the top compartment, opened and a notebook fell out.

I picked it up and saw that inside was written in a childish hand, "S.K. Her Book." This, I assumed, was the same S.K. who had scratched words in the cupboard and whose picture my mother had painted.

I flicked through the book, and some paragraphs caught my eye.

"I hate it here. I wish I could escape. I am supposed to be writing an essay called 'Life on an Island.' Miss Homer said I shall stay in my room until it is done, but I'm writing this instead. It is a secret and I shall not show her. She wants me to write about crabs and jellyfish and tides and scenery, but I don't care about those things. I'm going to write about Them and Myself. My father hates me. My stepmother doesn't like me very much either. Nobody likes me except Baby and she's too young and silly to know. My stepmother said to me, 'Look at your little sister. Isn't she a love?' I said, 'She's only a half sister. That's not a real one.' Everyone comes and looks at Baby and says how lovely and good she is, even if she has been screaming just minutes before. I bet when I was a baby they didn't say I was wonderful.

"I wish I could *see* my father. He doesn't want to see me, but he sees Baby now and then. The reason he doesn't like me has something to do with my mother. He didn't like her. I heard one of the servants say that. She died when I was seven. Then I became very naughty, like the time I threw Miss Homer's hair dye over the floor and she didn't want anyone to know she used it.

"When my stepmother came it was better for a while. But I knew my father only spoke to me because Stepmother asked him to. Baby came then and everybody made a fuss of her and nobody cared about me. My stepmother only cared about Baby and gave up trying to make my father like me."

I wanted to know more, but the remaining pages were blank. So I put the notebook back into its place and closed the desk. I was in no mood for writing to Esmeralda now.

I TOOK the oars and Jago sat opposite me. We were going to row to the bird sanctuary. It was a beautiful day with a still sea.

"It's the best time of the year," said Jago, "before the October gales set in. They can be very wild. On the other hand, they might not come at all. There's only one thing that's certain about our weather and that's its unpredictability. You row very well, Ellen. You're going to be quite a champion."

"If I'm going to stay here for a while that will be necessary."

"*If* you're going to stay. My dear Ellen, I hope you are going to stay here a very long time." I looked up and was disturbed by his intense gaze. "You're beginning to love the island, confess it."

"I'm finding it very interesting, yes."

Sanctuary Island lay before us, a green hump in the ocean. "Run her onto the beach here," he said.

I was proud that I was able to do so with competence, because I had an absurd desire to shine in his eyes.

Jago secured the boat and we started to walk up a slope to a sort of plateau. "Look at those choughs over there," he said. "There are hundreds of them. We get the occasional storm petrel. She just lands to lay her eggs and then departs."

"I'm surprised you find time to be interested in these birds."

"I find time for anything I want to do."

He put his arm through mine, ostensibly to help me up the slope, but I felt he was conveying the fact that he was going to find a great deal of time to spend in my company.

"Let's sit here," he said. He had brought a traveling rug, and now he spread it on the grass. We looked over the sea to Blue Rock Island, and I thought I could make out the artist's house. It was sheltered by tall trees and was not far from the beach.

"Tell me," I said suddenly, "who is S.K.? I think she must have occupied the room I'm staying in."

Jago wrinkled his brow, then laughed. "You must be referring to Silva Kellaway, your half sister."

"Then I'm the Baby referred to. Oh, you see, I found one of her notebooks, and she had written something about her stepmother and a baby. How strange! My sister!"

"Your half sister."

"You mean we shared the same father, and the stepmother she mentions is my mother?"

"Yes. Poor Silva, her life was tragic. And her death—for it's almost certain that she was drowned."

"*Almost* certain?"

"Her body was never found, although her boat was washed up on the island . . . empty."

"How very sad. How old was she when this happened?"

"It was about a year and a half ago. She'd be twenty-eight now."

"And she lived at the castle—in my room—until then?"

"Yes. No one knew why she took a boat out on such a stormy night, as she did. It was a crazy thing to do, but she was crazy."

"You mean she was . . . *mad?*"

"Oh no, just unbalanced. She'd be very docile for months on end and then suddenly she would create scenes."

"Do go on. I'm longing to hear everything about the family."

"There's not a lot to tell. Your father married twice. His first wife was Effie and she had Silva. Effie and your father used to quarrel violently. He was not fond of Silva. It might have been that he was disappointed because she wasn't a boy. I don't know. In any case, he could hardly bear to look at her. Then Effie died of pneumonia and after a year or two your father went to London on business and came back with your mother. She couldn't settle down either. Then you were born and that seemed to reconcile them, but only for a little while. Your father was not an easy man to live with. She went off, taking you with her. That was a surprise, for she had left no warning."

"Poor little Silva. No wonder she was unbalanced, as you say."

"I wish we could have known why she left, where she was going, and indeed could have some proof that she was drowned."

"If the boat was washed up empty, isn't that proof enough?"

"It is to some. But others will see an unnatural hand even in the most ordinary happenings."

"Well, if she is alive, I want to meet her. All those childhood years when I longed for a sister—and had to do with Esmeralda—I really had one! I wish I'd grown up with her in the castle."

He leaned toward me suddenly and gripped my hand. "So do I, Ellen. Then we'd already be firm friends."

A gull shrieked overhead as though he were mocking us. But Jago did not seem to hear. His expression had grown tender.

At that moment I was aware that we were being watched. I turned sharply and saw that a man was standing behind us. Jago noticed him too. "Why, it's our neighbor, the artist who lives on Blue Rock Island," he said.

We rose to our feet as the man advanced. "Ellen," said Jago, "let me present James Manton. Manton, this is Miss Kellaway."

He bowed. "I'm glad to meet you," he said. "I just rowed over here to make a few sketches. The light's so good today, and just look at that sea. I hope you're enjoying the island, Miss Kellaway."

I said I was finding it fascinating.

He watched a bird soar aloft into the distance, and then with a "Good day to you!" he went back the way he had come.

"Manton paints a lot of bird pictures. He's rather good with them. Well, Ellen, are you sufficiently rested to row us back?"

"Yes. I don't feel the least bit tired."

Taking my hand, he ran down the slope with me to our boat.

When we reached the Far Island, Jago said, "Before we go back to the castle I'm going to take you to old Tassie, the wisewoman of the island. She'll tell your fortune. You'll like that. All women do."

We walked up the incline to a small cottage surrounded by an herb garden. An old woman appeared at the door.

"Good day, Tassie," said Jago. "I've brought my ward along to see you. This is Miss Ellen Kellaway."

"Good day to 'ee, my lady." Her face was very wrinkled and her bright black eyes reminded me of a monkey's, sharp and shrewd; she wore a gray crocheted shawl, and the black cat who rubbed himself about her skirts fitted the scene perfectly.

We stepped into a cluttered room with a faint pungent odor. There was a chimney seat on either side of the hearth, and the cat, who had followed us in, leaped into a basket and sat watching us. There were pots and pans filled with mysterious substances, and bunches of herbs were hanging from the beams.

"Ellen is anxious to learn about the island, Tassie," said Jago. "And I told her she couldn't know much until she'd visited you. What have you got to tell her?"

"Come close and sit down near me, my dear," said Tassie. She held my hands and gazed into my face. Jago was watching her intently, and I was as much aware of him as of her.

"Oh my life, I do see much here for you. There's good and there's bad. You've had tragedy. Now there's two roads open to 'ee. You must be sure and take the right one."

"How shall I know which is the right one?" I asked.

"There's one beside 'ee to guide 'ee. You'm come home to your family and 'tis a good thing. You'm facing the right way now, but a little while back 'twasn't so. Your fate will soon be settled, for 'tis right at hand."

"You'd better listen to Tassie," said Jago. "She has special powers and is greatly respected here. All the girls come to her."

" 'Tis for the young lady to take the right course and she'll be happy for the rest of her days. She'll have fine sons and a daughter or two to bring comfort to her."

Jago was smiling at me now, his eyes gleaming, and I thought, He is really falling in love with me!

The prospect excited me and at the same time made me apprehensive. I knew that his emotions would be fierce, for there were no half measures about him. From the moment I had seen him at the Carringtons' I had been aware of him . . . physically.

Tassie was telling me what she did for the young people of the island. "If it's a love potion they'll be wanting, I give it to them. And I look into their futures." She moved closer to me. "I can help you to lift a spell that be cast on you, to turn aside an evil wish. So come to me, young maid, if you be in trouble."

"That's more than an invitation, Ellen," said Jago. "It means that Tassie accepts you as an islander." He placed several coins on the table, and I saw an avaricious gleam in the old woman's eyes. Then we came out into the autumn sunshine.

"She's a colorful character, our Tassie, don't you think? And you must admit she gave you a pleasant fortune," said Jago.

"She seemed to be well paid for it."

He looked at me sharply. "Well, didn't she deserve it?"

"If clients are going to pay according to what they're told, isn't that a temptation to the seer to be overoptimistic?"

"I don't think she was about you. In fact, I know you're going to have good fortune."

"Don't forget that rests with me."

"But you're a wisewoman, Ellen. I knew it from the moment I saw you. Joking aside, Tassie *is* a colorful character."

"Do you really believe in her special powers?"

"I'm like other people. I'm willing to believe that she helped me if I get what I want."

"And if you don't?"

"My dear Ellen, I always make sure I do."

We returned to the castle and I retired to my room. But when I lit the candles and the shadows began to form, I started to brood about the new aspect in my relationship with Jago. He hated my going to the mainland and did not want my friendship with Michael Hydrock to grow any more than Gwennol and Jenifry did; but was I right in thinking it was for a different reason?

Could it really be that Jago Kellaway wanted to be my husband!

THE next day I went to find Slack.

He was in the courtyard feeding an injured sea gull. "Her can't fly, Miss Ellen. Found her cowering on the cliffs, I did. Her wing be damaged and I reckon her had had no food for days. 'Twasn't only that—birds be terrible cruel one to the other. If one be maimed or be different, they peck it to death. People be that way sometimes. They don't always like them as are different."

"What a good thing you found it," I said.

"See, I've splinted her wing. But I don't want her flying yet. I want to feed her . . . slow-like at first. There now, my pretty, Slack 'ull look after 'ee, you see."

"I've come to ask if you'll come out in a boat with me," I said. "I'll do the rowing. I've promised Mr. Jago that I won't take a boat out alone . . . yet."

The fact that I trusted him enough to ask him to go with me delighted him. And as I got to know Slack I realized that his great pleasure in life was looking after people.

I rowed around the island.

"You be proper good with the oars, Miss Ellen," he said. " 'Tis safe enough if you don't go too far out to sea. But you do know how quick a breeze can arise; in fifteen minutes the sea can get all angry and ruffled up. That's what 'ee've got to watch for if 'ee be going to the mainland."

"Do you hear of many people drowning?"

Once again I saw the shutter come down over his eyes. "There have been," he said.

"There was Silva," I suggested. "You knew her, of course."

"Yes, I did know her."

"Just think. She was my half sister and I never knew her. I should love to have you tell me what you know about her."

"She were terrible fond of birds and little things," he said.

"Ah." So there had been a bond between them. I had guessed that. "Did she often come and help you feed them?" I asked.

He looked suddenly happy. "They'd perch on her shoulder. Kind and gentle she were to them. She'd talk and talk, like I wasn't there, and then she'd smile and say, 'I do run on, don't I, Slacky?' "

"And was she very unhappy?"

He looked frightened. "Yes, her used to cry and that was terrible. I never saw anybody cry like Miss Silva did. It was laughing and crying all at once, and she'd say she hated the castle and Mr. Jago and all of them."

"Do you know why she took the boat out that stormy night?"

He nodded, his lips pressed together. I believe he does know something, I thought.

"Did she go out in that boat because she was running away from something? You know, don't you, Slack?"

"You might say she were running away," he said slowly.

"If she went out on a wild night, she must have wanted to kill herself. No boat could survive in such a heavy sea, could it?"

"You can never be sure, Miss Ellen, what can happen to boats on the sea. . . . I pray she be happy in the new life."

His pale face was impassive again. I was convinced he knew more about Silva than he had betrayed. Perhaps when I had won his confidence he would tell me.

The "Ellen" Is Lost

JAGO was busy. He personally supervised the farms and arranged the island's business transactions, but he usually managed to spend some time of the day with me. We rode around the island, and he introduced me to the farmers and shopkeepers, the innkeeper, the parson, the doctor and all who made up the life of the island. We were growing closer. Almost against my will I began to feel I needed a strong dose of his society every day.

I had now become a good oarswoman, and he was delighted. One morning he took me down to the cove and there was a freshly painted boat with *Ellen* on the side. I was very proud of her.

After that I took the *Ellen* out by myself every day. I never went far out to sea, but usually skirted the island and put in at some bay which I had not visited before.

The island was growing on me. The people accepted me and I was beginning to feel that I belonged. But I could not help feeling that it was important for me to know what had happened to those vague figures of the past. I believed if I could discover what had happened to Silva, I would have a key to the whole situation.

Jago never wanted to speak of her. He had dismissed her as unbalanced, a foolish girl who had been unable to adjust to life and had found a dramatic way of ending it.

My father—who was hers also—had hated her. In fact, when I thought about it, he seemed to have disliked everyone, except perhaps his secretary-valet, Fenwick. Suddenly I had an idea: if I could have a word with Fenwick, I might discover something about my family. But how could I find him? When I asked Jago where he lived he said merely, "What can Fenwick tell you that I can't?" Perhaps he was right, but secretary-valets often know more about their employers than do their close relations.

Each day, weather permitting, one of the boats went over to the mainland to collect mail. One day, while I was pondering all this, I was delighted to receive a letter from Esmeralda.

She said the castle sounded wonderful and she longed to see it. Her parents had given several balls for her and she had met a very pleasant young man named Freddy Bellings. There was a good deal about Freddy—the color of his eyes, the kind humor of his manner and the way in which he could make jokes without hurting anyone's feelings. I could see that Esmeralda was delighted with him.

"We see a great deal of the Carringtons," she went on. "No one mentions Philip, but Lady Emily looks a little sad at times. She asks me how you are and hopes you are happy. Someone else asks about you. Rollo. He wanted to know where you had gone and whether you were settling down. I had just received your letter about the castle and everything. He was most interested."

I was so glad Esmeralda had found her Freddy. I was surprised, though, that Rollo should be interested in what I was doing. Perhaps he repented of his harshness to me. However, it was an indication of how much I had grown away from the past when my thoughts were almost immediately back with the problem of the moment: how to find Fenwick and talk to him about my family.

The Pengellys would be likely to know his whereabouts. So I decided to go to the inn and see what I could discover.

The sea was calm and I was now well practiced enough to row myself over to the mainland.

When I reached the inn Mrs. Pengelly brought out the inevitable homemade wine and saffron cakes, and I asked if she had any idea where I might find Mr. Fenwick.

"Well," she said, "he did leave the island when your father died. He retired to a cottage down in Fallerton, a small village but six or seven miles from here."

"I want to talk to him about my father."

She looked alarmed. " 'Twould only distress you, maybe, to hear how very ill he were at the end, Miss Ellen."

"Naturally I want to hear about my family. It seems so difficult to get people to tell me. Surely you must have known Silva."

"Oh yes. She were a strange girl. Wild-like—used to go out in the wind and lose herself for hours so we'd think something had happened to her. Seemed like she wanted to put us all in a turmoil. We did our best, your mother and I, and when you came along Miss Silva were better in a way. She were fond of you. But your father wouldn't have her near him; I never knew such a thing. Sometimes I'd hear her sobbing and I'd go and try to comfort her. Then she'd get up and dance around, laughing at me. My dear life, that were a time!"

"It was very odd that she should go off as she did."

A wary look came into Mrs. Pengelly's eyes, and I realized that even she knew something about Silva's mysterious disappearance, something that she was not going to tell me. But at the moment I was obsessed by the thought of finding Fenwick.

"I'll have one of the horses and go to Fallerton," I said. "What was the name of Fenwick's house, do you remember?"

"I can't tell 'ee that, Miss Ellen, but Fallerton be naught but a village. If you ask, someone will be bound to know."

Outside, as I was about to mount a horse, Michael Hydrock rode by. "Hello, Miss Kellaway, what a pleasant surprise!"

"I'm just off to Fallerton," I told him.

"Why, that's on my way. I'll come with you." He turned his horse alongside mine. It would have been rude not to accept his company, which, had it not been for those unfortunate scenes with Gwennol and Jenifry, I should have been very happy to accept. Well, they would both be on the island today, so I could give myself up to the pleasure.

"What do you want to do in Fallerton?" he asked.

"I'm trying to find a Mr. Fenwick who for many years was secretary-valet to my father. Perhaps I can find out from him why my father never got in touch with me."

"I have heard that Charles Kellaway had rather an unforgiving nature. Wouldn't it be better to let sleeping dogs lie?"

"I don't feel like that. I have a burning desire to know."

"Well, then, let's see if we can find Fenwick."

It was pleasant riding across the country which Michael Hydrock knew so well, and we soon came to the small village of Fallerton.

We saw a man fixing his horse's nose bag, and Michael called to him, "Do you know a Mr. Fenwick hereabouts?"

The man looked up. "Well, sir," he said, "if you do mean John Fenwick as took Mulberry Cottage, he have gone."

"Now where would Mulberry Cottage be?" asked Michael.

"Just follow the street and turn right and you'll see Mulberry. A bit of land there is to that place. He took over the market garden; but he weren't cut out for growing vegetables and flowers, he said. So he sold the place and moved away."

We thanked our informant and went to take a look at Mulberry Cottage. A rosy-faced woman came to the door. Yes, they'd bought the property from Mr. Fenwick, and they'd been here these past six months. No, she had no idea where he had gone.

Michael suggested we refresh ourselves at the local inn, which we found without any trouble. A sign creaking over the door said THE CORN DOLLY. We went in and ordered cider and meat pies.

When the innkeeper's wife brought us our food, Michael asked her about Mr. Fenwick, but she had no idea where he had gone.

"Not a very profitable morning," said Michael. "But never mind, I'll make inquiries. What do you think of the old Corn Dolly?"

"It's charming, but what an odd name."

"You saw the sign as we came in?"

"Yes—it looked like a bundle of corn tied up to look like a doll."

"That's exactly what it is. At the end of the harvest the people make these corn dollies and hang them in their houses. They're supposed to bring a good harvest the next year."

"This reminds me in a way of the Polcrag Inn. The open fireplace, the oak beams . . ."

"They haven't an earthenware lamp like this," said Michael, picking up a candlestick-shaped object from the center of the table. "See this hole at the top?" he went on. "A cupful of oil can be poured through that and then they insert a wick which they call a purvan. I like to see them keeping up the old customs. You don't see many of these Stonen Chills about now."

I picked it up and examined it. I said it was quaint, but my mind was really on Fenwick. I was bitterly disappointed that our search had been fruitless, and Michael sensed this.

"Cheer up," he said, patting my hand. "I promise I'll find Fenwick for you. When I learn something I'll send you a message by carrier pigeon. Gwennol and I often communicate that way."

"Thank you. It's good of you to be so helpful."

We left the Corn Dolly, and when we came in sight of the coast I was dismayed to see that a little way out the white horses were putting in an appearance.

"It's an offshore wind," said Michael. "Nothing much. They'll get you back, but it would be advisable to start at once."

"But I rowed myself over," I said.

"Oh." His expression changed and became anxious.

By the time we reached the Polcrag Inn I could see more of the white-crested waves, and Michael insisted that he would row me back. "You need a man's hands on the oars in this tetchy kind of sea," he said. He organized everything. He arranged for the *Ellen* to be taken to the island by one of the inn men, and he hired a slightly stronger boat than the *Ellen* and in it he rowed me over.

"You'll come to the castle?" I asked after we got out of the boat and were standing together on the shore.

"I don't think I will. I should get back."

"You've been so kind to me. Thank you."

"It's been the greatest pleasure," he said, and took my hand. Then he jumped back into the boat, waved, and took the oars.

As I went up the incline toward the castle I met Jenifry. I knew by her manner that she had seen our arrival and had watched him hold my hand when he said good-by.

I wondered if Jenifry would tell Gwennol what she had seen.

The next day Gwennol went to the mainland, and it occurred to me that I might call on Tassie. Perhaps she would have different things to tell me if Jago were not present.

She was sitting at the door of her cottage, and her wrinkled old nutcracker face screwed into a smile as I approached. "Come in," she said, and I followed her.

Logs were burning in the fireplace, and the pungent smell of herbs seemed stronger than it had on that previous occasion. "And what can I do for you today, miss?" she said with a smirk. "Would you like me to read the cards or look into the crystal ball?"

"You gave me a very good fortune last time I saw you," I replied. "Today I want you to tell me about someone else."

"Oh?" She cocked her head to one side.

"I want to know about my half sister, Silva," I said.

"Poor maid! Hers was a sad life. She often came to see me. Especially at the end. She had reason to then."

"What reason?" I asked excitedly.

"She was anxious about the future."

"People don't seem to want to talk about her."

" 'Tis natural. She could be lying at the bottom of the sea."

"Is that where you think she is, Tassie?"

She looked at me shrewdly. "The boat came in empty."

"Are you telling me she was really drowned?"

"I didn't say that, miss. I said the boat came back without her."

"What was she like, Tassie? Did she look like me?"

"Nay, she had a lot of yellow hair. She took after her mother. Nothing of the Kellaway in her. Can 'ee keep a secret?"

"Yes," I said eagerly. "I promise to."

"Her mother come to me afore Silva was born. She told me that she didn't want to bear that child. But bear it she did, and Silva was born to be unhappy perhaps and knew it."

"Tell me, Tassie, what happened just before Silva went away?"

"She came to see me, twice, in the week before she left. She said, 'Everything's going to change now. I shan't be here much longer, Tassie.' I read her palm, and I could find little for comfort there. But I didn't tell her that. If I see darkness hovering over someone, I don't always say so. 'You be watchful.' That's what I tell 'em to be. For who can say when the dark shadow of danger isn't hovering over us all, me . . . you . . . yes, you, Miss Ellen. And now there's nothing more I can tell 'ee about Miss Silva."

It was the signal for me to go. I put several coins into a bowl on the table and her shrewd eyes counted. "Come again, me dear, whenever you do feel the need," she said.

I thanked her and went out into the sunshine.

Two days later, as it was calm, I rowed over to the mainland once more. I was walking along the main street when a picture in one of the shopwindows caught my eye. It was a seascape—a sapphire-blue sea, and waves edged with white frills rolling gently on a golden shore—but what was so arresting was a cloud of white sea gulls rising and swooping above the water. The contrast of white and blue was dazzling. I must have that picture, I thought. It is so evocative of Sanctuary Island. Then it occurred to me that it would be an ideal Christmas present for Jago, and I was delighted.

I went into the shop and requested a closer look at the picture, entitled *The Gulls*. It was brought from the window and was reasonably priced. I would have it, I said.

While the transaction was taking place a man came from the back. It was James Manton, the artist. "Why, it's Miss Kellaway," he said. "So you are buying *The Gulls*. It's my painting."

"I am fascinated by it and I just felt I had to have it."

"You give me great pleasure. Are you taking it with you?"

"I thought I would."

"Did you come over alone?"

"Yes, and I'm keeping an eye on the sea so I don't get caught."

He laughed. "I have an idea," he said. "They can pack up the picture, and you and I will go and have tea at the inn. Then I'll carry the package to your boat."

So that was how I came to be sitting at the Polcrag Inn chatting with James Manton while we drank Mrs. Pengelly's strong brew and ate scones with jam and clotted cream.

"You knew my father, I believe," I said, for this seemed to me a heaven-sent opportunity to discover all I could.

His face hardened. "Yes, I knew him, but I would prefer not to talk about him to you. You could hardly hope to hear what you obviously want to from one whom he regarded as his enemy."

"He regarded you as such? I am sure he was wrong."

"Your father was a man who thought he was never wrong."

"I know his first wife died. . . ."

"Her life was wretched with him. He was a jealous and vindictive man. You can kill with cruelty, and that's what he did."

I shrank from the vituperation in his voice; he had seemed so placid before, a middle-aged man interested in his art. Now his hatred seemed to endow him with a vitality not apparent earlier.

"I knew his first wife and your mother too," he went on. "Your mother was an artist. She and I had a good deal in common, naturally. She could have been a fine artist, but your father despised that."

"Do you know what happened after my mother took me away?"

"He would never forgive her for running away, just as he never forgave Effie. . . ." He shook his head. "I shouldn't be speaking to you like this about your own father."

"What I want is to get at the truth, even if it's unpleasant."

"You must forgive me," he said. "I was carried away. Your father and I were not on speaking terms. He wouldn't have had me on the island. If I had put a foot there, someone would have been ordered to throw me off."

"Well, I hope that unhappy situation is over now."

"Oh, these family feuds get carried on for generations. They exist when the families don't know the original cause of the quarrel. I wouldn't go to Kellaway Island now. I'm content to stay at Blue Rock. I paint most of the time I'm there and then I go up to London to arrange exhibitions and see other people's."

"Well, I'm glad I saw *The Gulls* in the window and I'm glad it's your picture. I hope my appreciation of your work has done something to break through a little of the feud."

He smiled. "It's miraculous that you could be his daughter."

After I had rowed back I set up the picture in my room and studied it. Then I put it away, for if I was going to give it to Jago it would have to be a secret until Christmas.

IT WAS a golden afternoon later in October. I shipped the oars and let the *Ellen* drift on the tide. The day was so beautiful with the faint breeze on my face and that benign reddish sun up there. But then I began to notice that the clouds drifting slowly in the wind were taking on weird shapes. Dark shadows hovering over all of us, I remembered Tassie saying.

I had drifted nearly a mile out from the island, and as I moved the oars to prepare to go back, I stared down in sudden consternation. Water was seeping in.

I bent forward and ran my hand along the bottom of the boat. The water was still very shallow, and I felt something sticky, like sugar. As I watched, the water started to come in faster. The whole of the bottom was covered now. I seized the oars and frantically started to row for shore. How far off the island seemed!

Before I knew what had happened, the *Ellen* tipped to one side and I was in the water. By great good luck I managed to clutch at the keel as she turned upside down. She was floating and I was clinging to her with all my might. Temporarily I was safe, but I am not a strong swimmer and I could feel the water saturating my skirts. I could manage a few strokes, but could I reach the island, hampered as I was by my clothes?

My hold on the boat was precarious. "Help!" I shouted, but my voice sounded feeble.

"O God," I prayed, "let someone find me." And into my mind there flashed an image of Silva in another boat. I could feel my wet skirts wrapping themselves around my legs and dragging me down. I knew it would be disastrous to try for the shore, and yet with every passing second my hold on the *Ellen* was becoming weaker. My hands were growing numb. I can't cling much longer, I thought. Is this the end? No, no. Someone would come. Jago would come. Yes, it must be Jago. If only I could will him to be taking a stroll along the cliffs.

"Jago!" I called. "Jago!"

I would make an attempt to swim. I wouldn't die; I was going to fight for my life.

A shout came to me over the water. "Hold on, Miss Ellen. I be on the way."

Slack! He was near to me now. He swam like a fish.

" 'Tis all right, Miss Ellen. I be here now. . . . I be taking 'ee to the shore." His voice was soothing, comforting, as though I were a wounded bird.

I released my grip on the boat and for a moment was submerged. Then I was on the surface again and Slack's hand was under my chin, holding my head above the water.

The boat had moved away and the shore seemed a long way off.

How can this delicate boy bring me safely ashore? I wondered. Then I heard Jago's voice and knew everything would be all right.

I remember Jago's strong arms about me as he brought me onto the land and carried me to the castle. I remember being laid on my bed, then wrapped in blankets. Hot-water bottles were placed around me. I had had a terrible shock, I was told, and would have to stay in bed for a day or two.

I could not stop thinking of the terrifying moment when I had noticed that the boat was leaking.

Jago came and sat by my bed. "What happened, Ellen?"

"I was drifting away from the shore when suddenly I noticed that the boat was leaking."

"You must have struck something the last time you brought her in. The boats ought to be thoroughly examined before they're taken out. If anything had happened to you, my dear Ellen . . ." His face was distorted with emotion. "It's a lesson. We have to be very careful in future."

"I haven't said thank you for saving my life."

He rose and bent over me. "All the thanks I need is to see you safe." Then he stooped and kissed me.

I was glad that he went out then, for my own emotion was hard to hide.

Gwennol came to see me. "You don't swim very well, do you?" she said. "You must have been born lucky. You'll be more careful next time, won't you?"

"I really didn't realize I was being careless. Who would have thought a boat like the *Ellen* would spring a leak?"

"Any boat might," replied Gwennol. "She hasn't come in yet, so I expect she's drifting out to sea. I doubt she'll ever come back."

I sensed that she was longing to ask about that day I had spent on the mainland in Michael's company, for I was sure Jenifry would have told her she had seen us together. The restraint between us made us both uncomfortable and she didn't stay long.

Jenifry came, her face puckered into an expression of concern. "My goodness, you gave us all a turn. When Jago brought you in I thought you were dead."

"It would take a lot to kill me," I said.

"That's a comforting thought," she replied. "I've brought you a concoction of herbs my old nurse used to make. It's said to be very good for shock. Come, drink it. You'll be surprised how well you'll feel afterward."

I took the glass and set it down on the table beside my bed. "I couldn't drink anything now," I said. "I'm too tired."

"I'll leave you, then," she said. "But do take the tonic."

I nodded sleepily and she went quietly from the room.

There was something stealthy about her. I heard her footsteps going down the corridor and I picked up the glass and put it to my lips. I could smell the herbs and they were not unpleasant. Then I heard old Tassie's voice saying, "Be watchful."

I rose from my bed and took the glass to the window. I tipped out the liquid and watched it trickle down the castle walls.

The Island Necklace

THE next day I felt fully recovered and the first thing I did was to go to the dovecotes. Slack was there, as though expecting me.

I said, "Thank you for coming to my rescue, Slack."

"I may not be big, but I have the Power," he said. "I could have brought you in on my own."

"I'm sure you could, but Mr. Jago happened to be there."

"What happened, Miss Ellen? What did 'ee see?"

"See? Well, I suddenly noticed that the water was coming in. I thought there was something sticky there . . . like sugar."

"Sticky." His brows were wrinkled. "Like sugar, did 'ee say? I wonder what sugar could have been doing in the *Ellen*?"

"I expect I was wrong. I was so frightened. But I'm safe now. I can't tell you, Slack, how pleased I was to hear your voice."

" 'Twas the Power. 'Go along down to the shore. You be needed there,' I heard the voice telling me. 'Tis sometimes so when some little bird needs me. And don't 'ee fret, Miss Ellen. If you do need me, I'll know."

There was an almost fanatical look about the pale eyes.

The servants whispered of Slack, "Not all there." But there *was* something there, I was sure. I was glad he was my friend.

Understandably, for a week or more I had no desire to go to sea, certainly not alone. So I stayed on the island and took to going to the dovecotes when Slack was feeding the pigeons.

Once he said, "Did 'ee say sugar, Miss Ellen?"

I wondered what he meant for a moment; then I said, "Oh, you mean when the boat started to sink. Yes, I did think I saw what looked like sugar on the bottom of the boat."

His brow was furrowed. "How did sugar *come* to be there if it hadn't been put there? That's what I want to know."

"Slack, what are you thinking?"

"What if a hole were put there by someone 'as filled it with sugar? There's the Demerara kind . . . brown and coarse-grained, the kind that takes time to dissolve . . . specially in cold salt water. I've heard it said hereabouts more than once that it would hold a leak for a while if you happened to be not too far out to sea and supposing you had a packet of such with you . . . which is hardly likely." His eyes shone with the intensity of his feelings. "You wouldn't see it when you started out and when it did dissolve you have a hole, don't 'ee, what the sugar was bunging up. And the water could get in, couldn't it, where it couldn't before."

"You're suggesting that someone . . ."

"I don't rightly know, but terrible things can happen."

Did he really think that someone had tampered with the boat—*my* boat, which no one took out but me, knowing that sooner or later I should be at sea in it, and almost certainly alone! It was too farfetched, merely wild conjecture. Who would do such a thing!

"You must be careful, Miss Ellen. Mightn't be a boat next time."

"Next time?"

"I don't know what put that in me mouth, but I want to look after 'ee, you see . . . like I looked after Miss Silva."

"How did you look after her?"

He smiled. "She used to get fits of sadness and wildness, when she wanted to do things that would hurt her. Then she'd come and talk to me and the Power would show me how to soothe her."

"And that stormy night when she took a boat and tried to cross to the mainland . . . Did you know she was going?"

He hesitated, then said, "Yes, I knew she were going."

"Something must have happened to make her leave so hurriedly. What, Slack? You *must* know." He was facing my question with silence. I went on. "She was my sister. Just think of that."

"Her weren't like you, Miss Ellen. There couldn't have been two ladies who were so different. Her come to me afore her left and said, 'Slack, I be going away to a place where I'll be happy as I never could be here.' Then her gave me something. Her said, 'Keep these, Slack. Someone might want them someday.'"

"What did she give you?"

"I'll show 'ee."

He took me into the pigeon house, and in the cupboard there was a box which he unlocked and opened. Inside were two notebooks like the one I had found in the desk. A great excitement seized me. "Have you read them, Slack?"

"They be too much for me, Miss Ellen. I can read only little words. Then when you said about the sugar it was as though Miss Silva spoke to me. 'Let her read 'em, Slack.'"

He put the books into my hands. "I hope I be doing right."

"Thank you, Slack. I shall never forget what might have happened to me but for you," I told him earnestly.

"Master Jago were there, were he not? He just happened to be there. But I be mighty glad I were there too."

I did not think about what he meant until later. Meanwhile, I lost no time in shutting myself in my room with the notebooks.

The scrawly handwriting was a little more mature than that in the first notebook. It began: "Those were good days in a way when my stepmother was here with Baby, and when they went I was terribly lonely. At first I thought my father might like me more if there was no competition. How wrong I was! I found that out when he sent for me soon after my stepmother had gone. I was about fourteen. I had let myself imagine that he was going to tell me we would now become friends. All he wanted to tell me was that my latest governess had given notice. I was lazy, stupid and useless, but as he could not allow it to be known that he had a little savage in his household, he would engage a new governess. If he had any complaints from her, she'd be the last."

After a blank page the writing began again: "There is nowhere one can go without being aware of Jago. Since my father's stroke he has taken over completely. Yesterday I was in the garden picking roses. I turned suddenly and Jago was beside me. He always seems to be assessing me and that makes me nervous. He said, 'My sister, Jenifry, is coming to live at the castle with her daughter. They'll be company for you. You'll like that.' Jago has a way of telling you what you are going to like and daring you not to."

Another blank page. Then: "Gwennol is about eight. She is much brighter and prettier than I ever could be. I think Jenifry resents my being the daughter of the house. The idea of anyone's being jealous of me is comic! I'm glad they're here though. Gwennol shares my governess."

There was no more writing in that book. I picked up the second. "My life is so dull and I'm getting old. My father, I have been told, has said that he will not waste money on bringing me out. Jenifry always tries to push Gwennol forward in her social life. She has become quite friendly with Michael Hydrock, the most eligible bachelor in the neighborhood.

"She came to my room last night. She had been to a garden party at Hydrock Manor and she was all excited because Michael had been particularly nice to her.

" 'You're in love with him,' I said.

" 'Everybody's in love with him. Oh, wouldn't it be nice to have everyone in love with you?'

" 'As not one single person ever has been, I can't say.'

"Gwennol said, 'Poor Silva! I'm going to take you to Hydrock Manor. You know, *you* might meet someone there.'

"It's night and I can't sleep. So I'm writing. This room seems full of shadows. Perhaps that's because I've been so unhappy in it.

"Jago has changed. Two days ago we rode around the island and he talked about things in that way he has—as though it's the most important thing in the world. I was excited when we came back to the castle. Why is Jago suddenly becoming so interested in me?

"Yesterday Fenwick was sitting alone in the garden. 'Where is my father today?' I asked.

" 'He's having a day in bed, Miss Silva. He's a very sick man.'

" 'I'm sorry,' I said. 'I wish he would see me.'

"Fenwick shook his head. 'Whatever you do, miss, don't come to his room. That would just about finish him, the state he's in now.'

" 'Why does he hate me so? Did he want a son?'

" 'Maybe, but he's not one for children.' Fenwick shrugged his shoulders and seemed anxious to end our talk.

"I wouldn't *say* this to anyone, but I can write it. I think Jago is contemplating asking me to marry him."

Jago and Silva! The thought of it made me shudder.

I stared at the book in my hand. Why had Silva given the books to Slack? I read on: "I met *him* today. I went over to the mainland and he happened to come to the inn. He is so distinguished and handsome. I can't believe he could be interested in *me*. Why didn't we hire horses and go riding together, he said.

"What a day it was! I am so happy. We had cider and meat pies at the Corn Dolly, a beautiful, romantic place.

"He said, 'We must do this again.'

"Is it possible to be in love so soon, I wonder?"

Was it Michael Hydrock she was in love with? And was he really in love with her? Or was he merely being his charming self?

"Who wants to write when one is happy? He says he loves me. It is all so exciting. He says we shall be together and everything is going to be different."

Then I read: "The artist was on the mainland today. He asked the two of us to Blue Rock Island and he was very hospitable. He showed us his studio and his paintings. It was a lovely day, as it always is when we are together."

The rest of the pages were blank. Although I felt I had come closer to Silva, what had happened on that fateful night of the storm was more than ever a mystery.

He whose name she did not mention had told her he loved her. She was not the kind to imagine that someone loved her. In fact, I think it would be rather difficult for a man to convince her that he did. And then she had gone out in a boat to face almost certain death. Why? Had she, the child who had never felt wanted and who suddenly found someone she believed loved her at last, discovered that she had been bitterly deceived? Or had someone lured her to go out and risk her life?

My disquiet increased as a vision of Jenifry's face, when she had seen me saying good-by to Michael Hydrock after he had brought me home to the island, rose before me.

I put the books into a drawer and locked it. Then I asked myself if Slack, who knew something of Silva's story, had given them to me as some sort of warning?

JAGO rowed me over to Sanctuary Island.

"I've noticed you haven't been on the sea since the accident," he said. "But you don't feel afraid with me, do you, Ellen?"

"I've no doubt that if we overturned you'd bring me safely in."

We came to the island and he helped me out of the boat. He spread the traveling rug on the ground and we sat down.

"Ellen," he said very seriously, "I want to talk about the future."

"Your future?"

"And yours. In fact, I hope they will be intermingled."

I looked startled and he moved nearer to me.

"Since you came here, even the island has taken on a new meaning for me. I've always loved it, always been devoted to making it prosperous, but now everything seems so much more important."

My heart started to beat very fast. He put his arm about me and drew me to him.

"Ellen, I can't believe you're indifferent to me."

"Nobody could be indifferent to you, Jago."

"You mean they must either hate me or love me. Which is it for you, Ellen?"

"Of course I don't hate you."

"Then you must love me."

"I believe there can be a halfway feeling."

"I have no patience with halfway feelings. I love you, Ellen. I want you to marry me without delay. I want to go straight back to the church and put up the banns. I think it has to be three weeks before a wedding. Come."

He had sprung to his feet, but I remained seated. "You go too fast, Jago," I said. "This time last year I had not thought of marrying anyone. Then I became engaged and my fiancé was shot. Now you are suggesting that I marry you in three weeks."

He stared at me in amazement. "What has calculation of a year and weeks to do with it? I love you. You love me. Why wait?"

"Because I'm unsure."

"*You* unsure! You're not some silly simpering female who can be pushed as the wind blows."

"That's exactly so. Please, Jago, listen to me. I'm becoming fascinated by the island, but I don't want to hurry into anything. I don't *know* you well enough. You must understand that."

"Ellen, I thought you knew all you wanted to know about me. However, I know enough for both of us. I know that I love you, that nobody ever meant to me what you do, and that I wasn't really living until you came. Our marriage would be the best thing that could happen to us. Imagine us together for the rest of our lives on the island; we'd make it a paradise."

"Jago," I said, rising, "thank you for asking, but . . ."

He caught me and held me fast. The heavy lids had come down over his eyes, as though he did not want me to see all that was there. He kissed my lips then and I felt an immediate response to his passion. It had never been like that with Philip.

I broke free. "No, Jago," I said. "There's so much to consider. I still can't forget what happened in London."

"You'll soon see it as a fortunate release, my darling."

"It was not very fortunate for Philip."

"Let the past bury itself. You can't mourn him forever."

"No, I suppose all that will recede eventually, but I must be sure first. I love the island and I have so much enjoyed being with you. If we were never to meet again, I should be unhappy. When I'm with you I think I love you, but give me time to be sure, Jago. Let us go on for a little longer as we have been. Do this for me."

We were standing very close and he held my hands tightly. "Dearest Ellen," he said. "I will do anything you want." He picked up the rug and slung it over one arm; the other he slipped through mine as we went down to the boat.

He rowed me back in silence, and when we entered the castle he said, "Ellen, come to the parlor for a moment. There is something I want to give you." I went with him, and from a drawer he took out a necklace made of roughly hewn stones strung together on a golden chain. "It's the Kellaway Island necklace, and has been worn by our family's women for three hundred years," he said. "These stones—topaz, amethyst, carnelian and agate—were all found on the island, and similar ones can still be picked up if you search the shore at the right time."

I took the necklace in my hands.

"You will give it to our daughter and she will give it to hers, and so it goes on—a link through the ages."

"I think it is too soon for me to accept the necklace."

"That's not so." He took it from me and fastened it about my neck. His hands lingered there. "It becomes you. You are the rightful wearer. So wear it, Ellen. To please me."

I hesitated, for I thought of it as a betrothal ring. And I wasn't sure what I really felt about Jago. I wanted to be with him more than anyone else—yet I didn't really know him.

I left him and went to my room, and the first thing I did was to open my mother's sketchbook and look at the portraits of him. I had seen the kindly, protective Jago often. What of the other one?

Then I turned the pages. The book opened easily at the one I wanted. The room—the homely, pleasant room. Even as I looked at it, depicted so accurately there on paper, the feeling of doom remembered from the dream crept over me.

WHEN I went down to breakfast next morning Gwennol was there alone. She smiled at me in a more friendly fashion than she had done for some time, and I hoped that she realized that her jealousy regarding Michael Hydrock was unfounded. She asked if I had fully recovered from the accident; I told her I had.

"What an ordeal you've been through!" she said. "It's enough to put you off going to sea for a long time, I should imagine."

"Oh, I shall get over it. It doesn't do to give up just because something like that happens."

We chatted easily, and as we came out of the dining room, Slack ran into the hall holding a piece of paper in his hand.

"It's a message for me, is it, Slack?" Gwennol asked eagerly.

"No, Miss Gwennol. Not for you."

She looked bitterly disappointed and Slack stood uncertain for a moment. Then he said, "It be for Miss Ellen."

I took the paper. On it was written: "Fenwick found. I'll be at the inn this morning to take you to him. M.H."

I felt the color rise to my cheeks. If Fenwick would talk to me about my father, then I really would begin to learn something. I said, "Slack, will you row me over to the mainland this morning?"

"Why yes, Miss Ellen. In half an hour I'll be ready."

"Good." I hesitated, wondering whether to tell Gwennol what the message contained, but she turned and left the hall. It was too late to explain now, so I went to my room and changed.

Slack was ready with a boat and in a short time we were at sea, heading toward the mainland and the inn. Michael was there to greet me. "I've already told them to have a horse waiting," he said. "So we can start at once. The house is about eight miles inland, close to the moors. Shall we go?"

"Yes, I can't wait to see Fenwick."

We rode out of the courtyard together. It was a lovely crisp morning with a touch of frost in the air—rare in these parts.

"He wasn't easy to find. The man seemed determined to hide himself," said Michael. "But he has agreed to talk to you. I felt it best to warn him of your arrival."

We had left the sea behind and all at once the glory of the moors burst upon us. The bright wintry sun shone on the streams, which a few days before had been trickling over the boulders and were now frozen into immobility. We skirted the moor and came to the little hamlet of Karem-on-the-Moor. Fenwick's cottage was small but charming. Ivy climbed its walls, and a small path of

111

crazy paving ran from the front gate to the house. As we tethered the horses, the door was opened by a neatly dressed man.

Michael introduced us, said that he had business in the neighborhood and would call for me in about an hour.

Fenwick took me into a small room in which a fire was burning. We sat down and he asked, "Now what can I do to help?"

"There is a great deal you can tell me about my family. I can't understand why my father was so indifferent to us . . . to my half sister, to myself, to my mother."

"He was not indifferent to your mother nor to you. . . ."

"Why did she leave him?"

"She could not settle down on the island. She wanted him to take her away, but he said he had his duty there."

"But when she ran away he didn't care."

"He did. She had tried to go before but he stopped her. He ordered that no boat was to leave the island without his permission. We never discovered how she did get away. Obviously someone helped her."

"And what do you know about my half sister, Silva?"

"She was a morose girl who gave a great deal of trouble."

"Did my father not care for her? After all she was his daughter."

Fenwick hesitated, as though he were considering whether he should tell me what he knew.

I prompted him gently. "It is my family, you know. Even if there is something strange, I should like to know it."

He said, "Your father was not sure that Silva was his daughter. He discovered that her mother, his first wife, Effie, had had a lover in his absence on business, and he half believed that Silva was the result of that liaison. Your father was never positive and he could not bear to look at the child. Effie died of pneumonia when Silva was quite young. Self-righteous people are often cruel, Miss Kellaway. And I didn't think you'd really like to hear too much about your father."

"But I want to *know*. Then he married my mother. What of their life together?"

"He met your mother in London and he changed a little when

he brought her back to the island. But she found the place oppressive. They weren't compatible, and I think he was very disillusioned when he realized he had made another mistake. The fact is, Miss Kellaway, he was not a man for marriage. His temper was too short; he expected too much. It was the same with the island. He was not popular with the people. Now the island is a much happier place—and more prosperous—than it was in your father's time."

"Jago is for the island heart and soul," I said.

"Jago is a very ambitious man—in a great many ways more suited to rule the island than your father was. Your father resented him for this, and there was often tension between them. And Jago felt a certain bitterness because he belonged to the illegitimate branch of the family."

"But my father recognized Jago's superior ability to run the island by leaving everything to him."

Fenwick looked at me incredulously. "But by now you must be aware of the contents of the will."

"My father's will, you mean?"

"Certainly. *You* are the heiress of the island. You will be twenty-one next year, and you will come into your inheritance."

"*My* inheritance?"

"Of course. Your father was a man with a strong sense of justice. You were his daughter. He was sure of that. Jago was to hold the estate in trust for you until you were twenty-one, when it would become yours. If you died without heirs, your half sister—because after all he was not entirely certain that she was not his daughter—also was to inherit. In the event of your both dying without heirs, everything was to go to Jago."

I was astounded. I, who had grown up thinking of myself as the Poor Relation, had all the time been an heiress.

"Your father was a very rich man. With the price of land what it is and the prosperity of the island, you stand to inherit at least a million pounds. But surely Jago has informed you of this."

"I have heard nothing of it. Can it be that you are mistaken?"

"I should be very surprised if I were. Your father discussed it with me. I was more than a secretary. He trusted me. He thought it unfortunate that he had not known you since you were three. He said that on his death you must return to the island, learn about it and, he hoped, come to love it. He assumed that Jago's dedication to the place would become known—and necessary—to you. 'Of course,' he once said to me, 'she will marry, no doubt, and if she has a husband he might be able to do for the island all that Jago does. That will be a matter for her to decide.' "

I was speechless. This had completely changed my outlook. I said at length, "I thought I was Jago's guest. I was sure he was lord of the island. I am quite bewildered, not so much because I am an heiress—although I have yet to consider what that will mean. It is the fact that I knew nothing. . . ."

"Perhaps Jago had his covert reasons for not telling."

I felt myself flushing. Why, of course Jago wanted to marry me! The island would be mine, and I fancied he loved it with a passion he might not be able to give to anything—or anyone—else. The scene was falling into place, and my chief feeling was one of hurt.

"Your father was generous to me," Fenwick was saying. "He left me enough money to live on in comfort." He rose and went to a writing desk in the corner. He sat down and wrote something on a piece of paper, which he handed to me. On it was written "Merry, Fair and Dunn" and an address. "Your father's solicitors. It may be that they are looking for you. It's only a year since his death. They will confirm—or deny—all that I have told you."

"How strange that, having made such a will, he made no attempt to find me."

"He didn't want his life complicated at that stage. It's information which you should know now, however."

I thanked him, and told him he'd been ever so much more helpful than I could possibly have hoped. When Michael returned I showed him the address; he said he would take me there immediately. The solicitors' offices were in a town nearby.

And so, that afternoon, I learned that indeed they had been searching for me to inform me that I was the heiress to a considerable fortune which I should inherit when I was twenty-one. That was but a few months away. Until then it was held in trust, and

Jago Kellaway had the power to manage the estate; my father had strongly advised allowing him to continue to do so.

There was something else. It was true that in the event of my death without heirs, Silva Kellaway was to inherit the island. Since she was undoubtedly dead, Jago Kellaway was next in succession.

This last piece of news set the alarm bells ringing in my mind, but I didn't want to listen to what they were trying to tell me.

MORE than anything I was eager to confront Jago. I could not get rid of the thought that if I were not there, with Silva presumed dead, it would all belong to him.

Jago was not in the castle when I returned. Jenifry told me that he would not be back until dinnertime, and so I went to my room to change. But it seemed alien and filled with menace. When at last it was time to go down to dinner, my heart beat uncertainly.

Jago was there. "Have you had a good day, Ellen?" he asked.

"Very interesting, thank you. I went to the mainland."

Gwennol was eyeing me coldly.

"What! Deserting our island again!" said Jago.

Our island, Jago, I thought. You mean *my* island.

I wished we were alone. How long the meal seemed. As soon as it was over I said, "Jago, I want to talk to you."

His eyes lit up. Was he thinking that I had come to a decision? And being a man who could not imagine defeat, would he be certain that I wanted to marry him?

I faced him in the parlor. "Today," I said bluntly, "I have been to see Mr. Fenwick and he gave me the address of Merry, Fair and Dunn. Mr. Dunn explained to me the terms of my father's will."

Jago did not seem in the least embarrassed. "Then you know everything," he said easily. "How did you locate Fenwick?"

"Michael Hydrock found him for me."

"Oh? Is he interested in your inheritance?"

"What do you mean?"

"That he goes to a great deal of trouble for you."

"It was a friendly gesture. He is very rich, I should imagine, and would not possibly be interested in my inheritance."

"Don't be too sure. Often those who appear to be rich are in urgent need of money."

Jago is attacking, I thought, when he should be on the defensive. "You knew all this when you came to London," I accused.

"Ellen, let us not be melodramatic. As your guardian I wanted to get to know you and to inspect the man you were to marry. Philip's death made it possible for me to ask you here, so that you could come to love the island before you knew it would be yours."

"Why?"

"Because, my dear Ellen, if you had heard that you were to inherit a remote island which could, if sold, represent a great deal of money, what would you have done?"

"I should have come to see it, of course."

"And very likely have sold it at once—to some unknown person. That was something I dared not risk."

"And you thought I would marry you before I knew that the island was mine."

"That has nothing to do with our marriage, except that it will be profitable for you to have me here to work with you."

I looked into those heavy-lidded eyes; they held secrets. I felt wretched because I could not trust him, and yet I knew that whatever he had done, my life would be meaningless without him.

"Oh, Jago," I began, and he came swiftly to me and held me tightly in his arms.

His lips were on my hair. "I'll look after you, Ellen," he said. "You've nothing to fear with me to protect you."

I broke away from him. "It's all so unnecessary," I said angrily. "Why did you have to come to London so mysteriously—why?"

"I did not want the Carringtons to know that I was around, because, Ellen, I was making inquiries about them."

"About the Carringtons? They are a well-known family not only in England but internationally."

"Exactly. Then why should they be so happy about their son's marriage with a girl who was, it seemed, penniless?"

"They had so much money it was not important."

"Ellen, I believe they knew of your inheritance and that was why they were eager for the marriage. They wanted that money. The island would have been sold and the proceeds would have been used to back up the Carrington empire."

"This is wild speculation."

"Things are not always what they seem, my darling. I'll admit I did not want this island to pass out of my hands. The greatest joy I have ever known was when I met you and loved you on the spot."

"Your joy would have been less had I not been the heiress."

"Of course. But I was determined to have you for my own, and I would have found some means of saving the island too."

My common sense was telling me not to accept what he was saying, but common sense had no chance against such magnetism.

"Now, my dearest Ellen," he went on, "you will look at the island through different eyes. We'll work together. We'll have children, and we'll bring them up to love this place as we do."

"I have not yet said I will marry you."

"You are being perverse; you know you are going to do as I say."

"I think at times you believe you are a god."

"If you don't have a high opinion of yourself, no one else will." He gave me a steady look. "Why aren't you wearing the Kellaway necklace?"

"The clasp is weak. I'll get it repaired," I said, realizing he had talked himself out of a difficult situation.

I said I was very tired. But he held me against him for a time. "Good night, sweet Ellen. Don't be afraid to love."

Very firmly I said, "Good night, Jago." And I retired to my room. I could hear the wind rising and I went to the window and looked out on a sea just visible in starlight. The waves were beginning to have that white-crested ruffled look.

Could it possibly be true that the Carringtons had known I was an heiress? And Philip? I was sure he was without guile, but would his family have used him?

It was inevitable that I should have the dream that night. There was the room again—more familiar than ever. I could hear the whispering voices. The door was opening slowly. Then came the terrible realization that doom was just beyond it.

THE NEXT DAY I avoided Jago. I wanted to be alone to sort out my thoughts. The cool practical side of my nature must take command. I climbed to the top of one of the hills from where I could look down and see most of the island. How beautiful it was—very green, touched with the gold of the gorse bushes; and brooding over it all were the stone walls of the medieval edifice that had housed Kellaways for centuries. And this would soon be mine.

A man was slowly climbing the hill. There was something familiar about him. I must be dreaming. But how like—

"Rollo!" I cried.

"You're surprised," he said as he approached. "I'm staying at the island inn. I have business in Truro and I thought I'd look you up on the way. I've come to ask you to forgive me. I'm afraid I was quite obnoxious the last time we met. I've suffered many a qualm since. After all, Philip's death was worse for you than for any of us. And now that I can look at it more calmly, I agree—he could not have killed himself. I had to come and see you, Ellen, because I wanted to ask you to forgive me."

"I do understand. We were all distraught. I am so glad you no longer believe that I was responsible. How is Lady Emily?"

"The same as ever. She often speaks of you. By the way, the landlady of the inn told me you had an accident."

"Yes, my boat sprang a leak and overturned. I don't swim very well and stood little chance of reaching the shore. Fortunately a boy from the castle and Jago Kellaway rescued me."

"What a terrible thing to happen! Was the boat brought in?"

"No, it hasn't come in yet, and I suppose it won't now."

"My dear Ellen, you must take greater care. Tell me, are you going to stay here long?"

"It seems to have become my home. I never had a real home before. I like this place more and more every day."

"It's a rich and very profitable island, I imagine."

Just then I glanced down at the shore and saw Tassie. "Look," I said, pointing her out. "She's gathering limpets and crabs for her love potions and other concoctions."

"She appears to be a disreputable old crone."

"I hope she hasn't heard that. She'd ill-wish you. Oh, she's seen us." I waved a hand. She waved back and went on her way.

"Did she see me with you, do you think?"

"Certainly. Old Tassie sees everything. That's why her prophecies come true. Her eyes are open."

Rollo took my hand and said, "So I am forgiven? I can go on my way with a good conscience?"

I nodded. "Thank you for coming. Will you call at the castle?"

He shook his head. "No. I have to leave the island shortly. If I have time, I might stop by on my way back."

"That would be pleasant," I said.

As we went our different ways—he to the inn, I to the castle—I thought of Jago's suggestion that the Carringtons had been after my fortune. That seemed quite absurd.

It was two days later when Slack came to me in a state of great excitement. "Miss Ellen," he said. "The *Ellen*. She have come in. I were watching for her. I saw her and I swam out and brought her to my special cove where nobody goes. Come. I have something to show you. I don't like it, but we got to look at it."

He led the way down to the cove where the boat lay.

"That's not the *Ellen*," I said at once. "There's no name on her."

He looked suddenly sly. "I painted it out," he said.

"Why?"

He looked lost. "I can't rightly say. It seemed best. But look 'ee here." And he directed my gaze to the bottom of the boat. A hole was bored there.

"Miss Ellen, you did talk of sugar. Well, if a hole were bored and packed tight with a packet of Demerara sugar, 'twould take a little time to dissolve and that's what it did. 'Tis clear as daylight."

I stood there staring, and then I was aware of Slack beside me, gently laying a hand on my arm. "Miss Ellen, if you do be in trouble, come to me. I'll help you."

"Thank you, Slack," I said. "I'm glad you're my friend."

I can't bear it, I thought. Someone chanced that I would go out in that boat alone and saw to it that I would not come back alive.

In the Dungeons

FEAR was stalking me. I was certain now that whoever drilled a hole in my boat wanted to murder me. Could the reason be this beautiful, fertile island?

I went to the room on the ground floor which my mother had used. There was a certain comfort in sitting on the old settle and thinking about her. I could not get Silva out of my mind. Was her story in some way connected with mine?

Silva. Could someone have pretended to be in love with her—perhaps because she was her father's eldest daughter, who, it was thought, would inherit the island? And had that someone discovered that the island had been left to someone else—myself?

Jago's face rose before me, intense, passionate. I almost wished Slack had not found the boat, with the evidence of that hole.

I refused to think of Jago as the one who had made that hole in the boat, and my thoughts went to Michael Hydrock. What if he had been the one with whom Silva had fallen in love?

Then I thought of Jenifry and Gwennol. Jago might want the island, but Gwennol wanted Michael Hydrock.

And as I sat there brooding I heard a sound. A cold shiver ran down my spine. The door was slowly pushed open. It was only Slack.

"Oh, it be you, Miss Ellen," he whispered. "I knew someone was here like. It be a good spot to be when there's trouble about."

"What an odd thing to say. What's so special about this room?"

"Miss Silva, her did come here. You be watchful, won't 'ee?"

"Tassie also said that, Slack. It would be easier if I knew what to watch for."

"If you be feared sometimes, Miss Ellen, I'll be watchful for 'ee. Come to me first and then to this room. Then I'd know you was here. That would be best. 'Twas what I told Miss Silva."

"So she came here and then you came too?" I asked.

He nodded. "Miss Silva, her trusted me, her did. You trust me too, Miss Ellen. So you come here when the time do come."

THE SEA WAS BEING roughened up by the wind, and a boat was bobbing about on the waves. I left the cove and climbed the cliff, where I found a spot among the gorse and bracken. It was easier to think up here, away from the castle.

I was wearing a cape of greenish hue, and sitting there in it I almost merged into the landscape.

I watched the boat come in, and as a man stepped out into the shallow water the fancy came to me that I had seen him before.

Suddenly I heard Jago's voice and saw him ride down to the cove. Then he cried out, "How dare you come here like this?"

I couldn't hear the man's answer but could see that Jago was very angry. Then the wind dropped for a moment and I heard the man say, "I have to talk to you."

"What can you be thinking of . . . to come *here?*" said Jago.

The man was gesticulating and speaking earnestly, and I was frustrated because I could not hear his words.

"All right," said Jago. "I'll see you tonight. Keep yourself scarce till then. Meet me in the dungeons. We'll be out of the way there. Be at the west door at nine o'clock, but you're wasting your time. You'll get nothing more from me. Go back to the inn now and stay in your room till tonight. You'll be sorry if you disobey."

With that, Jago turned his horse and rode off. The man stood gazing after him. Then he looked up at the cliff. I shrank into the bracken though I was certain he could not see me. But as he lifted his face I realized with a shock that it was Hawley, the Carrington groom who had watched Philip and me in the park.

I sat still, staring out at the sea. What connection could there be between Jago and Hawley? A feeling of dread assailed me.

That Hawley was afraid of Jago was obvious, but on the other hand, Jago was so angry at the sight of him that he might have something to be afraid of too. Jago must have known he was coming—he had been at the cove to meet him and was anxious that Hawley should not be seen. By whom? By me perhaps. I was the one who had seen him in the Carrington household.

What had Jago to do with those horrifying events in London? And Hawley? He had come here to ask something of Jago. What did he know of Philip's death? It wasn't suicide; and if that was so, then it was *murder*.

I knew that I must be hidden in the dungeons to hear what Jago and Hawley had to say to each other. This was the only way to unravel the terrifying mystery.

It seemed as if evening would never come.

I put on a dress of biscuit-colored silk, and because Jago always looked to see if I had on the necklace of island stones, I decided to wear it. As I fastened it, I noticed once more that the clasp was not very strong, but it would hold.

Jago did notice the necklace. He said, at dinner, how becoming it was on that color silk, but I sensed that his thoughts were elsewhere. When the meal was over, Gwennol and Jenifry went into the parlor to take coffee. Jago did not join them, and I murmured something about having a letter to write.

I did not go to my room but slipped straight out of the castle and quietly made my way across the courtyard. I was terribly afraid that Hawley might already be in the dungeons, in which case I should be discovered.

It was a bright night, for there was a full moon and it touched the castle walls with an eerie light. I was full of trepidation as I descended the spiral staircase to the dungeons.

I stood in the circular enclosure surrounded by doors and looked about me. There was something repelling about the place, but I managed to push open a door and enter one of the cavelike dungeons. A faint shaft of moonlight filtered through a small barred window, but it was enough to show me the moist walls and earth floor. The cell was cold and smelled unwholesome. Nevertheless, I went farther in and half closed the door.

I waited. It must have been nine o'clock when I heard footsteps and the creaking of the enclosure door.

Through the dungeon doorway I saw a ray of light. Jago was carrying a lantern. "Are you there?" he shouted.

I cowered in my dungeon and wondered what his reaction would be if he discovered me.

Footsteps at last.

"Well, here you are," said Jago. "What do you mean by sending a message that you were coming to the island?"

"I had to see you," said Hawley. "I'm in debt and I need money. Just a little something. I did a good job for you."

"You were paid for what you did, Hawley. I'm no longer employing you. You made a pretty good mess of it too, I must say."

"It wasn't easy," said Hawley. "And after all the trouble I got into . . . I might have been accused of murder."

"You weren't. There was a verdict of suicide."

"It could have been different. Think what a tricky job I had to do. I had to get friendly with that maid Bessie and find out what your young lady was doing. Then I had to get the key cut for you."

"It was child's play," said Jago.

"I wouldn't call it that when a man was killed."

"You should have managed better than you did. Now listen, Hawley, you're saying, 'You pay me or else.' There's a name for that and it's blackmail. I won't have it, Hawley! I'll lock you up here and hand you over to the courts."

"I don't think you'd like some things to come out, Mr. Kellaway. The young lady—"

Jago interrupted. "If you think you can blackmail me, you've made a big mistake. Just remember what happened in Philip Carrington's bedroom."

"I was only working for you. . . ."

I felt limp with horror. I leaned against the wall, my fingers clutching unconsciously at my necklace. Could it be that Philip had been cold-bloodedly murdered by a man employed by Jago to kill him? And why? Because Jago knew that I was the heiress to the island and wanted to marry me himself.

There was a second or so of silence in the dungeons and during it I heard a slight clatter.

Jago heard it too. "What's that?" he cried sharply. "There's someone here. Did you bring someone with you, Hawley?"

"I didn't. I swear I didn't."

"I'm going to look," said Jago. "I'll search every one of these dungeons. You hold the lantern."

The light shifted and I peeped through the doorway. They had their backs to me and had started searching the dungeons on the other side. I waited, my heartbeats threatening to choke me, until they were as far as they could be from my cell. Then, while their backs were still turned, I slipped out silently. In a flash I was up the staircase, luckily unseen.

I reached the main building and forced myself to join Gwennol and Jenifry in the parlor. I picked up a magazine and leafed through it, my mind busy planning what I ought to do next. What I had heard this night had brought home to me one overwhelming truth: whatever Jago was, whatever he had done, I loved him.

I knew he wanted the island; but he wanted me too.

Jago was coming into the room now. I kept my eyes on the magazine, but I could feel his gaze fixed upon me.

He sat down beside me on the sofa and said, "Have you lost something, Ellen?"

I looked at him in surprise. His eyes were gleaming and there were conflicting emotions there—passion, reproach and a certain amusement. The amusement of a cat playing with a mouse?

He held out his hand and I stared down at it in horror, for there lay the necklace and I knew at once what that clatter in the dungeons had been. The catch was weak; I had grasped the necklace in my agitation and when I had let go it had fallen to the floor. Jago had found it; he knew I had been there and what I had heard.

"Ellen," he said gently, "what on earth were you doing in the dungeons? It takes courage to go there at night."

"I'm not afraid," I said, looking straight at him.

He put his hand over mine and gripped it hard. "I have a good deal to say to you. Will you come into my study?"

"I'll join you there shortly," I said.

"Don't be long."

I must consider what I have heard, I thought. I ran down to the hall and out across the courtyard. Slack was at the dovecotes.

"You look proper scared, Miss Ellen. Have the time come?"

I thought of Philip . . . shot. Had Jago really ordered that?

Slack was saying, "Don't be afraid. It'll be as it was with Miss Silva. Maybe there is no time to lose."

He took my hand and we went into the castle. He picked up a candle in the hall and lighted it as we entered my mother's sitting room. He approached the settle and lifted the lid. "Now you see, Miss Ellen, this ain't no ordinary settle." To my astonishment he raised the base, which came up like another lid. I could see down into darkness. "There be steps. Do 'ee see 'em? Go down 'em . . . very careful-like. I'll follow 'ee."

I got into the settle and lowered myself and my feet found the steps. I went down six of them. Slack handed me the candle and followed me, after shutting the lid and base of the settle.

"Where are we?" I asked fearfully.

"This be a great cave which do go right under the sea. 'Tis where I brought Miss Silva when she did fly away."

"What happened to her?"

"She did live happy ever after, as she told me she would. It goes down deep. Down and down and up again. 'Tis no more than a quarter of a mile long—the distance between Kellaway's Isle and Blue Rock. That's where it comes out. It's what they do call a natural cave, but the entrances was made in the old smuggling days. It weren't much used since then. I know about the cave from my mother, who knew of it from her father, who knew of it from his. Ships could come from France, and liquor would be unloaded and stored here until safe to bring it to the mainland."

"And when we get to Blue Rock, what then?"

"The artist will help us. He helped Miss Silva. He had a real fancy for her. Her went away to live happy ever after."

"And the boat that was washed up?"

"That were a trick like. Her weren't in it. 'Twasn't till later on a dark calm night when she did cross."

"How do you know all this, Slack?"

"Well, I helped her, didn't I? Her father had been terrible cruel to her, and she thought he'd laugh at her and try to stop her if he knew, so she ran away with her own true love."

"Where did she go?"

"That I never heard on, Miss Ellen. Be careful now."

Down we went, down a steep slope below the sea. It was damp and cold and we passed little pools of water; at times my feet sank into the sand and the surface changed to rocks. Fortunately Slack was surefooted and knew the way.

"Now," he said, "we are beginning to go up. It's a climb. But we'll soon be on Blue Rock and then Mr. Manton will be ready to help 'ee get to the mainland, if that be what you want."

I did not want to leave the island. I only wanted a day or two to think clearly about everything. I wanted to talk to Jago, to demand an explanation. But not just yet. First I wanted to try to stand outside the enormity of those emotions which Jago aroused in me and assess the situation dispassionately. I wanted to discover how deeply involved I was with an unscrupulous man who might well have been involved in Philip's murder.

I wouldn't accept the fact that Jago didn't at least love me a little; perhaps in time he would love me even more than the island. How obsessed I must be by him to be so ready to compromise.

But what if he did not love me? What if, after I had married him and willed everything to him, he'd have no further use for me? All I knew of Jago was that I loved him. That was all. But is it possible to love a man whom one can suspect of murder? The answer seemed to thunder in my ears: "Yes, yes."

There was one thing he was unaware of. He thought Silva was dead, but Slack assumed she had eloped with the lover of whom she wrote and continued to live happily ever after. If that were true, then on my death she would be the next in succession.

"Can 'ee hear the sea?" asked Slack. "We be nearly there."

Now we were right out in the open, pushing our way through bushes, and I could feel the fresh air on my face.

"There be the house," said Slack as he took my hand and dragged me forward. The door was open, and he went through, calling, "Mr. Manton. Mr. Manton. I be here with Miss Ellen."

There was no answer. We had stepped into a small hall, and Slack shoved open a door and we entered a room.

I felt my senses reel. There it was—the red curtains tied with gold fringe, the brick fireplace, the rocking chair, the gateleg table, and even the painting of the storm at sea hanging on the wall.

In every detail it was there—the room which had come to me so often in my dreams.

THIS was surely a nightmare. I had somehow strayed into the dream. "Slack," I murmured, "what is this room?"

"You'll be all right here," he said soothingly. "Miss Silva were . . ."

My eyes were fixed on the door which had been the center of the dream. It was not the one through which we had entered—there were two doors in this room.

The handle slowly turned. The door was beginning to open.

This was it—the moment when the terrible sense of doom had come over me—just as in the dream, except that this was not a dream but the actual moment of revelation. I was terrified of what the opening of the door would reveal. The artist! I thought. What has he to do with my life? Why should I fear him?

The door opened wide. A man was standing on the threshold. Not the artist, though. It was Rollo.

Amazement was quickly overtaking fear. Rollo! What could Rollo possibly be doing at Blue Rock?

"Ellen!" He smiled. "How good to see you here."

I stammered, "I—I had no idea. I thought the artist lived here."

"He's gone to London for a few days. He lent me his place. You look scared out of your wits. Come. Sit down. Let me get you some wine."

"I'm sorry," I said. "I'm so bewildered."

Slack was staring at Rollo. I heard him whisper, "Something terrible have happened to Miss Silva."

Rollo led me to the gateleg table and made me sit down in the chair which I had seen so many times in my dreams.

"You must tell me what happened, Ellen," he said. Then he poured something into a glass and put the glass into my hand. "Drink this. It will steady you. I can see you've had a shock."

"There's a tunnel from here to the castle," I began.

He did not express any surprise. "I was concerned about you, which is why I didn't leave the vicinity. I felt something was going on, and I couldn't get that affair of the boat out of my mind."

"You think someone was trying to murder me?"

He nodded. "I'm sure of it."

Not Jago, I thought. I won't believe it was Jago. "I want to get away to the mainland," I said. "I'll stay at the Polcrag Inn—at least until I've thought all this over."

"Of course. I'll row you across." Suddenly he seemed alert and distressed. "Where's the boy you brought with you?"

I looked behind me. Slack was not there. Rollo stepped into the hall, closing the door behind him and calling Slack.

Now that I was in the room alone I examined it with awed wonder. I went over to touch the window curtains. It was hard to believe that this was more vivid than even my most vivid dream.

My mother must have been in the room often, for she had re-created its every detail in her picture. Why and how it had played such a part in my dreams was what baffled me.

The door opened and the familiar feeling of fear began to creep over me.

It was Rollo, his face distorted in anger.

"I can't find the boy. Why did he run off? What did he say?"

"Something about Silva. She was my half sister. He said something terrible had happened to her."

"He's crazy, that boy."

"I don't think so. His mind works in a strange way, that's all."

"He's an idiot," said Rollo. "You haven't had your drink. You'll feel better for it, you know."

I took a sip. "I want to go to the mainland," I said.

"Finish your drink first, and I'll get the boat."

"I've left everything at the castle," I said.

"Why did you leave in such a hurry?"

"It seemed necessary then. Now . . ."

"You regret it?"

"Yes, I should have waited, should have talked to Jago. . . ."

My voice seemed to be coming from a long way off. Rollo was smiling at me and the room seemed to be dissolving about him.

"I feel very strange. Rollo, what's happening?"

"You're getting drowsy. It's the drink. A little sedative. You needed that—and so did I."

"You, Rollo?"

"Come. We're going to the boat. That's what you want, isn't it?"

I stood up, swaying unsteadily. He caught me.

"Now," he said, "it will be easy. Curse that boy, though."

He led me out of the house. The cold air revived me a little. "What happened?" I cried.

I heard Rollo laugh softly. "I didn't expect such luck. It'll be over soon. Come down . . . down the slope to the shore."

Something warned me. The doom feeling I had known in the dream was very strong. "I want to see Jago first. I *must* see Jago."

I slid to the ground. I was lying among the bushes. Rollo was trying to pull me to my feet, but I clung to the nearest bush with all my strength. For a terrible realization had come to me. The dream had been right. My doom had entered through that door, and my doom was Rollo.

The drink had contained more than a little sedative. I knew that now. Rollo meant to overcome my resistance so that he could do with me what he wanted. And something told me that what he wanted was to kill me. But why? Why Rollo?

Even at such a time I was able to feel relief, because I had been wrong about Jago. Oh, Jago, why did I run away from you?

Rollo was dragging me from the bush. He lifted me. "Don't struggle. It won't help you and will only make me angry."

It was hard going for him carrying me. I heard him curse against the sound of the breakers. And somehow I knew that he was going to row out and throw me into the sea; I would be unable to struggle because of increasing drowsiness.

I heard the boat scraping on the sand. He lifted me up and put me roughly inside. I tried to climb out, but he was ready.

"You've had a charmed life, Ellen . . . until now."

"Rollo, you came down here to kill me. Why?"

"You're in the way. That's all. If Philip had lived, this wouldn't have been necessary."

This was the end, then. My sleepy body would receive the embrace of the sea and my heavy clothes would drag me down.

But I was wrong.

There was a shout, and I heard Rollo's furious exclamation. And there was Jago himself on the shore, then wading out to sea. He knocked Rollo aside and snatched me out of the boat.

"Ellen." I heard his voice through the waves of sleepiness which swept over me and I was filled with exultation. "My Ellen."

I AWOKE in my bedroom in the castle. It was daylight and Jago was sitting by my bed. He bent over me and kissed me.

"All's well, Ellen. I love you; you love me, although I must say you didn't show it last night. I waited and waited for you to come to my study as you'd promised. Then I searched everywhere for you. By that time Slack had come back in a state of alarm. He said you were on Blue Rock with a man who intended to harm you."

"How did he know?"

"He'd seen him before on the island. Apparently, Rollo had had the house on Blue Rock for a week or more."

"So he could have tampered with the *Ellen*. Why . . . why did he want to kill me?"

"It's a simple reason. With you out of the way his wife would have come into a great deal of money."

"His wife?"

"Silva. You see, she's not dead. That boy Slack, pretending to be half-baked and knowing so much more than the rest of us!"

"Silva. Rollo's wife! Rollo wanting money. I can't believe it."

"The Carrington empire is tottering. They'd seen it coming and that was presumably why he married Silva. Then he discovered the contents of your father's will and that you came first. So they arranged for you to marry Philip, which would have made them sure of the Kellaway fortune."

"Philip. Oh, Philip! What happened to him? I heard—"

"Yes, I know. You were eavesdropping in the dungeons. The necklace betrayed you. But how could you have doubted me?"

"I had to know. I was afraid you might have done something. . . ."

"Which would have stopped your loving me?"

"The one discovery I made was that nothing can do that."

"Then your doubt was worthwhile. But if that devil had been minutes earlier he would have had you at sea. The worst could have happened."

"Tell me everything, please."

"I've had to piece a lot together, but it seems to me your father was not sure that Silva was his daughter; he suspected that she was James Manton's. So did Manton, because he and Silva's mother had been lovers. Rollo, who was interested in art, met Manton at a London exhibition and heard from him about the island and the Kellaways. He came, and met Silva on the mainland. He never crossed over to the island, so I didn't see him before that encounter in the house you were considering in Finlay Square.

He had discovered that Silva was the elder daughter and naturally believed that she would inherit the island. So he married her secretly—she was worried your father would object—and took her to London. Your father died and only then did the Carringtons discover that you were the heiress, so they devised the plan for you and Philip to marry. In the meantime, I came to London to see you and learned that all was not well with the Carrington interests. I understood why they were so anxious to welcome you. I engaged a private detective—Hawley, rather a shady character—to make a thorough study of their affairs. By serving in their household he found out more than I ever could. I gate-crashed the Carrington soiree, where I promptly fell in love with you."

"And what do you know about Philip's death?"

"It was an accident. A disastrous thing to have happened. Hawley was going through some papers in Philip's room when Philip disturbed him. Philip kept a pistol under his pillow and he threatened Hawley with it, demanding to know what he was doing. Hawley lost his head and struggled with Philip to get the pistol from him. It went off, alas, killing Philip. Hawley is a sharp character. He arranged it to look like suicide, and got away with it."

"Then you didn't hire him to kill Philip?"

"Certainly not. I was horrified by his death."

"But he was going to marry me, taking the island with me."

"I was planning to lay before you all the information I had gathered about the Carringtons, and I had a notion that you were at that time questioning the wisdom of rushing into marriage with Philip. I was counting on getting you to postpone the wedding for a while."

"And you got Hawley to have a key cut for you."

"Yes, I did. I thought that if we met in that house by chance I might be able to hint at something. I'd do a great deal to get you, Ellen, but I'd stop at murder. I was so anxious about you. I didn't trust those Carringtons. Then Philip's death changed everything. But that's the past. There's so much to plan for. Just think of it, Ellen . . . the two of us together on the island."

The Outcome

I MARRIED Jago a month later.

Everything was clear to me by that time. Rollo's body was found a few days later. After his encounter with Jago he had had no alternative but to try to reach the mainland. However, the sea was not in a benign mood that night. A few weeks later the collapse of the Carrington interests was announced in the papers; a great many people had lost money in the crash, and there was talk of a prosecution which might have taken place if Rollo had lived. It was presumed that he had deliberately chosen death by drowning.

I owed so much to Slack, who, when he had seen Rollo, had recognized him as the man with whom Silva had run away. But somehow he had instinctively known that this time he was there for no good purpose. So he had hastened back through the tunnel and summoned Jago.

Gwennol eventually married Michael Hydrock, and Jenifry went to live with them. Jenifry and I are quite good friends now— though we could never be close.

And I have found Silva. Her brief honeymoon with Rollo had soon ended and, when she realized that he was not in love with her, she had been more heartbroken than ever before. He had kept her shut away in a lonely country house while he sought to get his hands on the island fortune.

I brought Silva back to the castle. I call her my sister. And although it may well be that James Manton was her father, we both like to think it was otherwise. The artist is a kindly man, and we often row over to his island and have tea in my dream room.

It has not been easy to nurse Silva back to health. She was, at first, furtive and suspicious, and I taught her that there were people who love her. Slack has been helpful too. He is delighted to have her here and looks upon us both as his special protégées.

When my first baby came—Jago, after his father—Silva began to change. She adored the child and the others too. They love her dearly and I think that at last she is happy.

I never dreamed my dream again, but I think I know why it had haunted me. My mother had lived on uneasy terms with my father and was determined to escape. Her maid, Mrs. Pengelly, knew of the tunnel to Blue Rock, and one night, so I later learned from her, they escaped through it with James Manton's help. My mother carried me in the tunnel and to that room, and I would have sensed her fear that my father might come through that door to prevent her escape; I must have felt that fear so intensely that it haunted my dreams in the years ahead.

How I love the island! How I love my life here! Jago and I are full of contentment and plans for the future.

Often we lie on the cliffs and look down on the cove where I saw Hawley come in; we look up at the sky and see the pigeons now and then, perhaps carrying a message to Michael and Gwennol at Hydrock Manor; and sometimes we talk of the past.

"It's all yours now," said Jago.

"Ours," I reminded him. Yes, I thought, ours—this fair island, these beloved children, this good life. Ours.

Victoria Holt is one of several pen names used by a British novelist who has been writing professionally for more than thirty years. She is reluctant to reveal her true identity, but explains that she chose the name Victoria because her stories are Victorian, and Holt for the name of her London

*Victoria
Holt*

bank branch. It seemed a good omen. And, as it turned out, it was. Her first Victoria Holt novel, *Mistress of Mellyn* (a Condensed Books selection), was an international best seller. And its successors, of which *Lord of the Far Island* is the fourteenth, have all reached that same happy state.

Home for Miss Holt is a sunny flat with a terrace garden in her native London. Despite extensive foreign travel, Miss Holt still finds Cornwall, in England, one of the most fascinating, inspiring places of all. "I have spent many summers there," she says, "in a house right on the coast. On clear days I could look out my bedroom window and see a rockbound island. I would hear the sea thundering in the caves and wonder what it would be like to live on such an island. And so the story of *Lord of the Far Island* began to take shape in my mind.

"Another passion of mine," she continues, "is visiting castles and stately mansions. Recently I acquired an ancient house of my own in the town of Sandwich—a vital seaport during the Middle Ages. The house is called the King's Lodging, because Henry VIII stayed there when it was the local inn. In 1572 Queen Elizabeth visited the house and reviewed the fleet from my drawing-room window. I relish the rich historical background of my new home, and I expect to find rather special inspiration there."

ALEXANDER DOLGUN'S STORY

AN AMERICAN IN THE GULAG

A CONDENSATION OF THE BOOK BY

ALEXANDER DOLGUN with PATRICK WATSON

ILLUSTRATED BY JACK ENDEWELT

It happened so quickly: one minute Alexander Dolgun was a carefree American youth walking down a Moscow street. An instant later he was on his way to Lubyanka Prison—the first stop on a journey through hell. Dolgun's story is an extraordinary human document. Although it is a remorseless chronicle of suffering and degradation, it is also an inspiring testament to the power of the individual. Try as they would throughout the seven years of his captivity, Dolgun's adversaries were unable to break his spirit. Deprive him of sleep—he learns to sleep sitting upright; confine him to a dark cell— in his mind he paces across the face of Europe; beat him unmercifully— still he taunts his interrogator.

One of Dolgun's fellow prisoners, a doctor he loved and respected, said to him, "Whatever you do, write about us. Tell the world about us. People have to know."

He promised he would. With this unforgettable book he keeps his promise.

"A moving and impressive story of the strength of the human spirit."
—*Newsday*
"Impossible to pick out one passage and say: *this* is the most exciting!"
—Chicago *Tribune*

Alexander Dolgun in the American embassy shortly before his arrest.

CHAPTER ONE

ONE day late in 1948 a young American out for an innocent walk in the streets of Moscow was accosted by an operative of the MGB, the Soviet secret police. Had he been quick to run through the crowded streets to the American embassy, only two blocks away, he probably would have been safe. Instead, he paused to answer the agent politely. It was a fateful pause. Within seconds the young man was a prisoner of the MGB. He would live under their shadow for the next twenty-three years.

How it began was mundane enough. In the early 1930s, when jobs were scarce, a number of American technicians accepted offers from the Soviet Union to work in Russia for a one-year term. One of these men was Michael Dolgun, a Polish-born New Yorker, who went over in 1933 on contract to the Moscow Automotive Works. When his employers offered to help bring his family over if he would accept a second one-year contract, Michael Dolgun accepted. Much as he disliked Moscow, he thought he could stick it out one more year if his family was with him. Besides, things were still pretty tough in America.

But that one year stretched into two, and then four, and then 1939 came and with it the prospect of war. Michael Dolgun told the authorities he wanted to return home with his family. But endless bureaucratic barriers to his repatriation appeared. Since Michael was not politically sophisticated he didn't think of going to the American embassy for help. He had been dealing with the same Soviet officials for six years; *they* were his contact with the world of passports and money and travel arrangements.

Before anything was done for him war had come to Russia, and Michael Dolgun found that in the eyes of the Soviet government he had become a Soviet citizen, and he was drafted into the Red Army. For the rest of the war his family saw little of him. They had a terrible time finding food in the beleaguered city. Anna Dolgun and the teenage children, Stella and Alexander, yearned to go home to New York, but there was no way to do that.

Alex was a Catholic boy. He had been taught plenty about hell. But the searing realities of the pit in which he spent most of his twenties would soon make all that pulpit hellfire seem insipid.

I know about all this because I am Alex Dolgun.

Retracing my steps, I come back to that day in 1948—to the early hours of that day, between one and two in the morning, when I stood outside the apartment of my fiancée, Mary Catto, trying to say good night. Mary worked at the British embassy. I worked at the American. We were a lively, outgoing couple, and as a result we were invited to a lot of diplomatic parties that a twenty-two-year-old like me would not normally have been asked to.

Mary and I had been out very late that night. We were very close and very loving, but we had not slept together; that would wait until we were married. It was one of those nights when saying good night is almost impossible. We stood in her doorway with our arms around each other, very happy and very dreamy.

I remember that I felt kind of dramatic, and I said to her, "Darling, suppose something should happen to me and I should disappear for a few months." There was a look of genuine alarm on her face. I was enough of a kid, I'm afraid, to enjoy it.

I said, "Would you wait for me?"

"I would wait forever, Al," she said. "I love you, and I would wait for you. Are you serious about this?"

I said, "Listen, forget it. We're going to the Bolshoi tomorrow night—no, it's tonight—and I've got to get some sleep. I just had to know how serious you are." She held me very tightly. It was probably half an hour more before I left her and walked back to the American embassy residence with my head full of romance.

Now, I am not superstitious, but that remark to Mary about disappearing for a while was undeniably prophetic. . . .

Before coming to work that morning I had pocketed one of my guns, a really beautiful prewar Spanish automatic with a handsome brown bone handle. I wanted to oil it with typewriter oil, because I had no decent gun oil at the residence.

I also owned a Luger-shaped air pistol that fired darts, and that gun became an issue later on. It's a good thing I remembered to leave the Spanish gun locked in my desk at the embassy when I went out for lunch, or there would have been a very big issue over guns—I am sure of that.

Lunch was to be with Captain North, assistant military attaché at the Australian legation. We had agreed to meet at the Aragvi, a fine Georgian restaurant on Gorky Street. It would be a twenty-minute walk for me. I left the embassy a few minutes after one.

It was a bright, sunny day. The American embassy was opposite the north wall of the Kremlin then, and as I crossed Gorky Street, I could see lines of people in front of the Lenin Mausoleum, and lots of strollers out in Red Square. There was no snow in the streets, although it was nearly Christmas. The colored domes of St. Basil's were brilliant in the sunshine.

I turned left along Gorky Street, threading my way through the crowds of people in front of the Council of Ministers Building until I crossed the first street and started passing in front of the Diet Food Store. Shortly after I passed the store, I heard someone call my name loudly from a short distance behind me.

He was half running after me, but he called me Alexander Mikhailovich, a distinctly Russian form of address, and nobody ever called me that, so I didn't pay much attention. Now he put his arms out as if to embrace me, then said, *"Kiryukha"*—"Old buddy"—in a louder voice than made any sense for a man two feet away. "How wonderful to see you—it's been such a long time!"

I was completely mystified. I wondered if it was some nut. I had never seen this tall, grinning, good-looking man before.

He kept talking loudly, and took me by the arm and pressed me toward the edge of the sidewalk, by the road.

"Such a surprise, such a surprise, how wonderful we should meet again. Let's just come over here so we can talk!"

I said, "Look, I have never seen you before in my life. You've got me mixed up with someone else."

By now we were at the edge of the road. He said, "No, I don't think so. Your name is Alexander Doldzhin, isn't that right?"

Many Russians pronounced my name that way, as if it were *dole-gin*, like the drink, with the accent on the *gin*.

I said, "That's right, but who are you?" I was beginning to feel a little uneasy. I don't know to this day why I didn't catch on faster and just start running.

The tall man reached in his pocket and pulled out an ID card. His photograph was on it, and the name Kharitonov, S. I., Major, Operative Detachment, MGB—the Ministry of State Security.

I felt cold. But his manner was totally affable. He said, "Oh, don't worry, it's nothing important, we'd just like to talk to you for five minutes at the ministry."

I was going to get out of there. I pulled out my own ID card and said pretty brusquely, "Look, I am an employee of the United States embassy. I am not allowed to talk to any Soviet officials without permission. I'm sorry."

Kharitonov took the card. "You're the man," he said quietly. I held out my hand for my card. He just stared at me and slowly dropped his hand to his side without returning the card. That gesture turned me to stone. It was like a curtain going down. I hesitated one fatal moment, thinking, I better get that card back. Then I knew I couldn't and I tensed to run. But my elbows were seized from behind firmly, by two pairs of hands. I was trapped.

Kharitonov said in his broadcast voice again—for the benefit of the passersby, I realized now—"Well! Here's luck! Here comes my friend with his car. We can take a drive and have a chat."

A beige Pobeda pulled up beside me. The man on my right said in my ear, "Be quiet, now. Don't make any noise at all, please," and before I could even think, let alone react, I was squeezed in the back of the car.

In 1948 Dolgun was kidnapped by the Soviet secret police two blocks from the American embassy. This photograph of the building was taken that year.

I looked wildly around me at the street. The huge world clock on the Central Telegraph Building across the street said ten past one. As we drove away, I could see the lower part of a woman's body and the string bag that she carried. The bag was full of potatoes and a pair of women's shoes, with the toes sticking out. For some reason this struck me as funny and I giggled.

Kharitonov spoke in a very soothing voice. He said we were just going to the ministry for a little talk. "Don't worry," he kept saying. "Five minutes, that's all."

He was really smooth. I did stop worrying. I thought, They're going to make a pitch to me. Money, women, all that. They want me to be an agent. That was the only thing that made sense.

"Here we are," he said. "Do you know what this is?"

143

I looked out the window of the Pobeda as we drew up by a gray stone building. It was Lubyanka Prison, headquarters of the MGB.

I said, "Sure I know. It's the Government Terror."

Before the Revolution the prison had been the Government Insurance Hotel. It was called *Gos Strakh* for short. *Strakhkassa* means "insurance office." But *Strakh* also means "fear" or "fright," so for a while the prison was called the Government Fright. Then, after the purges, when it was constantly swallowing people who never reappeared, people began to call it *Gos Uzhas*—the Government Terror. It is an imposing building with great steel doors. Now, as we slowed down, they began to slide open. It was like a movie. I thought, Wait till I tell the boys about this!

The doors slid sideways into the wall with a grinding sound. Then they closed behind us and the doors of the car opened and we were in a big central courtyard, with Kharitonov very politely saying, "Look, don't worry, this will just take a few minutes, please come this way," in that soothing, reassuring voice of his. At the door he stood aside for me to enter first, and then skipped in front of me down the hall. There was no one else in sight.

We turned down a narrow side corridor. It was lined with doors strangely close together. Scarcely breaking the rhythm of his stride, Kharitonov opened a door and motioned me forward courteously. "This way, please," he said pleasantly. I walked in, still moving as quickly as we had been all along, and then suddenly came to a halt. I was in a box about four by nine feet. An empty box with a bench. I spun around.

"What the hell!" I said, really angry. But I said it to a door that was already shutting hard behind me. A door lined with iron, with a peephole in it. The peephole opened immediately. I went right up to it. I said, "This isn't funny, Major. Open up." The peephole closed again, but not before I saw behind it a dark eye with a dark eyebrow. Definitely not the light-skinned major.

I was very excited. Whatever mixed and unlikely thoughts were racing through my head, all of them meant adventure and great stories to tell. Here I was actually *inside* the infamous Lubyanka, the stronghold of the secret police of Soviet Russia. I was flash-fantasizing how I would reveal to the world the sinister plans of the MGB for buying off Americans. Maybe I'd be a hero and go on tour in the States. It literally never occurred to me that I was about to begin a prison term that might end with my death.

I supposed the guard with the dark eyes was going for Kharitonov. I turned around to look at the room I was in. The ceiling was high, almost ten feet. The walls were brown up to shoulder height, then whitewashed. Set in a recess over the door was a single bright bulb, screened by a heavy wire mesh. I looked back at the door. The peephole opened and closed again. Here they are, I thought, and waited for the door to open. Nothing. Silence. Then from somewhere close by a knocking sound and a muffled voice, pleading. I pounded with my fists on the door and shouted, "Let me out of this place! I'm an American citizen."

Immediately the bolt shot back. A blue-chinned man with heavy black eyebrows and a blue smock over his uniform stepped quickly into my cell. He whispered, "Now, please! Be very quiet. It is not allowed to shout in here." His manner was so polite that it put me off stride. He went on in a whisper, "Don't worry, please. It will only be a moment."

The knocking in the corridor started up again, and a woman's voice screamed out, "But there's no one with my baby! What's going to happen to my baby? Please! Please!" She was muffled by my door's being shut again. That really slowed me down. Despite the heat of the room I felt cold.

I was going to knock and yell some more, but the door opened and the blue-chinned man said, "Will you come this way?"

I thought, Okay, I'm sorry for that poor woman, but now whatever is going on with me is going to stop. Maybe I'll even make it to the restaurant before North decides he's been stood up.

I remember the face of that guard perfectly well. I saw him again years later when they brought me from camp for another interrogation, but he did not recognize me. Now he led me around a corner and motioned to another door. "Step in here." This room was quite bare except for a table and a straight-backed chair. The guard's manner changed. He was still polite, but there was no missing the absolute, quiet authority in his voice. The door behind us was locked.

"Take everything out of your pockets," he said.

I was going to refuse, but one look at his face made it clear there was no point. As I took off my watch and put my cigarettes and lighter and pen and everything else on the table, I explained to him that what was happening was in violation of international agreements, that it was a diplomatic mistake that would create very serious repercussions with the world's greatest power. And then I stopped. I understood, really, that he was just a functionary and I should save my breath for someone in authority.

He gathered up all my things and then said curtly, "Take off all your clothes and put them on the table." He left the room and the door was locked again.

"Boy!" I said tightly. "*Boy!* Just wait. Just you wait!" All the time taking off my shoes and socks, my shirt, my pants, until I stood in the middle of the hot room in my shorts.

I think I was there an hour before anyone came again. It may not have been that long, but the heat was getting me down and it seemed a long time. Then the door opened, and the swarthy, blue-chinned guy and a man in a colonel's uniform, MGB, came in.

The colonel had a piece of paper. He said, "This is a list of the property we are keeping for you. My name is Colonel Mironov. I am the commandant of the inner prison. If you need to go to the toilet or would like a drink of water, just call the guard." And he turned to go. I caught his arm, but he pulled away and gave me a very hard look. Before I could ask the questions that were welling up in me, he said simply, "Don't worry"—their favorite phrase—"you'll be fully informed very soon," and went out.

The swarthy guy pointed to my shorts. "Everything off." It was clear he meant it. I began to pull them off. When I looked up, he had my jacket on the table and was ripping the seams with a knife.

I said, "Just a minute there, fella. That's my good jacket." He went on opening the seams, as I knew he would. He felt inside the lining and the lapels. He ripped out the shoulder pads.

Then he picked up my shoes and went at the soles with his knife.

He pulled out the steel reinforcing shanks and put the shoes back on the floor, the soles flapping. Then he took my tie and shoelaces and belt and knocked for the door to be opened.

The door was unlocked again and a good-looking woman came into the room in a white lab coat over a uniform. I was terribly embarrassed. She had a clipboard and a pencil. She asked me if I had ever had tuberculosis, measles, malaria, scarlet fever, syphilis or gonorrhea (I was still composed enough to be insulted by this), diabetes, mental ailments, and so on. Then she walked up very close to me and told me to open my mouth. She examined behind my teeth and under my tongue. She looked in my ears and nostrils, under my eyelids, in my armpits, and even behind my scrotum.

"You can dress now," she said flatly, and left the room.

I was taken to a brightly lit room to be photographed and finger-printed. Then to another room, a dentist's office. Two guards stood by me, and a man in a lab coat opened my mouth and without a word drilled out a large filling from a molar.

By now I was red with fury but holding it, because I knew if I tried any physical protest they could stop me. I knew that before long I would be brought face-to-face with The Man. I had no idea who that would be, but I stored up scorn, arrogance, assurance, fury—a whole catalogue to dump on this poor guy, who would not have his job very long when they discovered how wrong they were.

A shower was next, too hot and no way to cool it down, and only a small bit of soft soap that smelled acrid and unpleasant. Somehow I knew I should take this shower seriously, so I washed my whole body thoroughly. I was in very good physical shape at this time. My weight was 186. I was five feet nine and a half, thirty two inches around the waist. My muscles were hard from exercise. I was an amateur acrobat, played a lot of sports, and for a couple of years I had been doing the Charles Atlas Dynamic-Tension muscle-building course, although I had never been a ninety-seven-pound weakling, like the guy in the comic book ads.

When I got dressed again after the shower, all I had left were my shoes, with the soles slit and flapping as I walked; my light gray navy-surplus gabardine pants, good heavy material; my navy-surplus shirt; two packs of Chesterfield cigarettes; and fifty-three wooden matches. My comb had been taken, but it wouldn't have been much use anyway, because the shower room had no mirror in it, and neither did the toilet when I asked to be taken there. In all the time I spent in prison in Moscow I would never see a mirror.

After my shower I was taken over by another guard. I followed his black boots along long gloomy corridors lined with doors, each door with its peephole and food slot with a sliding metal panel. The corridors were carpeted and almost the only sound as we moved along was the guard's clucking of his tongue—the signal used in Lubyanka that a prisoner was under escort. The effect of the silence and the gray doors repeating themselves down the corridors until they merged with the shadows was oppressive.

But I still could not take this thing seriously. When we came around a corner and I was put into another windowless box, I felt a bit nonplussed, because I thought I was on my way to see someone in authority and get things straightened out.

This box was longer and a little wider. The ceiling was high and the air was hot. Along one side was a narrow wooden bench. Above the door was an intense naked bulb, about 150 watts, I thought, in a heavy wire-mesh cage. The guard was closing the door when I said, "What happens now?"

"Don't worry," he said, "everything will be fine."

I walked up and down in the stifling cell. After a while I became completely parched in the heat under that glaring bulb, so I knocked on the door for the guard. The peephole opened immediately, and I asked for some water. He was back with the water in a moment. A pint-size metal mug. I drained it and asked for more. In a minute he was back with a refill.

Ten minutes later my bladder began to feel pretty full. Up till now I had not felt any physical needs; I think I had gone a bit numb. Anyway, I knocked on the door again, and again the peephole opened immediately. "I need to go to the toilet." The peephole closed and I heard the bolt being drawn back. The toilet was in a room across the hall, a trough urinal on the wall and a couple of holes in the floor, with metal footplates for squatting over. On the way back to the cell I said to the guard, "Listen, do you know what's going on here? I'm completely mystified."

He ducked his head and said in a whisper, "Don't worry. It will be all taken care of soon. Don't worry, now."

Sometime in the evening of the day of my arrest they came to take me for interrogation. No food was offered, but strangely I was not in the least hungry.

The guard opened the door and told me to follow him with my hands behind my back. We went through several corridors until we came to one with doors more widely spaced than in the cell corridors. The guard knocked on one and opened it without waiting. Inside was a huge barred window with dark brown curtains. I was staring at it to get some sense of the outside world when a voice said, "My name is Colonel Sidorov. I am your interrogator."

He was standing behind a large desk on the far side of the room. There was a shaded lamp on the desk, and bright overhead lights that gleamed on his face. Sidorov was tall, nearly six feet, with a kind of amused, easygoing, slightly cynical expression.

"Sit down," he said, motioning to a hard chair.

I sat down and took stock of this man before I said anything. He was about thirty-seven, trim and erect, with a lieutenant colonel's two stars on his shoulder boards. He sat down behind the desk and opened a file and read for a few minutes, looking up at me from time to time with an amused expression. Pretty soon I felt I had the situation cased well enough. The next time he looked up with this cynical half-smile I smiled back and said, "Well, I'm glad to meet someone in authority at last, Colonel Sidorov, because it would be just as well to get this little mistake straightened out."

Sidorov held up a finger, indicating that I should wait a minute, and went on reading.

I said, "Look, I'm sorry to interrupt your reading, but I think you should hear what I have to say, don't you?"

He put down the file. He said, "Yes, yes! That is what we are here for. At least that is what *I* am here for. Do you know why we have brought *you* here?"

"That's the point," I said calmly, smiling at him to show how confident I was. "I'm here for no reason at all. There is no reason why I should be here, and it will be very embarrassing for your government if I am not released right away—"

But Sidorov interrupted this speech with a wave of his hand. "Think!" he said sharply. Not angry. He still had that amused look. More like an algebra teacher who knows you are just a whisper away from the right answer and wants to encourage you. "Think about it for a moment. Look, I'm sure if you just think a little bit you'll understand why you are here. Then you can tell me about it and I will be glad to hear what you have to say." Quickly, and in a more serious style, Sidorov went on to tell me I was charged with espionage against the Soviet Union.

I said pretty emotionally, "There's been a terrible mistake! I've never engaged in any such activities. I'm a file clerk at the American embassy, for heaven's sake."

"Let's not waste time, Citizen Doldzhin," Sidorov said easily, still smiling. "You say we have made a mistake. I tell you we never make mistakes." He picked up the file. "It's in here. Places, dates, names of accomplices. All here. So don't worry about its being a mistake!" Then he leaned over the desk and looked at me sternly and said in a very quiet voice, "The MGB does not make mistakes, my friend. *We never make mistakes.*"

He thrust a piece of paper at me. It stated that under Article 58, sections 6, 8, 10, etc., of the Soviet Criminal Code I was charged with espionage, political terrorism, anti-Soviet propaganda. But the most impressive thing about this document was the signature: Rudenko. General Roman Rudenko was the chief prosecutor for the Soviet Union. I was shaken.

It began to look both preposterous and serious to me. I wondered if the embassy knew what had happened to me.

"I would like to make a telephone call," I said.

Sidorov smiled a tolerant smile and shook his head.

"Look here," I said loudly. "In my country even a common criminal is allowed to telephone his lawyer. I want to phone the embassy and get a representative over here! I want—"

"It really does not matter very much what you want now,"

Sidorov said paternally. "You should have thought about that before you undertook to be a spy in *my* country. Because that is no common crime, and you do not have the privileges of a common criminal. However," he went on, "maybe something can be done about that in the morning. It is too late to call there now, and I am required to get some basic information from you."

I took a big breath. I guessed I might as well resign myself to a night in Lubyanka. I thought, Cheer up, Alex, old buddy. They'll be here to get you in the morning. I nodded my assent to Sidorov.

"Where were you born?"

"New York City. East 110th Street."

"How did you get to the Soviet Union?"

"My father came here in the 1930s as a specialist at the Moscow Automotive Works. Later he brought the family over. He was drafted into your army. After graduation from the Anglo-American school, I got a job at the American embassy. That's all. I'm getting married soon and going back to the States."

Sidorov wrote all this down. At last he said, "Yes, we know about your relations with women here in Moscow, but I think your marriage seems pretty unlikely now, wouldn't you agree?"

I began to harden myself to deal as coolly as I could with whatever they threw at me. Stay on top, I thought. So instead of bridling at his taunt about marriage, I just smiled and waited for the next question.

He kept me at it all night. Everything he asked I answered easily. I knew a lot of time was going by, but I was surprised all the same when I heard doors opening up and down the corridor and caught a few muffled remarks from guards moving by to indicate that it was morning. Sidorov handed me the paper he had been writing on and said, "Please read these protocols, and if they are correct, please sign at the bottom of each sheet."

I said, "What is a protocol?"

"This is what we call the original notes I as an interrogator make on the interrogation. We can then refer to them as the weeks go by. . . ." He paused to let this take effect. "You sign to show your agreement that the notes reflect our conversation accurately." I signed the notes with a signature that bore no relation to my own except that it said Alexander Dolgun in English script, which is, of course, opaque to a Russian who knows only the Cyrillic alphabet and Russian script. Sidorov pressed the button for the guard.

The guard took me back through the maze of corridors to the cell and locked me in. I suddenly felt exhausted. I had only been in bed about three hours the night before. I wondered what Mary had done when I did not show up for the opera. I wondered why the embassy had not got through to me by now.

I stretched out on the narrow wooden bench, thinking I might as well sleep until something happened. I yawned hugely. Then I became aware of my heart beating fast and hard.

I believe that even at this early stage there must have been some suspicion in a distant part of my mind that things were worse than I would allow myself to be conscious of. In any case, that blessed mechanism that lets you sleep just did not work.

THE second day in Lubyanka began with a sort of quiet commotion in the corridor outside my cell. I could hear footsteps and hushed voices and the sounds of the panels of the food slots going back, and soon my own went back and a mug of hot tea and a small loaf of bread were placed on the shelf inside.

In Lubyanka they serve a complete loaf, and as I was to learn later, by comparison with the bread in other prisons it is quite tasty. On top of the loaf were two pieces of sugar. The tea was not real tea. It was colored water with a very faint smell of some leaf substance to it.

Although I had not eaten since breakfast the previous day, my stomach was tight and I was not at all hungry. I put the sugar in the tea and drank it slowly and pondered my situation. I looked at the bread and thought it did not look very appetizing and I could do without it—soon I would be eating bacon and eggs at the embassy.

About an hour went by and then the door opened and a guard I had not seen before took me along the corridors, *cluck-cluck*ing as we went, and left me again with Colonel Sidorov.

Now for some reason this second day of interrogation is less clear in my mind than what happened afterward. It was a jumble of questions about the most ordinary kind of family stuff. Where were my parents born? What relatives did I have in the United States? Where did they live? Sidorov kept on writing everything out in longhand. We worked at it all day. I remember seeing the light fade behind the curtains.

When I went back to the cell shortly after it got dark, there was a plate of cold soup on the food slot shelf, and later they brought some thin hot porridge and another cup of so-called tea. I drank the tea. That was all. Still no appetite. And still no ability to sleep, although by now I was feeling really ragged. Beat. And then, to my astonishment, at around ten they took me back to Sidorov.

More biographical research this night, although he seemed a little less interested now. From time to time he left the room. Finally, after one of these exits, he said that I was being transferred to Lefortovo Military Prison.

Around three a.m. the guard took me to a kind of lobby to what must have been the main exit of the prison. I was given a bundle and told that it was my jacket and other property that had been taken from me. Including my fine broad-brimmed fedora, which, I thought glumly, must be crushed out of shape in this parcel! I still was able to care about such things. Then they gave me the light topcoat I had been wearing when I was arrested, and we stepped out into the cold night air.

It felt refreshing and cleansing. In the yard there was a van with its back door open and a sort of ladder reaching to the ground. A colored advertisement on the side of the van read, DRINK SOVIET CHAMPAGNE, with a picture of the bottle and some fancy artwork. I had often seen vans just like it in Moscow. What I had not noticed before were the two rows of little ventilators on the roof, six in all.

One of the guards motioned me to go up the steps into the van. There were six small doors flanking a very narrow central passageway—no more than a slot, really. The guard held one open and motioned me into a box the size of a rabbit hutch. You could not sit down or stand up, just sort of hunker with your knees near your chin. I was shoved in and the door locked, and then the back door slammed and the van lurched off.

I could hear those sliding steel doors groan on their rails, then we moved forward again and I knew we were once more out in the streets of Moscow.

It took, I think now, fifteen minutes. It seemed longer then, because I was aching from the cramped position. A lot of my native cockiness was knocked out of me by the way I was hustled into this hutch like so much freight. I had to talk to myself to keep from losing control. "Easy, Alex, the last thing you need now is to get mad and bust a gut." By the time the van stopped I had stopped steaming, but my back and legs hurt like hell.

I heard the van door open. Then the guard unlocked my rabbit hutch. I crawled out and a guard led me through a dim corridor to a sort of office, where there was a man behind a counter.

"Name?"

"My name is Alexander Dolgun. I am an American citi—"

"Prisoner, be quiet!"

Prisoner!

I was given a spoon, a plate, a rolled-up mattress (very thin), a sheet, a musty old blanket, and a coarse pillow. Then I was taken to the cell that would be my home for the next ten months.

As my guard led me into the main body of Lefortovo prison, I stopped for a moment in astonishment. I had the uncanny impression that I had stepped into the bowels of a great steel ship. The guard hissed, "Keep moving!" He clanked his key on his belt—no tongue-clucking here. On both sides of us the walls rose up several stories, each lined with a narrow metal catwalk. In the space between the opposing catwalks, at every level, was a coarse wire mesh, stretching across the entire space. If anyone jumped or fell over the handrail, he would land unharmed on the wire mesh.

Lefortovo is shaped like a capital letter K—one straight long section, and two wings radiating from its middle point. The guard took me up worn stone stairs to the third level, and then along one of the diagonals.

At the end of the wing two heavy steel bars were pulled back on a cell door and I was motioned in. I noticed the number on the door as I stepped into the dark room. Cell 111. The walls and floor were painted black and the bed was a black iron cot. In the screened recess over the door was a little twenty-five-watt bulb.

Usually when you are dog-tired, and I was dog-tired, the physical touch of bedding makes you overpoweringly sleepy. But this thin, hard mattress and threadbare sheet and blanket smelled terrible, and I knew I was not going to sleep easily or soon. I recalled prisoner stories I had read. *Zenda. The Man in the Iron Mask. Les Misérables*. I thought, Well, better start a calendar. I took my spoon and made a single scratch on the hard black paint on the wall opposite the bed. As I stared at it something caught my eye: scratches that looked like words, heavily painted over. I ducked so that the meager light from over the door would make the scratches readable. I picked out a somber message from the past:

> *Who enters here do not lose hope.*
> *Who leaves do not rejoice.*
> *Who has not been will be here yet.*
> *Who has been here will not forget.*

I thought, Thank God I haven't done anything. I'd sure hate to spend a long time in this dump!

I looked carefully around the whole cell. It was seven feet wide, I guessed, and maybe twelve feet long. Beside the door was a conical cast-iron toilet with a wooden lid. It could be flushed by running water in the little sink which stood beside the toilet and drained into it. At the far end, if you stood on the bed, you could reach up to the frame of a small window with heavy, wire-mesh-reinforced glass. I was standing on the bed when the slot clanged open and the guard hissed in a loud whisper, "Prisoner, if you do that just once more, you will be taken to the hard punishment cells! Lie down on your bed. And if you use the blanket, keep your hands outside it where I can see them."

I was boiling with resentment. I took out a cigarette and lit up. The peephole opened. I wondered if this petty-minded slob would complain about the smoking. The peephole closed. Then, about a minute later, it opened again. Then closed. Soon I realized it was a rhythm, a peek once a minute.

The smoke was relaxing me. I felt sleep stealing over me. I pulled the blanket up to my neck and remembered what the guard had said about my hands, and then I drifted off in my first sleep in over forty hours.

"Podyom!"—"Get up!" There was a terrific bang on the steel door. *"Podyom!"* It felt as if I had slept ten seconds. In reality it had been, I suppose, an hour and a half. I pulled the blanket up over my face. The next thing I knew, the door burst open with an awful clang and a hard-eyed man ripped off the blanket.

"The prisoner will rise when he is told to rise. Hard punishment cells if you do not rise immediately. *Podyom!*" I rose.

I was quite vague in the head and blurry-eyed. I went to the sink and splashed water on my face. Suddenly, for the first time since they took me, I felt hungry. I remembered the smell of the small loaf of bread in Lubyanka and actually found myself looking forward to its arrival. Up and down the corridor I could hear doors clanging and bars and bolts being slid and shot home again. Soon the door opened and the hard-eyed man handed in a bucket half full of cold water, and a small gray rag.

"Wash the floor," was all he said.

I poured a little water on the asphalt and worked away at it and got it pretty well mopped up. Then I stood up in front of the peephole, and when it opened I held up the pail and rag so that he could see I was finished. The door opened. He looked at the floor, grunted, took the pail, and closed the door again.

And then, when breakfast came, I stopped being hungry, because the bread was a damp, coarse lump, sour-smelling and dirty brown. But, I thought, I may be here for a while and I'll need strength, so I took a bite of the dank stuff. The steaming cup looked like tea, but had no flavor at all. Still, the warmth was welcome.

My head hurt, and the piece of bread I ate made me feel sleepy again. I sat on the bunk and closed my eyes.

The slot banged open. The guard said, "Prisoner, you are not allowed to sleep in the daytime. You are not allowed to close your eyes. You may sit on the bed, but you must keep your eyes toward the door and keep them open. Please try to learn these things quickly or you will have a very hard time here. You understand?"

I nodded wearily. I was losing enthusiasm for this game. Let's get to Sidorov and get this stuff over with, I thought.

In Lefortovo a prisoner is taken to the interrogation building through a small anteroom. Here there is a large ledger. Covering it is a sheet of iron with a slit that is placed so that only the name of the prisoner signing in or out and the interrogator's name can be seen. There were two things I came to look forward to in the room of the iron book. One was to see the clock. This gave me a sort of time fix on the day. The other thing to look forward to was signing my name. To keep things a bit off-balance, I conceived the idea of signing my name differently each day, thinking up a new style of handwriting, either in the Roman or Cyrillic alphabet, and never giving them the same signature twice. Then, I thought, if they make me sign some goofy thing that incriminates me, I'll demand that they compare it with my real signature and I can claim it wasn't me. This was one of the first of many small techniques I devised for keeping a sort of sense of having the upper hand. Smiling at the interrogator all the time, being excessively polite, the changing signatures: these helped me retain a sense of being in charge of myself and human and not just a piece of meat these guys were shoving around.

So, hands behind the back, look straight ahead, parade downstairs to the first level, out to another building, and into the room of the iron book. Sign a flamboyant signature, feeling good. There will be news from the embassy today, I know it.

Down a hall, into the interrogation room. Sidorov is smiling.

"There is a letter from your embassy," he said.

"I knew it! That's wonderful!" I reached out for it.

Sidorov withdrew the letter. "It's nothing but a formal note of protest. They know nothing and they are not going to know anything. They wonder if we would be able to inform them. Hah!"

I was thunderstruck. I probably went a bit pale.

Then something happened; a light went on; I said to myself, "He's playing with you, Alex. Don't let him get to you. Get him!"

Out loud I said, "Well, of course you don't dare show it to me"—I smiled broadly—"because they are about to bring about my release through higher circles and you will be embarrassed. Don't worry"—I enjoyed saying that—"it will all be over soon."

Sidorov looked at me with that cynical look of his. I thought there might have been a bit of admiration in it. Then his face darkened and he snapped, "That's all you are going to hear from your embassy. That's the end of it. You will be here for the rest of your life. It's forever now, prisoner. So don't tease yourself with dreams about help from your stupid embassy."

He walked around to the back of his desk and turned away from me to let this sink in. It sank in, all right. I felt terrible. Cold. Sick. But at the same time I told myself he was probably lying (though as it turned out he was not), and I knew that at all costs I must not let his act work. When he turned again, I was smiling.

"Well," I said brightly, "let's get to work then!"

CHAPTER TWO

If I had known how hard that work would be, I might not have been so bright. I came back to my cell from that first day almost desperate to pick up my sleep where it had been interrupted. But when I lay down, the slot banged open immediately and the guard said, "Prisoner, you will not lie down until ten o'clock. Sit up and face the door!" By what I guessed was nine o'clock I was yawning uncontrollably. I wondered if I could last the hour. Then the slot banged open. "Prepare for interrogation!"

I could not believe it! I raged at Sidorov when he came in. I yelled that he could not expect me to remember anything if I could not rest my brain. He heard me out with a cynical smile and then went on with his questions. I realized that those first night-and-day grillings in Lubyanka had been just an opening blitz. This was going to continue for . . . for how long? I knew, numbly, that I was launched on the most terrific endurance test of my life. And I made a resolution. I stared at Sidorov and said, silently, with a deep, deep anger, "I won't break before you do, you bastard!"

The secret police in the Soviet Union are known as *Organi*—the Organs. The word is part of the national slang. It does not, however, carry any laughs with it, except in the occasional black joke. The Organs, whether referred to that way or by their initials as they changed over the decades—OGPU, NKVD, MGB, finally KGB—are a symbol of repression of such magnitude that the sight of their uniform with its purple stripes seems to take the will to resist right out of most Soviet citizens, and I guess to some extent that is what happened to me too, at the moment I was arrested.

Kidnapped is a better word. When regular police arrest you, they don't need to hide what they're doing. They have the law and the general support of the people with them, and they can openly say, "You're under arrest, charged with so and so," and that's it. But these people never did tell me I was arrested. "Come for a five-minute chat," they said.

Solzhenitsyn writes about the "rabbits" all over Russia. The ones who never protested. What's the matter with us? he wonders in *The Gulag Archipelago*. Why didn't we rise up and resist?

Well, I think I know why. It is *because* there is no legitimacy to the KGB. An illegitimate body that is really big and powerful is much more effective in its capacity to frighten people than a legitimate body. Because it is illegitimate, it answers only to the whims and appetites of its masters; and its masters are always shadowy, indistinct people or myths like Stalin, with infinite power and not answerable to any law or any system.

People adored Stalin. People want to love infinite power so that it will love them back. People knew that under Stalin millions disappeared in the middle of the night, but they said, "It must be for the best." My wife Irene's mother was married to a KGB officer. When she heard my story, she said to Irene, though she hated her husband, who had deserted her years before, "Alex *must* have done something terrible or they never would have taken him!"

I knew a pilot in the Soviet Air Force, Peter Bekhtemirov, who adored Stalin. One night he had a terrible dream: The Leader had died. Bekhtemirov woke up with tears streaming down his face. He awakened his wife and told her that he had just had the most terrible dream, that Iosif Vissarionovich was dead. When he went to the base that day, he was still haunted by the grief of that dream, and he confided it to some of his fellow pilots. One of the pilots gave him away, and the MGB charged him with an attempt to assassinate Stalin (political terrorism); a second charge was "an attempt to see an anti-Soviet dream." He got twenty-five years. His wife got ten for *not* denouncing him. Nobody believes me when I tell them this, but I know it to be true.

Now, after a few days with Sidorov, complaining as much as I could about the food and the lack of sleep in as cocky a way as I could muster, he began to get down to business. He would say, "You were employed as a clerk, chief clerk in the file room of the consular section, is that what you said?"

I would answer, "Of course, you know all that."

"That is correct. Now, a clerk is a very junior position. A clerk does not get invited to parties as the private guest of chargés d'affaires, or to dinners at major embassies. But we have dates in here"—he would slap the folder with the back of his hand—"of your dinner at the Australian legation—"

"The assistant military attaché is a good buddy of mine and—"

"The assistant military attaché! Indeed. A young clerk is an intimate friend of the assistant military attaché! Would you say that was normal? And here you are at dinner at the Canadian embassy, and here at the French. A junior clerk? Can you still maintain you were not in fact being prepared for a very special mission?"

He knew the name of every girl I had ever taken out. Most of them had been Russian, and I think most reported to the MGB.

One day, to change the subject, I said to him, "Your operatives are clumsy and obvious. They were following me and everybody else in the embassy all the time. I always knew how to give them the slip."

"I don't know what you're talking about," Sidorov said, showing a slight flush of irritation.

I said, "Okay, I'll tell you. I leave the embassy for lunch, right? A plainclothesman follows me to see what street I'm going to turn down. Now, he doesn't want me to know I've got a tail, right? So he drops behind and calls a phone booth a couple of corners ahead. 'Watch for a blond young man, one meter eighty, eighty-four kilos. U.S. embassy.' Or something like that, right? So I'm supposed to think I've lost the tail because there's nobody behind me. The tail is in the front now. Am I right?"

Sidorov did not say a word. Just stared at me.

I said, "Only I caught on and started watching the phone booths ahead, and as soon as I saw a guy in the phone booth a couple of blocks away, I'd wait until the guy behind had dropped off, and then I'd turn down a side street or go into a shop, and double back. I could always lose them if I wanted to."

I smiled at Sidorov. To my surprise he smiled back. "Please go on," he said a bit tightly. "This is very interesting."

I resisted the impulse to brag in detail about how I lost a car that was following me. I might want to use the same technique later. The block between the Bolshoi and a branch of the Moscow Art Theater was honeycombed with intricately connected courtyards, opening onto the street and to each other through narrow archways. I would lead a tail down Petrovka Street, going away from the Bolshoi, and before I got to the corner of Petrovsky Lane, where the theater is, I would suddenly wheel left into an archway. It was dark in there and slow going, if you weren't absolutely sure of yourself. I would turn off the lights, because I didn't need them. My followers would find themselves in alleys too narrow to go through. I would go back onto Petrovka through another arch, going the opposite way, while my pursuers were probably still backing out of some cul-de-sac.

Sidorov said loftily, "Of course, all of this is known to us. But since you have admitted these incriminating things, why not admit that you were engaged in espionage?"

"There's nothing incriminating about giving your guys the slip. I was trying to have a nice time with a girl. You can't feel relaxed with a girl when there is a carful of MGB following you."

"And why not, if you have nothing to hide?"

"Do you like being followed when you're out with a girl?"

Sidorov's smile dropped. He knew I had overheard him talking to his mistress on the phone in the interrogation room. He unlocked his drawer and pulled out a Tokarev revolver and placed it on the desk pointing at me. This must have been a night session. He would never have done that in the daytime.

He got up, taking the gun, and walked to the far end of the room, always pointing the barrel at me. He said, "I don't think you understand your situation. You're so stupid you keep giving yourself away and you don't even know it. This business of the cars. Every time you wanted a car you took it. Just *took* it! Do you think I don't know that a junior employee can't do that?"

There was no point in explaining. Sidorov would never be able to understand the attitude of an American kid who just takes the old man's car if the keys are in it. There were always half a dozen cars in the embassy yard, and if I wanted one, I just climbed in and gave the guy at the gate a wave as if I had an assignment. To Sidorov cars went with authority and official business. It was simply not comprehensible that you would use them for playing around. Unless you were somebody very highly placed.

And that is what he thought of me.

At least I think so. There were times in those early days when I suspected that he would take any credible confession, whatever it might be. At other times I felt he thought he was on to a really tough customer who was employing the most subtle kind of tactics.

My tactic was to try not to go crazy from lack of sleep, and I found the more I could irritate Sidorov, make him think he was getting somewhere and then let him drop, the higher my morale and the more nearly tolerable this terrible lack of sleep. I was beginning to be frightened about what might happen to me. There were periods when I could not recall what had happened in the last few minutes. Dropouts in my mind. Total erasures.

Even Sidorov would begin to sag in the small hours. Perhaps around three o'clock, after a lot of yawning, he would tilt back his chair and close his eyes and drift off. Then I would put my head on his desk and be asleep instantly. When Sidorov woke up, he would yell at me, "You're not allowed to sleep!"

"*You're* sleeping," I'd retort.

"*Never mind about me!*"

Later on I began to experiment with sleeping upright, to see if my body could learn to hold itself erect. If that would work, I might escape detection in the cell for a few minutes at a time.

And so it would go, snatching ten minutes here, half an hour there. But it was too little. Too little. I could feel myself slipping, getting looser and less disciplined every day. I dreaded going crazy almost worse—no, really worse—than dying. Dying would be preferable by far to this terrible thing of going nuts.

Try to go without water for a whole day. Then imagine that your thirst is a desire to sleep. Then you will have ten percent of what I felt. I thought of sleep all the time. I fantasized sleep as a lecher fantasizes the flesh of young girls or a shipwrecked sailor dreams about a steak and mashed potatoes. Often when they yelled *podyom* at six o'clock and I had been on the cot only five or ten minutes, I wanted to beat on the door and yell for them to bring Sidorov, that I would tell him anything, sign anything, if only I could close my eyes for a few hours of absolute peace.

Saturday afternoon came. Sidorov phoned his wife and told her he was on his way home for the weekend. Can you imagine what hearing that meant for me? When I got back to the cell, I ate the cold soup right away, all of it, as a celebration. Then, when the porridge and tea came at six thirty or so, I ate it all, taking time with each mouthful, to fill the hours until ten o'clock, when I would be allowed, I was certain of it, to crawl under the blanket (keeping my hands outside, of course) and sleep. And *sleep.*

I began to hear music playing. Pleasant, waltz-time music. I was sufficiently confused to wonder if I was imagining the music. But I went to the end of the gloomy black cell and listened carefully and was sure the music came from the window. It was quite clear. I could hear voices, indistinctly, calling out and laughing, and then an unmistakable rhythmic, whispering, scraping sound that I knew well: the sound of skate blades on ice! Somewhere close by the prison was a public skating rink, with music. I could see it in my mind. I loved music, and at that moment I loved it like Mary Catto, like a great dinner of roast chicken, like sleep.

I remember that I waltzed up and down the cell until bedtime. My floppy soles slithered up and down the asphalt. I held Mary in my arms and we spun around and around the ballroom at the Metropole Hotel. The peephole opened, rhythmically, every minute. I kept on dancing, bumping against walls occasionally, and humming under my breath. In a while I knew that nine o'clock had come and gone, and nine thirty. I sensed a settling down in the prison. I thought I would chance it. I stretched out on top of the blanket and kept my eyes wide open. The peephole opened, but the slot stayed shut. If the guard was going to yell and harass me, he would bang open the slot. I closed my eyes and listened for the peephole to come open again, but I never heard it. I dropped a thousand, a million miles into the most profound, world-banishing sleep I had ever known.

In the morning I was drugged with sleep. When *podyom* was shouted through the food slot, I knew I had to move, and I moved, but like a man underwater, in slow motion. By now I realized the importance of disciplined routine; I washed my face carefully. Then I took off my shirt and washed my upper body, cupping a little water in my hand and spreading it on, doing my whole trunk until I began to shiver with the cold. Then my lower body, taking off the baggy long prison underpants. By the time I had finished all that, I felt cheerful and hungry.

The breakfast ration never varied. Always it was four hundred grams of sour bread, a piece of which I usually forced myself to save for later in the day. Then the sugar and the imitation tea.

For a brief time I fell into the trap of imagining marvelous meals. I would spread a table with roast beef and baked potatoes and fried fish and bowls of gravy and white bread and green peas and ice cream. As I looked over all this stuff in my mind's eye, my stomach began to cry out with hunger. I salivated copiously and began to belch deep, sour belches. Then I realized that this was no good. I made a pact with myself that if images of food crept into my mind, I would force myself to think of something else, like hikes in the woods with Mary or poker games at the embassy. At first it did not work very well, because as soon as I went hiking with Mary, she would spread out a cloth and arrange cold sausages, cheese, and wine, and my mouth would fill with saliva again. So I had to try arithmetic or the names of ships in the major naval battles of World Wars I and II. I was absolutely determined that every task I set myself had to be carried through. Failure would be giving in to Sidorov, to *them*.

"Easy, Alex. Take it easy. You can do it." I constantly gave myself pep talks. "You've had almost no sleep for a week and you can do anything you want. You've got guts, boy. You're on to these Russians, aren't you? So as long as you're on to them they can't get you." And this is the way I kept myself going.

In the middle of the morning, that first Sunday, the slot opened and a guard dumped some books on the shelf. I rushed to pick them up. They were tattered and dirty, but they were treasures to me. I read every word with the greatest interest. I think I read those books four or five times during the next three weeks.

I have no idea whether the books were selected with a purpose in mind. One, *Political Prisoners in Czarist Russia*, was an account of the terrible indignities committed against the human person under the inhuman regime of the czars. The first thing I noticed was that none of the prisoners was ever prevented from sleeping. I was also fascinated to read references to a code called the prison Morse, used for tapping messages through the walls.

Another book was Dostoevski's *The House of the Dead*. Ninety-nine years before my own arrest this poor guy had been carted off to Siberia for discussing the theories of radical economists. He spent four hideous years there, "like a man buried alive, nailed down in his coffin." Reading of his troubles made me feel maybe mine were not so bad after all.

On this Sunday morning I read for an hour, then walked up and down in the cell for a while, then read some more, spacing it out so as not to finish the books too fast. Also, I knew I should have regular physical activity, so that I would not get too dependent upon fantasy. There was a tear in my navy-surplus shirt, and I decided that I would figure out some way to repair it. From reading old adventure books I knew that if you were a prisoner, you made needles out of fishbones.

When the thin soup came in the middle of the day, I saved three or four long fishbones from it and attempted to bore a hole in the flat part of the wide end with my teeth and then with my spoon. The bone, which was soft from being boiled in the soup, would either split or be crushed completely. Then I tried to sharpen my aluminum spoon to a point by scraping it on the floor, thinking I could punch a needle eye in tomorrow's fishbones. But a guard saw me sharpening the spoon and took it away, threatening hard punishment. I had been careless about the peephole timing.

I got the idea for making a more elegant calendar than my scratches on the wall. I thought I could mold some numbers and a base to mount them on out of the soggy bread they brought me every day, which went very hard when it dried out. That Sunday I started on the base. I kneaded some bread and rolled and pressed it until I had a small, solid rectangle. Then I bored my carefully hoarded matches about halfway through the top of the rectangle. These would be pegs to fit into the bottom of the numbers to hold them upright.

So, with reading and bread molding and my attempt at needle making, I passed away most of Sunday. Late in the afternoon a guard took me to the shower room. He pulled out an old pair of barber's clippers and reduced my week-old beard to a stiff stubble. Wordlessly he motioned me into the shower.

Even though the soap was the same foul-smelling soft stuff I had used in Lubyanka, the bath was welcome for the heat and because, despite my strict regime of morning washes in my cell, the cold water with no soap had left me a bit ripe. I used most of the soap. Then, when the guard was not looking, I pocketed the rest to take back to my cell. I was developing pack rat instincts automatically.

I thought about Mary Catto a good deal as the evening came on. I wondered for a while whether I should suppress those thoughts for the same reason I suppressed the food fantasies, but I decided not to. The memories of Mary and the other girls in my life were a vital part of my connection with the world outside. They made me feel better, not worse. So by the time I was once more allowed to put my somewhat less numb brain to sleep, I felt composed but lonely. Much as I detested Sidorov, I almost looked forward to the morning, just to have someone to talk to.

In the daytime Sidorov was easygoing and even chatty. Often he took time to read a novel or to write a report that had nothing to do with my case. In the afternoons he would lean back in his chair and talk about the only real enthusiasm I ever detected in him: soccer and the Moscow Dynamos. The Dynamos were a secret police–sponsored team, and Sidorov never missed their games. Sometimes he would spend most of an afternoon on that subject.

But at night he was always hostile and aggressive. His language was nasty, and he spewed out his words in harsh grunts and piercing yells.

The gun would come out a lot at night. He would brandish it in a wild way, and then sit at his desk and sight me calmly, aiming right between my eyes, and cock the hammer and twitch his finger as though he might fire at any time. This behavior made me pretty nervous. But I just kept smiling. Sometimes I would even wink at him over the gun barrel, and this made him furious.

Once during this second week I found myself unconscious on the floor, being yelled at by Sidorov. I had no memory of going off to sleep. One minute I was staring at Sidorov, trying to keep my eyes open; the next minute I was on the floor being roused.

In the cell I had to fight to keep awake with every bit of willpower I had. A few times I tried letting myself doze off while sitting upright on the bunk. If a decent guard was on duty, I might be left like that for a few minutes, perhaps even half an hour from time to time. But decent guards were few and far between. There was one young guard who would chat with me, and that was evidence that he was new at the job. Most guards, when I tried to make them talk to me, simply answered, *"Nye polozhna"*—"Not permitted." Speech was *nye polozhna*, sleep was *nye polozhna*, laughing was *nye polozhna,* anything human and simple was *nye polozhna.* I would ask a guard for something outrageous like a cigarette, so that I could enjoy saying *nye polozhna* before he did.

I made it through the second week. I was muddleheaded and anxious by Saturday night, but I also experienced a sense of satisfaction at having resisted every attempt by Sidorov to get me to admit to the fiction that I was a spy.

I sat on the edge of my bunk and read the poem on the wall, as I did most nights. *Who enters here do not lose hope. . . .* Then I checked the calendar. Twelve days since my arrest. It was . . .

It was Christmas Day.

In my confusion and exhaustion I had missed Christmas Eve. And in my anger and my urgent work of keeping sane and surviving I had scarcely given a thought to my mother, whose worried face now swam into my vision. She would have been expecting me for dinner. She would be pacing up and down wringing her hands. My father would be saying, "It's all right, dear. It's all right. He probably had to go on a trip somewhere. We'll hear from him tomorrow."

And then what would they do when tomorrow came and the tomorrow after that and still no word? I found the thought maddening. It made me tremble with fury at what seemed a worse affront to humanity than what was happening to me. I think when I finally settled into sleep my eyes were pretty damp.

For the rest of the week I worked at shutting out the images of Christmas and New Year celebrations when they crept up on me. I continued with my bread calendar, which went very well. When the base block got good and hard, it was a bit gray and rough on the surface. So I took off my shoe and rubbed the block with the sole until it began to look smooth, and then I polished it on my blanket every day. After a while it took on a gloss like polished wood. In the meantime I began to form the numbers. I made two ones, two twos, and one of everything else, so there were twelve of these little figures to mold. I made an elegant job of each one. Any that did not turn out just right I ate.

All this time the need for sleep was becoming more and more

intense. The busywork with making the calendar and a needle were desperate attempts to stay awake and to stay sane. Sidorov, at my request, had explained that the hard punishment cells were below-ground, unheated even in the depths of winter, had no windows and no bed, and that the whole day's food ration was what I was now getting for breakfast. So I was determined not to do anything that would land me in conditions that I could not stand up under.

Not that my own cell was in any way comfortable. In recounting what happened to me in Lefortovo, I am often afraid that people will forget what a hell I was living. I see them smiling and nodding cheerfully when I tell about making the calendar, for instance. But this was done in a cell purposely designed to create a waking nightmare for its occupant. It was even called a psychic cell, and Sidorov made no bones about the fact that it was intended to wear down my morale, because that was his purpose. "You won't last six months at the outside," he often said. "Nobody does."

Cell 111. The psychic cell. The black paint was neither flat, which might have had a velvety warmth to it, nor glossy, which might have had a few highlights in it, but just a hard black. The bed was black. The floor was black. The bulb over the door, which when I was allowed to sleep I had to face, was not bright enough to illuminate this black space, but bright enough to be an annoyance when I faced it.

The cell was cold. When the outside temperature dropped below zero, frost would form on the floor. I was warm only when they took me to Sidorov.

Memory keeps you alive. I firmly believe this. If I had not been able to remember faces, names, the plots of movies, words people had spoken to me, books I had read, restaurants I had eaten in, maps, the face of Europe, rooftops in Manhattan, I could never have survived the Moscow prisons. Labor camps, maybe. There you are with people. In Lefortovo prison, even though I spent nearly eighteen hours a day, five days a week, in interrogation with Colonel Sidorov, I was alone, and, next to the desperate need for sleep, aloneness was the most feared enemy.

Sometime in the third week at Lefortovo a new torture was

added to the cold and the black and the loneliness of cell 111. Early one morning a strange low rumble started somewhere outside my window and soon grew in pitch and volume until it was a gigantic roar. When I looked at my plate and spoon on the food slot shelf, they were visibly trembling. I was enraged. Even when I covered my ears, the sound drilled through my skull. I was relieved when they took me to Sidorov. I wryly complimented him on the inhuman ingenuity of the terrible noise. Irony was never Sidorov's strong point, and he didn't understand me. He said, "I know. It is terrible. They have an aeronautical research institute next door. That's their wind tunnel. Good thing my office is not on that side, I'd never be able to get my reports written."

So it was a wind tunnel and not a torture device. And yet it was going to get me down. I knew it. I decided I would have to train myself to be temporarily deaf, the same way I had trained myself to smile at Sidorov. However, almost as soon as I thought of that I also realized that I could use this noise to help me survive.

The guard brought me back to the cell at a quarter past five the next morning. I knew it was earlier than usual, because for the last couple of hours Sidorov had been yawning, and then, when he finally pressed the button for the guard, the doors in the other interrogation rooms were still closed and the corridors were quiet. When I got to the cell, I lay down on the cot and nobody bothered me and I had at least half an hour's sleep. Maybe three-quarters.

When they banged on the door and shouted *podyom*, I got up and started to walk back and forth in the cell, because as long as you were in motion they left you alone. And I began to count the minutes until the wind tunnel would start up, because I had decided how I would use it.

Breakfast would come about six thirty. I had figured this out by counting the number of times the peephole opened between *podyom* and breakfast. Then around seven a guard would hand in an old greatcoat, quite threadbare, and take me out into the yard for the exercise period.

The yard was divided by wooden walls. If I looked straight up, I could see the sky, and this morning, I remember, it was still dark and I could see a star. Is Mary looking at that star, too? I thought.

The guard came to take me back to the cell, and I waited for the wind tunnel to start up so I could experiment with making it work for me. I counted the times the peephole opened. When I guessed it was getting close to eight o'clock, I thought, All right, now. Maybe after this peephole but before the next one.

Finally the noise started. It was against the rules to talk in the cell or make any sound, but I turned away from the peephole, and as I strode toward the window, I opened my mouth as wide as I could and filled my lungs and I sang out loud:

> *"Mairzy Doats and Dozy Doats*
> *and liddle lamzy divey"*

Loud. I mean really full blast, everything I had. *Fortissimo.* Boy, it felt great!

At the end of the cell I turned and looked back at the peephole. I thought, On the way back, where he can see my face, I won't move my lips so much and I won't sing so loud, so even if he looks carefully, he won't know what's going on.

> *"A kiddley divey too, wouldn't you?"*

The effect was fantastic! I mean the effect on me. I was grinning to myself. I had discovered another instrument for my survival. It sounds crazy talking about this childish song as an instrument of survival. But this was a song from America, and back at the embassy residence was a phonograph with that record on it.

> *"If the words sound queer,*
> *and funny to your ear,*
> A *little bit jumbled and jivey,*
> Sing *'Mares eat oats and does eat oats*
> *and little lambs eat ivy' . . ."*

I immediately felt less tired. I knew I had to go back to the interrogation room in about an hour. Sidorov has had me three weeks now, and pretty soon I'll break down and tell him whatever he wants. But this morning I've got the bastard, because I can sing and that means I'm still in touch with the outside, and when he sees me, he just won't understand why I'm so damn cocky.

I remember that I walked faster and faster up and down the cell that morning, pivoting at the end, filling my lungs up and singing nonstop. "I'm the Lefortovo jukebox," I said to myself.

> *"Pardon me, boy,*
> > *Is that the Chattanooga choo-choo*
> > *Track twenty-nine,*
> > *Boy, you can gimme a shine . . ."*

The door of my cell opened and the guard handed in my bucket of icy water and a rag, and went out again. That meant about half an hour left before I would be taken upstairs. I began to scrub the floor. When I finished, I stood in front of the peephole with my rag and bucket. The guard opened the door without a word and took them away and locked me in again.

I was a bit light-headed. I would have to go three more nights with no sleep before it was Saturday—Saturday and Sunday nights they let me sleep while Sidorov went home or wherever he went. But somehow I knew that I would get through it.

The wind tunnel was still roaring. I grinned at it through the stone walls. "Thank you, friend," I said. And then I put my head back and filled the time I had left with a song I could really put my heart into.

> *"Oh, give me land, lots of land, under starry skies above,*
> > *Don't fence me in.*
> *Let me ride through the wide open spaces that I love,*
> > *Don't fence me in. . . ."*

The door rattled and swung open. "Prepare for interrogation," the guard said. When he looked at me to motion me out of the cell, his eyebrows went up, because I was grinning quite happily. But he didn't say a word.

Sidorov was not in the interrogation room when I got there. I sat on the chair and immediately went to sleep. I was beginning to learn how to sleep in a hard wooden chair without falling off, and to be ready to wake up again at the smallest sound. As soon as I heard the door opening, I woke up, and when Sidorov looked at me, my eyes were wide open. Sidorov sat down behind his desk and read for a while without looking at me, and pulled a pack of cigarettes out of his pockets and lit one.

After a while he said, "Prisoner, come over here."

I went and stood in front of his desk. He offered me a cigarette. "Here." I took it, and he lit it for me with a kind of courtesy.

"Your own are all gone, aren't they?"

"I told you that two weeks ago."

"In the labor camp where I will send you when I'm through with you, you can have your tobacco and you can smoke whenever you like. Wouldn't that be better than what you're getting here?"

I just smiled my simple smile at him and shrugged.

"Look, prisoner, I'm going to give you some advice. It won't get any better here. You think you're having a hard time, but it can only get harder if you don't cooperate. Now listen, it's all in here anyway"—he slapped the file—"all we need is a few details and a signed statement, and then you'll be able to sleep at night and smoke cigarettes and you'll probably get a very light sentence for cooperating."

I heard snatches of music running through my head. I laughed and said in English, "Is this the Chattanooga choo-choo?"

"What's that?" Sidorov said sharply.

I said, "If you know everything already, what do you need me for anyway? Why not just send me quietly off to camp? Then you could report you've got the confession you needed."

A trace of anger came into Sidorov's face. He picked up the paper. "You won't feel so witty later tonight," he said tightly.

All day I sat in the chair, shifting my shrinking buttocks from side to side, trying to blink away the burning in my eyes. Sidorov scarcely spoke. Around noon he left to get something to eat. I tried sleeping in my chair, but as soon as the guard saw my eyes close, he came and shook me. The high morale I had built up for myself with songs in the morning was beginning to wear off. There was a kind of pressure building up inside my skull. I knew it could only be cured by sleep. Before Sidorov came back I tottered and fell off the chair with my eyes closed. Somebody picked me up and shook me vigorously.

"Sleep," I said.

"Talk, and you'll get to sleep," Sidorov's voice said. I opened my burning eyes and smiled at him.

Back to the cell at six p.m. That night, or one night soon after, two things happened almost simultaneously. I noticed that my hair was falling out, and I found another use for my little towel.

In fact, my hair had started coming out at the end of the second week. When I washed my face and ran cold water through my hair with my fingers, a few hairs came away and I saw them in the sink. The next time I was drying myself after a shower I saw some more hair lying on my arm. This night I had brushed my hand across my head to try to ease the pressure in my skull, and I could literally feel a tuft of hair come loose. I brought down a bunch of blond hair and stared at it.

I felt a surge of panic coming on. I said, "Easy, Alex, that's what they want. To make you lose control." I was enormously tempted to feel my head and see if any more hair would come away, but I was terrified that it would, so I didn't.

I thought, I've got to get busy at something new, anything to keep my mind active. I decided to wash my plate very meticulously. Then my little towel caught my eye. It was woven pretty loosely of a fairly coarse cotton. I painstakingly pulled out threads until I had a long one that looked like about a meter, and then divided it up by sharp creases with my teeth into ten ten-centimeter lengths and then divided up the last of these into ten one-centimeter divisions. I now had a ruler.

First I decided to measure my cell. I said to myself, "I wonder how far I walk every day, up and down between these walls?" It was 227 centimeters wide and 351 long. I walked from the door to the opposite wall and back. Ten steps, five each way, which meant about seventy centimeters each step. If I could shorten the step to sixty-six and two-thirds, so that every three steps meant two meters, then a kilometer would take fifteen hundred steps.

I thought, I'll walk to the embassy.

The idea excited me strangely. In my dead black cell, isolated from everyone but the anonymous eye at the peephole, the fantasy of a walk across Moscow to join friends was totally seductive. I made the gates of the prison my first target and got up and started to walk as fast as I could up and down the cell. Now I am at the corridor of boxes; another thirty steps; lucky the door is open and no one is looking, and I'm out into the courtyard. It's dark enough. There is a van coming in with a prisoner. I'll just slip behind it and out into the snowy streets and freedom!

A nourishing fantasy. An energizing fantasy. I turned southwest and began to count my steps, up and down the cell. I walked past the skating rink, with the lights and music and the boys and girls whirling around, but I didn't look right or left, I just walked and counted. I began to recognize the streets of Moscow—streets I'd driven through with the boys from the embassy or with Mary.

Then I thought, Why not walk right out of this godforsaken country? Let's say it's only six kilometers from here to the outskirts of the city proper, then I can pick up a road west and just head right across Russia until I'm free! Only nine thousand paces to the edge of Moscow, kid. Pick it up now, pick it up!

The moon hung low in the west and I headed straight for that. No one in the nearly empty streets paid any attention to me, so I tucked my head down against the wind and walked and walked.

The door of the cell opened. "Prepare for interrogation." I thought, I'm only at 4150 paces. Then I thought, Why stop? I fell into step behind the guard and walked and counted, down the corridor, up the steps to the room of the iron book, signed my name with my feet still moving up and down. Might as well add in every step we can, kiddo, because we're walking home, and into the interrogation room, and I've got 4450 paces and Sidorov isn't here yet. Now if I can snatch another fifty paces before he gets here, I'm halfway to the edge of the city.

Sidorov came in on my second trip across the room. "Sit down, prisoner!" he barked. Three steps across the room to my chair makes 4475, so I have an extra twenty-five to make up in the morning. Now let me see exactly where I am and how many kilometers does 4475 paces make? Could I do that in my head? I wondered. Twenty-five paces is about sixteen meters. Sixteen meters short of three kilometers. Work that out in decimal places and see if we can get some kind of efficiency norm worked out for this. After a while Sidorov started shouting at me that he had put the same question to me three times without an answer.

"I don't get much sleep, you know," I remember saying to him.

It was not a very pleasant night. I fell off the chair at least twice, and the second time they woke me with cold water. I was shivering when they led me back to cell 111 at six a.m., and my legs were aching from the evening's crazy enthusiasm.

Although it is true that I was in interrogation sixteen to eighteen hours a day, one man could not really interrogate for such extended periods. Sidorov would begin each morning with a suggestion that it was time to confess, which he would repeat often during the day. The rest of the time he talked about other things.

Soon Sidorov began to stress my acquaintance with embassy military people, as if that proved something. And after a while he began to suggest that I was well acquainted with a good many Soviet officers, too. He would say, "Now, I'm going to give you one more chance to tell me about your attempt to recruit a certain Soviet officer into your espionage network," or something like that, and for a long time I just could not think what he was getting at. Then I had a sudden memory of an event that would be very hard to explain, and was in fact partly illegal. What had suddenly surfaced in my mind was a trip I had made in the summer of 1946. In the course of it I was caught trespassing, with a pistol in my possession, on the grounds of the dacha of the party secretary of the Ukraine, Nikita S. Khrushchev.

ONE of my father's friends was a Ukrainian named Michael Kovko. They had worked together in New York in the 1920s, and somehow in 1945 Kovko found out my father was in Moscow and came to see him. He was a captain in the army by then, posted in Kiev, the capital of the Ukraine, to run various peacetime transport pools. He was only in Moscow for a few weeks, but he visited my father fairly often, and I saw him several times. He was very strongly impressed with my working for the American embassy. I'm not sure exactly why, but he looked on me with some exaggerated respect. He said several times, "Why don't you come and visit sometime? Meet my wife and my children, see the Ukraine."

When Michael Kovko went home to Kiev, I forgot all about him for the time being. But one day in 1946, I thought of Kovko and decided very impulsively that I would go and see him when I got some time off from the embassy.

My current girl friend, Dina, thought it was a great idea for an adventure. She was a graduate of the Moscow Foreign Languages Institute and very bright and ready for anything.

To travel in the Soviet Union at that time, you had to have an official permit for each trip, and even Soviet nationals had a hard time getting them, to say nothing of foreigners. I thought, I've never seen any other part of Russia. I want to go, and I'll do it without a permit, somehow. Dina was all for this. So I started going to the railway stations to see what I could pick up.

I started talking with people casually, and I learned that a good many were traveling without permits and that the way to make arrangements was to find a sympathetic conductor and offer him a few rubles to fix you up. I went around the station until I found a conductor who said sure, he could get me on a train for a few rubles, but I'd better bring my own food, because food was scarce and rationed.

Dina and I were very excited. I packed a big suitcase with clothes and canned food, and a bottle of whiskey. I decided to take my two pistols with me in case we got to go into the countryside where I could do some shooting.

The conductor had told us how to get into the rail yards by a back way, and had set a time to meet him on the loading platform, a long way from the station proper. The agreement was two hundred rubles when we shook hands on the deal, and another three hundred when he got us on the train. Five hundred rubles was a very good tip to a Russian workingman in those days, but I overestimated his honesty and his goodwill. He promised me a good coach and ended up shoving us on a cattle car. I yelled "What about your promise?" but he just shouted that the train was pulling out, and sure enough we could hear the engine huffing and puffing and the cattle car was already pretty heavily populated.

"Take it or leave it!" he shouted. We climbed on.

It was a nightmare scene in that cattle car. People lay around on two layers of wooden shelves. The shelves were crawling with bedbugs and lice, but I had a can of DDT powder, and Dina and I made a sort of island of DDT for ourselves.

To try to get through the first night in a reasonably good mood, we drank the whole bottle of whiskey. Next day we were hung over and dying of thirst. The train seldom stopped. When it did I was able to go and fill the empty whiskey bottle with hot water, and we made instant coffee and ate our canned meat and fruit, while the others on the train ate dry black bread and looked at us with hostile eyes. We were three nights on that train.

It was five o'clock in the morning when the train pulled into the Kiev station. Dina and I were still full of adventure, even though we were pretty tired, and she agreed to wait in the station with the suitcase while I went off to find Michael Kovko. This was the kind of guy I was: I had not written to Kovko to tell him we were coming. After all, he had said come anytime. I found my way to his building on Levanovsky Street and climbed the stairs to his apartment and knocked on the door.

I heard his voice. "Who is it?"

"It's Alex!"

"Alex? Alex?" The door opened against the chain. "Alex! Alex Dolgun! Come in! Come in!"

Michael Kovko was in his underwear. He smiled amiably at me. "Listen, my wife's at the dacha with the kids. Come into the bedroom and tell me what you're doing here while I get dressed."

I followed him, saying, "Well, I've got a girl with me and . . ."

At the bedroom I stopped, because I was so shocked by what I saw. He was pulling on the uniform of the MGB.

He looked up and saw me staring at the purple stripes. "Yeah," he said, "disgusting, isn't it? Well, they needed a good car-pool man and they offered to make me a major and it's not so bad. Same job as the army. Better rank, better pay."

Even though he was an old family friend, the symbols of that huge illegitimate force made me cautious. I felt for the little Japanese pistol in my pocket. While Kovko belted on his own gun, he listened to the story of our trip and chuckled at the audacity of it. Then he said he would go and get a car and we would drive out to his country place. "Come on," he said, "let's get your girl."

We went out and walked a few blocks until we came to a large building. "MGB headquarters," he said casually. "Don't worry. I'll tell them you're my brother-in-law."

I kept my hand on the gun in my pocket. We walked right up to the checkpoint. Surrounded by MGB! Kovko told them I was his wife's brother and they issued a pass, just like that. We whisked into the garage. "I'm taking a car for the weekend," he said.

We took a green BMW and went to the station to get Dina.

Like many Russians with means, Kovko spent part of the summer in a couple of rented rooms in a small village near enough to rivers and woods to go hiking and picnicking. I began to relax once we got into the country, and Dina seemed completely at ease and surprisingly unaffected by the appearance of my friend in his uniform of the dreaded secret police.

We spent long evenings talking and drinking wine, and in the morning Michael and I would take his shotgun and his Tokarev pistol and go off to the banks of the Dnieper River for some shooting. I retained enough caution not to show him my own pistols, but I always had the little Japanese .22 in my pocket. Kovko was impressed when I shot some birds with his Tokarev.

Sometimes we would take a rowboat across the Dnieper and climb the high bank and roam the woods on the other side. What we did not know was that these woods were on the outskirts of the dacha being used at the time by Secretary Khrushchev.

One morning Michael shot two birds with the shotgun. We rowed across the Dnieper River and climbed the bank and threw the birds into the stream and took turns trying to hit them with the pistol. I could manage it, but Kovko couldn't. He was envious of my skill. Suddenly, as we were popping away at the birds, I heard a noise in the woods behind us. I turned around and got a shock. There were four plainclothes cops with pistols pointing at us.

The one who approached us talked with a tone of authority. "Why are you shooting here? Don't you know this is a forbidden zone?" Then he noticed the insignia on Michael's shirt. "Excuse me, Comrade, would you be good enough to explain? You see, you are on the grounds of Secretary Khrushchev's dacha."

Michael produced his documents. He was jovial, easygoing. It was very impressive the way he handled the cops. They became quite friendly and put away their guns, and we got out of there in a hurry, but not an undignified hurry. Kovko thought it was funny, but it took me a day or so to see the humor. After all, I had no authorization to be in the Ukraine, and if they had asked for my papers, it could have been pretty dramatic.

When it came time to head back to Moscow, Kovko got us on a first-class coach with excellent meals and comfortable beds. The travel restrictions had been lifted.

We had had a marvelous time. The walks in the woods, the exciting brush with the guards at Khrushchev's dacha, and lots of laughter and relaxed talk with Michael and his young wife, Valentina. Sometimes Dina had gone shooting with us, and she got to like the pistol. So when we got back to Moscow, I borrowed a .38, and we went into the woods on weekends and did some more shooting, trying to shoot the bottom out of a wine bottle, for example, by firing through the mouth of it. We continued to have a lot of fun together, and it might have gone on for quite a long time, even though it was not deeply serious, at least for me.

But one day I was walking in her street, Bolshaya Polyanka. I saw Dina ahead of me and decided for fun to walk up quietly behind her and take her arm and say, "Be quiet! MGB!" in a stern voice, to tease her. But she suddenly turned and went into a school building. I followed her up the steps of the building, and as I went in, I saw Dina ahead of me, going into a room down the hall.

There was an attendant by the door of the building and I asked him what that office was down the hall. Oh, he said, that's an MGB *spetsodel*, one of the briefing rooms where they hold informal meetings with their agents.

I was furious. My first instinct was to confront Dina when she came outside. But I realized that I was mad enough to smash her and that would be no good. So I just turned on my heel and walked out of that yard and never went to see her again. She called the embassy for a few days, but I never called her back.

So of course I was pretty sure that this was the episode that Sidorov had in mind when he tried to link me with a particular military man. It made me feel uneasy, because that trip to Kiev would be very hard to explain. The coincidence of turning up inside the boundaries of Secretary Khrushchev's preserve just would not be believed.

I said to Sidorov, "Look, you know I am really trying to remember. Can you tell me where these meetings with military officers are supposed to have taken place?"

No bite. He said, "I think you'd better tell me that. *I* know, of course, but if you want to save yourself trouble, you will tell me everything very freely."

So then I thought I would try to fix the time. I took a deep breath and said, "Now, I think you said we were talking about the summer of 1945," just to throw him off the Kiev trail, if there were any such trail.

Sidorov said, "That's right, 1945."

"Well," I said slowly, teasing him, because now I was perfectly relaxed. I would not have to tell him about going to Kiev in 1946.

"Well! Well?" Sidorov was getting impatient.

Fine. I just shook my head slowly and said, in complete truth, "No. I am sorry. I am trying, but I cannot recall anything from 1945. You know, I think you really have made a mistake this time."

Sidorov just slumped in his chair and looked disgusted.

Later that night he took it out on me, with rages and gun-waving and a renewed attack on my alleged relations with high-ranking military people. I could feel the tension rising and rising. I figured it would be only a matter of days before it spilled over.

CHAPTER THREE

Toward the end of the first month in Lefortovo things began to get very bad. Except on the weekends, I was never able to steal more than an hour of sleep every day. Effectively it was the same as no sleep at all, and my mind began to go blank fairly frequently. The effort to keep counting my steps and converting them to kilometers and remember where I had stopped walking the day before was almost more than I could summon up. My eyes burned and ached constantly. Sudden bright light was an agony.

Sidorov had increased the intensity of his questioning at night. He had begun to suggest that I was particularly interested in certain Soviet naval officers. He told me that my association with a naval lieutenant at our own embassy, Bob Dreyer, a guy I often went out with, was suspect, because they had long had him marked as an intelligence agent.

Sidorov would say, "We have indisputable evidence that you were engaged in espionage activities with Bob Dreyer. Why do you deny it?"

My answer: "I deny it, that's all."

He produced a collection of photographs, mostly of Soviet army and navy officers in uniform, and showed them to me one after another, demanding that I identify these men and cursing me when I said I did not recognize them.

Over and over again the same photographs, with the sense of violence coming nearer and nearer to the surface. "I'm giving you another chance. We know you know some of these men. Why do you deny that?"

My answer: "I deny it."

And then, around three in the morning, he handed me the photographs and yelled at me to keep turning them over until I was prepared to admit that I recognized someone in the collection. I said, "It's no use. I don't recognize anyone. Not one!"

I did not see him come at me until it was too late. His fist came in hard and caught me on the side of the face with enough force to spin me right out of my chair and onto the floor. I lay there, with the blow reverberating inside my skull.

Sidorov came and stood over me. "Get up!" he screamed. "Get up and go through them again and again until you confess you know him!"

"Who? Who?" I yelled back at him, still on the floor. "I never saw any of these men! None of them!"

Suddenly I felt as if my right shin had been cracked open. I sat up and grabbed for it, almost screaming, when the toe of his hard high boot landed on the other shin. I felt sick and my stomach began to heave. I pushed myself up somehow, breathing hard and fast to keep the tears back and to keep from yelling.

"The photographs!" he screamed.

I picked them up and bent over them again. My hands were shaking, but I started going through the photographs as quickly as I could, muttering, "I'll try, I'll try as hard as I can."

Sidorov paced the room. I worked at composing myself. Gradually my heartbeat slowed down, and my breathing got a good deal easier. I waited until Sidorov tired of walking and sat down, and then I looked right in his eyes and smiled a big smile. I said, "Maybe you've got some better pictures?"

His eyes went very narrow. I was taking the risk of another fist or a boot, but I knew this was the precise moment when I had to show him he was not winning. He did not get up out of his chair. He did not yell. He just stared. I think there might have been a faint hint of admiration in that stare.

Back in the frigid cell I rolled up my pants and looked at my shins. The left was angry, red, and bruised. The right was cut open, and when I pulled up the long prison underwear, a thin trickle of blood began to ooze. I washed it in cold water. My head was pounding terribly. I was shivering and nauseated. Breakfast made me more nauseated, but I worked at keeping it down. I prayed for the wind tunnel to start up so I could shout out some curses, tell some jokes, sing a rousing song. The wind tunnel did not start.

I wanted to continue walking to America, but I was too weak. I washed my face several times. I willed myself to sleep sitting up straight and probably caught a few minutes, but then I heard the slot open and the guard said firmly, *"Nye polozhna."*

Somehow I thought that was funny, so I laughed a weak laugh at him and said, "I know, I know," and waved him away.

Rubbing my head, I felt the bare patches and looked at the hairs on my fingers and suddenly got some energy from an idea that might save my mind. I knocked on the door, and told the guard that I had a serious scalp condition and needed to see a doctor. I bent over and let him look at my patchwork scalp. He went away and came back with the block supervisor, who also looked at my scalp. I could hear them confer outside. I remember being cheered by the arrival of a new idea for surviving, all the way back to the interrogation room that night. But the cheer did not last ten seconds inside the room.

Sidorov waded into me with both fists, yelling that if I did not tell him everything he would kill me with his bare hands.

He sent me flailing across the room trying to hold my balance, which was not very good to begin with. I hit the wall hard and went down on my knees. I thought, I must protect my shins! I must protect my shins! Sidorov picked me up by the shoulders and dragged me to my chair, screaming obscenities. He dumped me in the chair and slapped my cheeks hard, yelling at me to sit up.

"Are you going to identify the man?" he said, with a sudden quiet in his voice.

I did not trust my voice. I just shook my head and mouthed the words, "I can't."

The shock when his boot hit my shin on top of the first bruise made me gasp. The next kick made me yell out loud, "Please! Please! How can I tell you names I don't know! Please! I'll tell you any name! Boris, Andrei, anything, only please don't kick again!"

The fist lashed out again, and my consciousness just swam away. Then I was dragged down the hall to the cellblock by two guards holding me under the arms. I would come to and pass out as they dragged me up the stairs. They dumped me on the floor of my cell. I smelled vomit and realized it was on the front of my shirt.

My soaked shirt chilled my upper body. I began to shiver. The asphalt floor was terribly cold, but every time I tried to crawl to the bed I felt dizzy and sick.

For a long time I lay shivering on that floor. Then a strange thing happened. The pain receded. I was perfectly conscious. I was standing in the corner of the cell looking down at a shivering, vomit-covered wreck by the reeking toilet. There was blood on his face and his lip was swollen. He moaned with every breath. And I thought, Look how he suffers! But he doesn't cry. He won't give them *that* satisfaction.

I quite clearly stood outside myself and my suffering. It is my clearest recollection of that confused and agony-filled night. For a while I had clarity and peace. I watched my own body suffer. And when the suffering subsided a little and the moans stopped, I got back in the body and dragged myself to the bed and climbed in and blessed the warmth of the blanket, and left my hands outside, and slept without moving.

When *podyom* was shouted, I went to sit up, but my head was pounding again and I had to go very slowly. I found I could eat my bread, through a mixture of burning hunger and twinges of nausea. The hot tea seemed to help.

When the wind tunnel began to wind up, it startled me, and I was afraid that the noise would hurt my head. When it hit full volume, I felt a sudden sense of release and I had a terrible urge to cry. I thought, Quick! What's the most rousing song I know? And then I limped up and down the cell, feeling stronger as I worked some of the stiffness out of my legs, and I roared:

> *"Roll out the barrel—*
> *We've got the blues on the run—"*

A great song! A song I came to trust. I could feel the need for tears pushing hard from inside, but I pushed back with the song.

> *"Zing! Boom! Tararrel—*
> *Ring out a song of good cheer—*
> *Now's the time to roll the barrel—*
> *For the gang's all here."*

Stomping up the cell like a drum major, I brought my hand up and down with an invisible baton. To hell with them if they were watching. Let them watch. I stared hard at the peephole until it opened, and forced a huge smile as the astonished eyes peered.

Suddenly the door opened and a doctor came in. "What's all this about your hair?" he shouted over the wind tunnel noise. I shouted back. He motioned a guard and they took me out on the catwalk where the light was better, and shut the door against the noise.

I made up a story. I explained that this was an old ailment that ran in my family and was brought on by cold; that two of my cousins were said to have died of brain inflammation after all their hair had fallen out and that was why the whole family always wore hats all the time in cold weather. I said I had been wearing a hat when I was arrested, but it had been taken away. I must have been very convincing. When I came back to the cell in the late afternoon, my hat was on my bunk! My beautiful, wide-brimmed, American-made fedora! I savored the word. Fedora! The hat was a bit crushed from being bundled up, but I parked it jauntily on my aching head and sat on the bunk, facing the door. The brim shadowed my eyes, and in the weak light I was sure they would be invisible to the guard at the peephole.

When the peephole opened, I sat absolutely immobile. The guard seemed to wait a bit longer than usual, but finally he closed it. I thought, He's waiting to see if I move. I did not move. The peephole opened again in a minute. I sat motionless. Just before I thought he was going to open the slot and yell, I wiped the back of my hand across my nose. The peephole closed. I spent the rest of the evening conditioning the guard that way. Every time he looked in he watched a little longer, and every time I gave a sign of movement at the last moment.

I felt a hard knot in my stomach as the time came closer to go back to interrogation. I gingerly felt my shins and I knew I would scream if Sidorov kicked me again, as I fully expected he would. As it turned out, the next two nights were not so bad.

Sidorov, as he often did, stopped the interrogation early on Saturday, and when I got back to the cell, I had the consolation of the wind tunnel, which ran full blast that day until after six. I had another inspiration. I imagined Sidorov striding off down the street outside Lefortovo to his wife or his mistress, and I saluted his retreating back in my mind and shouted out loud, "Sidorov, you bastard, this song is dedicated to you!"

Then I sang all I could remember of

> *"Saturday night is the loneliest night of the week,*
> *'Cause that's the night that my baby and I*
> *used to dance cheek to cheek."*

It was my celebration of Sidorov's departure for the weekend, and for the rest of my time under his care I sang it every Saturday night. It was another of the little things that provided a growing mass of tiny, essential props for my morale.

My Saturday night sleep was long, dreamless, and a total escape. Stiff muscles on Sunday, but a vigorous walk in the exercise yard and through my mental road map, with lots more accumulated kilometers. And then came another immense lift to my morale.

I had become aware that I had a neighbor in the next cell. I could hear whispered remarks from the guard at mealtime and the sound of a slot moved back and forth. Then, on Sunday afternoon, while I sat working on a fishbone needle, I heard a series of taps on the wall, clearly coming from the next cell.

I tapped back with my knuckles. *Tap tap tap.*

He tapped back. Three taps. There was a pause. I heard the peephole in my cell open and managed to get up in one motion and walk about, concentrating on concealing my fishbone.

Then there was a pause for his peephole. Then another series of taps, quite rapid, but distinctly spaced in double groups: 2, 4. Then 1, 5. Then 4, 3. Then 1, 1. I knew Morse code well enough to recognize that this was not it. Then I remembered my book, *Political Prisoners in Czarist Russia*. This must be the prison Morse! Damn! Why hadn't that author explained the code! I began to answer in the same patterns, except that some of his groups were pretty long and I could not remember the entire sequence, so I would just break down and send a whole series of staccato taps. I was laughing out loud for joy. A fellow sufferer was next door, someone who would care and understand. I became totally absorbed in tapping, listening, tapping, laughing. I paid no attention to the peephole, forgot all about it. The slot burst open with an awful clang. The guard glared at me and said, *"Nye polozhna!* And if you do it again, it will be hard punishment cells. Tapping is a very serious offense!"* I said, "I understand," and went to my bunk and sat down. I heard the slot in the cell next to me bang open and knew that he was giving the same warning to my new friend. But I knew we could work it out, and I was ecstatic.

I went to work on the fishbone again, and being so full of high spirits, got a new idea. I split the end of the soft bone and twisted the two split ends around the point of a match. I thought that when it dried and hardened, I could remove the match and I would then have a workable needle with an eye cemented together by natural bone glue. It took a day for the bone to dry, and when I looped a thread from my towel through the eye and started to work on a rip on my shirt, the needle held together. A small success that seemed a triumph. I had lost several buttons from my shirt. I molded some buttons of bread, and when they dried, I sewed them on.

My neighbor and I continued our blind correspondence. The next time the wind tunnel started up I tapped as hard as I could on the wall, between peepholes. Back came the answer. Always in the groupings of two numbers. Now I realized that the same figure occurred over and over again like a musical theme. It went: 2, 4; 3, 6; 3, 2; pause. Then 1, 3; 5, 2.

I tried returning the same pattern, and this set off a terrific rattle of taps. I realized that my neighbor thought I suddenly understood the code. I answered with a simple pair of taps. He must have understood. A simple double tap came back.

We found we could get away with tapping while the food was being distributed; that was the only time when the peephole was not opened every minute. One evening I began to realize that a new pattern was emerging. My neighbor would start with the familiar 2, 4; 3, 6; 3, 2 . . . 1, 3; 5, 2.

I would answer with a single tap. He must have taken that to mean I didn't understand. Then he would begin the following pattern: 1, 1; 1, 2; 1, 3; 1, 4; 1, 5; 1, 6. Then a pause. Then 2, 1; 2, 2; 2, 3; 2, 4; 2, 5; 2, 6. Then a pause. Then 3, 1; 3, 2, and so on, to 3, 6. Then it would be 4, 1 to 4, 6. I knew there was some kind of key in this, but I could not get it. I would answer back a single tap. *I do not understand.* And patiently he would begin again, 1, 1; 1, 2, right through the whole sequence.

My friend kept up his attempts at instruction during every meal, but in the morning he would just tap simple taps that corresponded to the rhythms and routine of the day. No code; just an acknowledgment that we were sharing the same experience. Two taps: *Good morning,* as I came back from interrogation. (He was always there when I came back; he was not in interrogation then?) Two taps: *Going for my walk now,* when they came to take him to exercise. Two taps: *I'm back.* Two little human bits of caring.

Almost every day now I told myself the plot of a favorite movie or novel. And I continued to train the guards to believe I was awake under the shadow of the hat. I had to reach the point where they would not wait to see if I moved, where they would simply make a routine stop at the peephole, and go on.

Before long I began to give them their midterm tests and then their final exams. They all passed, and soon I could always get sleep in half-hour chunks.

At this point I can predict, I think, what a reader of this page will feel and say: "He's got it made. It's all right now."

Part of this is what I felt. Relief, certainly, and a certainty that I was now going to survive. But there was a grimmer side to it. As soon as Sidorov started to beat me, I realized that I was going to be in prison for a long time. I knew there would be more beatings and that I would suffer a lot. When they gave me back my hat, the hell I was living in became a hell I could survive, but it was still hell. I believe it was at that time that my eyes and mouth began to settle into a grim cast, which is still my normal expression when I am not excited or laughing. My iron mask never came off, and I can see that it never will.

I CAME TO LOVE THE invisible being next door who greeted me and said farewells. He tried every evening to teach me the key: 1, 1; 1, 2; 1, 3, and so on. I could not get it, but I felt his teaching to be a form of moral support. Even his simple double taps in the morning told me to keep up my courage, that I would get through.

The beatings came and went in waves, and I often had that experience of looking at myself shivering on the floor, doubled up with pain, bruised and nauseated, while I watched from outside. In the periods between beatings, when I was not in too much pain, I kept my clothes in repair by pulling threads from my towel and mending with my fishbone needles. From time to time the needles would disappear, but it took only three days for a new one to dry.

Sometimes I thought, I'm only twenty-two years old, and all this is happening to me! And I often thought, What a story I'll have to tell when I get out! Over and over, when something new and bizarre turned up, I would find some small satisfaction in the anticipation of telling the boys about it.

There came a time when I was afraid that Sidorov knew about my Kiev trip to visit Michael Kovko. He said one day, "We have definite proof that in 1946 you were being trained in terrorist activities."

I said, "What kind of training?"

He said, almost triumphantly, "In 1946 you were unmistakably observed practicing sharpshooting with a high-powered pistol. You see, our operatives have been watching you very carefully. Wherever you went in Moscow, we had you under observation."

In Moscow! Then it was *not* about Kiev. So what was it?

I sensed he had some kind of actual event in mind, but I could not imagine what it was. Whenever we had gone to the countryside to shoot, I had made sure to give any tails the slip—unless Dina was an agent after all. And if it was Dina, why would she have given me away about shooting bottles in the woods when she had a much better story in the Khrushchev dacha?

Again, Sidorov became violent. I would reel out of a night's session with half a dozen cuts on my face and both shins screaming with pain.

If I could have confessed to something at this point, I think I might have. Once, when I was dizzy from the blows on the head and the kicks in the shins, I shouted that I would confess whatever he wanted. I felt kind of crazy. "Put down I'm a Japanese spy!" I said. "I'll sign that! Put down I'm a Roman Catholic pope or a Chinese emperor. I'll sign that! Anything you want!"

He was furious. *Crack!* I could hear the boot hit my shin, and I thought it must have broken the bone. I doubled up with the pain. I lay on the floor roaring in pain and rage, and he came and smacked me on the back of the head with his fist.

And the next day he's all hockey news and soccer and the novel he's reading.

To my grief I could not resist any opportunity to tease or humiliate him. Once, when the interrogation rooms were all in use, I was driven in a DRINK SOVIET CHAMPAGNE van to Lubyanka and taken to an office that Sidorov shared with three other officers. I was feeling cocky, because it was an anniversary. Sidorov had told me, right at the beginning, that no one ever lasted six months under this kind of treatment. He meant only the solitary cell and the black walls and the sleeplessness; the beatings had not yet started. The reason I felt cocky this particular day was that it was June 15. I had passed the six months and I was still holding out. Thin and weak and a bit crazy sometimes, but still absolutely determined they would not get me and still able to smile at the bastard who was trying to beat me into the ground.

When I arrived in the Lubyanka office this June 15, two of Sidorov's colleagues were working at their desks. I started thinking about some way to make Sidorov look a fool in front of them.

"Going to talk today?" he asked.

I shook my head.

"All right, all right," he said easily. "We'll see if you change your mind later."

He began to work on his papers with his scratchy fountain pen. He cursed the pen a lot. "This lousy thing. It puts ink on me, it scratches like a cat, and it won't write!"

One of the interrogators laughed at him. "Well, you're a *durak*,

Sidorov, a fool. You can get a decent pen if you try. Look here. I have this American Parker pen. It writes like a charm."

Sidorov tried the pen and admired its smoothness.

I said out loud, "Fifty-eight point ten!"

Sidorov looked up. He had a little wrinkle of bewilderment on his forehead. I had come to relish being able to produce that wrinkle. "What's that?"

"Fifty-eight point ten," I repeated. "Fifty-eight point ten!"

The Soviet Criminal Code was famous for its Article 58, under which political prisoners were charged with everything from having an anti-Soviet dream to trying to overthrow the government. Section 10, anti-Soviet propaganda, includes a charge based upon bad-mouthing Soviet manufactured goods, even by implication through praising goods of foreign manufacture.

"Arrest him!" I said to the other interrogators. "He's committed anti-Soviet propaganda. Praising foreign goods. Arrest him!"

Sidorov just walked across the office, knocked me off the chair with a hard swing of his open palm, and left me on the floor.

After a while he said, "Get up." I got up on the chair. I stared at him and he stared back. He looked angry and tired. Six months, I thought, and this guy is working me over eighteen hours a day, and I'm tiring *him* out! I became aware that day that he had lost weight. Not, of course, anything like me. I must have gone from 186 pounds down to 130. But Sidorov's jacket hung loose, and his face was drawn. He was doing everything he could in this battle of wits, and while he was not exactly losing, he was not winning either.

I enjoyed the drive in the champagne van to Lubyanka and back, because I could hear the hubbub of traffic and could imagine people watching me spin along Kuznetsky Most. They thought I was a crate of champagne; and someday I would get out and tell them what I really was.

When I got back in my cell, I tapped two taps: *I'm back.*

Two taps from him: *Me, too.*

Using pieces of matches, I spread the tapping code out on my blanket and studied it. What *was* this 1, 1; 1, 2; 1, 3?

Then I thought, Should I read it as 11, 12, 13, 14, 15, 16? And if so, why does he skip from 16 to 21, from 26 to 31, from 36 to 41? Was there something in the interval of five? But there was also a grouping of six: 11 to 16, 21 to 26.

Five times six is thirty. So what?

Wait a minute.

Wait a minute!

If you leave out the "hard" sign, you could say that the Russian alphabet has thirty letters.

Five rows of six letters. Of course! That's what he sends me every night! The whole alphabet! How could I have missed it for so long? The numbers *have* to be coordinates on a simple grid. A checkerboard! My hands were shaking with excitement. I arranged thirty match pieces on the blanket and then I mentally placed a letter on each match. I checked out the well-remembered message:

2, 4;   3, 6;   3, 2;   1, 3;   5, 2
К   Т   О   В   Ы

Kto vy?—Who are you?

Oh, God! A pure rush of love in my chest for a man who has been asking me for three months now who I am. Quick. Piece out the numbers for Aleksandr Dolgun. It will be 1, 1; 2, 5; 1, 6; 2, 4; 3, 5 . . . I decided instead to surprise my friend with a question. I would send, *Kak vas zvat?*—What is your name?

I began to tap.

Tap tap, tap tap tap tap. Tap, tap. Tap tap, tap tap tap tap. . . . What is your name?

I heard a sound like a table falling over, and then a regular fusillade of taps from across the barrier of stone.

I looked at my checkerboard of matches, then tapped out *Medlenno*—Slowly.

And when I had it all out, back came in agonizingly slow taps so careful not to run away from me: *Dmitri Ragozin.*

I sent him my name.

We had some ten minutes of it. Pretty laborious stuff, at first. I often had to ask him: *Snova?*—Again? And watching my matrix carefully, I was able to pick up his story. Ragozin was an engineer, ten years older than I. He had spent some time abroad in the 1930s and, like so many Soviets who did so, got into trouble for it later.

Although I was eating up this human contact as if it were food, I knew that I had to conserve myself and take every precaution not to be caught. I sent him, slowly, painstakingly, *Sleep now.*

I composed myself on the edge of the bunk facing the door and let my burning eyes close gratefully. I'm sure that for the next hour or so, while I slept under my hat, bolt upright, the broad smile of achievement never completely left my mouth.

For the next several nights Sidorov looked exhausted, and from time to time he dozed off and so did I. Even though I was getting better than two hours of sleep every weekday, I was close to mental exhaustion and would nod off instantly whenever there was the slightest opportunity. We did little work.

I concentrated on my fantasies. Walking home, I had negotiated the prohibited zone at the border, dodged dogs and patrols of soldiers, and had made it through the woods into Poland. The heavy black line I was drawing across my mental map of Europe stretched longer and longer.

After several days Sidorov returned to the photographs. He tried being more specific. He reminded me that I had admitted drinking with some Soviet officers on V-E Day at the Metropole. I said, "That's right, but I don't recognize any of them in these pictures."

Sidorov finally showed me one man. "His name is Commander George Tenno," Sidorov said. "He tried to establish contact with you to give you information, don't you remember?"

I stared at the photograph. The face looked familiar. It would be easy just to say, "All right, George Tenno, that's right, I tried to recruit him and he tried to sell me information." Maybe all this could stop. As I stared at the face of this George Tenno, I decided that, yes, I did recognize him. . . . And then I caught myself. I silently did a couple of lines of "Beer Barrel Polka."

"What was your relationship with George Tenno?" he said.

I took a breath. I looked up at Sidorov. I said truthfully, "I don't know that name. If this is the man you're talking about, I might have had a drink with him or I might not. I don't remember. We all got pretty drunk that day. Didn't you?"

I knew the blow was coming. It loosened a tooth, and I went backward off the chair.

The beating that Sidorov hammered on me that night would become part of the cement, years later, of one of the finest friendships in my life. But this night the blows and the kicks kept raining down as I rolled and ducked and yelled for him to stop, until my head began to break into torn, terrible pieces and I lost consciousness. The next thing I knew I was on the floor of my cell, shivering and wet. The summer was gone. The crisp air of September was outside Lefortovo now, and they were letting it have its way with my cell. I had been in prison more than nine months.

I WAS not able to speak coherently for some time after that tremendous beating. I was so weak I fell off the chair in the interrogation room or fell over on the bunk in my cell almost immediately after I sat down. And so I would be awakened. Days went by when I got no sleep at all, days that I was simply not aware of.

When I could concentrate again, Sidorov showed me a protocol which made me laugh in a way that might have sounded hysterical to him but was just a relief for me.

I had made friends soon after the war with the Syrian chargé d'affaires. He was actually called Ali Baba. He was an amiable guy, and we had spent the Fourth of July together in 1946. We had a drink at his place and then went to my room, where I kept my air pistol that shot tiny darts into a target and looked just like a Luger. We had stayed in my room for some time while I showed Ali Baba what a great shot I thought I was. I remembered it very clearly. Sidorov had a whole protocol on it. Not from Ali Baba, but from an operative with binoculars, stationed on a rooftop, who had observed me through the window "training with a high-powered, high-accuracy hand weapon, possibly of German manufacture."

I told the story to Sidorov. He said, "How can you remember it so clearly, when you can't remember anything else I ask you?"

I said, "Because it was the Fourth of July, I guess."

He said, "What's distinctive about the Fourth of July?"

I said a bit snappishly, "How can you expect to interrogate an American citizen intelligently if you don't even know about our Independence Day?"

I don't remember the beating that followed. I remember him sweeping across the room at me. After that I only remember how I was later. Perhaps the next day. I stood in front of Sidorov's desk, thick-lipped and aching in every emaciated muscle. I don't recall what it was I had to sign. I just remember that, as I turned away from his desk to stumble back to my chair, I saw from the corner of my eye that he had picked up his rubber overshoe, and I thought, with a dim hope, Maybe he's going home early and I can get some sleep. Then, with my back turned, he brought the overshoe up between my legs in a really terrible blow. I had thought nothing could be worse than those repeated blows on the shins, but this traveled through my entire abdomen as if it were ripping open. I fell to the floor, vomiting. Sidorov just called in a guard. "Clean that up and get him out of here," he said sourly.

I was groaning on the floor but I managed to shriek at him—I did not recognize my own voice—"I will never sign another protocol for you!"

I don't know what the time sequence was next. It is terribly blurred. I know that I was standing in front of Sidorov's desk once again, some hours or days later, I don't remember. He had seven or eight protocols that had not been signed yet. I said, "I told you, I'm not signing any more protocols!"

I picked the sheets up and tore them in half and strode to my chair. Sidorov grabbed the overshoe and let me have it between the legs again. This time he was less accurate and I was not paralyzed by the blow.

I leaned against my chair. Sidorov was standing with his back to me at the desk, picking up the torn protocols. I called on every remnant of strength I had, and swung the chair at his head to kill him at last. But I was too weak; it was a poor blow, slow and badly aimed. He heard it coming and ducked, and I just grazed his forehead. Sidorov knocked me down. He looked a bit frightened. I said, "I'm going to kill you, you know."

Sidorov said, "No, you're not. You're going to the hard punishment cell for the maximum. That's twenty-one days and you'll never come out alive. I'm through with you!"

They dragged me across to the prison and down steep stone stairs. I remember being thrown in an absolutely bare cell. There was no bed, no sink, just a bucket with a lid. No window. Gray stone and black asphalt.

The temperature was below freezing. I had only a shirt and trousers. When they brought me water, my hands shook so hard that some of the water spilled on the filthy floor. The next time I looked it was frozen.

At night they brought in a wooden pallet for me to sleep on. There was no blanket. I was dying for sleep but shivering too hard to do more than doze off, wake up, doze off.

I knew with complete certainty that I could not last five days in that cell, let alone twenty-one, and I thought confusedly that I had better keep a calendar to see how long I did last. It never occurred to me that I would not know the outcome. I was too confused.

In the morning they brought me bread and a cup of water. I deliberately spilled a little more water in the corner. Later, when it froze, I skated on it, sliding around on my shoes for exercise and warmth. I sang all my songs at the top of my voice and nobody bothered me. I fainted often, and came to shivering on the ice. I believe I never stopped shivering, if that is humanly possible.

After a few days they brought hot soup made with salt herring. I drank it all down before I realized it was saturated with salt. By nightfall I was screaming for more water. Before morning I began to have hallucinations of swimming. I remember the shock of coming to my senses and realizing that I was on the floor of my cell stroking feebly. Every third day they brought the salt-herring soup, and I was so starved I ate it, even though I knew I would go mad for water.

The days passed in almost total confusion, except that I forced myself to mark the wall every morning, when they brought the bread. Incredibly the strokes passed five, and then ten. I shivered, slept a bit, skated on my rink; what else I don't know.

The strokes on the wall passed twenty-one. They passed thirty. I had been in the cell a month. I think some days I was delirious all day, but I am not sure of much except that I often said, "Hold on, Alex, hold on till the end!" I expected the end.

Forty-one days. A mouse has come into the cell. I will catch it and eat it. I salivate at the thought of chewing on the live mouse.

Then I watch myself lying, shivering on the floor, covered in filth, a skeleton waiting for a mouse. I watch for hours, but the mouse never comes to the man on the floor.

Fifty-two days on the wall, and I will die soon, and that's all right, but I still do not have a cold or a runny nose.

The door of the cell opens.

"Prisoner, get up!"

I can make it to my hands and knees. They help me. Not kindly, not roughly, just get the prisoner moving. I stand in the door of my own cell, 111, the psychic cell. At least there is a blanket and pillow here.

I did not understand their words. Wrap up the blanket and pillow? Will they take them away from me? I thought. Then I realized I was leaving cell 111. Something still alive inside me said, "Alex, they're moving you. You got through it. You're going to be all right!"

I think they took me to the sixth floor. When we reached the cell (it was 216, and I still see the number), the guard peered in the peephole. My chest caught in the way people describe as your heart skipping a beat. There could be only one reason for looking in the cell. There had to be another person inside.

The door was pushed open. The cell had a polished wooden floor and was bright and airy, with a big window. A man lay on one of the two beds. As the door was locked behind me, he got up and came toward me. He looked ferocious, and for a minute I thought they had put me in a cell with a murderer. He shook my hand firmly and gently, and said in a soft musical voice, "Let me please introduce myself. My name is Orlov. Captain Grigori Orlov."

CHAPTER FOUR

SEVERAL times during my interrogation Sidorov had tried to influence me with the promise of better meals, a full night's sleep, and company in the cell, if only I would confess. I was certain, whenever he mentioned putting me in a cell with someone else, that the person would be a stool pigeon and all of what I said would be reported. They knew that a prisoner kept alone for a prolonged period and then suddenly given company could not refrain from talking. They were right. I could not stop talking to Orlov. The expression "verbal diarrhea" is the same in Russian. I had it. I told Orlov my whole life story. I grew sentimental and expansive over my wonderful Mary, who would be my wife as soon as I got out. I boasted about the way I handled Sidorov. I remember that some feeling of caution made me withhold the story of the trip to Kiev, but I think that was the only thing I censored.

As I talked Orlov listened attentively. He was on extra rations, because he had come to Lefortovo from a prison camp to give some desired information. He always shared his extra ration with me. He had a few cigarettes and offered one from time to time.

"Well," Orlov said, when I had pretty well exhausted my story some days later, "I think you had better prepare yourself for camp, and I can be helpful."

I said, "But they are through with me now. They have nothing on me. Surely they'll have to let me out soon?"

Orlov looked a little embarrassed. He said, "I really am afraid you will have to face the strange reality you find yourself in. If they truly found nothing against you, your sentence will not be a very long one. But you will unavoidably be given a sentence. It is not possible for the Organs to arrest a man and then free him."

I just stared at him blankly.

He said, "Look. Cheer up. Camp is not fun, but after what you have come through with such shining courage, if I may say such words, you will do very well there. There are two kinds of prisoners in camp: the kind who die quickly and the kind who make life quite acceptable for themselves and survive very well. You are definitely not the kind who dies quickly, and I will give you some hints about how to manage."

I pulled myself together. I began to ask Orlov about his own background.

He had been a lieutenant in the army and he was captured by the Germans late in 1941. Some Soviet officers convinced him that he would be starved to death unless he agreed to work for the Germans. He finally consented and was assigned to a Colonel Krause, who specialized in recruiting Soviet POWs and deserters into the German Army.

He said, "I was in touch with all kinds of classified German material, in Krause's unit. And now I am beginning to justify myself a little, because they kidnapped Krause in the U.S. Zone in Berlin last month, and I am here in Moscow to confront him. To some extent I can truly redeem myself in the eyes of the state now, I think. But I felt so guilty at the end of the war that I went west instead of east, and ended up in Liège. I got married to a woman who ran an inn. It was a comfortable life, and I thoroughly and confidently expected to end my days as an innkeeper.

"One day a man came in who spoke Russian. He said he was an old émigré. We began to drink together. The next thing I knew I was waking up out of a drugged sleep on a Soviet plane. He was an agent, don't you see. I even paid for the drink that knocked me out," he finished ruefully.

For his collaboration, Orlov had been given ten years in labor camps. Now, because he had agreed to a confrontation with Krause, he was given extra rations and easy treatment. Because he shared those rations with me, I began to regain my strength quickly.

It was like a holiday in cell 216. Sunlight flooded in every afternoon through the frosted window. I wallowed in sleep every night, and the feast of talking went on and on. My muscles began to tone up, and I steadily gained weight, though of course not very much.

Orlov began to tell me about the life in camp, and gave me some survival rules that I never forgot. Some of them were inversions of the schoolbook sayings we used to get when we were kids. "Never do today what you can put off till tomorrow," for example. "Never tell the truth if a lie will do." He told me that it was important to find an income-producing occupation, that there was always some need to be met in every camp, and if you could find a way to construct or steal some needed objects, you did so and sold what you could in exchange for other survival items.

He warned me to watch out for common criminals.

"They are truly very tough boys, Alex. If you find yourself in a camp where political prisoners and common criminals are mixed, be careful, because the 'coloreds'—that's the name they are known by—live by stealing from the politicals. The coloreds call themselves *urki*."

"*Urki?*"

"That's their name. The *urki* come to prison ready-equipped for survival. They have lived underground outside in a way that teaches them how to cooperate against a hostile world, and when they come inside, it's not that much different for them."

He wagged a finger at me for emphasis. "They are a crude, hateful, antisocial gang, Alexander Mikhailovich, but they hang together and that makes them strong."

"And the politicals?"

"Entirely different! The politicals have no street experience in cooperating for survival. They distrust each other, so they are completely incapable of organizing. They are the perfect victims for the *urki*."

Occasionally a guard would take Orlov away, and while he was gone, I busied myself with exercise. I picked up my walking where I had left off, in Germany, west of Stuttgart, heading for the Rhine valley and the border with France.

It was about a month after my stumbling arrival in cell 216. I was much stronger now. My mind was alert and ready for anything. Orlov went out early one morning for another session at Lubyanka, and I was doing arm and chest exercises when the door opened and a voice said, "D. With all your belongings. Outside!"

They took me out to the courtyard. A butcher's van was standing there, with colored pictures of pieces of meat on it and six little ventilators on the roof. I was wordlessly motioned inside and we began to roll through the streets of Moscow. Outside I could hear traffic sounds, the bell of a trolley, and, best of all, the voices of free people talking as they jostled by the van at a stopping point.

At Lubyanka I was told to bring my bundle and follow a guard. I was amused to hear the tongue-clucking again. I followed him to a cell on the third floor, cell 33. To my pleasure the guard stopped outside the cell and looked through the peephole. I was to have company again. There were *two* strangers inside, a tall, rather courtly-looking man in his fifties with gray hair, and a short, dark man in his thirties. I walked forward briskly with my hand out and said, "Allow me to introduce myself. My name is Dolgun. I am an American citizen."

The older man gave a little bow and said, "Igor Krivoshein."

The dark-haired guy shook hands very warmly. He said, "My name is Feldman, and I bet I know all about you!" I raised my eyebrows. Feldman said, "Sure. I read about it in London. You were picked up outside the American embassy, right? I was a correspondent for *Red Star*," he added. "I used to get a bit loaded with my English friends and tell anti-Soviet jokes. One of my English friends turned out to be not so English and not so friendly, and here I am. Fifty-eight point ten."

Igor Krivoshein had fought in the White Army in the Civil War, and when they were defeated in the Crimea, he had found his way to Paris and settled down to work as a taxi driver. During World War II he served in the French underground and began to dream of going home again, because he was sure that things would change after the war. Sure enough, Stalin in 1946 announced that Russian émigrés were forgiven and invited home. Krivoshein was very happy. He set out with his French-born wife and child, got to Moscow, and was given a place to live and a job in a garage in Sverdlovsk, about fifteen hundred kilometers east of Moscow. One day his boss told him that he wanted Krivoshein to make a trip to Moscow with him to get parts. When they got to Moscow, the boss turned Krivoshein right over to the MGB, and the only puzzle is why they bothered with the Sverdlovsk honeymoon.

Neither man had had a rough time in interrogation. Feldman

said, "Dolgun, I don't know how you did it. I admire you very much. I thank God they did not take you to Sukhanovka."

I had never heard of it.

"To tell you the truth," Feldman said, "I'm not sure it exists. But the rumor is that there is a prison called Sukhanovka where they take only big cases. I've never heard of anyone coming *out* of Sukhanovka. I've heard of them going in, but never coming out."

I tried to get them to guess what was going to happen to me next. They would not. They said I should wait till I heard whether or not I was to get a trial, what the verdict was, what I was convicted of. "But I haven't done one thing!" I protested.

"Is telling jokes about the Soviet Union doing anything?" Feldman shot back bitterly.

I did not have long to wait. On the fourth day the door opened. "D. Come out." I was taken to an interrogation room, where an air force major was standing by the window. For a second I thought it might be a confrontation with one of the military officers that Sidorov was always referring to. But it turned out that Kozhukhov, this air force major, was really MGB and, like many of their officers, wore a uniform of the regular forces as a sort of disguise.

After the formalities of identification, Kozhukhov said, "We are going to resume interrogation."

He let that sink in. I felt very cold and a bit sick. I said in a low voice, "I'm not going back to Colonel Sidorov in Lefortovo, am I?"

"No," he said. "I will be your interrogator this time."

"Here in Lubyanka, then," I said.

"No." He looked at me with a very unpleasant smile. "No, I am transferring you immediately to Sukhanovka."

I FELT dizzy and terrified. I do not remember saying good-by to Feldman and Krivoshein, although I must have been taken back for my things. I do remember that it was a champagne van again.

Anger helped clear my head on the long, cramped ride. It took about an hour and a half, as far as I could tell. When the van finally stopped, I heard a squealing iron gate, then a moment later my cubicle was unlocked and I stepped out into very bright sunlight. It was January, cold and clear and fine. I caught glimpses of a high yellow wall with barbed wire around what seemed a good-sized compound, and a building that looked very much like a monastery, which is what it had been for a long time.

I was hustled inside. Someone, a guard, shoved me into a closet so narrow that standing straight up I almost touched the door and the back of the closet at the same time. There was no room to crouch or sit. After about an hour my feet began to hurt, and I tried resting my knees against the door and my back against the wall behind me. That relieved my feet for a while but hurt my knees; so I stood up again and moved from foot to foot.

Soon the food slot opened and a plate of soup was passed in. It was not much but it was delicious. I knocked in a moment, and the empty plate disappeared and was replaced by one with a tiny sliver of delicious veal cutlet and a spoonful of delicately fried potatoes, steaming hot and nicely seasoned. I could hardly believe it. I had not tasted food like that for over a year. I wondered what would come next. What came next was one cup of water. Then I realized what they were doing to me. There would be no more food. My appetite had been so aroused by those excellent teasers that I had given in to the kind of food fantasies that I used to suppress all the time in Lefortovo. Now I had to suppress them again.

I kept waiting to be taken to a cell. But nobody came. I became very sleepy, but there was no way to get any kind of comfort. I would lean my head against the door and angle my hip to one side. Then I would sleep for a few minutes and wake up with a terrible pain in my back. I tried it with my knees against the door but that was acutely painful. I asked for the toilet as often as they would take me, just to get a chance to sit down.

On the third morning I began to keep count of the days. I could not believe it when the morning of the fifth day arrived. I would lose consciousness and wake up to intense pain in my kneecaps, extending through all the muscles of my legs. That evening I was taken to a cell, shaking, my legs terribly swollen, my knees a total agony. A folding bed was pulled down from the wall and I was given a clean blanket and pillow. But the pain was too great to sleep more than a few minutes. My feet and lower legs had gone numb, and as sensation returned they at first prickled lightly and then began to be very hot and to ache with a deep, dull ache.

I was overwhelmed. I could believe that nobody ever came out of this hellish place. My one-day-at-a-time attitude, which had gotten me through before, was gone. I came near to panic.

Sometime toward morning I must have regained some of my composure. I still had my measuring string, and I began to measure the little cell. It was exactly 1.56 meters by 2.09, just long enough for the two narrow beds that were made of heavy wood, reinforced with iron, and hinged to the wall. My bed, when it folded up into the wall in the morning, had a spring lock, which was opened with a key at ten thirty at night. Between the beds, and under them when they were down, was a narrow table somewhat the shape of an ironing board, mounted on one-inch pipe sunk in the concrete floor. At opposite corners of this table were round stools on pipes, less than eight inches across. That was what I had to sit on during the day. If your buttocks are not well-cushioned, it is painful.

I began walking and counting again—I was almost across the border of France by now—but walking was slow and difficult because, with the stools and the table and the cramped size of the cell, I could make only two steps to the end, a half step sideways around the end of the table, two steps, a half, and so on.

The next morning I was taken into another building, where the interrogation rooms were. I thought as I walked and counted, If everything else about this place is horrible, what in the world will the interrogation be like? Kozhukhov gave me no time to speculate. As I came into the room, he tripped me and sent me tumbling to the floor. As I tried to get up on my hands and knees, he put his big jackbooted foot between my shoulder blades and roughly shoved me down again. I turned and stared at him. Wide Mongol cheeks and a cruel leer. He said harshly, "You will find that Sukhanovka is nothing like the Sunday picnic you had in that kindergarten called Lefortovo! Now, start answering questions."

I said to myself, "Well, here we come."

THE HUMAN MIND HAS A number of safety valves, and most of mine have worked well and often. I am not even sure safety valve is the right expression, because while there is the release of pressure that comes with jokes and fantasy, there is also the suppression of things that you cannot tolerate very well. I suppressed for a long time, working on this book, my suicide plans in Lefortovo under Sidorov. The perception of myself as someone who coolly and deliberately planned the destruction of his own life is something that I "forgot" until I had to deal with it. I was able to keep it forgotten in reviewing the Lefortovo experience; I cannot do so in the case of Sukhanovka.

In Lefortovo I decided, very simply and straightforwardly, that if I became convinced that I was going to break down and become a tool for Sidorov to use as he pleased, I would simply step up on the iron cot and throw myself headlong off the bunk with my arms firmly at my sides, in a dive that would bring me down headfirst onto the cast-iron toilet. I was sure that my skull would be caved in by the impact and that I would die quickly.

It was not a good concept, because by the time I began to feel seriously that I might have to use it, I was far too weak to have any assurance of launching myself at that ring of rough iron with enough force to do the job.

Here in Sukhanovka the plan was more elaborate. The bed that was unlocked and let down every night was terribly heavy. At some point I realized that if I could find a way of unlocking the bed myself, I could use it as a weapon for my self-destruction.

When I was taken to the toilet, I was given a tiny scrap of toilet paper. Instead of using it I washed myself and palmed the paper. I slowly began to accumulate quite a few of these little scraps. I had decided that I could make papier-maché out of them and use it to block the hole the latch sprang into, so that when the bed was put up, the latch would *appear* to spring, but the bed would actually stay in position only because it was vertical. I had noticed that it stayed balanced in the vertical position before it was latched. When the guard left, I would pull the heavy iron and wood frame toward me until it was just barely balanced on its hinges, then quickly kneel and place my temple on the stool so that several hundred pounds of falling wood and iron would instantly crush my skull. It was not pleasant, of course, to make such a plan and to begin to hoard paper in aid of it, and yet it gave me an escape route, if what was happening got beyond the point where I could bear it.

VERY soon after the brutal Kozhukhov once again began the long review of my personal history, I woke up one morning and realized that my cheeks were hot and my lips dry. I asked for the doctor. She came—middle-aged, tired, sympathetic—and shoved a thermometer under my arm. It read over 40° C.—nearly 105° F.—and I was very frightened. The doctor told me sadly there was nothing she could do but give me aspirin. I was stunned when I realized that meant no relief from interrogation.

In fact, Kozhukhov treated the fever like a joke. I pleaded with him. I told him I was sweating and that the fever was dangerously high. He said, "I'll help you to cool down, then!" He stepped to the window and threw it open. Outside, the late February air must have been below freezing. Kozhukhov put on his army greatcoat and his fur hat and heavy gloves. Then he just laughed hugely at me. He tried to continue the interrogation, but I was shivering too much to answer him. He finally closed the window, not out of any humanitarian intention but because the shivering and the chattering teeth slowed down his work and made progress impossible.

I am not surprised that chronological recollections of Sukhanovka scarcely exist. I went downhill quickly, losing weight and losing clarity. I remember that Kozhukhov tried to get me to say that I had attempted to persuade a Soviet employee of the U.S. embassy, Morris Seltser, to defect to the United States. I denied the charge. Kozhukhov told me he had been a boxer and would demonstrate a few of his punches to help me remember. His favorite was a hard jab on the biceps, repeated to the point where my arm would be swollen and completely useless. I said I remembered Seltser all right. He was a messenger and handyman who made a good living selling secondhand goods, some of which he bought from embassy employees at good prices. A carton of cigarettes would bring two hundred rubles around Moscow in those days.

I had never played this black-market game. I thought it was bad stuff. But Morris boasted to me during our one and only conversation that if he had been living in America, he would have been a millionaire, because he was so good at buying low and selling high. And it turned out that this was the only source of the accusation that I was helping him escape to America.

Every day Kozhukhov would hit me. I was so weak that one or two blows would keep me in agony for hours. Sometimes Kozhukhov would smash me with the edge of his open hand right under my nose. I would go temporarily blind from such a blow, and sometimes my lip would bleed. And all the time I denied and denied trying to persuade Morris Seltser to defect, until one day Kozhukhov brought me a protocol that showed my room had been bugged the day Morris and I had talked.

I was furious with Kozhukhov through my fear and weakness and fever and pain. I yelled, "Is *this* what's supposed to prove I was trying to make Seltser defect? Are you serious?"

I even laughed at him. My self-respect would not let the opportunity go by, even though I might suffer for it. Kozhukhov did not hit me for laughing. I suppose he had been told to see if there was anything behind that innocent conversation, and in the end he probably felt not sheepish, but a kind of what-the-hell feeling.

By the end of February, 1950, my buttocks had shrunk to wrinkled skin, and sitting anywhere was painful. I probably weighed less than Charles Atlas's famous ninety-seven-pound weakling by this time, but I was much too feeble for any Dynamic-Tension exercises. I walked a little in the cell and continued to move across France toward the border of Spain.

I would pass out with increasing frequency, sometimes coming to on the floor of the interrogation room with a doctor peering at me, sometimes on the floor of my cell with a guard's key tapping at the food slot. As time went on, I became more and more useless to Kozhukhov. Because I was losing consciousness so frequently, he would terminate interrogation at one or two in the morning, and I would be allowed to sleep until six. Then, just before six, I would hear others being led back from interrogation, some screaming for help, some moaning, some—from the faint sounds of dragging— unable to walk. I knew what that was like. It was like me.

Did they take me for baths at Sukhanovka? I do not remember. What I do remember is that somehow I was naked. It must have been at the bath. I looked at my shrunken body and I saw a devastating thing: my knees were thicker than any other part of my legs! The terrible thing that swam into my mind was a photograph in *Life* magazine of some survivors of one of the Nazi extermination camps. The creatures who stared out of deep, dark sockets were not really people. I believed they could not see or comprehend anything, and I thought that such a life was worse than death and was more obscene than anything that could be imagined. Now I was in that photograph. I shook with my fever, and I thought, Is this a life that is better than death?

I know that I came very close to plugging the bed's spring lock. I remember that, sometime in late April or early May, I knew that the end had about arrived. I was able to be almost dispassionate about it. I could say to myself, "Alex, you did everything you could. Now it is time to rest, forever."

Hazy and delirious much of the time now, I am aware one morning that a woman in a physician's smock is in my cell and that someone has told me to get up and get my things together. I think I try to do this, but I cannot raise myself.

I am in a van, on a bench. The van lurches, and I look up and see that trees in early leaf are going by. The lurch almost knocks me off the bench, and a guard beside me holds me up. Not kindly, not roughly, just an object: keep the prisoner off the floor.

But the prisoner slides gratefully onto the floor and loses his senses. Then the sound of car horns and tram bells, and I force myself awake and pull up and catch a brief glimpse of the streets of Moscow, and of people.

We stop and someone tells me where we are. Butyrka Prison. Orlov, my Lefortovo cellmate, had spoken of Butyrka. "A slack place," he said. I remember nothing of arriving there, only that after some days I became aware of waking up in a firm comfortable bed, white-smocked medical people moving about, tubes taped to my arm, and of the marvelous sense that I was not hungry and that my mind was emerging from fog into clear light again.

ONCE I was conscious again and the fever subsiding, they began feeding me sweet tea and eggs and cod-liver oil, and every day I felt a tiny increase in strength. An astonishing wave of confidence and optimism returned. I *knew* that I would survive because I had survived.

Every day I got glucose and vitamins, and when the fever started slipping back, I began to worry that I would be shipped out, so I learned how to keep my fingers in my teacup when a medical assistant, called a feldsher, brought the thermometer in the morning. I would hand it back with my hot fingers on the bulb. That maintained my apparent temperature around 39° C. (102° F.) and so kept me in the hospital.

One day they took me to a sort of interrogation room. The civilian behind the desk asked my name, and corrected it to Dovgun-Doldzhin. Somewhere along the line they had given me a second name, Dovgun, which they hyphenated to their version of Dolgun. No one ever explained this appendage. He then went on to read away the next quarter century of my life, as if he were prescribing cough medicine: "Alexander M. Dovgun-Doldzhin, by decision of the Special Committee of the Ministry of State Security [the MGB], on the basis of your espionage and other anti-Soviet activities, you are deprived of freedom for twenty-five years in IRT." ("Corrective labor camps," he explained.)

He presented the order to me and told me to sign. I refused—signing that thing would mean agreeing with it.

"Sign!" he said. "Otherwise it's the hard punishment cell!"

I shook my head.

He brandished the pen at me.

I shook my head again and said, *"Nye polozhna!"*

I never did get the hard punishment cell and I guess, having gone to the trouble of putting me back together again with drugs and vitamins, they probably thought it would be illogical to turn around and murder me right away. But it is hard to say, because everything in this crazy system seemed illogical. Maybe my avoiding hard punishment in Butyrka was only bad management.

From the hospital they sent me to a crowded cell that had twenty-five beds and more than twenty-five people, so there was sleeping in shifts and much lying on the floor. I went around the cell and asked every man what his sentence was. One man had ten years. Every other person had twenty-five years' corrective labor, five years' exile, and five years' deprivation of civil rights. All around the packed cell: "Twenty-five, five, and five." "Twenty-five, five, and five." I was the only one who had not been given the extra "five and five."

The men in the cell talked about *etap*, a shipment of prisoners to labor camps anywhere across the huge eastern expanses of the Soviet Union. I was told that from now on, as we moved through transfer prisons and on and off trains, we must learn to recite the prisoner's "prayer." A guard would call your initial: "D!" Then all the initial Ds must come to the door of the cell and recite their prayer, consisting of full name, date of birth, length of sentence, and section of the criminal code under which they were convicted.

Receipts for confiscated belongings were issued to incoming prisoners. Dolgun concealed this memento of Butyrka Prison as a way to "beat the system."

Hence, "Dovgun-Doldzhin, Alexander M., 1926. Twenty-five years. Fifty-eight point six. Fifty-eight point ten." That was my prayer, and I would recite it hundreds of times in the next years.

On the second day in this crowded cell a guard called for the Ds, and two or three of us recited our prayers. I was told to bring my bundle and follow him for the *etap*. I was shoved into a Black

Maria and taken to the train station with a dozen other men.

Stolypin railway cars are masterpieces of the deception of the security system of the Soviet Union. They are painted to look like mail cars. They were designed to the orders of a czarist minister, and they carry his name. They are converted from old coaches, and in place of four-bunk compartments giving onto the corridor, there are four-plank cells, ostensibly meant for a maximum of sixteen prisoners but in my experience seldom carrying fewer than twenty. At each end of the corridor there is a toilet. Guards patrol the corridor. You are not allowed to talk to prisoners in the next cell, but you can talk all you want to the men in your own, and I enjoyed that. I was lucky to be one of the first to board the train and to occupy the plank across the top bunks before the cell was filled. "Filled" is the right word. Arms and legs and bodies were mixed together.

The stink and confusion were terrible. I think we were two or three days on the first part of the trip. The dominant smell was urine, and the floor was always wet. Sleep was a haphazard affair, but at least, if you could find any way to drop off for a while, the guards did not bother you. The weather was warm and got warmer as we traveled east and then south. Once out in the open country, where curious civilians could no longer see what kind of mail was being carried in such mass loads, the guards threw open the windows and we could see the countryside sliding by.

Before boarding the train we had been given rations: two days' supply of bread, sugar, and several pieces of salt herring. I warned everyone against eating the herring. Some understood. Others knew I was right, but were too hungry to do without it.

Within two hours there were cries throughout the car, begging for water. The guards strolled up and down and laughed at the poor pinched faces pressed against the bars, pleading for a drink. All the guards on the trains were cruel and abusive. In prison the guards did their job in a straightforward way and left the abuse to the interrogators. But these men on the train were brutal by temperament. Perhaps it was a requirement for the position. Usually their brutality was expressed in the crudest, most direct form, with kicks, rifle butts, and curses. Sometimes it had a kind of low-grade ingenuity. This group on our car withheld water until the screams became a constant wail and then brought all the water anyone wanted, and sat back to watch the fun as bladders began to cry out for relief and people went into silent agonies or else humiliated themselves by wetting their clothes at last or urinating on the floor.

Kuibyshev is about six hundred miles east of Moscow, almost in the foothills of the Ural Mountains. I have been told it is a fine city, but all I saw of it the morning we arrived was cobblestoned streets and poor, shabby houses. The guards made no attempt to conceal us from the population there. We were simply dragged out between lines of armed soldiers, with huge German shepherd dogs snarling and pulling on their chains, and marched through the town while people stared or more often went indifferently about their business. The march was perhaps two kilometers, and by the end I was being dragged, because I could not walk.

When they marched us in the prison gates, I became aware that there was an immense group in this convoy—several hundred men and women. Some were vigorous and sleek, though most were thin and weak like me. Some of the women were carrying babies that were a few days old. We all sat on the ground, waiting for the next order. Some of the prisoners, particularly women, went from person to person seeking news. "Where did you come from, brother? Potma? Have you seen my husband? Vasili Grigoryevitch Kravchuk? No? And you, brother, where have you come from? Lubyanka? Did you hear any news of Vasili Kravchuk?"

After an hour or more had passed, we were taken into a large barrackslike building with showers rigged along one wall and told to undress and put our clothes on the floor in front of us. The women screamed and protested, but the guards smashed them in the face if they hesitated. Soon we were all naked, three hundred skeletal, vulnerable human bodies. A file of fifteen or twenty guards stood laughing and joking about the physical characteristics of the naked bodies in front of them. We were told to take a step backward while they moved forward to search our bundles.

Soon we were led to a long, low table where two trusties with hair clippers came along and clipped our armpits, our heads, our beards. Then we had to step up on the table while they went to work on our pubic areas. The women were almost all crying with terror and humiliation. After the shaving we were herded to the showers, men and women together. There were screams and yells of rage as we were scalded with terribly hot water for several minutes. Our clothes were hung on wheeled racks like those in the garment district in New York, and rolled into a huge oven, where they were disinfected. Afterward we had to scramble through jumbles of clothing to try to find our own. Then the men and women were finally segregated into groups and taken outside again.

The cell that I and about fifteen others were led to opened directly on the yard. It was cell number 12. At the door we formed a line and one by one repeated our prayers and were roughly pushed inside. I grabbed a space to sit down on a sort of long bunk.

My first impression was of bedlam. The cell reverberated with chatter. Later I counted 129 people in a cell about sixteen feet wide and forty feet long. Two layers of bunks, which were nothing more than hard plank platforms, ran along each of the long sides and across the far end. At that end was a large window, open in the warm air, with bars on the outside. By the door, opposite the window, was a large wooden barrel that served as a urinal.

Several people came up to me to hear news from outside. The first question was always, "Are you from freedom?" And when I explained that I had been in prison for a year and a half, many still wanted to know what it was like outside; they had been in prison for five years, ten years, some for twenty years.

For some reason I was standing up. Perhaps I had been squeezed off the crowded bunk. The talk around me went silent suddenly, and I saw three ragged young men advancing toward me, grinning wickedly. They stepped up to within a couple of feet of where I stood hanging on to a bunk support, and looked me over with insolent eyes. I still had my navy-surplus gabardine trousers, and even after a year and a half of prison they were in much better shape than most prisoners' clothes. These toughs were *shobla yobla*, the lowest of the *urki*, or criminal class.

The one in the middle said to the others, "Look, brothers, he has my trousers on!"

I said, "What are you talking about? These are mine. Hands off!"

The leader kept pushing at me roughly. "Now, look at this, brothers! A common thief wearing my pants! Well, well!" Then he grabbed a bundle of rags from one of the other young jackals and held it out to me. "*These* are your trousers," he said between his teeth, holding them under my nose and pushing his face very close. "Now give me mine and give them to me quick," and he thrust out two fingers as if to jab them in my eyes.

I had been up against tougher guys than he for a year and a half, and I was certainly not going to take this lying down. I was too weak for a good swing, but I held tight to the post with my left hand and brought my right up from below in the hardest uppercut I could manage. It connected beautifully, and the kid went down on his back. He looked astonished and he looked ready to kill.

The room went absolutely silent. The guy on the floor got up, rubbing his chin. He spread his hands and held the other two toughs back. His eyes looked murder. "I'll take him," he said. He took a step toward me.

But it never happened. A loud call from the back of the room stopped the *shobla yobla* cold.

"Off!" this voice said, with great authority. "Lay off, now. That man is a *dukharik!*" *Dukh* is the word for "soul." In this context it means pretty much the same as the English word "guts."

"Bring him to me," the voice said, more quietly.

One of the *shobla yobla* said, almost deferentially, "The *pakhan* calls you," and then he led me to the other end of the room.

Pakhan is underworld slang for "the chief." In rank and authority this man had the status of a robber king. To meet such a distinguished, high-class *urka* is a very rare event.

The man I saw on the lower shelf at the end of the cell was impressive in every way. He was well over six feet tall. He sat cross-legged on the bunk in boots of fine black soft leather, with blue trousers tucked into the tops. His whole suit was a rich blue and made of good cloth. Perhaps the most astonishing thing of all was that this man had in his hand a large polished hunting knife. With the absolutely classical manner of a movie tough guy, he sat there slicing pieces of smoked meat from a big chunk and popping them in his mouth. Not only that, but he had *white* bread, which I had not seen since December 13, 1948, almost eighteen months earlier. He looked me over with an amused smile.

The *pakhan* said, "Here, sit." I made a cushion out of my jacket and sat down beside him. The *pakhan* looked me over, and I looked over all the people around him. There was a short, fair-haired guy sitting at his right, and from time to time someone would come up and whisper to him and he would whisper back, or just nod or shake his head. He looked like the *pakhan's* grand vizier, and that is almost exactly what he turned out to be.

The *pakhan* cut off some smoked sausage and put it on a slice of white bread and handed it to me. I gobbled it down. I had not eaten such good food since my last breakfast at the embassy.

My benefactor opened his eyes at the speed with which his gift disappeared. He made another sandwich and offered it, and while I gobbled it down, he waved his hand, and a mug of water appeared. He waited until I had drunk, then he said simply, "Well?"

I said, "I'm an American citizen. I was kidnapped by the Organs. I've just come from Sukhanovka. My name is Alexander Dolgun."

"Then I call you Sasha the American, okay? This"—indicating the grand vizier—"is Sashka Kozyr. He is my deputy. My name is Valentin Intellighent. You can call me Valka."

I said, "Thanks for the food. I really don't understand how you get all this stuff . . . and the knife. What's going on here?"

Valentine the Intelligent just laughed. "I will explain it to you sometime," he said in a very good-natured way, but also in a way that made clear that *he* was the chief and *he* would decide the order in which things were to be done. "Listen," he said, "if you're an American, you must have seen lots of movies, yes?"

I nodded.

"And you read a lot of books? Read novels a lot?"

I nodded again.

"Good. We may be able to have a business relationship."

The *pakhan* grinned widely at my bewilderment. Then he became very serious and peered at me directly. "Now listen," he said. "Can you squeeze a novel?"

I said, "What do you mean, squeeze?"

He said, "Squeeze is slang for tell. We have no storyteller here. Can you tell us novels, narrate the stories? The same with movies?"

I said eagerly, "Sure I can. I've spent the last year and a half telling myself all the movies and novels I could remember."

"That's excellent!" Valentin said. "I'll call the brothers around and we can get started."

I said, "Valka, wait one minute. I've just come in on *etap*. I'm exhausted. I've been starved for a long time, and I hardly had any sleep on the train. I could do a much better job of squeezing movies if I could get a good long sleep first."

He looked disappointed for a moment. Then he nodded decisively and said, "Of course. You sleep, and when you are ready I will feed you some more and then we can get started."

He made them clear some space on the top shelf at the side of the cell near the window so I would have air. Some of the *urki* looked pretty ugly about giving up their space to me, but they did not dare let the *pakhan* see their anger. He got some coats and helped me make a sort of pad to stretch out on, and a soft pillow of crumpled cloth in a small sack. He put his head close to mine and said, "Sasha, you look terrible. Sleep as long as you want. Nobody can hurt you, because I am looking after you."

I could not speak—there was a lump in my throat at so much kindness in such a cruel place. Valentin Intelligent turned around and said quietly to Sashka, "I want silence."

Sashka jumped up and whistled sharply through two fingers. The chatter in the cell died down quickly.

Valentin Intelligent looked around the cell to make sure everyone was attentive. There was not a sound. "Good," he said. "That is the way it is to be until I say so." He pointed at me. "I want silence in this cell because a *man* is sleeping!"

He had used the word *chelovek*, which is like *Mensch* in German. The way he stressed the word, it meant a man with a capital M, a person. I felt elated by the compliment. I looked around the cell with my eyes half closed. Just before I drifted off to sleep I got some insight into the prosperity of my newfound protector. Over in the corner two of his *urki* serfs had engaged three new Estonian arrivals in earnest whispered conversation. The new arrivals were obviously politicals, fresh "from freedom." Their characteristic Baltic sacks on the floor beside them were quite full. They were totally unaware of what then happened. A third hoodlum sat on the bunk behind the Estonians. He took off his shoe and pulled from some mysterious hiding place a tiny strip of broken razor blade. Later I learned this was called a *moika*, that it was a standard weapon among the pros, and they could almost always conceal one well enough to get through any search. As I watched, the third *shobla yobla* deftly gripped the *moika* between two filthy toes, extended his foot, and silently slit the Estonians' sacks from top to bottom. Then, with a continuing deftness that I found a delight to watch, he retrieved with his agile foot several sausages, a loaf of bread, some handkerchiefs, and several paper packets of tea.

I had an inward chuckle and said to myself, "Business as usual." Then I closed my eyes and went off into a very happy sleep.

CHAPTER FIVE

VALENTIN Intellighent was as good as his word. Throughout my stay in the cell, where he ruled like a feudal duke, no one tried to do me harm, no one stole from me, and I found that Valentin was not only a benefactor but a subtle and fascinating talker.

When I woke up, I smelled porridge. The evening meal was coming in, served from big barrels. The pros got theirs first, of course, and the political rabbits hung back meekly and waited.

"Hungry, Sasha?"

It was Valentin. I said, "Very."

"Want some extra porridge?"

I said, "Sure I do. Wonderful."

He sent word to the door. The trusty on the barrel passed in twelve extra portions of the watery gruel, and they were brought over in relays by the criminals. For the first time since I was kidnapped I ate until I was full. When I finished I was terribly sleepy again.

Valentin came up and looked at me expectantly. Then he said, "Not ready yet, eh, brother?"

I shook my head.

"Sleep," he said.

When I woke up again, it was dark in the cell, but I felt bright and optimistic and interested in company. I sat up and looked for the *pakhan*. Valentin caught my eye and smiled warmly to see me looking rested and alert. He cut me off some bread and smoked meat and said, "Do you feel like a cup of real tea?"

Tea was forbidden in prison, but I nodded eagerly.

Valentin signaled to one of his *shestyorki*, deputies of rank just below that of Sashka, and the *shestyorka* began to build a curious bonfire on the concrete floor near the window. The principal fuel was plastic toothbrush handles, stolen from the politicals. The plastic smoked and stank, but the deputy held a tin cup full of water over the fire until the water boiled. Then he put in a chunk of pressed tea, like a plug of tobacco almost. "It's called *chifir*," Valentin said. "It'll wake you up."

Wake me up! It nearly blew my head off! Soon my heart was beating very fast. Valentin grinned at me. "Ready?" I nodded. The deputies and some of the more civilized *urki* gathered around. A few politicals came nervously to the edge of the little group, but kept a respectful distance.

I started. "During the war there was a house in Occupied France that contained one of the deadliest Gestapo units the Nazis ever had. The address of this house was thirteen, Rue Madeleine."

I had told myself the plot of *13 Rue Madeleine* so many times that I could see individual shots in the movie as I told it. With my extended descriptions and the talk about the inner feelings of the participants, I managed to talk all night.

When I had finished, the *pakhan* stood up and shook me warmly by the hand. He opened a pack of strong Russian cigarettes and offered me the first smoke. My head spun a bit from the impact of

the tobacco. It was already spinning with the feeling of security
and success that I was catching from Valentin Intellighent.

When breakfast was brought, Valentin turned my portion of
black bread over to his *shobla yobla* and gave me some more white
bread and smoked bacon. After breakfast we were taken out to the
yard for exercise and to go to the latrine building. Next to the
outside wall of the prison was a fire zone filled with rolls of barbed
wire, and Valentin explained that if a prisoner stepped inside the
fire zone, the guards on the watchtowers would shoot to kill.

The two of us walked together, my arm about his shoulder for
support, around and around the big yard, sharing our life stories.
He was a safecracker, he told me. That put him in the top professional class. To rob an individual of even a large sum of money
would be beneath him. His real love and the great opportunity for
an elegant job was an "unbreakable" safe, and he claimed he had
broken many of them. I believed him. He was one of the most alert
men I had ever met. He had been orphaned as a boy of ten, but he
had never lost the manner of speaking he had learned from his
father and mother, who were both professors. That is why his
professional name was Valentine the Intelligent.

He explained to me the differences between the *urki* and the
politicals. "The *urki* are loyal Soviets," he said. "We don't want to
overthrow the system. We just happen to be in a different field of
endeavor. We get a very good living from it. We don't stir up
trouble like these other worthless scum"—waving an arm at the
groups of politicals—"we just stick together, and if there is another
war, we'll help out the best we can. But the *urki* are organized and
the politicals are not. We get the guards to sell the stuff we liber-
ate from new arrivals, and we split with them, and they buy us
good food and tobacco and make sure we have what we need."

"By the way, that's a very fine hat you're wearing," he said
parenthetically. "Is it American?"

I told him the story of the hat and how it had saved my life.

He tried it on. "I certainly like that hat," he repeated.

I was not feeling bright and I failed to get the message.

The exercise period tired me out badly, and I took a nap when we got back in. When I woke up, I saw a lot of expectant faces looking in my direction. I asked for a drink, and a deputy brewed some more explosive *chifir*. Then Valentin gathered my audience and nodded to me to go ahead. I told them a story I knew they would love, about a movie company coming to New York to make a film about a bank robbery. They negotiate with a major bank to get permission to film the bank. They arrange with the police department to provide lots of cops to keep traffic and passersby from bothering them, and on the appointed day they calmly rob the bank under the unconcerned eyes of New York's finest.

Hardly anyone in my audience moved as I spun out the story, and when I came to the punch line, the getaway, and the picture of the cops standing around with their faces getting redder and redder when they finally found out what had happened, there were deep chuckles of satisfaction. They clamored for another story right away, but Valentin intervened and decreed that I should rest my voice and build up my strength. So I sat quietly with Valentin for the rest of the afternoon and nibbled white bread and bacon and listened to his bits of lore on prison life.

He said, for example, that if I ever heard guards in a transfer prison talking about India, to avoid going there because that was the cell where the *urki* were who collaborated with the guards. Politicals would be put in it for a few minutes "by mistake." By the time the "mistake" was discovered and rectified, the poor political would be very much poorer.

I said, "And if I can't stop them putting me in such a cell?"

"Oh, that's easy."

All the other *urki* listening to this chuckled and exchanged knowing looks. "Go ahead, *pakhan*, tell him," one said.

"Now, Sasha," Valentin said to me, "if you saw a clean white handkerchief lying in the mess by the barrel over there, would you wipe your dirty feet on it?"

"Of course not," I said. I wondered what he was driving at.

Valentin said emphatically, "Of *course* you would!"

"Listen, Valka, is this some kind of riddle? I don't get it," I said.

"Just remember what I said," Valentin answered.

When supper came I was again offered extra helpings, and again I ate them greedily. I slept for an hour or two, and then I started an Ellery Queen mystery, and it lasted through the night.

The next day Valentin made a further gesture of confidence. He told me about his escape plan and invited me to join it. The plan was to hide in the latrine building and at night use some iron pipes that were lying beside it to pole-vault from the roof over the wall. I said I would have to build up some strength first, and he agreed to wait, because he really wanted my company.

"I'll tell you why I admired your hat so much, Sasha," he said. "I wanted it for my escape. I figured with a hat like that I would look like some big party official and nobody would ever accost me. But if you come along, it will work for all of us."

I thought about that for a while. I said, "What kind of a life could I have outside, though? I'd be a fugitive all my days."

"I've been a fugitive a lot of my days, you know," Valentin said. "It's not so bad. I escaped from the orphanage when I was eleven."

"Valka," I said, "how much time have you done in prison all together?"

"If you count the orphanage, which I certainly do, almost twenty years."

"And you're not forty yet."

"Thirty-eight, that's right."

"But isn't that a terrible life?"

"I miss my women. And wine. I miss wine a great deal. But you can see that I live very well in prison. It never lasts long. And when I get out, there is no way that I can have the women and the wine and the good suits unless I live my life with the *urki*."

I said I would go along with him and we shook hands on it. We walked the yard hand in hand. In the Soviet Union good friends do this openly, and it is perfectly natural.

When we came back to the cell, rather than telling stories as such, I answered questions about crime in America, the electric chair, the FBI, weapons, the careers of outstanding criminals, the techniques of safebreaking. (I was hardly an expert, but Valentin expressed polite interest, so I kept on with it.)

Then Valentin told one of his exploits, how he had stolen a whole carload of sugar—I think it was sixty tons—and sold it at a very good price. Others recounted some of their adventures.

Several of the younger guys talked sadly and sentimentally about their mothers. Most of these men were tattooed, and many had MOTHER on the back of a hand or a forearm. Valentin asked me about my mother. I said, "I don't know. I have no way of communicating with her. She may not even know what's happened to me."

"Write her a letter."

I laughed bitterly at the cruel joke.

"I'm serious," Valentin said. "Listen, don't you think I can get it out? Write her a triangle. Now! Come on." And he told Sashka to get a piece of paper and a pencil.

A triangle is just that: if you are too poor for an envelope and stamp, you fold your letter into a triangle and the Soviet post will carry it anyway. This started during the war, as a way for soldiers to send mail, and it was still accepted in the 1950s. I wrote, telling my mother that I was fine, that I was going to be in Central Asia, at Dzhezkazgan 292. (I had seen that on my transport file.) And I asked her to get in touch with Mary and say that I was fine and that she should not feel compelled by her promise to wait for me.

Valentin gave the letter to Sashka, who slipped it to a guard.

That night I began my longest tale, Victor Hugo's *Les Misérables*. I think these men, many of whom had lived outside the law all their lives, were caught up in the story of Jean Valjean and his relentless pursuer. It was easy for them to see themselves rowing in the galleys. The story was utterly real to them.

From time to time in the days that followed I was slightly feverish, and I began to worry about getting up enough strength to go with Valentin and Sashka. I could not imagine pole-vaulting from that latrine roof and the long run at top speed afterward. I confided this to Valentin one day. He looked terribly disappointed, and I believe he really was. I said, "But if I can't go, I want you to have my hat." He was pleased. But he insisted on holding out a little longer.

It was no use. My fever began to rise daily. I also had bouts of diarrhea and began to be a bit dehydrated. Then news came in one morning that the *etap* was to go on to Dzhezkazgan. I was to be on it, and so was one of the *urki*, a young man named Vasya.

"I'm not going *there!*" he said. He then got a needle and a piece of fine thread. He ran the thread between his filthy teeth until it was well coated with plaque. Then he ran the thread just under the skin on his thigh, and drew it out again.

Valentin said, "Tonight you'll see. He'll be really sick. And you'd better be too, because you're in no shape for the *etap*."

I said, "I don't have to fake it. I'm sure my fever is pretty high. I haven't told you, because I didn't want you to worry."

He looked me hard in the eye. He said, "It's too bad, my brother. We could have had a good life."

We shook hands. Then I lay down and began to moan and clutch my stomach. Valentin pounded on the door and told a guard to get a doctor, there was a sick man in here. He was right. My stomach was cramping, and I was covered with cold sweat, and shivering. By early evening I was good and sick. Around suppertime Valentin brought Vasya over to me. His face was flushed and his eyes were very bright. He peeled back his trousers. "Look," was all he said. His thigh had swollen and it was terribly discolored. The infection was raging but there was no sign of the wound that induced it. "Did you ever see such a *mastyrka?*" he asked me proudly.

I had heard those terrible tales about what prisoners did to themselves to avoid transportation, so I guessed at the meaning of the word. "Congratulations," I said feebly.

The doctor came. Vasya had a fever by then and was incoherent. They took us to the hospital on stretchers.

The second night in the hospital I heard a fusillade of shots echo among the buildings. Later that night I was shaken awake by one of the prisoner orderlies. "Wake up and hear what I have to say, *chelovek*," he whispered. "The *pakhan* and Sashka and a guy called the Tiger made their try tonight. You probably heard shots?"

I nodded weakly, fearfully.

"The Tiger is dead. Sashka got it in the leg, but he made it over the wall. The *pakhan* made it, too."

Parasha, the prison telegraph, confirmed the escape of the *pakhan* and Sashka, and the death of the Tiger.

The doctor kept me on for three or four days after my fever had subsided, and did his best to feed me up and restore my strength. When the next *etap* was formed, there was no avoiding it. We were lined up in the yard, and while we stood there, a man came over and handed me a letter.

I could not believe it. It was from Moscow, from my mother. I was so excited I tore the letter getting the envelope open. There was not much news. She said that she was glad to know I was all right, and that she would try to get a food parcel sent to me. The weather is fine, she wrote, and that was about all.

And yet it was like nourishment, like a warm bath, like a drink of wine. A wave of hope swept over me. I grinned as we marched through the streets to the train. Now someone could start working on my behalf; now they knew where I was.

That hope kept me buoyant as the train worked its way east and farther east into the Urals and then across them.

It took slightly more than a day to reach the next transfer prison, in a small city called Chelyabinsk, and the memory of my first hour inside that prison will never leave my mind.

There were eight political prisoners in my group, and we were lined up, as usual, and segregated from the professional criminals.

A couple of guards came out of the building and said to the men who had searched us, "Where to for these?"

Someone said, "India."

I fell down on the ground clutching my stomach. I rolled around and said, "I've got a terrible fever; I think I'm dying."

Suddenly there was a terrific blow from a boot in my wizened buttocks. I leaped up yelling. The guard who had kicked me laughed coarsely and said I would have a long wait for a hospital bed when I could dance like that. He cuffed me into line and herded us along a corridor until we stood outside a cell marked 49.

There was a terrific noise from inside, a constant chatter like a collection of animals. At the door the guard heard our identifying prayers one by one and then shoved us inside. I was number five in the line. When the first man walked in, there was a pause and then a cheer went up. Then the second. A pause. A cheer. As the third man went through, I was able to peek inside the cell. It gave an impression of enormous confusion, of bodies milling about. But what struck me was that on the floor by the urine barrel a gleaming white handkerchief was spread out. The number three political walked in and daintily sidestepped the handkerchief, and then a cheer went up. I remembered Valentin's riddle. I remembered him telling me that *of course* I would wipe my feet on it. Now I guessed why. I stepped up and I thought, Well, okay, here goes.

I carefully wiped my feet on the handkerchief.

No cheer. Then I looked up.

What I saw was exactly like an overcrowded monkey cage in a big zoo. What seemed like hundreds of bodies were hanging by an arm or scrambling up and down like young apes, eating with their fingers, chattering and gesticulating, and all of them naked except for underpants, and all of those naked sweating bodies tattooed, it seemed at first, from head to foot. Three or four dirty, ugly men ran to me as I stepped away from the hankie. One helped with my bundle: "Here, let me take this off your shoulders, brother, you look like a wreck." They led me to a bunk.

I wondered how long I could keep up the deception. I certainly was in no way a brother to these disgusting hoodlums.

Tattoos are a cultural mark of those members of Soviet society who pursue, as Valentine the Intelligent had said, "a different field of endeavor." Here I saw a complete gallery of elaborate designs on exposed flesh. One man had his whole back covered with an elaborate floral design supporting the proud motto: I WOULD DIE FOR MY MOTHER. One had a different girl's name on each of his fingers and on each of his toes. Another had SLAVE OF THE COMMUNIST PARTY on his forehead.

I won some time, before they started asking me about my own career in crime, by telling them how the *pakhan* had escaped from Kuibyshev. Many of them knew Valentin well, and all of them knew his reputation. They looked at me with great respect when I told them that I had been invited to join the escape. By now I thought I had gone about as far as I could with my masquerade. I let my shivers become a little more pronounced and I said, "Brothers, I'm afraid I'm desperately sick; the fever is coming back; I hope I don't infect anyone!"

They fell away from me. But one bold fellow felt my head with the back of his hand. He called out, "One of the People is close to death, brothers. He must have a doctor, quick!"

Some of these monkeys ran to the open windows and began to yell. Others pounded on the cell door, yelling, "Help! Help! A *chelovek* is dying! A doctor! Help!"

Pandemonium.

Amid all the other yells I could hear screams. The *urki* were turning their attention to my fellow politicals. Here it was no discreet bag slitting. They simply knocked the poor fellows down and stripped off their clothes.

Shortly the cell door was unlocked, and a senior officer came in with three guards. He shouted, "There has been a terrible mistake!" Then, "Get these political prisoners out of here, you fools! Don't you know this cell is only for coloreds?" As the guards shoved the seven men out into the corridor, the officer stuck his head back in the cell and winked at the *urki*.

As soon as this performance was over, the *urki* set up their cry for a doctor again. "One of us is dying!" There was at least another ten minutes of this, and then the prison doctor came in. I was dragged off to the hospital, where he gave me some quinine and aspirin and discharged me, and I was taken to a cell for politicals. I felt sick, but I was relieved to be out of India.

I was in that cell less than a day before the next leg of the *etap* began. It was long enough to get a sinister foretaste of the next period of my life. There was a tall, emaciated man in the cell who paced up and down, incessantly coughing. He wore a black cotton jacket and trousers and a black cotton cap. A rectangle was cut out of the left breast of the jacket and a strip of white cloth sewn in with letters and numbers on it, something like CB 551. The same patch and numbers were sewn on both arms, on the front of his cap, on the left leg of his trousers, on the back of his jacket.

I asked him his story. He stared at me out of cavernous, miserable eyes for a long time before he answered.

They were sending him to Spassk, he said finally, a camp for the dying. He had silicosis from the copper mines and knew he could not last long, but death could not be worse than the living hell of Dzhezkazgan. I was horrified and told him in a kind of gasp that I was going to Dzhezkazgan. He just shook his head and coughed heavily, but said nothing more.

This walking dead man made me deeply afraid. I had stopped shivering from the fever after the drugs I had been given. Now I quite literally started to shake from fright. Somehow I got hold of myself, and began the old pep talks. "Remember what Orlov said," I reminded myself. "There are two kinds of prisoners in camp: the kind who die quickly and the kind who survive very well. You are not the kind who dies quickly."

By the time we were loaded back on the train I had pulled myself together. I was still physically weak, but I felt morally tough and even a bit adventurous once again.

Soon the green-treed hills were left behind and the train began to climb through grassy steppeland. Then the grasses began to thin out and there was nothing but flat expanses of rock and sand. We were very high. This land is all more than two thousand feet above sea level. At night the car was freezing; in the daytime it was unbearably hot.

At three o'clock on the third morning the train stopped at a station that seemed to be in the middle of empty space. When we came out, there was nothing but flat rock reaching off into the darkness, and milling dogs pulling at their leashes, and dozens of guards in tropical uniforms, shivering in the cold.

When we got to the camp, it was beginning to get light in the east. When the sun came up, it was hard and sudden—like a stab; only the warmth was welcome. Almost immediately after the sun appeared, the gates swung open.

I began to feel as though I was hallucinating again because I could hear music, a band playing some kind of bravura march. Then out of the gate came a column of walking corpses in black cotton jackets with white number patches. Their faces were pale and they stared straight ahead. Somehow I learned that they were from a hard punishment barracks called BUR. They marched, or shuffled, into the distance surrounded by guards and dogs.

We were formed into columns of five and marched through the gate. Inside the walls the camp appeared to be a village of low stone buildings, with a barren dirt road running between them. The music, when I found it, peering around in the shadows inside the walls, came from a pitiful little band of prisoners sitting on a bench, playing away, with desperate eyes—a tuba, a trumpet, a drum, an accordion, and a violin. The whole picture was so bizarre I still felt myself in a kind of dream state. Am I really seeing this? Human ghosts playing a lively march.

In the supply room we were given our black clothes and numbers. My number was Ess Ya 265—in Russian letters: СЯ 265.

The next several days passed uneventfully except for talk. This was the quarantine. I was glad of the rest. After that we were sent for medical examinations and then assigned to our barracks. The medical examination consisted almost entirely of having your buttocks squeezed. If you had buttocks, you were assigned to the copper mines, which meant silicosis and early death. If you had no buttocks, you were too weak for the copper mines, so they would send you to outdoor construction or the rock quarry. I was assigned to barracks number 5. When I got there, I was supposed to look for the chief of the quarry brigade I was assigned to, known simply as the brigadier. His name was Vtyurin, and he showed me where I was to sleep, on an upper bunk in section 1 of the barracks.

The first person I got to know in the barracks was a Moscow biologist named Vladimir Pavlovich Effroimson. As soon as I told him my story, Effroimson said, "Well, you're in luck. There's a man from the U.S. embassy here in camp."

My jaw must have dropped. I said, "Tell me! What's his name?"

Effroimson said, "Victor S."

"Victor! Impossible. He was shot in 1941. I never met him, but I heard his story."

"Well," Effroimson said, "then you'll have the pleasure of your first conversation with a dead man, because there he is over there!"

He pointed out the window, and I looked across the street to where a tall, lanky guy was in conversation with a shorter man. He had a very low number, which meant he was one of the first lucky ones to get to Dzhezkazgan. I dashed out into the street.

I came up behind him and said formally, "Mr. S.?"

He turned around and looked at me curiously. I immediately said, "You're from Moscow?"

"Yes."

"You worked at the American embassy?"

"That's right."

"Well, so did I. My name is Alexander Dolgun"—and I launched into the prayer and other elements of first meeting.

After we'd talked for a while, I said, "Listen, I heard all the time that this was a death camp, but you look in good shape. How come?"

He laughed. "For some reason or other my dossier was marked EXTREMELY DANGEROUS when I first came down here. They never dared let me out of camp to go to work. *Pridurka*, that's a soft-job worker, from the first day. Always in camp, always a chance to steal food. Now they know I'm not dangerous, so I get some hard assignments. But I know my *tufta* now. I get along."

"*Tufta?*"

"*Tufta* means filling your work quota without really doing any work. I can give you some hints, but mostly you'll have to figure it out for yourself, depending on the job you're on." Then he said, "Who's your brigadier?"

"Vtyurin."

"Well, I don't know him. But you better make friends with your brigadier. That's the beginning of successful *tufta*."

It seemed strange standing there in the hot sun chatting easily with Victor, who seemed almost an old friend, even though I had never seen him before. He was a Soviet citizen, but his English was perfect, and hearing and speaking my own language gave me an enormous boost. Despite the reputation of the camp, I began to sense again that conviction that I could handle anything.

It took me some time to find Vtyurin. He said that it was very hard work in the quarry and that he was insistent about the quotas being filled, so I thought I was not going to have much luck there.

That first night in barracks number 5 we were locked in at ten o'clock. I scrambled up to the top bunk that Vtyurin had assigned me. I was very tired and even the flat boards felt good.

Then I sat up with a start. I had been bitten on the leg. I threw off the blanket. A bedbug ran out and disappeared. Then I was bitten on the foot, then on the arm, then on the back. I began to thrash around. My next bunk neighbor sat up and said crossly, "What the hell are you doing?"

I said, "I'm going to kill these bloody bugs!"

"Don't be crazy," he said. "Look at the wall."

I stared at the whitewashed wall. It was not white anymore. A mass of black insects was migrating down it. I screamed and jumped off the bunk. Angry prisoners snapped at me to shut up. The wall seemed to move. I began to shiver again.

I sat down at the table by the door and stared at the bugs on the wall. I put my head on my arms on the table and tried to sleep. There was a sudden touch on the back of my neck and I started up, terrified. There were bedbugs on the ceiling, and now and then some dropped off on me and on the table. From time to time I dozed off, but even if I was not awakened by bites, I would start up, imagining that another bug had landed on my neck.

The bedbugs seemed to thin out toward morning. I dozed off for a while with my head on my hands, and then at about four o'clock guards opened the doors and began to curse and yell *podyom*.

The brigadier organized us for breakfast. One man was dispatched to the kitchen to get the soup bowls for our twenty-five-man group, another to the bakery for the day's allotment of seven hundred grams of bread per person. Then into the mess hall. By a quarter to six we were forming columns of five inside the gate, and the sorrowful orchestra was beating out its up-tempo march.

It was a long, long march to the quarry. Five kilometers, perhaps five and a half. The first view of the worksite was of a pair of watchtowers silhouetted against the yellow sky. Then a barbed-wire fence that seemed to stretch forever in both directions. When we came to a gate, we were led inside and taken to the lip of the biggest excavation I have ever seen in my life. It must have been nearly two kilometers across and about one kilometer wide, oval in shape, with a spiral truck road winding down to the bottom. I was given a sledgehammer I could hardly lift, and led to a rock face deep down in the pit. The unbelievable daily quota of rock was three cubic meters for each person. My heart sank.

I looked around me. Everywhere men were wearily lifting their picks and sledges and slamming them feebly against huge rocks. I tried to lift the huge sledge and it slipped sideways and pulled me over with it. I lay panting on the ground until a Muscovite student named Boris Gorelov helped me to my feet again.

"You better stick with me for the day," he said. "Anybody in your shape who actually tries to lift a sledge is either crazy or too young to be outdoors by himself."

We both laughed. "Anything you say," I told him.

Thank God for Gorelov that day! He had received some food parcels from home, and had shared them with the brigadier. This got him a blind eye to his *tufta*, his cheating on the quota. Gorelov could build a hollow mound of stone that looked like three cubic meters, but which really contained only about a third of that amount. Taking pity on me that first day, he built the hollow square mound, and when the sun became unbearably hot, he put me in the shade to rest and went on working on his own. The sun made the rock so hot we had to wear gloves to avoid blisters.

At noon we were led to a primitive field kitchen: an iron stove on wheels, with a simmering kettle of porridge. It smelled delicious, but it was so thin you could drink it like water.

Gorelov had secreted a package of white bread and greasy smoked bacon, and he shared it with me. The bacon made me anxious. I thought that it might have been too much of Valentin's greasy meat that triggered my diarrhea the first time. But it was eat meat or starve.

Soon my diarrhea started up again, as I had feared it would, and I began to feel terrible. Gorelov told me that I just might be able to talk my way into the hospital by claiming it was the fever again.

And so, after another night fighting off the bedbugs, I grabbed my bread when it came and went straight to the hospital.

The doctor, a Latvian—and a prisoner, of course—shoved a thermometer under my arm and asked me my story. "I think it's another malaria attack," I said, trying to sound very sick.

The doctor looked at me carefully. He said, "You're not Latvian, by any chance?"

"No. I'm an American."

"An American!" He seemed delighted. He immediately started speaking English, almost without an accent. "I've been dying to find someone to talk English with," he said warmly. "Now, we are not allowed to put you into the hospital for diarrhea and . . ." He looked at the thermometer. "Hmm, no fever. I guess you knew that. Let me see." He began to examine me. My legs had been swollen for some days; he pressed the puffiness along my shinbones and a depression remained when he took his finger away. "That's got to be connected with something," he said quietly. He did a most meticulous examination of my heart, and then he wrote out a very extensive history, always speaking English.

The doctor's name was Arvid Atsinch. He liked the colloquial ways of the language, and he announced right at the beginning that he would call me Al, if that was all right with me.

"Al," he said, "with the edema in your legs and the way your heart sounds, I can make you out to be a real mess. But you'll be able to walk around and do light work, and if you like, I'll give you some medical training, because I need another assistant."

"Wait a minute," I said, "what's all this about my heart?"

"Let me ask you about your treatment before you got here," Atsinch said. "It seems to me that you have been very badly abused recently, am I right?"

I told him about the beatings and the sleeplessness and the cold and the starvation.

"Perhaps that explains it," he said. "The left ventricle of your heart is quite enlarged. Without an X ray I can only estimate how much, but it seems to me to be about four and a half centimeters. I think you have what we call congestive heart disease, and with your diarrhea and your general weakness it means that we will have to start some very extensive therapy."

That meant rest and food. I was given a bed and a hospital gown and started on vitamin injections and intravenous glucose.

Arvid Atsinch began my medical training later on that very first day. He asked if I felt up to making rounds with him, and gave me a white smock and a stethoscope to wear around my neck. We saw men with tuberculosis and silicosis, men with dysentery. We saw a great variety of wounds from the mines and the quarry and the construction sites. Fractured skulls and limbs, eyes and fingers and toes lost, lacerations and scrapes and burns. Atsinch taught me how to sterilize the skin with alcohol and give injections.

Atsinch said, later in our first day together, "You know, Al, I think you have the makings of a physician. I'm going to teach you as much as I can while you're here with me. It may be the only way you will ever survive camp, with that heart of yours, to have a skill that will keep you out of the mines."

What an irony that was. Arvid Atsinch's own exquisite medical skill would be, not too many years later, the very thing that took him into the mines and to his death. I would see a lot of deaths in my years in Dzhezkazgan. I would feel grief for only a very few, but Atsinch's would be one of them. He was the first man I became strongly attached to in camp.

Although he was only a few years older than I, I found myself accepting his teaching unreservedly, whether it was medicine or philosophy or politics. I had never done any serious thinking before I met Atsinch, and the person who starts your mind working in a serious way is someone you remain grateful to. He believed that a man deprived of liberty tends to degenerate morally, so he kept stressing the point of survival with decency. He tied that theme into the whole of history. It was as if I were taking off dark glasses for the first time and finally getting a clear look at the world.

Atsinch for his part seemed to be fulfilled by having a pupil— maybe even disciple is not too strong a word.

He asked me if I was squeamish at the sight of blood. I said I didn't think I was, and he said that he would like me to learn to assist him in surgery, which was his real specialty. Our first case was a mine injury. A man was brought in with a messy head wound. Atsinch handed me a straight razor and told me to shave around the wound while he got instruments and dressing ready. My hands were a bit shaky. The man was conscious, but dazed and very frightened. That made two of us. When I first applied the razor, it cut into a bit of loose flesh. He said in a very loud voice, "If you don't know how to do it, don't do it." Atsinch quickly took the razor, and I watched him shave the man gently and cleanly in about thirty seconds. Then he cleaned out the wound and put on a dressing and sent the man away to a bed. I had begun already to fancy myself a budding physician, but the amazing skill and sureness of my friend's hands took some of the cockiness out of me. I knew I had a long way to go to achieve *that* kind of perfection.

In order to get a week or two of rest, many of the people we operated on had committed *mastyrka*. There were frequent amputations of fingers and toes. Several people came with suppurating arms or legs that showed no wound, and I often got them to admit that they had infected themselves. I asked Atsinch how this met with his standards of morality. He said he could not fault these people, and even admired the ingenuity of some of them. "I do think amputation is foolish, though," he said. "That really does dishonor to the human body."

On the third or fourth day Atsinch took me to the morgue and began to show me how to make superficial incisions. The incising and draining of abscesses was so common, he thought I should be able to do it on my own. He gave me a handbook of anatomy and began to guide me through it.

When a patient died, Atsinch was required to perform an autopsy and write it up. He insisted I attend. I found the first few pretty hard to take, but as Atsinch showed me a diseased liver, a tubercular lung, and all the myriad manifestations of the body's disintegration, my distaste soon gave way to an intense interest.

During this time my edema began to go down and my muscles to build up. I began Dynamic-Tension exercises again, and plenty of fast walking up and down the corridors of the little hospital. Atsinch continued to give me intravenous glucose and vitamins, so even though the food ration was not generous, I was able to build up some flesh again. But when the MVD administrator made his regular visit, I was always in bed looking miserable.

Westerners find it strange that in a prison camp where life was held in such low value there should have been a hospital at all, and one staffed with such a dedicated and skilled doctor. I have to explain that the hospital does not represent any concern over the welfare of the prison inmates. It represents only one concern: that regulations be met. It is laid down in Soviet law that within any prison there must be medical facilities for every so many prisoners; that a person with a fever of more than 38° C. is to be hospitalized, and so on. Someday a bureaucrat who wants to find fault with another bureaucrat may investigate to see whether these regulations are being met—so they are maintained purely for bureaucratic reasons.

My only regret about the hospital was that my comfortable and interesting life there had to come to an end. My edema was gone. My dysentery had stopped. Even my heart sounded better. Atsinch could no longer keep me hospitalized, and at the moment he could not get me an official job as a feldsher trainee. "You're strong enough to handle a great deal, I think," he said. "I'll put on your sheet that you are to report for examination every day for the next two weeks, and we can keep some glucose coming. And vitamins. And then we will see what happens after that. Good luck, my friend."

So I regretfully packed my little sack and went to the administration office to pick up my new job assignment.

Vtyurin's brigade was assigned to the railroad station unloading bricks and cement and lumber. It was hard work and *tufta* was difficult to invent. My friend Gorelov had gone to the hard punishment barracks and I had not found a way to bribe Vtyurin.

It was not long before my confidence began to slip again. The work was much too hard for the amount of food and rest we got.

Two or three people died every day, and as the weather got colder, the rate of deaths increased. At those altitudes, with no bodies of water and no vegetation to moderate the temperature, September slips into winter very quickly.

Now it was dark when we stumbled out of the gates at six o'clock in the morning. The convoy guards stood around with machine guns cocked. The dogs steamed and barked continually. You had to take off your mittens and open all your padded clothing for a search, no matter how cold it got. Many men collapsed in uncontrollable trembling during the search and had to be dragged along by their fellow prisoners until their blood got moving.

The soldiers who guarded us wore thick felt boots, fur mittens, and sheepskin greatcoats. They would steal wood from construction projects and make fires, and when it got down below 0° F., they allowed us to make fires too, if we could scrounge some wood. The guards did not care where the wood came from. I remember a very cold day when we burned half a carload of window frames.

The cold made us more fatigued, because our bodies burned more food to keep warm, and of course it was terribly hard to walk out of a barracks that was above freezing—if only barely—into the bitter, dust-laden wind or blowing snow at five or ten above zero.

One night I was asleep on my bunk, when I felt my leg being tugged. It was an MVD. "You СЯ two sixty-five?"

I said I was.

"Get your stuff and come with me."

He took me across the frozen compound to the dining hall. Several MVD were there, and they searched me thoroughly. I kept saying, "What is this all about?"

"You'll see, don't worry," they said.

They took me to the bread window. "Seven days' allotment," the captain in charge said. I was given several loaves of bread, ten lumps of sugar in a newspaper twist, and two salted herrings. I realized this meant *etap*, and I asked where.

"None of your business," the captain said.

Eight more prisoners were brought in. Some were given five days' allotment, some three, some four. I was the only one with

seven. I deduced I was going to Moscow. This made me terribly
excited, because I thought perhaps I would be released. Then I got
scared, because they might be taking me there to shoot me.

I was dying for confirmation of my guess about Moscow. I said
quietly to the captain, "It's the center for me, isn't it?"

He smiled then. "Good guess."

I said, "In that case I should get the rest of my personal belongings. They're in the hospital." That was a lie, but I had to say
good-by to Arvid Atsinch.

I was taken across to the hospital. I found Arvid and woke him
up and told him. His eyes shone. He said, "Dear friend, they're
going to let you out! I know it!"

He made up a package of tobacco and soap and sausage and
matches. He said, "Whatever you do, write about us. Tell the
world about us. People have to know." I promised I would.

CHAPTER SIX

AT THE station I was put on a Stolypin car attached to a waiting
train, and into a cell of my own. The door was opened after the
train began to roll, and two guards stood outside with a master
sergeant and a senior lieutenant. The officer said, "Prisoner, you
must understand that you have nothing in common with the general convoy on this coach. I am the only one allowed to speak to
you. If soldiers in the general convoy speak to you, ignore them."

So. There was a special escort assigned to look after me!

Somehow this confirmed my fear that I was going to Moscow to
be shot, and I began to shiver again, although the cell was very
warm. Soon I talked myself back into a tentative optimism and
went to sleep. It was pleasant to sleep in a warm place, I told
myself; I like the sound of a train at night, and I had lots of room
to stretch out. With various reassuring thoughts, I slept pretty well.

Finally, early one morning, I was taken off the train in Moscow and put in a plain gray van. After a few minutes the van
stopped and I heard the familiar doors of Lubyanka. The sound
gave me pleasure, strangely enough. I was searched by the same

blue-chinned guard who had searched me in that same room almost two years earlier.

I was taken to an office where a man of medium height sat writing at a desk. I studied him very carefully—I remember doing it, but I cannot remember his face. I have every reason to remember this man, General Ryumin, but he has no face for me, no features at all.

Finally he said, "Why do you suppose we have summoned you?"

I said I had no idea.

"Well, of course, you have your twenty-five-year term, and in a sense we are through with you. But we are very much interested in the operations of American intelligence here in the capital and throughout the Soviet Union. We believe you can supply some important links. We expect you to talk very freely, because two years have gone by and all your American friends have dispersed to other posts. So tell me, what do you say?"

I just stared at him silently.

"I suppose you are able to recall Sukhanovka Prison," General Ryumin said.

I had trouble getting my voice to work. I said, "Very well."

"Of course," Ryumin said levelly. "Of course you do. I have to congratulate you on your passing of that test. I know your endurance and I know how to break it down very rapidly. I am quite prepared to beat you to death, if I do not get your confession."

He put his fingertips together and waited. I just stared at him until my throat came out of spasm. Then I said, "What confession? I thought you just wanted some links in your picture of United States intelligence in this country."

"Ahhh," said Ryumin. His fingers were still together.

"You mean I am supposed to be one of the links?" I asked him.

"Ahhh," said Ryumin.

I said, "I will tell you what I know. It's not much. I had nothing to do with intelligence operations. I can't say what I don't know." I was trying hard to keep the fear out of my voice.

"It is altogether up to you," Ryumin said after a while. "I will give you a few days to think it over."

He pressed a button. A guard came. I went to my cell in a daze. The next day at noon I was taken to Ryumin again.

"Will you cooperate?"

"I told everything in the interrogations. There is no more."

"It is your life."

Back to the cell.

Next day at noon. "Well? What about it? Nice cell here in Lubyanka? Nice food? Nice companions? Or torture and death at Sukhanovka?"

"Let me ask one question," I said.

"Ask it, then."

"Why? Why did you bring me back? Why all the special treatment on the train? What do you hope to gain?"

"Ahhh." Ryumin got up and walked back and forth for a minute. "All right, I'll tell you," he said. "We are going to have a public trial to expose certain Soviet citizens who have collaborated with you and your colleagues. You know who they are."

I said, "Witnesses at public trials usually disappear afterward. They are shot so they can never recant."

He looked angry for a moment. Then he said, "I don't need you as a witness. I need you to lead me to those traitorous officers."

I said, "I really have told you everything I can think of."

"It is not good enough," Ryumin said flatly.

I tried a last, hopeless gambit. "I'll make something up if you want. Would that help?"

Ryumin flew up out of his chair and yelled at me. "We have no desire to be misled by your phantasmagoric inventions! We want the truth and we will have the truth!" He pressed the button so hard that his finger bent and went white at the knuckle. He said, "So! I will see you in Sukhanovka! You can blame only yourself for what happens next!"

There was snow at Sukhanovka when I got out of the van. My cell was number 18. I truly believed when I came into it that it would be my last home in the world. I was deeply, terribly afraid.

It must have been eight thirty or a quarter to nine when the cell was opened. "Prepare for interrogation."

General Ryumin was not in the interrogation room. The man waiting for me was an MGB colonel with a chunky humane face. He said, "Please sit down. My name is Colonel Chichurin."

Chichurin's technique was consistent with his appearance. At the beginning of each session he would say, "Are you going to confess today?"

I would say, "There is nothing to confess." The rest of the session was small talk.

There was no sleep except Saturday and Sunday nights, and soon I began to go unconscious and fall off the chair again. I had lost the knack of sleeping while sitting up.

Several weeks went by uneventfully, except that I acquired bruises from falling off the chair. I no longer had that urgent sense of fear, but I still felt that the sleeplessness and the tiny meals would finish me off. It was just a matter of time.

I became terribly agitated one day when Chichurin told me that the Organs were planning to arrest my parents if I did not confess. He was lying; they were already in prison. But of course I had no way of knowing that. I told him I would confess anything, make up anything to save my parents, but he said that it had to be the truth. Fabrication would not do.

Then one night Chichurin just shook his head and sighed when I came in. Finally he told me that General Ryumin was coming that night. He smoked nonstop and coughed a great deal. He sent me away with two guards. By now they had to hold me up; I was not able to walk by myself. We came to a room with the number 13 on it. I was too stupefied even to think at the time how corny that was. Inside there was a thick Persian carpet with a thin runner lying on it. There were dark stains on the runner.

Ryumin came in and said, "Well, well, so here you are. Would you like to change your mind and talk?"

Chichurin came in and Ryumin told him to pull the drapes.

I simply repeated that I had nothing to say. Ryumin opened a drawer and took out a rubber club about two feet long and an inch thick, with a leather strap which he turned around his wrist. He said, "This will advance the process of changing your mind."

I felt no fear. I think I believed I would feel nothing. I stayed on the chair, dull and inert. Ryumin knocked me off the chair with a blow to the head. It hurt like hell. I roared as I fell on the floor.

He told Chichurin to sit on my legs. He said, "I have a Cossack method of beating. You will never have felt such pain!"

The thing was terrible. I broke my fingernails on the rug. The blows went right on the sciatic nerve, blew up inside my head, all over my body—total explosions of pain. I passed out.

Water splashed on my face. A stethoscope on my chest. "How's his heart?"

"I think you may continue, General."

"Prisoner, will you confess now?"

"To what? Anything, just tell me what! I have nothing to—"

The terrible explosions again. Total pain throughout my body. I must have yelled but I have no memory of it. When I came to again, they were sitting on chairs. "Take him away," Ryumin said.

I had about three hours to sleep but there was no way to escape the pain. They put up the bed at six. I was left all day in the cell.

At nine thirty they dragged me to Chichurin's room again. He said, "Don't you think you had better confess now? You don't want any more of *that*, do you?"

"Please! Please! Don't let him do that anymore," I pleaded with him. "I have told you everything I know. Please! *Please!*"

Ryumin sent for us at midnight and they began again. I cried and pleaded and lost consciousness several times. A doctor applied a stethoscope and told Ryumin he could go on. Then unconscious again, and somehow back in the cell, lying on my stomach, drifting in and out of oblivion, then fiery pain, then oblivion.

At some point a woman doctor examined me in a clinic of some kind, and they left me alone for a while. A few days, or perhaps only one day. I was fuzzy and blanked out most of the time. Then Chichurin started at me again, and for a month or so I saw him every night and spent all day in the cell. He pleaded with me to do anything to avoid the terrible beatings. I am sure he was sickened by my condition.

Some weeks later Ryumin began again. After the first blow I

knew I was through. I screamed, "All right. I'm ready. I'll confess!"

He kept hitting me.

I screamed, *"I'm ready! I'm ready to confess!"*

He stopped hitting me. I was dragged to another room. They left me with a guard for about forty minutes. I worked my mind harder than I ever had. It had to be a story about my friend Bob Dreyer, and that George Tenno they had been talking to me about before. When they came I told them Dreyer and I had been trained together and Dreyer had tried to recruit Tenno. I made up code names for both of us. Ryumin and Chichurin both took notes like mad. When I had told everything I could safely fabricate, they praised me warmly.

I was allowed to sleep all night. For ten days I had all the sleep I wanted. My welts began to heal.

Then one night, "Prepare for interrogation."

At least it was not room 13 I was taken to. But when Chichurin came in, his face looked genuinely anguished.

"You are in worse trouble than ever now," he said gravely. He said nothing more, and I was too frightened to ask.

At midnight we went to room 13. Ryumin came in. "You tried to cheat us, did you!" He knocked me flat. "Confess that you lied!"

After two or three of those explosive blows with the rubber truncheon, I said, "Yes! Yes! I lied."

He kicked me in the jaw. There was a tearing pain right through to the back of my neck. A stream of blood poured onto the carpet. I could see that there were two teeth on the runner.

I had spent those ten days in the cell working up yet another story. They did not like the new one. So the beatings began again. I was sure I would die. I was rolling about so hard to escape the blows that twice I rolled too far and the truncheon landed on my belly. There was a ripping sensation and a deep pain that would not go away.

I screamed out a third version. The blows stopped; I passed out several times. Each time a feldsher listened to my heart. Finally he said it was too weak to continue.

I woke up in Butyrka. A tube was taped to my arm. I was stiff in every joint and my skin felt like parchment that would tear if I moved. I began to examine my body. I had a terrible shock when I looked between my legs. My scrotum was swollen to the size of a child's football. A part of my intestines had descended into it.

After two weeks, during which I slept almost all the time, I was taken in a wheelchair to an interrogation room. There Chichurin gave me a fifteen-page confession to read. It was cleverly done out of all my fabrications, and I could see that it would probably withstand scrutiny and satisfy Ryumin.

Chichurin had composed it himself. There was a litany that went: Q. "Is it true that prior to your arrest the American intelligence service was preparing to spring you into action?" A. "Yes." Q. "Were you assigned to strike up acquaintances with military personnel?" A. "Yes." Q. "For what purpose?" A. "For the purpose of persuading them to divulge information." And so on.

I handed it back. I said, "That's very interesting, but I'm not going to sign it."

For the first time he became really violent in his manner. "Sign it, you stupid son of a bitch! Sign it or Ryumin will be here tonight, hospital or no hospital! Sign it! Sign it! Sign it!"

I thought, I have twenty-five years anyway.

I thought, No one will ever believe this pack of lies anyway.

I signed.

BACK at Dzhezkazgan I was disappointed to find myself in a strange compound, several miles from the first camp I had been in. I had to resign myself to the probability that I would not see my old friends again.

However, in the quarantine barracks I met a young Muscovite with whom I felt comfortable from the first moment. His name was Edik. He had been a student at Moscow University. Once, in a study hall, he overheard a group at a nearby table telling some of the anti-Soviet jokes that have always been around underground. Example: A rabbit is caught trying to flee across the border. The MGB interrogate the rabbit. "Why did you want to leave the Soviet Union?" his interrogator asks him.

"Because," says the rabbit, "I heard that all camels are going to be castrated."

"But you are a rabbit!" remonstrates the interrogator.

"Sure," says the rabbit, "but just try to prove that after they've castrated you for being a camel!"

This is the kind of thing these students were giggling over at a table near Edik's. Three of that group were arrested soon after, because the fourth was an MGB informer. Edik was arrested for *not* having informed. He was tried and got twenty-five years.

They brought a sort of personnel questionnaire around the quarantine barracks one day. On the forms where my profession or trade was to be entered I put down boldly: physician. Then, since we were offered three options, I put down mechanic as number two, and out of some strange whim I can't explain now, locksmith as number three.

On the second Sunday we were released from quarantine. I said so long to Edik and went out in search of the hospital. There I made myself known to the physician in charge, a man named Shkarin, and within a few minutes he had brought his two colleagues, Kask, the laboratory man, and Adarich, the surgeon, to meet and to examine me. I was still in appalling condition. In addition to the scrotal hernia and general debility, I had an exudative pleurisy and a very high fever, so I qualified for admission. They were interested in my description of the training Atsinch had given me, and discussed the possibility of adding enough training to qualify me as a feldsher. While I was mending in the hospital, Adarich began where Atsinch had left off, and on days when I was feeling up to it, I went to the morgue with him and learned how to make an appendectomy incision and how to suture it up, and how to amputate toes and fingers.

I was discharged from the hospital after two weeks. Adarich said he was trying to get me assigned to the hospital, but he warned that it might take some time. In the meantime I was put on a construction brigade, working on buildings near Krestovaya village.

My brigadier was an easygoing guy and had the *tufta* well organized. When he saw how feeble I was, he helped me to goof off for the first week. So I prowled around and acquainted myself with everything that went on. I watched men operating metal lathes and thought that looked like a soft touch. I watched the arc welders and it looked as if you could make a few rubles at it, if you could think of some things in demand, like spoons, to manufacture on the sly. The locksmith's shop looked like a soft touch, too.

Tufta could stretch only so far; I would have to do some work. This turned out to be carrying stone for the masons, and it nearly killed me. I had to find something else as soon as possible, so I approached the brigadier in the machine shop, a man named Zyuzin. He was an accomplished guitarist, and I asked him to teach me to play. He began to teach me simple chords so that I could play what he called "dog waltzes": rudimentary tunes like "Dark Eyes."

After we had made friends over the guitar, I expressed a sort of offhand interest in joining his brigade. He thought the idea was just fine—we could do music together every night—and somehow he was able to arrange the transfer.

I was assigned a job on the drill press. I connected it up incorrectly the first morning. The electrical cables got tangled in the drill mechanism and I shorted out the whole shop.

If it had not been for Zyuzin's skill in *tufta*, I might have died. That must sound like an exaggeration, but this is how it works. If you made your norm, you were given a basic food ration, known as one hundred percent, and this was sufficient to keep you going. If you dropped below your norm, you got a lower ration. With lower rations you would be too weak to maintain whatever percentage of the norm you had been achieving, and so your ration would be lowered again. Finally it would be reduced to the starvation ration. Somehow Zyuzin kept me and all his brigade at least at the base rations by satisfying the MVD that his norms were being met when they were not, juggling books, and keeping his brigade loyal to him so that no one would be tempted to turn informer.

Informers were usually killed. There was a prisoners' committee called the People's Council of Justice that undertook to execute these destructive people. The standard practice until mid-1953 was for a nominee of the council simply to walk up to the condemned man in the yard, say quickly and quietly, "The People's Council has condemned you to death," and stab him.

In 1953 a declaration came out that any prisoner known to have killed another prisoner would be summarily shot without trial. After that the execution of informers went underground. Once a hoarse whisper reached my ears from a nearby bunk: "Ivan Sergeiyevich Rostov, you are condemned to death by order of the People's Council," and then some unpleasant gurgling sounds. After that I heard the soft padding of bare feet as the unknown executioner slipped back to his bunk.

I was falling dangerously below my norm, and it was difficult for Zyuzin to cover for me. He sent me to the blacksmith shop. "There's always a demand for apprentices," he said.

I was assigned to help an old Estonian blacksmith named Arnold cut metal. I was to wield the hammer, but could hardly lift it. He held the chisel. I had a knack of somehow striking the chisel in a way that would cause the handle to break off and the hot blade to fly through the window.

Arnold was shocked. "How did you do that! That never happened before!"

I went to get the chisel. It had smashed through the glass window and disappeared in a snowdrift outside. Then Arnold set up for another try. The bar of hot metal was laid on the anvil and he seized the chisel and signaled me to strike. The big hammer came down at an angle, and the chisel disappeared. We both looked around. There were no new panes of glass broken. The chisel was not on the floor anywhere. Finally, knowing it was crazy, I went out and looked in the snowbank. There it was, and it must have gone through the already broken windowpane.

Arnold said, "How can anyone so sloppy be so accurate?"

We tried again, and for a while I managed to hit straight on. The next day I broke a couple of handles, and the next day a couple more. They quite often went through the same window. Arnold the blacksmith was too kindly to complain, but he looked increasingly pained each time I shot a chisel out the window.

One day, coming back from the supply room with a new handle, I saw a commotion out in the arc welders' yard. The door opened and they carried in a dead guy with burns up the sleeve of his jacket. He had electrocuted himself.

I had been practicing arc welding in spare moments, because it looked like a soft job. Now I ran to Zyuzin and pleaded with him to give me the dead arc welder's job. Zyuzin called the chief engineer, a civilian. "Can you do a figure-eight bead?" the man asked me.

"Sure, easy."

"Can you make a double seam on two pieces of rail?"

"That's baby stuff," I said indignantly.

"All right, come outside and show me," the engineer said.

He gave me a mask and a machine and the two bits of rail I was to weld. "Call me when it's done," he said, and went inside.

I looked at the eleven other arc welders. They were all looking at me. Suddenly I felt embarrassed, so I pulled on my gloves and shoved the mask down over my face. I couldn't see a thing. Sweat kept getting in my eyes. I would lift the mask to wipe it away, catch the amused looks from the other guys, shrivel up with embarrassment, and try again.

It took me nearly an hour to make those two seams.

I called Zyuzin and he called the engineer. He picked up a sledgehammer to see if he could break open my weld. Suddenly he put the hammer down again without using it. Then he swung his boot six inches and gave the weld a light kick. It fell apart.

I was mortified.

The engineer laughed. "I'll show you how to do it right," he said. "You've got the basic idea, but there's still a lot to learn."

Actually I learned welding quickly and moderately well. My job was to make components for a basement staircase—cross-gridded steel plates for the steps, and I beams for the sides. Although by the end of the day I was exhausted, I found the long march back to the barracks a cheerful time, because it meant going home, to rest and food and friends. I would carry stolen boards and studs home for the fire, and when the guards confiscated the wood, I was philosophical about it. I understood that there were certain costs you had to pay for survival.

One day Arnold the blacksmith came into the yard and stood watching me work. "Things are not the same in the forge anymore, Alexander my boy," he said. "I have had the same chisel handle for three weeks now, and some of the spice has gone out of life."

We both laughed over this, and we rolled ourselves a smoke and sat on a snowbank for a short break.

"I've been watching you work, Alexander," Arnold said. "I am surprised at how well you are doing. Please don't be offended."

I said there was no offense.

Arnold said, "I have an idea for making some money to buy extra food. Do you think it would be difficult to set aside a few round bars and some angle irons from time to time?"

I said I thought not.

Arnold explained that he had been talking to some of the civilians who had been lured by the government to work in Dzhezkazgan. They were disgruntled, because when they arrived here in the town, they found cold, half-finished apartments, with no furniture.

What they hated most was the lack of beds, which meant sleeping on the floor. Arnold figured out that we could collaborate on making bootleg beds. I would weld together a rudimentary frame and he would make ornaments in the forge.

So we entered into a partnership. I had to give up lunch breaks for a while, but we could finish a bed in a week and we got about four kilos of bread for each one, or occasionally a piece of meat.

My morale was good. I could even claim overproduction on the job and get extra rations, but I still found the carrying too much for me. I staggered under a sheet of steel as though the wind were blowing me around. So I persuaded Zyuzin that I could increase my output a lot if he got me an assistant, and to my delight he somehow got Edik, my friend from quarantine, assigned him personally to me, and moved him into our barracks.

So now, in the evenings, I had Edik to talk with and Zyuzin's guitar to listen to, and I began to think of studying the guitar seriously myself.

Despite being competent at welding, I still had a talent for blunders. Shortly after Edik joined me, we were given a pattern for big office safes made out of thick sheet metal. We cut the sides and top and bottom and the door, made the hinges, then had to weld the hinges to the door, and then the hinges to the frame. Edik held the sheets in place while I welded them. The first one was a bit awkward and we had to cut apart one seam and reweld it, because it was crooked, but by the time we got the doorframe in place, we were getting the hang of the job and moving at high speed. Too high, as it turned out. Edik stood inside to hold the door in position while I welded the hinges to the doorframe. It took all his strength to hold it precisely, so he told me to hurry.

I hurried. I slapped the seams on one after the other. Soon the last seam was on, and I said, "That's it." We had finished our first safe and it was still early afternoon. I was sure that we could, with appropriate cheating, make over our norm and get extra rations on this job, so I immediately ran to the stockpile to start chalking out new sets of bottoms, sides, doors, and so on.

Amid all the clatter I became aware of Edik's voice calling, with a hollow sound. He was still in the safe.

"Come on out! Let's get going," I yelled.

"I can't!" he yelled back.

I had welded the door on backward! The hinges would only bend inward and the door was bigger than the inner lip of the doorframe. I ran for the torch. Edik screamed that he was roasting as I started to cut the hinges. I cut as fast as I could, but by the time I got him out he was unconscious from the smoke and the heat, and it was some time before we got back on friendly terms.

CHAPTER SEVEN

IT WAS the spring of 1952. Soon I would be twenty-six years old. Memories of the freezing dungeon at Lefortovo and the horrors of Sukhanovka had somewhat faded, although my jaw still ached where Ryumin had broken it and I still had and have scars from Sidorov's kicks and Ryumin's rubber club.

Spring on the desert steppe is the only time when there seems to be any life on it. For a very brief period, measured in days, the melting snows leave behind enough water for wild red tulips to blaze out across the otherwise dead land and wild garlic to grow in profusion. If we were on an outside job, we picked the wild garlic and took it home for its vitamin C content.

For a brief period during this sudden bloom the death rate would fall off. Sometimes more than a day would pass without a death in our little town of several thousand slaves. Fantasies of an American invasion, preceded by airlifts to drop arms to us, bloomed along with the desert flowers, and my spirits were as high as anyone's, although I did not share that particular fantasy.

I kept pleading with Zyuzin to show me more chords on the guitar, and he somehow found a beat-up old guitar which I could buy for a couple of loaves of bread. Now, when the singing started in the evenings, I would accompany the singers with my dog waltzes.

What I really aspired to was learning to play classical compositions, like Zyuzin. I resolved that I would have to have a classical Russian guitar, which has seven strings instead of six, and after a while I found an old woodworker who said he could make one. I watched him make it over a period of months, and in the meantime asked all my friends to try to find me some real guitar music. When my guitar was finished, some music turned up: Rachmaninoff's "Italian Polka" and some Chopin waltzes. Zyuzin started to teach me how to read music.

It was a painstaking business. I still cannot imagine how the rest of the men in the barracks were so patient with my fumbling attempts. I found it immensely difficult, but totally absorbing, which was what I needed. Working away at my music, I could forget the howling winds outside on winter nights and ignore the bedbugs for a while. I buried myself in pages of Chopin and Rachmaninoff and in the constant exercising and training of my fingers.

Marching to work and drumming thirty-second notes against my chest, I would daydream escape plans. I wanted to escape, but the more I heard about the failure rate the less I believed in the possibility. Any normal escape was doomed. There was no place to hide in the open desert, and if you did not die of exposure, you were beaten up or shot, and then, no matter how great the distance, you were brought back for hard punishment. Nobody ever came to me with a credible plan. And while attempts were made every few weeks, they almost all failed.

So all through the spring and into the early summer of 1952 I worked away at welding during the day and music during the night, and while I dreamed of freedom and prayed for it, I was really resigned to the fact that for the time being at least I was a slave in a slave labor camp and there was no point pretending otherwise. Then in the middle of that overwhelmingly hot summer there was a development that looked bad at first but that soon changed my life radically for the better.

MY SCROTAL hernia began to strangulate. Adarich, the surgeon, had said to try to live with the hernia until I was stronger, but I had let it go on too long. I spent several very bad nights in pain, and Adarich and Shkarin said that I would have to have surgery within hours or face the risk of serious peritonitis. Adarich put me on the operating table and gave me a spinal. I said, "Couldn't I have a general anesthetic? I'm frightened."

Adarich said, "Listen, with your heart we'd never wake you up again. This is going to be an easy operation, because your abdominal wall is so thin I'll be through it in one cut. There!"

Adarich was fantastically quick. Within minutes it was over and I was carried to a bed.

I felt quite triumphant, despite some pain, because I had remained conscious through the whole thing. Adarich helped take my mind off the pain by telling me that he could justify the need for another feldsher in the hospital and it would make sense for me to resume training. He said, "The medical administrator is an MVD captain named Lavrenov. He's a drunk, but not a bad guy in some ways. You'll have to get on his good side. He's agreed to meet you, and you've got to give him a present."

"A bribe?"

Adarich winced. "You'd better be very sure it doesn't look like a bribe. You have to find something he would like to have and give it to him in a way that looks completely innocent."

I had a Parker 51 pen and a Ronson lighter in my little sack in the storeroom, along with my civilian clothes. I told Adarich about them and he agreed that they would make ideal presents.

At the end of six days my sutures were taken out. On the twelfth day Adarich let me go out of the hospital, and very stiffly and carefully, expecting something to unzip at any moment, I walked to the storeroom to claim my pen and my lighter. That afternoon Adarich and I went over the material that Lavrenov would quiz me on.

When I met Lavrenov walking in the compound a few days later, I went up to him and said, "Citizen Chief, could I have a word with you?"

"What is it, prisoner?"

I said, "I have found it very interesting to be a patient in your hospital. It seems very well supplied and managed compared to the hospital I worked at in the previous camp."

In 1955 fellow prisoners smuggled a camera into the prison hospital. Using film from the electrocardiograph, they photographed Dolgun.

He accepted the compliment noncommittally. Adarich had made it clear that I should not come right out and ask for the job, just indicate my background and get a conversation going. Lavrenov asked a lot of questions to explore my understanding of routines, hygiene, postoperative care. I felt I was doing pretty well. Then I said, "Citizen Chief, I want to ask you a small favor."

His face darkened a little.

I said, "I brought with me from Moscow a couple of cherished items that I am afraid are going to be stolen if I try to keep them here. I would rather give them to someone who knows how to appreciate them than have them stolen. I wonder if you would accept them." I told him what they were.

He looked around carefully to make sure nobody was watching, and then he said he would be glad to have them, pocketed them quickly, and said that he appreciated the gesture very much.

In three days he turned up in the hospital and told me to come to the operating room. There he quizzed me in detail about injections, sterilizing instruments, and the uses of intravenous glucose. Fortunately, most of the questions touched on procedures I had been taught or had experienced as a patient. Then he called in the patients due for injections that morning and made me demonstrate.

I felt quite confident. I had developed a knack for working very fast. A split second after I had sterilized the area with alcohol, I had the needle in, and the patient hardly felt a thing. Lavrenov nodded with approval.

Then he took me to the morgue. This was harder. A patient had died of TB and he told me to begin the autopsy. I had never done one on my own, but I had watched both Atsinch and Adarich and had had some instruction from Kask, the laboratory man. I was very nervous, but I put on a good show, and acted as if I did this sort of thing all the time. Finally, Lavrenov said, "I'm satisfied."

And that was it. I was a feldsher!

At first I was assigned to another feldsher, Vasya Kargin, to learn the routines of the duty shift. Then after a few days I took my first full assignment, which was a twenty-four-hour shift. I took one day, eight a.m. to eight a.m., Vasya took the next. We could usually grab a little sleep in the afternoon, but we were on duty for the full period. From midnight until four a.m. it was usually quiet. Adarich and Kask and the others slept in the hospital and I could call them if there was an emergency.

At four thirty I would go to the outpatient clinic to meet the first hopefuls looking for rest, for a chance to malinger, or for more serious help. Sympathy and the chance to spend a few days in bed were the big draws. There was an outer room where I, as the feldsher, would put iodine on scrapes and cuts, bandage light wounds, hand out aspirin and stomach powders. If it was something more serious than that, I had to refer the patient to the doctor, who usually arrived at about five thirty. I wore a white lab coat and all the prisoners called me "Doctor" automatically.

On my second or third day alone in the outpatient clinic, a patient walked in as soon as I had opened the place. He was a hard-looking man with tattoos on almost every centimeter of exposed skin. A professional.

"Doctor," he said grimly, "I have a terrible stomachache."

"Where?" I said sympathetically.

He motioned me to come close. "Here," he whispered fiercely, pulling back his shirt. His right hand was inside his shirt, holding a wicked curved knife like a miniature scimitar. "I want opium. I am always treated very well here. You're new. You might as well know that if I don't get my opium, you get the knife."

We used tincture of opium for extreme diarrhea. Five or six drops in a glass of water.

I was in a quandary because I knew if I refused him, he would probably kill me, and if I gave him what he wanted, I would never get rid of him and he would have a certain amount of power over me. I got out a cone-shaped beaker and told him to show me how much he usually took. He indicated a little over a centimeter. I quickly grabbed an iron solution, and threw in a few drops of bitters that we kept for appetite, and then stirred in some water and gave it to the addict. I moved to put the table between me and him as he drank it, and felt behind me for a scalpel, in case he should pull his knife.

But he just tossed the mixture back and said, "Thank you very much, Doctor," with a big mischievous grin that transformed his grim features, and went out.

I thought, I'll see him again. So I made up a bottle of my spurious mixture and put a TINCTURE OF OPIUM label on it and shoved it to the back of the case where no one would use it by mistake. The same man came back the next time I was on duty and I poured him a dose from the same bottle. The next time I saw him he complained that he wasn't getting much of a lift from opium anymore. He looked at the label closely and then asked for a triple dose. After I poured it, he walked around the dispensary for several minutes looking disconsolate. Finally he heaved a big sigh and said, "Well, I don't know . . ."

Then he went out. I never saw him again.

THE morgue was the domain of an orderly called Nye Russki. Guards never went in there, partly because the hospital staff spread the story that all corpses were highly infectious. Nye Russki told me that there was a cache of forbidden books and other contraband under the autopsy table, perfectly safe, and if I wanted to conceal any small articles, I should put them in the morgue.

One morning Nye Russki came to me and said, "How many corpses are we supposed to have?"

I checked the book. "Nine," I said. "Why?"

"Oh, it's all right. Thank you." He went away.

The next day Nye Russki asked me again. There had been no deaths in the night. I said we still had nine and pressed him to know what the trouble was.

"I'm either having eye trouble or trouble with my head," he said unhappily. "I know you are right about the nine, but two days in a row I count ten. Please." He motioned me to go with him.

We went to the morgue. I counted nine corpses, stretched out on the packed earth floor. Nye Russki counted nine.

"Okay now?" I asked him.

"No. I counted ten a few minutes ago. I *know* I did."

The next day he came to me looking terrible. "I need some medicine," he said in a panicky way. "We have twelve corpses!"

"Eleven," I said.

"That's just it. There should be eleven, but I'm counting twelve. Please come with me again!"

I went. We counted. Eleven corpses.

Poor Nye Russki felt terrible. I think he was really worried about his mind.

The next day he came to me looking very much relieved.

"Please," he said with a big smile. "I know where our extra corpse comes from. Come! Come! I want to show you!"

He took me outside. We had a ladder leading to the roof of the hospital, for snow removal in the winter. He motioned me to follow him up the ladder. The morgue roof had a small skylight. We looked through. There was an extra corpse, all right. It was sitting up reading one of our contraband books!

Something clicked. I knew that there had been a search on for several days for an *otkazchik*, one of a group of conscientious objectors who would not work on their Sabbath and were always being beaten up for it.

I said to Nye Russki, "You watch the outside door of the morgue. I'll go and talk to the corpse."

I had recognized him. His name was Valka; I had treated him in the hospital. When I unlocked the door, he was lying among the corpses trying to look like one. I walked right over and stood staring down at him. He could not stand the suspense, I guess. He opened his eyes after a bit and grinned at me sheepishly. "Hello, Doc," he said.

IN THE hospital I developed a strenuous program of exercise once my general health was in top shape again. I had done some minor acrobatics when I was a kid, and now I began to practice walking on my hands again, usually up and down the hospital corridor. One night as I was grunting along on the return trip—which I had never accomplished yet in full—I was interrupted by a scream from the end of the hall. I jumped to my feet and saw an old Polish professor we were treating for hepatitis reeling around the corridor with his hands to his head. As I ran to him, he tripped on the coal box, fell, bumped his head, and went out cold on the floor. I dragged him to the operating room and began to treat the scratch on his head. In a few moments his eyes flickered and opened. He looked quite panicky. "I am going to die, Doctor. Please tell my family. Oh, God have mercy on my soul, God have mercy!" And on and on so fast I could hardly understand him.

Finally I seized him firmly by the shoulders and gave him a sharp shake. "Stop all this," I said. "Tell me what the trouble is!"

"I am going to die. I am dying of liver dystrophy. I know the symptoms are hallucinations, and oh, Doctor, when I came into the corridor I saw you walking on the ceiling!"

Memory brings all these things quickly to the surface. They were the things that created life in the midst of death, and humanity in the midst of a constant and diabolical oppression. But these comic incidents were rare—small bright spots almost obliterated by the gloom and terror out of which each day was built.

As healthy and productive as the hospital was, in terms of my physical recuperation and my growth as a human being, when I force my memory to be accurate, it reminds me that my life was surrounded by death. I had become hardened in some ways, to protect myself. But grief sometimes broke through the barriers I had built around me.

There were so many men who would never go back to their families, who died in tears of loneliness. Most of these men would have raised children, loved wives, done some work they could take satisfaction in, made some choices about the direction of their lives, except that a state wanted their slave labor and to obtain it had elaborate machinery for the creation of guilt where guilt did not exist. Almost no one I knew in Dzhezkazgan had committed an offense that would be recognized as a crime by any democratic government. They were innocent men. I took their deaths to be murder, whether they died of bullets or fever or despair.

There was a boy named Arkadi, a poet from Moscow. I call him a boy, although he was a year or two older than I, say twenty-seven or twenty-eight, because he was boyish in his enthusiasm and his humor until the day he died.

He was one of those young dissidents of the late 1940s who got into trouble with his eyes wide open. He had written savagely satirical poems about the regime and about the Leader, and circulated them privately. To anyone else that would seem to be folly or self-destruction. To Arkadi it was the only honorable thing to do, to fight the injustice, the waste, and the inhumanity he saw. He loved Russia, but not what was happening to her.

When they brought him to the hospital, he had bilateral pneumonia. We had no procedures for surgical treatment when a lung abscessed, and we had no antibiotics except sulfa. He was going down every day, and yet he was always gay, always making new poems, love poems and poems about a bright future.

Arkadi was a tall, lanky guy who liked to stride around the ward in his prison underwear, with his bony knees poking through the cloth, reciting verse and telling funny stories. At night we sat together for hours. I would bring cool cloths for his forehead. He had a constant high fever and he coughed a great deal. We sat close together and talked about how the world could be if all nations put their faith in parliamentary democracy. He believed it could work in the Soviet Union, although it would take a long time and a lot of education. I scrounged some fine white paper and had it bound in book form, and he filled the book with poetry, some his own, some he knew by heart from Russian poets he loved.

Adarich told me that Arkadi could never survive. I suppose Arkadi himself knew that privately; he never showed it. In another camp not far away there was a chest surgeon who could have done the surgery, and one of the few things I have to hate Lavrenov for is that he refused to transfer Arkadi to that camp. For four months he went down steadily while we watched.

I gave him extra ampules of glucose intravenously whenever I could; they gave him a little more strength to breathe, but the abscess in his lung was suffocating him, and we both knew it. One night I was sitting on the edge of the bed beside him. We were not talking; he was too choked, too short of breath. After a while I said, "Well, Arkadi, you want to sleep now, don't you? Shall I leave you, and come back in an hour to see how you are?"

He did not answer. I bent over him and felt his chest. It was still. Arkadi was dead.

I said to myself, "This is a hero's death, but I have no way to honor him."

He died because he believed in something fine and refused to hide it or to compromise it.

I went outside. There was a friendly guard on duty around the hospital, and he made no objection if we wanted to take a little walk at night, as long as we stayed close by. Behind the morgue was shadow, where the floodlights from the walls could not reach. I could see the stars. I looked up and said good-by to Arkadi, somewhere in the stars. I tried to recall Mary's face. It was too far away. I felt a sadness that was like a deep burning in my gut. I did not want the sadness to go: it was the right thing to feel then.

I yearned for living people to love. One I loved had just died, another was so far away her face was fading from me.

ONE morning a man in the lineup clearly had a raging pneumonia. His fever was very high. His cheeks were flushed and he had a bad cough. Clearly a sick, sick man. And yet, looking at him made me want to laugh. He had a round bald head and his face was a clown's face. He seemed to have a spirit to match. Despite the illness he smiled and joked while I examined him. He was Ukrainian. His name was Marusich.

I took Marusich along to the ward to show him his bed. The minute we entered the ward a loud voice boomed from the back of the room, "Well, for heaven's sake! Who do I see? It is his worship, the governor of Zhitomir!"

Marusich stared for a moment, then said, "Look at that! The governor of Odessa!"

The two men embraced each other warmly. I took it for a joke, of course, but I soon found out that both men had indeed been the equivalent of mayor in those considerable cities, and because they had stayed in their posts during the Nazi occupation, they had been convicted of collaboration and treason and sentenced to twenty years. Marusich was still in politics: in camp he was one of the key figures in the western Ukrainian "community," and he wielded a good deal of power. He was very grateful for the careful attention I gave him and told me that if I ever needed a little muscle to help me over a trouble spot here or there, just to call on him. His lung healed quickly and I was sorry to see him go, because he was a source of cheer in the gloomy ward.

There was a crazy Kazakh named Shargai in our camp. Shargai always sang in a very loud voice, day and night, and he seldom slept. He kept his barracks mates awake most of the night, and there was no way they could shut him up. So the prisoners all complained to the administration, who decided Shargai was insane and had to be hospitalized. That made him our problem.

We discovered that in addition to singing he had two passions: smoking crude, strong Kazakh tobacco, and helping other prisoners, especially those in trouble.

So I did two things. I canvassed all the Kazakhs I knew in camp, and explained that we had one of their brothers in dire circumstances in the hospital and that they could help by making sure that he had lots of tobacco. They responded like true brothers, and although the hospital began to take on a heavy smell from the tenacious smoke, we had periods of quiet.

I then decided to make Shargai the water boy. All our water had to be carried by hand from a central reservoir. So I explained to Shargai that there was a serious need for fresh water all the time, that the patients were too weak and the staff too busy to carry it. He was delighted. Ten hours a day he carried water and at night collapsed, exhausted, and slept like a dead man.

Shargai had a vision, a premonition about Stalin.

Adarich and the other doctors often met in the evenings for political discussions. Shargai heard of these meetings and begged to be allowed to sit in. He had a great respect for the doctors. Anyone with a white coat was included in his worship of the magic of medicine. Because we were fond of him, we let him attend the meetings. We did not know then that he had a huge brain tumor, but we did know that his mental condition was weakening.

In the meetings he was usually silent. However, in the middle of February, Shargai said that he had an important announcement to make. He looked around at each face very gravely. "My dear, dear friends," he said. "I know that I am going to die shortly. Very very soon. A few days at the most." His manner was quite lucid. He wasn't interrupted. "But that is not my announcement. My statement is that soon after my death the lives of all you prisoners will change radically for the better. In fact, before many years after my death, all of you will be free men. But as soon as I am dead, things will begin to change for you."

We all humored him. "Well, Shargai, that's wonderful, tell us more about it. What will cause the change?"

"There will be a single occurrence in the Soviet Union of the greatest importance."

"What occurrence, Shargai? Is it connected with your death?"

For a long time he would not tell us. Then he said, "My dear friends, I love you all so well, and I shall be so sorry to leave you all. . . ." Tears formed and ran down his long, bony nose and dripped onto his huge mustache. "The event is this. Almost as soon as I am gone, you will learn that the Leader is dead!"

Although there had been a few rumors of ill health in the Kremlin, there was no indication of anything seriously wrong with Stalin. But even though it was preposterous, there was something very powerful in the way Shargai told us his fantasy.

A few days later Shargai started to rave and to complain, when he was lucid, of terrible pains in his head. A day or two later he lapsed into a coma. At ten thirty at night on the second day, during my duty, he died. I was relieved to see him out of his pain.

Shargai died on February 28. Five days later there were cries and yells of celebration throughout the camp; news had come in that Stalin was dead.

Shargai had prophesied. The Leader was dead. And within a very short time things indeed began to change very much for us.

Soon there were rumors of mutinies in camps all over the Gulag Archipelago, which is the name ironically given to the entire network of Soviet prisons and labor camps: islands in a sea of oppression. The only immediate result was a sense of anxiety among all the custodial personnel. In some cases this was shown by an unbelievable demonstration of friendliness toward the prisoners. After all, we might soon be freed, and it would be very unhealthy to be remembered by so many ex-prisoners as a tyrant and a sadist.

The medical administrator, Lavrenov, had almost always been pretty easy to get along with, and now he was even easier. He still drank too much, but he was in the hospital a great deal more, trying to be helpful.

He took me aside one day and explained that I had already overstayed the regulation period for the assignment of an uncertified medical person to a hospital job. Almost all *pridurki* assignments were allowed to continue for only a short period—I think it was six months in most cases.

"You're a first-class feldsher. I've seldom seen anyone learn so fast," Lavrenov said. "I'm going to recommend that you be sent out as a feldsher. They'll put you in a tough job, you know, maybe even the mines, but if you go as a feldsher, you'll be okay."

Months before, because of my enlarged heart, Arvid Atsinch had been able to get me listed as Medical Category Two, so that I would not be sent to the mines. The doctors had conferred over my heart periodically and now declared their amazement that the original enlargement had spontaneously reduced itself. I was healthy again.

Lavrenov said, "Whatever happens, if they want you, it won't be in mine fifty-one for a while. It's closed down. They had a terrible accident. Elevator cable broke."

I said I had heard that everyone was afraid to ride the elevators in mine 51 because they were prone to mechanical failure.

"This one was the worst in a long time," Lavrenov told me. "Twenty-seven people aboard. There was a doctor killed, too. His insides were wrecked. They brought him back to his own hospital and he knew he was going to die. So he begged his colleagues not to operate on him, said he was going anyway."

There was only one other hospital in the area. I had a chilling premonition. I said, "Try to think of his name, Citizen Chief."

"A Latvian doctor," Lavrenov said.

I felt sick. "Atsinch," I said.

"That's the name," Lavrenov said. "Of course! I forgot. You were trained by him, weren't you?"

In the space of a few weeks two of the people I had come to care for intensely were dead, Arkadi and Arvid Atsinch. It made me feel hard. I felt hatred. Lavrenov was trying to be nice and could not possibly have understood the grimness in my face.

It got grimmer. Within a few days the camp *naryadchik* sent for me. The *naryadchik* is the trusty prisoner, who makes work assignments. He got out my file. "You're leaving the hospital," he said.

"Where will I be working?"

"Mine fifty-one. But take it easy, brother, you're lucky. You're to go as feldsher."

"But listen," I said hotly. "Mine fifty-one is supposed to be

Copper mine 51 in Dzhezkazgan was visible from the labor camp gates. And frequently so was a camel, due to the proximity of the desert steppe.

closed. The elevator crashed. A friend of mine was killed in it."

"Catch them closing that mine!" He snorted. "Anyway, the elevator is fixed again. The repair should last a week at least!"

The summer had come. Walking just the short distance to the mine with my little satchel of supplies was the hardest part of the day. It was often 110° in the shade, and there was no shade. The hot sun turned my face and neck a dark copper color in a few days and my hair bleached almost to the color of wheat.

It was a relief to go down the mine at first, because it was cold and I wore my padded jacket down there. I had a niche next to the machine shop, near the elevator, and I painted a big red cross on the little table and bench they gave me. The mine had many accidents; I expected to be busy.

Silicosis had been the scourge of the mines before I came there, but after Stalin's death they introduced wet mining. A hose attached to the drilling machine sprayed throughout the drilling, so the dust settled out of the air and the incidence of lung diseases began to go way down. All the digging used to be by hand. Thousands and thousands of lives were lost to exhaustion. Now they had brought in huge electrically powered scrapers that vastly increased production and cut down on deaths.

Most of my work was on crushed fingers. At home in America you would be hospitalized for a crushed finger. But all I could do was apply a dressing and distribute a handful of aspirin. The patient had to go back to work. If a whole arm or leg was crushed, he would be excused from work, but unless I yelled and screamed that he was bleeding to death, he would have to wait to go back to the barracks with everyone else at the end of the shift.

Almost every evening I played guitar with Zyuzin, and my music was advancing well. I was also continuing to learn medicine. I borrowed some medical books from Adarich and read pharmacy and physical medicine and even obstetrics and gynecology. The atmosphere in the camp grew easier every day. There were no drastic changes, just a little easing of attitudes. Rations were still terrible. The less skillful at the craft of survival still died quickly, but fewer died, because survival took a little less skill.

As part of the "thaw," the hours of work were shortened from twelve to ten, and so, because people had more rest, the poor rations were more nearly adequate. And there was more time in the evenings for rest and recreation.

Sometime in November, 1953, I was told again to see the *naryadchik*. There was a rumor that he had a friend in another camp who was a feldsher and had been eyeing my job.

"You have been assigned to Zheldor Poselok," the *naryadchik* told me. "Your brigadier's name is Ivanov. You'll be on construction. Hard labor. Extreme hard labor, in fact."

Zheldor Poselok was a huge railway construction project and a notorious man-killer. I said to the *naryadchik*, "I'll look forward to meeting you outside someday."

He said, "Go pack your stuff and meet the convoy here in half an hour. You're being moved to the KTR."

Camp number 1, the KTR. I felt a real chill. The death rate from exhaustion was spectacular in the KTR.

Leaving my old barracks was a blow, too. No more musical evenings with Zyuzin. No more long chats with Adarich. Oh well, I thought, it's been a lot worse.

It was still early in the afternoon when I moved over to the KTR. I slung my sack of belongings on the floor and waited for the work brigades to come back from Zheldor Poselok so that I could find Ivanov and be assigned a bed. When the convoys returned, I was struck by the fatigue etched in the faces of most of the men.

Ivanov, the brigadier, was a surly, black-haired man in his early forties. He just scowled when I introduced myself and told me he would find a bunk for me when he was good and ready. I sat at the table and waited. Suddenly I heard a loud familiar voice call out, "Well, look at that! It's his honor the doctor!" I looked around and saw a merry clown's face. Marusich, the governor of Zhitomir! We ran and embraced each other.

"My dear Doctor!" he exclaimed. "What good fortune brings us together again?"

"I'm not sure it's all good fortune, Marusich," I said glumly. "I've lost my medical status. I'm here on extreme hard labor for some reason. I'm assigned to Zheldor Poselok."

"And so am I! And so am I! Cheer up! Cheer up! We old hands know how to manage these things, don't we?" He winked a huge wink and grinned. "You will be my bunkmate."

Marusich arranged it, and I also discovered that he had been assigned as day cook, which meant he had sacks of coarse-ground grain to make porridge with and to give to his friends. "Just come over to my brigade at noon," he said. "I'll see you get all you need to eat. What a great pleasure to see you, dear Doctor!"

That evening Marusich was in constant demand. The barracks was full of western Ukrainians, and he was sought out as a sort of magistrate to settle disputes. It was clear that he was a man of some substance in the brigade and in the barracks.

In the morning, when we got to the project, Ivanov started handing out assignments. He was flanked by two real toughs, his assistants. I just walked off and spent the day roaming around the worksite, watching men lay bricks and mix cement and carry lumber. I tried to look as though I were on my way from one job to another and to keep out of sight of Ivanov and his thugs.

At one end of the project there were half a dozen apartment buildings going up for the civilian workers. As I walked among them, I came around the corner of a building and bumped right into a tall man who was walking fast. I was about to yell, "Why don't you watch where you're going?" when I realized who it was—my friend Victor S.! We both started shouting at once.

Victor told me his story. After I left him in that first camp, when I was taken back to Moscow for interrogation, Victor had found out that he would be sent off to hard labor. Then he heard of an ingenious technique for faking silicosis.

In his sack of personal belongings in the storeroom Victor had a small silver ring. Following instructions he had heard about, he filed a small quantity of silver dust from the ring and mixed it with tobacco into a number of cigarettes. He smoked the cigarettes, inhaling as deeply as he could. The theory was that a microscopic film of silver dust would build up in the lungs in a way that would show a strong shadow in an X ray without seriously impairing the lungs. Victor smoked the cigarettes, wondering all the time whether he was committing suicide. Then he went to the hospital, coughing in the way he had seen silicosis victims cough, and demanded an X ray. Sure enough, there was a terrible shadow on the lungs, and he was disqualified from hard labor. He was sent to Spassk, the camp for incurables. Then the government granted amnesty to all incurables, and Victor was freed. These invalids were all expected to die soon and were not given travel rights, so they all stayed on in Dzhezkazgan, and Victor applied for an engineering job at Zheldor Poselok. They took him on in the planning and design office. Victor was sure he could get me assigned to it. He had a lot of friends among the engineers, who worked closely with the camp administration on the labor assignments.

Victor was as good as his word, and within a few days he had me moved into the office with him as a blueprint planner, which was pure *tufta* and meant nothing at all.

In camp it was a confused period. A number of amnesties were granted. I think the first one was freedom for children under the age of fourteen. There were only about six in the whole area and their going did not change things for the rest of us, except to cheer us up somewhat, because it was a sign of change. Similarly, all prisoners with sentences of five years were released and pardoned. That accounted for maybe three men out of three thousand.

The gates between the KTR and the adjoining camp were opened, and the inmates were free to move between the camps and visit each other until lights-out. It was rumored that reliable prisoners were to be given passes to come and go between camp and their work assignment, without having to march in convoy. Soon a list was posted of those prisoners who would be issued passes, and every day we saw a few new smiles on the faces of those men who had this experience of imitation freedom.

The numbers were finally taken away. I came out one morning to find hundreds of prisoners yelling and laughing and ripping the linen patches off their sleeves and caps and trouser legs. The air was filled with a snowstorm of number patches. For all the prisoners of Dzhezkazgan the numbers were the prime symbol of our slavery, of our demotion from human being to object. Their disappearance was like the beginning of a fresh new day.

There were new rumors of labor camp mutinies, and the guards and administration became noticeably more friendly, in a sickening way, every day.

A "culture brigade" was formed to give camp entertainments. I signed up as a musician. The brigade practiced in the mess hall.

One of the acts was an acrobat named Grigori Levko. I showed off one night and walked the length of the mess hall and back on my hands. He suggested that we do a partner act, and began to train me to do a number of routines with him. There was a fine, trained Ukrainian baritone, and an accordionist and a mandolin player, and we rehearsed an orchestral number together.

After several weeks of practice we staged our first concert on a Sunday afternoon. It was probably pretty ragged stuff, but we thought we were just fine, and so did the starved audience. The applause was deafening.

Then a movie projector was brought in and Saturday night, once a month, we had a movie. They were terrible propaganda movies about heroic tractor drivers, but we loved them. Two brothers named Boyko, who were professional electronics technicians, were put in charge of the projector and its sound system, and they requisitioned tubes and other parts and began to build radios. Soon the Boyko brothers had built some excellent radios, which they tied into a sound system with a loudspeaker in each barracks, so that the whole camp could have music.

One day in the early spring of 1954 I stopped to read the news on the bulletin board at the administration office. Suddenly my name hit me in the eye from the middle of a long list. I looked at the top of the list. It said, "Prisoners Eligible for Passes: Apply at Administration Office."

I ran to the office, certain that I would be told it was a mistake. It was no mistake. I was expected to go out of camp with the culture brigade to perform for other camps, so a pass had been issued that would allow me to move about without convoy. This might have seemed an invitation to escape, but of course there was still no way to cross the desert without dying of exposure, and the issuing of these passes had generated very few escape attempts.

I HEARD that there were plans for the construction of a new village, and the *parasha*, the prison telegraph, said that there would be jobs for technical specialists like electricians and bricklayers. If you were lucky enough to get such a job, you would have a permanent pass and would live at the project virtually as a free man. I went to the *naryadchik* and put my name down for the project. He told me it was called Nikolsky Project, and gave me a form on which to register my specialties. I put down arc welder, of course, and then plumber, although I had never touched a pipe.

The culture brigade was still touring the camps, and we were busy practicing and increasing our repertoire two nights a week, when we got the news that we were to be combined with a similar brigade from a women's camp in the Dzhezkazgan area, and that in fact two women performers would work with us at the next rehearsal. This was tremendously exciting.

When the night arrived, we found that both the women were singers. One was a radio operator from Minsk named Zoya Tumilovich. The other girl was an Armenian named Nadya, and I never got to know her very well, because something snapped when I met Zoya, and all those years of repression and deprivation threw up an enormous, irresistible need to be close to this woman. I just had to hold her hand when I could, flirt with her, look in her eyes.

The guards were very easygoing, and by the second or third rehearsal Zoya and I were exchanging very frank gazes and sneaking touches. It was immensely arousing but frustrating, because there was no conceivable way of being alone together.

The first mixed concert was held in our own mess hall. I really do not remember much about it, except that Zoya sang beautifully and that I was swept by desire for her. We still had no way of finding privacy, but I felt sure a way would come. Zoya told me that there would be another concert the following week at a different camp, and we would see each other again soon.

The next morning I was ordered to go to see the *naryadchik*. When I went to the administration office, he said, "You signed up for a plumber, didn't you?"

I looked blank. I'd forgotten about that.

"Nikolsky Project," he said. "Here's your pass. Here's your work assignment. Meet the convoy at the gates with your things at two o'clock. There's four hundred going from this camp, so try to get there early."

It was the strangest sensation. I was to be almost free! I would live in an area I had never seen before and once again have to tackle work I had absolutely no knowledge of. Suddenly I felt terribly excited. I was sad to be losing Zoya and sorry there was no way to communicate with her, but that was a feeling that got lost somewhere in a jumble of vibrant new hopes for the future.

CHAPTER EIGHT

WE WERE led through the gates in the wall to trucks which were waiting outside. There was a mood of elation in the group of four hundred who were going to Nikolsky.

Weeks before, a plumber named Margolinshch had told me about the proposed new project. Now he was sitting right here in the truck with me. I moved over beside Margolinshch and told him I was counting on him to show me something about his trade.

"Don't worry about a thing," he said cheerfully. "I'll show you everything I know. And if they give us any choice of partners, we'll just say we've always worked together." Margolinshch was a skinny, good-humored guy.

In about half an hour we arrived at the town of Nikolsky. It was a jumble of half-constructed buildings. We passed a sewage or water trench and suddenly cheers went up from hundreds of workers digging it with shovels and pickaxes. All of them were women! Soon we realized that most of the workers already on the project were women. A terrific buzz began to run through the truck. We stopped outside a high barbed-wire fence with four watchtowers. Inside the fence was a grouping of several two-story apartment buildings. That, we learned, was the women's enclosure. To our surprise we were sent across the road to a group of similar buildings that had no enclosure at all.

In the morning we were given our assignments. Two plumbers were to install cold-water plumbing for one building in seven days. There were eight apartments in each two-story building. It meant nothing to me, but Margolinshch was shocked. "How they expect us to do such a thing?" he wanted to know in a thick Latvian accent.

But there was clearly no time to sit around and grouse. We had to get our norm fulfilled or work some smart *tufta*, and so we got to work, bending pipes on a crude hand-operated pipe bender, hacksawing off the proper lengths, and threading them.

At the end of the first day we had scarcely started on one apartment and we were totally worn out. We got up at the first light on our own. We were convinced that the only way to hold on to these "free" jobs was to meet our norms or come pretty close. At breakfast Margolinshch drank so much tea that by the time we left for work he was quite high and terribly cheerful.

"Wait till you're catching on to it! We never make eight apartments in one week, but we come close."

When at the end of the first week we had completed only two apartments out of the eight, I suggested to Margolinshch that we measure up five buildings, cut all the pieces and mark them, and then do all the assembly at once. I was sure we could increase our output considerably that way. Margolinshch simply poured himself another cup of tea and said, "Let's go then."

We never came close to doing a full building in one week, but we pulled well ahead of our first week's miserable twenty-five percent of the norm. We were so tired that our original excitement over the presence of women virtually evaporated, although I often thought of Zoya.

Gradually we arrived, Margolinshch and I, at an understanding that we could work only so much. We knew we were doing better than the other teams, because of our system, and we began to take life a little bit easier.

When Margolinshch and I began to install our preshaped plumbing units, we ran into an electrical crew at the second building. I was fascinated to see one woman, whose figure was lithe and graceful, wield the wire and the cutters with immense speed and deftness. There was a wisp of pale blond hair hanging out of her cap. She stopped for a moment and took off her electrician's glove to wipe the sweat from her forehead. She must have sensed me watching from behind, because she turned around for a brief moment, and in that moment I saw a wonderful face: cool, aloof, frankly appraising, with eyes that were dark blue—almost black.

I was hooked. I had to get to know this woman. I found out that she was a Latvian named Gertrude. Half the men in camp were in love with her, without having spoken to her. She had the reputation of being cold as ice.

I purposely extended my work in her building. I found ways to pass near her, or to install pipe where she was wiring, but I never spoke with her. One day, while I was standing on a box trying to attach a connector above my head, a wrench slipped out of my hand. I was standing on one foot, holding the pipe, and Gertrude dropped her work and ran to hand me my wrench. I thanked her in a matter-of-fact way, and went on with my work.

At the lunch break we sat on the floor together and ate our bread silently. Suddenly she said in a clear, soft voice, "Where are you from?"

I told her I was an American from New York City. She looked wistful. She said she had always dreamed of living in a country where you could determine your own future. We immediately fell into a political discussion. Gertrude was passionate about leaving the Soviet Union. Her parents had been arrested for being dissenters, and Gertrude, who was only fourteen at the time, had routinely been arrested with them. She was only eighteen now.

"I am very cynical about people," she said. "Many men have tried to make friends with me and I have trusted them until I found out all they wanted was to sleep with me. I know everyone says I am very cold; well, it's true. I have been hurt a great deal in my life and I am going to be very careful from now on."

And yet, as the time went by, when I did not seek her out as a lunch companion, she sought me out. We began to talk, in an oblique way, about a future in which we were both out of the Soviet Union. There were just the faintest shades of suggestion from both of us that this might be a future we could make together. But it was perfectly clear that our relationship in camp was to be one of the spirit only. I was falling in love without reservation, and yet I had to be reserved. It was an exquisite dilemma.

For a day or two I was distracted by another fortunate turn of events. When I got back to my room one night, Lavrenov was waiting for me. "How is it going?" he asked.

"Pretty well, Citizen Chief. How about you?"

"Well, we have some problems. There are so many little accidents and infections here at Nikolsky that we are using up too much transport to bring those people over to the hospital. The women's camp at Kingir has sent a physician over to handle the women's enclosure. Now I want to assign you to look after the men. Will you do it?"

Would I! It meant less fatigue, more interesting work, much more freedom to move around. Besides, I had come to love medicine and, frankly, to enjoy my role as the doctor. I got busy right away setting up and stocking a clinic in the apartment block.

Gertrude and I began to talk more and more about finding a way to be together "after." I had endless fantasies about bringing her to America, about seeing the Great Lakes with her, and Niagara Falls, and of course exploring the streets of New York City. In none of this fantasy was there any sex. Gertrude to me had a purity of person that somehow stood outside of sex. We talked with growing intensity every time we met. She became animated and warm with me, but we never so much as held hands.

IN THE clinic I relied heavily upon the therapeutic value of injections. But syringes were in short supply, and one day I decided to go to the town of Dzhezkazgan and see if I could buy some at the pharmacy there. I found out that an ambulance would be making the round trip that day, and I asked for a ride into town. The driver dropped me off in the marketplace and we agreed to meet there again that night at five o'clock.

I spotted the drugstore across the square and headed for it. It was late morning. Just as I came up to the drugstore, I met two men I knew: Felix Zaporozhets and George Zhorin. They hailed me very warmly. They were serving in Dzhezkazgan as free workers. "Hi, Doc. Where are you going?"

I said, "The pharmacy. I've got to buy some syringes."

"Ah, syringes, let's go get a drink and celebrate."

I felt a warning inside me, but I said, "Sure. Let's go."

Zhorin led the way to a Georgian *mors* vendor, and my friends seemed to be his favorites from the way he welcomed them. *Mors* is sweetened fruit juice. The Georgian poured glasses of it and then said, "Now, brothers, I also have some very fine *cha-cha*." *Cha-cha* is Georgian moonshine. We all said yes to *cha-cha*. The Georgian ducked under the counter and came up with a bottle of milky-yellow stuff. He poured a big slug into each glass. It tasted awful.

We had some more, and by and by Zhorin asked the Georgian to give us a couple of bottles we could take with us. We went to George Zhorin's apartment and got happily, stupendously drunk.

I suddenly remembered five o'clock. The boys helped me find my way to the marketplace. I was quite cockeyed and fell down in the street in front of the ambulance. Fortunately it had good brakes. I pulled myself up and said to the driver, "Going back?"

He had a funny expression on his face, but he said, "Hop in."

After about forty minutes we stopped, and the driver called, "Destination. Everybody out."

I practically rolled out the back door and then I heard the ambulance drive off. I was on a paved road. I could not remember any paved roads in Nikolsky, only dust. I wandered around for some time and I finally found out I was in Kingir. Dzhezkazgan was twenty-seven kilometers away, and Nikolsky somewhere in between.

It was getting dark. At nine there would be a roll call. I would be counted missing and that would be the end of my pass.

A convoy of trucks came along. Dazzling headlights. A truck stopped. A voice said, "Hop in."

I hopped in.

Then a look at the man. I suddenly felt quite sober. He was an MVD colonel.

That was the end of my pass, and I never went back to Nikolsky again.

The worst part was not seeing Gertrude. Back at camp I wrote to her every chance I got. I sent off the letters with truck drivers, and she wrote back: sad letters about how long it seemed before she would ever see freedom, and how committed she was to finding a way to leave the country. Occasionally there would be oblique references to a future in which I appeared.

They put me to work running a five-speed lathe, making machine parts. It was not bad except that once again I had to march in a forced convoy, with guards and dogs.

In the fall of 1954 there were many indications of change. A wage system had been introduced, and if you saved carefully, a couple of rubles a month, you could treat yourself to some candy or cigarettes or toothpaste and other small but, to us, rare luxuries. Prisoners were paying attention to dress. Men cut wedges out of the bottoms of their trouser legs and inserted gussets, and so, fifteen years before it was a big thing in America, we were cheering ourselves up in Dzhezkazgan with flared pants.

After a while Lavrenov asked for me back in the hospital, and I went back to my old job as a feldsher. It was pleasant in the hospital. The incidence of severe infections and other illnesses related to extreme fatigue and malnutrition was way down, and so was the mortality rate.

It was rumored that a commission would come from Moscow to review our cases, and that perhaps many of us would be released. Then another amnesty was announced. The thousands and thousands of prisoners of war, Russians who had been captured by the Germans and then imprisoned for treason when they returned home, were released and forgiven. The camps began to look distinctly underpopulated. I thought that Gertrude had somehow been let out with this group, because her letters suddenly stopped coming. But friends reported that she had gone into a depression and was speaking to nobody.

Soon we heard that the long-awaited commission from Moscow had begun its work, and that thousands of prisoners were being released every day. Since there were about seventeen million political prisoners in the Soviet Union in the early 1950s, it would take some time before the wave of releases would get to us, we assumed, but that was not the bad part. The bad part was that those who had been sentenced by committee or special procedure would not be released. Gertrude had been sentenced by committee. Now, friends reported, she assumed she was going to be in camp for the rest of her twenty-five-year sentence. That was why she was so depressed. I tried writing to cheer her up. But I had a hard time knowing what to say. I had been sentenced by special procedure myself.

From the beginning I had been forbidden to send or receive mail. Suddenly, on August 20, 1955, I got another letter from my mother. Her handwriting was weak and irregular, which made me think she must be sick. But she said that she was all right, that the MVD had given her my address, and that she wanted news of my state of health. I quickly got a copy of my pass photograph and sent it off to Mother with a short note saying that my health was good, that I was thrilled to hear from her, and that if there was any chance of a food parcel, I would enjoy a few treats.

Before long a parcel came. Obviously my sister, Stella, must have sent it from America, and my mother forwarded it to me. It contained Maxwell House coffee! In a vacuum-packed tin. There were canned butter and canned bacon, and a whole carton of Chesterfield cigarettes. I lost most of those to the guard who inspected the parcel for contraband. He let me keep two packs out of the ten.

I shared the cigarettes with Pavel Voronkin, an artist acquaintance from camp, who was becoming a very close friend. At one of the culture brigade concerts I had met Yulya, an attractive young woman from Harbin, where Pavel had lived as a child. She and Pavel started to correspond and without ever setting eyes on each other fell in love. Then, after a few months, they managed to meet and found that a real and tangible affection had grown. They agreed to marry if they ever got out alive. Yulya was released in an early amnesty, but she stayed in the area and vowed to wait for him. Her letters really kept Pavel alive at this period, because he had begun to feel, like my beloved Gertrude, that he might never be released. Pavel too had been sentenced by committee.

I had convinced myself that the refusal to release those sentenced by committee made no sense at all and would soon be corrected. Although of course there was a deep fear, which I suppressed as well as I could, that I might be wrong.

In January of 1956 we heard that the commission—*the* commission—had arrived in Kingir.

Every day the news came that hundreds of prisoners had been released. The excitement in our camp was almost unbearable. Discipline became very lax. Even the dumbest, coarsest guards started trying to behave like human beings. By late February the air was electric. First one camp and then another in Kingir had been closed. Then the really dramatic news was released: the commission would arrive in Dzhezkazgan on March 1.

On the first day the stories came back as the first free men returned to camp. A man would go up the steps of the administration building to the room where the commission met. The door would close. In minutes he would be back out, stumbling like a drunk, grinning, maybe jumping up and down, maybe just stunned.

Some lay on their bunks. Some sat in a trance. A few packed up their stuff, shook hands with their friends, and then marched to the gates and were free, just like that. The first groups of free men had to wait several days before their passports, train tickets, and release certificates were arranged.

By the third day it was clear that many of them had no sense at all of how to manage on the outside. There were many deaths from drunkenness, or because people just stepped in front of trucks without seeming to see them, when they had not been drinking at all. Careful warnings were made to all the men walking out free.

Pavel Voronkin's name came up very early. He came out looking shattered, and he wept openly and told us that, because he had been sentenced by special committee, he was to have his case reviewed again at some unstated future date. My stomach knotted at the news. I was almost sure I was in for the same thing.

I went to the administration building. I stood in front of the commission with my heart beating so loud it would break windows. The four men looked very tired. One of them, a General Todorov, said, "We can't review your case, Doldzhin. We have nothing but a slip of paper with your charges. We have to send to Moscow for your full file from the KGB. It will take between one and two months, and we will call you back. That's all."

That was it.

As the weeks went by, Pavel began to believe that the commission had been lying to him when they told him his case would be reviewed again. He lost his appetite and got very thin and weak.

One day I came back from work and found him looking very

strange. He was shaking his head and waving at me and opening and closing his mouth, but no words would come out.

Finally I detected the word "cable" forming dryly in his mouth. I said, "What cable?"

He managed to croak an answer. "Cable from Moscow." He looked quite disoriented. He shook his head in amazement and fell against me and embraced me so violently I could hardly breathe. Then he said, "Alex, I'm a free man. A *free man!* The decision was made even before the commission came here. I've been free for three months only nobody remembered to tell *me!*" We stared at each other. Suddenly we began to laugh, and Pavel skipped about like a child. He said, "I'll be with Yulya tonight, Alex! Do you know what that means?"

I nodded. I was trying not to show what it meant to me that my last friend in camp was going. But Pavel saw my thoughts. "You'll be next, and then we'll all be free."

Pavel Voronkin skipped out the gates of Dzhezkazgan, and I went slowly back to a dwindling barracks that now contained not one human being that I knew well or really cared about.

Soon the sixty or seventy of us left in the old camp were loaded into trucks and taken across the hill to another camp.

When I climbed down off the back of the truck, Lavrenov was waiting for me. He told me he was working in another camp near Dzhezkazgan. He wanted me to accept the assignment as chief of the hospital. I was too gloomy to be delighted with the assignment. But I knew that it was just what I needed to help me survive however much longer it was going to be in this lonely existence.

One day a man from Nikolsky came into the hospital to see me. The camp had shrunk again, to a few hundred. I was just sitting in the practically empty hospital looking disgustedly over the littered yard. The man seemed embarrassed. He looked at the ground.

Finally he said, "They asked me to come and see you."

I said, "Who asked?"

"At the women's enclosure. Nikolsky. They said you're a close friend of Gertrude's, maybe her only close friend."

I felt an instantaneous cold panic.

He licked his lips before going on. He said finally, "She was very depressed, you know."

I think I pleaded with my eyes to have it finished.

He said, "Well, yesterday she was up on the high-tension line, connecting the main service. She just took off her gloves. They saw her—she very calmly and deliberately reached inside the box and took hold of the two terminals."

I just stared. My eyes were dry.

He said, "It was six thousand volts, you know. It was over right away. She wouldn't have felt anything."

He waited for a while. I think he must have been a very decent man. When he saw I could not possibly speak, he got up quietly and went to the door. He said, "I'm sorry, Doctor."

And when he was gone, I sat and stared at the empty copper sky. It got darker and I still stared. There was no one in the room, no one in the camp, no one outside the camp, no one in the Soviet Union, no one in the whole world. I knew the feeling of being utterly, totally alone. And in the morning I saw the dawn come up and I knew that nothing had grown or been born in that night.

CHAPTER NINE

It was July, but I was scarcely aware of the heat. I have little recollection of the days as days; they were empty and forgettable. I knew now I would never be released. I knew that somehow I would work out a way of living through my remaining years in camp, but for now I was wallowing in disgust and self-pity.

I slept most of my free time. I heard that the commission was back again. Every day there were fewer and fewer prisoners around. One morning I was roughly shaken awake by a guard. He said angrily, "Are you Doldzhin?"

"Yeah," I said, "I'm Dole-gin. What do you want?"

"We've been trying to find you for three days. Don't you ever look at the bulletin board? They've been calling for you at the commission. Get dressed and get over there on the double!"

I did not rush. I washed and had some breakfast and went out to see for sure that my name was on the board. It was. I heard a voice call out, "Say, Doc!" It was feldsher Vasya Kargin. He had a special committee sentence like me.

I asked him where he was living.

"Right here, Doc. How about you?"

I had been moping so much, I had not even known there was one of the old gang around I could have spent some time with.

There were about a hundred men waiting outside the administration building. When I finally stood before the commission I scarcely looked up.

The chairman said, "Tell me, where would you like to go?"

"What do you mean, where would I like to go?"

He said easily, "I mean where would you like to live? Do you have any relatives?"

I said, still not allowing myself to believe what was happening, "Well, my mother lives in Moscow."

"Would you like to go to Moscow?"

I just looked at them for a long time. Then I said in a choked way, "Would you let me go to Moscow?"

The chairman said, "Yes, we will release you to Moscow, but it is a conditional release. You must sign this document."

The statement declared that during my years in camp I had been naturalized (without having been consulted, let it be clear!) as a Soviet citizen. That if I went to Moscow, I must never try to contact the American embassy. That if I did try to make that contact or tried in any way to leave the Soviet Union, I would immediately be put in a closed prison, not a camp, for life. That I would be under constant surveillance by the KGB.

Was that fully understood?

I said yes, it was fully understood. I signed.

The chairman said, "Yes—well, you can go now."

It was July 13, 1956. I had been kidnapped December 13, 1948.

I was in shock. I stepped to the side of the building and sat down on the hot earth. No one paid any attention. They were used to it by now. My mind was racing crazily.

A voice brought me back. Vasya Kargin.

"Say, Doc! I'm free! You, too?"

I nodded at him dumbly.

"Well, what the hell!" he said. "Let's . . . let's just *go* then!"

We went off arm in arm. By and by we began to giggle. We headed toward Dzhezkazgan, toward the town. We began to sing different songs. I don't know what Vasya sang. I bellowed out,

"Oh, give me land, lots of land, under starry skies above,
Don't fence me in."

EDITORS' EPILOGUE

Upon his release Alexander Dolgun was sent to Moscow by train. His mother met him at the station, and he was shocked by her aged appearance, although she was only fifty-seven years old. She seemed nervous and forgetful, and Dolgun soon learned that she had been arrested by the KGB in 1950, after she had received his message from Kuibyshev. She had been tortured in efforts to extract evidence that would incriminate her son. This treatment had resulted in a mental collapse, and she had spent three years in a prison insane asylum. When she was released in 1954, she found that the KGB had confiscated all of the family's belongings except the kitchen table.

Two days after Alex's mother had been picked up his father had been arrested and sent to a slave labor camp for remarking that Soviet cars were inferior to American cars. When he returned home in 1955, his wife raged at him for subjecting his family to the horrors of Russia, and they became totally alienated. He now lived in the town of Istra, about fifty-five kilometers from Moscow, and worked as an auto mechanic. His son began to visit him often and they were on the best of terms.

Back in Moscow, Alex found a job as a typist in the Ministry of Health publishing house. Eventually he became an editor in charge of English-language editions of Russian medical publications.

The housing situation was very tight, so Alex and his mother shared a small room. Shortly after his return his mother attacked him with a hammer, convinced that he was a KGB agent under orders to kill her. Eventually she became unmanageable and was hospitalized until her death in 1967.

Soon after his release Dolgun received permission to contact the American embassy in order to collect his belongings and money owed to him. He was given what struck him as a very cool reception and the sum of one thousand dollars—his accumulated retirement benefits. His sister, Stella, had authorized the embassy to give his personal property to the Red Cross.

Former political prisoners called themselves the Trade Union, and at one of their parties Alex met George Tenno. Tenno was notorious for having tried two spectacular escapes from the camps. In prison he and Alex had been repeatedly and painfully questioned about each other. Although they had never met, the KGB had been convinced that they were co-conspirators. Now they became close friends. They spent a lot of time planning their escape from the Soviet Union. However, the terms of their release forbade any attempt to leave the country, and they were under KGB surveillance.

Tenno introduced Dolgun to the writer Alexander Solzhenitsyn, who was working on his monumental book, *The Gulag Archipelago*. Solzhenitsyn was most interested in interviewing Dolgun, as he had never before met a sane survivor of Sukhanovka Prison. George Tenno's history was used as a base for one of the characters in Solzhenitsyn's novel, *One Day in the Life of Ivan Denisovich*.

With money saved from his salary and earned by free-lance translating jobs, Alexander Dolgun was able to buy a used car. He often drove to Istra, where his father helped keep the car in shape. His father died early in 1968.

Over the years Dolgun managed to integrate himself, on the surface, into the daily life of a Moscow bureaucrat. He points out that in Russia many people lead a sort of double life in order to cope with the extremely restricted and regulated way of life imposed by the government. However, he discovered that the prison camp technique of *tufta* served him well in civilian life, and enabled him to avoid political or military service. (It will be recalled that while in prison he had, involuntarily, been given Soviet citizenship.)

In 1964 Alexander Dolgun met a gray-eyed Russian girl named Irene. They were married in 1965 and a son, Andrew, was born within the year.

Stella Dolgun, Alexander's sister, had left Russia in 1946, and gone to New York, where she worked for the United Nations. In 1948 she heard of Alexander's disappearance from his former fiancée, Mary Catto. Stella contacted the State Department, but was told that relations between the United States and Russia were so touchy that if any approach were made on Alexander's behalf, he might be shot.

Stella had very little more news of her family until 1955. In that year she received a letter from her mother, and sent the food parcel off to Alexander. In 1956 she heard of Alexander's release. They began to correspond, but it was impossibly dangerous for him to hint to her that he would like to leave Russia.

In 1966 Dolgun sent word to Stella, through a friend, that he was counting on her to get him and his wife and son out of the Soviet Union. With this her efforts began in earnest, and after contacting many top U.S. officials, she enlisted the help of John P. Humes, then ambassador to Austria. Humes brought the case to the attention of Secretary of State William P. Rogers. Finally, on December 21, 1971—after many maddening delays and bureaucratic complications—the Dolguns were allowed to leave Russia and fly to Vienna. In January they boarded a plane for New York. Painted on the nose of the airplane was its name: *Great Hopes.*

A Talk With Alexander Dolgun

An infectious smile lit up his face as Alexander Dolgun leaned forward, savoring the memory of that day in January, 1972, which marked the realization of his own American dream. "Coming home," he said emphatically, "was the happiest event of my life."

The vivid blue eyes turned sober as he began to discuss his book. "I am

Alexander Dolgun

not a political man, and my book is not a political book. It is a pledge. It *had* to be written. But in a way it was one of my most difficult ordeals.

"About a year after I was released from prison I began to put my experiences on tape. It took me two years. Then my friend George Tenno was arrested on what turned out to be a false charge, and the MVD called me in, too. At the end of two days they let me go, but I was apprehensive they would come to search my room. I spent that night shredding the tapes with scissors and then, not trusting the garbage system, I drove into the country and threw the pieces onto the country roads.

"When I got back to the States, I started the book again, but it was too much to try to relive alone. I needed a compassionate listener. My publisher suggested Patrick Watson."

Compiling the book took a year and made heavy demands on both men. Each weekend Watson, a leading journalist and licensed pilot, commuted from his native Canada to Washington for two days of grueling twelve-hour sessions with Dolgun. For Alex, reliving his experiences was an emotional agony. "Everything came back so vividly that at times I would start shaking and couldn't go on." He still hasn't read the finished book.

He talked about his life today. Home is in a quiet suburb near Washington, D.C., where he works as a program analyst for the Department of Health, Education and Welfare. His wife, Irene, a tiny, vivacious brunette, is busy becoming an American, and their son, Andrew, is immersed in the day-to-day doings of any ten-year-old boy.

Alexander Dolgun sat back, a satisfied grin on his face. Life as an ordinary citizen clearly agrees with him.

MINNIE SANTANGELO'S MORTAL SIN

A CONDENSATION OF THE NOVEL BY
ANTHONY MANCINI

ILLUSTRATED BY ALEX TSAO

For Minnie Santangelo, widowed Italian mamma living in New York's Little Italy, times of hardship have never smothered a buoyant good humor and natural conviviality. Now, as the neighborhood prepares for the annual Feast of Saint Anthony, Minnie looks forward to celebrating her favorite festival with joy made even more special by the home-coming of her son, Remo. Her excite-ment, however, takes a sinister turn when a local murder portends danger for the Santangelos.

Thus begins an adventure casting peaceable, pious Minnie in the un-likely role of sleuth, matching wits with mafiosi, suspecting her own friends and neighbors as she tracks a crafty killer. Sustained by her faith, .guided by plucky determination, her talent for detection surprises even Minnie herself.

Suspenseful from beginning to end, Minnie's story is also rich in warmth and humor, blending a delightful assortment of characters in a setting as charming as it is unique.

Chapter 1

JERRY Tedesco's head had been bashed in with a statue of the Virgin Mary.

Down at Curcio's pork store the women shopping for chains of aromatic sausages squawked like parrots over the event. They seemed more dismayed over the sacrilegious than the homicidal significance of the news. Men gathered at the Sons of Sicily Social Club and traded knowing looks. Old men in the boccie court on Mott Street bit on their *toscani* cigars and grunted with disapproval. The kids who hung out in front of Nunzio's candy store wisecracked about it. And in St. Theresa's, by the flickering candles, old women in black mumbled prayers for his soul. Little Italy was clucking its tongue over the murder of one of its own.

Not that they were surprised. Everybody knew that Tedesco was connected to—call it the "honorary society." So the community gave a collective shrug.

They had a theory down at the precinct: Tedesco had a reputation as a maverick in the organization. Informants said that he disobeyed the local prohibition against dealing in drugs and that he failed to pay his "taxes." But the cork had them baffled.

They found Jerry Tedesco on the linoleum floor of his religious-articles store. His curly gray hair was matted with dried blood and his right shoulder was broken. The weapon, wearing a carved smile, lay beside the body. It was not one of the fragile plaster statues that lined the shelves, but an ebony Virgin whittled by mission craftsmen in Cameroon. There was a cork in the dead man's mouth.

A cork—probably from a wine bottle. The detectives wondered what it meant. Was it just to confuse them or was it a real clue? They knew the answers would be hard to get. The neighborhood was made up mostly of Sicilians, Neapolitans, and other southern Italians—people with many talents. There were those talented at cutting a fine suit, fashioning beautiful mosaics, cooking a tasty *zuppa di pesce*. But the people had very little talent for talking to the police.

MINERVA Santangelo had been hitting the Marsala bottle. With an apologetic glance at the statue of Saint Anthony on the sideboard, she took another swig. Then she poured the rest into the skillet, making the beef slices bubble up. Glowing with wine and anticipation, she jostled the meat with a fork and hummed a song.

The kitchen was the soul of Minnie's four-room apartment on Hester Street. It was a cheerful place, though in need of paint. The walls were gleaming with copper pans, festooned with strings of red peppers and hanging garlic. The blue linoleum floor was waxed glossy. The old refrigerator and stove were covered with decals of Walt Disney animals. Thumbtacked over the refrigerator was a calendar showing a movie star Jesus pointing to his exposed Sacred Heart, circled by a crown of thorns.

City noises rose from the street below, where fruit and vegetable sellers were dismantling their stands for the night. The men, tanned and muscular, carried crates of tomatoes, fennel, spinach, and grapes into their stores. They swapped jokes and friendly insults, eyeing the girls who sauntered past. One man wiped his brow and bellowed up at Mrs. Santangelo's window, "Eh, Minootch."

Grimacing, she shook off the effects of the Marsala, pulled herself up to her full five feet one inch, and looked out. "My father named me Minerva," she scolded her neighbor. "You have no right to change it after fifty-four years."

Arturo Longo bowed with exaggerated gallantry. "Forgive me. I only want to find out if Remo is home yet."

"No," she said, mollified. "Not yet." Minnie wiped her chubby hands on her apron and looked nervously at the wall clock. She was famous for her pasta and her piety but not for her patience. "He should have been here by now." She smiled at Arturo. "Come up a little later. For coffee."

His gold tooth glittered through his grin. "Okay. But I was going to ask him down to the club for espresso and *sambuca*. Some of the boys wanna welcome him back too."

"Never mind the club."

He shrugged. "It ain't such a bad place, you know."

"It's no Sunday school," she answered firmly.

He laughed and drifted back into the store. Minnie liked Arturo. But she disapproved of most of the men who hung out at the Sons of Sicily. They used the place to get away from their wives, and the younger men imitated gangsters. Remo wasn't their type. Minnie had raised her son not to have any romantic notions about mafiosi. Her attitude had been forged in experience. But she refused to think about Sicily today or about what had happened in Porticello twelve years ago. The pasta would overcook and Remo liked it *al dente*.

Hiccuping, she padded back to the stove as Bruno warbled a greeting from his cage suspended from a curtain rod in the window. *"Finalmente,"* Minnie said, with an affectionate wave of a wooden spoon. "You finished napping." The parakeet continued to chatter while his stout mistress stirred the spaghetti sauce. Minnie had thick dark hair streaked with gray and combed back into a bun. Her figure, never slender, had ripened to full-bodied middle age. But she still had good legs, which she never missed an opportunity to display, and a freshly pretty face. Her hazel eyes did not reveal any particular spark of intelligence; the lines in her olive face did not tell of vast experience. Yet there was something solidly charming about the way she looked.

She wore a touch of pink lipstick as a concession to her son's long-awaited return. She turned off the burners, and as she removed her apron she heard the whistling.

At first she thought it was Bruno, but she knew the bird couldn't whistle "Bandiera Rossa." She whirled around and called, "How many times have I told you not to whistle that revolutionary song in this house? What will the neighbors say?"

"They will say that weirdo Ray Santangelo is home!" said Minnie's son, dropping his bags in the entryway.

Minnie tried to fight back the tears. She lost the battle.

"Ah, come on," he said. "It hasn't been that long." He came into the kitchen and put his arms around her.

She shook her head in mild reproach. "Oh, yes, it has been a long time," she protested, sniffling. "Seven months!" She made it sound like a century.

THEY had *cannoli* for dessert, washed down with espresso and anisette. She looked at him and said, "You didn't eat much."

"Now don't exaggerate," he chided. "I had extra helpings of pasta, meat, salad. I haven't eaten this well in a long time."

"I can see that," she said, frowning. "You lost weight."

"Yeah. Don't I look great?" He broke into a wide, immodest grin, exposing a chipped front tooth that blended well with his irregular good looks: nose broken on the college boxing team, lips finely sculpted, large ears, heart-shaped jaw, gray eyes (legacy of the Norman reign in Sicily), and dark curly hair.

The lopsided grin melted her. She patted his arm and watched him bite into another pastry. It was hard to believe that he was twenty-six years old. To her he was a mixture of boy and man. A lawyer who wore crew-neck sweaters and studded jeans. An amateur but proficient scholar of Italian history who spent hours in a playground with a basketball. A self-taught gourmet cook who ate peanut-butter sandwiches. A man-boy who liked milk shakes and, on occasion, downed bourbon boilermakers.

He grabbed another *cannole*. Thin or not, he hadn't lost his Sicilian laborer's appetite, inherited from his father. But one side of him baffled her: he had spent seven months teaching school to Apache Indians in New Mexico as a VISTA volunteer. Working to help total strangers was something Minnie didn't understand. Apaches were not even Italian, much less Sicilian or relatives.

Ray ("Remo") Santangelo had an ambivalent standing in the neighborhood. People liked his friendly manner, but they also mistrusted him. After all, why didn't he set up a law practice, make a lot of money, and allow others to defer to him? Even as a youngster he had been different: he studied hard in high school and didn't hang out on the corner much, went to City College when it was attended mostly by Jewish boys, and then to N.Y.U. Law. Maybe he thought he was better than his neighbors?

But these suspicions were offset by his unabashed Italian chauvinism. Ray spoke Italian. He sang Italian songs. Before he left for New Mexico, he had been very visible in the community, eating at local restaurants and attending socials. He had just the right dash of irreverence for authority, yet he had managed to escape the kind of cynicism that could close him off completely from the outside world. He was a funny kid, this Ray Santangelo.

But then he had a funny upbringing. There had always been whispers about the way his father died. And his mother was sort of different too. She had books in the house, never remarried, kept to herself, more or less. No one could fault her friendliness, though. Or her housekeeping, her morality, and piety.

Ray lit a pipe and looked around. "Nothing much has changed," he said. "Gotta get the slumlord to paint this place."

"Don't talk that way," she scolded. "He's your father's cousin."

Ray bit on the pipestem. "A slumlord is a slumlord."

She shrugged. "Now that you're back what are you going to do?"

He ignored the question. "Were Papa and this slumlord friends?"

"You gonna join a law firm? Set up a practice?"

"You never like to talk about him."

"Who?"

"You know who." He sighed. "Are you ever going to tell me what happened to my father in Porticello? I'm a big boy now."

"Please," she said with an imploring look. "What's past is past.

297

Let's talk about you. Tell me what it was like in New Mexico?"

"That's past too." He looked at her, his face wreathed in pipe smoke. "It was something I felt I had to do."

"I was all alone here," she said, with no note of grievance in her voice. It was a simple statement of fact.

"I know. But I'm back." There was a pause. "What do you think about me going into politics?"

"What do you mean? You wanna be mayor?"

He laughed. "I'm only interested in this neighborhood."

She looked concerned. "There's no mayor here."

"I know," he said dryly. "But there's a boss, eh? There's Bert Marrandino."

"Better we mind our own business about that."

He knitted his brow. "It came to me in New Mexico. 'What am I doing here?' I said to myself. 'The people back in my own neighborhood need help too.' I want to run for the City Council. What do you think?"

Before Minnie could answer, the doorbell rang.

AFTER Arturo Longo had gone through the greetings, the backslaps, and the broad hints about Indian women, he sniffed his brandy and said confidentially, "It's not really a surprise."

"What?" asked Minnie.

"About Jerry Tedesco." Arturo figured that they had not heard. This was his way of bringing up the subject.

"Okay," Ray drawled. "What about him?"

"Killed in his store," Arturo said. "Hit over the head with a statue. He must have crossed somebody."

They were silent. Killings in Little Italy, though they didn't happen every day, were not unprecedented.

"God punished him," Minnie finally declared sadly.

"And how does Marrandino fit in?" Ray asked.

Arturo looked nervously out of the corner of his eye. He shrugged without saying anything.

"They won't get anything on him," Ray said, waving his hand in disgust. "Well, Tedesco was no rose, either."

Minnie thought of her late husband. Stefano had been a rose; a rose trampled underfoot.

"There was a very funny thing about this killing," Arturo continued. Minnie and Ray looked up with interest. "Nobody knows what it means, but they found a cork in Tedesco's mouth. You know—a cork from a bottle. Right in his mouth."

Ray looked bewildered. But Minnie crossed herself and kissed the crook of her index finger.

EARLY the next morning Ray went out to stroll the neighborhood and renew acquaintances. Minnie was alone with Bruno, her statue of Saint Anthony, and a growing disquietude. She smoked a cigarette, a secret vice. She didn't inhale and the smoke left her lips haphazardly.

Remo had left whistling "O Glorizia Tu Sei Maledetta," an antiwar song. She chuckled; her father used to sing it years ago in Abruzzi. Ah, how they would have loved each other.

Giorgio Monfalcone, Minnie's father, had been a great bear of a man. Under his thick eyebrows had burned the most piercing eyes in the whole province of L'Aquila. His mustache was no stubby Hitlerian brush as was fashionable those days in Fascist Italy but a proper arabesque, as assertive as his personality and his politics.

He had been a schoolmaster in a village at the foothills of the Gran Sasso. The first few years of Minnie's life there were happy ones, but then her world collapsed. Her father said disparaging things about Mussolini in the classroom. He was drummed out of his job, and Minnie's playmates treated her like a pariah. At first her father was not discouraged. He took a job on a small newspaper and held his head high as he walked through the piazza each morning to take his coffee and *frulatti* in Guglielmo's Bar. Then the newspaper folded. Minnie's mother carped and wailed about their low estate, and soon, instead of coffee and *frulatti*, Giorgio was taking coffee and anisette every morning. And soon he skipped the coffee and switched from anisette to brandy.

In five years he was dead.

Minnie, dull with grief, retreated into her fantasies and her father's books. She dreamed of writing plays or being an actress. In fact, she did play in a school production of *Antigone*.

Minnie's mother remarried. Her new husband, a wealthy farmer, did not think it seemly for a young girl to read books, and had them sold or destroyed. He forced Minnie to leave school and work in the olive groves. In 1939, when she was nineteen, she was sent to the United States to live with her father's sister. There was a mutual feeling of good riddance between Minnie and her mother. They never set eyes on each other again.

Stubbing out her cigarette, Minnie burned the tip of her index finger. She was distracted. The news of the cork . . .

Twelve years ago they had gone to visit Porticello, Sicily, Stefano Santangelo's birthplace. Minnie's husband, fourteen years her senior, had wanted to see the town again before he got too old. They held hands through the citrus groves, drank local wines, made excursions, and basked by the sea under a blood-colored sun.

There hadn't been much time for holidays before. Their life together in New York had been roughly fashioned and, in the beginning, unromantic. Their first son had died of meningitis. When she had fits of crying in the middle of the night, Stefano's strong hands smoothed her hair, massaged her shuddering shoulders, and prepared her cups of mulled wine. This man whom she had not loved in any romantic way, this unlettered carpenter, gradually showed his mettle. Soon Remo was born. Things got better, and by the time they visited Porticello, Minnie was in love with her husband. That is just when he was taken from her.

The cork. She shrugged; it means nothing. She crushed out another cigarette as if to squash out her fears. It didn't work. Jerry Tedesco's death had unlocked the old demons of revenge.

The statue of Saint Anthony seemed to gaze at her reprovingly. Revenge was not the thought of a good Catholic woman. But she was tired of letting life push her around. She bit her lip and crossed herself. "Sant' Antonio, give me strength."

Arturo stuck his head into the foyer. "Anybody home?" He smiled and waved a jug of homemade wine. "Brought something."

With three strides he was in the kitchen, and a wooden chair creaked as he settled in. He unscrewed the bottle top. "Why the long face? Wait'll you taste this." The amber liquid gurgled into a tumbler. He shoved the glass over to her.

She smiled wanly as she sipped the wine.

"Pretty good, eh?" He searched her face for signs of approval. Minnie nodded, feigning enthusiasm. *"Ottimo."* Excellent.

He smiled again, baring beaver teeth and covering small brown eyes with wrinkles of contentment.

Arturo Longo was a chunky man of around sixty who liked brandy, eggplant, and soccer matches. A bachelor, he worked late afternoons and evenings and spent much of his time alone in his two-room rear apartment on Mulberry Street, watching game shows and soap operas on television. He had kidney stones and a touch of psoriasis, and almost always wore a soft cap. He had once worked on a hydroelectric dam project in Mozambique, and took pleasure in recounting his African adventures. He consulted the family-doctor column and the astrology chart in the *Daily News* every day. He was extremely strong and was forever challenging other men to arm-wrestling contests.

Minnie liked Arturo and was touched by him. He too was lonely, and he had been kind to her in the three years since he had moved into the neighborhood. And she was amused to have a suitor.

"It's good for the blood, eh, Minnie?" Arturo said of the wine.

"It tastes very good too." She gulped more and it started going to her head. She hadn't had anything but coffee that morning.

"Wanna come to the Fulton Fish Market tomorrow morning?"

"No thanks, Arturo."

He inspected her closely. "Something wrong?"

"No."

He shrugged. "Police been asking questions about Tedesco. Nobody's saying anything. Nobody knows anything."

The wine and the need to confide in someone had loosened her tongue. She blurted, "I think I know something."

Arturo set down his glass. He wore a skeptical look. "What do you mean?"

"First pour me more wine. Not even my son knows this." The

wine sloshed into the glass. She took a gulp. "You know my husband, Stefano, was killed?"

"I heard. I felt you never wanted to talk about it, Minnie."

"Killed while we were on vacation in the old country. He was walking alone near the house where he was born. Bandits, they said. But he didn't have much money on him." Minnie looked fixedly at Arturo. "He was found with a cork in his mouth."

His eyes widened. "Eh?"

"Just like Tedesco."

"We-e-e-ell," he said after a long pause. "How come nobody knows about this?"

"First the Sicilian police said the cork didn't mean anything. Then they told me not to tell anybody about it, for the good of Sicily. I didn't tell. I only wanted to come home to Remo."

"It must be just a coincidence," Arturo decided.

"Should I tell the police about it?"

He looked startled. "Oh, no. There's probably no connection. The police will just give you trouble. You know how suspicious they are."

"Maybe it could help them find Stefano's killer."

"They won't care what happened in Sicily years ago. They'll say you had something to do with Tedesco's death, that your husband was mixed up with the Mafia. That wouldn't be good for Ray."

"You think so?" She was worried. The scandal might destroy Ray's political career before it got started.

"Sure," Arturo continued, knowing that his argument was sinking in. "And don't forget, if you go to the police, your friends and neighbors will say you are an informer and a traitor. That you go against our ways." He patted her arm. "There must be a good explanation for the cork. Don't get yourself involved in all this. You'll get in trouble with the law and with other people too."

Minnie, though she was not Sicilian, was still a southern Italian and understood what Arturo meant. Yes, she told herself, she was letting her imagination run wild. But the caution rang hollow.

"Take my advice," he said, rising and stretching. "Put it out of your mind and don't worry."

"You're a good friend, Arturo."

"Sure," he said, looking at her with what could be interpreted as longing. "A good friend."

As his footsteps receded on the staircase, she sighed. She decided to take her problem where she took most of her problems.

FLAMES danced in crimson glasses at the foot of the side altar. Minnie dropped a quarter into the slot before picking up a wick and lighting two candles. Some people put their money in after lighting the candles. Others lit more than two. But Minnie observed protocol and didn't try to get a bargain for her money.

She knelt at the altar rail and prayed. She looked up at the statue of Saint Theresa, cradling an armful of marble lilies and smiling. She waited a full five minutes for some signal that her prayer was being heard. Saint Theresa continued to smile.

Minnie's religious faith had survived, either despite or because of her troubled childhood and rebellious spirit. Something in her responded to practices which relied more on symbols than reason. Some call it superstition. Others call it mysticism. Minnie called it nothing. It was her faith.

Saint Theresa was still smiling. Minnie thought, inwardly cringing at the blasphemy, that the saint looked silly. Her favorite was Saint Anthony. She had named her first son after him, and devotion to the monk of Padua kept her from being bitter about his death. Minnie thought she'd try Saint Theresa this time, though, since the church was named after her.

She moved to the opposite side altar. Had the marble smile faded or was it just her imagination? She lit two more candles and thought, with a guilty conscience, how expensive all this was getting. She prayed hard to Saint Anthony. In a little while she felt better.

Minnie rose and walked to the center aisle, genuflecting as she passed the tabernacle. She decided to make the stations of the cross. She liked the sad pageantry of the story. Jesus meeting His Mother on the road to Calvary struck her with particular poignancy right now. She was enjoying a warm glow, thinking about

Simon's offer to help Christ shoulder the cross, when the wail of a baby distracted her. An afternoon baptism.

The mood had been broken. Hurriedly, Minnie finished the stations. In the lulling silence she had begun to forget her troubles. Now they slowly seeped back.

Forehead and forefinger damp with holy water, Minnie emerged into the clear sunlight of Elizabeth Street. She was removing her kerchief when a black biretta bobbed into view.

"Ah, Signora Santangelo," the priest called out. *"Buon giorno."*

"Buon giorno, Don Giacomo," she said with a polite nod. "I would have greeted you first but you were reading your breviary."

He smiled indulgently. "I've been reading this breviary for forty years. I welcome interruptions."

She looked a trifle scandalized.

"Social contacts are good," he went on. "They are oases in the desert of duty. Even Christ in the wilderness had angels come to minister to Him." She blushed at the implied compliment.

Don Giacomo's aristocratic features were those of a prelate, not a padre. Yet he was just a simple priest, without even a parish. In his sixties, he was retired from a ministry in Sicily and living with an older sister in the neighborhood. He was a spare, stooped man whose cassock hung from his scarecrow shoulders like wash on a line. He spoke to Mrs. Santangelo in a flowery, textbook Italian. He may have been low in the Church, but he was high in Minnie's affections.

They started down Elizabeth Street together. He smiled at her shyly, a little conspiratorially. "You haven't been over for a game in a long time."

Flattered to be a partner in his secret passion for card playing, she flashed him a warm smile. "Maybe I'll come Wednesday night," she said, suddenly thinking that it would be a good chance to question his sister on the matter of corks. Concetta DiPalma's memory went back a long way. She was nearing ninety and was revered in the neighborhood as something of a folk historian.

"Meraviglioso," he cried. Marvelous. He whispered from the corner of his mouth, "There's nothing wrong with a little fun now

and then. And even Saint Paul, that old puritan, said, 'Never censure an old man.' "

Laughing, the old priest shambled along with Mrs. Santangelo. From the back they resembled a crow and a partridge with their heads together. Don Giacomo, his talent for small talk as prodigious as his taste for sweet liqueurs, jabbered on. "I hear that the prodigal son is back."

Minnie cast him a disapproving glance. "You make it sound like he did something wrong to go help the Indians."

"Don't worry, signora," he said, chuckling at his own sense of irony. "God loves repentant saints."

Minnie's sense of competition was awakened by the man's wit. "What do you know of saints, Don Giacomo? Priests are experts on sinners."

He chuckled again. "Quite right. People think we deal in goodness, but human failure is our stock-in-trade."

"In any case, you deal with human beings and that is a good thing."

"Yes." He looked at her. "You are a perceptive woman."

Minnie had an idea. "You are sort of psychologists. And psychologists are useful on a politician's staff."

"Experts in human relations. Every politician could use them. What are you driving at?"

"Remo is going into politics."

"I see. Wants to save the world."

She smiled wearily. "Not anymore. Just this neighborhood."

"I see." He pondered as they turned a corner. "That could be tougher than saving the world."

"Will you help him?"

"Me? What could I do?"

"Be his adviser or something. He has few relatives. His friends are scattered. I would feel better with you helping. Running against the organization can mean trouble. Having you at his side would make it safer."

"What is he running for?"

"City Council. In the Democratic primary."

Don Giacomo frowned. "Anthony Regale is hard to beat. He has Marrandino's full support. And the people like him."

"He can be beaten. And he *should* be beaten."

"Yes. An unsavory person." They stopped at the corner where their homeward courses divided. He stood musing. "It would be nice to be really involved in something again."

"I'll ask Remo to come over the night of our card game. You can talk about it."

"It will be a pleasure."

As she walked to her apartment, Minnie was oblivious to the evening spectacle of Hester Street. She didn't hear Mrs. Cavallo bellowing her nightly dinner call from a third-floor window to her son. She didn't notice Angelo Leonforte brandishing a broomstick at kids pitching pennies in front of his store. She was deep in thought. Don Giacomo could be a great help to Ray. And his sister might be able to help with that problem of the cork. Arturo had convinced her not to go to the police. But she would at least investigate on her own. Her desire for revenge flared.

She didn't notice the man sipping coffee in the café across the street. He quietly watched Minnie and stroked a curiously old-fashioned handlebar mustache.

Chapter 2

RAY Santangelo remembered Joe DeSimone's tough-guy manner and the cigarette permanently dangling from his lower lip. When they were kids, Joe had shown Ray his drawings and designs, reluctantly at first, then with open enthusiasm. He had been pleased when Ray told him he thought he had talent. He confessed that he wanted to be an architect.

But Joe DeSimone didn't have a chance. His father was alcoholic, his mother retarded. One thing led to another, and Joe's talent, his very life were squandered. It ended with an overdose.

Calvin Paguate, that sullen Athapaskan Indian with a face like a totem, had reminded Ray of Joe. The same sad face and high cheekbones, the same sense of fatalism. Calvin drank.

"Go home," he had told Ray. "Go home, white man. Only a Geronimo can help us."

Ray had packed his bags and said adios to his own misplaced idealism. Ray had been duped by the 1960s, by the mystique of a protest movement which saw only blacks, Chicanos, Puerto Ricans, and American Indians as oppressed people and sometimes saw them *only* as oppressed people.

Ray said adios to the Calvin Paguates and *salve* to the Joe DeSimones. If he couldn't be Geronimo, he would be Garibaldi.

He turned the corner at Mott Street. It was a blustery spring day. When the weather turned in Little Italy, the streets budded with humanity. Old ladies propped pillows on windowsills. Storekeepers dragged folding chairs out on the sidewalk. Dropouts clustered around Nunzio's candy store.

He stopped to chat with four old men playing boccie in the vest-pocket park. They greeted him effusively. "Look who's back," said Pietro Ricci. "Longo says you want to be a politician."

"That's right, Pietro. You gonna vote for me?"

"Sure," he said, with a shrug of indifference. "You can't be worse than the rest of those crooks."

"I think we need a piece of the action," said Ray. "Money for school programs, drug-rehabilitation services, things like that."

Pietro Ricci looked skeptical. "We can help ourselves."

Vito Moresca squinted in annoyance. "We playing this game or no? You can talk politics when it gets dark."

"I'm through," announced Leo Fossi. "My wife's gonna murder me if I don't get home. If I don't listen to her, she makes me sleep on the couch."

The other men guffawed. "Who's gonna be my partner?" shouted Vito. "How about it, Ray?"

"Yeah, sure." Ray hefted the bowling ball and walked up to the line. "What do you men think of the way Regale does his job on the City Council?" he asked. "Has he done anything for you?"

"Of course," said Pietro. "He got my nephew John a good office job with the sanitation department."

Ray completed his shot. "I mean, has he done anything for the community as a whole?"

"Sure," said Jimmy Carbone. "He doesn't let them push us around at City Hall. You know, he's a karate black belt. You gonna run against him?"

"I was thinking of it," Ray said.

They gave him pitying looks. Ray had his work cut out for him.

AFTERWARD he stopped in at Ferrara's for an espresso. The store was thronged. He sat near the front window, watching the copper glow of the setting sun.

Valentina Corvo walked up to him as he fiddled with his cup. "Well, Ray. How are you?" she said, hand resting on outthrust hip. He looked up at her.

Tina Corvo had the kind of face one would see on an Etruscan sarcophagus—long nose, brown eyes like huge almonds and fringed with long lashes. Her limbs were slender, almost spindly. The look was softened by generous breasts and a sleek curve of the back. She had a rich, dark sensuality. The photographers who hired Valentina liked her mixture of roiling Vesuvian looks and icy demeanor. At twenty-four she was on the brink of becoming a top model. She was also Umberto Marrandino's niece.

"Tina," he said, rising. His eyes swept over her. "Dynamite. I saw your picture in a magazine a couple of weeks ago. How are you?"

They sat down and she inspected Ray with curiosity. "Nice tan."

He shrugged. "A fringe benefit."

"Get it all out of your system?"

He laughed. "Oh, I'm incurable." He studied her. She wore no makeup, a white sweater, and blue sailor pants. Her hair was pulled back, showing a high forehead and prominent cheekbones.

She said, "I missed you, you creep."

He raised his eyebrows. "I'm sure you kept yourself amused."

"You understand that I'm no angel, no matter what my uncle thinks. But I still missed you."

He sipped the espresso. "Me too," he admitted grudgingly.

Her smile had a hint of triumph. "Come see me. I still live in the Village." She scribbled a Bleecker Street address on a napkin. "Say, day after tomorrow at about six."

"What's the point, really?"

She searched his gray eyes. "We can try."

His mouth went dry. "Okay."

"Gotta run. Till day after tomorrow."

Every man in the place watched her glide out. Including Ray.

Two men sat in the back, drinking orange soda. The fat one, Petey Ianucci, looked at his sleek companion, Dominic Saraceno.

"So the kid is back," Petey said.

CONCETTA DiPalma was sitting at her usual station by the window, in a creaky wooden rocker padded with layers of cushion.

"Luck isn't with you, Mrs. Santangelo," the priest said, triumphantly slapping down the winning card.

"You play too well," she conceded, while looking at Concetta.

The old woman was enveloped in nodding gloom. Her sightless eyes were rheumy and the trace of a bitter smile was on her lips. Although it was almost June, she was bundled in layers of coarse clothing, with which she now and again fidgeted.

Don Giacomo poured *sambuca* with a flourish. The clear liqueur oozed into the glasses, emitting a strong anise odor. Minnie held up her hand. "I've had too much already. I'll talk to your sister for a while." She rose and tentatively approached the old woman. "How are you feeling?" she inquired politely.

Concetta cackled in Sicilian. "Eck, eck. How should I feel? One-quarter here." She indicated the sky with a bony finger. "Three-quarters there." The hand plopped back into her lap, as if the result of a superhuman effort.

"Old age is a blessing from God," Minnie said formally.

"And a curse," Concetta snapped. "Bah. I'm blind and useless."

Minnie tried again. "Age has its compensations. Like wisdom." She rested her bottom on the window ledge. "Your mind is still quick. And your memory."

"Ahhh." Concetta nodded in satisfaction. "I often cannot remember what happened yesterday. But happenings of seventy years ago are sometimes clear as visions."

"She speaks the truth," said Don Giacomo. "She remembers things better than I." He sniffed his drink sadly.

"He remembers nothing," Concetta said gruffly. "My half brother is only sixty-three, and he forgets the names of our cousins."

"I hardly even remembered you when I first came here," he said. "I was just a child when you left for America."

Concetta sat in glum silence. Then she said, "Some things are best not remembered."

"Like what happened to Jerry Tedesco," Minnie said.

True to her admission, Concetta did not remember the recent event. "What happened?"

Minnie recounted the killing, saving the cork for the last detail. When she finished the story, she took a deep breath and folded her hands in her lap.

Concetta sat silently for a while. "The *stoppaglieri*," she finally announced.

"The who?" said Minnie.

"The *stoppaglieri* of Monreale, where I was born. The cork was their mark."

"I am from Abruzzi. I don't know about such things. Who were the *stoppaglieri?*"

"A Mafia," Concetta replied. "A group of families who joined together for protection in the old days. *Cosche*, they were called, like the leaves of an artichoke. But they have not existed for years."

"What happened to them?"

"Oh, things got out of hand. Bloody. Finally the government in Rome cracked down. Jailed the leaders. And the people got fed up, especially after the feud between the *stoppaglieri* and the *fratuzzi*. That one caused a lot of bloodshed."

Minnie sensed that she was on to something. "The *fratuzzi* were another *cosca?*"

"Yes. Their feud began so long ago that people forgot what started it. But that didn't matter. Only vengeance mattered. One killing led to another, until it became nearly impossible to end."

"So the victims of the *stoppaglieri* were all left with corks in their mouths," Minnie reflected. "Where were the *fratuzzi* from?"

"I think from Bagheria." Her old face was screwed up with the effort of remembering. "Yes, Bagheria."

Minnie looked up sharply. Bagheria was only a few kilometers from Porticello. Was the Santangelo family once in the *fratuzzi?* "Could this feud still have been going on twelve years ago?"

"No. The carabinieri cracked down when I was young."

Minnie looked grave. "Do you remember some of the families?"

"Not in the *fratuzzi*, they were from another town. But the Santinis, Guerras, and Bencis were the main *stoppaglieri* families."

"Did some of them come to America?"

She shrugged. "Some from every family eventually emigrated."

"Maybe the Tedescos were in the *fratuzzi*," Minnie said.

Don Giacomo approached the women with a frown. "You take a morbid interest in this murder," he said to Minnie. "Surely you don't think this old story has anything to do with Tedesco's death."

"But the cork, Don Giacomo," Minnie said.

He drained his glass. "Maybe one of these American mafiosi was familiar with the old story and decided to revive the tradition. Maybe in his perverted way he felt that all the color had gone out of the Mafia business."

It sounded plausible. Still, Minnie wasn't convinced.

Concetta had not been listening. She plucked a live ember from the ashes of her memory. "Teodoro Guerra." She spat the name like sour milk from her mouth.

"Eh?" said Minnie.

"Oh, he was a bad one. A don of the *stoppaglieri*. And a cold-blooded killer. He was consumed with hatred for the *fratuzzi*."

"What finally happened to him?" asked Minnie.

"He was old when I was young. He would have been long in his grave by now, even if the police hadn't executed him."

"Then he *was* executed."

"Eventually. They had a big trial for all the leaders. Even members of the *fratuzzi* gave evidence against him. To save their own skins, they cooperated with the police. A great scandal."

The rocker creaked as she talked in a slow, somber monotone. "The Guerras were a bad lot. Teodoro's father, Don Marco, had also been a leader before he was shot. There was a son as well. Marco, named for his grandfather. He was just seven years old when they took his father, Teodoro, away."

"Marco Guerra," Minnie said slowly, thoughtfully.

"I still see him in my mind," continued Concetta, "even though it was nearly sixty years ago. The carabinieri had his father in shackles in front of his house. The entire town was there to witness the arrest. Young Marco's mother and sisters wept behind their hands. But the boy didn't flinch. He didn't turn away. His eyes were dark and steady. I remember it well. That was just before I left for America."

Don Giacomo said, "They must all be dead by now."

"I was there and I am not dead," she reminded the priest.

The awful implication was not lost on Minnie.

The long black robe swished as Don Giacomo edged closer to his neighbor. "Tell me what is troubling you," he said, laying a hand on Minnie's shoulder. She knew that she could unburden herself to him, that the priest would be helpful and sympathetic. But instead, she stored his offer in her mind. Concetta excused herself and went to bed just before the doorbell rang.

After he was let in, Ray placed a white box on the kitchen table. "Thought you'd like some pastry from Ferrara's."

"I'll make the coffee," said Don Giacomo. "I've been hearing all about your good work with the Indians. I myself was never cut out for the missions."

"I wasn't a missionary. I was in VISTA, a government program."

"Is it really so different?"

"I suppose not," he admitted.

Don Giacomo set the espresso maker on the stove. "Your mother seems to think I can help you in your attempt to get into politics."

"I can use help," Ray said. "It's going to be tough to beat Regale."

Don Giacomo shrugged his stooped shoulders. "Tough, yes. But not impossible. How will you get started?"

Ray's face livened up. He lit his pipe and began. "My first step is to get the Camillo Benso Cavour Reform Club to back me. I'll make my pitch at its candidate's night next Tuesday. The club's support means financial help from the New Democratic Coalition and workers to carry petitions. I need a thousand signatures to get on the ballot. Once that's accomplished, it's still an uphill battle. Regale has the district leaders in his pocket and regular organization support. Insurgents don't do too well in this neighborhood."

"But that won't stop you, eh?"

Ray sucked on the pipe reflectively. "No, it won't. I know I can reach these people, with a couple of breaks."

"What kind of campaign do you plan?"

"You may be able to help me there. Get me access to church groups, the Holy Name Society, the PTA. I'm going to base my campaign on two themes: drugs and dropouts. Italians have a relatively high school-dropout rate and a high drug-addiction rate among white groups. What does Regale do about it? He talks tough, that's all."

Don Giacomo frowned. "We don't like politicians to stress our shortcomings. And the Italian-American has little interest in meetings or political activities." He sat opposite Ray and poured himself another glass of *sambuca*. "You will have to bend your ideals a little to have even a slight chance of winning. Do a little rabble-rousing. Condemn the powerful."

"I won't go that route. Then I'd be just like Regale. But I can condemn City Hall for ignoring our needs. And there's nothing wrong with Italian pride. We've got a lot to be proud of. There's a great waste of human resources in this neighborhood."

Minnie looked at Ray admiringly. "You understand the people."

"Mamma, that's why I'm back. What do I know about Indians?"

Don Giacomo stroked his chin. "A messiah must come from his own soil."

Ray nodded. "I don't claim to be a savior. But I do believe that an outsider can't do the job of a native son."

Don Giacomo smiled. "I agree. The people are like bison who follow a strong leader from among the herd."

Ray grimaced. "I don't like the idea of a herd. The people are not mindless animals. In fact, their independence is a big problem to anybody who wants to organize them. You've got to appeal on a direct personal level. I intend to be very visible in the neighborhood, to talk to everybody I can."

The coffee was ready. Don Giacomo poured while Minnie set the pastries on plates. "And you have to do favors," he said.

"I'll do all the favors I can," Ray replied, biting into an éclair. "But I'm at a disadvantage. Regale can do more because he's in power."

Don Giacomo cleared his throat. "I'm an old man, Remo. I was once respected back in Italy. I was a fairly good priest. My talents are not great, but I have some knowledge of how Italians' minds work. I would be honored if you would accept my help."

"With pleasure," Ray said. Minnie beamed as they shook hands.

"How do you say it?" asked Don Giacomo. " 'Power to the people.' "

Chapter 3

UMBERTO ("Bert") Marrandino studied himself in the mirror. The years had left their mark, that was true. But at fifty-seven he was still a handsome man with a flat stomach.

His toupee sat on an oblong head, and he had large ears, pointed at both ends. The jaw was also pointed but had a suggestion of strength. The nose was thin and curved, the sideburns speckled with gray.

Bert was naked except for a towel wrapped around his torso. He turned on the ornate gold faucets in the bathroom sink, scrubbed his hands and face vigorously, and reached for a monogrammed towel. He was getting a little pale and could use a trip to Puerto Rico. He sighed; not now, too many problems. He cursed under his breath. That Tedesco got what he deserved. Still, it was troublesome for him. It turned up the heat.

Marrandino padded out of the bathroom. His clothes were laid out on the bed. He didn't go in for a stereotyped image: no silk suits, pinkie rings, and white-on-white shirts. Marrandino dressed rather like a tasteful diplomat—stylish but understated. On the bed were white boxer shorts, black socks, pigeon's-egg-blue broadcloth shirt, wine-colored silk tie, and a three-piece suit of gray gabardine with deep center vent and cuffed trousers. At the foot of the bed stood a pair of oxblood cordovans.

There was a knock at the door. "Come in."

Petey Ianucci shambled his bulk across the deep carpet and held out three packs of cigarettes and one package of Sen-Sen.

"Throw it on the bed," said Bert.

"Yes, sir," the fat man said. He placed the articles down and eased himself into a wing chair with a sigh. He mopped his brow with a handkerchief. "Getting hot. How'd it go with the DA?"

Marrandino was buttoning his shirt. "You think they could keep me any longer than it takes to call my lawyer? Hand me that tie."

Petey rose and, breathing heavily, did as he was told. "The air conditioning in the Lincoln is on the blink," he announced.

"Never mind that. Did you find out anything?"

"Nothing definite, but a few good theories."

Bert shot him an angry look. "Keep your theories, you cucumber. I want facts. Who iced Tedesco and why?"

Petey sulked for a bit and then said, "I can't help it, Mr. Marrandino. Even our friends in the precinct haven't got a clue."

Bert pondered this. "The DA seemed to be splashing around too.

315

But we can use methods they can't." He cursed and gingerly touched an inflamed mole on his breastbone. It had been bothering him lately. Then he began to knot the tie. "What theories?"

Petey rubbed his pink hands together. "The boys from Long Island say Tedesco was doing some free-lancing out there, dealing in heroin and prostitutes. They say he got iced when he got too greedy."

Bert belted his pants and put on his jacket. "What's with this cork business?" He flicked lint from his sleeve.

"No one knows for sure. Maybe just something fancy, like the mark of Zorro, you know."

Bert jogged his memory. "I seem to remember my father telling me something about corks. Long time ago in Sicily."

Carmen the manicurist entered the room after a discreet knock. Bert nodded, sat on the divan, and stuck out his right hand, which she dutifully began to buff.

Umberto Marrandino had the hands of a harpist—smooth palms, curved knuckles, tapering fingers. He was born in Catania, in eastern Sicily, where his father was a prosperous exporter of olive oil. The business had failed and the family came to the States, where Bert's father worked in a textile factory—a job he always considered beneath his dignity. His son was never to work with his hands. That was fine with Bert. But he didn't use them to thumb through medical books, as his father had urged. Instead they caressed dice, flicked cards, and—infrequently—held a revolver.

In New York the kid from Catania became a go-fer, a street rat on the periphery of the local organization. Young Umberto, ruthless and intelligent, soon came to the attention of Luigi Castelbianco, an elegant don with ascetic tendencies. In a few years Umberto's tapering forefinger squeezed off a bullet as he executed his first rubout. It was a rite of passage set up by Castelbianco.

Carmen gently touched his palm, signaling for Umberto to switch hands. She buffed the left one.

"I'm going to a meeting tonight," Bert informed Petey. "You know how to get in touch with me in case something comes up."

"Sure. You know that Santangelo kid is back?"

316

Bert reflected. "Minerva's son. So he's back. So what?"

"He wants to run for City Council against Regale. They had a candidate's night yesterday at the reform club and he won their support."

"Fat chance he has." Bert arched his brows. "Still . . . Maybe we should have a chat with him."

"I don't think he'll talk to us. He made a speech about reforming things around here, about how the Mafia gets kids to drop out of school and get hooked on drugs. He said he's gonna change things."

"Hasn't he heard that the Mafia doesn't exist?" Bert hissed.

"Maybe *he* shouldn't exist," the fat man ventured.

Bert looked fixedly at Petey. "You know better than to think that. You have to use finesse with politicians. See what turns him on. Make him a proposition."

"I think I know one thing that turns him on. Your niece."

Bert suddenly pulled his hand away from Carmen's feathery control. "Valentina? What does she have to do with him?"

Petey shrugged. "I saw them together in Ferrara's. They acted like old friends."

Bert pondered. "So maybe they are old friends. That may be good." He gave his hand back to Carmen. "We may be able to handle him. In fact, some local opposition may make Regale look good. As long as the opposition is not serious."

Carmen sniffed, hearing nothing. She thought that Marrandino was a pretty man but that he had an unpleasant sweet and sour odor about him, like overripe fennel. Still, he paid well.

"Watch the kid," Marrandino said. "He shouldn't give us much trouble. But we ought to keep the situation under control."

Petey nodded. "I'll take care of everything."

SHE liked absinthe and acid rock. He liked beer and blues. She bought her clothes in fey thrift shops and kinky boutiques. He went to the army-navy stores and Brooks Brothers. She took Zen archery lessons. He attended hockey games. She dropped acid at the movies. He cried at the movies. Yet they were drawn to each other like lodestones.

Ray glanced around the apartment. It was airily furnished in wicker chairs, expensive prints, Iranian throw cushions, and hanging plants. The liquor cabinet was stocked with everything from ouzo to the Wild Turkey now gurgling into his glass.

"You seem to be doing well on your own," he said.

Valentina handed him the drink. "The TV commercials pay good residuals." She smiled. "Not that I have to depend on them. Uncle Umberto would see that I was comfortable."

He cringed at the mention of Marrandino. Some mafiosi were likable despite their activities. But he loathed Marrandino.

Tina did not like her uncle, either. Although she was bound to him by family ties, she had reason to hate him. Her father, Vito, had been in prison for the past thirteen years on Marrandino's account. Vito had married the Mafia chieftain's sister to get a cushy job in the rackets. He developed a taste for Puerto Rican women. Okay if he had been discreet. But he broke a cardinal rule; he was not careful about appearances. Bert asked Vito to carry out a contract. It was a setup, and Vito got twenty years to life.

With a blend of indulgence and authoritarianism, Umberto took over the raising of Valentina. He gave her clothes, jewelry, European trips, and a college education. She had to be home at eight p.m., and he screened all her friends and activities.

At twenty-one she rebelled. She took an apartment in Greenwich Village, working as a waitress in an actors' hangout. Soon she began getting bit roles and modeling jobs. But her independence was not absolute. She was still in some ways a protectorate of Umberto Marrandino, and she even took pleasure in watching people's faces when she told them who her uncle was.

Her brown eyes appraised Ray Santangelo. She wondered why he turned her on. He was too straight-arrow, too involved and committed. She walked across the room to a drawing board. "Want to share a joint?"

"No, thanks." He watched her from behind as she rolled the cigarette paper.

She chuckled. "You're afraid of me, I think. I awaken the sleeping playboy in you."

She threw her weight on her right leg and her right hip jutted out. She had always had an overpowering physical effect on him. She was wearing a halter and jeans that exposed a taut midsection. Below her rib cage was a small tattoo of Donald Duck. He thought, The sleeping playboy? Maybe she was right. Dammit, why did he find her so attractive? He took a slug of bourbon.

She sat down on the corduroy couch and patted a spot next to her. "So sit."

He hesitated, then came across the room and sat down. "Sorry I'm acting so distant."

"Don't talk." She nuzzled his ear, tapering fingers gliding over his cheek. His mouth sought hers. Her hand traced along his thigh as he held her close.

"Nice Sicilian girls don't behave that way," he said.

She moved away from him and stretched languidly. "I've never behaved that way with a politician before."

"I'm still an amateur."

She laughed. "I wouldn't say that. Oh, you mean as a politician. My uncle Bert could help you get experience."

"Thanks, but no thanks."

"Don't be like that. C'mere." She sighed and began unbuttoning his shirt.

"I'm nothing to you but a sex object," he said.

"You know your place."

"You took me," she said. "Now you must-a make me your wife. Tomorrow I will-a shave my upper lip. You put on-a clean-a shorts and we see the priest."

He was laughing. Suddenly her demeanor grew serious. "Live with me," she said. "Forget politics. I want you."

"Wait a minute. I like you a lot, but . . . we're too different."

"We could really get it on, you know," she said.

He shook his head. "Listen, I'm running for office. I shouldn't even be seen with you, but I'm not going to blame you for your relatives. That isn't it. We're like oil and water. We don't mix."

"I could tell my uncle you seduced and abandoned me."

"Sure. But you won't."

"How can you be so sure?"

"I'm a good judge of character."

She looked wistful. "Okay. We'll just have this kind of thing."

"Let's not program it."

After he left the apartment, she sat on the bed puffing a cigarette and watching the plumes of smoke drift out of the window
and dissolve.

Chapter 4

A RAGGED patch of cloud doused the sun briefly just as Minnie
emerged from the tenement on Hester Street. She headed toward
the river, a bag of bread crumbs tucked under her arm, turning the
whole affair over in her mind. Did the killing of Tedesco have
something to do with the *stoppaglieri-fratuzzi* feud? What of Stefano's murder? Bizarre coincidence?

Minnie had been on the verge of telling Remo the whole story,
but she feared he would tell the police and that might throttle his
political career. There was no need to involve him. After all, there
wasn't any real evidence.

She reached her favorite bench in the park by the East River.
There were few people around and she could be alone with her
thoughts. The yellow and blue umbrella of a frankfurter stand was
visible near the highway. The whine of an outboard came from the
river. She scattered the bread crumbs on the brownish grass. The
pigeons dived to the feast. Inexpertly she lit a stale filter tip.

A man appeared on the concrete path to Minnie's left. His stride
was leisurely but purposeful. He wore a brown woolen suit and a
checkered vest. The white handkerchief in his breast pocket looked
luminous against the dark suit. He had a dated look which was
enhanced by a jaunty handlebar mustache, and his continental air
seemed out of place in the surroundings.

The man made his way toward Minnie and sat tentatively on the
far corner of her bench. A look of indecision flickered across
a face which strove to be handsome but was a few years past

succeeding. He spoke in mellifluous Italian. "A fine day, isn't it?"

She glanced at the stranger. He tried a smile, but it wasn't enough to conquer her suspicion.

He persisted. "A good place to think, eh? Forget your troubles."

Minnie was becoming alarmed. She was on the point of asking him what he meant, but chose instead to remain silent and glower at him.

"So you decided not to go to the police with your story, Signora Santangelo?" he said.

Her pulse raced and she started to rise, but he reached over and laid a gently restraining hand on her wrist. "Sorry I frightened you. You're not in any danger." Minnie froze. "My name is Professore Gaetano Conti." He stood and gave a slight bow. Dumbfounded, she settled back on the bench. "I flew here from Italy a few days ago, after I read about the Tedesco murder in the newspaper."

"What have I to do with this murder?"

"Let's be frank with each other, eh? I am well known in Italy as a journalist and historian. My specialty is the traditions of Sicily. Particularly of the Mafia."

She rose from the bench. "This is no business of mine. I have nothing to do with the Mafia."

"I know about your husband. I know about the cork."

The words hit her like a blow. She sat down. "But how?"

"It's my business, after all."

"Do you have credentials?"

He flashed
a smile. "Of
course." He

reached into his breast pocket and produced a tan leather wallet, from which he extracted press credentials with Italian government markings and a photo of himself. "I free-lance, write books, appear on television."

She handed the credentials back. "What do you want from me?"

"For beginners, let's talk about the connection between your husband's death and Tedesco's death."

"You think there's a connection, then?"

"Indeed I do."

"And with the old feud? The *stoppaglieri?*"

He appraised her. "So you know about that. Good. Yes, I think it does have something to do with the feud."

Minnie's eyes flashed. "Do you know who killed my husband?"

"Not for certain, but I have my suspicions."

"It was because the Santangelo family were members of the *fratuzzi*, wasn't it?"

"Yes, but your husband was an innocent victim. He was too young to have been involved in that mess."

She clenched her fists. "Then why? Why?"

"I think your husband and Tedesco were victims of a madman."

"Marco Guerra," she said, almost inaudibly.

He looked impressed. "Yes, Guerra. You obviously have a talent for detective work."

"My husband never did anything to him."

"No, he didn't. But to Guerra's mind your husband's very existence must have seemed an insult. Guerra had been taught from birth to hate the *fratuzzi*. His father had been executed, his family, leaders of the *stoppaglieri* for generations, had been dishonored. Then you and your husband showed up on vacation, perhaps more prosperous than those who stayed behind. The name Santangelo mocked him. So he struck out against your husband."

Minnie's doubts about this man were swept up in her excitement. She wanted to know more. "Why did the police in Italy tell me not to mention the cork?"

"The old Sicilian code of honor still existed. They were afraid that some member of your husband's family would take revenge."

"But my husband had no family left there."

"Then another family in the old *fratuzzi*, perhaps. They weren't taking any chances on a bloodbath." He hitched up his trouser leg in order not to wrinkle the crease, and crossed his legs. Minnie noticed his scant growth of hair and tried to judge his age from it and the lines in his tanned face. The neck muscles sagged under traces of after-shave powder.

A few pigeons strutted by, but Minnie had forgotten about the bread crumbs. "Didn't the police try to catch the killer?"

"They worked on it. But they had no proof."

Her face darkened. "If I only had a chance at Guerra."

"Maybe you will get your chance. You seem to have a spark, Signora Santangelo. Intelligence. Spirit."

She was flattered. She was not unaccustomed to compliments on her housekeeping and cooking, but on her intelligence, her spirit? She savored the thought. Perhaps the real Minnie was just beginning to emerge full force. Still, she wouldn't let this person flatter her off her guard. "What do you mean, I might get my chance?"

"To catch Guerra. We could work together. As a journalist I am pretty good at the art of detection. So are you, I think."

Minnie shivered slightly as the sun dipped lower over the downtown skyline. "How can we be sure it is Guerra?"

"Nothing is certain in this life. But Guerra is psychologically suited. It was like a congenital disease with Guerra, this sense of vendetta. Soon after his father was executed he was sent away to a Jesuit school, but came back to Monreale. He was living there twelve years ago when your husband was killed. He was questioned by the police. But, as I said, they had no evidence."

"They simply let him go?"

"They watched him, but he kept clean. Then four years ago he disappeared."

Minnie sat bolt upright.

"Just like that." He snapped his fingers. "Without a trace."

"Until this cork thing and Jerry Tedesco."

"He must have gotten to New York somehow. Shall we walk a bit? It's getting chilly."

Minnie distractedly scattered the remainder of the bread crumbs as she rose from the bench. A flurry of pigeons swooped down.

"There is no record of his immigration, but there are ways of getting into the country." He cast her a sidelong glance. "How about it, then? Will you be my co-detective?"

She hesitated. She would like to punish this Guerra, but she was no detective. She was a scared, simple woman. "I want no part of this," she said. "I don't want to get involved."

"You *are* involved. Don't you understand that?" He threw up his hands in exasperation. "If Guerra killed Tedesco because he was a member of the *fratuzzi* families, do you think he'll stop there?"

"Tedesco is nothing to me," she said, almost sobbing. "I don't want to put myself and my son in danger."

"But he is in danger. He's a Santangelo."

This is what Minnie had been fearing, but she still refused to admit it. "No, no. How do I know who you are? Leave me alone."

He stuffed a slip of paper into her hand. "My phone number. If you change your mind, get in touch with me."

She whirled away and rushed up the steps of the highway overpass. He stood there, arms folded, watching her go.

A breeze tugged gently at Minnie's dress as she walked the mile or so to Little Italy. The risks of action were too great, she told herself. What about the risks of inaction? Her son. Would another man be taken from her as she stood idly by?

The breeze skittered trash in the crooks of curbstones, and a man on a tall ladder battened down a soft cap with the palm of his hand. They were putting up arches of colored lights for the Festa di Sant' Antonio. The *festa* had always been a special occasion for her. Now she was not exactly in a festive mood. She mumbled a quick prayer to Saint Anthony and entered her apartment building. Her door was ajar, and mentally scolding herself for forgetting to lock it, she entered the apartment.

The fat man was sitting on a kitchen chair. Another, younger man was leaning against the refrigerator.

A leer spread across the fat man's face. "Hello, Mamma," said Petey Ianucci. "Close the door behind you, huh?"

PETEY IANUCCI's balding crown and long hair gave him the look of a jolly fat friar with the perpetual grin of a porpoise. The pockets of his loud sport jackets were always stuffed with snacks and betting slips. He specialized in the organization's growing pornography business. He had in his lifetime killed four men.

Dominic Saraceno was a quiet youth of twenty-eight. He had tightly curled hair like that of a Roman bust, a Cupid's bow mouth, and a cleft chin slightly upturned toward an altogether perfect nose. His large brown eyes did not betray his ruthlessness. His voice was the giveaway. It was a throaty, raspy, thoroughly disagreeable instrument and he knew it. Out of his own cruelty he drew a pure, almost sexual pleasure. He had killed five people.

Minnie's fear suddenly dissolved into anger. "What do you want here, Mr. Ianucci? You have no right to break into people's houses." She felt bolder as her fist closed around the scrap of paper upon which Conti had written his number.

"Now take it easy, Mamma. This is just a social visit. All the people in this neighborhood are my friends, right, Dominic?" The younger man did not answer.

"Friends knock before entering," she said.

"We knew you wouldn't mind. You're our kind, right?"

She speared him with dark eyes. "You are not my kind."

He clucked his tongue. "Shouldn't talk that way, Signora Santangelo." He hefted his huge bulk from the chair and shambled nearer. Minnie stood there stonily. "You know, you remind me of my own mamma. She's fixed up nice now. Big house in Bayonne, two color TV sets, a big backyard, even a swimming pool." He looked around with distaste. "You should have all that too. Sit down, Mrs. Santangelo. You'll get tired."

She sat down. "I have to make the novena," she lied. "Why don't you tell me what you want and leave, eh?"

"Aha, so you're religious too. My mother even goes to church on weekdays. I got respect for the Church. Look at the Vatican. They got more money and power than . . . than Russia, maybe."

"Money's very important to you, Mr. Ianucci."

"Sure." He let out a high-pitched laugh. "Ain't it to you?"

"Other things are more important."

His eyes, already almost lost in folds of flesh, narrowed even more. "I agree. Like respect. And relatives." Minnie was getting frightened. "Mr. Marrandino wants to see you about your son."

"What does he want with Remo?" Panic edged into her voice.

"Your son's been going around the neighborhood with a very loud mouth. Mr. Marrandino sent him a message that he wanted to see him, but Ray wasn't very polite. He didn't even answer it. So, being that you and Mr. Marrandino are old friends, he thought you might come for a chat."

"My son has a mind of his own," she said evasively.

"Can it hurt to talk? There's a place for him in politics if he cooperates. We'll let Mr. Marrandino explain all that."

Minnie felt her cheeks burn. Who did he think he was, a courier from the baron? This wasn't Sicily. This wasn't the old days. "If he wants to see me," she said defiantly, "let him come here."

"He won't like this."

"Get out," she said evenly. "You think everybody in this neighborhood has to do what you say?" She stood up and waved a finger at him. "I'll tell you something." He recoiled. "You're not as frightening as you think. Your kind killed my husband. Hoods like you killed my father too. Your kind survive when people shut up. Maybe you will find the Santangelos very talkative." Minnie, drained by the emotional outburst, sat down.

Petey's face was twisted. "I think you will be sorry for this."

"I said get out." She did not waver outwardly. But inside, her defiance was melting.

Dominic shuffled away from the refrigerator. He grinned at Mrs. Santangelo. The teeth were white and even, like a movie star's.

"Oh," said Petey. "I haven't introduced you. This is Dominic. I think you might be seeing more of him from time to time."

The handsome face blushed with suppressed pleasure.

MINNIE made the novena after all. She decided it was not the kind of thing she should lie about even to the likes of Petey Ianucci. On the way home she brooded. Were all these crazy things really happening to her? She mistrusted Conti—he seemed too plastic. She feared and hated Marrandino. And this avenging madman Guerra—was he real? She hadn't the strength to fight all these forces. She was just a woman.

A phrase from a song she had learned from her father stole into her mind: *"Sebben che siamo donne, paura non abbiamo."* Even though we're women, we're not afraid. The words stirred Minnie. But her mother and stepfather mocked her in her mind's eye. *"Sei una figliuola semplice. Devi stare a casa."* You're a simple little girl. You belong at home.

Minnie reminded herself that everyday things must be attended to. She stepped into Angelo Borgia's butcher shop.

"Hey, signora," said Angelo, punctuating his greeting with the thwack of a cleaver on the side of lamb chops.

"I wanna nice chicken."

"You bet," he said jovially. "You look a little sick, if you don't mind my saying so. Your son giving you trouble already?"

"No trouble," Minnie said quickly. "Just couldn't sleep too good last night. That chicken looks too fat."

The butcher held the chicken above the scales. "It's gotta be plump," he said. "Like a woman." She gave him a disapproving look and he laughed. "Howzat?" he asked, weighing another chicken. "Three dollars even. Some sausages? A little flank steak?"

Minnie shook her head. Ray wasn't bringing anything in right now, and the pension and insurance check didn't stretch very far.

"Buona festa," the butcher shouted as Minnie went out the door.

That's a laugh, she thought. *Buona festa.* Yet, despite all her troubles, she began to feel a little more cheerful. What could Marrandino do, after all? They didn't go around killing politicians anymore. They killed only their own kind nowadays. Yes, she was starting to feel better. Getting out, seeing people. *Sì. Buona festa.*

Arturo stood by the vegetable stand, waving to her. "Hey, Arturo," she shouted, almost happily.

Arturo adjusted his cap as Minnie approached. He puffed out his chest a bit. He was on his own turf, in his element. "Want some nice 'scarole?" he said, beaming. "Just in fresh."

"Sure. And tomatoes and peppers. Throw in some lettuce too."

He shook open a brown paper bag like cracking a whip. "You look good, Minerva. Like always," he said.

Minnie jabbed a knuckle in his ribs. "You're good with the talk."

He put the escarole on the scale. "I'll give you good weight." He threw on a few more leaves. "I was thinking," he said with forced nonchalance. "There's a party at the club tomorrow. They have one every year, you know, right before the *festa*. Uh, you wanna go with me maybe?" He counted out a few tomatoes and looked into the bag. "How many you want?"

"Six." She fidgeted with her hair and smiled to herself. Why not? She needed a little fun. "Sure. I would love to go, Arturo."

Chapter 5

THE party was held in the clubhouse on Baxter Street. The afternoon sparkled like wine. It was Sunday, a day to dress in satin and serge, a day to forget the boss and esteem good food. Dance the *saltarella*, sing a *stornello*, flirt, tell stories, swill the wine. The landlord never comes on Sunday.

Three bridge tables were covered with a long white tablecloth and blanketed with Italian and American dishes all spiced by the old recipes. There were kaleidoscopic antipastos and great round loaves of bread; pots of spaghetti and meatballs, peppers cooked with anchovies, eggplant parmigiana, chicken with lemon and bay leaves, hamburgers cooked in olive oil; almonds, walnuts, tarts, *cannoli*, spumone, tortoni, grapes, oranges, cheeses, kegs of beer, wines from Tuscany and the Piedmont, figs and raisins, ginger ale and orange soda, Scotch, rye, gin, bourbon, vermouth, bitters, anisette, *sambuca*. And Brioschi.

People sat in folding chairs, eating and jabbering. People stood by the coffee bar under the mounted swordfish, drinking and bantering. People lounged by the Coke machine, flirting and complaining. John Carbone and Stefano Curto played their guitars. The room was festooned with red, white, and green crepe.

Minnie and Arturo walked in. Arturo, holding a porkpie hat in his hands, bared his beaver teeth. The right collar point of his shirt was folded up. His brown wing tips were shined to a high gloss. Minnie's hand rested in the crook of his elbow. Her smile was a sunbeam of pleasure. Minnie loved parties.

She was dressed like a flagship about to be launched: white shoes, a floral print dress, garlands of costume jewelry, a gold wristwatch that Stefano had given her, and a felt hat with an ostrich feather sticking out of it.

They joined the festivities. The talk and the good-natured wisecracks flowed easily. Minnie, her cheeks flushed, her hazel eyes flashing, was surrounded by men.

Grazietta Lecco was there, giving Minnie a sullen eye. Her husband, Nicola, appraised Minnie. "You're a good-looking woman, Minerva Santangelo. It's a wonder you never caught a new husband."

She smirked. "Who said I was fishing?"

He winked. "With bait like that, they would bite anyhow." Grazietta Lecco frowned at her husband as the other men roared with laughter. Minnie grinned widely.

The musicians struck up a tarantella and three men asked Minnie to dance. She chose Arturo.

Minnie whirled, switched partners, and stomped again to the staccato music. People clapped and formed a circle around her. A yell went out: "Amaddeo! Amaddeo!" Amaddeo Girelli entered the circle in a spirited pas de deux with Minnie. Another yell: "Arturo!" With a whoop, Arturo drained a glass of wine and jumped into the circle. Cheeks red, eyes glistening, he locked elbows with Minnie and twirled her like a top.

Later they caught their breath under the cool revolutions of the ceiling fan. Arturo mopped his brow. "I never knew you could dance so well."

"You're not bad yourself."

Arturo looked reflective. "When I worked in Africa, we danced every Sunday. Men with men. There was nothing else to do."

Minnie was touched by this glimpse into Arturo's lonely past. She wondered why he never married, never mentioned his family. It was unusual for a Sicilian to be adrift like that.

The music began again. It was time for *stornelli*. These were not merely folk songs, but a good-natured competition among neighbors. Gathering up the folds of her long skirt, Grazietta Lecco walked over to the guitar players and whispered a request. She was a Tuscan who felt superior to her southern Italian neighbors and proud of her rich contralto. She sang a piece from Tuscany, and when she finished, everyone clapped heartily. Arturo yelled, "Minnie, sing an Abruzzese song."

A general shout went up: "Sant' Antonio, Sant' Antonio."

Minnie smiled, appreciating the rivalry. She rose with great dignity and took her place in front of the guitarists. Her voice was a nasal soprano, but she had power, range, and imagination. She motioned for everyone to join in the refrain, which they did. Then she basked in the applause and whistles. Grazietta Lecco clapped politely. Arturo glowed with pride. *"Brava!"* he shouted. Minnie sat down beside him. Arturo raised his glass to her and drank. He felt mellow and sentimental. He was humming.

"What's that, Arturo?" Minnie asked.

"An old Sicilian love song."

Stefano Curto picked out the tune on his guitar. "Come on, Arturo. Sing it for us."

Arturo took a swig of wine and nodded, then sang effortlessly and beautifully. To everyone's surprise, the voice that emerged from this homely man might have belonged to an archangel. It was a side of Arturo that no one had ever seen. When he finished, the room was silent. There was no clapping—just quiet nods and murmurs of appreciation. Arturo poured more wine into his glass. He wore a contemplative look.

He rose, a little wobbly on his feet. "Who took the floor out from under me?"

Minnie steadied him by grabbing his elbow. "You okay?"

"Sure, sure. Just too much wine, that's all. Think I'll go home."

Minnie frowned. "Sure you'll be all right?"

Carmine Balducci shouted, "Eh, Minnie. Let's have 'Lu Caccia-tore Caietane.'"

WHEN she got home that night, Minnie began to make a late-night salad for Ray. He had spent the evening at his campaign storefront on Elizabeth Street and was due back soon. She sliced a tomato and sang to herself: *"Sant' Antonie, Sant' Antonie, lu ne-mice de lu demonie."* Saint Anthony, Saint Anthony, the enemy of the devil. The party had left her glowing.

As she minced garlic, something made her feel uneasy. She had a vague feeling that something was wrong in the apartment. She shrugged it off, doused the salad bowl with olive oil, and added salt. She identified the feeling more exactly. It wasn't that something was wrong, but that something was missing.

Whatever it was, it would turn up. She washed the lettuce and radishes, chopped up a carrot, and made curlicues of a green pepper. But the feeling crept back.

She walked into the living room and glanced around. Everything seemed in order. Her eye fell on the yellowing wedding picture sitting on top of the television console. How formal and uncomfortable Stefano looked in the starched collar, she thought with affection. She went back into the kitchen. What was missing? What? She wiped her hands on her apron, eyes resting momentarily on the garment's design: big daisies and little birds, gay singing birds. . . .

She turned slowly and looked in the place she was reminded of. The blood rushed to her head and she stifled an urge to cry out. She rushed to double-bolt the door. What a fiend he must be, what a scorpion.

331

What she had missed was a familiar sound, the cheery warble that had filled the apartment every day for the last five years.

She looked again. Bruno lay amid the gravel and seed on the floor of the cage, wings flattened against the frail body.

The cork looked absurd clamped in Bruno's beak.

Chapter 6

MARCO Guerra sat in his room, his face obscured by the night. Hunched by the window, he gazed at the crosshatch of fire escapes and luminous banners of hanging wash. He had the dark shape of a sulky buzzard, a patient bird of prey.

He listened to the strangely human sound of the alley cats. Their mating cries inspired his scorn, like people squealing for their shoddy pleasures. Marco Guerra hated cats. They were too sensual. That's why he couldn't stand Minerva Santangelo. That's why the role he played for her was so difficult to sustain. She was so . . . earthy. But he had the silly woman fooled.

He laughed. Killing the bird had been a stroke of genius.

He rose from the straight-backed chair and sat on the cot. With a cold eye, he took in the bedroom: a chipped mirror on a wall from which paint peeled; a plastic wastebasket; a cheap wardrobe. His lips curled. The Guerras had come to this.

What would Don Teodoro have thought of the squalor? That lordly man, with long white beard, courtly ways, and chilly smile. The memory of his father and grandfather fortified him over the long, unrewarding years. He did not have the trappings of the power they once enjoyed in Sicily. No villa, no bodyguards, no people kissing his hand in the piazza. But the trappings were so much garnish. What counted was the righteous exercise of power. Marco Guerra was still a worthy son, with sway over life and death. To him murder was a detached act of duty. He let himself remember. . . . A bell had jangled as he walked into the store. Jerry Tedesco emerged from a back room, smiling. He knew Marco Guerra, but not as Marco Guerra. The victim, descendant of the traitorous *fratuzzi*, smiled like an innocent cherub.

Guerra had asked to see the African statue of the Virgin. Still smiling, Tedesco took it down from the shelf. The statuette had been carved by a black artist who, like Guerra, was an ancestor worshipper. It was fitting.

Now Marco Guerra shivered in his room. Dawn was approaching. He went back further in his memory. . . . He had confronted him along the river outside Porticello. The man had stopped to pick up a few glossy pebbles. When he straightened up, the pistol was pointing at his head. Stefano Santangelo was more baffled than terrified. "What do you want, *amico*? Money? Put that pistol away." Santangelo was a worthy enemy. Courageous.

The sultry sun formed a nimbus around the victim, giving an incandescent quality to the event, like a holy vision. Guerra felt a rush of beatific transport. He screamed exultantly, *"Viva la famiglia Guerra."*

Crows shrieked as the shot rang out. Blood brimmed over Stefano's lips, frozen in a puzzled smile. He fell. Guerra lowered the muzzle, savoring his satisfaction. He knew the purpose of his life now, a life which had rung hollow until the reverberation of this gunshot. He remembered the long nights without his father. He would go to America. He would track down every one of them.

He walked over to the wardrobe and fished the old locket from a jacket pocket. In the twin ovals were the yellowing photos of his father and grandfather, his icons. She is not a Santangelo. But I will kill her too. Perhaps before I kill the son.

Smiling, he lay down and was soon engulfed in dreams.

MINERVA Santangelo gently lifted her parakeet's body and placed it in a sandwich bag. She stored Bruno in a small empty section of the refrigerator until she could give him a proper burial. All the while she thought of revenge.

It was not Bruno so much whom she wanted to avenge. He was just a bird. But her father, her husband, and her own lifetime of enforced passivity. Revenge was said to have a sweet foretaste and a bitter aftertaste. But she wanted it anyhow.

Marco Guerra. She could visualize him, a faceless specter, smirk-

333

ing with pleasure at her writhings, her useless prayers. No, Marco Guerra. You have underestimated the enemy.

Her sense of competition was awakened. Yet she knew that this was no *stornello* contest. This was life and death. And she would not stay in the wings anymore. She remembered when Stefano was killed. She had seethed inside, but had carried out her prescribed role like an obedient dog. Like a woman. It would not happen again.

Minnie would act the detective, as Conti wished. She would pretend to work with him. But she wouldn't trust him. She would work alone. She would track down this man Guerra. She felt confident, like an actress who had prepared herself.

THE coffeehouse was decorated in the mezzotint tones of the cinquecento, and Gaetano Conti fitted in as neatly as the final piece in a jigsaw puzzle. "A pretty touch, killing Brutus," he said.

"The name was Bruno," said Minnie. "What do you mean, a pretty touch? The bird was my friend."

He patted her wrist. "Forgive me. I was speaking in the abstract. In a way I admire his criminal aesthetics."

She shuddered. "Don't make him sound like an artist. He's a fiend."

Despite her mistrust of the man, Minnie was impressed with Conti's high-flown language and intellectual style.

He gave her a warm smile. "I'm very glad you decided to be my co-detective, Minerva. May I call you that?"

She nodded. "It is my name."

"If we put our wits together, Guerra won't stand a chance. He's smug right now. But we have advantages. He doesn't know that we are even aware of his existence. Also he doesn't know about me."

Minnie was reading everything he said two ways, in the light of the possibility that he was who he said he was, and the possibility that he himself was Guerra, baiting a trap for her. She must be nimble-witted. "How do we go about catching him?" she asked.

"I think that Guerra is personally known to you, probably to most of the people in the neighborhood."

She sipped her coffee reflectively. "Then you think that when he disappeared four years ago he came to Little Italy, made friends, and waited to take his revenge?"

"Very likely. Jerry Tedesco was big and fairly young. Not a person to be bludgeoned to death by a man in his sixties, unless he was caught off guard. He wasn't likely to become careless with a stranger coming into his place." Conti signaled a waiter for two more cups of coffee. "We should not be seen together. He's probably observing you pretty closely. He might even recognize me."

"You have met Guerra?"

"No. But I am fairly well known in Italy."

"It would be helpful to know what he looks like."

"Descriptions are useful only to a point. If a man has a harelip or stands six feet nine, a description is indispensable. But with someone like Guerra—medium height, sixtyish, balding, moderate build, dark eyes—it is not much help. And I wouldn't overlook disguises. A toupee, perhaps? A few added pounds? A slouch? They could do wonders." He waved a coffee cup in front of his aquiline nose. "He could even disguise his hate."

Minnie's gaze shifted outdoors. "Why, there's Arturo," she said. He was emerging from a stationery store across the street.

Conti swung his head around. "Arturo? Arturo who?"

"My friend. Wait a minute and I'll ask him to join us." She started to rise.

"Don't do that." His hand restrained her. "We cannot trust anybody. Who is he and how much does he know?"

She sat down slowly. "Arturo?" Minnie knew that Guerra could be posing as a friend, but sweet, gentle Arturo a killer? She stammered, "He . . . he knows only about Stefano's death and about my suspicions that the same person killed Jerry Tedesco. He does not know about you."

Conti stroked his chin. "How long have you known him?"

"For three years. He came to the neighborhood from Boston. Originally from Sicily, from Catania." Her voice and face were grim. "He's a bachelor, lives alone. I've never heard him talk about his family. That is strange for a Sicilian!"

"Now let's not make too much of this," he cautioned. "All of these things are circumstantial." He looked at Arturo. "Hmmm. He looks a bit heavier than the description. Somewhat shorter too."

"He could have gained weight." Minnie was trying out her detective skills. "He does slouch a little."

Conti settled back calmly into his chair. "I will investigate his background. Meanwhile, be careful. Don't make him sense that you suspect him. What did you say his last name was?"

"I didn't. It's Longo. Arturo Longo."

"Of course, you will not tell him about me. And urge him not to tell anyone else about how your husband died. If he is not Guerra, there is no sense having him tell the man who is that we're investigating." They both glanced around, to see that Arturo had gone. Conti turned to Minnie. "You were telling me that you and Marrandino were once friends?"

"Good friends. We came to the neighborhood at about the same time. His people are from Catania too, a good family."

"Then he is certainly not Guerra," Conti surmised. "That doesn't necessarily mean he wasn't involved in Tedesco's death in some way." As he concentrated he toyed with his mustache. "He may be useful to us. Capitalize on your relationship with him."

Minnie considered this possible, though not probable. Umberto had been fond of her once, a long time ago. Still, she would try. She was turning things over in her mind. Now she had two suspects: Conti and, although she was loath to admit it, Arturo. It occurred to her that on the night Bruno was killed, Arturo had drunk too much and left the party early. Had it been a ruse?

Conti suggested that they leave the coffeehouse. As they parted he favored Minnie with one of his more dazzling smiles.

Chapter 7

ANTHONY Regale had the style of a locomotive churning with compressed energy, blowing off gusts of steam. He was squat, with curly hair and waving arms. His face was homely, brown eyes slightly crossed, eyebrows seemingly parted in the middle. Out of a mouthful of discolored teeth came the malapropisms of the street kid who had risen in the world. He was a city councilman.

He came to politics by way of his position as president of the neighborhood chapter of the Italian-American Civil Rights League. In his first run for the council he had based his campaign on physical prowess, particularly his expertise in karate. He stressed his ability to "fight for the neighborhood" against outside forces, including other ethnic groups and the power brokers at City Hall. The pols snickered. The people voted for him.

Now he was running for his second term against an "upstark" named Ray Santangelo, a reform candidate whom he was belittling from the podium as "this child progeny who's still wet behind the ears." He wore a theatrical look of contempt. "What does this bookworm, this *idealist* know about the real world? The world where, if you don't get the other guy first, he'll get you. That's politics. You need a city councilman who knows the ropes, one who's not afraid to stand up for you at City Hall." A murmur of approval went up from the audience. "A councilman is a symbol of the neighborhood he represents. Do you want your symbol to be a kid or a man? Ray Santangelo is a nice kid. But a kid."

He stepped down to a burst of applause and whistling. The debate was being held in the basement of St. Theresa's and was sponsored by a joint committee of the Holy Name Society, the Italian-American Civil Rights League, and the PTA—familiar, friendly ground for Regale and no-man's-land for Ray. About sixty people were in the audience, including local merchants, working-men, civil servants, and a total of seven women.

Umberto Marrandino was applauding Regale. He thought, A little bit of overkill, but the audience goes for it.

Ray sat beside the old priest, Don Giacomo. He rose and walked to the podium, nervously clearing his throat. He waited for the whispers to quiet. He began. "Most of you know me already, but for those who don't, I'm Ray Santangelo. I am a candidate for nomination to the City Council from this district. This means you will have a choice when you go into the voting booth on primary day, a choice you should consider very carefully."

Ray spoke in measured tones and used gestures sparingly, a style deliberately antithetical to Regale's. He knew he lacked his opponent's panache, but Italians liked dignity too.

"I was born and raised in this neighborhood and I love the place—its shops and restaurants and the people. I love the fact that you can buy an Italian record here or good mozzarella, and I will fight for zoning laws to preserve the neighborhood's character." The audience was becoming more attentive. "I want to get trees planted and have buildings declared landmarks. I believe this should stay an open area for our Chinese and Puerto Rican friends, but I want to keep the flavor Italian, like basil leaves in tomato sauce. I am proud of this neighborhood. I am proud of my people." He paused and scanned the faces in the audience.

"But I am not proud of rats and neglect. I am not proud of slumlords and organized crime. I am not proud that there are no health facilities, and that no new housing has been built here in half a century. I am not proud that our kids drop out of school in such great numbers. Our girls are encouraged to do nothing but become housewives. Our boys get strung out on drugs. What has Regale done for you but talk tough and show off his black belt? We need services, money, a piece of the action. We need education, health, and housing. We have a right to it.

"We are hardworking people with great talents and serious problems. We are religious and philosophical. We don't want to lose the greatness of the old country, but we don't want to neglect the opportunities of the new country. We like turkey on Thanksgiving. But first we eat lasagna. We want to learn from Americans how to use education and technology. We pay taxes and send our boys off to war. We want what's coming to us. As city councilman I won't have the power to change everything overnight. But I'm going to fight for these things with everything I've got. Thank you."

Don Giacomo, sitting in the first row, burst into applause and, after a lull, was joined by many others. Florence Fauci whispered to Gloria Maglia, "He sure is cute." Marrandino glowered. The kid knows how to make a speech; that's unfortunate, he thought.

Dr. Enrico Lucca went to the podium. "Now, if the two gentlemen would come up together and take questions from the audience."

This was the part everyone was waiting for: the joust of wit, the clash of styles. The contest.

Joe Tasca, a bricklayer, rose. "What about secure jobs? I'm always getting laid off and so are other guys in the neighborhood."

Regale spoke up. "I agree that we don't get our share of the pie here. You people know as well as me that it's not what you know, it's who you know. And I know everybody downtown. I can see that construction contracts come to the neighborhood. What can my opponent do? Who does he know? Nothing and nobody."

A few members of the audience laughed.

Ray addressed the questioner. "Here's more talk about what Regale could do, not what he has done while he was councilman. Did he attract new housing here which skilled neighborhood residents could work on? No. He built a chain of karate schools in the city. Did he get a job corps program set up for our young workers? No. He gave speeches against campus radicals. I intend to do more than make speeches. I will fight for a bill to renovate the tenements in the area, with federal and state funds, making them low-income cooperative apartments so that the workingman can eventually own his own place. The bill would specify local labor for the renovation work."

Regale frowned. "That's just rhetoric. He—"

Dr. Lucca interrupted. "I'm sorry, Councilman. There is no re-buttal. Frank Gioberti, you had your hand up."

"Yeah. Talk about education, I don't know if I want my kids to go to college where girls and boys live in the same dormitory and streak around with no clothes on and smoke pot and throw bricks. Education can make you crazy instead of smart. It can cause men-tal problems." Gioberti got a few nods of agreement.

"Was that a question?" asked Dr. Lucca as Gioberti sat down.

"That's good enough," said Regale. "Let me answer that."

"You have the right to answer last this time," said Lucca.

"That's okay," said Regale. "I wanna point out that I have very little formal education myself. I didn't bury my head in a book when I was a kid. I worked on the docks to help support my family. That doesn't mean we're dumb, us guys without college educations. And just because my opponent went to law school doesn't make him smart. I don't care if he was born here. He knows nothing about people and how to make things work in this neighborhood." He stepped away from the podium.

Ray moved forward. "I agree that education itself does not make a man good or wise. But it is a useful tool that many of you, through no fault of your own, have been deprived of. Most of you bettered yourselves despite this handicap. But don't you want your children to have the option of going to the best schools possible? We should have good trade schools for those who want to be auto mechanics or electronics specialists. And those who want to be doctors or lawyers should have the opportunity too."

Ray received warm applause. He was scoring points. The session went on with questions about traffic lights, civil service exams, and the Columbus Day parade. Here Regale showed his advantage as an incumbent by promising to grant specific favors. Then Lucca called for the final question.

John Fiorentini stood up. He was the owner of numerous neigh-borhood buildings and executive secretary of the civil rights league. "I have a question for Mr. Santangelo. You know that Italian-Americans are often depicted as gangsters, or as cowardly or over-sexed. What are your plans for improving this image? And won't your emphasis on dropouts and drug addicts make matters worse?"

Ray cleared his throat. "I agree that we have an unfair image and an unfair press. At the same time, I don't believe in censorship of movies or television. But we can act as a pressure group, as consumers. This can be accomplished with organization and political activism, which I will try to promote."

Ray's hands gripped the lectern. "As for the second part of your question, I can only answer by telling you about a friend of mine. Or should I say a former friend. His name was Joe DeSimone. Maybe some of you remember him. Joe DeSimone was a talented young artist. I can't say that he had Michelangelo's genius, but he might have had. He was never allowed to find out. If he had lived, he might have done more for our image than fifty thousand demonstrations in Columbus Circle. But because we have no adequate counseling or addiction services here, because the people in City Hall don't pay attention to us, Joe DeSimone died at sixteen, a junkie. Talk about cultural heritage, what about our cultural future? We have to preserve our Joe DeSimones, and the only way to do that is to call attention to them, not hide them away. If we let such young men flourish, our image will take care of itself."

The audience was silent. Lucca approached the podium. "Time is up. Thank you, gentlemen. Thank you, everybody."

Don Giacomo came to Ray's side. "You did well, young man."

Regale thrust out his hand. "Not bad, kid. If you want a job with me after I win, come around and we'll talk."

Ray smiled. "Thanks for the offer. But I intend to win."

Marrandino sat stony-faced in his chair. This kid was no pushover. He turned to Petey and Dominic and whispered instructions.

MINNIE's hands shook as she shoveled coffee into the espresso maker. Don Giacomo had told her about Ray's performance last night. She knew that the better her son did, the more trouble he could expect from Marrandino.

The Santangelos were now threatened from the one side by a fanatic of the old Mafia, and from the other by its descendant, the new Mafia. It made Minnie bitter. It wasn't fair.

She put the coffeepot over a blue flame. She told herself Minerva Santangelo would fight back. She would not lose a second son.

She went to the refrigerator for milk. Her hand froze on the door handle. Bruno's body was still inside. That spider Guerra. That *demonio*. He was a faceless symbol of all the cruelties and disappointments that had blemished her life. Could she, like Saint Anthony in the desert, beat the devil?

She took out the milk carton. In a few minutes she was sipping coffee and looking moodily out the window. Banners, lights, and signs for the *festa* were already up. The fruit store across the street made her think of Arturo. It seemed incredible that he might be Marco Guerra and not a jovial fruit vendor, not a mellow companion who enjoyed a taste of wine and a salty story.

As Professore Conti said, the evidence was circumstantial. She savored the word. It evoked her detectiveship. She was no longer just Minerva Santangelo, aging Italian mamma. She was a sleuth.

Minnie trudged over to the sideboard and extracted a hidden package of cigarettes from a drawer. She lit one in her usual clumsy way. She fetched a bottle of anisette from the cupboard and poured a healthy dollop into her coffee.

"Don't move," said a voice. "Just stay right where you are."

She whirled around. The man she saw was Arturo Longo.

"I always knew it, Minootch. You're a secret alcoholic."

She must act calm, she told herself. A forced smile thawed her lips. "Come in, Arturo. Want a drink too?"

"Did I frighten you? I shouldn't sneak up like that. But you shouldn't always forget to lock your door."

The admonition, which could have been innocent advice, seemed like a threat. She tried to look casual. "I didn't expect you."

"Is everything okay?"

"Sure. Why shouldn't it be?"

"I mean this cork business."

Minnie froze. She read twenty sinister meanings into everything he said. Yet his questions could be innocent and natural. "I don't want to involve you, Arturo."

He frowned. "Look, I am your friend." He cast his eyes down. "I

342

had hoped that maybe I was even more than a friend. You are like my own family. I am . . . I am alone in the world."

Minnie felt a twinge of doubt. This was the old Arturo. He couldn't be a killer. With sympathy she said, "You are very kind to want to help. Of course you are like one of the family."

He broke into a wide smile. "Tell me what's troubling you."

She sighed and told him about Bruno. As he listened his tiny brown eyes narrowed. She did not tell him about Conti.

He shook his head in consternation. "Then there must be a connection. Maybe you should go to the police after all."

"No."

"Anyway, I will protect you from anybody who tries anything." He gripped the table edge in a gesture of determination.

Minnie's mind raced. He gave up the police idea quickly enough. Yet somehow she couldn't persuade herself that Arturo was a maniacal killer. "It's comforting to know that."

He glowed. "We'll think of something."

Later Minnie did a lot of thinking. Was Arturo really Guerra? Or was Conti? Or was Guerra neither of them? If he was Arturo, why hadn't he tried something just now or, indeed, during the last years? Perhaps he anticipated a symbolic moment and was toying with the Santangelos sadistically. Perhaps . . . Who can fathom the mind of a murderer? She must investigate.

IT TOOK a long time for her call to get through to Signor Squinzano at the United Nations press office. She had been referred to him by the Italian consulate.

"Conti, Conti," said Squinzano. "I am looking through a directory of journalists and writers. Sorry, no Gaetano Conti. Sure you have the name correct?"

"I am sure. Have you never heard of a writer of that name? A man about sixty, an expert on Sicilian customs?"

"Impossible, signora. I would have heard of him. I used to specialize in Sicilian problems myself."

She frowned. "Thank you. I'm sorry to have troubled you." She placed the phone back in the cradle. Conti had lied to her, had said he was so famous in Italy that he might be recognized by Guerra. He must really think her stupid not to suspect she would check up on him. Clever of him trying to shift suspicion to Arturo. Now what would she do?

The doorbell rang. Minnie left on the chain as she opened the door a crack, and was startled when she saw who was standing there in the dimly lit hallway fidgeting with his hat.

"May I come in?" asked Umberto Marrandino.

THE tense waiters hovered around the table. Umberto scooped up a clam from the half shell and popped it into his mouth. Minnie sipped white wine and felt conspicuous.

"Remember the clams we used to have at Frankie's in the old days?" he asked. "Well, they didn't taste nearly as good as these. Why do people always talk about the good old days? These are the good old days. Cars are faster, men walk on the moon."

He had taken her to Hoboken for seafood, to an old restaurant on the waterfront. "You're not eating," he said, pointing his fork at her plate.

Minnie forced herself to smile, and speared a clam. She was half listening to Marrandino's rambling as she watched Petey Ianucci sullenly sipping beer at the bar. Beside him two burly longshoremen gestured broadly in conversation.

Minnie inspected Bert as he continued talking. His years made a difference. As a young man he had been able to be cruel, but he had also been generous and even tender. Beneath the surface she had sensed a softness, a vulnerability. But no more. Now inside he was like an old alley cat, scarred and wary.

"So," he said as the waiter set a plate of fried fish before him. "It's been a long time, eh?"

Minnie eyed her fillet of sole without appetite and said, trying to sound amiable, "Too long, Umberto. What made you look me up after all these years? Still carrying a torch for me?"

"You were the only woman ever to turn me down."

"That's a pretty good average," she said lightly. From his tone it was clear to Minnie that he wasn't regretful, but his pride still hurt. The thought rankled him that she had preferred a simple carpenter to Umberto Marrandino.

"You know why I looked you up," he said finally.

"Why didn't you come yourself the other day," she said, casting a contemptuous glance in Ianucci's direction, "instead of sending your friends?"

"I should have," he admitted. "But that's over with. I'm sure we can settle our differences."

Minnie looked directly at him. "What differences, Umberto?"

His eyes narrowed. "Don't fence with me, Minerva. Your son is behaving foolishly. But I'm sure you can convince him to meet with me about his political plans. He could have a bright future, that kid, if he would only wait his turn, show some respect for the traditions of the neighborhood."

"You mean he should pledge allegiance to you."

"Not pledge allegiance. Cooperate."

"Young people are different nowadays. Like you said, times have changed," she added mockingly. "And everything is better now."

He seethed, making a visible effort to control himself. "You shouldn't ridicule me, Minnie. You always had this rebellious streak." Umberto was annoyed with himself. In the organization, he ruled with cool authority. On the streets he was treated with respect and deference. But this woman, this nobody, unsettled him.

Minnie sensed his discomfort and grew frightened of angering him. She lowered her eyes. "I'm sorry. Old friends can tease."

He grunted. "Okay," he said grudgingly. They were both conscious of their diplomatic missions.

Minnie fiddled with her fish, affecting nonchalance. "Everybody's talking about the Tedesco murder. Wonder why he was killed."

He shrugged. "Who cares? He was a snake. More wine?"

"The cork was strange, wasn't it?"

"Such things are not for women to think about. Tedesco got what he deserved. Take it from me."

"But why—"

"I don't want to talk about it anymore," he snapped. "It's none of your affair. You always lacked *discretezza*."

If only he knew how much it was her affair. Or did he know?

Umberto snapped his fingers and a waiter rushed over to the table. "Coffee," he ordered, without consulting Minnie. "Bring me some cigars." He waved the waiter away and turned to Minnie. "Did you enjoy the meal?"

"Fine," she said without enthusiasm.

He took two cigars from a box the waiter was proffering like a jeweler holding a selection of fine gems. He lit up. "So you will remind Remo of the traditions of the neighborhood. I will take good care of him."

"I can't do that," she replied evenly.

Umberto clamped down firmly on the cigar. "You can't?"

"I don't mean any disrespect," she said dryly. "He would never follow my advice. He has his own ideas about the neighborhood."

Marrandino touched his breastbone through his shirt. The mole was still inflamed and painful. He cursed this stubborn woman and her do-gooder son.

"You are making it very difficult," he said. "I tried doing this the decent way. But there are other ways."

The menace was not lost on Minnie—and what good would it do to anger him? "I will talk to Remo," she promised. "But I can't guarantee he will listen."

He rubbed lemon peel on the rim of his coffee cup. "We'll see."

Minnie's hand shook as she raised her cup to her lips. There was nothing she could do but play for time. Remo would never give in, and she would not want him to. The Santangelos were not serfs.

"I'll take you home," he said, snuffing out the cigar.

RAY was washing dishes when the Lincoln, glittering with chrome, pulled up in front of the tenement. A light rain was falling, giving an extra iridescence to the big car. He raised his eyebrows when he saw Marrandino get out. Then Marrandino was holding Minnie by her elbow. Ray grabbed for a dish towel. He waited quietly by the door as their footsteps sounded on the stairway. When they reached the landing, he heard her whisper, "I don't know if he's home. In any case, I want to talk to him first."

"Why waste time?" Umberto asked.

"That's right. Why waste time?" Ray said contemptuously, swinging open the door. "You have something to say to me?"

"Just wanted to say hello," Marrandino said amicably.

"The pleasure is all yours," drawled Ray, stepping aside as they entered the apartment. He shot his mother an angry look. "Have a nice evening?"

Minnie wearily took off her raincoat and said, "We had dinner. We know each other from the old days."

"Gonna offer me a seat?" Umberto asked.

"I guess you're going to take one anyway."

"Show respect, young man." He sat down in an armchair, resting his elbows on crocheted doilies. "I just want to have a little chat. I heard your speech the other night. Impressive."

"Thanks."

"Believe it or not, I agree with a lot of the things you said. It's about time we get what's coming to us from the powers that be. You have a good point."

"So you support me."

"A kid with your education and looks could go far around here. If you learn to be patient, I would give you my blessing."

"Thanks all the same."

"Think of me as a consultant. Somebody who knows the people and their problems, commands respect, can get things done for you."

"Pull a few strings," said Ray.

"Nothing wrong with that. It's an old practice in politics."

"Of course, you want nothing in return."

"I have everything I need."

"Virtue is its own reward."

"Right. You could be President someday, the way you understand things."

Minnie had been listening breathlessly, hoping that Remo would say nothing to inflame Marrandino. Still, she was proud of her son's defiance.

"Got any coffee?" Marrandino asked her.

"Sure," she said, rising from her perch on the arm of a chair. Ray gave her a look of extreme disapproval. She sighed and went into the kitchen, watching them from the open door as they conversed, now rather idly. Marrandino's right hand massaged his breastbone.

Minnie brought the coffee in as Marrandino was saying, "I hear you're friendly with my niece Tina. You're a clean-cut kid. She could do worse."

"We're just friends."

Marrandino mused. "I could groom you for the State Senate. Forget about the council. Then you and Tina can get married."

"Got it all figured out, haven't you?"

"What's the matter? You too good for my niece?"

"That isn't the point. Things just aren't that way between us."

Marrandino reddened and said, "Wanna have your fun with no responsibilities, is that it? Lead on an innocent girl and—"

"Innocent?" Ray laughed. "Tina is about as innocent as Myra Breckinridge."

Marrandino shot up from his chair. "You better watch it, kid!"

Ray softened. "Look, I'm sorry if I said anything that sounded demeaning. Innocence isn't valued anymore. Ask Tina."

Minnie was shaking with fear. "Just leave him alone," she said coldly to Marrandino.

"I will. For now. But if he doesn't watch his step, he'll end up like Tedesco." He grabbed his hat and made for the door.

"*Arrivederci,*" Ray said as the door slammed. He turned to his mother. "Sorry I chased away your boy friend."

"He's not my boy friend. I had dinner with him for your sake."

"My sake? I don't need that kind of favor. How often have you seen this guy since my father died? Or did you even wait until he died?"

"God forgive you for talking that way."

"You never talked about his death. Like you felt guilty."

"Is that what you think? Is that what you thought all these years?"

"It was no heart attack. He was killed, wasn't he?"

"I didn't want to tell you. I wanted to spare you."

"What did Marrandino have to do with it?"

"Marrandino? Nothing."

"People say he was angry when you married Papa."

"Your father was killed in Sicily. Years afterward. You don't really think I know who did it?"

In stony silence he went to the closet for his raincoat.

"Where are you going, Remo? I have things to talk to you about."

"I don't want to hear." His hand was on the doorknob.

"But, Remo—"

No use. Minnie watched him from the window as he made his way down the sidewalk. He waved at a figure who emerged from the shadows, and they continued down the street together. At first Minnie could not make out who it was. She was just glad that Remo was not alone, that he had a friend with him.

It was raining harder now, blotting out the two figures. Minnie sighed and turned from the window. Abruptly she realized that the figure had looked like Arturo. Her prime suspect was now Conti, but she couldn't take any chances. She rushed to get her raincoat.

EACH shadow took a nightmare form as Minnie hurled herself down the slick streets, looking for her son. A segment of the pavement ahead was bathed in light from the Sons of Sicily Social Club. There was a chance they had stopped in there.

She entered the club. At the far end of the bar Arturo sipped a drink, alone. He looked surprised to see her, cheeks flushed, hair soaked with rain. "Look who's here. Anything wrong?"

"Where is Remo?"

"I just saw him. He headed for the subway. Is anything wrong?"

She searched Arturo's face for clues to whether he was lying. There were none. "Which subway?"

349

"Uptown IRT. Anything I can do?"

She turned and left.

He called after her. "Wait, Minnie." But she was already heading for the Canal Street station. If Arturo were telling the truth, Remo might still be waiting for a train.

She plunged down the subway stairs and fished in her purse for a token. The machine sucked in the coin and she swiveled through the turnstile. There was no sign of Remo.

A train pulled into the station. She got on, caught her breath, and asked herself where she was going. As the doors clapped shut, she caught a glimpse of a straggling passenger who had just made it into the next car.

She decided to try Tina Corvo's place. She knew that Tina lived somewhere in the Village. At Bleecker Street she got off to check the phone book in the station's booth, but most of its pages had been torn out. Frowning, she looked around, deciding what to do. A passenger at the far end of the platform abruptly buried his face in a newspaper. Minnie didn't notice. She left the station.

In a candy store two blocks away she looked up the address. It was nearby. A vague apprehension swept over her when she reached the street again. She set her features grimly and walked west on Bleecker Street.

Tina's apartment was on the third floor. Minnie stopped wearily on the landing to catch her breath and heard angry voices coming from 3C. She edged closer to the door.

"You couldn't keep your hands off of him, could you? Why couldn't you leave him alone?"

"You don't know what you're talking about, Mrs. Tedesco," Valentina said.

"I know your kind. You filthy—"

"Oh, so your husband had nothing to do with it? How long do you think he chased me with his tongue hanging out?"

"You're lying." Mrs. Tedesco broke into sobs. "Why did you have him killed?"

"You can't come here and talk to me this way," Tina said. "Just get out. I've had enough."

Minnie ducked around a corner in the corridor. In a few seconds she heard the apartment door open, and Mrs. Tedesco's footsteps receded down the stairwell. This new knowledge opened up a whole frontier of speculation. But Minnie was too fearful for her son to sort it out right now. She knocked on Tina's door.

"I have nothing more to say, Mrs. Tedesco. Go home."

"It's not Mrs. Tedesco," Minnie responded.

She heard the jiggle of the peephole. Tina's expression was a mixture of suspicion and curiosity as she swung open the door. "Come in, Mrs. Santangelo."

Tina was dressed in a short Japanese robe, nipped in at her slender waist by a sash. Her legs tapered down to graceful, slim ankles and bare feet, buried in the deep pile carpet. She stepped aside to let Minnie enter. "What can I do for you?"

"I am looking for my son."

"Care to sit down?" Minnie sat on the edge of the couch. "I haven't seen your son for nearly a week."

"Do you know where he might be?"

Tina shrugged. "He doesn't check in with me, signora. *Vuole qualcosa da bere?*"

Minnie declined the offer of a drink. The faultless Italian reminded her that Tina had had some schooling in Italy and had traveled widely there and in Sicily as well.

"Has something happened to Ray?" Tina asked.

"Maybe you can tell me that."

Tina sighed, the memory of her confrontation with Mrs. Tedesco still vivid. "Not another one."

"Couldn't you tell your uncle to leave Remo alone?"

"I could, but he wouldn't listen. I wish your son would stop trying to be the Martin Luther King of Italian-Americans. I'd feel a lot better if he could just unwind, relax."

"He does what he has to do. What good is life if you don't fight for something, believe in something?"

"Oh—it might still be good. In any case, if he wants to be a hero, you'll have to expect some very rough times." Tina sat down in a basket chair.

Minnie had been watching her move easily around the room. She had grace, and Minnie understood her son's attraction to the girl. She thought Tina was a little sad beneath the cool façade.

"What are your feelings about my son?"

Valentina flushed. "What's the difference?"

"Could his friendship with you cause him trouble? Look what happened to Jerry Tedesco."

Tina realized that Minnie had heard her argument with Mrs. Tedesco. "I want you to leave, Mrs. Santangelo. Tedesco is no business of yours. You're asking for trouble."

"I just want to protect my son. If anyone tried to hurt him I would—"

"You would what, Mrs. Santangelo?"

Suddenly, Minnie found herself on an obscure terrain of consciousness. She knew she was capable of murder. "I would kill them."

"I thought you were a good Catholic," Tina said with a touch of mockery. "Murder is a mortal sin, you know."

"A good Catholic walks a tightrope. I believe in the devil. I know I am capable of evil."

Tina had a feeling of disquiet.

"I'll see you to the door," she said.

IN THE subway, Minnie took a seat for the short ride home, hoping that Ray would have returned. She thought about Tina and her possible connection with Tedesco's murder. From her travels in Italy she easily could have learned of the cork killings.

The train pulled into a station. As the doors closed again, she looked up and saw that she was going uptown instead of downtown. She reproached herself for the error and at Fourteenth Street crossed over to the downtown side and waited for the local.

The platform was thronged with a Saturday-night crowd. Passengers paced impatiently. A couple standing near Minnie embraced languorously. As the rumble of an oncoming train grew louder, Minnie found herself, like everyone else, jostling for a spot close to the platform's edge. She felt an elbow in her ribs and someone scuffed the heel of her shoe. She grunted in disapproval.

It all happened in two or three seconds. She had two distinct memories. Briefly she felt a hand in her raincoat pocket. Then there was a sharp shove at the base of her spine. She caught sight of the train filling the mouth of the tunnel as she fell to the tracks.

Her hands, automatically thrown forward for protection, touched the ground first. Knees and right hip crashed hard on the tracks. The bruising pain was blotted out by fear. In the brief moment of horror and panic her senses, like indifferent computers, continued to register impressions—the screams of passengers, the look of terror on the face of the motorman as he tried to slam on the brakes. It was too late.

Chapter 8

It was another shimmering Sunday morning. The clear bells of St. Theresa's summoned the residents of Little Italy to Mass. Louis Monti on Baxter Street paused during his weekly shave to wink at his foamy reflection. Benny Suino on Grand Street cursed and thrust a pillow over his head. Men promenaded in suits or sipped bitter espressos while their wives were in church, praying for health and a winning lottery ticket.

In her apartment on Hester Street, Minnie was praying too. She shifted her body and felt a sharp pain in her hip, but at least she was all in one piece. Minnie's was a prayer of thanks.

She had reacted quickly on the subway tracks, hugging the greasy, littered underground like a long-lost friend. The rumbling monster passed over her. It never even touched her. She had refused an ambulance, brushed herself off, and come home, escorted by a policeman. It wasn't until much later, after she had taken a warm bath and downed three glasses of Marsala, that she remembered the hand thrust into her pocket before she was shoved.

She discovered a cork in her raincoat pocket. He had left his trademark again.

She was shaken but safe. More important, Ray was safely asleep in his own bed. He had apologized when he got home, explaining

353

that he had been tense about the campaign. He was unaware of her ordeal. It was better that way.

The clangor of the church bells rose again. Minnie tried to decide whether she should go to Mass. Surely the threat of being murdered was a legitimate excuse for missing services. But she was safe enough in church, among friends and neighbors. Or was she? She thought of the religious statue that had been used to bash in Tedesco's skull. Did the killer have a religious fetish? Who could tell with a madman? She thought, It must be Conti. He must have followed her and pushed her to the tracks. She shuddered at the thought of how close she had come. Yet she was dimly aware that the whole bizarre episode was like a rite of passage for her. She had faced death and come through. She would beat this fiend and she would do it alone.

She thought with a glimmer of triumph how Guerra must be cursing his luck at this moment. He had tried to kill her and had failed. She had to do something drastic. Fast.

MINNIE rather fancied the pearl-handled Smith and Wesson .38. "The pretty gun in the middle."

The clerk squinted at her, not his usual type of customer. "You have a permit, lady?" She didn't. "You can't just walk in off the street and buy a gun in this city."

Minnie was flustered. The man treated her as if she were buying pornography. She almost walked out, but steeled herself. She would need a weapon to get her adversary to confess. She hoped it would come only to that. "Where can I get a permit?"

"You can't do it just like that," he said, snapping his fingers. "You gotta be investigated and all. It takes time."

She looked dejected.

"What do you want a firearm for? Somebody bothering you?"

"Not exactly." She improvised. "The city is so dangerous. Muggers, burglars, rapists. A woman my age, all alone . . ."

"Yeah. I know what you mean."

She looked conspiratorially from side to side. "Think you could stretch the rules a little?"

"Nothing doing," he said. "I'm not risking my license." She started out. He beckoned her back. "Why not buy a rifle?"

"I wouldn't need a permit?"

"In Yonkers you could even buy a howitzer without one."

"Okay. I'll get one of those, if it doesn't cost too much."

He laughed. "A howitzer's a cannon. I was exaggerating. Take this." He handed her a business card. "My cousin has a place in Yonkers. Out of the city you don't need a permit for a long gun."

She brightened and asked him for directions to Yonkers.

MINNIE unwrapped the brown paper package and laid the weapon on the kitchen table. The man in the store had sold her pellets and shown her how to load and shoot. She should not aim, but point it down at the ground. It would kick up, he said. Her shoulder hurt just thinking about it.

Experimentally she hefted the weapon and looked down the long barrel. With a twinge of guilty excitement she placed her finger on the trigger.

"Don't worry about a thing," he had told her. "Get a firm grip, point it a little downward, and squeeze the trigger. Don't jerk it. Just squeeze it firmly. Like squeezing your husband's hand on a roller-coaster ride."

Squee-eeze it. She was beginning to feel more confident.

She walked into the living room and propped the shotgun against an armchair. She sighed and sank into the chair.

Hours later she was wakened by the sound of ringing. In a fuzzy state she stumbled to the phone and picked up the receiver. It was Conti. Her eyes caught sight of the shotgun, still propped up against the armchair. She had been waiting for his call.

THEY bought hot dogs and sat on a bench, eating silently, gazing at the old sailing ships anchored in the South Street Seaport. The East River was veiled in mist, like a mourner. Sea gulls cawed, and somewhere a boat blew its siren.

She bit into her frankfurter, churning inside but keeping her outward composure. She had told him of her conversation with

Tina and the plunge to the subway tracks. Not to tell him would have tipped him off that she knew who he was. She studied him— the powdered neck, weak chin, thin sensuous mouth, curved nose, ferrety eyes, dyed hair—the profile of a killer.

It was Tuesday, the day after she had bought the shotgun. This meeting was supposed to be a strategy session, to share information they had gathered about Guerra, to plan the next course of action. But Minnie was plotting her own strategy.

He said, "You could have been killed and yet you seem almost revitalized. Perhaps you thrive on adventure, Minerva. On danger."

"No. I don't enjoy it one bit."

He raised his eyebrows skeptically. "It's not enjoyment exactly. But the contest, the struggle. It's vivifying, isn't it?"

She looked at him. He did actually take pleasure in all this. "I just want to catch Guerra. To protect my son."

"Don't worry. We'll get him. I've been investigating."

She thought, I'll bet. "We have many other suspects now," she said. "Besides Guerra."

"Yes?"

"There's Valentina. She could have had something to do with the Tedesco killing. She may have found out about the cork tradition in Italy. And she had an affair with Tedesco."

"It's worth exploring. But I still think it's Guerra."

"There's Bert Marrandino himself," she added, wanting him to think she was still searching for the killer. "Marrandino had reason to kill Stefano. I jilted him for my husband. And he had reason to kill Tedesco too. For fooling around with his niece."

"I still think it's Guerra."

"And you think Arturo is Guerra?"

"Possibly. I have another bit of information. It's quite interesting. When Teodoro Guerra, Marco's father, chose a bride, he picked a dark-eyed beauty with a good dowry. The young girl's name was Beatrice Longo."

Who did he think he was fooling? But Minnie's face registered surprise. "No!"

"Yes."

"Then that settles it." Make him believe she believed him.

"Let's not be hasty. Longo is a common name."

"But everything else fits."

"We have no real evidence. But whether Guerra is Longo or not, I think he will strike again soon. If we don't stop him."

"What should we do?"

"Tomorrow the *festa* begins. And Thursday's the *processione*. Something makes me think he will choose the religious celebration, with the crowds and confusion, to strike again. I will keep a close eye on Longo for the next few days."

And who will keep a close eye on you? Minnie thought. She said, "I have a plan. I will ask Arturo to come to my place Thursday night to watch the *festa* from my window. You can come earlier and hide somewhere. I will confront Arturo with what I know about Guerra. I will insult the Guerra family. It may enrage him enough to make him give himself away. Perhaps he will even attack me. Then you can come out of hiding and—"

"Good idea. We'll do it."

Minnie sighed with relief. Her real plan was to get Conti up to the apartment and safely away from Remo. Once there, she would train the shotgun on him and make him confess to everything, on paper. Then she would call the police. It could work.

A gull snatched up a crumb of hot-dog bun floating on the fetid surface of the water. Minnie shivered. It wouldn't be long now.

They said good-by.

GAETANO Conti buried his chin in the upturned collar of his raincoat and walked through the gathering fog. He entered a building on Mott Street just short of the corner of Hester and climbed five flights to an apartment situated above a warehouse.

His home away from home, a soulless place with washstand, hot plate, dingy walls. He threw his raincoat on the bed and walked over to the window. The field glasses lay on the sill.

He focused them on Minnie's apartment. As usual, she was bustling around the kitchen, barely visible through the mist. He idly watched her for a while.

He went to the phone and dialed. "It's me," he said. "I've got a list. There are several possibilities, but I've got a hunch about one in particular. It'll all be in my report."

He hung up the phone and, yawning languidly, went to the desk. He took up a pen and a sheet of correspondence paper, and headed a letter, "Ms. Lenore Conti, Worthington School, Cambridge, Massachusetts."

He bit his thumbnail, wondering how to begin. He set the pen to paper. "So you finally decided to work for a living." He hoped she would understand the gently mocking tone. "I was beginning to think you took after your great-grandmother on my mother's side. She lived in the Piedmont. . . ."

As he wrote, the door of a closet behind him opened soundlessly. At first just a crack. Then an inch more.

"Actually, I'm glad you got the chance to see a bit of the world. We had knapsacks in my day too, and I remember a trip I made to eastern Europe. . . . Work continues to keep your mother and me apart. . . ."

The door was now open enough to allow a man to slip out.

"You can see that I'm learning. Notice I used 'Ms.' . . ."

The man gripped the blade.

"I miss you so much. . . ."

The knife thrust entered Conti's back between the shoulder blades, making an odd, dull sound. The victim groaned, swiveled around, and faced his attacker, who punched him hard in the face. Conti fell to his knees. The man got the victim in a headlock and pulled the knife free. Conti struggled weakly. The man drove the blade into his chest. He was dead in a second.

Breathing shallowly, the man stood up. He went to the washstand and cleaned the blood from the knife. Then he washed his hands and face and wiped them on a towel.

Marco Guerra sat down on the bed and smiled in satisfaction. He dug into his pocket and drew out the locket. It was cold in the palm of his hand. He flicked it open and gazed at the oval photos. The visages were stern, but the descendant read approval on the ancient, yellowing faces.

THE SHOTGUN WAS HIDDEN in the broom closet behind the Hoover upright. Minnie went over the plan in her mind. When Conti arrived on Thursday night, she would tell him that Arturo was not due for an hour. She would leave him in the living room and come into the kitchen on the pretext of fixing coffee. She would fetch the shotgun and surprise him. It couldn't be simpler.

She boiled water for a late supper of spaghetti. Ray sat at the kitchen table, scribbling notes for a speech. The candidates would talk from the bandstand on the night of the *processione*. Wearily he put his pen down. "Hey," he asked Minnie. "Where's Bruno?"

"You just noticed?"

"I've been busy. What happened to him?"

"Dead."

"Too bad. How'd it happen?"

She shrugged. "Birds die. They get fed up with life, I guess. How's the speech coming?"

Ray walked to the window. The fog was lifting. "Not bad, I guess. Have to keep it short."

She studied her son. "Promise me you'll be careful. Don't go anywhere alone these next few days."

"Marrandino can't do anything to me. It's too risky for them to harm a political candidate."

"Just don't go anywhere alone. As a favor to me."

He smiled indulgently. "Okay, okay. I'm never alone anyhow." He peered at her. "You don't look so well. Anything the matter?"

She frowned and took a container of leftover tomato sauce from the refrigerator. "It's nothing."

"It's the strain of my campaign, isn't it?" He laid his arm on her shoulder. "I know, I don't give you enough attention. Too busy being a savior or something."

She held a handful of spaghetti over the boiling water and looked at him. His eyes were red, his hair tousled. "I'm okay. You been getting enough sleep?"

"Some."

"But not enough." She shook her head and dropped in the spaghetti, gently separating the strands with a spoon. "It'll be ready in no time. I've already fixed a salad. Why don't you take a break?"

"Good idea. I'll watch the late news."

She dumped the sauce into another pan and put it on to heat. "Turn the TV up so I can hear from the kitchen."

She stirred the sauce, thinking of happier times. She hadn't had a chance really to enjoy having Remo home again. He was watching television, she fixing a late supper. She savored the moment of domesticity like a rare truffle.

Dousing the salad with dressing, she daydreamed about how it would be in a few weeks when the election was settled one way or the other and, more important, when Guerra was caught and she could relax. Would she ever see the day?

The reverie was interrupted by the voice of the TV announcer. "On Mott Street tonight there was another bizarre cork killing."

Minnie stopped her work in stunned silence. "The victim was found with a cork in his mouth, recalling the case of store owner Jerry Tedesco, who was bludgeoned to death two weeks ago."

Ray called from the living room. "Hear this, Mamma?"

"Police said that the latest victim was Gaetano Conti, a federal agent who was working on the case. The victim was found in an apartment he was using in the neighborhood. . . ."

Minnie gripped the sideboard for support. It shook and something crashed to the floor.

"What the hell was that?" Ray shouted from the living room.

The statue of Saint Anthony lay shattered to pieces on the imitation tiles.

Chapter 9

LITTLE Italy was decked out like a *grande dame*. Lampposts and trash receptacles were painted the green, white, and red of the Italian tricolor; multicolored lights arcaded the streets; banners of religious societies stretched between tenements; music blared from loudspeakers. The *festa* had begun.

Celebration meant food. The streets were lined with tables, booths, and vans with side openings. Pizzas, sausage and pepper heroes, clams, watermelons, hanging garlands of nuts and candy, Italian ices, frankfurters, even blintzes. Lots of food.

Celebration meant games of chance. Break a balloon with a dart and win a stuffed Snoopy. Throw a dime in a dish and win a parakeet. Pick a number and win a coffee urn, or whiskey.

Celebration meant noise. Screams from the Ferris wheel in the parking lot. Hippies hawking costume jewelry. Dogs barking. Bands playing. Mothers shouting at their children.

Don Giacomo sat by the window in Minnie's apartment, gazing at the scene with distaste. "There must be a Protestant somewhere on my family tree. It all seems so commercial and hedonistic."

Minnie smiled tolerantly. "I don't think Saint Anthony minds if people profit a little from his feast day." She added quickly, "Of course, you know best in these matters."

"You're right," he conceded. "Only puritans think that fun and religion don't mix. I wouldn't turn down a cup of coffee."

She sprang to her feet. "Where are my manners?"

"Don't worry about your manners. This *is* a business call."

She flushed, not used to priests making ironic references to their duties. As she prepared the coffee, he asked, "And Remo? How is he doing?"

"Okay. He wrote his speech for tomorrow night. Will you help him with it?"

"Of course. Not that he needs me that much. He has a way with a speech. But I can go over it with him." He peered at Minnie. Something seemed to be troubling her. "You don't seem well." He paused. "Do you want to talk about it?"

She sat down, slumping her shoulders. "Is this a confessional?"

"Talk to me not as a priest, but as a friend."

"Can you separate the two?"

He smiled. Without answering, he said, "I know that you are worried about something. Some struggle with your conscience."

"It's hard to know what to do sometimes. But I have done nothing wrong, Don Giacomo."

"One can sin in thought as well as in deed."

"Are thoughts of vengeance always sinful?"

361

He shrugged. "I am a poor theologian, especially in the abstract. Why don't you just tell me what's bothering you?"

She was tempted. But why involve anyone else in this mess? "I must work it out for myself. I will fetch the statue."

As she went into the other room, Minnie stole a glance at herself in the hall mirror. She did look haggard. The news of Conti's death last night had left her distraught. She thought of Arturo. She must come up with another plan.

She took the new statue out of the bedroom closet for Don Giacomo to bless. She had gone uptown with Ray that morning, and they had bought it in a shop near St. Patrick's Cathedral. When the clerk showed it to her, she had said, "It looks different somehow. He looks Irish or something."

Ray said to the clerk, "Got a Saint Anthony who looks more Italian?"

The clerk bared his teeth in a sarcastic smile. "Perhaps one dressed in an undershirt?"

"A comedian, huh?"

"Never mind," said Minnie. "I'll take this one."

"No." Ray fixed his eyes on the clerk. "It looks too Irish to me."

"Now that I look at it again," Minnie replied, trying to avoid an argument, "it looks Italian. Just like a cousin I remember. I'll have it blessed at St. Theresa's."

"The statue," the clerk said with hauteur, "has already been blessed by the cardinal."

"Sure," Ray sneered. "In an assembly line."

"I think I'll have it blessed again," Minnie said softly.

"By an *Italian* priest," said Ray.

"All the same to me." The clerk shrugged. "Shall I wrap it up?"

"No." Ray leaned his elbows on the counter. "We'll eat it here."

Chuckling now at the recollection, Minnie went back into the kitchen. She said to Don Giacomo, "The man said it was already blessed by the cardinal. But I would feel better if you do it."

"It can't hurt," he said. She handed him the statue. He raised his hand and sketched a blessing, murmuring the prayers. The sun from the window glinted off the gold ring on his finger.

When she had the statue back in her hands, she beamed and said, "He's my favorite saint."

He smiled. "He's a fine saint. But I've always had a fondness for the martyrs. Saint Stephen, who was stoned to death for his faith. Saint Damien working with the lepers. They seem more in tune with the world of suffering that we know."

"Yes," she said soberly.

"But may your saints, Mrs. Santangelo, always carry lilies in their arms and have sparrows perched on their shoulders."

She poured coffee. "Saint Anthony is not a sissy saint."

"Indeed he isn't. A handy friend to have around, especially with Satan still in business."

"Yes. He's a good fighter." She looked directly at Don Giacomo. "He's a good ally for someone who is fighting against something, wouldn't you say?"

"Let's say he has had some experience in such matters. Are you fighting with the devil, signora?"

"In some ways, I think so."

"In some ways, we all are. He's a formidable enemy."

After Don Giacomo left, Minnie chewed a fingernail and mulled over their conversation. The devil was a formidable enemy. It seemed to her that she was pitted against a whole company of demons—Guerra, Marrandino, her own thirst for revenge.

She gazed at the statue of Saint Anthony. There was no reassurance there. Instead, she had a funny feeling. She supposed a new statue took getting used to. But she couldn't shake the feeling that some useful secret was hidden behind the plaster smile.

On the following evening Don Giacomo was in his bedroom getting dressed to go out. He and Ray planned to meet in the sacristy of the church to run through the speech. With slow movements he put on a clean undershirt, trousers, and a freshly laundered cassock. He looked into the mirror and straightened the Roman collar. The act caused him to smile. His piety was askew.

The sounds of celebration outside grew. Despite the noise, he felt serene as in a cloister. The papery face, wrinkled and wattled like parchment, looked peaceful, reposed. He had good feelings about tonight. Very good feelings.

He walked over to the window. The *processione* had begun. Good. It was time. He thought, I'm coming, my son. Be patient. Whistling, he went out the door. He whistled a requiem.

La processione, highlight of the *festa*, began on Elizabeth Street in front of St. Theresa's. People pressed against police barriers to watch the event, a mixture of pageantry and piety, like a nun in stage makeup. The normally boisterous streets were hushed, echoing with the hypnotic beat of drums and the chiming of bells.

A squad car led the way. First came children dressed in Communion outfits. Their hands were joined in an attitude of prayer, and from the corners of their eyes they searched out their parents on the sidelines. Next came brown-robed Franciscans from a neighboring church; two altar boys in white surplices and red cassocks holding up a large crucifix; acolytes with lighted candles; drummers and buglers; young boys in velvet Renaissance costumes.

A blue station wagon pulled a float upon which rode Saint Anthony, a mannequin in a brown robe. Cradled in the statue's left arm was a Christ Child doll in white dress; in his right arm were white lilies. From time to time, onlookers detached themselves from the crowd, pinned money on the statue, and, after swift genuflection and the sign of the cross, melted back into the throng.

Now the neighborhood people came: old couples locking arms and mumbling beads, housewives carrying lilies, and men with blessed loaves of bread. Bringing up the rear was Bishop Fauci, his golden miter gleaming in the fading sun. He held aloft the monstrance containing the holy wafer.

The parade turned the corner at Grand Street, passing the Trevi Fountain restaurant. Piero Ciardi, the owner, clucked his tongue. "They march while people are getting killed."

"Eh," said his nephew Richie. "The procession has to go on."

Ciardi shook his head. "I hope my kid gets home okay."

The procession approached Mulberry Street and the Mare Azzuro bar, where Vince Delaney, an off-duty plainclothesman, drank his rye and remarked, "The neighborhood is uptight. Never experienced anything like it."

"How's the investigation coming?" asked his drinking buddy.

Delaney shrugged. "We have men all around. I'm not in on it."

"They expect something?"

"I think so." He drained his glass.

The participants in the procession began to sing: *"O Saint Anthony, pray for me."* Among them, her nasal voice raised in supplication, was Minnie. No matter what her troubles, she never would have missed the procession in honor of her favorite saint.

As they turned the corner at Baxter Street, Minnie caught her breath at the sight of two familiar figures. Petey Ianucci, rocking on his heels, was chatting with Dominic, sulkily propped up against a lamppost. She shaded her face with her hand. The sight of the two hoods rekindled her fears for Remo.

She started as a hand touched her shoulder. "Arturo!" she exclaimed, frightened, but keeping her composure.

He smiled at her. Or was it a leer? "I never thought you would march in the procession without me." He grabbed her hand. It was clammy with fear, but he didn't seem to notice.

A knot was tightening in her throat. *O Saint Anthony, pray for me.* She looked at the saint floating down the street like the ornamental prow of a ship. Her thoughts raced. Arturo wouldn't try anything with all these people around, would he? But if he were insane? Another song coursed through her mind, *Saint Anthony, Saint Anthony, the enemy of the devil.* She glanced sideways at Arturo. He was looking straight ahead, singing the hymn.

The sun dipped below the tenements, and the trellises of lights were turned on, casting an eerie glow over Arturo's beaverlike features. She thought, At least he's here and Remo is safe.

She prayed to the image that glided tiltingly down the street. If only you could talk, she said to herself, trying to fathom his smile. I feel you have something to tell me.

The drums beat in her ears. Arturo whispered, "What do you think about that federal policeman getting killed?"

Her eyes flashed at him. She was sure he was taunting her. She wrenched her hand free and ran, losing him in the crowd of worshippers, but she remained in the procession.

Catching her breath, she thought, That was a mistake. Now he would suspect that she knew. But she could not stand his leer, the taunting undertone in everything he said. Yet he had looked genuinely puzzled when she broke away from him.

She continued to sing: *"O Saint Anthony . . ."* Her knees were weak, but the fear was slowly ebbing. Images tumbled through her consciousness. She again gazed at the statue. She was in her kitchen and Don Giacomo was raising his hand in blessing. Blessing. Blessing. . . . Then it came to her. A blessing in disguise.

Minnie shuddered with pleasure at the tangible result of her faith. Saint Anthony had answered her. Maybe it was just a coincidence that she remembered what had been bothering her just at the time that she was praying to her patron saint. But the clue was related to the saint in a direct way as well. She was convinced that she had experienced spiritual intervention.

She had to leave the procession. But before she separated from the crowd she raised her voice, chanting above everyone else, asking her saint's protection.

THE whistle of the calliope could be heard dimly in Concetta DiPalma's kitchen. She thrust her beak out the open window and muttered, "Those pagan noises make life impossible. Sleep, like everything else, comes hard at my age." She sighed. "Ah, well. I'll soon get more than enough sleep. The deepest sleep."

The old woman dragged her stiff body over to the rocking chair. "Now what are you so excited about?"

"I just want to ask you some questions," said Minnie Santangelo, who sat nervously in a corner chair.

Concetta settled back, blinking her sightless eyes. "Ask away. I don't know much about anything anymore. But ask away."

"I am going to ask you to search your memory."

Concetta grinned with satisfaction. "Ah, yes. A memory which goes back almost ninety years can be valuable. It's the only thing I have left." With her gnarled hands she sketched a gesture of mod est acquiescence. "You are so agitated. This has something to do with the *cosche*, doesn't it?"

"Indirectly. I want to ask you about your brother. What was Giacomo like in the old country? As a child."

The old woman wheezed. "We were almost strangers. He was only three when I left Italy. And he is the son of my father's second wife. I only began to know him when he came here four years ago." An electric organ from the bandstand outside all but drowned out her feeble voice. "Ah," she lamented, pressing her hands to her ears. "If only I were made deaf instead of blind."

A disturbing thought struck Minnie. She continued. "Then you have never even seen Don Giacomo as an adult."

The old woman cackled. "I have never seen anyone at all for a long time. Why are you so interested in him?" She felt along a side table for a cup of *camomilla*, and guided the brew to her lips.

"There is a point to this questioning, although I myself don't quite know yet what it all means. Is your brother left-handed?"

Concetta DiPalma looked puzzled. "Left-handed?"

"Please. Try to think."

"I don't really remember. But he must have been right-handed. It was considered disgraceful in the old days to be left-handed. Why don't you ask him yourself?"

Minnie's heart was beating like a runaway metronome. Don Giacomo had used his left hand to bless the statue. She remembered the sun glinting off the gold ring which she was certain he wore on his left ring finger.

Even left-handed priests are trained to use the right hand in ritual. It becomes second nature to them. Minnie hastily put down her cup. "Where did they go?" she asked, rising.

"Who?"

"Remo and Don Giacomo, of course," she said impatiently. "*Where did they go?*" she implored.

"I believe to the church. To go over the speech in privacy."

"I must get there quickly." Minnie headed for the door.

Concetta seemed not to hear. "He was a beautiful boy, I remember that much." Her voice had the musing tone of far-off recollection. "Auburn ringlets, striking blue eyes, like an angel."

Minnie stiffened with fear. There was now no doubt; the eyes of the man she knew as Don Giacomo were copper brown.

She clambered down the stairway. Why did they have to live on the fourth floor? Every second was precious.

Minnie kept telling herself that it wasn't possible, but she knew that it was. It made her feel sick to her stomach. Her insane compulsion to solve this affair alone had made a mess of everything. If anything happened to Remo . . .

She bounded down to the second-floor landing, gasping. The light bulb on the stairwell leading to the first floor had burned out. She plunged into the darkness down the last flight.

Her hands were groping for the doorknob when the blow fell. It landed hard on her left ear, making her head ring with pain and her teeth clamp together. She fell to her knees, tearing nylons and skinning flesh. She seemed to be falling down a children's slide. She felt giddy. Then she felt nothing.

RAY Santangelo glanced uneasily around the sacristy of St. Theresa's. "Haven't been in this place since I was an altar boy. Sure we won't be in the way?"

Don Giacomo sat in a Gothic-style chair with a high back and a purple cushion. "There will be no services until tomorrow. We will be disturbing no one and no one will be disturbing us."

The smell of incense hung in the air. "Still, seems a funny place to edit a speech." Ray ran his hand through his thick wavy hair.

"But I guess we better get to it. I'm due on the speaker's platform in a little more than an hour." He handed four sheets of paper to the priest. "Why don't you just read this through first?"

"Good." They both fell silent as Don Giacomo's eyes flickered from line to line. As he read he thought, Slowly now. There is no hurry, no hurry at all. Savor the moment.

When he finished he said, "You have a way with words."

"It's short, at least. How do you think it will go over?"

"It's clear, reasonable. But it isn't emotional enough."

"I want to appeal to reason. To better instincts."

"You don't condemn the powerful enough, threaten the Establishment with reprisal."

"That's rabble-rousing."

"Words don't have to lead to violent behavior, but the people in this community have to be convinced that you know how to impress the outside world with flaming rhetoric."

"Just sound good, look good, while the problems fester. I am trying to change that."

"Nothing changes in the end."

Ray frowned. Priest or no priest, he didn't think he liked Don Giacomo's code of morality. "Yes, I know. And you think the people are like a herd of bison."

"If the leader runs off a cliff, they will follow. So the leader must be strong and show them the way to survive."

"A patriarch, right? I don't buy this benevolent dictator mentality." Ray wore a sneer of displeasure.

"These people are used to nothing else. They want nothing else. They come from villages where they were told what to do."

"Baloney," Ray said, choosing a word he could utter in church. "They have a healthy streak of rebellion in their tradition too. When leaders exploited them, they fought back. They fought French interventionists and the Papal States. They fought Normans, Saracens, Greeks. This is the spirit I want to appeal to."

"A modern Garibaldi, eh?"

"You bet your life. Garibaldi went to Brazil and Uruguay to fight in civil wars. But he came home eventually. So did I. Italians do not quit. Every one of them I know has a fierce sense of independence and doesn't want anybody to tell him what to do. Don Giacomo, that's what's known as freedom."

"License, not freedom."

Ray's face flushed with anger. "How can you, a priest, talk so cynically?"

Don Giacomo rose and smiled condescendingly. "We're human."

"You're educated. I thought you were enlightened as well."

"By my standards, I am." A bitter tone crept into his voice. "But I'm not as clever as the Santangelos. Such a noble family."

Ray didn't understand why the discussion was taking this turn. There was so much grievance in the old priest's tone.

Don Giacomo continued. "My father and grandfather were leaders of men. They commanded respect, played upon fear."

Ray grimaced. He asked, "Was your family in politics?"

"In a way, they were."

Ray felt queasy. Something was very wrong with the mood of this meeting. "You don't have any specific suggestions?"

"About what?"

"The speech, of course."

"No."

Ray was beginning to suspect that the man was unbalanced, perhaps senile. "I'd better leave."

"No. No, don't." Don Giacomo grabbed Ray's forearm roughly. His grip was stronger than Ray would have expected. "Forgive me. I enjoy being disputatious. It stimulates the brain. I was merely playing the devil's advocate."

Ray relaxed. "So that's it. You had me going for a while."

"It's actually a fine speech. Brilliant." Don Giacomo smiled. "Now I think we should pray. For the success of the campaign."

"I am not very religious, you know." Ray regretted the apologetic tone that crept into his voice.

"But I am. Humor me." With a swirl of the cassock he swept out of the sacristy. Ray followed in his wake. He noticed that Don Giacomo seemed taller than usual, showed more certainty in his stride. The priest appeared gripped by excitement, like someone on the brink of a highly pleasurable experience. Perhaps he luxuriated in prayer.

The two men paused to genuflect at the main altar. At the far side altar, with its statue of Saint Theresa, Don Giacomo motioned Ray to a cushioned kneeler. Coughing uneasily, Ray knelt.

He looked around. The empty church was shrouded in darkness. Every rustle of sound was amplified, bouncing off the stone pillars. The monstrance was covered in garish brocade. Candles and vases of gladioli were placed everywhere. He tried to pray.

Don Giacomo stood slightly behind and to the right of Ray, breathing audibly. Ray turned to look at him and saw that his eyes were shut tightly, presumably in silent prayer. Ray coughed again and said, "I'm ready."

"Have you forgotten how to pray?"

Ray shifted the weight on his knees, recalling how uncomfortable he had always felt on kneelers as a boy, how he furtively used to rest his bottom on the pew ledge to relieve the discomfort. "Yes," he said. "I think I have forgotten."

"Turn and face the altar. Concentrate," the priest rasped. "Ask God's forgiveness for your sins."

"But—"

"Please. Do as I say."

Ray felt that there was a special significance to this occasion, at least for Don Giacomo. So he tried again to pray.

There was something strange, unidentifiable but palpable, in the air. The back of his neck began to tingle. He whirled around in time to catch sight of the flashing blade.

MINNIE's eyelids fluttered open and she focused on a blank wall with cracked plaster. Oh, how she hurt! There was an odd sound. She looked around cautiously. Dominic and Petey were playing darts.

Dominic chortled as his dart hit center black. Petey scowled, jowls sagging. "Damn," he hissed.

Dominic sneered. "Not too good at this game, are you, Petey?" The darts clattered as he dropped them on a table.

Minnie had taken in the scene and figured out what kind of spot she was in. She must not show any signs of consciousness until she had decided what action to take.

She was lying on her stomach on a musty sofa in a dimly lit cellar, from the smell of it. Her hands were tied behind her back. She could hardly see anything but the cushion against which her nose and mouth were pressed. She moved her head an inch.

She saw that Petey had sunk into a tattered armchair and was sucking on a lemon ice. Dominic was standing moodily near the table. The opposite wall was lined with shelves stocked with cans of olive oil. She remembered that Marrandino imported pasta, oil, and cheeses in one of his quasi-legitimate enterprises.

Minnie lay wondering why they had captured her. She concluded that they hoped to persuade Ray to stop speaking against Umberto. They knew that if they threatened Ray directly, he would react with moral indignation and ignore them.

Nothing mattered now but saving Remo from Guerra. She moved her head another inch. Her captors didn't seem much concerned with the possibility of her getting away. It wasn't what they expected from a middle-aged mamma. So Minnie reckoned—small consolation—that she at least had surprise on her side.

She surveyed the scene. The sofa was about fifteen feet from a door that was double-bolted from the inside. The only other furniture in the room was two chairs and the table.

Petey tore open a bag of potato chips. The crunching in his mouth came closer to Minnie. Through half-closed eyes she caught a glimpse of him leaning over her.

"Still out like a light." He shook his head in disapproval. "You always beat them up too much, Dominic, to get your kicks. I feel bad about it. You know, she reminds me of my mother."

Dominic moved to the couch. "I'll stick a gag in her mouth."

Petey waved him away. "Let her scream. No one can hear her from down here. Let's play cards." He shambled over to the table, sat down, and began to shuffle a deck of cards. Dominic dropped lazily into the chair opposite the fat man and shoved the darts to one side. One of them toppled off the table, rolled across the floor, and came to rest about two feet from the sofa. To Minnie, its progress across the stone floor sounded like thunder. But her captors didn't seem to hear a thing.

Her mind raced. Could she use the dart to cut the rope? It was time to act. She groaned softly and rolled off the couch, hitting the floor with a hollow thud. Groaning again, she rolled over onto her back. She felt the dart pressed against her left buttock.

"What's she up to?" Dominic was on his feet.

"Take it easy," Petey said, keeping his chair. "She just fell. She's probably all shook-up. Doesn't even know where she is."

Her plan was working. She shifted her weight until she clasped the dart with both hands, continuing to hide it from view.

Dominic left the table and hovered over Minnie, eyeing her suspiciously. Petey labored to his feet, breathing heavily.

"Okay, Mamma. You're not badly hurt. Don't try anything funny and we'll get along dandy. Help her up, Dominic."

Dominic lifted her roughly by the biceps and shoved her into a sitting position on the sofa.

Petey walked over and aimed a masklike smile at Minnie. "I warned you to play along with us, didn't I?"

She whined, "I hurt all over. I've done nothing. Let me go."

"In due time. Just before your son goes up to make his little speech tonight, he'll get a note explaining the whole thing. Then maybe he'll lose his voice or something. Know what I mean?"

Minnie groaned again to give herself time to think. The dart was pressed against the rope around her wrists. She would have to pluck at the weave with the point. To keep her shoulders from bobbing, she pressed them against the back of the sofa. It wasn't working well. Her shoulders were moving perceptibly.

Dominic squinted in suspicion. Minnie sobbed, and with each sob her shoulders shook. She plucked a few strings loose.

"Ah, quit bawling," Petey said disgustedly.

Minnie's sobs grew more intense. A slap stung her cheek. "He said to quit crying," Dominic rasped, his eyes shining.

"Cut that out. Mr. Marrandino said not to hurt her unnecessarily."

Minnie kept sobbing and plucking away, but she was getting

nowhere fast. The rope was too thick. She had to think of another way.

Petey's face grew softer. "Go ahead and cry," he told Minnie. "It's good for you." Then he turned to Dominic. "Let's have another hand."

As the card game continued, Minnie maneuvered the dart near the knot, hoping to wedge it in and loosen it. Her fingers were growing numb. After four tries, she still couldn't get the dart wedged in properly. A bead of perspiration trickled over her eyebrow.

She was near despair. She held the dart in her left hand while massaging the fingers of her right hand with her thumb to bring the circulation back. Then she switched the dart over to the right-hand fingers and began to try again.

"Gin," announced Dominic.

"Damn," said Petey. "My deal this time."

Minnie shut her eyes with concentration. She pointed the dart up toward the knot and jabbed at the loops. This time it slipped in between. She sighed in relief and massaged her fingers again. Then she gripped the shaft of the dart with both hands and focused all the will and strength of fifty-four years into those ten fingers. Nothing.

She relaxed, caught her breath, shut her eyes tightly, and pressed hard against a loop. It moved slightly.

Dominic flicked off another card.

"I've been waiting for that one," Petey said, chuckling.

"Yeah?" said Dominic. "Gin."

The thickest portion of the dart was now between the knot loops. Minnie continued tugging, and with each tug the knot became a little looser. Finally it gave.

She slipped the rope down over her fingers, taking care not to move her arms noticeably.

Minnie plotted furiously. A dart was not much of a weapon against two armed men. If only there were just one armed man.

"I'm hungry," she announced feebly.

"Shut up!" Dominic shouted.

"Keep quiet, Dominic. She probably hasn't had anything to eat for

374

hours." Petey moved to his feet. "Could use a bite myself. You hold the fort while I go over to the grocery store." He made for the door. "Be back right away," he said, shutting it behind him.

Minnie hoped that Dominic would neglect to bolt it again. Come on, Saint Anthony, stick with me just a little longer, she thought.

Dominic removed his jacket and hung it over a chair. No shoulder holster. Minnie scanned the room. On a coat hook in the far corner was Dominic's gun in a shiny black holster.

He started playing solitaire, nonchalantly turning over the cards with his right hand while drumming the table with his left.

She hadn't much time. Insecurity whispered to her: It was useless. What match was she for a strong young man? *Sebbene che siamo donne.* Even though we are women. Minnie clutched the dart and rushed the table.

She didn't see Dominic's doelike eyes widen in astonishment a split second before they were shut tightly in pain. She didn't see anything but the drumming hand, clumps of silky hair between the knuckles. She concentrated all her energy, psychic and physical, on plunging the dart through the back of the hand and impaling it to the table.

Dominic let out an animal scream.

She didn't look back, but threw herself at the door. Dominic was bellowing with anger and with the agony of separating his hand from the table as Minnie slammed the door behind her. She bounded up a flight of stairs and, panting, looked around. She was in an alley. At the end of it, streetlights shone, and the muffled sounds of the *festa* rose to greet her. She knocked over a trash can, made for the lights, and rushed through the crowds, gasping. She should have felt revulsion for the act she had just committed, the most violent in her life.

Instead, she felt drunk with triumph.

THE knife pierced Ray's skin below the left shoulder, plunged in deeply, and was withdrawn viciously. Blood gushed forth and was blotted up near the breast pocket of his blue suit.

Guerra, his face contorted, was raising his arm, ready for the second strike. Ray tumbled clear. The blade shredded the crimson carpet of the altar steps.

Ray struggled to his knees, clutching the wound. Guerra whirled around, poised for another lunge, his heavy breathing echoing eerily in the empty church. Ray scrambled to his feet, reeling backward, knocking over a vase of gladioli. With an animal grunt Guerra lunged again. Ray grabbed the killer's wrist, forced the knife hand backward, and brought his knee up. Guerra howled and the knife clattered to the floor.

The young man dived for the weapon and was kicked in the ribs. The knife went skidding over to the main altar. Guerra began to run after it, but Ray grabbed his foot and capsized him. Guerra fell on a kneeler, sending it crashing into the altar rail.

Guerra cursed. Panting, he regained his feet. Ray was getting weaker. The blood kept pouring forth. He made a run for the knife.

They grappled for the weapon beneath the tabernacle under a large crucifix. Guerra brought a fist down on Ray's face. Ray reeled with pain, and blood squirted from his nostrils. He managed to fling a nearby chair, and part of it caught Guerra on the head.

Guerra, his cassock spattered with blood, lay sprawled beneath the statue of a seraph. Finally he raised himself to a crouch. Ray stiffened but couldn't muster the strength to move.

Flushed with excitement, Guerra rose. His hoarse warning resounded like an incantation: "Santangelo, you are about to die."

Holding a heavy candelabrum, he moved slowly, with the sweeping gestures of ritual. He relished the moment, the end of his odyssey, climax of his sweet passion, the culmination of centuries.

Ray tried to stand but slumped down again. Guerra advanced. "Why?" asked Ray, stalling. "What have I done to you?"

Guerra stopped and broke into a tittering laugh. "Your father asked me the same thing before I killed him. I have waited a long time for this. It is my duty."

"You're—you're out of your skull."

Guerra whirled to face the altar, raising the candelabrum high above his head. "Before both God and Satan, I avenge the Guerras and the *stoppaglieri cosca*."

The first blow cracked the bones in Ray's right forearm.

"Marco Guerra!" The shout echoed through the church.

Candelabrum raised above his head, the killer hesitated.

"Marco Guerra, don't move!"

Guerra slowly turned around and faced Minnie. She stood just outside the altar rail, leveling the shotgun at his middle. "Put that thing down," she ordered him.

He looked at this woman with the gun. Such a creature was not going to spoil his consummate moment. Why hadn't she died when he pushed her onto the subway tracks?

The trigger of the shotgun felt cool. "Squeeze it like you would squeeze your husband's hand on a roller-coaster ride," the man had said. She wavered. "Put that candleholder down."

Ray was frozen with terror and disbelief. He looked at his mother, then back at Guerra. The hand holding the candelabrum began to shake violently. Minnie tightened her grip on the trigger. Froth showed at the corner of the killer's mouth and a low moan came from the depths of him. The moan turned into a hoarse croak: "Long live the Guerra family! *Viva la cosca!*" The candelabrum started down toward Ray.

Minnie's mind resounded with the admonition: It is a sin to kill, to kill, to kill. She fired.

The spray of lead entered Guerra's body around the shoulders and head. He toppled noiselessly as the echo of the blast reverberated from the choir loft to the sacristy. Minnie saw the statue of Saint Anthony, eternal understanding written on his beatific features.

With a clatter Minnie Santangelo dropped the shotgun to the tiles. "I killed him." She began to sob. "Forgive me, Lord. I killed him in Your presence."

Ray was dazed, aflame with pain. His eyes turned from his mother to the still body of Guerra, a great, black, blood-soaked vampire bat, cassock billowing, arms spread-eagled, face down on the tiles. He looked at his sobbing mother and tried to speak words of comfort. Nothing came from his vocal cords but a groan.

Epilogue: One Year Later

THE priest of St. Theresa's raised his hands and intoned, "May his soul and the souls of all the faithful departed rest in peace. Amen."

"Amen," murmured Minnie, stirring in the front pew at a memorial Mass she had arranged for the soul of Lieutenant Gaetano Conti of the U.S. Strike Force on Organized Crime. Balm for her guilt. Saying the Mass, Father Mancuso occupied the very spot where Guerra had fallen. Holy ritual on profane ground. Yet she realized that killing Guerra had not been profane but inevitable.

In the past year she had learned details about the man she once believed to be her adversary. Conti had been sixty-one years old, born in Rome, a naturalized U.S. citizen, and an undercover agent. His story to Minnie was as close to the truth as his mission allowed.

He was an expert on Mafia history and knew of the *stoppaglieri*. When he read about Tedesco's murder and the cork, he asked permission from his superiors to work with the local police on the case. It didn't take him long to learn about the Santangelo killing, which led him to Minnie. He didn't tell her who he really was, because he knew about her reluctance to cooperate with police. Also, there was a chance that the Santangelo family was responsible for Tedesco's death in some way. But his main suspect was Guerra.

Somehow, before Conti could make his suspicions known to his superiors, Guerra found out about him. He had probably been following Minnie and observed them during one of their rendezvous.

"Lord have mercy on us," said Father Mancuso.

Minnie gazed at the spot in front of the altar where the bloodstains had been scrubbed away. Memories flooded her senses. Patrolman Corallo had shaken his head in total disbelief. He had seen many unusual things during his eleven years on the force. But this one took the blue ribbon: an Italian mamma guns down a priest on the altar.

"Get an ambulance," Corallo had told his partner. "The young guy's still breathing." Squatting beside Guerra's body, he shook his head slowly. "Forget about the priest here. He's finished."

Minnie sat outside the altar rail, sobbing.

An ambulance and the detective squad were sent for by radio. Before long, Mrs. Santangelo found herself in the back seat of the police car. Other policemen were holding back the crowd surging to catch a glimpse of her. Familiar faces in the throng wore incredulous looks. But Minnie could only think of her son.

"Is Remo all right? I have to see him."

"He's being taken to the hospital," Corallo said. "You are going to be booked."

The nightmare had not lasted long. In a few hours Minnie Santangelo was freed. The detectives pieced together an account of what had probably happened by checking her story against Conti's notes. But the full story wasn't known until weeks later. The passport office had a photo of the real Don Giacomo, and the police in Bagheria had a mug shot of Guerra. They were not the same man. Copies of Guerra's fingerprints matched the ones taken from the body of the man Minnie had shot.

Some five years ago everyone in Bagheria must have known that Don Giacomo was emigrating, to retire in Little Italy with his sister. Somewhere between Bagheria and the port of Palermo he met his end. The rest had been easy for Guerra. He knew that the Roman collar would inspire deference in immigration officials. He also correctly reckoned that, to many people, priests were like Chinese waiters. They all looked alike. He was to join a sister who was old, blind, and didn't really know him. Years in the Jesuit school had given him a background for impersonating a priest. It had been all too easy.

Holding the host aloft, Father Mancuso said, "All of you take and eat of this. For this is my body."

Minnie went to the altar rail to receive Communion, followed by three old women and a young woman she had noticed earlier. She was about twenty-four, with dark hair, a translucent complexion, and the delicately formed features of a Renaissance Madonna.

After most of the worshippers had filed out, Minnie stayed behind for an old habit—to make the stations of the cross.

Beads in her hands, she stopped at the first station. She was reminded of her son's suffering. He had sustained two broken ribs, a fractured forearm, a broken nose, a knife wound that needed eighteen stitches, and serious loss of blood. But no vital parts were touched and he mended quickly. The emotional wounds took longer. Despite hopes of a sympathy vote, Remo lost the primary by two thousand ballots. Soon afterward, Valentina Corvo moved to Chicago, and Ray went into a deep blue funk out of which he only recently was emerging.

One event had perked him up: the indictment of Anthony Regale on charges of taking contract kickbacks from private carters with Mafia connections in the neighborhood. There might be a special election, and Remo already was talking about running again.

At the second station Minnie's thoughts focused on Umberto Marrandino, who himself was beginning to know suffering. A mole on his breastbone turned out to be skin cancer.

Another station. She thought of Arturo, a friend in need. Why hadn't she trusted him? But at the time she couldn't trust anybody.

After she made the stations, Minnie walked down the center aisle to the font and dipped her fingers into the holy water. The young woman who had received Communion with her touched her on the arm. "Signora Santangelo? I am Lenore Conti."

Minnie felt a surge of happiness. "So you did come."

Lenore nodded. "Thank you for the Mass. I liked your letters. They were a comfort."

Minnie took her arm and began to walk out of the church. "I liked yours too."

The door opened onto Elizabeth Street, astir with morning movement. Street cleaners swept up the debris of the *festa*. The old men, who were always up early, greeted each other and lighted up their first cigars of the day. A babble of radios came from the open windows of the tenements.

Minnie turned to her companion. "Come up for coffee. I want you to meet my son."

Anthony Mancini is well acquainted with the milieu he describes so vividly in his novel of Italian-Americans. He was born in 1939 in New York City, both his parents having emigrated from the Abruzzi region of Italy, and his mother served as partial prototype for the story's engaging heroine. The Mancinis made their home in the Bronx, where the author attended a Jesuit school, then went on to Fordham University while working nights as a copyboy on the New York *Post*. After earning his degree and serving in the army, he continued a career in journalism, working on a GI newspaper in Germany in the mid-1960s and spending varying amounts of time in Italy over the years. He now lives in New York and is a reporter for the *Post*, covering everything from music reviews to political stories, as well as contributing articles to a wide variety of other periodicals. Mr. Mancini's wife, Patricia McNees, is a free-lance writer and editor, and his twin brother, Joe, is also a writer.

Anthony Mancini

Minnie Santangelo's Mortal Sin is Anthony Mancini's first novel, written during "spare time" in the past few years. He is an avid fan of suspense stories and decided to write in the form of a mystery, since he felt its rigid structure would provide helpful discipline for a novice fiction writer. He has plans for a sequel, in which Minnie Santangelo will find further adventure.

A
SPORTING
PROPOSITION

A CONDENSATION OF THE NOVEL BY

James Aldridge

ILLUSTRATED BY BEN WOHLBERG

When the son of a poor Scots immigrant and the daugher of a wealthy rancher laid mutual claim to a mischievous Welsh pony, the Australian outback town of St. Helen was split asunder. The confrontation of the two indignant young people reveals long-smoldering resentments beneath the town's deceptively tranquil surface.

The spirit with which this boy and girl gamble for the love of a wild pony becomes contagious.

It is not easy to tell the story of what happened to Scott Pirie and his pony that summer in the 1930s, because it is more than the story of what happened to a boy and his horse. It is, in fact, something of the story of our town of St. Helen, in the state of Victoria, and in putting the story together I have often been tempted to go off at a tangent and describe some of the other dramas that our town went through at the time: how a local private airplane crashed while trying to fly under the town bridge; how a bushfire crept dangerously near the plains of wheat that enrich the town; and how four men were wounded in accidents while shunting railway trucks or driving sheep through the town.

But these events, after all, had nothing to do with Scotty Pirie, who, with his pony, Taff, divided St. Helen that summer into his defenders and attackers. And considering that Scotty was then thirteen, it was no mean feat. To me it had always seemed inevitable that something like that would happen, for Scotty could be stubborn as well as mischievous and troublesome. But for most of our Australian bush town he was just another wild colonial boy who was always worth blaming for something.

And perhaps that is the real starting point of this story, because all our local dramas were the result of the kind of life we led, bordered by bush on one side and a hundred thousand acres of wheat on the other, cut right down the middle by a wide, exciting river that flowed full and fast in winter but dried to a trickle in summer. There was a smaller stream, just above the town, which joined the big river and formed an island where we boys would "go bush" from time to time. Both rivers played a part in what happened that summer. So did the vast, wealthy sheep and cattle station, Riverside, across the big river in the state of New South Wales. Its owner, Ellison Eyre, became Scotty's chief opponent in the division of the town.

Even though we had good schools, a cinema, a newspaper, six pubs, a racecourse, a golf course, and a main street under the raglike leaves of peppercorn trees, we had such a variety of pressures on us and such different levels of self-interest that we were never cohesive. Or ever dull. We were rich and poor, cultured and ignorant, mean and generous, country-minded and town-minded. I suppose that is why we split down the middle over Scotty.

In St. Helen, Scotty Pirie counted as a bushboy because he lived five miles out on an arid, salty-earthed farm with his Scottish mother and father. When I think of Scotty I always see him crouched low on the bare back of his wild Welsh pony, Taff, and fleeing down the side streets of the town. As a rule Scotty would ride boldly down the main street when he came, but he always seemed to leave the back way, as if he had been up to something. Boy and pony seemed to flit in and out of the gum trees as if they weren't there, fading clean out of sight before you actually saw them. I never knew anybody who could appear and disappear the way Scotty did.

One story about Scotty comes to my mind. There was a big bend in the river just before it reached the town. The railway line from Benbow to St. Helen went straight for the bend and then made a turn with the river. This was where Scotty, on his pony, would race the old A3 steam engine of the passenger train as it slowed down. It was rough ground, but Scotty and Taff were really one animal, and the potholes and rabbit holes were no real danger to the galloping pony. The danger was a high barbed-wire fence that joined the edge of the railway line to the bend in the river.

Usually Scotty just scraped across the tracks in front of the train before it came to the fence, and every time he did it, the engine driver, J. T. Crimean, and the engine fireman, Andy Anderson, said they sweated like mud-caked dogs, because the train missed Scotty by inches. But this time they had been going faster than usual, and Scotty clearly couldn't make it.

J.T. leaned out of the driver's cab and shouted angrily. Scott had the galloping pony scalloping up air with its four hoofs. He slackened his elbows a little more, which was all the message Taff needed. But though the pony was now flat out, mane flying, it was still clear that he would not make it.

"Put on the steam brake!" Andy shouted to J.T.

"Too late. We're turning."

The A3 entered the bend. "He'll hit the fence."

"No. He'll go into the river."

But, in fact, Taff dug his hoofs into the dry, caked earth and suddenly stopped dead. The boy on his back flew over the pony's head and landed in the river with a noisy smack.

J.T. and Andy leaned out of the cab until they saw Scotty come up and start to swim toward the bank. They were so unnerved by the incident that they reported it to the stationmaster at St. Helen, who told the police. Sergeant Joe Collins visited the school, and Scotty was called in to the headmaster. After a lecture and a warning he was given four cuts of the leather strap on his hand.

We all knew that the strap hurt, morally as well as physically, but Scotty had never been dismayed by punishment. Or rather, he didn't show that he was. He was always reluctant to show any reaction or even to talk about it.

This time he was angry with Taff. "He'll never go near the water," Scotty complained. "Last winter, in the floods, he was caught on a clump of dirt in the paddock and we couldn't get him off. Water and goanna lizards—that's all he's afraid of. Taff'd die before he'd jump into the river. He'd sooner throw me off. Otherwise," Scotty said with a puzzled shrug, "he's game for anything."

Like Scotty himself.

That race with the train was typical of Scotty. He was always pitting himself silently and daringly against unbeatable odds. He did not openly challenge all of St. Helen all the time, but he challenged a particular part of it a lot of the time, and this obviously had something to do with his poverty and the isolation on the Piries' hopeless farm.

Angus Pirie and his wife (we never discovered her first name) had come to St. Helen in the early 1920s direct from some grimy Glasgow slum. They had been shipped out to Australia by one of the organizations that helped poor British emigrants to exchange British poverty for Australian poverty. It was called the Big Neighbor movement. Agriculture was almost the only thing Australia could offer these people, so they were often settled on farmlands even though they had never been on a farm in their lives, and the land was often too poor to support a cat.

Angus and Mrs. Pirie had been settled on a low-lying block of land which had been sold to the Big Neighbor movement for just such poor, ignorant emigrants. It was like iron in summer, and in winter it was muddy, salty and swampy. Since Angus knew nothing at all about growing things or about cattle and horses, it was like asking a child to fly a complicated airplane.

Yet this small, hungry Scot *did* fly the airplane, and he and his thin-armed, pale-eyed, lonely little wife somehow survived, though nobody knew how.

As the years passed, Angus became harder and grimmer and thinner. He also became more silent, more cut off, the longer he had to fight the mud and the salt and the weather to get milk from his four dairy cows and alfalfa from his fields.

My mother told me that when Scotty was born nobody in the town knew anything about it until months afterward, when Angus was charged by the police for failing to register within two months the birth of a child. My father, a barrister-solicitor (an amalgam in the Australian legal system), got Angus off by a technicality which said that in outlying districts the period could be extended, providing there were extenuating circumstances. My father, an Englishman in this self-consciously Australian town, made an angry plea; a day spent away from his farm to register his son's birth, particularly at that time of the year, would have been impossible for Angus, who worked from four in the morning to ten at night on the place some land speculator had saddled him with. If the magistrate didn't consider those to be extenuating circumstances, my father said, he would look into the whole question of why such hopeless land had been given to Pirie in the first place. The magistrate, a land speculator himself, quickly dismissed the charges.

Scotty was not actually seen by St. Heleners until he was about four years old. Then, one summer day, Mrs. Pirie came into town with her husband and son. They walked the full five miles there (one mile from farm to road, four miles on the road). Nobody was sure why they all came in that day; perhaps it was some sort of celebration. Pirie himself sometimes came in to the grain and feed store, or to the butter factory to be paid for his milk, but Mrs. Pirie was a rare sight. On this Saturday, market day, the town was full of farmers' trucks, buggies and cars; full of town and country youth parading the crowded main street. Angus went off to do his business and left Mrs. Pirie and Scotty to walk along the main street. They went the full length of it, looking in every window. Then they sat on one of the benches along the footpath under the peppercorn trees and waited.

For what? For people to greet them? For neighbors to talk to? Mrs. Pirie didn't know anyone in St. Helen. She had no near neighbors except some Chinese market gardeners. She simply sat still, a tiny figure with her thin arms and pale, Scottish, city-bred eyes; and she kept her gaze firmly ahead, as if she were dreaming of some black stone street that was forever sunk in the mists of loch and dale and smoke and soot.

But not Scotty. He didn't resemble either his dark-eyed thin father, or his mother with her faded, innocent, distant face. Scotty had bright, challenging, watchful blue eyes and a restless, silent way of inspecting everybody as if judging and sorting them out.

My mother saw the Piries that day. Later she described Scotty to me as a vigorous little sun-scorched boy with no shoes or socks, wearing black velvet short pants, obviously made from a cast-off dress someone had given Mrs. Pirie. I remember those velvet pants three years later, let down but still wearable, though patched. And by then Scotty fought anyone who mocked him for them.

"You could see even on that very first day," my mother added, "that the little boy was looking after his mother. He wasn't going to let anyone sit down near her or touch her. You could see it in that stubborn little face and the fists: *Don't touch!*"

That may have been one mother's sympathy for another, but later Scotty proved willing to fight anybody who insulted him, laughed at his father or mocked his silent, patient mother. And he had to fight, because his father was the sort of man some considered fair game. Every now and then when he came into town on Saturday, Angus would go into the White Swan Hotel, put four shillings on the bar and ask for that amount of beer. He would drink the beer and then leave, drunk on his feet, and the town larrikins would follow him home, mocking him and aping his incomprehensible Scots burr. They also tried to undo his bootlaces while he staggered on, oblivious of the fun he was provoking.

When Scotty was old enough to realize what was happening, he would walk in frustration beside his father, and if the ruffians came too near he would hit out wildly, although they were twice his size. Once, when two boisterous brothers named Southby (they were a little drunk themselves) found a woman's old straw hat somewhere, they imitated Angus and his wife walking into town. Scotty threw rocks and horse manure at them and then flung his seven-year-old barelegged body at the nearest Southby boy. Fortunately the Southbys were not vicious. It was simply their Australian fascination with mockery: have a go at anything, no matter what. They held Scotty off and made a drunken joke of it, but they didn't do it again. I think Scott never passed them in the street without sending them blue-eyed reminders of his long memory.

My father disapproved of Angus Pirie's occasional drunkenness. My mother asked what else could a man do every now and then to forget his misery, but my father thought drunkenness was admitting moral defeat and was a waste of hard-earned money. The

Piries had to live most of the time without money, bound in debt to two merchants who gave them credit: Dorman Walker, the grain and feed merchant, and Flannigan, the grocer. The Piries didn't buy clothes, and they used oil lamps, but Pirie was so much in debt that Mrs. Pirie would not see a penny on her kitchen mantelpiece from one month to the next. She baked her own bread from flour bought on credit, and she made the little butter they ate from the scant amount of milk they kept for themselves.

After his first visit Scotty next appeared in town when he was left at the school gate one morning at eight o'clock by his father. He was only seven, but it was left to him to go into the school and tell the headmaster who he was. School didn't start until nine, so Scott sat down against the gatepost and waited, ignoring all taunts, until he guessed it was almost nine. Then he went inside.

After that he was brought to school every day by a neighbor's son, Beebe Dancy, who came from a farm farther along the road. He was three months older than Scott, and they both came to school riding on the broad back of an old mare, their four bare legs dangling. They were both so small that they could only mount by climbing up on the school fence, and since there was not even a trot left in the mare, it took them more than an hour each way.

These conditions may seem rather hard now, but at the time they were not really noticeable. There was considerable poverty in St. Helen, although it was the center of one of the richest sheep, wheat and citrus countries in the world. Nobody thought it real hardship when, at age eight, Scotty had to do an hour's work on the farm (cutting wood for the kitchen stove, swinging a full-size axe, cleaning out the dairy shed, washing the milking buckets and filling the water troughs) before seven forty-five to get to school by nine. He had to do the same chores again when he got home at five fifteen. His lunch, which his mother gave him in a cloth sack made from a sugar bag, was a boiled egg, two thick slices of homemade bread and sometimes a tomato or a cucumber.

Scotty got into the scrapes we all got into. He was nearly drowned at nine trying to swim in the fast river before it was low enough. He was bitten by a goanna lizard when he was ten, and it

391

nearly killed him. Being a bushboy, with country habits, he put frilled lizards (frightening-looking monsters but harmless) in the teachers' desks. And because he never wore shoes (few of us did), he always had a smashed toe from stumbling or kicking it on something. He also had trouble with his patched velvet pants, and the shirts his mother made from other people's dresses.

Then Beebe's old mare was frightened by a goanna, tried to leap a canal, fell on Beebe and killed him, and broke her own front legs. The mare had to be shot, and thereafter Scotty walked the five miles to school. At his age it was obviously impossible to do it every day, so he began to stay away more often, until the headmaster informed the state inspectors and they informed the police.

Again Angus faced the magistrate, accused this time of failing to send his son to school. Again my father got him off, threatening to sue the state government for failure to provide Scotty with an education in his own home, a state law in Victoria if children were unable to reach a school. Angus escaped a fine, but it didn't get Scotty to school, so my father approached the Big Neighbor movement and told them they had to do something about Scotty.

My father had made them so nervous about the Piries' salty farm that the Big Neighbors did not want a new clash with him. They appealed to Ellison Eyre, the owner of the sheep and cattle station across the river. Riverside was famous for its homebred mounts; there were the Thoroughbreds Eyre used for himself and his family, and also the wild horses bred for his drovers and stockmen. He kept the tough little herd running wild in the open bush along the river, for a rough-bred horse when broken could do the difficult work expected of it on a sheep and cattle station.

As well as these horses, Ellison also kept a herd of wild Welsh ponies. The original Welsh breed had been mixed with Thoroughbred and Arab to make them very beautiful and daring animals, well-shaped, tough, handsome-headed ponies with long tails and thick golden manes. The Eyre ponies were all a chamois color, and so absolutely identical that you couldn't tell one from another. They were also remarkable for their spirit: rebellious, independent, stubborn, intelligent, willful, gay and good for anything—town riding, rough riding or simply pulling. There were about a dozen broken-in ponies from Eyre's herd in the town, and every year one or two of them disappeared, stolen by someone passing through.

Ellison Eyre offered one of these Welsh ponies to the Big Neighbor movement for Scotty. They took it, unbroken, to Angus, who said he would not accept it from them as a gift. Angus was still very bitter about the Big Neighbors, and he told them in his hard Scots burr that his son would walk a hundred "guid miles" to school before he "w'd take a gift a that daft beast." So my father persuaded Angus to buy the pony for three pounds—a lot of money for Angus to pay, and, in fact, another debt that stitched him still tighter to Dorman Walker, for Angus had to borrow the money from the grain and feed company.

That was how Scotty got his pony, Taff. When he had spent a couple of months being thrown off the wicked little beast, he got it reluctantly to school. It kicked down the little shelter there the first day, fled and had to be recovered by twenty yelling, joyful schoolboys. Taff bit two of them and lashed out with his hoofs, but Scotty got a grip on the bridle and leaped on. Or rather he got as far as the neck, and the pony galloped off with Scotty somehow getting around the back, where he simply sat it out until the pony had galloped himself out of breath.

That was the way he left school every day for weeks—at a gallop, clinging to little Taff's rippling, straining body.

Soon you could not think of Scotty without thinking of Taff. They seemed to be utterly preoccupied with each other, though it was not a smooth relationship. Scotty would press Taff into impossible situations, demanding fearless and instant obedience. In return, Taff would never wait for Scotty to be properly mounted, and he would bite or run away when he felt like it. But they seemed to have developed an almost instinctive sense for getting each other out of trouble.

Our barber, Jock Linnear, called Scotty "the four legs of Rob Roy" one day when a customer, Mr. Jacklin, the timber merchant, was complaining that he had nearly been knocked down by boy and pony on a footpath near his timber yard. "Practically cut me in two, galloping across the path. Then he turned and shouted at me that he was late for school. I ought to tell his old man."

"And his old man would tell you something so ripe you wouldn't understand it," the barber said, and everybody laughed.

Indeed the most common complaint about Scotty was that he never used the road. "He just cuts through backyards and alleys," Mr. Stone, the iceman, said. "And he comes out of places that even I didn't know existed. The other day I saw him coming out of the back of the *Standard*. Then he cut across the back of the fire station and came out next to Rolls, the tractor agent!"

Later, Jock the barber would take Scotty's side in the issue that was to divide the town, and Jacklin the timber merchant would be on Eyre's side.

In general, Scotty's sort of mischief was expected of bushboys, who were supposed to be a bit wild. But one day Scott was caught dipping into the bin at the back of the *Standard*, where the lead slugs of used type were thrown after the newspaper had been printed. The slugs could be melted down and used again, but to Scotty they were throw-outs, useful for fishing-line sinkers.

"You were stealing," Barney Phillips, the printer, said, holding Scotty firmly, while Scotty held on to Taff.

"I didn't know I was stealing," Scott said boldly.

"Like hell you didn't!" Phillips relaxed his grip a little and in a flash, Scott was in midair between ground and pony, and Taff was already in motion. They were down the alley and through the Baptist churchyard before Phillips had turned around.

But Phillips had obviously let him go, and in the eventual division of the town he was on Scotty's side.

In explaining Scotty, I mustn't sentimentalize him. He wasn't all good or all bad, but he was never mean, and I never knew him to cheat or steal, although he didn't mind acquiring anything that happened to be lying around. He had his own likes and dislikes in the town, and if there was a pattern to them, it was that he never took sides against anyone who was as poor as his own family. He liked our family, or rather tolerated us, and one Saturday he came

to us on little Taff's bare back and called out at the back door as we were eating breakfast.

"Mrs. Quayle! My father sent you some . . ." and he used the farmyard term for horse manure. That was the sort of language my father would not normally tolerate. He hesitated, with a spoonful of egg on the way to his mouth, but my ten-year-old brother, Tom, laughed until he was sick, and my mother had to suppress laughter, it was so innocently said. She went to the back door and asked Scotty how much it would cost.

"Nothing." Scott said his father had told him not to take anything. It was Angus paying my father for his help in court. "Where do you want it?" Scott asked.

My mother said, "Over near the rhubarb, under the peach tree."

Scotty let Taff pick his way in and out of my father's pampered vegetable beds and, without getting off, tipped the bags of manure into a heap under the tree by swinging Taff around on his hind legs. Then he picked his way out, like a cat in a rosebush, while we all watched Taff breathlessly. But he hadn't trampled anything.

"Spread it out at night," Scott advised my mother confidentially, "then it won't stink so much."

"Don't you want to wash?" my mother asked him.

"No need, Mrs. Quayle. I'll go home by the river. . . ." He was gone before my mother could offer him peaches, jam or a biscuit.

THERE was one whole street in town that Scotty detested. It was, of course, the most prosperous one. All the houses in Wilson Street were hidden behind high fences. They had large gardens with thick lawns, palm and orange trees and flower beds. Almost every one of them had a snarling, teeth-baring dog that ran along the picket fence as you walked past, barking and snapping at you.

One by one Scott eventually turned all those dogs loose, usually by plaguing the dog to get mad, then unlatching the gate and flying down the road on Taff, with the dog at his heels. Scotty was inclined to free anything that was locked up, even if freedom was dangerous for it. One day, for instance, Scott let out a family's pet kangaroo and tried to chase it to freedom. But dogs appeared from nowhere and began to attack it, and Scotty had to chase it back into its cage. On the other hand, when Scotty let out an aviary of about a hundred of our native budgerigars (small, colorful parrots) in Wilson Street, they knew exactly where to go. They flew squeaking and screeching to liberty in the bush. But that was a piece of personal revenge, for the house belonged to the family of Clara Alexander, who had once pinched her nose in class and said, "You smell, Scott Pirie."

Actually it was true that Scotty usually did smell of cows and hay and horse: that was a country smell you expected on bushboys; still, the girls giggled when Clara said it. One of them, Doris Dowling, the doctor's daughter, who was a tomboy and always in trouble like Scotty, told Clara that she smelled awful herself.

"And your old man makes his sausages out of dead cats and dogs," Scotty added.

Clara's father was a butcher, and Scotty was merely repeating the usual insult that sausage makers the world over have to put up with. Clara seemed untouched by it, so Scotty let the Alexander budgerigars out. In the division of the town over Scotty, Mr. Alexander naturally chose the other side, as did most of Wilson Street.

One by one the incidents that made up the town's picture of Scotty were recorded, and the effect depended on whether you were one of Scotty's victims, or an amused onlooker, or a sympathizer. But then came a crisis that involved much more than Scott. Taff suddenly disappeared, and that changed everything.

His disappearance was a mystery. It was late winter, the river was still high and full, the ground was still soggy, and one night Taff—apparently—broke out of his halfhearted enclosure and went over to the river paddocks, presumably looking for something to eat. Like Scotty, he was willful and always hungry. Feed for Taff was difficult in the winter, for the Piries could not afford to buy hay, and that whole winter Scotty's friends had been helping him to find patches of long grass to cut, dry and store. We even used to take bundles of it to school. But whenever there was a shortage of feed at home, Taff would break out and go browsing.

That morning Scotty shouted to his mother, "Taff's knocked the rail down and gone down by the river." So he went out to the flat muddy ground toward the river, sure that he would find Taff on one of the patches of dry grass. But Taff was nowhere to be seen, and things suddenly looked serious. Scotty searched every inch of the farm and the riverbank to make sure that Taff had not fallen and broken a leg; the Chinese market gardeners, in their calm way, organized their own search. But there was no sign of the pony.

That left the river, and the possibility that he had fallen in and drowned.

Scotty walked upstream and downstream to see if the banks were broken anywhere, though with Taff's neurotic terror of water, there was little chance that he would go near the edge. His fear also precluded any idea that he would recklessly plunge into the water and swim downstream, though Eyre's wild horses sometimes did that. The only remaining explanation was a thief. The Piries kept no dogs, so anyone could have taken Taff away quietly.

After two days' absence searching the bush, Scotty turned up at school without Taff. We all began to speculate, but to every suggestion Scotty had one caustic answer: "You don't know Taff."

"He would never go away with *anybody*," Doris Dowling said, always loyal to Taff and Scotty.

Certainly nobody but Scotty had ever been able to get near him. He particularly disliked men and boys, but on occasion, with Scotty's help, he would permit a girl to approach him. We therefore concluded that whoever had stolen Taff had known the Piries' farm and Taff, and had a reason for taking him away. Suspicion pointed in the direction of Dorman Walker, to whom Angus Pirie owed a hopeless debt. He was unpopular with all of us. It seemed ridiculous, of course, that a prosperous merchant should steal a horse, but he had often sent one of his tractors out to a farm to pick up unpaid-for farm machinery or harnesses. Perhaps he had done the same with Taff, the only thing of value that Angus could part with. The pony was now worth about twenty pounds, because he was such a beautiful little beast. But Walker would have picked him up secretly, with no court order, since he knew that my father kept a close watch on what happened to the Piries.

At first Scotty seemed sure that Taff would turn up, and the more we argued with him about it the angrier he became. But finally our concern began to persuade him that Taff had really been stolen, with no way of finding his way back.

I'll never forget the sight of Scotty walking to and from school. The four legs of Rob Roy reduced to two, the top without a bottom. It was an unsatisfying sight. In fact, Scotty seemed to move along with a pounding, lurching movement, as if Taff were a solid ghost under him.

THE original Eyres were squatters on the vast open grasslands across the river, but in the eighty years of their proprietorship of Riverside they had become wealthy and powerful. In fact, they were the aristocracy, with a sense of being above anything that could touch them—anything that came from the town of St. Helen or the state of Victoria anyway, since on their side of the river they were subject only to the laws of New South Wales.

Ellison Eyre was the latest of the Eyres to work the beautiful old Riverside homestead. Educated by a governess as a child, he had then gone to an English public school and Oxford. He had married the daughter of a wool and wheat broker, and they had a daughter named Josephine, who was about the same age as Scotty.

Josie was as separate from the town as Scotty was. She was being educated by a governess, and if she ever did appear, it was because her father had something to do in St. Helen. And that would be an event for some of the women to talk about. "Did you see the little Eyre girl with her father?"

The remarks about her were flattering or not, depending on who made them. Josie was either a stubborn or a handsome little girl, with a hot temper or a will of her own. She was either a snob or an intelligent girl, full of character. I myself remember her then as a poised little girl who always wore jodhpurs and who spoke and walked briskly, as if she knew what she wanted and expected it to be forthcoming. Rather like her father, in fact.

When Josie was about eleven she caught infantile paralysis. We had full reports about it from Bluey Waters, one of the Eyre stockmen, who came into the White Swan Hotel every Saturday for his beer, from Dr. Dowling, and from the town telephone operators, who listened in on all Riverside calls. At one point we heard that Josie would probably die, and for weeks there was a lot of sorrow and sympathy in the town for the Eyres. Specialists were flown in, and two nurses also arrived from the city.

Like every other mother in the town, my own mother was not only concerned for the girl but worried that my sister and brother and I might catch polio. But my father put it into perspective. "The Eyre girl might as well be living a million miles away. Her family has almost no physical contact with St. Helen. It's a terrible thing for them, but Josie won't give up easily. She'll fight."

Josie fought and Josie survived. It was six months before we heard in what condition she had survived. She had escaped any damage above the waist, but one leg was paralyzed from the hip down, and the other had only a little movement above the knee.

It was a year before anyone actually saw Josie. After that she came into town more often, sitting upright in her father's car, the same independent-looking little miss. She would not allow anyone to see her useless legs. That was the early period of Sister Kenny's methods of massage and exercise, and there was a nurse permanently at Riverside working on Josie's legs.

One Saturday when I saw her in the family car, waiting for her father, I said, "How are you, Josie?"

"Very well, thank you, Kit," she replied firmly, warning me off more questions. She was still a very determined girl.

If it had not been for those useless legs, Josie, now thirteen, would already have been sent away to some exclusive school. Since that was impossible, she remained a self-disciplined girl, almost alone on a vast sheep and cattle station despite visitors from the city and the few local girls who were now encouraged to come to see her—daughters of other landowners or of our member of parliament. Sometimes my sister, Jeannie, went there. She said that Josie, who had more or less been born on a horse and had always ridden, was frustrated and miserable with her immobility. So Ellison had decided to find some means by which Josie could get around on her own. He flew to the city, and a month later a little dogcart arrived at the railway station.

Blue Waters, the stockman, explained its odd size and shape to us when he came to pick it up in a truck. The yellow cart was wide, with a very low center of gravity, so that it would be difficult to tip over, and it had strong but light wheels. The polished shafts ballooned out, then narrowed down to an end far ahead of the cart. That also made it difficult to tip over. The cart had two beautifully upholstered wraparound seats designed to keep you in, and two armrests which folded back so you could get in and out easily. It also had folding steps and a folding handrail so Josie could pull herself in and out. All it needed was a pony to pull it.

Ellison Eyre sent his stockmen out to catch three or four of the wild Welsh ponies so that Josie could choose the one she wanted for the dogcart. Rounding up those wild-running ponies was not easy. We all believed that a wild horse that is caught is the one that *wants* to be caught, that some wild horses will die before they allow themselves to be captured. Almost always the Welsh ponies stuck together. Sometimes the whole herd would get lost deep in the bush, and it would take some serious riding to get them back into open country. On one occasion, when the herd got into a part of the bush the stockmen couldn't reach, Eyre had to get help from a local pilot who had been a fighter ace in World War I to buzz the horses out with his noisy little Sopwith.

The stockmen had a difficult time cutting out ponies for Josie to choose from; they all seemed particularly cunning that year. It was also early summer, when wild horses are in their best condition and at their most independent. But they finally managed to cut out four of them, and Josie was wheeled in her chair to take a look. Being Eyre ponies, the four that Bluey Waters had selected were more or less identical in coloration and height, so there was nothing in their general appearance to govern Josie's choice. She kept shouting at Blue to make them run around faster.

Blue chased them on foot, though he was only five feet two and his bowlegs could have straddled a barrel. When they split up, Josie called to Blue to follow one of them and keep him away from the others if he could, but the wild pony always outran Blue and returned to the other three. Finally one of the ponies turned on Blue and faced him. Head down, he backed away while keeping an aggressive stance: a pony who was going to face the trouble.

"Keep him, Blue," Josie called out. "Don't let him go!"

This was the way the Eyres tried to pick the most spirited mounts among the wild horses—the gamest, the most determined, the most intelligent. But this time Ellison Eyre objected and said to Josie, "You want a pulling horse, Josie, not a riding horse. That's a different temperament."

"No! I want this one," Josie insisted.

"He'll give you trouble," her father warned her.

"I don't care. I want him."

It is said that anyone choosing a horse usually chooses one that is a reflection of himself. "All right, sweetheart," Ellison said, and the pony was marked with a daub of tar.

When Josie had been wheeled inside the house, Ellison Eyre began to annoy the pony to see what sort of temper it had: hot and mean, or simply willful and unafraid. The pony was obviously both afraid *and* unafraid of Ellison, but for the most part it trotted irritably out of the way, its eye fixed on this man with a long switch in his hand. Finally Ellison cornered it. It pawed nervously, lowered its head and kept its eye on Ellison's feet and hands.

"Watch his teeth," Blue called to his boss. "He's a biter."

"They're all biters," Ellison said. He went nearer to the pony. When his hand went out to touch its shoulder, it suddenly lifted its head, butted, knocked Ellison over and broke free. Blue laughed.

"Well, at least he's quick and clever," Ellison said, picking himself up. "And he doesn't defend himself with his hoofs. Stake him out and we'll look at him."

The pony was driven into a paddock, haltered, tied with soft cotton ropes, and held firmly by the stockmen while Eyre felt his legs, flanks and chest and looked gingerly but carefully into his dribbling, furious mouth.

"His mouth's rather soft," Ellison reported. Which was all to the good, for when driven by Josie he would be light on the rein. "All right," Ellison said. "He'll do. She's picked one like herself: a bit quick-tempered but clever. Get him cleaned up."

Ponies coming in from the bush were dirty and *felt* dirty. If a horse had to change its habits, there was no better way than to start by changing its feelings. You combed and cleaned a wild pony so that it knew something extraordinary and satisfying had happened. After that the real taming could begin.

Josie wanted to shaft-break the pony herself, but that was not possible. Bo (a corruption of Beau, the name Josie gave him) didn't take kindly to shafts at all. Josie got up every golden dawn when the crows were cawing and went down across the dew-soaked fields to the saddling yard with her kelpie dog, Max, who was trained to creep up on ponies inch by inch, like a good sheep dog, thus getting them used to something domestic. Josie also insisted that she wheel herself into the saddling yard, so that Bo could feel free to inspect her. But when Blue finally attached a pair of soft willow shafts to Bo's canvas girth, Ellison kept Josie away while Bo ran around furiously trying to get rid of them.

Once, trying to free himself, Bo got stuck in a split-rail fence. Josie approached him and stroked his jaw and scratched his nose until Blue grew nervous. "Don't trust him too much, Josie," he warned her. He had hardly said this when Bo's teeth snapped like a snarling dog's. Josie pulled her hand away, only just in time.

"That's enough," Blue said, but Josie studied Bo, and Bo studied her. He snapped at her other hand, but it was merely a nip, like a friendly cat's, and almost affectionate.

"It wasn't a bite," Josie insisted when Blue later reported it to Ellison. "It *wasn't!*"

When Bo was finally taught to open his mouth to a bit, Josie, in the wheelchair, was simply too low to bridle him. She wept with frustration when she tried, but she persisted; and Bo lost his wild temper and began bending his head so that she could do it. The final step was putting Bo into the shafts of a buggy.

There is a psychological moment in breaking a horse when it stops resisting and begins to adapt itself to what is asked of it. One day Blue decided that Bo had begun that mysterious adaptation.

Blue told Eyre that the pony was ready, and Bo was put into the shafts of a buggy.

Josie wheeled her chair to the buggy, and Blue lifted her up beside her father. She took the reins unceremoniously from him, and Bo trotted off obediently. All went well until, as the road made a bend, they met Josie's mother, Pat, in her Chrysler, returning from a visit to a neighbor. At the sight of the car Bo swerved and ran on confidently, missing the Chrysler by inches as Josie tried to stop him. Ellison snatched the reins and, standing, pulled fiercely. Bo's front legs left the ground as he stopped dead.

Ellison told Josie that Bo still did not allow for the width of the buggy he was pulling. "You'll have to know where you can get through, because he can't judge yet."

"I know, I know," Josie said, impatient to go on.

"And he's got a little devil in him, Josie. He'll play tricks on you if he can, for fun. *Never* let him play."

Finally Bo was put between the shafts of Josie's cart, the specially made yellow buggy, and she was allowed to go off on her own. The little buggy was so much lighter than what Bo had been trained to pull that the pony pounded down the dirt road at a busy little trot. Ellison was delighted and Josie in ecstasies.

"She won't be content until she's got that buggy off the road and into the open country," Pat told her husband. "Look at that." Josie had driven the buggy at full speed through the gate. "She's going to try to use that buggy as if she were riding it, not driving it."

From then on we could see Josie driving around just across the river or bouncing wildly across the Eyre paddocks. The yellow buggy, Josie and Bo became as much of a piece as Scotty and Taff had been, and as daring. Josie took that buggy into the bush and across broken fields. When they went after sheep or rounded up horses, Josie would follow the drovers and the stockmen. Farmers reported seeing the little yellow buggy appearing and disappearing in the most extraordinary places. By now Bo had completed the final stage of his adaptation: he was enjoying himself.

Yet we never saw the yellow buggy in town. When Josie appeared in town it was still in the front seat of one of the Eyre cars

or trucks, upright, with her pigtails neat on her shoulders, her eyes
alert and bold, and her legs hidden, although it was reported that
massage was improving her legs a little.

IN THE meantime a sense of loss seemed to have gotten the
better of Scotty, and one day he disappeared, the way Taff had
disappeared. Angus Pirie finally went to the police and reported
that Scotty had not come home for four days.

"That poor woman," my mother said, knowing that Mrs. Pirie
must be in agony, no doubt spending half her time looking out of
that house in the middle of nowhere, watching for Scotty.

The first thing we thought of was the river—he might have been
caught in a snag while swimming. Or perhaps he'd been bitten by
a snake and was lying somewhere dead. But my brother Tom said,
"Not Scotty. He's gone off somewhere, looking for Taff."

"It's months since Taff disappeared," my mother said.

"That's what he's done," Tom insisted.

And, in fact, that was what Scotty had done. He had gone to the
next small town, Tasco, and had been seen there around the vine-
yards. There were four or five Welsh ponies in Tasco and he
looked them over. One night a fruit grower caught him in the
corrugated-iron shed where raisins were dried. He had eaten nothing but the half-dried grapes and had stomach pains because of it.
The grower brought him to the police in town, and after they had
told him he was a nuisance and slapped him on the backside with a
billy, he was sent home.

Two weeks later he disappeared again, going upriver because
someone had told him that an itinerant rabbit trapper had been
seen on a Welsh pony. There were always one or two of these
semihermits who had gone bush. They would only appear in town
when they had bundles of rabbit skins to sell. When Scotty reappeared he said he hadn't found the trapper with a pony.

Scotty plunged through the town every night on his way home,
but he always looked as if he were hurrying somewhere else. He
disappeared again one Tuesday. That Friday his mother walked
into town and asked my mother if Tom and I would go and look

for Scotty in the bush that was part of the Eyre property. When Tom and I came in from school we found the women drinking tea, Mrs. Pirie in a black dress, black stockings, and shoes that had been soled—probably by Scott—with slices of used car tires. She wore a faded straw hat with a narrow crinkly brim. It had two cherries on it, and under the cherries her eyes had the look of someone who was not only alone but who spent most of the time preoccupied with something far, far away.

My mother told us what Mrs. Pirie wanted us to do, and Tom was instantly full of plans for swimming the river. But when my father came in and heard about it he said, "It's simpler to ask Eyre to tell his stockmen to keep a lookout."

He rang Ellison Eyre and told him that the Pirie boy was missing, possibly in that patch of bush upriver from him.

"I'll send Bluey Waters down that way tomorrow," Ellison told my father, who hung up and asked Mrs. Pirie if that helped. Mrs. Pirie nodded, but she looked at that impersonal telephone as if it had robbed her of all her hope. Then she got up, and Tom and I and my mother walked her to the gate.

"Where does he eat and sleep?" she said, as if we might know.

"He may be on Pental Island," I suggested, though I really didn't believe it.

This time Scotty was found in Lyah, where there was a Visitors' Meeting. In such country meets there were always pony races, and Scotty hung around the paddock, inspecting the ponies as they came in from outlying districts. Jorrocks, a man who traveled around with goat carts, gave him two shillings a race for sitting behind a billy goat in a sulky and racing against half a dozen other goat carts. The drivers urged the billy goats on by pulling their tails and shouting well-tried goat language at them. The winning driver got five shillings—which wasn't bad.

Scotty won, and stayed with the goat carts for the rest of the four-day event. He won two more races, because, he told us, he only started pulling the billy goats' tails when they were fifty yards from the finishing post.

He came home finally with a traveling salesman, and a few days later he was back at school. But he was a subtly different Scotty. My father said one night at dinner, "The Pirie boy is going to become a larrikin if he goes on like this." He added angrily, "Sheer waste." And making a moral case of it to Tom and me, he pointed out that personal rebellion and casual vagabondage were sisters under the skin. "Nothing but self-indulgence," he said between mouthfuls of Yorkshire pudding. He hated self-indulgence.

But at the moment we boys envied Scotty his adventures, although it was hard to forget the picture of Mrs. Pirie walking home along the road that led to nothing, in her black shoes with tire soles. After all, Scotty wasn't simply indulging himself. He was still looking for little Taff, and he was not a natural vagabond.

He disappeared once more, and this time he went fifty miles into New South Wales to a town where there were horse and pony sales every year. By now his mother and father had resigned themselves to his disappearances, although we knew that every time he came back Scotty got a hiding from his father. Scotty was also having trouble at school. He was bright, even clever, in his solemn way, but school had nothing to offer him at the moment. The headmaster had once shouted angrily at him, "How do you think you'll ever get a job in the post office or the railway if you go on like this? Tell me that, Pirie."

Pirie couldn't tell him.

The headmaster did his best, but most of the teachers simply gave up. It was becoming hopeless to try to rescue Scotty.

It must have been that fifty-mile walk home that somehow got to him. He decided, finally, that little Taff had gone for good. The problem that remained was what to do about it.

In ALL this time Scotty had never blamed Dorman Walker for Taff's disappearance, the way most of us did. Or at least he had not so far looked for revenge. But he spent more time in town now, wandering around the familiar back alleys and shortcuts, where he would pick up anything that happened to be lying around. Finally the idea of doing something to Dorman Walker corrupted him, and Scotty began to slip through a high window into Walker's grain and feed barn. The long, dark, cool shed filled with farm machinery, tractors and fertilizers fascinated us. There, to satisfy his smoldering anger and frustration, Scotty, who simply wasn't a destroyer, would run around on the stacked hay or in and out of the rakes, harvesters and tractors doing what mischief he could.

Then, one evening, Scotty started one of the tractors in the barn. Walker, sitting in his office, was so afraid when he heard the clattering roar that he wouldn't go and see what had happened. But the noise also startled Scotty, who fled. The next time Dorman Walker saw Scotty near his place he gave chase. In fact, Scotty rarely went through town now without someone taking off after him, and he would tear up the road and then suddenly disappear the way only he could disappear.

Even so, Scotty still had his friends, and sometimes when he was being chased he would hear an encouraging shout: "Keep it going, Scotty. Don't let them catch you!" Surprised, Scotty would turn around. Hello, Mrs. Whoever-it-was, he would shout. Then he would scramble over some nearby fence.

It was becoming clear that the town could no longer discipline Scotty, or hold him. And that was when he accidentally met Josie Eyre and her pony—a meeting which changed everything.

St. Helen held a big agricultural show every year. Inside the spacious fairgrounds were a full-size arena, a grandstand, and a dozen buildings for the usual exhibits of wheat, wool, butter, fruit, vegetables and homemade jam and cakes. The arena held cattle and sheep competitions, but most important, the horse shows— jumping events, best horse-and-buggy competitions, dressage and, above all, those thundering contests of power and speed, the trotting races, in which trotters and pacers could compete against each other. All the horses had to trot, but the trotter pulled a sulky with a driver in it, while the pacer carried a rider.

Most of the pacers and trotters in the St. Helen show were owned by out-of-town professionals, who traveled around the country competing in all the local race meetings. But this year Ellison Eyre had entered two of his Thoroughbred pacers. He had also brought in Josie, and, between trotting heats, she would compete with Bo and her yellow buggy in the best-turnout event for pony and trap.

The best horse out of the three heats was the winner of the trotting event. From under the grandstand—unseen by the track stewards yet near the thundering horses—Scotty and Tom and I were now watching the first trotting heat. Ellison Eyre, in his custom-made jockey silks, boots and skullcap, rode onto the track on his beautifully groomed Thoroughbred pacer, Flick, and out of admiration and sheer local chauvinism we hoped he would win.

A trotter puts each of his hoofs down individually, beating the earth with a powerful, disciplined rhythm. When the race began we were up on our feet as the horses came flying by, sweat pouring off their legs and backs. The competitors raced wheel to wheel, horse to horse, and in the last circuit, when Ellison Eyre achieved half-a-head lead, we shouted ourselves dizzy. But in a brief, violent maneuver he was squeezed out by two sulkies which went on to finish first and second, inches apart. Ellison Eyre was third. It would have surprised that wealthy landowner to learn that we three patched, barefoot supporters actually felt sorry for him as he trotted, embarrassed at defeat, out of the arena. Half an hour later, though, we would have different feelings about him.

The next trotting race would not take place for a while, so we left the arena for the saddling ring, where competitors were preparing for the best-turnout contest for pony and trap. Sitting outside of the ring, we watched a frisky black pony being persuaded into buggy shafts by two sisters, Miss Elsie and Miss Gwen Stern, who kept a dairy farm. This was their spoiled-pet pony, and we all laughed as they pushed and begged him and he dodged the shafts. Then we saw Josie Eyre in her yellow buggy, to which beautiful little Bo, brushed to golden perfection, was harnessed, and in sheer admiration we hoped Josie would win.

Suddenly Scotty got up. "That's Taff," he said, pointing at Bo.

He crawled into the ring and ran to Josie's rig. Gripping Bo's bridle, he pulled at the bobbed hair that flopped between the pony's eyes, as he had done with Taff.

"Taff," he said.

They say that animals respond to a tone rather than to a specific word, so maybe it was Scotty's tone, but Bo definitely flattened one ear and shook his head playfully, as if to free himself. We had often seen Taff do that. But we also knew that almost any pony would do the same thing.

"Take your hands off him!" Josie shouted at Scotty.

"You've got my pony," Scotty said, still holding Bo.

Josie slapped the reins to make Bo move. By now Tom and I had crawled into the ring and were pulling at Scotty's arm. "That's Josie Eyre's pony," I said nervously.

But Scotty, who had been feeling the pony's head and neck, pulled free and held on to the bridle as if his life depended on it. The pony, caught between the two, let out a sharp whinny.

"Stop him, stop him!" Josie screamed at her father as Scotty began to undo the harness straps that attached Bo to the shafts.

Ellison Eyre had gone off briefly. Now he walked up to Scotty, lifted him off the ground and tried to swing him out of the way. Scotty kept a struggling deathlike grip on the bridle and fought to free himself. Bo, meanwhile, began to back away nervously.

"Get Josie down, someone!" Ellison shouted. "Get her off."

Blue Waters leaped on the buggy and picked up the protesting Josie. He handed her down into the arms of the Misses Stern, just as Ellison broke Scotty's grip. Bo, now in panic, moved off.

But Ellison kept a firm hold on the kicking Scotty, who was still shouting that it was his pony, it was Taff. Finally Ellison managed to get Scotty down on his stomach, and told Tom and me to go and get Constable Peters. But though Scotty had gone mad, neither Tom nor I was going to get a policeman to help Ellison hold him.

"Let him go," said Tom boldly.

When some of the track stewards arrived, Tom and I knew that we must get out of the way. We were urged on by a flick of Blue's long buggy whip, and we left a captive Scotty yelling on one side of the ring while a furious Josie sat helpless on the other side, with Bo—or Taff—somewhere between the two of them.

Everyone who had seen the incident at the saddling ring knew that if Scotty got free he would go straight for the pony again. So the angrily weeping boy, now held firmly by Constable Peters, was taken home. Tom and I watched from a safe distance as Josie, flushed with anger, insisted on participating in the turnout event. Bo, now shying nervously at everything, was disobedient in the competition and Josie didn't win. She was given a consolation prize, but she was furious with disappointment.

By the end of the day everyone had heard about Scotty's utter certainty that Bo was, in fact, little Taff. Was it possible that Bo and Taff were the same pony? Many people, Tom and I among them, argued about it.

"It's Taff," said Tom with a ten-year-old's conviction.

"How could even Scotty know that?" I argued.

"He just knew," Tom said with the opinionated anger that would soon become typical in St. Helen as the town began to divide fiercely over the issue.

The next morning was Saturday, and Tom and I, anxious to see Scotty, were up at six and soon on our way to Scotty's place. We found him glowering with resentment, piling up mud on the banks of the little drainage canals with which Angus had been trying to drain off salt from his land.

"How do you know that Bo is Taff?" I asked him.

"How do I know?" Scotty repeated indignantly. "I know who you are, don't I? I can tell just by looking at him that he's Taff."

When I pointed out that Blue Waters had told everybody how he had caught Josie's pony in the wild herd, Scotty insisted, "I don't know how they got him, but he's Taff."

"Even if Bo is Taff, Josie Eyre will never give him up," I said.

"Well . . ." Scotty said menacingly. "If she doesn't . . ." and he left it at that.

The incident also deeply affected the Eyre household. All our information came from Ark Arkright, whose father owned the White Swan Hotel. He told us about an argument he had overheard in the bar. Blue Waters, beer soaking his shirt sleeves where it trickled from the overflow of froth, reported that Ellison had questioned him nervously about how the pony had been picked out from the wild herd, and where.

"But he didn't have to ask," Blue said. "He saw Bo himself the day we brought him in with the others from the rough herd. He *knows* Bo was one of the herd."

Doubty Andrews, one of the town's skeptics, said, "Maybe he was. But it's been a couple of months since young Pirie lost his pony. Maybe Taff went back to the herd and turned wild again. He was half wild anyway, the way that little devil used to ride him."

"But you couldn't get near Bo when we brought him in from the bush," Blue said positively.

I suppose this was the beginning of the town's division, although at this stage it was still only an argument over a horse. Horses still mattered in St. Helen, probably because they implied a lost link with the outback. In actual fact, like most Australians, ninety percent of our townspeople knew nothing about the outback or about horses, even though they were not far from both. It was one of those myths, still current, that imagines the Australian character to be somehow derived from the stockman, the drover and the outback roustabout. Whereas the real outback type was never more than a few of our total population, and the real Australian character is urban and suburban. There is much playacting in the so-called Australian character.

So a dispute over the ownership of a horse was ideal for a good noisy debate at the long White Swan bar, which by eight o'clock was as wet as the edge of a swimming pool. And the same arguments were repeated over and over, until finally they degenerated into insults, and Scotty and Taff were forgotten.,

On Monday night my father reported at home that Dorman Walker had dropped into his office to ask what the legal position was regarding ownership of the pony in a situation like this.

"I told him there was no legal position at all," my father said. "But Josie's got the pony, and under these circumstances possession is certainly nine-tenths of the law."

"But it's Scotty's pony," Tom said.

"You think that because you sympathize with him," my sister Jeannie said. "Well, I sympathize with Josie and I say it's hers."

So our own family was divided.

THEY WERE THE LAST long days of that summer, and school was about to recommence. The river was then at its lowest, and those of us who lived by it clung to our river's fading joys as long as we could, diving deeper and deeper in the mudholes, or leaping off the cliffs over the rapids, or simply skidding on our chests in two inches of pale water.

At night I would lie in my bed on the veranda and hear ten million frogs in the swamps of Pental Island—not singing but simply raising an enormous volume of distant night sound, which blocked out for me all the emptiness and space around us.

I loved all that space in daylight, but I was utterly unnerved by it at night. I wondered how Scott Pirie felt when he spent nights alone on that frog-laden island. He had disappeared again. Then one afternoon, when I was fishing near the island, a barefoot, sunburned Scotty, his fair hair long and wild, suddenly appeared out of the bush and asked what day school started.

"Next Tuesday," I told him. "Where have you been? Your mother's frantic."

"How many more days till Tuesday?" he asked, ignoring my question.

"Four days from today," I told him.

He glanced at the two perch and the small Murray cod I had caught. "There aren't any fish here this year," he said. "Why don't you try—" He stopped. Scotty knew the river better than any of us and usually he was generous with his information, but something was on his mind this time.

"All right," I demanded. "Where should I try?"

"Ah, it's all the same, Kit," he said with a shrug.

So far no mention of Taff or Bo, and I decided that Scotty had resigned himself to defeat. But his bright blue eyes should have told me otherwise.

"Are you coming to school on Tuesday?" I asked.

"It depends," Scotty said mysteriously. He was leaning on a stick he carried in case he met snakes. "I guess your father knows what I did at the show. What does he say about the pony?" Scotty thought of my father as a sort of oracle on the law.

"He says that in a case like this, possession is what counts. Josie's got the pony, and you haven't."

We looked across the river at Ellison Eyre's wild pony herd, which was crowded together under some tall, shady gum trees.

"Don't you believe that the pony she had was Taff?" Scotty suddenly demanded.

"I'll only believe it," I said, "when I know that Taff swam the river and joined the Eyre herd again, because there's no doubt Bo was brought in wild. There's no other way it could be him."

Scotty shrugged and said nothing, and I wondered then if he had been wandering up and down the river to see if there was anyplace where Taff might have crossed it without getting his feet wet, for Taff would never have gone into the water. But when I asked him he merely shook his head, told me he'd be seeing me and disappeared again in the bush along the riverbank.

On Tuesday, Scotty turned up at school. He wore a shirt we hadn't seen before, made, perhaps, of a woman's blouse, and on his feet a pair of socks and thick shoes, soled—like his mother's—with slices of tire. All day he behaved like the old Scotty. But when school was over he simply walked through the town with Tom and me without any of his usual mischief.

"He must be sick," Tom said as we watched him disappear down the road to his home.

I had to admit that I too was surprised. Scotty's behavior seemed significant, but of what?

That evening at dinner my father told us the clue. On Saturday night Josie Eyre's pony, Bo, had disappeared.

"He did it!" Tom shouted, almost leaping out of his chair. "Scotty got his pony back!"

Jeannie told Tom to be quiet. "Well?" she demanded, the only member of the family who could demand anything of my father. "Tell us what happened."

My father told us that Josie had first missed the pony on Sunday morning. Ellison and his stockmen had looked for him all that day and Monday, but couldn't find him anywhere. So this morning Ellison had reported his problem to Sergeant Joe Collins.

"Will they blame Scotty for taking the pony?" I asked.

"If they find it on the Piries' farm."

"Will they take it back?" Jeannie asked.

"Probably. . . ."

"Can Sergeant Collins search the farm and tell Scotty, 'This is Josie Eyre's pony,' and give it back to her?" Tom demanded.

"That's what he'll try to do," my father told him.

"Then they'll accuse Scotty of being a horse thief," I said, wondering if I had unwittingly encouraged Scott to snatch the pony by reporting my father's legal opinion on possession.

"How can they call him a thief for taking his own pony?" Tom protested.

Surprised at the intensity of our feelings, my father put down his knife and fork and looked thoughtful. "Nobody will cheat the Pirie boy out of his pony—if it *is* his pony," he said. "The law can quite easily see to that." Then he was silent, and we knew that he had finished talking about the matter.

In fact, the pony was not at the Piries' farm. Sergeant Collins and Ellison Eyre drove out there and, without consulting Angus or Mrs. Pirie, walked about the place, obviously expecting to find Bo (or Taff). But there was no sign of him and nowhere to hide him on that barren farm. Angus was in the fields working on the drainage ditches when they arrived, but he had seen the car, and sticking his spade in the hard ground, he walked across to face the two men— money with the law beside it. Scotty, listening from the house, reported their conversation to us later.

"What do you glib-gabbets want?" Angus growled, like a dog protecting his battered kennel.

"My daughter's pony," Ellison answered. "Your son tried to get hold of it at the agricultural show two weeks ago."

"Well, he hasn't got your pony here," Angus said.

"But you know where it is," Collins persisted.

Angus had simply stared at them in his shriveled way and refused to answer.

"You're a fool, Angus," Collins told him. "If I find that you're hiding the pony, I'll take you in, and your boy too."

"Just get off my land," Angus snarled at him. "And the muckle devil blaw ye south!"

Joe Collins said menacingly, "We'll be back, Angus."

That was really how the hostility between Scotty and the Eyres began, and by the end of the week arguments had developed in the town about whether or not Scotty had snatched Josie's pony. But one question remained unanswered for all of us. If Scotty had taken the pony, where was he hiding it? Sergeant Collins had failed to find any trace of the animal in the area around the farm, but there were hundreds of places in the bush along the two rivers where Scotty could have hidden him—and the Eyres, with police help, had already begun to search them all.

We at school argued more about *how* Scotty had snatched the pony, for none of us doubted that he had taken it. Apparently a dog belonging to one of Ellison's drovers had discovered someone on the Eyre side of the river the night before the pony disappeared. The drover, Skeeter Bindles, had given chase to a figure about Scotty's height, but whoever it was had plunged into the river and escaped. Skeeter hadn't told Ellison at the time, because the Eyre drovers often ran into swagmen along the riverbanks who were up to no good and who fled if they were discovered.

"All right. But how did Scotty get into Bo's paddock? It's only a hundred yards from the Eyre house. And what about the dogs?" the garage owner's son, Peter Pullen, asked.

We finally decided that Scotty must have crossed the river upstream, coming on the Eyre house from the back. He had caught one of the broken horses from a large paddock some distance from the house, smeared himself with manure to confuse the dogs (we believed this to be important) and walked with the horse to the rail, where he was able to slip into the paddock where Bo was kept. We differed on how he got Bo away, but most of us agreed that he had put Taff's bridle on Bo, removed a rail at the far end of Bo's paddock, mounted the pony and jumped him into the adjoining paddock. He had then replaced the rail and ridden the pony to the end of the second paddock, where he had repeated his earlier performance, and then gone back the way he had come.

But if he had persuaded Bo to cross the river, then Bo was not Taff. Had Scotty found a place where the pony could cross without getting his feet wet? I remembered that just before Bo had disappeared, Scotty had changed his mind about telling me where to fish; maybe that was the place of the dry crossing, and I decided to look for it, but in secret, so as not to jeopardize Scotty.

But then my father came into the affair.

Sergeant Collins got Scotty out of class one day, took him to the police station for three hours of questioning, and then charged him with suspicion of theft and concealment of a pony and with obstructing a policeman in the performance of his duties. Scotty had tried to run away when he was taken from school, and I think he had also kicked Sergeant Collins in the shins. Finally he was taken home, Angus Pirie was told of the accusations against his son, and since no one else in town would take such a hopeless case, Angus came to my father.

If SERGEANT Collins had known at the outset how seriously my father would treat Scotty's defense, he might have acted differently. To my law-loving father, statutes and the just administration of the law were the only true constants in life, and when the police misused the law or misinterpreted the statutes he was as incensed as if he had caught someone stealing.

In dealing with Scotty, Sergeant Collins was breaking two cardinal rules of police responsibility, my father told us one night at dinner. "Ellison Eyre is breathing down his back, so without really exhausting the means at his disposal for finding the pony, Collins is hoping to frighten the Piries into producing the animal."

Against anyone but a fanatic on justice like my father, Ellison Eyre would easily win his case. But once my father got his teeth into an issue like this he fought like a tiger.

"Ellison Eyre just wants to boss everybody," Tom said, voicing an instinctive Australian hostility to our squatter aristocracy.

My English father saw that a native was putting an immigrant at a disadvantage, and he was determined that Scott Pirie was going to be equal to Ellison Eyre before the law. First he would try to persuade J. C. Strapp, Eyre's lawyer, who would be the prosecutor, to have the charges against Scotty withdrawn. The law was being used too casually against a minor, guilty or not.

"He won't agree to it when he knows you're going to defend Scotty," Jeannie said. She and Strapp's daughter, Ellen, went to St. Helen's only private girls' school, and they often quarreled bitterly about anything concerning their rival fathers. But Jeannie believed (like most of the girls at her school) that Scotty had stolen Josie's pony and ought to give it back.

I could sympathize with Josie Eyre. We all did. Blue Waters had reported how miserable Josie's life was without Bo, since she not only missed him, but also the freedom of movement he had given her. And she refused even to consider replacing her beloved Bo with another pony. "You've got to find him," she begged her father. So naturally Ellison had to try to recover Bo. Yet my loyalty was more and more to Scotty, who was obviously going to be the real victim in the matter—unless he got expert legal help.

"When will the case be heard if it comes to the magistrates' court?" my mother asked.

"Next week."

"How long will it last?"

"I can't really say, Hannah," my father said a little irritably, knowing what was on her mind. The Piries could not pay him, and he wouldn't ask them to.

My mother shrugged in resignation and gave us dessert, a rice pudding with not enough sugar in it, for she had run out of sugar and money at the same time. But we were used to that by now. My father's insistence on principles usually meant a financial loss, and that was why we were poor.

ON THE Sunday before Scotty's case was due to come to court, Ellison Eyre drove out to the Piries' farm and told Angus and Scotty he wanted to talk to them.

"Say what you want and then get off my land," Angus said sourly. My father had told the Piries not to talk about the case to anyone, particularly to someone from the other side.

"Will you come down to the road?" Ellison asked persuasively. "My daughter Josie is waiting there in the car."

Angus hesitated on the veranda of his barren house, Scotty and Mrs. Pirie behind him, confused for a moment by Eyre's politeness. "What for?" he asked suspiciously.

"My daughter wants to talk to your son," Ellison said.

Perhaps Ellison had forgotten that he himself was responsible for the charges against the boy, but Scotty hadn't. "Don't go, Dad. It's a trick," he said.

Angus told him to be quiet. "What can your daughter say that you can't?" he said to Eyre.

Restraining his exasperation, Ellison said, "She simply wants to explain what that pony means to her."

"Whose pony are you talking about?" Angus said angrily.

Ellison's patience cracked. "Come on, Pirie, be sensible!"

Scotty began to back away then, and Ellison realized his mistake. "Just a minute, son," he said quickly. "Josie can't walk here," he went on, "so I thought you wouldn't mind going to her."

Even Scotty knew that by asking them to face Josie with her useless legs Ellison was counting on a certain kind of charity. Scotty said, "I'm not going anywhere with you."

"All right," Eyre said resignedly. "I'll put it to you myself. You can have any pony you choose from the herd, if you'll hand over the one you took. And," he said to Angus, "I'll throw in twenty pounds and see that the charges against your boy are dropped."

"I haven't got your pony!" Scotty cried.

"But you know where it is," Ellison said sharply. "We'll find it eventually, and then you'll get nothing."

"My son isn't a thief," Mrs. Pirie said.

And then, with the worn edge of whatever pride he had left, Angus turned on Ellison. "It's no use coming here with your money and your daughter, Mr. Eyre. Twenty pounds won't persuade me that my son is a felon. Whatever he has belongs to him."

With that, he and Mrs. Pirie walked into the house. For a moment Ellison and Scotty looked boldly at one another, each recognizing the other's determination to pursue this to the bitter end.

On Monday, Angus reported Eyre's visit to my father and so did Ellison himself. Ellison tried to persuade my father to make the Piries accept his offer, but my father refused. "The offer implies the boy's guilt and provides a reward for admitting it," he told us later. J. C. Strapp had refused also to have the charges against Scotty withdrawn, so the case would still go before the magistrates. "Strapp argued that the Piries' refusal of a generous offer left him no choice but to allow the charges to stand," my father said.

The search for the pony went on, but by Wednesday, the day our local magistrates sat, Bo was still undiscovered. A magistrates' court, the lowest in the state system, could deal with cases summarily. J. C. Strapp had revealed that he intended to call three witnesses. My father had decided to call none at all. He would try to destroy the prosecution's case with their own material.

The morning of the trial Scotty came to our house as we were going off to school, and together he and my father walked down to the office. My father could not talk to children, or at least he couldn't unbend to them, and so far he had not exchanged a word with Scotty about the pony. But, as it turned out, on that walk my father got more out of Scotty than any of us had, including Scotty's own father. I think it must have been the violence of my father's honesty that either attracted or awed the boy.

Though it was unusual, Scotty was not present for his own trial. My father sent him to school, telling him to come to court only if Constable Pete Peters came to get him.

The chief magistrate, Mr. Cross, and Mr. Strapp wanted to know, in very sharp language, why Mr. Quayle, Scotty's representative, hadn't produced him. Had the boy absconded?

I was sitting at the back of the court, absent from class because I was determined to see what happened.

My father too spoke sharply. "I suggest to the court that there is no need for the boy to be present during the prosecution's attempt to blacken his character."

Mr. Cross rebuked my father, and I noticed that the rebuke was delivered rather ostentatiously just as Ellison Eyre walked in. Mr. Cross (we called him Crisscross) was a retired solicitor who held mortgages on many local farms and was trying to achieve intimacy with "fellow landowners." The other magistrates, Jimpson and Jardine, were insignificant men whom everybody ignored.

My father took Cross's reprimand calmly. "There are precedents, your Worship, for a juvenile defendant to be absent while the case against him is presented." And with his lawbooks and notes he produced half a dozen examples in Australian law, going back to colonial times, when a governor's son and sons of other important citizens had been spared the horrors of the court when charged. "If the case is proved against the boy, we will gladly produce him."

"Your point is taken, Mr. Quayle," Mr. Cross said irritably. "Mr. Strapp, do you want the boy here?"

Strapp was a very stout man who always wore wonderfully clean white shirts, and sometimes a bow tie. He looked warily at his unpredictable opponent, then said a little too casually, "Oh, I think in this case we can allow our wild young outlaw to stay out of it for the time being."

My father slapped the table in protest. "Your Worship, I strongly object to counsel's defamations against my client. The boy is of good character, and nobody here should forget it."

"Oh, never mind," Strapp said. "I withdraw the remark, so let's for heaven's sake get on with it."

"Go ahead, Mr. Strapp," the magistrate said quickly, a nervous little lift in his voice, as if he were still trying to impress Ellison Eyre but was no longer sure he could do it.

Strapp outlined his case. He told of Bo's capture and training; of how the pony had become Josie's pet and the means (the very precious means) by which she could get around. He went into detail about the trouble with Scotty at the show, and told of the sighting of a boyish figure on Eyre property and his escape into the river the night Bo disappeared. More important, Strapp had a witness who had seen Scott Pirie riding a pony along the riverbank in the early morning hours after Bo's disappearance.

My father listened impassively as Strapp spoke of Josie Eyre's pain and hardship and asked for the pony's return. Finally Strapp called his first witness, Sergeant Joe Collins, who told of investigating the pony's disappearance. He had discovered a corral by the river, and in the sand were the prints of a barefoot boy and an unshod pony.

When he had finished, Collins started to step down, hopefully, but my father raised his hand and kept him on the stand. After a silence my father asked, "Was the Piries' farm the first place you thought of when Miss Eyre's pony was reported missing?"

"Of course it was."

"So you went straight to Mr. Pirie and his son and asked what they had done with the pony. If you had found it there, what would you have done with it?" My father was sitting very upright at the worn, ink-spotted table reserved for counsel.

"I would have returned it to the Eyre family, of course."

"And did you go out to the Piries' because you were doing your duty? Or because Mr. Ellison Eyre told you to go there?"

Strapp objected to the questions, and the magistrate told my father that he was not in order. I saw my father flush angrily. "If Sergeant Collins wants to reply that he was simply doing his police duty, then let him say so."

"It was duty," Collins said.

"Now, a few months earlier, Sergeant Collins, when Mr. Pirie reported that his son's pony was missing, did your sense of duty cause you to rush to the Eyre place and ask Mr. Eyre what he had done with that pony?"

Sergeant Collins looked unhappy. "Of course not," he said.

"Is there some special difference between Mr. Eyre and Mr. Pirie that can explain your inconsistent behavior, Sergeant?" But my father didn't give him a chance to answer. "How would you have known that the pony in question was Mr. Eyre's?" he went on, getting up from the table and coming around to the witness box. "Had you ever seen the Eyre pony?" Collins admitted that he hadn't. "Yet if you'd found a pony at the Piries' farm, you were going to turn it over to the Eyre family?"

"Under the circumstances it was fair to suppose it was theirs," Collins said, collecting his wits.

Again my father flushed angrily. "Who are you to decide what belongs to anyone? Were you setting yourself up as an arbiter above the law?"

I realized then that my father was having it all his own way, because neither Mr. Strapp nor Sergeant Collins really believed in what they were doing, and I sympathized with both of them for being forced by Ellison Eyre into a situation they didn't like. My father was taking full advantage of this, but Strapp knew the law too and managed to protest that the court was not there to measure Sergeant Collins' duty. The magistrate warned my father not to pursue his "innuendos." But my father had one more question. "What did you do about finding Scott Pirie's pony, Sergeant?"

"I couldn't do much other than put up notices and ask the police at nearby towns to keep a lookout for it."

"You didn't ask Mr. Eyre to see if it had somehow got back into his wild herd?"

"No."

My father threw up his hands, shrugged and said, "Pity. . . ."

The next witness, the Eyre stockman Skeeter Bindles, reported that his dog had found a boy on the Eyre station the night before Bo had gone. The little devil had immediately plunged into the river and had swum like a fish to the other side, but Skeeter knew Scott Pirie by sight and he was definitely that boy.

My father, who had been listening with exaggerated attention, asked, "What color is Scott Pirie's hair, Mr. Bindles?"

"Light brown, I suppose."

"I could produce half a dozen boys with light brown hair in St. Helen who swim like fish and behave like little devils," my father said. "The boy you saw—was he wearing braces to keep his trousers up?"

Skeeter screwed up his eyes. "Maybe. I didn't notice."

"Then what *did* you notice that would irrefutably identify the figure you describe as Scott Pirie?"

"It's difficult to pick out one thing," Skeeter said boldly. "But it was him all right."

My father went on tying knots in Skeeter's story until Skeeter stepped down.

The last witness was Alan Smith, the state inspector of canals and rivers and a respected irrigation and flood authority, important to the riverbank farmers. A tall, thin man with gray hair and mustache, he had been visiting St. Helen once a month for years.

He knew Scott Pirie well, he said, and had last seen him riding a pony along the banks of the river about five in the morning after Bo had been stolen. He had shouted a greeting, but on hearing it the boy had dug his heels into the animal's flanks and had taken flight into the bush.

"Was there any doubt that the boy in question was Scott Pirie?" Strapp said.

"None," Alan Smith said.

My father took up the questioning. "What were you doing on the riverbank that day, Mr. Smith?"

"Inspecting it for erosion."

"You've spent a lifetime studying water systems and are an expert on them. Are you also an authority on boys and ponies?"

"Hardly," Mr. Smith answered.

"As an amateur on boys, then, how could you tell at five o'clock in the morning, from a considerable distance, that the youth you saw was actually taking flight?"

"It seemed obvious," Smith replied.

"Ah. It seemed obvious. Did you get a good look at the pony?" He had. "Was its mane clipped? Its tail cut short?"

Smith hesitated. "I don't think so."

"You're sure of the boy's identity?"

"Yes."

"What about the pony?" my father snapped with sudden ferocity. "Was it the one stolen from Mr. Eyre?"

Mr. Smith blinked. "It was one of those Welsh ponies Mr. Eyre breeds, but I don't know if it was the stolen one or not."

"You're an honest man, Mr. Smith. In your own judgment, if you had actually examined the pony, could you then have sworn in this court that it was the one stolen from Mr. Eyre?"

"No, Mr. Quayle," he answered. "I couldn't."

My father signified with a wave that he had finished his cross-examination, and in effect that was also the end of the prosecution's case. The evidence against Scotty had been reduced, even ridiculed, but the chief magistrate did not intend to let him off yet.

"Do you feel that it would now be justified to allow your client to appear before us?" Mr. Cross asked my father sarcastically.

"Why not?" my father said offhandedly.

So Constable Peters was sent to school to fetch Scotty. Mr. Strapp was asked if he had any final remarks.

Strapp said, "We'll rely entirely on the evidence, your Worship. Not on clever argument or tricky cross-examination. We don't like prosecuting a boy, but I think we have shown here that he took the pony. And however painful, the law cannot relax its duty."

That was well said, for the less Strapp said now, the better for his position. I felt that my father was by no means yet the victor.

"Well, Mr. Quayle?" the magistrate said sourly. "Have you something edifying to say in conclusion?"

"My learned friend Mr. Strapp has said in effect, Let there be law," my father began. "But the law has been abused in this case from the outset. Two ponies are missing—an immigrant boy's and a rich man's. When the boy loses his pony, the police do no more than their routine duties. So when the boy believes his pony is in Miss Eyre's possession, he tries forcibly to get it back. His efforts are naturally resisted, and the police rightly escort him home. Later Miss Eyre's pony disappears. But this time, clearly using the law unequally, the police, prompted by Mr. Eyre, charge the boy with theft. The police act hastily to recover the Eyre pony. They are set, on Sergeant Collins' own admission, on prejudging the case. He, not this court, was going to decide that any pony found at the Piries' farm belonged to Mr. Eyre.

"But the proper course should have been for the police to find out if the boy had a pony, to ascertain if it could be proved conclusively that it was the Eyre pony, and only then to bring the matter to court. Instead they tried to frighten the boy into surrendering a pony they could not prove was not his own.

"The real issue here is not the boy, but the pony. We have only one pony and two people claiming it," my father said slowly.

Strapp leaped up. "Is counsel deliberately withholding evidence? You have been denying that you have the pony."

"I've never denied that we have a pony, merely that it was a stolen pony. Is it Bo, belonging to Ellison Eyre? Or is it Taff, belonging to Scott Pirie? That is how this matter should have come before the court, with both claimants equal before the law."

"I object with all the force at my command." The words came tumbling out of Strapp's mouth. "Mr. Eyre has had to face the distress of his daughter—"

My father turned on him savagely. "Miss Eyre isn't being prosecuted as a felon. It is a barefoot thirteen-year-old boy you are prosecuting. Isn't that distress? I will not produce the pony," he added, looking straight at Eyre, "until the prosecution withdraws the criminal charges against Scott Pirie, without prejudice. Then Mr. Eyre can begin some other form of litigation to test the real point: whether the pony in my client's possession is Bo or Taff."

Ellison Eyre sent Strapp a silent message of assent, and the prosecutor, sighing his defeat, stood up and reluctantly agreed to my father's suggestion, on condition that he produce the pony. At this, there was laughter and clapping in the court.

But my father had not yet finished. He would surrender the pony to the police pound for safekeeping, he said, only on Sergeant Collins' guarantee that there would be no unauthorized access to the animal by either side. Collins assured the court that he would do so. The magistrate said, "Is this case withdrawn, Mr. Strapp?"

"Yes, your Worship. We withdraw."

The case was thus ended, and just then Constable Peters arrived with Scotty, who looked hot and bewildered but still fighting.

"Good for you, Scotty!" Peterson, a night watchman in the timber yard, shouted to him, and in the odd melee which followed, four people clapped the boy on the shoulder, while others, in the first real demonstration of the town's divided factions, circulated around Eyre, which embarrassed and annoyed him. As the court was clearing, the supporters for Scotty or Ellison Eyre—or rather for Scotty or Josie Eyre—were very noisy. I was amazed at how much feeling Scotty's predicament had already generated.

A Sporting Proposition

I GOT BACK INTO MY classroom undetected, between periods, when none of the teachers were about. I announced that the case against Scotty had been withdrawn and that the court would decide whether the pony was Taff or Bo. There were shouts of approval from some but catcalls from others, and the rival groups immediately began a bitter argument over who would get the pony and how the court could even decide such a thing.

Then we noticed our English teacher, Mr. Cannon, standing in the doorway listening. "Did you report to the headmaster that you were in court today, Quayle?" he demanded.

"No, sir," I said.

"Well, I won't report you, but you can write out fifty times, 'I must not take sides against the law, even when it appears to be wrong.' " Obviously he was against my father and Scotty.

When Scotty came back at lunchtime, twenty of us collected around him in the schoolyard to ask where he had hidden the pony and what secret sign he would put on it so that it couldn't be switched with another.

"I don't have to mark him," Scotty said. "I know Taff."

At the end of the school day he was out and away before anyone could stop him. But as Tom and I were walking home he appeared from somewhere near Dr. Taplow's place. He told us that in the morning he would meet my father at the police pound with the pony. But how, he worried, would my father prove it was actually Taff? He hadn't liked to ask him.

I promised to try to find out, though I didn't think my father would tell me anything. But I said, "Don't worry, Scotty. He knows what he's doing."

When I got home I did everything that was considered my duty with particular care, in case my father had seen me in court and was going to punish me for missing school. I didn't want to add to the suffering, so I chopped the wood, filled his kerosene lamp, cleaned out the kitchen drain and washed the dog and cat bowls. My father came in at six and I was looking ostentatiously at my homework. Dinnertime came without my being told to bend over the arm of the sofa to get four of the best, and I knew I was safe.

But I also guessed that he knew where I had been that morning and was merely closing his eyes to it.

At the table he explained briefly what had happened in court, adding that the pony case, as the town now called it, would probably be tried in two weeks.

"Those children will have a painful wait," my mother said. "I'm sorry for them both."

"*I'm* sorry for Josie," Jeannie said, but she was in a dilemma, for she was the one my father was closest to and now she was taking the opposite side.

"You can't be sorry for Josie Eyre," Tom said indignantly. "She's got hundreds of ponies and now she's trying to get Scott's too."

"That's enough!" my father said sharply. "Neither of you has any proof whose pony it is."

I saw my chance. "How will you prove it's Taff?" I asked.

"By internal logic," he said. "If it's young Pirie's pony, it'll reveal itself."

My father firmly believed truth had a quality of its own which could not be measured but which always revealed itself when it was attacked from all sides. "Truth will out," he would say. He believed that everything in man was man's idea, but originated from the cosmic mind—God. So everything had its inner logic. But I knew that he really discovered his own truth in legal cases by hard work and knowledge of the law.

Next morning, half an hour before school, Tom and I, the Eyres and some townspeople were at the police pound to see Scott arrive with the pony. Both of them looked as if they had been hiding in a brier patch. The pony was covered with burrs and mud, his mane and tail were tangled, and he limped, making him and his barefoot rider seem part of the same soreness.

"It's Bo!" I heard Josie shout from an Eyre horse truck near the gate, upright and neat as always, and very sure of herself in her pigtails. She had insisted on coming. In fact, Blue reported later that she had wept and banged her wheelchair into a wall when her mother had said that she couldn't come.

"You'll only upset yourself," her mother had told her.

"But I'm upset already," Josie had said with irrefutable logic.

Scotty didn't even look at Josie as he rode through the open gate and into the pound. There were two other horses there, but they had been divided off and the pony had a piece of the paddock to himself. Scotty had slipped off his back as if removing his own skin, and with the same movement he slid away the bridle.

As Sergeant Collins was closing the gate, Ellison Eyre jumped down from his truck; he was heading toward the pony when my father, who was inside the paddock, held up his hand and stopped him. "Wait until Mr. Crisp looks at him, please."

An arthritic old man who had been a drover and a noted horseman in his day, "Crispie" now was responsible for seeing that the stock waiting at the railhead did not stray where it shouldn't.

As he approached the pony its ears went back, its head shot up, and Scotty, gripping the mane, was almost lifted off his feet. That was a Taff gesture. On the other hand, the pony allowed Crispie to hold him as he said gently, "Whoa, boy. Steady." And that wasn't at all like little Taff, who never stood still for strangers.

Crispie lifted the pony's sore leg, looked at the hoof and told my father, "It's a crack that's gone into the flesh, but it'll be all right with a bit of pomade." Then he opened the pony's mouth and inspected his teeth carefully. The pony still did not object, looking even more unlike Taff. But then most animals will accept an expert's handling.

When the old man had finished, my father explained to an angry Ellison that Mr. Crisp was his consultant. "He tells me he will know this pony anywhere from now on, which is, of course, a guarantee for us both that strangers will not interfere with him."

"Then am I permitted to approach the animal now?" Eyre said sarcastically.

"Of course," my father said. "Let him go, Scott."

Once released, the pony flung up his head and trotted away. "Come up to him from his quarters," Josie shouted to her father and Blue, who had joined him.

The pony waited for them, tolerating this approach. When they got to his shoulder they petted him, and Blue suddenly slipped a rope halter over his nose. Scotty flew at the two men. "They're taking him away," he choked. "Let him go!"

Sergeant Collins caught the kicking, struggling boy in midair. "None of that," he shouted.

My father spoke sharply to Scotty, and then he called me. "Kit, tell him it's all right."

"It's all right, Scotty," I assured him. "They won't take him. My father won't let them."

But I couldn't blame him for misunderstanding the situation. In his expensive clothes, with Blue at his side and a truck waiting nearby, Ellison Eyre seemed about to seize all before him.

"If you do not object," Ellison said to my father, "I simply want to take the pony to my daughter."

"Of course. Kit, open the gate for him."

Ellison and Blue led the pony to where Josie was sitting in the truck. Josie was too proud to cry in public, but though she disciplined herself, we could see two very undisciplined tears rolling down her cheeks when she got her hands on the pony's head.

I looked at Scotty. Wide-eyed, caught for the first time in the rivalry of pain between them, Scotty stared at the emotion-filled girl, who must also have understood by then that they were sharing the same misery.

Mrs. Stout, an ardent Christian from one of the minor sects, who did a lot of charitable good in the town and disliked disorder, shouted to Ellison, "Put the pony in the truck and take it home."

"And take Mrs. Stout with you," someone added. That was Mrs. Maddy, who dressed and spoke like a man.

Everybody laughed then, breaking the tension which had gripped us, and the pony seemed to relax as well. It nudged Josie in that nose-bumping way ponies have.

"Take him back now, Blue," Mrs. Pat Eyre said anxiously.

As Blue led him to the paddock, more tears splashed down Josie's face. "Shame," someone said.

It was almost nine o'clock, and my father ordered Tom and me to school. Scotty had disappeared, so we left with the dozen or so other pupils who were there. Leaning on the rails of the pound, the adults were arguing about the pony, looking for identifying characteristics to prove it was Taff or Bo.

Miss James, who worked in the sweetshop and sometimes gave us presents of stale, hard snowballs, said that she had seen Scott Pirie's pony dozens of times and she was positive this was it.

On the other hand, Jack Diamond, who delivered kerosene to the Eyre place every month, said that the pony was Josie's, because like Bo it had thick back legs, whereas Taff's were inclined to taper near the fetlock.

As we headed for school at a jog trot, Tom said indignantly, "Did you see Dorman Walker?"

I nodded. He had not been in court for Scotty's trial, but it wasn't Scotty he was interested in. It was the pony.

"He thinks he'll get hold of the pony if Scotty wins. But we'll see about that," Tom said as we puffed along. He was taking up his usual posture of moral indignation, already planning a second battle even before the first had been won.

OVERNIGHT it became an excursion for half the town to go and see the pony in the pound. Not a day passed that Tom and I didn't go there, and by the time the case came to court again, we could identify everyone in St. Helen as for or against Scotty.

Scotty could not walk through town without someone shouting encouragement or opposition. And bewildering things happened to him. One day he was given a suit of clothes by Mr. Wilson, the draper: pro-Scotty. He was accused of stealing oranges by Mrs. Sims, wife of the town surveyor: anti-Scotty. Dr. Taplow called out to him an unprecedented "How are you, son?" from his Buick one day: pro-Scotty. At school we were ferocious in our partisanship, with sentimental pity for the crippled Josie or the barefoot Scotty.

The day Scotty brought the pony to the pound, he kept watch all night against the police station wall, convinced that Eyre was coming back for the pony with his truck. Sergeant Collins found him there at three in the morning, when he went outside to make sure everything was all right. Later he rang up my father to complain, and my father told me for heaven's sake to reassure Scotty.

But nothing I told him would undo his suspicion that Collins and Eyre were in collusion to steal or switch the pony.

Scotty didn't see what I saw in the process: that Ellison Eyre was an honorable man. Scotty saw only Eyre's arrogance and his conviction that the law was there for him, not for Scotty. Tom agreed. "He's rich and can do what he likes," Tom said.

"That has nothing to do with it," my father told him angrily. "Eyre is a gentleman and Collins knows his duty. That's what counts. Not whether they're rich or poor."

But my father was disappointed with Eyre for abusing the privileges of his wealth. Even so, what he was really nervous about was Scotty, not Ellison, trying to steal the pony. He took Scotty into his office one morning and talked to him for half an hour, and he went to the pound every day to see that the pony was all right.

What the situation did was to reveal Scotty and Josie to each other, and Josie herself to the town. It must have been difficult for Josie, who hated to be seen in her wheelchair, but the day after the pony was impounded she came to the paddock in the truck and let Eyre lift her into her wheelchair in front of at least a dozen people. Everything about the pony was now done with an audience. She wheeled herself right up to the pony, who stood his ground, ears twitching, muscles quivering. But as she started to pat him, she leaned forward too much and the chair tipped over and flung her out. The pony ran away.

"But she wouldn't give up," my sister Jeannie said later. In temper and bright eyes Jeannie resembled Josie. "Her father picked her up and put her back in the chair, and this time she wheeled around to the side of the pony. She had a currycomb and she combed out his mane and even his legs."

The restless pony for the most part tolerated this. The incident extended the pony argument considerably, because the town now saw Josie close up for the first time, not only with the pony but in the way she looked and behaved. And she was a very impressive little girl. Jeannie said, "I actually forgot that she was crippled, even though she was in that chair."

Scotty had few attractions that would appeal to anyone except

for his silent, barelegged, brown-faced surface and his stubborn
mouth and mischievous eyes. But he had his own success with the
pony. Sergeant Collins was glad to have him come once a day to
fill the water trough. Scotty carried the water in a kerosene tin
that was so big he could hardly manage it, and the water slopped
all over his legs. Technically it was his duty to provide feed as
well, since he was the defendant, but Eyre generously sent hay and
oats, which my father accepted on condition that Scotty give it to
the pony himself. Later I realized why he had insisted on this.

Scotty was most impressive when he groomed the pony. His way
was neither affectionate nor rough. It was simply a natural contact
of his body with the horse, done with such confidence that any
pony would probably have accepted it. He combed out the tail
with his old currycomb, and though the pony kept walking away,
Scotty followed, never letting go, holding him or shouldering him
into the fence to keep him still. When the pony tried once to
squash him against the fence, Scotty was under the belly and out
the other side before the pony knew what had happened.

Between them, Scotty and Josie soon had the pony perfectly
groomed. Scotty would be at the pound before nine and after four,
and Josie, not confined to school hours, would go there at eleven,
or sometimes at three in the afternoon. Normally Eyre was strict
about Josie's schoolwork, as was her governess, Miss Steele (a stern
young woman with a bun of golden hair). But sometimes Miss
Steele herself would come with Josie and sit in the truck. "Keep
away from the fence," she would call out nervously to her pupil in
her wheelchair. Or, "For heaven's sake be careful of your hands."

Inevitably the day came when Josie and Scotty overlapped.
Scotty was late one morning, because he had to milk for his father,
who had an infected hand. He was struggling with the water tin
when Josie arrived, and she and Miss Steele sat in the truck and
watched him pour water into the trough, then fill the tin with hay
and tip it into the feed bin. And finally, rake manure into a corner.

"I was washing my face and hands in the horse trough," Scotty
told us indignantly, "and the governess said that someone ought to
tell me that wasn't hygienic."

"Why didn't she tell you herself?" Doris Dowling asked him.

"Because Josie Eyre told her not to talk to me," he replied.

Scotty had finished what he was doing, then leaned on the fence as Josie wheeled into the paddock to groom the pony with a proper horse brush. She talked to the pony all the while and lavished affection on her Bo. Scotty was sure that the pony didn't like it, for he had always treated Taff as he would treat himself.

They met at the pound on one other occasion. Ellison Eyre brought Josie early one day and stood at the gate watching Scotty fill the feed bin with hay. "You're giving him too much," Ellison said. "He's not getting enough exercise, so one portion of hay and one of oats is quite sufficient."

"He doesn't eat oats," Scotty argued. "He doesn't like them."

"Nonsense. . . ."

"But he doesn't," Josie shouted from the truck. She and Scotty exchanged words through Ellison Eyre as if he were a lightning conductor for them, but they never talked directly to each other. I thought what a pity that was. After all, it seemed extraordinary that they both claimed a pony who didn't like oats.

"Tell him not to pull the mane like that," Josie called.

Scotty, trying to get the pony out of the way while he filled the feed bin, was pulling the mane as if he were lifting an anchor.

"Why do you pull on him like that?" Ellison said sharply.

"You tell her it doesn't hurt him," Scotty said indignantly. "If you take your hands off him, he plays tricks on you."

I saw Ellison smile to himself. I think he admired Scotty for standing up to him, in his bare feet, and a velour shirt that might have been cut from someone's curtains.

We were now confused, for the pony obviously responded to both Josie and Scotty. "Animals know when they are the center of attention, and this pony is obviously enjoying every moment of it," my father told us over dinner. And I believed it. I saw that wicked little Welsh pony bite Scotty one day, and I saw him tip Josie out of her chair another day. I saw him follow Scotty around the paddock like a dog, and then put his head in Josie's lap and nuzzle her as she caressed him from her chair.

"You dirty dog," I said disgustedly in his ear one day when I was sitting on the fence and he came near. And I swear his ear twitched and his eyes responded like a dog's.

Meantime the court papers had been served. The case would be heard at the next session of a higher court, before Mr. Laker, a visiting judge who was renowned for never saying much in court and even less outside the court, but who was a passionate visitor to country race meets and a well-known judge of horseflesh.

The day before the case came up, my father told us over dinner that, Mr. Strapp, representing Eyre, had four witnesses, some of them expert ones. My father also had four witnesses, including his own expert, Mr. Crisp, the old drover. He didn't tell us what his case would be, but he did say that he would try not to put Scotty in the witness box. He'd made it clear that if Strapp asked to question the boy, he would then ask to question Ellison Eyre.

By the time the case was heard, you could lay a bet in the barbershop at eight to four against Scotty, but in the bar of the White Swan Hotel, where the real sports were, you could get seven to five that the court would rule for him. The Saturday before the case, Blue bet four pounds on Josie's chances, because, he informed everyone, Mr. Strapp would put Josie herself in the witness box. We all knew the sympathy Josie would get.

"Why won't you let Scotty into the witness box?" Tom asked my father.

My father looked over his spectacles at both of us and said, "It is a principle of advocacy that children in court may win sympathy— but often lose cases."

The day for the court case began with a startling telephone call from Sergeant Collins at seven thirty, reporting that the pony was gone. "Somebody put a crowbar into the padlock and pried the latch clean out of the post," Collins said angrily.

"Oh, no . . ." my father groaned.

"I'm not accusing the boy," Collins said quickly, "but I'd like you to see my position. I'll have to go to the Piries' to look."

"I see my client's position," my father said sharply, "and I won't tolerate anything that prejudices it." He hung up, stood still for a moment, then turned to me. "Borrow a bicycle and get out to the Piries' farm, *quick*. Find out if the boy is there, and if he had anything to do with taking the pony from the police pound."

I rushed across the street to the Phillipses to borrow a bike. It was a lady's bike, ancient, almost four feet high and hell to ride, but Barney Phillips said I could take it. I jumped on and, sawing my way across the empty space between the handlebars and seat, headed for the Piries'. I had only gone about a mile and a half when Sergeant Collins passed me in the police Chevrolet and stopped to offer me a lift.

"No thanks," I said, feeling rather sorry for him in his wretched dilemma. "I'll get there on my own."

"Please yourself, Kit," the sergeant grumbled as he started the car. "Your old man's going to skin me alive in court for this, but I don't know what else I can do."

Long before I reached the Piries' place, the sergeant was on his way back, with Scotty beside him. I called out to them, but Collins only shouted something and drove on. I turned and followed. Puffing and red-faced, I reached home and told my father what had happened. He thought for a moment, then told me to get down to the police station and get Scotty. He would telephone, and I was not to leave without Scotty.

I got back on the bike, pedaling like a boat on a storm-tossed ocean. When I got to the station there were cars and motorcycles, people talking and arguing, and there in the pound, calmly eating from the feed bin, was the pony. Scotty was pouring water into the trough. I asked him what had happened.

"Somebody found him down by the power station."

"But who let him out?"

"I don't know," Scotty said, puzzled and fed up with the complexity of it and with the onlookers, arguing all around him.

It was obvious that some local larrikins had been playing a joke on the town. Or someone who didn't like Scotty had done it. Or someone who didn't like Josie Eyre. I took Scotty back with me, and my father told him to go home and put on his best clothes and be at the courthouse, with his father, at ten o'clock.

I had been excused from school for the day by the headmaster himself so that I could report back about the trial. "I hope," he said, "that this will curtail some of the wilder elements who plan to miss school and go to the courthouse." He was being rather sour, but I thought I recognized a pro-Scotty influence in the idea.

It was clear from the outset that every claim made by one side, and proved by witnesses, could be made equally well by the other side, and disproved by witnesses. This, it turned out, was my father's tactic: to make absolute judgment impossible.

Mr. Strapp set out vigorously to prove that the pony in the pound was Bo. But whenever he tried to mention the vital part of his argument—that Scotty had stolen Bo—my father objected. Scotty was not on trial for theft. Finally Strapp gave up all hope of making that point.

He called on Blue to explain how the pony in dispute had been caught from the wild herd. "Objection," my father said quickly. "There's no proof yet that the pony in question is the same one Mr. Strapp is talking about. So let counsel and witnesses refer to *a* pony, not *this* pony."

The silent judge, in his silent wisdom, simply nodded, and thereafter all of Strapp's evidence had to refer to *a* pony. Blue was allowed to explain how *a* pony had been selected, broken and trained by young Josie, under considerable difficulty and with real courage, and how it had become a substitute for the girl's own legs.

I was sitting on one side of the courtroom behind my father, next to Scotty and Mr. Pirie, both in jackets that smelled of mothballs. On the other side of the room were Ellison Eyre, Josie and Mrs. Eyre, who was stunning in a hat with a fine veil into which a butterfly had been worked. Ellison had carried Josie in, but she wanted no sentimentality. The moment he put her down she adjusted her legs with her hands, sat up straight and with a look forbade anybody to pity her. When Strapp referred to her condition, she swished her braids impatiently and, for a moment, looked hard at Scotty. He was sitting on his hands, embarrassed, staring straight ahead, his hair hopelessly alive all over his head. But then

Josie caught my eye. Realizing that she was also being watched, she blushed and looked angrily away.

"Now, Mr. Bluey," Strapp was saying, and when everybody in the court laughed, Strapp looked a little bewildered.

"I'm Mr. Waters," Blue drawled.

"Of course. I'm sorry," Strapp said.

More laughter. For most of the people the trial was rather like a good horse race in a country town that loved horse racing. But indignation and sympathy were also present. And I noticed on many faces a determination to see justice done.

When Blue had finished, my father asked him if he had ever seen the pony, Taff, which Mr. Pirie had bought thirteen months ago.

He had, and had even caught and delivered him.

"Exactly how high was he?" my father asked.

"About thirteen and a half hands," Blue said. "I never really measured him."

"Did you or anyone else at Riverside record the distinguishing marks of the pony you took to the Piries'?"

"No, I don't think so."

"So you have no exact information on Mr. Pirie's pony, then, and you could not say scientifically that the pony we have in the pound is *not* that pony. Did you ever measure Mr. Eyre's pony, Bo, or record his markings?"

"There was no need to."

"So you really couldn't say, either, with records used in bloodstock identification—measurement, height, and distinguishing marks or coloration—that the pony in the police pound is Mr. Eyre's. In fact, to prove that in this court, Mr. Waters, you would have to produce such scientific records. Unfortunately," my father went on, "your word by itself isn't quite good enough, because I can produce equally reliable witnesses to say that in their opinion the pony is Taff."

"Well, they're bloody well wrong," Blue said.

But my father had finished with him. I could see that Strapp was puzzled at the way things were proceeding and so was Eyre. Wouldn't it have been better to undermine the Eyre case and

439

prove Scotty's? Even the judge put on a pair of pince-nez and looked solemnly at my father, as if trying to estimate his intentions.

The only real evidence Strapp had to prove the pony was Bo, not Taff, was the evidence of his unshod hoofs, his affection for Josie Eyre, two horny marks on his back legs, and his coloration. Strapp had two witnesses for these facts—Blue and the stockman Skeeter Bindles—who had handled both ponies. But though they made some distinction between the two ponies, they had to admit again that they had no recorded proof that the pony in this pound was one or the other.

Mr. Strapp's final witness was Josie herself. When she was called to testify, the judge asked her if she wanted to sit in a chair at the front of the court.

"No. I want to sit there," Josie said, pointing to the box, and when Ellison had carried her there and somehow got her into it, she again made that impressive, impatient little gesture which commanded everybody to ignore her disability.

"Now, Josie," Strapp began when the rituals of procedure had been completed. "Let me ask you: Do you believe that the pony in the police pound is your own pony, Bo?"

"Yes," Josie said boldly.

"How do you know?"

Josie bit her lip. "Well, I know my father is my father, and my mother is my mother. And I know Bo is Bo. I can't tell you how."

The gallery liked the answer, and even my father raised his eyebrows appreciatively.

"What sort of a pony is your Bo?"

"He's stubborn, clever, and sometimes he's wicked. He doesn't like anybody except me to touch him much."

"And what sort of things does the pony in the police pound do that Bo also does?" Strapp asked.

"Well, he jerks his head up like that"—she jerked her head up—"when you get too near him. He lets me brush him under his jaws, and a lot of our ponies don't like that. He puts his head down and pushes me in the chest when I tickle him, and he also bends his head to let me brush him."

440

Judge Laker seemed fascinated, as if he had finally heard something worthwhile.

Strapp went on. "When you called the pony in the pound by the name Bo, did he come to you?"

"Yes, instantly."

"Are Welsh ponies—the Eyre breed—inclined to kick or bite?"

"They kick at each other, but they don't kick people much. They do bite a lot."

"Did the pony in the pound ever try to bite you when you held his head or tickled or brushed him?"

"Bo never really bit me. Ever. But he bit him!" Josie pointed to Scotty, and the two of them looked at each other for a gray and cloudy moment in the court. I saw Josie gulp, and Scotty, embarrassed by the fuss and overwhelmed by the court proceedings, blushed to his ears. He stared wide-eyed at Josie and, as if they were twins, tightened his lips the way Josie tightened hers.

"Objection," my father said gently, without standing up.

Strapp agreed not to press the point. "One final question, Josie. You love your pony. What would you do if you lost him forever?"

"I'd *die!*" Josie said vehemently.

The judge smiled at such a healthy conviction, but women all over the little courtroom were almost applauding. My father frowned, and objected to children being led into a question which pointed to an emotional answer like that. The judge nodded agreement, and Strapp turned the witness over to my father.

Josie sat there like a queen as my father stood up and said, "Miss Eyre. . . ."

Josie liked that. She straightened up and became a little miss, throwing back her pigtails.

"Did the pony in the pound come every time you called him?" he continued.

Josie hesitated. "No, he didn't."

"So sometimes you called him and he didn't come."

"Yes, but that's only because he's wicked."

"One more question, and then you can go back to your mother and father."

"I don't mind being here," Josie said. Another good answer.

Everybody laughed, and I think the judge nodded his silent approval. But my father didn't like it.

"You may not mind, Miss Eyre, because you're an intelligent little girl. But I mind, and so should others in this court. Now, one more question. Did your pony ever bite anyone at home?"

"No," Josie said. "He just nibbled sometimes."

"So your pony wasn't a biter, whereas this one seems to be."

Catching the meaning of her answer, Josie said quickly, "That's because he liked everybody at home, but not him." Again the finger shot out at Scotty.

"We'll have to see about that later, Josie," my father said, almost to himself, and sat down.

Josie was carried back to her seat, and the stiff silence in the court reflected the sympathy she had won.

It was my father's turn then to present his case. He began by saying that Ellison Eyre's Welsh ponies were famous for their identical coloration and height, and their stubborn and sometimes unpredictable humor. So without exact records you could not say accurately that any two-year-old pony was Bo or Taff or any other.

"I make these preliminary remarks," he concluded, "aware that my evidence is no better and no worse than that of the other side."

Again everybody was puzzled, including the judge. "Frankly," he said, "I don't quite see your direction, Mr. Quayle."

"It will become clear in a moment, your Honor," my father said. Then he called his own expert witness, Mr. Crisp, to show that in age and characteristics the pony could indeed be Taff.

Mr. Crisp said he remembered Taff well. Scotty had brought him in for free treatment for hoof trouble, and he was convinced, as an experienced horse handler, that the pony was Taff.

Then Strapp questioned Mr. Crisp, suggesting that it was impossible for him to be absolutely sure. But Mr. Strapp was clearly aware now that the more he looked for doubt, even on the other side, the more he was playing somehow into my father's hands.

The next witness was Mrs. Maddy, the one who dressed and spoke like a man. She said she knew all about horses, for her father had been a horsebreaker. She had inspected the pony thoroughly, and she was convinced that it was Taff.

Strapp had to question her, and again the argument went back and forth. Then my father brought in one of the Piries' neighbors, and the milk collector for the butter factory. Finally he called Angus, who described bitterly how he had bought the pony, and how Scotty had broken it in until the boy and pony were one.

Strapp was stumped. He did not know what my father was working up to. As a result his questions had no direction. My father told us later, "Even if you can't decide what is in the other man's mind, you must always persist clearly with your own case. That was what Strapp should have done—although it probably wouldn't have made any difference."

Finally, to everybody's surprise, Scotty was called. While Strapp was questioning Mr. Pirie, my father had spoken quickly to the boy, so Scotty knew what was expected of him. He got up and walked cautiously to the box, like a soldier walking through a minefield. His startled look was a funny mixture of fear and hostility, of puzzlement and grim determination.

"Now, young Master Pirie," my father said. "Is the pony in the pound your own Taff?"

"Yes," Scotty said, head down.

"Son, forget all this"—my father waved his hands at the court—"and talk to me as you would to your friends at school. Did that pony come to you in the pound when you called him?"

Scotty raised his head. "Yes," he said.

"Every time?"

"No. Not every time."

"Did that pony ever bite you, as Miss Eyre said?"

Scotty was slowly unbending, but his eyes were fixed on my father, as if he dared not look anywhere else. "A few times."

"Is that unusual for Taff? Did he often bite you?"

"Yes. Taff was always waiting to catch me off guard. When he did he'd whip his head around and nip my legs. And then he'd laugh, the way horses do when they've played a trick on you. But I didn't mind. I was always playing tricks on him too."

"What do you do to him when he plays tricks?"

"I whack him," Scotty said.

"You mean with a stick?"

"Oh, no. With my hand."

"Hold your hand up so we can all see it." Scotty held up his squat, small hand.

"Nothing much to worry about there," my father mumbled, and then he sighed and said, as if he finally had to come to it, "If you were to lose your pony, Taff, by one means or another, would you want to have another?"

"No, I only want Taff," Scott said grimly.

"Mr. Eyre has generously offered to give you any pony you want from his herd. Why do you only want Taff?"

"Because he's my pony," Scotty said indignantly.

My father sat down, and Mr. Strapp began to question Scotty. I think we all waited for the one question he had to ask. "How did you get the pony that is now in the police pound?"

"My father bought him," Scotty replied.

"Didn't you get him some other way more recently?"

"Objection," my father said. "Counsel is asking the boy to incriminate himself."

"You cannot ask a self-incriminating question, Mr. Strapp," the judge said. "You know that."

Strapp shrugged angrily. Since he couldn't ask Scotty straight out if he'd stolen the pony, it was pointless to ask him anything at all. Scotty was allowed to step down.

It looked as if the case were over, and despite my father's neutralizing of the evidence, I felt that the decision would be given to Strapp. After all, Scotty had lost his pony months ago. Then, suddenly, he had admitted having a pony again, only a short time after Josie's had been stolen. That could not be ignored.

But my father had not finished. In summing up, he said that there was absolutely no hope of either side proving to the satisfaction of the court that the pony in the pound was Bo or Taff. A decision either way, based on the evidence, would be patently unfair, indeed impossible.

"Then what, Mr. Quayle, are you asking the court to decide?" the judge demanded.

"Nothing," my father said. "Bear with me a moment, your Honor," he went on quickly. "St. Helen is horse country, and here we are still part of what one could call Australia's horse culture. This is a country court, and issues about horses and sheep and cattle are part and parcel of its business. So I think we have to consider this case in our own special way, according to our own special circumstances." He paused for effect.

"What exactly were you thinking of?" the judge asked, as if warning that it had better be good.

"Well, first of all, your Honor, it is a well-worn part of all British justice that justice must not only be done, but be *seen* to be done. Since it is clearly impossible to choose fairly between the two protagonists, I think we must look for natural justice to help us."

"What are you getting at?" Judge Laker demanded.

"Natural justice is a silver thread that runs through our common law. I am proposing that we ask natural justice to help us. Since even a Solomon could not decide fairly whose pony this is, I propose that this court arrange a situation in which the pony itself can make its choice."

The courtroom exploded into laughter and confusion. Strapp was on his feet, the judge was banging on the wall behind him with his pencil, and the court officer, Mr. Cuff, was calling for order.

When order was at last restored, the judge told my father to outline the conditions he envisaged for a pony to make up its mind.

My father spoke as if he were taking the judge into his confidence. "Let us say a roped-off area for the pony to wait in, then a passage for him to walk down, leading to an open space with our young protagonists at opposite sides there. Let them both call the pony, and let the pony decide which one he will go to."

The judge looked down at my father with a gambler's eye. "The idea is intriguing, Mr. Quayle, but will Mr. Strapp and his clients agree? Will your own client agree?"

"I think I can persuade my young friend," my father said. Then he looked at Josie. "I'm sure everybody concerned has been impressed with the intelligence and character of Miss Eyre, who, I am sure, would agree that this is a fair way of deciding it."

Mr. Strapp stood up. "I shall have to consult my clients."

Eyre had been explaining the suggestion to his wife and Josie, and now Josie was nodding vigorously, saying, "Yes, yes."

The murmur in the courtroom was like a train coming busily into a station, but the judge let it go on, while Strapp talked to Ellison Eyre and my father explained it to Scotty and Mr. Pirie. Scotty tightened his lips again and said, "I'll do it if she will."

"Your Honor." The noise subsided as Strapp addressed the court. "While this is not a well-tried procedure, my clients agree to the suggestion, provided it is properly organized by the court and is in fact a genuine sitting of the court itself."

"Does your client agree, Mr. Quayle?" the judge asked.

"Unhesitatingly," my father said, "and I think Mr. Strapp's remarks are well taken."

The judge had a grip on his upper lip, as if he were pleased himself but under strict self-discipline. "Well, I suppose it is a fair sporting proposition," he said.

I realized then that my father had cold-bloodedly counted on the Australian fascination, almost the Australian instinct, for the sporting proposition. Looking around the court, I could see the gambler's glint in every eye, and I had to include in that Josie herself, her parents, Scotty, Mr. Strapp and myself. But not my father. He had planned it that way; it came out of inner logic.

"In that case," the judge said, "I will adjourn this matter now and ask Mr. Quayle, Mr. Strapp, Sergeant Collins and Mr. Cuff to consult with me in chambers. We will have to choose a venue and set up some ground rules. Then I will convene this court at a proper place, where we can seek the help of what Mr. Quayle has so rightly called the silver thread of natural justice."

HAD my father ever asked himself, I wondered, if Scotty really *did* swim the river and take Josie Eyre's pony? My father's honesty was irreproachable, but lawyers never asked themselves certain questions when defending a client. When my father walked along the street he never looked at anything immediately in front of him. He was always looking at some unknown point far ahead, and I think that little gap of blindness just in front of him was his moral safeguard. Self-protection aside, he enjoyed playing the Australians at their own game. The split in the town now was almost like that in the partisan crowd around a boxing ring.

Judge Laker, Mr. Strapp and my father chose the local fairgrounds for the scene of the big decision. Surrounded by a high fence, it would permit easy control of spectators. The court would convene there in one week's time, and meanwhile neither Josie nor Scotty was to go near the pony. A square where the pony would wait was to be erected in the arena, and a narrow passage would lead to a large, fenced-in square with Josie in one corner and Scotty in the other. The pony's choice would be decisive only when, without either youngster's moving, he came near enough to be touched. The judge's decision would be final.

"What if the pony doesn't go to either of them?" Tom asked, when we heard at dinner what the arrangements would be.

"They'll stay there until he does," my father said.

Jeannie protested. "If Josie loses, she'll never get over it. It doesn't matter so much with Scotty. He's a boy."

"It will matter to both," my father said. "That's the pity of it."

"Is it necessary to make it so public?" my mother asked.

"Justice should always be as public as possible, Hannah. Otherwise it doesn't speak with the loud voice of public conscience."

The loud voice of St. Helen's public conscience was already making itself heard. Betting on the result was so passionate at school that the headmaster had to totally forbid it, but the school was only a reflection of the town itself, and we still bet anything we could—money, pocketknives, marbles, slingshots, fishing rods. I bet the two top sections of my father's fishing rod against a new reel, although one without the other was useless. A girl called Sandy Williams tried to bet Scotty himself that he wouldn't win, and Scotty, in tears, flew into a temper and pushed her over and pulled her pigtails until she ran screaming for help. It was one of the few times I ever saw Scotty in tears.

On Saturday (the test would be on Wednesday) I saw Josie in town, sitting in her father's car outside the house of Mr. Strapp's law partner. "Kit," she called. "Kit Quayle. Come here." I approached, and her brilliant eyes accused me.

"Everybody in town is betting," she said. "What did you bet?" I refused to tell her, and she demanded, "Why does everybody in your school hate me?"

Surprised, I told her we didn't hate her. In fact, we mostly admired her, but she said, "Doris Dowling hates me!"

"Doris likes Scotty, that's all," I said.

"What does *he* say?"

"Scotty? He won't even talk about it."

"I won't either," she said vehemently, and whatever had inspired Scotty to knock Sandy Williams down was also affecting Josie. "Why don't any of you believe it's my pony?"

I told her that a lot of us did believe it.

"Mostly girls and town boys," she said grimly. "Country boys are on his side. So are you, although you are a town boy."

I could not explain to her all my complex reasons for supporting Scotty, and I knew already that I was going to be very sorry for either loser. So I said, "You've got a lot more ponies, Josie. You can take your pick."

"But it *is* my pony," she said angrily. "If I was at your school . . ." The sentence trailed away. Josie knew all about our school rivalries and longed to be in the middle of the fray. "If he gets the pony, I'll never come into town or talk to anyone here again," she threatened, almost in tears.

I left then; I had no desire to see anyone in tears—anywhere, at any time, or for any reason. Least of all Josie Eyre, who was not the tearful type.

By now I knew the emotional mechanism of both Josie and Scotty, and could not help feeling that both were secretly aware, above all, of each other.

Scotty seemed to be waiting to see which way his life would go, as if it were all out of his hands. He had always been a fighter, but now he didn't know whom or what to fight. And I knew that if he lost the pony, he was going to plunge into a reckless personal revolt which might lead him in a wrong, wasteful direction.

"Kit," he said to me, appearing over the garden fence eating an autumn orange, "would you ask your old man if I can take my bridle with me tomorrow?" Tomorrow was the day of decision.

"All right," I said, knowing that he was too proud to ask my father. He could ask me, for I was one of his own. "I hear you were talking to that girl yesterday," he went on.

"You mean Josie Eyre? Yes, I was talking to her."

We were walking by the Pickering place, where once he would have teased the dog behind the fence. But even the teasing part of him seemed to have gone. Only his old habit of appearing and disappearing remained, and that was an instinct by now.

"What did she say about me?" he asked.

"Nothing," I said. "She wanted to know what *you* said, but I told her you wouldn't talk about it."

"She thinks she's going to win, doesn't she?" he said.

"She's not so sure, Scotty."

"All those people in court are on her side."

"What are you talking about? A lot of them are on your side."

Scotty shrugged. "Anyway, I'm not going to lose, Kit. That's my pony, and when I whistle, or click like this, or hold up the bridle, he'll come. *She* can make any noise she likes, or call him Bo, but it won't make any difference."

"Too true," I said.

"I suppose she'll be sitting in that chair, but I don't care," Scotty said grimly. "I'll bring my bridle, and if they won't let me use it, I'll put up my hands and shake them, just as if I've got it."

Neither he nor Josie could know what that pony would do, but unlike Josie, Scotty did not threaten the town with permanent absence or silence if he lost. He seemed instead to be somehow threatening himself.

It was a fine autumn day. The headmaster had intelligently faced the fact that the whole school was passionately involved with the affair and had therefore allowed twenty-four pupils, Tom and myself included, to go to the fairgrounds to see natural justice at work. So that we could report back without too much distortion, we were about equally divided into those who supported Scotty and those who supported Josie. We walked in twos to the arena behind two teachers who were themselves antagonists in the same rivalry that had split the children and the town.

When we reached the large old wooden gates of the fairgrounds, shaded by gum trees, we were surprised to see some fifty people waiting to get in. The gates were only half open, held that way by Mr. Bell, the owner of the bicycle shop, who had been deputized as gate controller. We were allowed to march in ahead of the others to an area that had been set aside for us near where Josie and Scotty would wait. All of us crowded up close to the rail.

Soon the little grandstand of the fairgrounds was almost full; the arena was surrounded by townspeople waiting and arguing. And Sergeant Collins, magnificent in his trooper's uniform, was parading around the area on his black Thoroughbred to keep order.

Within the arena was a small roped-off square, where the pony was walking around fretfully, and a lift-out gate which led to a narrow passage twenty yards long. This led to a larger fenced square with a chair in one corner and space for Josie in the other. Outside the fence stood a table and half a dozen chairs and the judges' stand usually set up at the trotting races. That, we guessed, was where the judge, my father and Mr. Strapp would be.

Scotty was in his corner. He had been sitting there alone since nine o'clock. It was now ten o'clock, the appointed hour, and there was no sign of Josie Eyre. The pony was becoming more and more restless in response to the tension and excitement around it.

I noticed Scotty's bridle was on the chair (my father had said he would consult the judge and Mr. Strapp about it). "Scotty has a secret trick," I told my friends mysteriously. "You'll see."

Just then Josie arrived in the car with her father and mother, and in the horse truck behind was her chair. Blue lifted it down, and Josie, by some extraordinary balancing, got into it without help.

"Good for you, Josie," someone shouted.

There were cheers and countercheers, but whereas Josie ignored them, Scotty, sitting on his hands, looked around at the crowd and probably added this situation to all the other indefinable pressures that were interfering with his life. Josie wheeled herself into the enclosure and over to her corner. The pony was now tossing his head and cantering nervously around his little square. Once he rushed forward as if to jump, but swerved off at the last moment, almost tangling himself in the ropes.

Some sort of consultation was going on between Judge Laker, my father, Mr. Strapp and Ellison Eyre. Then Mr. Cuff, the court officer, walked over to Scotty and spoke to him, and Scotty handed him the bridle, which Mr. Cuff put on the ground just outside the fence. There was a shout of dismay from the Scotty supporters.

"Unfair," someone shouted. "You've cut his arms off!"

Sergeant Collins, on his Thoroughbred, shouted angrily, "Order! This is a court."

Finally the judge, followed by bulky Mr. Strapp and the very neat figure of my father, climbed into the judges' stand, followed by Mr. Cuff, who raised his voice and shouted that the court was now in session. Then he turned to the stands and bellowed, "There must be absolute silence in this court. If there is any shouting or distraction, the judge will order everybody out and the matter will be decided in quieter circumstances."

"Good for you, Cuff," someone shouted. But so many people told the man to shut up that obviously there would be no real disturbance, not even from the larrikins.

Constable Peters was at the gate to the pony's compartment, and the judge was standing with a handkerchief in his raised hand. An expectant silence fell on the crowd. Josie leaned forward tensely in her chair, gripping the sides, and Scotty had his fingers up to his mouth, waiting to whistle.

"Are you ready?" The judge's voice wafted thinly over the arena.

I suppose they said yes, for the judge dropped his hand, Constable Peters opened the gate and, hesitating a moment, the pony looked at the opening and then galloped out. He ran down the narrow rope lane. Now we could hear Scotty's frantic whistle and Josie's desperate voice. "Bo. Bo. Come here this instant!" she said.

"Taff," Scott said. "Come on!" And he made his little clicking noise. He too was sitting down. Obviously he had been told that it would be unfair for him to stand up.

The pony burst into the square, cantered a few yards, tossed its head, stopped and looked around, ignoring both of them.

"Bo! Bo!" Josie clapped her hands. "You're so wicked. Will you come here!"

"Taff!" Scotty was shouting and lifting his hands above his head as if he held a bridle. "Eight o'clock, Taff. Eight o'clock." That was the time they normally set out for school.

The pony looked at Josie and took his first steps in her direction. She redoubled her shouting. "Come, Bo! Come on!"

Scotty was whistling frantically.

"I can't bear it," Doris Dowling said. She put her head down and stared at the ground. I felt the same way, but the fascination of it was impossible to resist.

The pony turned off toward Scotty. "No. No," Josie shouted. "This way!" The pony stopped again and looked across the gap at the court table. I felt that he was not only aware of all the attention, but was playing the fool to drag it out.

Finally he turned and trotted irritably away, and for a moment Scotty and Josie both waited to see what he would do. He stopped and turned toward them, and Doris Dowling looked up as they began calling again. This time there was anguish in Josie's voice. "Bo! Bo . . . please come, or I'll never forgive you. Ever."

Scotty was trying to keep from bouncing up and down on his chair as he called, "Eight o'clock, Taff. Time to go." Then he yelled, "Taff!" so loudly and desperately that someone laughed— the only time there was any sound at all from the public.

The pony ignored the two of them now and walked around the square as if he wanted to get out of the whole thing. As he passed only five feet from Josie, she appealed hysterically, "Bo! You're so wicked. Come when you're told!" The pony simply stood still and looked at her. Then he walked on as she called desperately after him, beating her hands on her chair in a frenzy.

Scotty was now clicking and slapping his chair. He was already hoarse, and sounded tired. Suddenly he gave up. The pony stood fifteen feet away looking at him, and Scott stared back at the pony with a blank, resentful look, as if sending him to hell.

"Bo. . . ." It was a last cry from Josie. The pony lifted his head and shook his neck.

He walked straight up to Scotty and pushed him off the chair. When Scotty picked himself up, clinging to the pony's neck, the pony flung up his head, lifted Scotty clean off his feet and dumped him on the ground in the well-known rough play that boy and pony had always enjoyed.

The whole arena burst into shouts and whistles. The judge's mouth opened and he pointed at Scotty, but I could hear nothing except the noise from the gallery. Doris Dowling was shouting passionately, "I knew it!"

But Scotty had been unable to hold the restless, excited pony, who now trotted away determinedly. And then, with its own kind of cynicism, it went straight up to Josie, who had been watching miserably, and began to nuzzle her.

The entire arena fell silent as Josie lavished her own kind of affection on the pony, who nuzzled her and took little nips of her sleeve, and I knew she was saying, "You're so mean. Why did you go to him?"

"It's Bo," someone shouted.

Of course it was Bo. It was Taff *and* it was Bo. There were arguments, and later some fighting, but there was no doubt that Scotty had won. The pony had gone to him first, and the judge had already given him the decision.

The gallery had now broken into the arena and were on their way to the pony. But Scotty snatched the bridle from the ground, ran across the enclosure, pulled the bridle over the pony's head as it jerked away from Josie, and was mounted and racing down the narrow alley into the little square. There he pulled on the ropes until he got one of the stakes out of the ground. He jumped the drooping rope and was across the fairgrounds before anyone could order him back. Everybody, including Josie, had watched, electrified. Josie, in fact, had somehow raised herself on her useless legs, and then had toppled over. A hundred people were on the way to her, but Ellison got there first and picked her up.

"Put me down!" she cried angrily, and her father quickly put her in the chair as some of her unknown supporters reached her.

"Poor Josie," Doris Dowling said unhappily.

There was nothing else one could say, and since Scotty and the pony had now galloped through the main gates and were well on their way home, the Eyre entourage also began to leave. I was standing near enough to say to Josie, "Don't let it get you. Everybody's sorry about it."

But Josie stared straight ahead, face white, lips compressed—her emotional discipline admirable. She was not going to see or hear anything as they drove away.

I DON'T think it ever occurred to my father that justice that day rode on the whim of a horse. He refused to discuss the case and forbade us to refer to it again. As far as he was concerned, there was nothing more to be said. But outside the house we had to solve the questions among ourselves. The Saturday after the decision, as we headed for Scotty's farm, Tom and I tried to work it out.

"Taff must have been frightened by a goanna, fallen in the river, swum across and joined the wild herd," I said.

Tom refused to believe that. "If it was the same pony, Bo would not have been wild when the Eyres caught him."

"It doesn't take long for an animal to return to the wild," I argued. "And Scotty kept Taff half wild anyway."

"But Taff was used to people," Tom said. "So if he was also Bo, why did they have so much trouble breaking him in?"

"Nobody ever tried to *ride* him," I pointed out. "They were trying to break him to shafts, and Taff had never been in shafts."

"What about his hoofs—no nails and no shoes?" Tom persisted.

I explained that Scotty had never shod Taff, nor had Josie shod Bo, because her pony was driven on soft ground, where naked hoofs were better.

"If it's one and the same pony," Tom said finally, "that means that Scotty *did* swim the river and take him back."

"Of course," I said. "That's why we can't talk about it at home. It's one of those things that lawyers just don't want to know."

We were the children of a legal-minded household, but whereas Tom respected and believed in absolute law and justice, I never did. Something made me look for the twist of fate and for human complexities, because like everything else, justice was human, not absolute.

"I don't know," Tom said, trying to keep his absolutes intact. A week ago he had been pleased to believe that Scotty had swum the river and taken the pony. But now that he had seen how much it hurt Josie, he didn't want it to be the same pony. That, in fact, was what bothered everybody who had been at the fairgrounds.

When we reached the farm, we found Scotty and Mr. Pirie building a new enclosure for Taff out of fence wire and old railway ties. "Hello, Mr. Pirie," Tom said. "Do you want any help?"

"Aye," Angus Pirie said. "You boys dig the holes and put the posts in, if you will, while I do something more useful. I'll put up the wire later." Then he stuck the crowbar in the hard ground, took a large bag of fertilizer, humped it on his skinny back and staggered like an ant across the dry paddock.

Scotty was watching us, as if we had come out to warn him of some imminent danger, and Taff, standing in the old enclosure, stared over our heads the way horses do (maddeningly) sometimes.

"What's up?" Scotty asked suspiciously. "Are they going to come after me again for Taff? Is that why you came?"

"He's yours," I told him. "It's all settled now."

"As long as they don't try it again," Scotty said aggressively.

Mrs. Pirie came out and called to us, "Hello, Tom. Hello, Kit. Would you like a lemon drink?" The friendly Chinese market gardeners must have sent her a bag of their lemons.

"Thanks very much, Mrs. Pirie," I said quickly. I knew she was making a gesture of gratitude to my father.

We were working hard digging the postholes when Mrs. Pirie reappeared with two glasses of lemonade for Tom and me and a cup for Scotty. She had lavished a tablespoon of her precious sugar in our glasses, and it was marvelous stuff on that warm autumn day. "Before you leave I'll give you some griddle cakes for your mother," she said.

Mrs. Pirie had always been small, but each time I saw her she seemed to have shrunk. Obviously I was getting bigger, but that day she seemed especially tiny. I think it was her dress, probably cut from a checked tablecloth, which made her appear almost pretty, rather like a demure Scottish lass, though a lass grown old and dry in our barren wastelands. She watched us as we went back to digging holes, undoubtedly happy to see Scotty there with his friends. I knew what hell she must have been through every time he had disappeared or gone bush over the river.

We were still digging at the hard, salty earth when we heard a truck. We stopped and looked down the rough dirt road to see a horse pickup bouncing mercilessly over the ruts and holes.

"It's them," Scott shouted.

It was indeed Ellison Eyre, and there was someone in the front seat with him and another figure bouncing painfully in the open back of the truck. Scotty looked around for his father, but Angus was out of sight. He snatched up the bridle, had it on Taff in a second and would have been off if Tom and I hadn't stopped him. "Scotty, they won't take Taff," I said, holding him back.

"Yes, they will," he said, trying to push us away.

Tom let go, but I held on. If Scotty ran now, he would always disappear in the face of a threat, an authority, a law, a rule, a demand. I said, keeping a grip on his shirt, "Scotty, you've got to face up. You can't just take off every time they come near you."

I think Scotty knew that if he fled once more from riches and authority, he would never have the true strength to stand up for himself. "All right," he said grimly, "but don't hold me." He shook me off. "And drop that rail over there, Tom. Just in case."

Tom dropped one of the fence rails at the back, giving Scotty a quick exit if he needed it. We stood like three musketeers watching the horse pickup come nearer, and it was almost on us before we saw that Josie was in the front seat next to her father. Blue was in the back. He waved at us as the truck negotiated a huge ditch, which, on the face of Josie Eyre, was a punishment.

"Hello, Tom. Hello, Kit," Ellison said. And to Scotty, "Hello, son." We recognized a reluctance to compromise on a class difference by using his name.

"Hello, Mr. Eyre," Scotty said boldly, and I could have clapped him warmly on the back for that act of self-confidence.

"My daughter wants to talk to you," Ellison said stiffly. "Can I put her over there on the veranda? After that jolting she needs to get out of the pickup for a while."

"All right," Scotty said, hostile but firm.

Josie was staring at Scotty, who stared back at her, Taff's bridle in his hand and Taff's nose nudging at his back.

"I don't want to go to the veranda," Josie said. "Put me there." She pointed to the stack of ties we were using for posts. Ellison Eyre lifted her out of the truck and put her on the ties, and moved away from her quickly so as not to annoy her.

Josie had not taken her eyes off Scotty and Taff, and obviously Taff sensed it, because when she had settled herself the pony obligingly and cynically moved a couple of feet in her direction. Scott held him back. But when it was clear that Taff wanted to approach Josie, he moved with the pony toward her, although he would not let go the bridle. They were now face-to-face, and Josie, in better command of herself than any of us (we were nervous or embarrassed) said to Scotty in her trim, deliberate voice, "I just wanted you to know that I'm sorry we got your pony by mistake. We never knew it was yours." She hesitated as Taff nuzzled her; then she pushed her face calmly into his nose. "That's all," she said.

Scotty wasn't equal to it yet. "I suppose you didn't know."

"And he *was* wild when he came in with the others," Josie went on. "And I'm sorry. That's all."

Scotty was blushing now. "It wasn't your fault," he finally managed. "It was his." He jabbed a finger in Taff's ribs.

"No," Josie said, with her world of confidence all around her like a solid shell. "It just happened. That's all." The pony was nipping at her sleeve, and without saying anything Scotty handed her the bridle. That was when Josie had to control herself with her admirable discipline. In fact, Josie had to rise above having everything,

458

just as Scotty had risen above having nothing. And she did it well.

"You see," she said quickly. "He *is* Bo. So couldn't you ride him over to Riverside on Saturdays or Sundays? If it isn't too far?"

Scotty was now cracked from top to bottom in confusion, probably with admiration too, because he knew as she knew that they were equals in this. What had hurt one had hurt the other, and what had given Scotty his victory had also given him an insight into what Josie had suffered in defeat.

"I didn't want to take your pony," he said. "But I knew he was Taff the moment I saw him."

"I don't care about that now," Josie said, determined not to be upset. "But couldn't you come over sometimes? You could ride him around in the paddocks with me."

Scotty looked around for help, not knowing what to say. Finally he said, "If it's all right with you, Mr. Eyre, I'll do that."

"Of course," Ellison Eyre said.

"Will you come next Saturday?" Josie pressed.

Scotty dug his bare toes into the earth and said with his old stubbornness, "No. But I might the Saturday after."

Josie knew she had met her match and didn't argue. Just then Mrs. Pirie came out of the house with a jug of lemonade and glasses. "It's fresh," she said. "Do you want to come inside?"

Ellison, with his serious courtesy, said, "You're very kind, Mrs. Pirie. But it's pleasant out here in the morning sun."

He took a glass, and Josie took one and thanked Mrs. Pirie in her Riverside voice. Blue was given one. The three of us watched them sipping politely until it was finished. Mrs. Pirie stood perfectly still. Her eyes were neither for nor against them, and I think both Ellison and Josie were only now realizing what this plot of barren land meant. Mrs. Pirie and her dress were so eloquent of it.

"Thank you very much, Mrs. Pirie," Ellison said, giving her the empty glass. Then he told Scotty, "I brought you a couple of bags of hay for the pony. Blue'll unload it for you."

Scotty's blue eyes flashed angrily, and Josie recognized the mistake. "We just happened to have it in the back," she said quickly.

Scotty was proud enough to have refused, but he did Eyre the

459

favor of accepting it to avoid embarrassing him. The gap was still there, but Scotty was clearly not going to be a victim of it again.

"We'd better go, Josie," Ellison said. "Where's your father?" he asked Scotty.

Scotty pointed to the paddock by the dirt road, where the small black figure of Angus Pirie was plodding back to see what was happening. "I'll talk to him on the way out," Ellison said, and he walked over to Taff, ruffled the pony's head and ears and said grimly between his teeth, "You little brute."

Taff tossed his head. And as Josie handed Taff's bridle back to Scotty, that little master of irony, the pony, bit Scotty hard on the rear. Josie laughed delightedly, calling Taff wicked as her father carried her back to the truck. Scotty followed, and he stood with her for a moment while Taff-Bo nudged his back.

"Have you got another one now?" he asked her awkwardly.

Josie nodded, as if words were dangerous on that issue, and Ellison Eyre started the motor and called out good-by to Mrs. Pirie. Josie bit her lip and gripped the side of the truck as she prepared for the painful journey back. We watched and winced with every jerk and bounce as they went along the dirt road, and we saw them stop for five minutes while Ellison Eyre talked to Angus Pirie. What was he saying? What was he offering? What was Angus accepting? It didn't matter anymore, and when they reached the asphalt road we heard the truck accelerate, and after that there was nothing left for any of us but the future.

That too had its problems, its dirty tricks and its unpredictable fates. And the only one who had the right to laugh at it was Taff-Bo, who, with the stupidity, cunning, lack of principle, deviltry, intelligence and cantankerousness of a horse, obviously knew a good sporting proposition when he was offered one.

James Aldridge, born of English parents in Australia, grew up in a small town on the Murray River. He had a typical Australian outdoor boyhood—fishing, exploring—sometimes at Pental Island. *A Sporting Proposition* is loosely based on recollections of his happy boyhood.

James Aldridge

Aldridge left Australia in the late 1930s as a very young man, and got a job as a reporter in London. When World War II began he became a correspondent for the North American Newspaper Alliance, a syndicate which employed many distinguished writers. He met his Egyptian wife, Dina, in Cairo in 1940. After covering the war in Greece, he lived in New York for some time, where he wrote his first novel. Later he returned to active war reporting and covered the Russian front from the siege of Leningrad to the battle of Stalingrad.

Since the war the Aldridges and their two sons have lived mainly in London, but they are constant travelers and could just as well be found in Egypt, Switzerland, Russia or France.

James Aldridge is the author of nearly twenty works of fiction and nonfiction. His worldwide popularity has led, among other honors, to the whole family's having been officially invited for a fascinating visit to China.

The explosive saga of the Grangers—a family torn
by its heritage, wealth, and the responsibility of

POWER

A CONDENSATION OF THE NOVEL BY

RICHARD MARTIN STERN

ILLUSTRATED BY DAVID BLOSSOM

El Rancho del Norte sprawled across 775 square miles of northwestern New Mexico. Old Tully Granger had carved the vast holding out of the wilderness; his son Matt had inherited the empire and defended it against all comers. Now it was young Tom Granger's turn to be *el patrón*—the boss. Tom was not at all sure he wanted to be tied to the land, and his playboy brother, Will, was urging him to sell.

At the ranch was Matt Granger's stepdaughter, a young woman called Tish. She, among others, was depending on Tom. And so were the villagers, who feared the atomic reactor being built on Granger property and were terrorized by the mysterious scourge of shootings and cattle rustling that had invaded the family domain.

The ranch had become the prize in a deadly power game, and like it or not, Tom must play to win. In a fast-paced adventure the author of *Stanfield Harvest* and *The Tower* captures the romance and reality of the new West.

THE cross hairs of a 4X scope followed the man in the meadow. He was unaware of this, his concentration fixed on the topographical map in his left hand and the opened magnetic compass in his right. He wore an aluminum-frame backpack; his binoculars were secured to one shoulder strap. He was unarmed.

The man did not hear the shot that killed him; at three thousand feet per second the bullet far outdistanced the sound. And the echoes died unnoticed, except by a hawk, which, frightened by the sound, flew off down the valley. The man fell face down, arms outstretched, the map and the compass just beyond his hands.

There was an early snow that night, and the wind piled great drifts against the fence in the meadow. By noon of the next day not even the green of the man's backpack showed.

1

EL RANCHO del Norte sprawled over 775 square miles—496,000 acres of mesa, high desert, plains, valleys, and mountains—in the sovereign state of New Mexico. One man, old Tully Granger—Granger the First, as they sometimes referred to him—had put together the vast holding and held it against all comers, Indian, Spanish, Anglo.

Most of the entrances to the ranch were protected by stout gates, all by cattle guards. At the main entrance a gatehouse was occupied by José Valdes, his wife, and their brood of six. José, otherwise known as Joe, was the third Valdes to preside over the gatehouse. The .30-30 behind the door had been a gift to Joe's grandfather from Tully Granger well before statehood.

The main house, crenellated, turreted, bay-windowed, in all ways both massive and hideous, stood a mile inside the main gate. The house was very quiet now. Matt Granger—Granger the Second—Tully's son, aged eighty, was on his way out. "Fighting every foot of the way," young Dr. Harry Walker said in the downstairs hall. He smiled at Tish. Your stepfather's a character, his expression said.

"I'll go see him," the girl said. "Sometimes he listens to me." She was tall and slim, with calm eyes and short reddish brown hair. She wore faded jeans, a flannel shirt, and deerskin squaw boots. Crossing the hall, lightly climbing the stairs, her feet made no sound.

The old man was propped up in the bed. He was shrunken now, merely a husk, but the big hands on the coverlet and the wide shoulders against the pillows told what he once had been. He could smile faintly at the girl, showing teeth that were still his own. "The little pipsqueak sent you, did he?" The words were without rancor. "He wants to stick needles in me to keep me going, and he isn't going to. I'll go out my own way."

The girl's smile was sham; she was close to tears. "Haven't you always done it your way?"

The old man's face softened. "I'm cantankerous, honey," he said. "I've been that way too long to change. Even for you."

"I wouldn't ask you to." Words were difficult. She took a deep breath. "Tom phoned from Chicago. He has a charter plane waiting for him at Albuquerque."

The old man nodded faintly. "Give me a kiss and then beat it. I'm going to sleep."

Tish bent over the bed. The old man was unshaven and the

white bristles were rough. She kissed him gently. "I'll stay."

"No, you won't." The voice was suddenly stronger. "It takes two to bring somebody into the world, but you leave it all by yourself."

She crossed the room slowly. At the door she looked back. He lifted one hand in a gesture of dismissal and farewell.

THE plane took off from Albuquerque and headed north by east. "Rancho del Norte," the pilot said. "I've heard a lot about it, but I've never been there. They'll let us land for sure?"

"They'll let us land." Tom Granger was a big man, as tall and as broad as his grandfather. He sat quietly now, watching the approaching mountains. You didn't know how much you missed the bigness of this country, he told himself, until you came back to it.

"That's Los Alamos over yonder," the pilot said, "where what they call the Atomic Age got started."

Tom looked down at the river as it wound from the mountains into the mesa. It was partially obscured by a brownish haze.

"Our local smog," the pilot said. "We can't compete with Los Angeles and the big cities back east, but we do the best we can with what we have. That haze comes from those coal-fired generators up at Four Corners—where Utah, Arizona, Colorado, and this state meet. And you know the worst of it? The smog is all we get. The electricity goes to LA and Phoenix."

"I've heard."

"I flew another fellow named Granger once," the pilot said. "Missed his commercial flight in Albuquerque, and hired me to fly him to Dallas same way I'd take a bus into town. Him and his wife, real purty lady, he called her Sweet Sue." He gave Tom a sideways glance. "Kin?"

"My brother." There would be talk back in the Albuquerque hangar, Tom thought, even though there was nothing really to talk about. Grandson coming home because aged grandfather was dying—where was the news value in that? But he knew the answer; the Grangers were talked about, whatever they did.

"You know about that dead fellow they found?" the pilot said. "Two, three weeks ago it was. Been under the snow all winter."

"I hadn't heard," Tom said. "Who was he?"

"Well." The pilot grinned. "They haven't done much about it yet, because they can't decide which county he was shot in. County line runs through the meadow where they found him."

The line between Grutas and Jicarilla counties almost bisected the ranch; since statehood that fact had caused problems. Two sets of commissioners, two sheriffs, the inevitable tug-and-haul over jurisdiction. It was no wonder that Tom's grandfather had once threatened to secede from the state.

The tale was legend. "I'm easy to get along with," Matt Granger had told the governor. "Most times, that is. But if I have to, I'll shut up the ranch tighter than a drum and shoot at anyone that sets foot on it from either county. You hear me?"

The whole town of Santa Fe had heard, Tom thought now, producing one of his rare smiles. He roused himself and pointed to the right. "That bald peak," he said. "Head straight for it. There's a meadow at its base. We'll land there."

Once, when he was a boy, he climbed that sheer rock face on a dare from his brother, Will. It had taken almost two days, and he had spent the night huddled on a narrow ledge.

Came morning and he had stretched cautiously, stomped his feet to speed up circulation, tightened his belt against his hunger, and started up again, one handhold, one foothold, one more heave.

Old Matt Granger was waiting at the top, just himself and two horses. "I ought to whale you, boy," he said. "Just why did you do a fool thing like that anyway?"

All Tom said was, "I wanted to see if I could." But it had been Will's dare, of course, made with his sly smile.

The old man raised his big fists and let them fall to his sides. "Get on your horse," he said. "If you can."

Tom got on the horse and followed his grandfather down the back hump of the mountain in silence.

Long ago. Things remembered. Home. Home? Think about that, he told himself. Because in the life he had made for himself in the East, there were a job and a girl. And did they not spell home?

The girl's name was Grace, and she was eastern-bred, city-oriented, at ease in her surroundings. She saw Tom as a modern-day Lochinvar out of the West; large, strong, frighteningly direct. "I want to be wooed," she said once, "not taken by storm."

"There isn't time for wooing. I'm in a hurry."

"To get where?"

"Wherever I'm going."

Even Tim Jonas, his boss at Jonas Construction Company, registered mild protest at Tom's devotion to his work. "Boy," Tim would say, "it may sound strange, but I wish you'd slow down."

"You want this bridge built, don't you?"

It was just a small bridge across a nameless New Jersey creek, but it was a beginning, Tom's own. He knew every beam, every truss, every rivet. Once he had taken Grace out to the site. She had said, smiling, "This is my competition?"

"You were expecting another George Washington Bridge?"

She should have known better, she told herself, than to tease this man about his work. "I was only joking. Don't be cross."

"I'm not cross."

"Just disappointed. I understand." Grace hesitated. "What I don't understand," she said at last, "is why you are even here in the East at all." She waited for Tom's reply.

"The general idea," Tom said slowly, "is to make a life for myself, of my own. This"—his gesture took in the absurdly small structure spanning the tiny waterway—"is a beginning."

But now, because his grandfather was dying, he had walked out and left the bridge half done. It was, he thought, somehow symbolic, the first time he had ever walked out, even temporarily, on anything he had set his hand to.

"A ranch this size," the pilot said, "must be tough to run."

Tom's smile was grim. "It is," he said. "It sure is."

TISH had parked a jeep in the meadow and tied a silk scarf to the antenna. "That," the pilot said, "is using the old head." Watching the fluttering scarf, he kept on around the meadow and landed upwind. Tom wrote out a check, handed it to the pilot, grabbed his bag, and stepped out.

Tish was slowly untying the scarf. "Hi."

"Hi." Tom swung his bag into the jeep. "Thanks for coming."

"It's a long walk." She stood uncertain, the scarf still in her hands. "You want to drive?"

"Not unless you want me to."

She got in behind the wheel, and for a time they drove in silence. Then, "He's gone," the girl said. "He went to sleep. I think he knew he wasn't going to wake up."

Tom nodded. "A good way to go."

"And you don't care, do you?" There was anger in the question. "You and he never got along."

"That's right. We never did."

"But you were the one he told me to send for." She turned to face him. "Why?"

He smiled. "Probably because I was easier to find than Will. He and Sue flit around too fast."

"They're in Gstaad. I sent them a cable. And I telephoned Seth Porter in Santa Fe. He's driving up with the legal documents."

"Good."

"Wayne Carter wanted to see Matt," Tish continued.

"Who is he?"

Tish said, "He's the physicist in charge of the atomic reactor they're building in Long Valley."

"On ranch property?"

"Matt leased the land to them." Again a silence as they bumped out of the meadow onto a dirt road. The scent of pines was strong.

Tom said, "I understand they found a man dead. Shot."

Tish nodded.

"Do they know who he was?"

"He was identified as Walter Borden, a geologist. Apparently he was a conservationist, but he was where he had no right to be."

"I don't recall," Tom said, "that we shoot trespassers on sight. Or do we?"

The girl was silent.

"The old man," Tom said, "had been ailing for how long?"

"Six months. Longer."

"Who's been running things? Clyde Burley?"

"Among others."

They pulled up to the big house, and Tish switched off the engine. "I'll have your bag taken up to your rooms," she said, and then she hesitated. "I haven't said it yet, but welcome back."

HE STOOD in the office, looking at the desk that had been his great-grandfather's and then his grandfather's. Once as a boy he had perched in the big chair, laid his hands flat on the desk top, and pretended that he was the man in control. When he heard old Matt's footsteps he had jumped down.

"Trying it for size, boy?" Matt had said. "Maybe a little big for you right now." He had seemed amused.

Now Tom walked around the desk, hesitated, and then pulled out the chair and sat down. Maybe still too big for me, he thought, but there is no other way than to try it. Someone has to. He looked around the remembered room.

It was larger than life-size, as were all rooms in the main house, and paneled in straight-grained ponderosa pine from trees felled on the ranch. There were trophies on the wall: a massive grizzly head, a snarling cougar, a bearded mountain goat, a record rainbow trout. All taken on ranch property.

There were pictures too, which Tom had studied as a boy. There was young Teddy Roosevelt beaming at the camera through tiny round glasses, and there was the Russian grand duke who had come ten thousand miles for his grizzly bear.

There was also a picture of Tom and Will's parents, their father in his lieutenant colonel's army air force uniform, wings and ribbons prominent. Tom thought his grandfather had chosen this picture for the office wall because it caught the spirit of those few years when Bill Granger was actually doing something useful. Somewhere too, probably buried in a file, was a newspaper photograph of the *Andrea Doria* with the great hole torn in her side, final memory of Bill and Liz Granger.

There was a gun cabinet—shotguns, rifles, handguns, scrupulously cared for, carefully kept under lock and key. In the heavy drawer beneath the glass doors ammunition was stored. Fly rods, reels, and boxes of tied flies shared the cabinet with the firearms.

On the conference table near the wall was the tantalus Tom remembered from his earliest days. Its two decanters were no doubt filled with the fine bourbon shipped to the ranch by the barrel direct from the distillery in the East.

Tom looked at the far wall, where the pieced-together fifteen-foot series of topographical maps showed the outlines of the ranch in black crayon, all seven hundred and seventy-five square miles of it. Accumulated honestly? Maybe, maybe not.

Tom roused himself at the knock on the door and called. When the door opened he said, "Hello, Clyde. Come in."

Clyde Burley, the ranch foreman, was a big man who rolled as he walked, as if his boots were too tight. He sat down and stretched out his legs. "Sorry Matt's gone," he said. "What now?"

"We'll have to see. Seth Porter's on his way up."

"But you're in the saddle?"

"Maybe."

Burley said, "Matt wanted to give me a contract. I said no, if a man needs a piece of paper to hang on to his job, he'd better quit."

Tom studied the man. "Is that a question?"

"In a way."

"I don't want you to quit," Tom said, and paused. "If and when I do, I'll tell you."

Burley nodded. "That's good enough." He started to rise.

Tom raised his hand. "Nothing's official until Seth Porter gets here, but I'd like a few answers. The dead man they found in the meadow. Was that up by the old mine shaft?" That was the only meadow he could think of that was bisected by the county line.

"That's the one. Juan Valdes was riding fence and found him. Saw the backpack in the snow. Pepe Martinez wants it to be that one of our people shot him just for going through a fence." Martinez was the district attorney in Grutas County.

"Tish mentioned an atomic reactor in Long Valley."

"Yeah." Burley's voice was carefully expressionless. "Fellow named Wayne Carter. Big words. Big ideas." At last expression showed: amusement. "He looks at birds through field glasses. Seems he looks at Tish too."

It was Tom's turn to smile. "You and Carter get along?"

"Enough. He stays pretty well out of the way. His problems aren't with us."

"Who are they with?"

"Sheep die," Burley said, "and the first thing anybody thinks of is radioactivity." He paused. "A Chicano kid in Las Grutas has leukemia. They never had any leukemia before that they know of. Maybe radioactivity again." Another pause. "Some fish float downstream, belly up. Me, I think somebody used dynamite, but they're saying radiation is killing the fish."

"Matt knew about this?"

"Some." Burley hesitated. "He was tired. He didn't reach out for trouble anymore. If it came at him, that was one thing. But this—" He shook his head.

Tom sat on at the desk after Burley had gone. From the walls the trophies and the pictures looked down on him. As they had looked down on Matt, and on old Tully too. That figure of speech of Burley's stuck in his mind: "He didn't reach out for trouble anymore." Tom guessed that pretty well summed it up.

Because they *had* reached out for trouble, Tully and Matt, those two progenitors of his; they had grabbed whatever happened to be lying around and squeezed it with both hands until it hollered. The outline of the ranch on the map was the proof.

There had been an editorial in the Santa Fe newspaper once, Tom remembered, that referred to El Rancho del Norte as an "empire" and a "foreign country." Well, it was an enclave, separate and distinct from the two counties that contained it, an inevitable source of envy and annoyance.

Was water low in the stream that wound through Grutas County to the big river? Then somewhere on El Rancho del Norte they were diverting too much water for their own selfish purposes. Did one of the Gonzalez boys turn up missing one fine day? Then he had been caught taking a deer out of season on El Rancho del Norte, and the ranch people had seen to it that he never had another chance. (No matter that the boy eventually turned up in Los Angeles; the story persisted.)

In one of his rare times of easy talk with Tom, old Matt had made the point: "We're the biggest man in the bar, boy, and whenever somebody wants to make trouble, we're the natural target. They'd purely love to cut us down to their size. The only thing is"—the old man's smile was wicked—"in all this time they haven't figured out how to do it."

There was another knock on the door, and Tish walked in. She closed the door quietly. "You're the *patrón* now," she said.

"That isn't settled."

"You know different." There was strength in Tish, a willingness to speak out. Her mother, Helen Wilson, had been thirty years younger than Matt when they married; Tish had come with her and had grown up with Tom and Will on the ranch. "Hadn't you better say hello to your people? They know you're back. They're waiting. I'll go with you. You've probably forgotten names."

The people waiting were Pepe and José and Juan, Inocencio and Consuelo and Dolores, Lupita and Luisa and María Victoria. . . . They spoke a soft slurred Spanish with English words interspersed, and they smiled and shook the hand of *el patrón* in welcome.

Walking back to the office, Tom said, "I'm being managed."

"I'm trying to pay my way," Tish said.

"But this is your home. You're part of the family."

"No." At the office door Tish stopped. "Mother was, because Matt married her after your grandmother died. I just came along with her. Matt would have had to adopt me to make me part of the family. He didn't."

Tom tried to make it light. "Then maybe I will."

"If that's an offer," Tish said, "it is declined. I'll send Seth Porter in as soon as he gets here."

SETH Porter was well into his sixties; a man with white hair, a round face, and an easy, almost perpetual smile—as if running the state's most prestigious law firm was the easiest thing in the world. "It's been a long time, Tom," he said.

Tom went to the tantalus and poured two drinks. "I don't think," he said as he raised his glass, "that I've ever even seen you with a briefcase."

Seth raised his own glass. For a moment he was solemn. "Good hunting, Matt," he said, "wherever you are." He took a long sip. "There are papers in the car. They can wait. What's important is you—what you're fixing to do."

"I don't know yet." Automatically he walked around the desk and dropped into the big chair. "I've got a life in the East."

Seth nodded. "The East is where the action's at, no doubt about it. We're just a backwater." The easy smile showed. "And some of us like it just that way."

"It's a good act," Tom said, "and when I was growing up, I believed it. The country-boy role."

"It's more than an act. I was born here. I grew up here. I went away to law school—and I couldn't wait to get back."

Act, or a matter of conviction, Tom thought, it made no difference. Seth Porter was a rare being—a man at peace with himself. Tom felt a sense of impatience that the same could not be said of him. "All right," he said, "what do those papers in the car say?"

"Why," Seth said, "they put you in the catbird seat. You and Will share alike, but you're the man in charge. If you'll take it, that is. The ranch, the paper, the radio station. Taxes will take a big bite, but we prepared for this as best we could. The cash position of the estate is sound."

"What about that atomic reactor?"

Seth sipped his whiskey. "That was Matt's idea. But I made sure it's a lease that can be broken—for cause."

"If, for example," Tom said, "there are radiation leaks, radioactive pollution, that kind of thing?"

"Exactly."

Tom thought of what Burley had said about leukemia, dead sheep, and dead fish. "Why did Matt lease the land?"

Seth took his time. He said at last, "Matt purely hated that smog that's creeping down from those Four Corners coal-burning power plants. That was one reason. Another was that he knew some of the people who are sponsoring the project. It does look as if they've come up with a safe, efficient reactor design, and we need all the new sources of energy we can get." Seth paused. "They wanted an isolated location, and Long Valley was ideal." He paused again. "There is probably one other reason. This place has always been ahead in mining, cattle breeding, land conservation, reforestation, you name it. I think Matt wanted the ranch in on the ground floor in atomic power generation too.

"You know," Seth went on, "there are some folks who aren't exactly wild about the idea of safe, economical power generation from atomic fuel. Stands to reason, when you think on it."

"Oil people?" Tom said. "Coal operators?"

"A man with a lot of money invested," Seth said, "purely hates to see his business undercut. You think on it, son. The whole thing. Sitting behind that desk just might give you more action than you bargained for. Old Tully gathered in the land. Matt held it together and added a few flourishes. Keeping it is going to present lots of problems." With that Seth got up.

Tom said, "You're not leaving?"

Seth smiled as he shook his head. "I have an idea a few fish might be hungry, so with Granger permission . . ."

"Help yourself," Tom said. He too was smiling. "We'll have your catch cooked for breakfast."

He sat alone again. Now, for the first time, he could actually feel the permanent absence of the decisive, fierce old man in the upstairs bed. Tom had been left a responsibility impossible to avoid.

2

THERE were only five passengers in the first-class section of the 727. The Will Grangers sat on the cabin's shaded starboard side, far enough forward for a good view, far enough aft for a smooth ride. These Grangers were knowledgeable air travelers.

Sue had the window seat. She was deeply tanned, small-waisted, full-bosomed, a blond girl who had known from childhood that the world would always be good to her. Will Granger preferred the aisle seat, where he could stretch his long legs. He was as tall as his brother, Tom, but of a less bulky, more elegant build.

"He was really rather a dear," Sue said. She was speaking of old Matt. She glanced at Will. "You don't agree?"

"He was fond of pretty girls." Will was smiling. "But there were other sides to him too. Things always ran *his* way."

"*You* seem to have had what you wanted."

"Most of the time." Smiling still, his defense against the world. "I wanted to be an artist. My mother thought it was a great idea. She saw me in terms of Rembrandt or at least Picasso." He was mocking himself, but it was true. "All those drawings I did. Birds, snakes, landscapes. I think I was pretty much what they call a natural. Then in 1956 my art career went down with my mother in the *Andrea Doria*. Matt took a dim view of artists."

Sue smiled. "Never mind, darling, we'll be artists at living." The smile disappeared. She said slowly, "Did you miss your mother?"

"That's a funny question." Will paused for reflection. "And I don't know the answer. She was just—gone, no longer there. I think Tom missed her more."

"I would have thought less."

"Don't let him fool you. He doesn't always show what he thinks." Or give warning of what he is going to do, Will thought. And then, Face it, he told himself, you're still afraid of Tom.

"Excuse me." Will and Sue turned to look up at the big man in the aisle. His smile was easy. "You're Will Granger, aren't you?"

Will nodded.

"Farley Wells." The big man held out his hand. "We met a few times in Houston. Petroleum Club, among other places. And the little lady, as I remember, is Sweet Sue. A real appropriate name. May I buy you folks a drink?"

They sat together at the table in the lounge. "I heard about your granddaddy's death," Farley said. "I'm right sorry."

Sue said, "You knew him, Mr. Wells?"

"No, I never had the pleasure, ma'am. But I knew *of* him, of course. One of the big ones, he, and his daddy before him. Not many ranches like that left." Farley tasted his drink. "You folks being met at Albuquerque? Because if you aren't, I'd be right pleased to carry you as far as Santa Fe."

Sue looked at Will. Will said, "Thanks, but we have a charter plane to fly us to the ranch."

Tish met them with a station wagon, and they bumped along in relative silence through the forest with its heavy scent of pines. Finally Will said, "Tom is here, I gather. Has he taken over?"

"In a way." Tish's voice held nothing. "I don't think he's made up his mind yet whether to stay or go back east."

At the house Will and Sue left Tish to cope with the luggage and went up the broad steps into the front hall. There was the carved office door. How often, Will thought, have I been summoned here to await old Matt's judgment? There was the same feeling of dread now as he knocked and opened the door.

Tom was in jeans and boots and a flannel shirt. As he came out from behind the desk Sue had to admit that he was impressive.

They shook hands. "You made it," Tom said. "The funeral's tomorrow. Just the family and Seth Porter and our own people."

"And then?" This was Will. "You're staying here?"

"I don't know. Right now I've got to run down to Las Grutas to see my old friend Pepe Martinez. He's DA now and I don't want him up here with a posse on account of Walter Borden, that man who was shot."

"The charter pilot told us about the shooting," Will said. "If you don't come back, we'll send out the dogs."

"I'll come back," Tom said, and walked out.

Las Grutas had once had a population of ten thousand, and weathered houses to accommodate most of that number lined street after deserted street. The present population was closer to thirty-five hundred, but the town was still the county seat and the center of Grutas County activity. There was some agriculture, and some sheep raising and cattle grazing on nearby U.S. Forest Service land. There was no industry.

A few houses boasted TV antennas, aimed hopefully in the direction of distant Albuquerque. There was a local radio station, Granger-owned, which broadcast Spanish-language programs, country music, news, and weather reports. There was the weekly newspaper, the Las Grutas *Bugle*, also Granger-owned, which covered the area in a mixture of Spanish and English.

Pepe Martinez, county district attorney, held forth in the county courthouse. He was Tom's age, twenty-eight, with his eye on the governor's chair down in Santa Fe. "And you may get there yet, Pepe," Tom said, sitting loose and easy in the DA's office, "but not by going out of your way to twist Granger tails."

"I'm talking about murder on ranch property," Pepe said mildly.

"What was Borden shot with?"

Pepe hesitated. "It was a heavy-caliber sporting rifle."

"Our people," Tom said, "don't go around carrying expensive heavy-caliber sporting rifles. If anybody carries anything, it's a saddle gun, a thirty-thirty carbine most likely, and then only if there's reason to think a cougar is causing trouble." He paused. "You know the man was a geologist. What was he after? There's your starting place."

"He could have been on the track of gold, maybe. Or uranium."

"Let's assume he was," Tom said. "Then why would any of the ranch people shoot him? If he found anything, we'd benefit. We own the mineral rights." He stood up. "You're brighter than that, Pepe. If anything turns up, I'll be available."

He left the courthouse and started for the ranch pickup, then, on impulse, turned away and walked to the office of the Las Grutas *Bugle*. For a wonder the office was open, Kelly Garcia apparently taking a breather between news gathering and ad peddling. "Well, well, well," Kelly said. "Will you look who's here! Seeing how it looks from ground level—or below?"

"More or less," Tom said.

Kelly was the older man by twenty years, a failed city newspaperman, uncompetitive, comfortable in this isolated world. He leaned back in his chair now and put his feet up on the desk. "Well, the lead story is the dead man, Walter Borden, the mysterious walker. I even had a call from the LA *Times*. His family had been wondering what happened to him." He shrugged. "All I could tell them was that he got himself dead. Pepe Martinez—"

"I've talked with him," Tom said, and left it there, apparently wanting to change the subject.

"Okay," Kelly said. "There's other news. That little girl with leukemia. You've heard about her?"

"And about dead sheep and dead fish." Tom paused. "Any proof that the reactor is to blame?"

"You don't need proof. All you need is rumor." Kelly smiled suddenly. "You know about a bill in the state legislature to raise funds to buy El Rancho del Norte?"

"I wasn't aware anybody had said the ranch was for sale. You know who introduced the bill? Who's behind it?"

"Sam Waldo introduced it. I don't know who's behind him."

"Then find out," Tom said. "And call me." Sometimes a faint warning bell began to toll and a man did well not to ignore it.

WAYNE Carter arrived at the ranch house in a gray four-wheel-drive pickup. Tish met him and walked with him up the broad steps. "Tom isn't here," she said, "but he called from the village and he's on his way. Let's wait in the office."

Wayne was a middle-sized man in his early thirties, solid and fit, dressed in chino trousers and an old tweed jacket. He had been in the office before, but never with time to look around in leisure. He walked from picture to picture, and then turned to smile at Tish. "Fascinating," he said. "A family ledger." He pointed at the picture of Bill and Liz Granger. "Who are they?"

Tish told him. "They must have been a lot like Will and Sue, scurrying around the world amusing themselves."

Wayne sat down in one of the leather club chairs. "But Tom isn't like that?"

Tish smiled as she shook her head. "Tully, then Matt, then a skipped generation—and Tom."

"You like him?"

Tish studied the toes of her squaw boots. "I don't know," she said. "Sometimes I've leaned on him." She paused. "I was fourteen and there was a hand here on the ranch, an Anglo, who gave me a bad time. I didn't want to go to Matt. And I didn't know how to cope by myself. Then Tom came home on vacation from school in the East. He saw what was going on and told the hand to quit bothering me. It didn't take, so Tom called the man out of the bunkhouse and in front of all the other hands he beat him until he couldn't stand. Tom was just sixteen, not even full-grown."

Carter said slowly, "And I would guess that when Matt heard about it he said that Tom had done right, but that next time he had better clear it with Matt first?"

It was exactly what Matt had said, but how could this man have understood? "They never got along," Tish said.

"No." Wayne was thoughtful. "I shouldn't think they would."

Somehow the subject made Tish uncomfortable. "How's the bird-watching?" she asked.

"Only what I happen to see. I've been—busy."

Tish hesitated. "Is there trouble at the reactor?"

"We have a few problems." Just then Tom walked in and Wayne stood up to greet him. They shook hands briefly.

Tom smiled at Tish. "How about having a couple of beers sent in?" Dismissal. "Sit down," he said then to Wayne Carter. "Apparently we have things to talk about."

"Obviously," Carter said, "you know about the reactor."

There was a knock at the door, and a maid came in with the beer. Tom handed Carter a bottle and a stein, took his own, and began to pour carefully. "You wanted a place," he said, "and Matt liked the idea. But Seth Porter attached conditions."

Carter ignored his beer. "Nobody pretends, Mr. Granger," he said, "that any kind of atomic reactor is foolproof. There is a chance, only a chance, mind you, of a runaway reaction. There is the problem of heat dispersal. And there is the problem of radioactive-waste disposal." He paused. "With appropriate design and normal care in operation, the chances of a runaway reaction are practically nil."

The man had to have faith in what he was doing, Tom thought, and found no fault in that. "Go on," he said.

"Heat dispersal," Carter said, "can be handled in a number of ways, and I can assure you, as I assured Matt, that the local environment will not be harmed. It will even be benefitted. I'm an environmentalist myself, Mr. Granger, and I subscribe very strongly to the thesis that if we don't stop looting this planet of ours, we are headed for catastrophe."

A trifle pedantic, but clear, Tom thought.

"Disposal of radioactive waste," Carter said, "can be a stickler; we have to be careful where we put it. We are exploring some of the abandoned mines near Long Valley. One of them, an abandoned lead mine, seems close to ideal."

Tom set his stein down on the desk. "Leukemia, dead sheep, and dead fish," he said. "I've been hearing little else."

Carter smiled. "The fact of the matter is that all we have done so far is basic construction. There is no radioactive material on the site, and there hasn't been. We're far from ready for it. All these rumors have nothing—absolutely nothing—behind them."

"Who's starting them?"

Carter looked puzzled. "Rumors don't have to be started deliberately. Atomic physics is mysterious to most people and probably seems dangerous as well. They think of Hiroshima and Nagasaki and the H-bomb tests. Every reactor built in this country has been surrounded by rumor."

"I believe that." Tom paused. "How do the oil, gas, and coal people feel about atomic reactors generating power?"

Carter was smiling again. "Some oil companies are looking into atomic power generation on their own. But, of course, some are against it." He dismissed the possibility of chicanery with a gesture. "Those people don't start rumors, Mr. Granger. They have other, more powerful weapons."

"They wouldn't stoop to rumor, you mean?" Tom shook his head in wonder. "You had something else in mind?"

Carter now was clearly uneasy. "A rifle," he said. "It turned up on the site one morning last week. Nobody knew anything about it. I thought one of your ranch people had lost it."

Tom kept his voice unconcerned. "What kind of rifle?"

"Like that." Carter was pointing at the gun case. "The one on the right with the telescopic sight."

Tom was recalling Pepe Martinez's description of the weapon that killed Walter Borden—a heavy-caliber sporting rifle. Well, that fit the rifle in the gun case. "What do you mean," he said, "it turned up one morning?"

"It was leaning against a wall," Carter said, "as if someone had put it there and forgotten about it. But it doesn't look like the kind of possession anyone would forget indefinitely."

"And you don't like it."

"There are a lot of things I don't like," Carter said. "We had a fire some time ago. It could have been accidental; spontaneous combustion isn't out of the question."

"But you don't think it was." Tom stood up, walked over to the gun case, unlocked it, and took out the rifle Carter had pointed out. Automatically he worked the bolt and verified that the weapon was unloaded. Wordlessly he handed it to Carter.

Carter turned the rifle over in his hands. "It looks a lot like the other," he said. "I'm no expert."

"That," Tom said, "is a three-fifty magnum. If I were you, I'd take the rifle you have into Las Grutas and turn it over to Pepe Martinez, the DA. He'll ask you a lot of questions. I suggest that you answer them." He replaced the rifle in the cabinet and locked the door again. The key went on top of the cabinet, where only a tall man could reach. He walked back to his chair and sat down.

Carter said, "With Matt gone, what happens here? Will the ranch be broken up? Sold? Our lease—"

"I can't tell you what is going to happen yet," Tom said. "But consider your lease secure—as long as there isn't too much trouble because of your presence. We've existed with these mountain villages for a long time, and we won't jeopardize our position now. If we have to break the lease for cause, we will."

Tom stood up and walked to the door. He said gently, "I've been told of your interest in Tish. She is part of the family."

"And you," Carter said, "are head of the family now that Matt is gone, is that it?" He paused. "I'm being warned off?"

483

"Just warned to bear in mind that I want her happy, not hurt."

"That I will do." Carter walked out of the office.

I'm getting in deeper and deeper, Tom thought.

THE phone call was from Grace, and the connection was bad. "I miss you." Her voice was faint and distant. "And it's raining and the whole world is gray."

"It's nice here," Tom said, and instantly realized how inane the remark sounded. Grace's voice sounded again.

"I didn't hear you," he said.

"I said, 'I love you.' " This time overloud. "And I want you."

What did a man say to that? "I'm sorry," Tom said.

"I thought you might be." A pause. Then, quietly, "Good-by, Tom." The line went dead.

He called back, but there was no answer.

THERE was the new inn, where he could have stayed, but Farley Wells had known Santa Fe for a long time and he preferred the old La Fonda Hotel when he was in from Texas on law business. There was a message for him at the desk. His face was thoughtful as he carried it upstairs. In his rooms he took off his jacket, loosened his tie, and went slowly to the telephone. The number he called was in Houston, the private unlisted line, of course, and to the voice which answered he said merely, "Farley here, J.R."

J.R.'s was a quiet voice, a voice that expected and always received full attention. "I just got back, Farley. I have your report, and I wanted to make sure that we understood one another."

No comment required. Farley waited.

J.R. continued. "Our position is somewhat anomalous. Or let us say flexible. We own uranium deposits, so obviously we are not against atomic reactors per se. And we would not like to be placed in the position of openly impeding progress. On the other hand, in that state we also own high-sulfur-content coal deposits. And with the need for energy as great as it is now, those coal deposits should be mined."

"Yes, sir." Elementary, Farley thought; but it was one of the old boy's many strengths that he liked things spelled out. Then if you stubbed your toe, there was no excuse.

"So," J.R. said, "I approve your ideas, but I want no adverse publicity, and above all no trouble. Given that understanding, Farley, you have a free hand."

Farley hung up and walked slowly to stand at the windows looking out at the two asymmetrical towers of the cathedral. They were truncated, even blunt, and the impression they gave was that of strength rather than beauty. When you get right down to it, there is no substitute for strength, Farley thought. Or power.

The old man on the telephone was proof of that. A word from him and drilling began in a new field, production was increased or decreased, a ten-million-dollar contract was signed. Or he, Farley Wells, was given carte blanche and he had better not fail.

There was one thing to remember: J.R. was a great believer in what Farley thought of as overkill. He frequently sent two representatives to work in ignorance of each other to reach the same objective. It was something to bear in mind.

The telephone rang and Farley went to answer it. "Sam Waldo here, Mr. Wells," the voice said. "I'm in the lobby."

"Come up." Farley's voice was cordial. "I brought along some sipping whiskey I'd like your opinion on." As he hung up he made a wry face. He took no pleasure in Sam Waldo's company.

State legislator Sam Waldo was short and fat. He wore a brown-and-gold striped suit and a Fort Worth stetson, which he laid carefully on a table before he shook Farley's hand. "I'm mighty glad to see you," he said. He accepted a shot glass of whiskey and sniffed it appreciatively. "This liquor's been keeping real fine company," he said. "*Salud!*"

Farley sat down. "How are things going, Sam?"

"Real fine, Mr. Wells, real fine. Here's the bill I've sponsored." Sam took out sheets bearing official stamps and a quantity of signatures, most of them illegible. He started to hand them to Farley.

"I'll take your word for it, Sam," Farley said. "If you say it's right, then I know it's right." He watched the flush of pleasure in the fat cheeks. "Will it pass?"

Sam sipped his whiskey, his little finger well extended. He set the shot glass down with delicacy, and leaned forward confidentially. "I'll tell you how it is, Mr. Wells," he said. "It'd be real fine if I could tell you it was going to be like shooting fish in a rain barrel. But I'm just not sure. I'm purely not."

Nothing showed in Farley's face, and his voice held no edge. "How much, Sam?"

Sam licked his lips. "Well, maybe five thousand more."

"A lot of money, Sam."

"I know it is, Mr. Wells, a lot of money."

"But under the circumstances I think we'll put another five thousand in the pot. Wait here." Farley walked into the bedroom and returned with a thick bundle of bills. "We expect results," he said. "We don't mind spending money. But we like for it to buy something." He turned toward the door. Interview ended.

Sam stood up. "All the bill does is appropriate the money to buy, *if* the Grangers will sell. And maybe they won't."

"Maybe."

Sam hesitated. He took a deep breath. "I pushed this, Mr. Wells. I been telling everybody we ought to buy the ranch, keep it for the state, for a recreational area."

"A mighty fine idea."

"You suggested it, Mr. Wells."

"I don't rightly remember that, Sam," Farley said. "I remember it as your idea, and like I said, a mighty fine one. You'll have the conservationists behind you, and everybody who likes to fish and hunt or just walk in the mountains. You'll be a mighty big man."

Sam took another deep breath. "I'll look awful foolish too, Mr. Wells, if the Grangers tell us to go to hell, they're not selling."

"Let me worry about that, Sam," Farley said, and opened the door. "Thanks for coming up."

When Sam Waldo had waddled off down the corridor, Farley closed the door and went to stand again at the windows facing the cathedral. Beyond the two towers the Sangre de Cristo Mountains looked huge against the sky; Lake Peak still showed a sizable patch of snow beneath its summit. It was big country.

Big country, big stakes. Farley's own estimate of the value of El Rancho del Norte was thirty million, give or take a couple. And if the state would pick up the tab, so much the better, but one way or another the ranch was going to be—neutralized.

3

MATT's funeral was a brief ceremony, sparsely attended. Clinging to the old customs, Father Enrique spoke the words in Latin, while Tom, Will, Sue, Tish, Seth Porter, Clyde Burley, and the ranch people stood silently around the grave. The ranchwomen wept. The hands began filling in the grave. Tom stood for a few moments in silence, conscious of the great mountains looking down, changeless. Then he thanked the padre and walked slowly with Tish and Seth Porter back to the house. Will and Sue followed.

Inside the house Tom considered the propriety of conducting a business discussion with the old man's grave not yet filled in and found himself thinking how Matt would snort in derision if he were here. "Boy, you do what has to be done. There is no point in putting it off." Tom opened the office door. "Come on in," he said. "Seth will explain the situation."

Seth wore his easy smile. "There is very little to explain. With the exception of a number of relatively small bequests, Tom and Will inherit everything. Tom is named executor along with the Santa Fe bank and myself. In effect that puts Tom in charge." He paused. "If he wants to be, that is."

Tish was looking at the floor. No mention of her in the will, Tom thought, and what did that mean? That Matt had assumed she would be taken care of? So be it.

Will said, "Then all we have to do is sell and split the loot."

Tom looked at him. "Maybe we don't want to unload."

"Maybe you don't," Will said, "but I do. A feudal estate in the mountains has no appeal for me. The place is an anachronism." He was holding himself under tight control. It was difficult. "Sue and I want to live our life," he said to Tom.

"You can. Just as you have."

"And you'd stay here?"

"About that I don't know. I haven't decided yet."

"All right," Will said in a changed voice, "tell me why."

Tom nodded. "I'll give you several reasons. The village. The ranch people. The power plant." And, he thought, that visceral feeling that had been with him ever since he looked at the mountains and felt that he was home.

Will took a deep breath and let it out slowly. "I don't think we owe the village a thing," he said. "We've kept it alive. Maybe it's time it was allowed a decent death. There's no future for those people back here in the mountains. And what do we owe the power plant?"

"You want money," Tom said.

"Exactly right. My share." Despite himself, Will's voice was rising. "And if you think—"

"Don't threaten me," Tom said. "I'll make up my mind and I'll do what I think is best." Why was it, he thought, that always he had had to put down his brother? Why could he never make his point without inflicting pain? "I'm afraid that's how it is," he said.

Will looked at Seth Porter. "Suppose I sue for my share?"

"Why, you could try, son. We lawyerfolk love litigation. But I think you'd be wasting your time and money."

Will turned to Tom. "I lived out my purgatory as a kid here on this godforsaken ranch. Now you want to keep it up, play emperor the way Tully did, and Matt." He shook his head. "I said it. I want out." He paused. "And I'll find a way."

When Will and Sue had left and closed the door, Tom looked at Seth Porter. "I went to see Kelly Garcia at the paper. He says there is a bill in the legislature authorizing the state to buy the ranch. Do you know about that?"

"Sam Waldo's bill," Seth said, as if that explained all.

"Did he think it up?"

"He says he did. But I'm not sure I'd believe Sam if he told me the time of day. More likely somebody thought up the idea and fed it to Sam in little pieces he could understand, possibly well-buttered little pieces. Sam has an appetite."

Tish said suddenly, "You don't want me anymore, do you?" She got up from her chair and stood for a few moments, looking at Tom in silence. She said at last, "I'm glad you're staying for a little while, anyway." She was close to tears. "It isn't going to last, is it?" She hurried to the door and went out.

"In my experience," Seth said, "problems come in batches. Maybe litters is a better word. Like hound puppies."

Tom was staring at the closed door. "She says that Matt never adopted her."

"I suggested it to him once," Seth said. "He said he'd think about it. Probably it slipped his mind." He was silent for a little time. "What could be behind Sam Waldo's bill," he said presently, dismissing Tish, "is an honest effort to put the state in a position to bid on the property if you decide to sell; to keep it as recreational area and out of the hands of developers. That could be it."

"But you don't think so."

"I don't see honest conservationists contributing to Sam Waldo's private pension fund just to get him as a front man," Seth said.

"Then what is your guess?"

"Guess is what it is, son. I'd say the bill's *against* something rather than for it, but I've got one of our bright young boys nosing around to find out more."

Tom said slowly, "The only thing we're doing that we haven't been doing all along is to allow the building of that reactor."

"My thoughts had been running the same way." Seth stood up and walked around the room. "A new kind of reactor. Breeder type. Experimental. As I understand it, it generates fuel instead of just using it up."

"What if it's successful?" Tom said. "One power plant?"

Seth said slowly, "What about a gaggle of them, a whole atomic TVA up in these mountains, generating power for the entire Southwest? But power generation isn't the end of it, if you listen to young Wayne Carter." He walked slowly back and forth as if before a jury box. "In a reactor you've got heat to get rid of. Suppose you pipe that heat into the ground? A network of buried heated water pipes? What happens?"

"You raise the ground temperature."

"Exactly." Seth was smiling as at a bright young pupil. "And when snow falls it melts, and instead of ten-foot drifts you have moist growing land. And with all the sunlight we get even in winter, you'll have turned Long Valley, and maybe adjacent areas too, into year-round agricultural land. But what chance would there be for the AEC or anybody else to set up a number of atomic generators *and* develop fertile ground on land the state had bought and devoted to recreation?" Seth paused. "I'm a suspicious fellow by nature, son. I'm guessing that Sam Waldo's bill is a pressure move—and I'm guessing that the pressure has just begun."

IN A WAY, Tish thought, she was somehow kin to the wild creatures who roamed the mountains, because her instinct when she was hurt or frightened, as now, was to seek solitude. One of the ranch jeeps was handy. She drove it away from the big house.

For a time the dirt road led through piñons and junipers, chamiza shrubs, sparse grama grass, and occasional clumps of prickly pear cactus in chartreuse bloom. Then, climbing, the road entered the ponderosa forest, and suddenly the scent of the big pines was all around her.

She stopped the jeep at the edge of the road, got out, and began to walk. In the shelter of the trees there was an almost cathedral hush. She came to a small stream and paused to admire a clump of tiny pinkish violets. Farther on, Indian paintbrush caught her eye. She was alone in familiarity, strangely soothed.

She had lived most of her life in these mountains and meadows, mesas and valleys, but it would not last. That was the recurrent, devastating thought. She blamed herself for having failed to understand that the vast ranch actually was, as Will had said, an anachronism, as out of tune with the times as the feudal states she had once loved to read about.

As long as Matt had lived—even in old age keeping her world intact—she had seen no reason to question her own place in the scheme of things. Only once had Matt urged her to leave. "Honey," he had said, "this is no place for a young female. Go on up to Denver. Take an apartment, get a job, meet some people your own age. What is it they say? Live it up a little."

And so she had gone to Denver, and from the beginning she had hated it. She missed her solitude, her long quiet walks and glimpses of life even more shy and retiring than herself: the flitting shadow in the forest that could be a deer, a scuttling badger, otters at play, a single soaring eagle, a mother bear with her cubs. . . .

She met people her own age in Denver, bright, interesting people. They had projects, schemes and speculations. They were a bustling part of a bustling scene, but their interests were not hers. After six months she had gone back. "Please, Matt, let me stay here with you."

They were in the big office. "Honey," the old man said, his voice unnaturally gentle, "this is your home, and if this is where you want to be, then this is where you stay. It's just that I purely hate to see anyone as good as you go to waste."

The trouble was, of course, that she was Tish Wilson, sometimes erroneously called Tish Granger; and only she herself knew what an insufficient being she was and had been: insecure, constantly wary, knowing that in any crisis she would be found wanting.

She had never discussed this with anyone. She had been twelve years old when her mother died, and there had been only Matt, Tom, and Will left surrounding her. The children of the ranch people viewed her, as they viewed all Grangers, with a kind of unshakable awe, a barrier through which one could not pass.

When she was little she had invented a twin sister, and at night alone in bed she had made up stories in which the two of them faced problems, even dangers, and together emerged triumphant. But in reality she was and always had been alone.

She came to a large fallen tree and hoisted herself up to sit on its rough bark. The trick was to blend into the landscape with total immobility. She breathed slowly, silently, and waited.

A small wood mouse came first. He stood on his hind legs studying her, and as she watched he raised both forepaws and daintily cleaned his whiskers. Satisfied at last, he dropped to all fours and went on about his business, digging here, poking there.

How long she sat on the fallen tree she had no idea. She saw three deer and a single elk, a bobcat silent as the night, two more mice, and a red fox. When she let herself down to the ground again, she felt refreshed. She walked back to the jeep. Maybe things *would* remain the same, with Tom instead of the old man sitting behind the big desk holding her world together. Maybe.

THE northwestern half of the ranch lay in Jicarilla County, the most mountainous county in the state. Dos Piedras, the county seat, was in an upland valley long since denuded of timber. There were few cattle and only an occasional field under cultivation. For as long as Tom could remember, it had been so.

"We endure," his friend Tito Abeyta had told him once. "What else can we do? It's an Anglo world, your world, and we don't fit in it. There's no way out."

"You got out," Tom had said.

"I got to college, if that's what you mean, because I was big and strong and good at knocking people down on a football field." He patted his right knee. "But after this, no longer good enough for the pros in Houston, so here I am, back again."

"You could have stayed away. In Albuquerque, even Denver."

"You miss the point. Out there I don't fit except on a football field. I'm a part-Chicano, part-Indian freak. Back here I'm King Tito among his own."

Tito wore the sheriff's star now, a .357 magnum on his hip, and a battered and sweat-stained hat pushed back on his black hair. "You came back too," he said. "To stay?"

"For a while," Tom said.

"I always figured that you'd take over after Matt. You're the same kind of guy. What can I do for you?"

"What's the feeling in Jicarilla County? I'd like to see what I'm up against."

Tito got out of his chair and prowled the office, a big man, tall, solid, moving easily despite the weak knee. "You've had problems on the ranch. No skin off my back, because it all happened in Las Grutas County, near as we can tell."

Tom said quietly, "What kind of problems?"

"Rustling. Good old-fashioned rustling. With big semitrailer cattle trucks that can be two hundred miles away by daylight. Clyde Burley hasn't mentioned it to you?"

Tom shook his head in silence.

"Well," Tito said, "it's not the kind of thing a man likes to boast about. I don't like the feel of it. It's big-city professional stuff. You Anglos are bringing the rear end of your culture back into our mountains, and we don't like it."

"I don't much blame you," Tom said.

"Look," Tito said, "there's more. It's different, but in a way it's all part of the same thing. Hippies, yippies, flower children, call them whatever you want. They've set up a commune. They work. I'll give them that. But what they don't see is that the free and easy life-style they're so proud of is just plain insult to my people. We believe in the Church, in the family, and in women who run the home, raise the kids—and behave themselves."

A man exposed to two cultures, Tom thought, not entirely at home in either. "Go on," he said.

"A pickup truck comes into town," Tito said. "There're two, three guys with beards and long hair, black hats, and dark glasses. There are a couple of women too, and they're wearing the tightest, shortest cutoff blue jeans you ever saw, and they wiggle and waggle when they walk. And you know what?"

I could guess, Tom thought, but I won't. "Tell me."

"The pickup truck gets stopped out in the hills, and the chicks get raped. I round up the *macho* punks who did it, and they say, 'They asked for it, didn't they?' "

"In the East, the Middle West, or out on the Coast," Tito said, "it's different. The people who come there want to learn the American language and the culture. They want to fit in, that's why they came. But with us Indians, Chicanos—we *were here*, and you people ran all over us. So we live in your world, but we don't have to like it."

Tom drove slowly back to the ranch. Clyde Burley was in his office, which was a combination tack room, lounge, and closed-circuit TV center. He listened quietly while Tom told what Tito Abeyta had said about the trailer trucks and the rustling. He nodded. "We lost altogether about fifty head. Good stock."

"Fifteen, twenty thousand dollars' worth of beef," Tom said. "Any ideas?"

Burley shook his head. "But if you want to blame me—"

"Get the chip off your shoulder." Tom turned and walked away. He thought, I'm looking for a fight, and wondered why.

"Because you don't want to be out here in the first place, luv. Simple as that." Sue's voice behind him.

Had he spoken aloud? Turning, he made himself smile. "Does it show?" he asked.

Sue tucked her arm through Tom's. "Take me for a drive. Show me some of this feudal domain. I think you could use a little relaxation."

Tom hesitated. Then he nodded. "Let's go," he said.

After they left the ranch the road climbed in wide swinging curves, following the contours of the great mountain. They passed an abandoned mine, crossed a dry ravine, and Tom stopped to shift down into four-wheel drive and low transmission. "Hang on," he said, and turned off the road onto a dirt track.

They were above timberline now. Ahead as far as they could see, mountains rose in tumbled mass, and the high clear air was chill. Involuntarily Sue shivered.

"Cold?" Tom said. He stopped the jeep. "We'll go back."

"No." He was considerate, this big man. "I want to go on."

Tom smiled and put the jeep in gear.

Sue said, "Are you still looking for a fight?"

"Are you baiting me?" He knew little of his brother's wife. He knew little of women, he thought, period.

"That's part of the game," Sue said. Automatic coquetry. "We can't compete on even terms so we pick our tactics. And our times and places." She was not sure exactly what she had in mind, but she had watched Tom put her husband down almost without effort, and it was a scene she would not forget.

They topped a last steep rise and Tom braked the jeep to a halt.

495

On the horizon a single peak rose plain in the sun. "Mount Taylor," he said. "It's a hundred and twenty-five miles away."

"Fascinating." Sue's voice and smile mocked him. "Why are men always looking at distant things?"

"Instead of at you?"

"Since you mention it—yes. Am I worth looking at?"

"You are."

"But I don't think you ever noticed before."

"Wrong. At the wedding I took one look and wondered how in the world Will had managed to catch you."

"Maybe I wanted him to catch me." Sue paused. "But maybe if I'd seen you first, it would have been different."

"That is nonsense, and you know it." His tone was sharp.

Sue shook her head gently. "You're the original. He's the not very good carbon copy. It doesn't take long to see that."

"What I ought to do," Tom said, "is put you over my knee and paddle your bottom."

She had a feeling of exhilaration, of flirting with danger. "If that's your idea of fun, I'll go along." Her smile spread.

Tom turned in the seat, caught her shoulders in his hands and shook her. "You're my brother's wife," he said. His voice was low-pitched, angry. "We'll both remember that. Is that clear?"

Sue was smiling, the female triumphant. She took her time. "We'll see," she said at last. "We'll just have to see."

4

WILL Granger drove into Las Grutas, where Kelly Garcia waited in the newspaper office. "Long time no see," Kelly said. He shook hands briefly and sat down to wait in silence.

"Nothing special on my mind," Will said, a statement only partially true. "But if anybody knows what's going on, you do."

"What kind of goings on?"

Will fidgeted in his chair. He disliked demeaning himself before this newspaper bum, but he had no choice. "Is the ranch for sale?"

Kelly's eyebrows rose. He had no desire to say anything Tom

Granger would disapprove of. On the other hand, Sam Waldo's legislative bill was open knowledge. "There's some," he said, "who apparently think it is. Or will be." He explained about the bill. "If you want to talk to somebody," he added, "there's a dude up from Houston, name of Wells, Farley Wells, and the word is that he knows more about that bill than Sam Waldo does. . . ."

EXCEPT for guests, people in the ranch house breakfasted early. This morning Seth Porter was there with Tish and Tom.

Over bacon and eggs, "I'd like a guide," Tom said. He looked at Tish. "Are you available?"

"You know every inch of the ranch."

"But I want to see exactly where that body was found." Tom paused. "And anything else that's new since I was here last."

"Of course," Tish said. "You're the *jefe*." She stood up. "I'll see to the house chores and be right with you."

Seth Porter drank his coffee. His face was expressionless.

"All right," Tom said, "whatever it is, say it."

"Nothing on my mind, son, except what kind of fly I'm going to try. I purely resent having that big trout laughing at me."

"You had a phone call last night."

Seth smiled. "Don't tell me this house is bugged." He had another sip of coffee. "Incomplete information," he said, "so there was no real point in telling you about it. But Sam Waldo has a kind of sponsor, an oil lawyer from Texas, name of Farley Wells, and he's in Santa Fe right now."

Tom thought about it. "Your idea of pressure still holds?"

"Son, if it's pressure," Seth said, "then this is just the start. I know of Farley Wells, and he's not a boy they send out on a man's errand." He pushed back his chair. *"Permiso?"*

Tom smiled up at the placid face. "Good fishing."

He sat on over a cup of coffee laced with fresh ranch cream. It was probably Tish's doing that his old silver napkin ring with the grizzly bear on top had been polished until it gleamed and then placed at the head of the great table—and he had automatically seated himself where it was. He looked around the room smiling.

The table would seat twenty without crowding. The ceiling was beamed with great timbers cut and sawed on the ranch, rack-dried and finished out by imported adzmen. The heavy wrought-iron wall sconces, originally for oil lamps, had long since been electrified, but their past-century appearance was intact. Things well built and lovingly tended endured, he thought, and for the first time understood Matt's possessiveness and pride in this empire.

Sue walked in, Will behind her. Sue was in jodhpurs and a short-sleeved cream-colored silk shirt. Will wore loafers and slacks and carried a light jacket. "It doesn't look as if you two are going in the same direction," Tom said.

"Will is driving to Santa Fe on a mysterious errand," Sue said. "I'm not all that fond of Santa Fe, so I'm going riding." She paused. "If you would like to ride with me—"

"Sorry." Once alone with her was enough.

Tish came in, and Sue said immediately to her, "I'll have fruit juice, tea, and toast." For a moment the words hung in the air.

Then Tom said, "Consuelo's coming. She'll take care of you. Ready, Tish?" He smiled at them all.

"Anything you want in Santa Fe?" Will asked carefully.

Tom shook his head. There was something strained in Will's manner, something sly and a trifle furtive. Tom followed Tish out to the waiting jeep. "You drive," he said. "I'll be back in a moment." He trotted into the house.

When he returned he carried a .30-30 carbine, which he set in the rack across the rear window. Tish watched him in silence as he tossed a cartridge holder into the open glove compartment. "Don't ask me why," he said, "because I don't know."

WILL drove into Santa Fe, parked in the municipal lot, and walked the two blocks to La Fonda. On the house phone, "Will Granger here. If you have a few minutes, I'd like to talk to you."

"Delighted," Farley Wells said. "Come up. We can talk here."

Riding up in the ancient elevator, Will wondered exactly what he was going to say and, as far as that went, what it was he actually had in mind. Sooner or later confrontation with Tom?

Well, if that was what had to be, so be it, but Will would rather have someone else leading the charge. Maybe Farley Wells.

Farley Wells shook hands in a strangely gentle manner, as if he knew his strength and understood the necessity of keeping it under control. "Good to see you again," he said. And when they were seated, "How is the little lady?"

"Sue is fine." Sue would always be fine. "What I came for . . ." Will began and wondered how to continue. He was used to making his wants known, but it occurred to him that he was now engaged in a very different kind of negotiation, one that required finesse. "I understand Sam Waldo has a bill in the legislature, authorizing the state to buy the ranch. I have also heard that you know more about the bill than he does."

Farley's face remained unchanged but his eyes turned expressionless. "Now I wonder where in the world you heard that."

"From a newspaperman." Had he said something wrong? The tension in the room was palpable.

"Newspapermen get funny ideas," Farley said. He studied Will carefully. "You don't like the idea of the bill. Is that it?"

"I think it's great. I want the damn ranch sold. To somebody, and I don't care who—the state, the atomic people, anybody."

A trace of a smile lifted the corners of Farley's mouth. "I've never believed," he said, "that the time of day had anything to do with whether a man took a drink or not. And I have some bourbon I'm right proud of. Maybe you'd care to sample it?"

The tension was gone from the room, friendliness replacing menace. Will felt a strong sense of relief. "I'd be delighted."

THE road they had taken from the ranch house rose steeply. At the top, "Stop here a moment," Tom said, and stepped out of the jeep to look down at the scattered ranch buildings. Tish shut off the engine and came to stand beside him.

There was the isolated main house, a mass of stone. There the enormous wooden barn, neatly painted, with its hay storage, its milking stalls, its separated stalls where the blooded cows were brought to calve. Clyde Burley's office and breeding files were there, adjacent to the breeding pens. Over yonder was the smithy where Tom had spent hours turning the blower crank at the forge, watching the farrier fit horseshoes to the ranch's riding stock.

"I still have the knife you made me," Tish said. He'd made it from a worn Nicholson file, heated, hammered, heated again, the blacksmith's hammer draining the strength from Tom's young arm. "It was a birthday present, do you remember?"

"I remember it," Tom said, his eyes on the buildings below. The windmill still stood, but it was no longer used. Diesel generators now provided electricity for lights, pumps, barn equipment. Power lines could have been run into the ranch from Las Grutas, but Matt had preferred his independence.

There were clusters of small adobe houses for the ranch families. Here and there was movement: children playing, a man on horseback, a ranch pickup raising a plume of dust, two colts in the far pasture racing in wide circles. . . .

A living, breathing, functioning organism, the ranch, Tom thought. "First let's go to where they found Borden."

Tish parked in the shade of a ponderosa and led the way along the fence line into the upland meadow. "It was a wet winter," she said, "more snow than usual. This is the result." She pointed to blue iris, scattered buttercups, and orange Indian paintbrush.

"Not the kind of place where you'd expect violence," Tom said. "Can you locate the spot where they found Borden?"

Tish could. "He was lying here, face down, his arms stretched out. He had been shot from behind."

Tom turned to face the ponderosa forest. "Two hundred yards," he said, estimating the distance. "Shooting fish in a barrel. Now, what was there about his being here with compass and map to cause somebody to gun him down?"

Tom had turned back. He studied the fence line. He looked around the meadow. It told him nothing. "Let's go," he said. "Where was the rustling?"

As the crow flew it was not far, and the same barbed-wire fence separated the pastureland from the county road.

"It would be no trick at all," Tom said. "Cut a section of fence, drive the beef through, up ramps into the trucks—and away you go." He was looking at Tish. "You look skeptical."

"Fifty head," Tish said. "You don't find that many together very often, and to round them up at night— Unless somebody came before dark, on horseback, say, and rounded up the fifty head and held them in those trees until the trucks came."

Tom nodded slowly. "And when the trucks were loaded, what did your rider do? Turn his horse loose and go off in a truck?"

"Or stayed." Tish's voice was quiet. "If he was local, he would stay, wouldn't he?"

"You mean somebody on the ranch." Tom's voice was angry. "When was this, do you know?"

"It was only a day or two before the first big snow. By the time Clyde and the hands really got into studying what had happened, the snow came along and hid everything."

"Any other ranches been hit?"

"Not around here that I've heard of."

Why not? There was no immediate answer except old Matt's: "We're the biggest man in the bar, boy. When somebody wants to make trouble, we're the one he comes after."

They got into the jeep and Tish started the engine. "The commune?" she said.

"Have we had any trouble with them?"

Tish shook her head. "Clyde drove over when they first settled. He showed them the ranch boundaries and said that if they wanted to go on ranch property, they'd have to have permission."

"No point in my going there, then," Tom said. "Let's just drive around. I don't have the feel of the place yet."

As they reentered the ponderosa forest they saw a Chicano boy of perhaps eighteen stumbling through the trees. He held one hand pressed to his cheek, and blood oozed through his fingers. He saw the car, looked around wildly, and then waited, his eyes sullen.

Tom had the door open. "What's happened?"

"Nothing."

"That's a pretty large nothing."

"So, okay," the boy said, "I'm on your ranch. You—"

"We'll take you to Dos Piedras," Tom said. "Somebody'd better look at your face. What's your name?"

"Abeyta. Luis Abeyta."

Tom smiled. "You're one of Tito's cousins?"

The boy hesitated. "You know Tito?"

"We're old friends."

The boy sat in the back seat, hand still pressed to his cheek. Tish drove out to the country road and started to turn right. The boy said, "The other way." His voice was hard, angry. Tom turned in his seat and looked straight into the muzzle of the .30-30. The boy's forefinger rested on the trigger. The hammer was cocked. "Like I said, the other way—turn left," Luis said.

Tish spoke in a voice that was not quite steady. "But that's toward the commune."

Tom's voice was quiet. "So that's what happened, is it, Luis?"

"Four of them jumped me." The boy's voice was a snarl. "I followed one of the chicks, and they were waiting. Now I'm going to show the slobs. Let's go."

"There's no shell in the chamber," Tom said.

The boy's eyes dropped automatically to the rifle. Tom caught the barrel of the gun and pushed it up. In the enclosed car the sound of the shot was deafening, and a hole appeared in the roof. Tom wrenched the rifle out of the boy's hand. He let out a long breath and looked at Tish. "Head for Dos Piedras," he said.

When they got there, Tito Abeyta was sitting in his office, hat pushed back on his head. He looked at Luis and then at Tom.

"I didn't bang him up," Tom said. "Apparently he went snuffling after one of the commune girls and she set him up for a beating." He paused. "And Luis was going back there to start a civil war—with my rifle."

Tito scowled at Luis. "Damn young stud. I ought to show you what a real beating is." He stood up and Luis ducked. "But what I'm going to do," Tito said, "is tell those damn hippies that if they don't behave themselves, I'm coming at them for real. And that goes for you young Chicano punks too, *comprende?*"

"Okay," Luis said in a scarcely audible voice.

Tito looked at Tom. "You want to meet your neighbors?"

The thought had been in Tom's mind. "I think it might be a good idea," he said. "Tish can wait here for us."

THEY had come from the points of the compass—from Burlingame and Brookline, from Madison and Mobile, from Seattle and Shaker Heights—to meet in this small commune. The shifting population was currently nine men, eleven women, and four small children. The children played in front of an adobe structure from which a thin smoke column rose. A young woman who wore sandals and a skirt that trailed the ground stared at the visitors.

" 'Take me to your leader,' is that it, man?" This was Joe, in a black hat with a red feather perched on wild dark hair, a full beard, dark glasses, jeans, and sandals, naked and tanned to the waist. "Man, we don't have a leader. This is a free society." Joe had a master's degree in sociology. "If it's a bust—"

"No bust," Tito said. His voice was quiet. "Just a warning." He told Luis's story briefly.

"That one," Joe said. "Yeah. Look, man." Joe gestured at the adobe building and the children playing in the bare dirt. The woman in the long skirt had been joined by another, this one in tight cutoffs and a brief halter top. "What have we got to get a bunch of Chicano kids all uptight? Why can't they leave us alone?"

"Your women get the Chicano kids all uptight," Tito said.

"Man." Joe shook his head. "Man, we're living in the twentieth century. You don't keep chicks under lock and key."

"The only trouble with that," Tom said, and surprised himself by the saying, "is that it isn't the twentieth century in these parts, and God knows if it ever will be."

Joe was looking at Tom with a strange new expression. "You just think that one up?"

"You," Tom said, "had better think it over."

DRIVING back to Dos Piedras, Tito large and silent beside him in the jeep, Tom said, "How do they live?"

"If you mean," Tito said slowly, "are they maybe rustlers, the answer is no. Some of them get monthly checks from home. One of them has a bank account I'd like to have."

Back in Dos Piedras, Tito swung out of the jeep and stood fingering the hole in its roof. He bent down to speak through the open window. "You were lucky, amigo." He straightened and held the door as Tish approached. "Take care. I've noticed that people who ride around with guns sometimes end up having to use them."

Tom drove off in silence. He was thinking of the commune people, the local people, and the Anglos like himself. Taken together they formed an explosive mixture, and precisely what might come of that was anybody's guess.

THE Long Valley road leading to the reactor construction site was blocked by a gate over the cattle guard. On either side of the road Cyclone fence stretched into the trees, its top guarded by three strands of barbed wire. A uniformed guard came out of the gatehouse as the jeep drew up. "You have passes?" Polite, but firm.

"Call Wayne Carter," Tom said. "Tell him Tom Granger is here. With his sister."

Tish waited until the guard was back inside the gatehouse. "I'm not your sister." Her voice was low-pitched, angry.

"All right." Tom was smiling. "What do you want to be? Your mother married my grandfather, so that puts you in my parents' generation. What do I call you—Aunt Tish?"

"Oh, damn you, Tom!" Tish drew a deep, unsteady breath.

"I don't pretend to understand females," Tom said.

"That's nothing but a pose. The whole trouble is you see more than enough and you always have."

"You underestimate yourself."

"Matt kept saying that, and it isn't true. Nothing's worse than being told that you're smarter or prettier than you know you are."

"Maybe," Tom said, "it's about time you started believing it." His voice was gentle. He seemed about to say more, but the guard came back and gestured them through the gate. They entered the reactor site on a blacktopped road that curved through the trees.

The trees ended and the Long Valley vista opened to view:

grassy meadow, stream, and at the far end the majestic mountains plain against the sky. "I always thought," Tish said, "that this would be an ideal place for a house. Instead—"

"Instead," Tom said, "progress. Think of all the electric can openers and electric carving knives and portable electric hair driers this valley will supply power for."

Wayne Carter was waiting in the doorway of a construction trailer. Behind the trailer was a long, low, windowless building of unpainted concrete. Men in hard hats swarmed in the area amid the inevitable disorder of a construction site.

"It is not very pretty, is it?" Wayne Carter said. "Maybe one day there will be some provision for beautification in the budget." He shrugged. "Come in. I can offer coffee."

There were drawings spread on a drafting table, along with a desk-top computer terminal. Wayne gestured toward the drawings. "I don't know how much you know about reactors."

"Assume," Tom said, "that we don't know a thing."

Wayne leaned against the drafting table. "I guess the first thing to understand is that the purpose of a nuclear reactor is to produce heat. That heat is used to change water into steam to drive turbine generators that actually produce the electricity. Same principle as the fossil-fuel power plants—oil or gas or coal. Consider the reactor as a furnace."

Tom saw the interest in Tish's eyes, not only in what the man was saying, but in the man himself as well.

"The fossil fuels," Wayne was saying in his slightly pedantic way, "produce heat by combustion. We do it by bombarding atoms of fissionable material with neutrons, so that the atoms break, releasing neutrons to collide with other atoms at enormous speeds, breaking them up and thus setting up a chain reaction that produces the heat we want. It was the same reaction in the atomic bomb, but by controlling it we keep it within usable bounds."

"Controlling it how?" Tom asked.

"We can slow down the reaction by pushing graphite rods, which absorb neutrons, into the midst of the fissionable material."

"What is fissionable material?" Tish asked.

Wayne smiled faintly. "That is the heart of the matter. There are four materials available that are capable of sustaining the fission process; all four are rare, hence expensive, and as a matter of fact, only one of them—uranium 235—exists in any quantity in nature. We have to produce the other three artificially if we want to use them." He paused. "But there are ways of getting around at least some of the rarity and that is what we intend to do here."

The man really knows his stuff, Tom thought, and found a measure of resentment rising in him. Ridiculous, but there it was. "Explain that," he said.

"It isn't all that complicated," Wayne said. "We can artificially produce enough uranium 233, a fissionable isotope of uranium, to start and sustain our chain reaction. And in the reactor we also put some thorium 232, which we call a fertile material. It absorbs some of those free neutrons that are flying around, and by absorbing them, the thorium is converted into the very same uranium 233 that is running the chain reaction. So we produce more fuel than we use. For that reason the kind of reactor we are building is called a breeder reactor. If you'd care to look around—"

Tom shook his head. "I just wanted to see the general layout." He hesitated. "Any more—accidents?"

"Not since the fence went up."

Tom said, "You took the rifle to Pepe Martinez?"

"That same day." Wayne paused. "He didn't seem to want to believe my story of how I came by it."

"Pepe wouldn't." On that, at least, they agreed. "How about completion? When will you be in operation?"

"We have months of construction still ahead. We won't be in actual operation until well into the late fall of next year."

Ample time, Tom thought, for that bill in the state legislature to be passed. He wondered if he should tell Wayne about the bill, and decided against it. "We'll go along," he said. "Thanks for the explanation."

Driving back to the ranch with Tish, Tom felt again a presentiment of trouble. "How would you like to spend a few days poking around for me in Santa Fe?" he said.

"Why me?"

Spoken aloud, Tom thought, the words were going to sound strange. And yet they were true. "Because I can trust you," he said.

"Is it that?" Tish said slowly. "Or is it that you want me tucked away in a safe place—just in case?" She looked up at the hole in the jeep's roof and shivered faintly.

Tom was smiling. "So you feel it too," he said. "I was beginning to wonder if I was the only one."

5

SUE was luxuriating in a large marble bathtub when Will returned from Santa Fe. He perched on the bath stool to admire the sight. "The story is," he said, "that Tully bought two of those tubs at auction when a plush Denver bawdy house was torn down."

"And I fit the picture?" Sue was quite aware of her body's splendor, and she enjoyed its effect on her husband. She smiled up at Will. "Don't start pawing the ground, sweetie. All in good time. What did you do in Santa Fe?"

It was a game they played of tease and tantalize, and not for the world would either have broken the rules. In their lives all pleasures, great or small, were to be savored to the full.

"I saw a guy," Will said.

"How fascinating." Sue sat up and leaned forward. "Do you want to soap my back?"

Will took off his jacket and knelt beside the tub. Sue's back was silky and deeply tanned. His hands moved slowly, sensuously spreading lather on the smooth skin.

"It was Farley Wells, the man we had a drink with on the plane." Will dried his hands and went to perch again on the bath stool. "He's coming up here," he said.

Sue sank back into the water, her face and eyes thoughtful. "Why?" she said.

"Maybe it wasn't entirely by accident," he said slowly, "that we were on the same flight." The coincidence had not occurred to Will until this moment.

"Sweetie." Sue's voice held a faint edge. "You haven't told me yet why he's coming."

"It's called unanimity of purpose," Will said. "You and I want the ranch sold. Farley Wells wants the ranch sold. So we join forces right here. Doesn't that make sense?"

In many ways, Sue thought, he was a small boy with a small boy's love for intrigue. On the other hand, he was the man she had chosen, and so far she had had no reason to regret having chosen him. She smiled, and her body stirred gently, sending small ripples against the sides of the vast ornate tub.

THE next afternoon Tom, Will, and Farley Wells sat in the downstairs office. "This," Farley said, "is sipping bourbon." He rolled a small taste around on his tongue. "I've always said you could tell a lot about a man from the whiskey he drinks."

Tom smiled. "You and Will just happened to meet on the plane and then again in Santa Fe?"

Will shifted in his chair.

"Well, now," Farley said, "the fact of the matter is that if I hadn't run into your brother, I'd have come right up here to see you anyhow. Now that's plain talk, isn't it?"

Seth Porter had said that Farley Wells was not a boy they sent on a man's errand, Tom remembered; and he decided that as usual Seth was right. "Obviously," Tom said, "it's about the ranch and what's going to be done with it."

"Well, now," Farley said, "there aren't many large holdings like this one left intact, and when it appears that maybe there will be some changes, a lot of folks start sniffing the wind." His tone was friendly. "You can see how that would be."

"You tell me," Tom said.

Farley leaned back in his chair. "Over in the Four Corners area not too far from here there's coal, lots of it. That's energy that's needed now and will be needed more in only a little time."

"There is also," Tom said slowly, "atomic energy."

Farley had another sip of whiskey. "Coal, oil, gas—those we know how to handle. Maybe they're dirty, but they can be cleaned up. But when you go messing around with the atom—" He shook his head gently. "Oh, I know it's being done, reactors at work and so far no big troubles." He paused for emphasis. "But one reaction that gets out of hand and there is hell to pay."

"I've heard the warnings," Tom said.

"Why, now, of course you have." Farley was smiling. "And I do sound like an old-time evangelist, don't I, a real Bible banger? I'm sorry about that." He had another small taste of his whiskey and leaned back again. His gesture took in the pictures on the walls. "A lot of history in this room," he said. "Young Teddy Roosevelt, isn't that one? Friend of old Tully's?"

The man was very good, Tom thought; never pushing too hard, shifting ground with ease, handling himself like a boxer with a good left hand. "They hunted together," he said.

"And I'll bet they talked a lot too," Farley said. "About this big country and whether it would ever settle down; or whether a man out here would always be able to make his own decision, and not have to kowtow to some pipsqueak from government."

"Or," Tom said, "a man named Sam Waldo with a bill in the legislature?"

The office was still. Will sat motionless, watching both men, almost holding his breath. But the tension was quickly gone.

"You know Sam?" Farley said easily.

Tom shook his head.

"A self-important little guy with now probably the only good idea he ever did come up with." Farley gestured again at the Roosevelt picture. "Teddy would have approved. Country like this kept just the way it is, wild and wonderful, not cut up into little pieces fit only to support a jackrabbit, let alone a family moving out here from the East thinking they've bought a piece of heaven because a New York newspaper ad said so."

"And," Tom said, "not a place for an atomic TVA project either. Isn't that really what you're saying?"

Farley's voice was still easy, friendly. "I've always liked a man who said what was on his mind. Maybe one day you and I will have to go around and around scratching like two tomcats in a gunnysack. I kind of hope not. But if that's how it comes out, why, it will be a real pleasure."

Tom too was smiling. "Fair enough," he said. "We'll see how it works out."

EDITOR Kelly Garcia could recognize a story for the *Bugle* when he found one. As now, the morning after the new incident. His pulse quickened as he began to gather his facts.

First from the Grutas County district attorney, Pepe Martinez: "How many head rustled this time?" Kelly asked.

"Who can tell?" Pepe was scornful. "How can you get an exact tally on a ranch that size?"

"All right," Kelly said. "But when did it happen, and how do they even know?"

"The fence was cut sometime last night. Cattle tracks lead to the highway. There are oil drippings where apparently the trucks were waiting. And there's a man named Archuleta in the hospital in Santa Fe with two broken legs. The state police got him out of his pickup. Two big cattle trucks ran him off the road less than a mile from the cut fence." Pepe shrugged. "It's too much coincidence to think they weren't loaded with Rancho del Norte cattle."

Kelly was taking notes. "Archuleta didn't manage to pick up a license number, did he?"

Pepe shook his head. "But he said the trucks that came at him had plates; it was dark and he couldn't read them. New Mexico cars and trucks have plates only on the rear, so they must have been Colorado plates. He also said both trucks were full of cattle."

Kelly tucked away his folded copy paper and pencil. "I'll see what they say at the ranch."

When Kelly arrived out there, Tom was in the big office, angry, but under control.

Kelly said, "The wire services will want a story on this. You have any objections?"

"No. Just don't make us look any sillier than we are."

When Kelly was gone, Tom summoned Tish. She sat down in a chair against the wall and said nothing. Old Matt had treated her like this on occasion too, and rather than resenting it, she felt flattered. "Even if I don't say anything to you," old Matt had told her once, "I know you're there, honey, and that's what counts. Times when you have to make decisions, it's a lonely world."

Was it the same now with Tom? Tish didn't know, but she hoped so. There was a likeness between grandfather and grandson that was above and beyond mere physical resemblance.

Tom said at last, "Santa Fe it is." He paused. "If you'll go."

"Of course I will."

"I want you to see Marty Romero of the state police. I'll give him a call. Get as much dope as they have on rustling anywhere in the state. Method of operation. Possible destination for the stolen beef. That kind of thing."

Tish nodded.

"Then have one of Seth Porter's bright young men help you out. I want whatever Seth's people can find out about Sam Waldo's bill. And stay at La Fonda. I want to be able to reach you."

Tish stood up. "On my way."

Tom waited until she was at the door. "One more thing," he said. "Take care of yourself, you hear?"

Tish smiled. "And you take care of yourself too," she said. She hesitated. "You're the only one who can hold it all together." She turned then and walked out quickly.

Tom sat on, motionless. Could he hold it all together? He was not sure he could, and he was still not sure he wanted to. He pushed back his chair and stood up. The important thing right now was last night's rustling. Out in the hall he told Consuelo to pass the word to have a horse saddled for him.

A young Chicano boy led up a big sorrel gelding that Matt had ridden often. Matt's working saddle and handwoven saddle blanket were on his back. Tom took the reins. How long had it been since he had been on a horse? Two years? Three? It felt good, easy, natural. He lifted the gelding to an easy trot that could cover mile after mile without strain.

He came at last to the scene of last night's rustling. The same spot as the other time, he thought; a winter separating the two crimes. Now that good weather had returned, were they in for a rash of thefts? He sat quiet on old Matt's saddle, noting the trampled ground where the cattle had been held. The quantity of droppings argued a considerable period of confinement.

His eyes caught a glint from something—a piece of metal?—in the trampled earth, and he bent to look more closely. Suddenly something buzzed above him like an angry hornet, and simultaneously the explosion of a shot echoed in the trees.

Tom shifted his weight forward and banged his heels hard against the gelding's sides. They took off at a dead run, across the open ground, away from the direction of the shot.

When he was into the trees, and safety, he reined the gelding down and turned to look back. No one had followed. He thought about going back on foot to see if he could catch a glimpse of the shooter—and decided against it. Lucky once, he told himself; don't crowd it. At a steady trot they headed toward the ranch house.

FARLEY Wells borrowed one of the ranch cars and, alone, drove to the Long Valley atomic site. To the guard at the gate he said, "Tell Dr. Carter, please, that Tom Granger sent me."

What Tom had actually said was, "You might as well meet him—and he you." Farley parked the car and stood for a few moments studying the reactor building. He turned to see Wayne Carter in the doorway of the construction trailer. "I'm a guest at the big ranch," Farley said easily, "and my business is gas and oil."

Wayne nodded. "Come in."

Farley had been in construction trailers without number. Like offices and libraries, he thought, they tended to reflect the character of their owners. This one was neat, orderly, and in its sparse way comfortable. "I've heard tell," Farley said, "that what you're doing here is in the nature of a pilot project."

"In a sense," Wayne said, "all breeder reactors are pilot projects. There is a great deal we don't know about them yet."

"Sort of like running before you learn to walk. Only, if you fall down, everybody gets skinned." Farley smiled suddenly. "Strike that, Dr. Carter. I'm sure you try not to stumble."

"We take precautions," Wayne said, "just as you do when you're drilling a well or laying a pipeline or unloading a supertanker." He paused. "You are against atomic reactors, is that it?" he said.

Farley smiled gently. "Well, now, let's just say I think they have their dangers."

"Is that all it is? Or are you against reactors on principle, because they threaten the fossil-fuel monopoly?"

"That would be pretty shortsighted, wouldn't it, Doctor?" Farley said. "We're already in a bind for energy, and that won't automatically cure itself. Some folks think we won't ever whip our energy problem until we start using sunshine to develop power."

"I happen to be one of them," Wayne said. "But in the meantime breeder reactors like this one are going to have to carry some of the load. We have oil enough to last perhaps fifty years, and coal for about ten times that. But coal might foul our atmosphere beyond recovery. At least fission reactors don't do that."

"A true believer, Doctor." Farley smiled again. "I like to see a man with faith in what he does. Even if I don't agree with him."

"I get the impression that I am being warned."

"Now whatever gave you that idea, Dr. Carter?"

"Somehow I don't see you taking the trouble to come here out of simple curiosity." Wayne paused. "Men like you don't do things without reason."

"I am flattered."

"Tom Granger told me that rumors don't start without someone behind them. I didn't believe him. Now I'm beginning to wonder."

"Rumors get started in a variety of ways."

Wayne nodded. "And for a variety of purposes." He was slow to anger, but his temper was rising now. "Once when I was a kid I watched two scorpions drowning in a horse trough, but they were still trying to fight each other. It's true that if we aren't careful, we'll make this planet uninhabitable. It's also true that we're running out of the energy we have to have for survival. But instead of trying to work together, too many people are grinding their own axes, storing up wealth and power they may never get to enjoy." He paused. "I think you are in that category, Mr. Wells."

Farley's face had lost none of its easy friendliness. "Like I said, Doctor, a true believer. They are rare."

Farley said good-by and drove slowly back toward the gate. He liked Wayne Carter, and there was, of course, a great deal in what he had said. But a man was less than practical if he failed to keep his eye on his own interests.

At the gate he hesitated briefly and then turned toward the village of Dos Piedras. After all, he thought, a man had every right to see an old friend in Jicarilla County, didn't he?

Sheriff Tito Abeyta was in his office when Farley walked in. He had a spur on the desk in front of him, with a loose rowel lying beside it. He saw Farley, did a slow take, and then pushed back his chair and stood up. "How are you, Mr. Wells? And what are you doing here in the boondocks? You're the second person I've seen from Houston since I got back here."

"We miss you, Tito. We'd like to win more football games." Farley wondered who the other visitor from Houston had been, and what he was doing here, but those questions could wait. "I'm staying at the big ranch," he said.

"With Tom Granger? I've known him since we were kids. Used to hell around together—but he's a hard-nosed—"

"I'm Will Granger's guest."

"You interested in the big ranch, Mr. Wells?"

"I find it interesting. Straight out of the Old West. Rustling and everything."

"I heard." Tito's voice was expressionless. "That's Grutas County, not mine."

Farley said slowly, "And is the atomic reactor in your county?"

Tito shook his head.

"I was hoping," Farley said, "that it might be." He was silent for a little time. Then, "Let's say that I'm interested in Dr. Carter's project, and I would be happy to be kept up-to-date on its progress or its problems. Of course I'd be willing to pay for somebody's time and trouble to keep me informed."

"A lot of people are interested in that reactor," Tito said. "Before they put up that fence they were having plenty of problems."

Tito hesitated. "Like I said, it's outside my jurisdiction. Still, I expect I could manage to keep up on things."

"I will appreciate it," Farley said. Then, "You said I was the second one from Houston to drop by. Who was the other?"

Was there a change in Tito's face? Hard to tell. "Joe Harlow," he said. "Remember him, Mr. Wells? He's been off in Saudi Arabia doing chores for the old man. Happy to be back, he said."

Chores for J.R., Farley thought. "What was he doing up here?"

"Hunting. They come to these mountains from all over."

Long after Farley had driven away, Tito sat on at his desk. Twice he opened the drawer and looked at the three one-hundred-dollar bills Farley had left with him.

SETH Porter sent one of his young assistants over to meet Tish upon her arrival in Santa Fe.

Jimmy Thomas was redheaded and bubbly, a product of Stanford University Law School, where he had edited the *Law Review*. Together he and Tish walked to La Fonda.

Jimmy was in love with Santa Fe. "It's probably old hat to you," he said, "but I can't get over the clear air, with no smog, and mountains close enough to reach out and touch. In thirty minutes from the office I can be on any one of half a dozen trout streams."

Tish was smiling. "I like your enthusiasm." She enjoyed Santa Fe. Sometimes in winter she came to ski the nearby basin, and in summer she sometimes came for the opera.

At the hotel Jimmy hesitated. "Are you going to be in Santa Fe for a day or two?"

"At least."

"Then," Jimmy said, "maybe we could have dinner?"

"That would be very nice," Tish said. It was strange how relaxed she felt with Jimmy. Usually she felt insecure and uncertain in the presence of men who took more than a casual interest in her.

At the desk Tish found a message from Lieutenant Romero of the state police, and she went up to her room to call him back.

"Tom asked me to tell you everything we know," the lieutenant said. "If you want to come out here, I'll do my best."

It was the new state police complex out on the Albuquerque highway, low, massive, glaringly gray against the brown landscape and the jagged Ortiz Mountains. She was shown immediately to the lieutenant's office.

She had met Marty Romero once or twice. He was a wiry man with dark hair and dark angry eyes, a mixture, it was said, of Anglo, Apache, and Spanish—and one of the few remaining Apache trackers around. He was college-educated, and it was also said that he might have been head of the state police had he not spoken his mind to everybody, including the governor.

He was polite now. "We had a rash of cattle rustling last fall, when beef was scarce and high-priced in the markets."

"We had that one strike then too," Tish said.

"But only that one." The lieutenant paused. "South and east, ranches a tenth the size of Rancho del Norte were hit half a dozen times. And your hit came just before the first big snow, long after the other action had petered out. I don't know what I'm implying, if anything, but when you find something that stands outside of a pattern, you wonder about it."

"Ours might have been local, not organized, is that what you're thinking? But we're pretty sure the trucks were from Colorado."

"Actually, after you left for Santa Fe, Tom went out to see for himself," Marty Romero said. "Somebody shot at him—"

"Oh, no!"

"They missed." Marty saw the relief in Tish's face. He tucked it away in his tracker's mind, as he tucked away all signs. "So," he said, "it would seem that not everybody connected with the hit went off in the Colorado trucks."

Right back to my first guess, Tish thought. "Somebody local could have rounded up the cattle and held them," she said. "But Tom was shot at today, and it all happened last night. Why would a rustler still be there?"

Marty Romero nodded. "Maybe he came back. Maybe he had left something. Tom said there was something metallic on the ground, but he didn't have time to see what it was." He smiled without amusement.

517

Tish stood up. "Thank you."

The lieutenant rose too. He watched her walk out—tall and slim, mountain-bred, he thought; in an odd way not unlike himself. He sensed in her a feeling of not belonging almost as strong as his own. We're two misfits, he thought, but each of us—in our own way—is thoroughly competent.

JIMMY Thomas sat in Seth Porter's office. "Yes, sir," he said, "that's the word: Sam Waldo is passing out a few hundred here and a few hundred there. It's not easily proved, of course."

Seth smiled. "We're not after legal proof, son. Have you talked with the conservationists—Sierra Club and the others?"

"Yes, sir. They're high on the Waldo bill. They never expected it from him, but they're all for it. And they aren't in favor of the atomic reactor project. I'd have thought they would be. It's either that or smoky fossil-fuel plants like those up at Four Corners."

"I'm not too happy about atomic power plants, either," Seth said. "On the other hand, what are the alternatives? Fossil-fuel plants will run out of fuel in not too many years. There's geothermal power—not just from geysers and hot springs but from tapping deep underground sources of heat, steam. But that isn't something that will happen tomorrow. Some think solar energy is the only solution. The fact is that we have to have more energy, and as matters stand now, we have to have either pollution or risk in order to get it. I'd rather take the risk of that reactor than the stink of more coal-fired plants and the strip mining that feeds them."

"I guess I see your point, sir," Jimmy said.

"Back to Sam Waldo. What's your head count on his bill?"

"It will get a do-pass in committee," Jimmy said. "And it will go through the House without trouble. In the Senate it may be closer, but I think there'll ·be enough horse trading to get it through."

"What about the governor? Will he veto—or will he sign?"

"There'll be a lot of pressure on him to sign," Jimmy said. "People I've talked to think this story might get nationwide attention. Hunters, fishermen, conservationists from all over the country may be interested, not to mention local pressure."

"It's local pressure I'm thinking of," Seth said. "The governor counts votes, and votes don't come from out of state."

Jimmy said, "But will the Grangers sell even if the Waldo bill does pass and get signed by the governor?"

Seth took his time. He said at last, "If they aren't willing to sell, the state could exercise its right of eminent domain, have the property condemned, and buy it at the fair market price, whether the Grangers liked it or not."

6

Tom had been in no hurry to tell anyone on the ranch about the shooting episode. He had ridden straight back and shut himself in the big office to call Marty Romero. They discussed the cattle rustling and the shooting. Then, "What are the chances of your coming up?" Tom asked. "We could use a tracker."

"Big cattle trucks don't leave tracks, amigo."

"Men do. And horses. Among other things, I'd like to know who shot at me."

There was a silence. Then, "We'll see," Marty Romero said.

Tom hung up and rang for Consuelo to bring him a beer. When she returned with it, Tom asked her to shut the door and sit down.

Consuelo perched uncomfortably on the front six inches of a chair. She smoothed her skirts and waited patiently.

Tom poured his beer. "After I rode off this morning, did any of the others leave? My brother or his wife? Or Señor Wells?"

"Only Señor Wells. He wished to visit Valle Largo."

Long Valley, Tom thought, the atomic site. It was in the opposite direction from the site of the cattle rustling.

"Have the goodness to ask Señor Will to come in."

While he waited he studied the contents of the gun cabinet. No rifles missing.

"Going hunting?" Will's voice from the doorway. "I was told *el patrón* required my presence."

"Close the door," Tom said. "You want a beer?"

"In a little while a Bloody Mary." Will sat down and stretched his legs. "I understand we've been rustled again?" His tone implied that he could not have cared less.

"It's your money as well as mine."

Will shook his head. "I won't think of it as money until I have it in my hand. Until then it's just beef on the hoof, no more interesting to me than it ever was."

Tom said as offhandedly as he could, "Somebody tried to kill me this morning. Rifle shot."

"If you're serious, and I assume you are, are you pointing a finger at me? Because I haven't seen you all morning until now." Will paused. "What price a hunter wanting to take a deer off-season, firing at something that moves? It happens."

It did happen indeed. But Tom thought the possibility did not apply this morning. "I doubt it," he said.

Will nodded as if he had expected nothing different. "Then I have exhausted my theories." But he made no move to rise. "I was planning to have a talk with you," he said. "There is a bill down in Santa Fe to appropriate state funds to buy the ranch. You know about that?"

Tom merely nodded.

"So what does it mean to you?" Will asked.

"I don't know yet."

"Sooner or later you're going to have to make up your mind. In the meantime Sue and I—dangle. Is that how you like it?"

"You're not hurting for money. You can go wherever you like, and do whatever you want, just as you always have."

"And what if you decide to put a tether on us?"

"I won't. After taxes, things are going to be a little tighter than they were, but not so tight that you'll feel a pinch any more than I will. Matt always gave you whatever you asked."

"It was his to dole out as he wanted. What you're controlling is half mine. I want it. All of it."

"Don't work yourself up," Tom said. "I'm not going to break up this ranch just to make you happy. Go have your Bloody Mary. I've got work to do."

Will expertly mixed two Bloody Marys and carried the drinks

out to the terrace, where Sue lay on a chaise lounge in the sun. She said idly, "What did Tom have in mind?"

Will's voice was quiet. "Someone shot at him this morning."

Sue sipped her drink slowly. "Could it have been an accident?"

"Tom says no." Will wanted to drop the subject; just talking about it made him uncomfortable. "If I do say it," he said, "this is a superb Bloody Mary."

"You can always bartend, darling, when we run out of money."

"We aren't going to run out of money." Damn it, Will thought, he and Sue had never quarreled over money. Why should she raise the subject now?

They were silent in the sunlight for a time. Sue spoke at last. She was looking, not at Will, but at the distant mountains. "What did Tom say that upset you?"

Was he that transparent? He supposed he was, and the realization did nothing to restore equanimity. "I told him about the bill down in Santa Fe to buy this place. He knew about it already."

"Of course. Your brother isn't stupid, darling. And why do you suppose he sent Tish to Santa Fe?"

"All right. So he knew. I asked him what it meant to him and he said he didn't know yet." He paused. "That's all."

"No, it's not. Then you told him you wanted your share and you were going to get it." Sue paused. "Didn't you?"

"What if I did?"

Sue said, "Darling, do we need the money? I mean really need it. Isn't just knowing it's there enough?"

"No."

"Do we owe money? Is that it?" Sue paused. The silence this time was eloquent. "How much?"

"Enough."

"Have you told Tom?"

"No. Do you think it would do any good? Basically he's like old Matt. You're supposed to earn your way in this world, but since I don't do that, the least I can do is stay away from gamblers and loan sharks and be a good little citizen."

"I see." Her tone was quiet, somehow decisive.

Will studied her. "That means what?"

Sue said slowly, "Tom isn't about to sell the ranch, at least not in a hurry and maybe not at all. And you are not about to go to him with your problem." She paused. "I assume it is a problem?"

"It is." It was not a very heroic role he was playing, Will told himself. Well, he had never thought of himself as being like old Matt or Tom, larger than life-size.

Sue spoke, her voice totally calm. "Someone tried to kill Tom this morning, you said. What if he had succeeded?"

Will had a long pull at his drink. "Then we'd get the bundle." He stared at Sue. "Just what are you thinking?"

"Why, nothing at all, darling. I was just—wondering." She sat up, swung her legs from the chaise, and got to her feet.

FARLEY Wells drove back to the ranch from Dos Piedras in a thoughtful mood. What Tito had told him—about trouble at the nuclear reactor site before the fence was put up—was disquieting to Farley because he did not understand it. Was Joe Harlow involved? But J.R. had said that he wanted no trouble.

Tom was in the big office and he called, "Come in," to Farley's knock. "Sit down, Mr. Wells. What can I do for you?"

Farley closed the door and took one of the leather visitor's chairs. "I've been to see Wayne Carter. A very able man, I should say. Then I went into Dos Piedras to have a little visit with an old friend from Houston, Tito Abeyta." All open and aboveboard.

Long Valley was in the opposite direction from the rustling site, Tom thought, but the road to Dos Piedras went right past it. He could not see Farley as a bushwhacker. Still. "I'm a little jumpy this morning," he said. "Somebody took a shot at me."

"Any idea why?"

"Ideas," Tom said, "but that's all." He made a gesture dismissing the subject.

Farley accepted it without comment. "I understand," he said, "that there have been—problems at the atomic plant."

Tom studied the man. "So I've heard." His voice was expressionless. "And rumors," he added. "Dead sheep, dead fish, a little girl in Las Grutas with leukemia." The more he thought about it, the angrier he became. "And there hasn't been any radioactive material anywhere near the site."

Farley nodded. "It didn't look as if they were very far along."

"There is also," Tom said, "the matter of that bill in Santa Fe, authorizing the state to buy the ranch. Add it all up and it seems pretty clear that somebody doesn't want a breeder reactor in these mountains."

Farley smiled easily. "I imagine quite a few folks don't." He paused. "Although I don't really see the connection between a few rumors and a bill in the state legislature. I've heard about the commune. That's where your rumors might come from."

Tom nodded slowly. "I hadn't thought of that."

"Folks on the back-to-nature kick don't like a lot of things. Maybe I don't like some of them myself. I don't like smog over Los Angeles or New York or, for that matter, Houston. I don't like rivers or lakes that stink from pollution."

Tom was smiling now. "And you don't like atomic reactors."

Farley seemed to relax. "True enough."

"Because with oil and gas prices what they are now, atomic power is competitive?"

The antagonism between them was almost out in the open now, Tom thought. "You wouldn't have had anything to do with the rumors about the reactor?" he asked. "Or Carter's problems?"

"No." Farley took his time. "And you can believe that."

"Sam Waldo is your only approach—so far?"

Farley said slowly, "You're doing a lot of guessing."

Tom nodded. "About a lot of things."

Farley sat quietly, thinking. He said at last, "I've answered your questions; how about a little quid pro quo? Are you going to try to keep the ranch as it is?"

"Maybe."

"Your brother—"

Tom's smile was wicked. "My brother is a spoiled brat. He is married to a spoiled female. Neither of them has ever done a useful thing in their lives. I'll make the decisions here, regardless of them

525

or, for that matter, the legislature in Santa Fe." The smile spread recklessly. "My grandfather told the governor once, and I quote: 'If I have to, I'll shut the ranch up tighter than a drum and I'll shoot anyone who sets foot on ranch property.' " Tom paused. "I'm beginning to know how he felt."

LIEUTENANT Marty Romero drove his own pickup truck from Santa Fe to El Rancho del Norte. He drove without haste, enjoying the day, which was bright and clear, and the views of mountains, meadows, and streams, which were spectacular.

At the ranch Marty found Tom waiting in front of the big house. They shook hands. "Thanks for coming," Tom said.

"*De nada*—no sweat." Marty paused. "You're looking good, amigo; big and mean." He showed white teeth in a quick smile.

Tom gestured at the pickup. "Care to take a ride?"

Facts were what he needed, Marty thought. "Let's go."

They parked off the blacktop road. "The trucks were apparently loaded right there," Tom said, pointing. "That was where the fence was cut. I was on my horse there when the shot was fired." It was all he needed to say.

Marty went through the barbed-wire fence in one easy stooping movement. Then, motionless, he began to study the ground.

It was not black magic, Tom thought, but it smacked of it when you watched a real tracker at work. It was, rather, what some had described as genius: an infinite capacity for detail. Bit by bit the picture was assembled and brought into focus.

He roused himself at the sound of Marty's voice. "If you can get through the fence, I think I can tell you a few things."

The ground looked to Tom exactly as it had looked in the morning, but now it was about to reveal its story.

"Your horse," Marty said, "has a loose shoe on the off fore. You're lucky he didn't throw it when you took off." He pointed. "One other horse has been here. Tracks and partial tracks there and there and there. The rider gathered the cattle and held them. Then he got off his horse over here. Now why would he do that, I wonder? He tied the horse to that branch and walked over here,

just about where you were when the shot came and you took off."
Marty was watching Tom's face. "What does that suggest?"

Tom shook his head.

"Think about it," Marty said. "Suppose you've got tracks of his horse made at two different times? One set while he was rounding up and holding the cattle, and the other set maybe this morning when he came back? And that second time he got off his horse. He's a big man, incidentally, big as you are."

Clyde Burley came to mind. And Farley Wells.

"In this ground, pine needles and all," Marty said, "the tracks aren't good, but he is big, you can tell by his stride." He paused. "You said you saw something on the ground. Would he have gotten off his horse to look for it? Because he had lost it in the dark the first time he was here? How about that?"

Tom nodded slowly.

They drove back toward the ranch house in silence. Tom said at last, "Will you know his tracks if you see them?"

"His horse's tracks, but not his. Those pine needles, amigo—" Marty shook his head. Then, "Why can't you remember what you saw on the ground? That's the trouble with you Anglos: you look at things but you don't see them." He paused and the white teeth showed in a half smile. "One of the troubles."

"Okay," Tom said, "lay it on. It was something metallic. Round, I think, but I'm not even sure of that. I bent down to look closer and he fired, and then I was thinking of other things."

Back at the big house Marty took a worn pair of saddlebags from behind the seat of his pickup truck, and a rifle from the window rack. He walked with Tom up the broad steps.

Tom called for Consuelo. "Connie will show you to a room," he said. "When you're ready, come down to the office."

He sat behind the big desk and stared at the trophy-laden wall for inspiration. As Matt had, he thought, and probably old Tully before him. The door opened and he turned to look. It was Will. "What's Marty Romero doing here?" Will asked.

"It ought to be obvious," Tom said. "Cattle rustling is still a crime. Why are you uptight about it?"

"I don't like fuzz, particularly half-breed—"

"Hold it right there." Tom controlled himself with effort. "This is as much your place as it is mine, but if you start throwing your weight around like a snotty red-neck Anglo, I'll kick you all the way down to Albuquerque and aboard an airplane heading east." He paused. "Is that clear?"

Will's face was white. He hesitated, seemed about to say something, changed his mind, and turned away.

"And the next time you want to come in," Tom said, "knock!"

The door slammed. It had been slammed many times, Tom thought, and it hadn't broken yet. He found himself smiling as he realized he was even beginning to sound like Matt.

He was still smiling when Marty knocked and came in. "I see cream on your whiskers, amigo. *Qué pasa?*—what gives?"

"I don't think I could explain." He stretched out an arm for the tantalus, poured two shots, handed one to Marty.

Marty held the glass and looked slowly around the room. "I've never been in here before," he said, and smiled at Tom. "I've never been in the office of one of those big board chairmen in the East either, but I imagine it has this same kind of feel. Power, amigo, the power to make things happen. Are you going to stay?"

"I wish people would stop asking that."

"They won't until you make up your mind." Marty studied his whiskey for a little time in silence. Then he looked up. "Something maybe you haven't thought of, amigo. Somebody shot at you. We think we know why: because you saw something on the ground he didn't want you to see. You didn't really see it, but he doesn't know that. So maybe he'll have another try, no?" He nodded toward the gun cabinet. "It might be an idea if—at least for a little while—you keep looking over your shoulder, and have something to shoot with where you can reach it."

JIMMY Thomas was prompt; his phone call from the lobby of La Fonda came at precisely seven o'clock. "I'll be right down," Tish said. Together they walked out to Jimmy's little red sports car. "I hope you like Spanish food," he said.

"I do." Tish was smiling.

Jimmy started the engine. "Then away we go," he said. He swung the little car onto the highway and began to accelerate. "Look." The moon was rising behind the mountains. "It's full tonight." They topped the rise and began the long swoop into the valley. "Do you ski?" Jimmy said suddenly.

"Yes."

"How about the opera?"

"I come down for it every summer." I did, she thought, but how will it be now? She put the question aside. "You too?"

"It and the skiing are two of the reasons I'm here." Jimmy glanced at her profile. "Don't tell me you fish too?"

"My stepfather gave me a rod when I was nine." And Tom, then eleven, cut the hook out of my shoulder; we never told Matt. . . .

"Fishing," Jimmy said, "is the third reason I'm here." And, he thought, it's beginning to look as if I have a fourth.

"There's good fishing on the ranch," Tish said. "I could ask Tom to invite you for a weekend." Why this sudden boldness? But Jimmy was sweet, easy to be with. "I mean, if you'd like that."

All that Jimmy allowed himself to say was, "I'd like that very much."

WHEN they came out of the restaurant the moon was high, casting deep shadows in the nearby hills. Jimmy held the door for Tish, walked around, and got into his own seat, and then, reluctant to start the return drive, just sat, his hands resting on the wheel.

"It was a lovely dinner." Tish's voice was quiet.

"I don't remember what we talked about," Jimmy said.

Tish was smiling now. "Neither do I."

Jimmy was silent for a time. Then, "When are you going back to the ranch?" he asked.

"I don't know. It depends on Tom."

Jimmy said slowly, "Granger the Third, is that it?"

"Don't be bitter."

"Not bitter," he said, "so much as jealous. He can order you around and I can't. That's what bugs me."

"What orders," Tish said, "would you give me, if you could?"

"How about this for a start?" He drew her to him and lifted her chin. It was a long kiss, tentative at first, but gaining increasing urgency. Afterward they sat in companionable silence.

"I think we'd better go back now, Jimmy."

"Yes." He made no move. "The trouble is I don't have any place to take you. I have two roommates, both lawyers, and—"

"It doesn't matter."

"It does. I ought to have a splendid pad to show you."

"With etchings?"

He squeezed her hand gently. "The question is, would you come? Or would I need the king's permission?"

"I'm over twenty-one, Jimmy." Another long kiss.

"Will I see you tomorrow?" asked Jimmy.

"Maybe. Probably. I—hope so."

"Unless you hear from—the boss." Jimmy sighed and started the car; they sped down the drive in the bright moonlight.

At La Fonda there was a message telling Tish to call Mr. Granger at El Rancho del Norte.

Tish called Tom in the morning. "I'm going to see Seth Porter," she said. "He'll give me the latest on Sam Waldo and his bill."

"Good." Pause. "You were out last night."

"Yes, with one of Seth's young men. Was there something you wanted?"

"Just to see that everything was all right."

"Everything is fine. Tom . . . I think I may be in love."

There was a silence. It grew, stretched. Tom said at last merely, "Take care." And that was all.

7

THROUGH his window Tito Abeyta watched Marty Romero's pickup truck roll to a stop outside his door. From the open doorway Marty said, "Hi," and walked in.

"What brings you to these parts?" Tito said. "The rustling was in Grutas County."

As Marty sat down he noticed a spur and loose rowel on Tito's desk. "Since I'm here, I pay my respects. Besides, the cattle trucks came from Colorado, which means they came through Jicarilla County, no?"

Tito scowled. "Maybe," he said. "You want me to ask around up toward the state line? Did anybody getting up during the night see a couple of cattle trucks heading north?"

Marty smiled. "That might help." The smile disappeared. "And somebody on horseback took a shot at Tom Granger yesterday."

Tito sat up. "Why?"

"Anybody's guess."

Tito studied Marty's face. A waste of time. "What's yours?"

Marty shook his head. "I'm reserving it." His tone changed. "How're things? Benny Baca behaving himself?" Benny Baca was the state policeman in the area.

"We get along," Tito said. He lifted his big shoulders, let them fall. "Things are quiet. We keep them that way."

Marty was looking with amusement at the .357 magnum on Tito's hip. "You're still attached to that thing?"

"I even fire it off now and then. It impresses people."

Marty stood up. "Mind if I look in on the hippie commune?"

Tito got up too, large and solid. "Help yourself. Just don't let those chicks take your eye off the ball."

"Thanks for the warning," Marty said.

A BATTERED pickup and a superannuated school bus were parked near the adobe building of the commune when Marty drove up. He got out of his own truck and looked around.

There was no corral that he could see, and no stable. No horses? Probably not. These were city people for the most part.

"Looking for something?" A female voice behind him.

Marty turned to look at her. She was young, how young he could only guess, but he doubted that she was eighteen. He wondered if one of those pitiful bulletins on runaway children applied to her.

"Have you had a good look?" The girl was smiling. Then the smile faded. "You're some kind of fuzz. I can smell it."

"That's a pretty sharp nose," Marty said, and he added almost offhand, "particularly for such a young chick."

"I'm eighteen. And it's none of your business anyway."

Marty shook his head slowly. "It could be, *chica*, if we found you were, say, fifteen or sixteen. So don't push it."

He turned away as Joe walked up. "Something you want, man?"

"He's fuzz," the girl said, losing some of her belligerence.

"I can tell," Joe said. "What are you after?"

"Do you have any horses?"

"No horses. We're not the horsey set."

"Do you have a rifle?"

There was hesitation this time.

Marty smiled. "Never mind. Most people do. There's no law against it, only against using it the wrong way."

Joe said slowly, "Like what?"

"Like shooting at a man yesterday. Not far from here."

"You think we're mixed up in it? Far out!"

"No," Marty said, "since I've seen you, I don't think you had anything to do with it, but the chance was there."

Joe's smile was weary. "Why pick on us, fuzz? Answer me that? Why is it always us?"

"Because you're asking for it. And in your own way you love it, because it means somebody is paying attention to you." Marty turned away and walked to his pickup.

He had one more destination in order to touch all bases: the reactor site. He had not known about the fence and the guarded gate, and he whistled softly when he saw them. A lot of money involved.

He thought he recognized the guard: Pete Baca, one of Benny Baca's family. After identifying himself he drove in, parked by the construction trailer, and got out to look at the building.

"Lieutenant—Romero, is it?" Wayne Carter's voice from the trailer door. "Come in. What can I do for you, Lieutenant?"

"Tell me about your fence," Marty said, and sat down to listen.

"We put it up for the usual reasons," Wayne said dryly.

"Vandalism?"

"I suppose you could call it that." Wayne shrugged. "The kind of thing that happens at every construction site."

"In cities," Marty said, "not out in the mountains. Mountain people think differently. I think the vandalism you had was just intended to annoy you. The question is, why? I'm trying to find a— pattern."

"What kind of pattern?"

"You have a big ranch and two villages that have lived together a long time, a stable situation. Then you add a hippie commune and a nuclear reactor, and things begin to happen. Suddenly rustling comes back. A stranger turns up shot, dead. Vandalism at the reactor site. Yesterday an attempted murder on ranch property. Add rumors about radioactivity—"

"Where there isn't any radioactive material," Carter said.

"Okay. Then stir in a bill down in Santa Fe to buy the ranch when the ranch isn't even for sale." Marty cocked his head and smiled. "Things happen because people want them to happen. I want to know which people, and why."

"That's out of my line, Lieutenant."

"Maybe, but you're part of it." Marty gestured toward the open doorway and the organized bustle around the concrete structure. "I've heard some pretty wild things about what you're doing here, and what might come out of it. A generator network and a power grid, climate change. That's pretty far out. Me, I always get a little uneasy when the Rain Dance ends in a cloudburst."

"The rumors—are you talking about the little girl with leukemia?" Wayne Carter was frowning now.

"I'm talking *beyond* the little girl with leukemia, Doctor. Are the rumors just malicious mischief? Or are they part of a plan?"

"To do what, Lieutenant?"

"To get you out of here." Marty paused. "Even if it means taking over the ranch. And the first step in a power play like that might be to persuade people that they're a lot better off without atomic power on their doorstep."

He drove back to the ranch, thinking that he probably had not accomplished a thing. On the other hand, sometimes when you were hunting, your mere presence stirred up game; and he had let himself be seen in a number of quarters.

At the doorway of the big house he watched a ranch car drive up and stop in a shower of gravel. Will got out and came up the steps two at a time. To Marty, "Caught anybody yet?"

Marty smiled. "There's a question cops ask themselves in almost every detective story," he said. "It's 'Who benefits from the crime?' " He watched surprise come into Will's face. "If Tom were shot, killed," Marty said, "how could you be affected? Aside from being grief-stricken, I mean?"

Will, shocked by this bluntness, said, "You have a dirty mind."

Marty nodded and walked past Will into the big hall.

KELLY Garcia drove his dusty VW beetle at a moderate pace, never shifting into top gear. Like Marty Romero, Kelly had been struck by the strange events which had followed the appearance of the reactor project and the commune. Unlike Marty, he had an uneasy visceral feeling that there were awesome forces at work.

From the wire service people in Santa Fe he had picked up a fair amount of background on Farley Wells. "By all accounts a nice guy," the wire service man had said, "but he is J. R. Benson's man, and that says it all."

As far as Kelly was concerned, it did indeed say it all. It was a far cry from that shadowy old man in Houston to cattle rustling here in these remote mountains, and Kelly had no proof that there was any connection. But Farley Wells *had* come to the ranch, and by so doing he *had* in a way brought J. R. Benson here as well.

The VW came around a bend in the road and stopped precisely where Marty Romero's pickup had halted. Kelly gazed at the barbed-wire fence that had been cut for the cattle to be driven into the trucks. He got out of the little car, ducked through the fence, and stared at the ground. It told him nothing, and he wondered why he had even bothered to look. He started to turn away and saw a man watching at a distance of no more than fifteen feet. Behind him a horse stood patiently, its reins wrapped around a small branch.

"I thought I'd find you here," the man said. His voice was easy enough.

"Just trying to figure a few things out," Kelly said. "And getting nowhere," he added.

"But you had some reason for coming here in the first place. And that makes it bad. Too bad."

"Look," Kelly said, "why shouldn't I come here? Why—" He stopped and stared unbelieving at the gun pointed at his chest. "Now look," he repeated, more in protest than in panic.

"Too bad," the man said again.

Panic took over. "Look!" Kelly said. "I don't know anything! Not a thing!" But now of course he did know entirely too much.

The shot echoed briefly in the trees, and after that there was no sound. The man walked without haste to his horse, undid the reins, and swung aboard. He rode off at an easy running walk.

It was Benny Baca, the state policeman, who saw Kelly's VW the next day and recognized it. As he got out of his patrol car to see what might have prompted Kelly to stop in this remote spot, four turkey buzzards flew heavily out of the trees. Benny Baca went through the fence to have a look.

His normally swarthy face was pale when he came back to the patrol car and made his report on the radio. "Tell Lieutenant Romero I'll wait here," he added.

Tom Granger rode in the pickup with Marty Romero. Tom's face was set, angry. "Kelly Garcia," he said. "He didn't have to die like this—for no reason."

"You said he was poking around, no?" Marty said. "Then maybe he found out a little too much."

There was an ambulance that doubled as a morgue wagon and a Grutas County sheriff's car parked with Benny Baca's patrol car. Marty got out of the pickup. "Stay here, amigo. There's nothing you can do, and I don't want your big feet walking around on the scene." He disappeared into the trees.

When Marty came back his face was bleak. "I would say our

same big man, amigo. Again his tracks in the pine needles are unclear. But it was the same horse, tied to the same branch."

Tom said, "Kelly—"

"Maybe he knew what hit him," Marty said, "but not for long. One shot." He touched his chest. "It went clear through him. We'll look, but I don't think we'll find the slug."

"A rifle again?" Tom said. "From a distance?"

"From fifteen feet, and he was shot from the front. He probably recognized the man, but he can't very well tell us who it was." Marty opened the pickup door. "Let's find out where Clyde Burley was." His voice was cold. "And that big dude from Texas."

"He went back to Santa Fe."

"Maybe he stayed there, and maybe he didn't." Marty hesitated. "And just on a wild hunch, amigo, I'll want to know where your brother was all day yesterday too."

WHEN they got there, Clyde Burley was not in his office. As Tom and Marty started to leave, Clyde rode up on his big buckskin. He swung down and looked from face to face. "Trouble?"

Marty said, "You ride this horse much?"

"He's my top horse. Why?"

Marty merely nodded and walked a few steps to the horse's rear, stood quiet studying the tracks in the dirt. Then he came back. "Where were you yesterday afternoon?" he said.

Clyde shrugged. "I spent the afternoon with Emilio, trying to save a cow and her calf." He looked at Tom. "We managed. Mother and child are doing well. Now, what's it all about?"

Tom told him. Clyde whistled softly. "Same place," Tom said, "and probably the same man who took a shot at me."

"I want to call Santa Fe," Marty said. "We'll have a few questions asked down there."

Santa Fe, in the person of a state police sergeant, listened respectfully. "Will do," the sergeant said. And then, "Kelly Garcia. Who would do a thing like that?"

"That," Marty said, "is what we're going to find out. You can call me here." He hung up and got out of his chair to prowl the big office. At the gun cabinet he stopped. Over his shoulder, "One of your guns is missing, amigo." He turned to look at Tom. "Sporting rifle, bolt action, looks to be the thirty-aught six. Will?"

"Probably. He knows where the key is, and none of the ranch people would touch the cabinet." Tom was scowling. "But there are all sorts of reasons why he might have taken it."

"*Claro.*" Marty's voice was calm. "Some people like to shoot at tin cans or jackrabbits. Is he a good shot?"

Tom made himself relax. "He's a good shot. Or was. But it doesn't take a good shot to hit a man from fifteen feet."

"True." Marty walked back to his chair and sat down. "Anything you're not telling me, amigo?"

The man was implacable, Tom thought. "No," he said. And then, "Clyde's horse was not the one?"

"No. If the boot tracks were only a little plainer—" Marty shrugged. "But we'll find him." There was finality in his tone.

SETH Porter sat in the governor's office in the new state capitol known locally as the Roundhouse.

"My people tell me," Seth said, "that Waldo's bill will pass easily in the House and probably squeak through in the Senate. What will you do then, sir?"

The governor was ranch-bred, more at home on a horse than behind a desk. His strengths were a blend of shrewdness, political sagacity, and a feel for popular sentiment. "Well, now, I'd have to ponder a bit on that." His voice had a Western twang.

"Sam Waldo doesn't usually do things out of the goodness of his heart," Seth said.

"What do you think he really wants?"

"To stop that atomic reactor. There is a lot of coal up in the strip-mining country that somebody would like to see used, somebody who has enough money to buy Sam Waldo and half the legislature, and will maybe put pressure on you to go along."

"I don't buy easy, Seth."

"I know you don't. But this pressure can be applied in other ways than money."

The governor's faint nod was acknowledgment.

"If that reactor works the way some people think it's going to, my friend, a power grid can be established right here in the state, supplying a good share of the Southwest with its electrical energy. The state could pick itself up and get out of the poor-neighbor class, and wouldn't that be fine for whoever sits in that chair?"

The governor was silent. Seth heaved himself to his feet. "I've taken enough of your time."

"Always glad to talk with you." The governor stood too.

"Ponder on it," Seth said. "And when somebody comes around to do a little arm-twisting in favor of Sam's bill—"

"Nobody has come yet, Seth."

"Somebody will. I'll bet my bottom dollar on that."

WILL Granger carried a rifle when he left the car and went up the steps to the big house. He found the office empty, and the key on top of the gun cabinet in its usual place. Will unlocked the cabinet and was about to replace the rifle when Tom's voice stopped him.

"Did you fire it?"

"I was sighting it in," Will said.

"Where?"

"In the blind bend of the big arroyo. Where we always did."

Tom made himself relax. "Tell Connie. She'll have someone clean it for you." And then, puzzled now, "Sighting it in? What for? Going hunting?"

"I might. Why?"

Tom told Will what had happened to Kelly Garcia, and could see no reaction other than incredulity. He nodded toward the rifle Will had leaned against the wall. "That could have done it."

"Do you think it did? Is that it?"

"No."

"And what does the gestapo think?" Will said.

"If you're talking about Marty," Tom said, his voice cold now, "I don't know. He keeps his opinions to himself."

Will thought about it, nodded shortly, and went upstairs to his room, where he stretched out on the daybed. The .30-06 rifle he had been firing had needed no sighting adjustment. It held fine, just the way he liked it, and although he had not touched a rifle in a couple of years, the old skills remained intact.

He told himself that he had nothing specific in mind, and knew that he lied. Looking through the sights of the rifle, he had tried to imagine what it would be like if instead of a small spot on the dirt bank he was looking at a man. Would his finger be as steady and gentle on the trigger, his body as relaxed? When he squeezed off the shot, how would the man react? Would he stagger and lurch? Or would he go down all at once, forever ignorant of what had happened to him?

And then what? Obviously lay the blame on the unknown sniper. Or should it be an accident, one of those hunting tragedies? After all, there were such things as ballistics tests. Lying there staring up at the ceiling, Will let the questions echo and reecho in his mind.

He roused himself at the sound of the door's opening. It was Sue. She wore the Chinese silk robe he had given her, and she was barefoot. She was smiling that secret smile that could infuriate. Slowly she crossed the room and stood before him, unmoving, knowing exactly her power over him. He reached for her. . . .

WILL lay on his back, spent and defeated. The male might be the dominant sex, he thought, but at a time like this he was at the female's mercy until he had gathered his strength.

Sue lay on her side, propped on one elbow. With her free hand she traced patterns on Will's chest. "Another shooting," she said. "The wild, wild West." She paused to kiss his shoulder. "But not at Tom this time." Another pause. "I wonder why."

Will said slowly, "What do you mean?"

"Somebody shot at him once, darling. Doesn't it stand to reason that somebody might shoot at him again?"

It did make a kind of sense, Will thought. Hadn't he been thinking along exactly the same lines when Sue came in?

"You must have thought about it," Sue said.

"Naturally. He's my brother."

"And you are your brother's keeper. Of course."

"That," Will said, "was what you had in mind, wasn't it? Good old brotherly concern."

"Why, what else?" Her lips touched his while she spoke. "And you'll keep thinking about it, won't you, darling? In just the same way." Her mouth on his prevented reply.

8

SPRING was ripening, and the air was warmer than it had been. Tom rode again the big gelding and sat old Matt's working saddle. Remembering Marty's warning, he had taken the .30-30 carbine. It was beneath his right leg now, resting in a worn leather scabbard.

He had no particular destination, merely a desire for solitude. As a boy he had often taken long aimless rides, something old Matt had understood, if Will had not.

He came to the fence line and followed it to the meadow where Borden's body had been found. There he reined in the gelding and sat thinking for a time. Two rustlings. Three shootings; one here, the other two where the cattle had been held and loaded into the trucks. The odds were that the last two shootings were connected with the rustling. Marty thought so, and Marty did not jump to untenable conclusions. What, then, if the shooting of Borden had followed the first rustling?

Borden might have been close to the scene. Perhaps even in his sleeping bag in his tent when the trucks rolled up and the cattle were loaded. Had he seen the man on horseback who had rounded up the cattle? Or, more to the point, had the man seen Borden? Was that why Borden was eliminated?

Tish had said that the first big snow had followed the first rustling. The dates should be checked to verify her memory. Then to talk with Marty Romero about the idea. Marty and Pepe Martinez could carry it from there.

After her last talk with Seth Porter, Tish had called. "Sam Waldo's bill is almost sure to pass," she had said. "And that leaves it up to the governor."

Unwelcome news, but no excuse for open lament. "How's your love affair going? Am I going to have to give a bride away?"

"I'm sticking my tongue out at you," Tish had said.

Now, riding slowly across the meadow, Tom wondered if he had made a mistake in sending Tish to Santa Fe. In many ways Tish was shy, even unworldly. But then there was an indomitable quality in her that emerged at unexpected times.

Tom remembered that colt Matt had bought her years ago. Tish had loved and tended it, and had allowed no one but herself to train it to bridle and saddle. Tom had appealed to Matt.

"Leave her alone, boy," Matt had said. "She'll be thrown, but that won't hurt half as bad as not being allowed to try."

"She's a girl."

"You've finally noticed? All right, so she's a girl. This is something she has to do. It's her own decision."

And so Tish climbed aboard the colt and was promptly bucked off. She picked herself up and climbed aboard again. This time she lasted a little longer, but the end result was the same.

When Tom helped Tish to her feet she shook his hand away. "Leave me alone!" There were tears in her eyes.

"You heard her, boy." Matt was leaning against the fence.

Tish walked slowly to the colt. She collected the reins, put her foot in the stirrup, and swung again into the saddle.

The colt promptly buckjumped sideways and kicked out with both hind legs. He jumped again, but Tish stayed on his back, and all at once he stopped and stood still, shivering.

Tish reached down and patted his neck. "It's all right," she said gently. She touched his barrel with her heels and clucked to him. He hesitated and then moved off at a walk.

Tom was smiling as he remembered. Yes, he thought, indomitable was the word. He reached the far edge of the meadow, crossed a small stream, and began a slanting climb up the mountain's flank. At the top of a small rise, movement caught his eye, a flash of light color, another. Pronghorn antelope were sailing off through the brush as if on springs. He reined in and, smiling, watched the beautiful little beasts.

He nudged the gelding into movement and almost simultaneously something buzzed behind him; the crack of a rifle followed. He bent low over the horse's neck and dug both heels into the animal's flanks. They took off at a run, down the far side of the rise, heading for a rocky outcrop, and there Tom grabbed the .30-30 and dismounted, diving into the shelter of the outcropping.

He studied the terrain. There was no one in sight. The shot could have come from below that small rise to his right. Or from above. Either way, high ground was the place for him. Bending low, the rifle in his right hand, he began moving up the slope.

From the outcropping ahead he would have a commanding view of the far side of the ridge. He covered the last little distance at a run, rifle now at the ready, hammer cocked, finger on the trigger.

He ducked behind the rocks, then moved forward to look down. He saw no man at first, and he made himself study the entire area slowly, clump of brush by clump. And then he saw the legs. The body had to be there, hidden by the chamiza bush, angled in the direction of the rise where Tom had sat and smiled at the antelope.

Kneeling, he took careful aim and squeezed off a shot. Dirt flew about a foot from where the man's head had to be. Automatically Tom levered another shell into the chamber as he shouted, "Drop your rifle and stand up slowly!"

The legs moved first, with infinite slowness. Then the man stood up and turned uncertainly, not knowing exactly where to look. It was Will, the rifle still in his hand.

"Drop it," Tom said. His voice was cold. He stood up from the rocks, the .30-30 at his shoulder aiming at Will's belly.

Will's hand opened. The rifle dropped to the dirt. "Look," he said. "It wasn't what you thought!"

Tom came down the slope without haste. "And just what did I think?" he said.

Will moistened his lips. "You seem to think I shot at you!"

"I don't think it. I know it." The words were slow, pitiless. "But you made a mistake. You missed."

"I was shooting at the antelope!"

"There are antelope," Tom said. "But you can't see them from here. They're on the other side of that rise." The anger was turning to contempt. "Among other things, you're a damn liar. But, then, you always were, and you always expected to get off scot-free. This time you're not going to."

"I tell you it was an accident!" Will took a deep breath. "And you can't prove it wasn't!"

Slowly Tom nodded. "You have a point there." He saw the sudden relief in Will's face. "So," he said, without change of expression, "we'll consider this an accident too." He slammed his fist into Will's face. Will dropped to his knees.

"In case you get the idea of trying again, you'd better not miss," Tom said, "because the first shot I fire then won't be a warning." He picked up Will's rifle and walked away.

MARTY was at the ranch house when Tom rode back. He followed Tom into the office and watched as he leaned the two rifles against the wall and then poured two drinks.

"Will tried to bushwhack me," Tom said finally. He drank half the shot glass of whiskey in one swallow. "And," he said, "I came close to killing him."

"Maybe you should have."

Tom studied what was left of his drink. "Maybe you're right. But I'm glad I didn't." He finished the drink.

The office door burst open and Sue rushed in. "What happened? Damn you, what happened?"

Tom's face was bleak. "Ask Will."

"I did. You smashed his face and he isn't making sense."

Tom pointed silently at the two rifles leaning against the wall, and Sue turned to look. "I see." Her voice was quiet. She looked at Marty and then again at Tom. "Are you going to—what is it you say?—press charges?"

"No. It's finished. But if you want him alive, keep him under control. That's a warning."

Sue's eyes narrowed. "You think I'm the one in charge?"

"Yes."

"How do you know it wasn't an accident?"

"I know. So does Will."

"I'm taking him to Santa Fe. His face has to be looked at. His nose is broken, I think."

"He can always say he walked into a door," Tom said.

Sue stamped her foot. "Doesn't anything—touch you?"

Nothing changed in Tom's face. "Attempted fratricide makes me unhappy. Will and I aren't all that close, but we are brothers, and that is supposed to mean something."

Sue was silent for a long time, her eyes steady and contemplative on Tom's face. "And you think I am responsible?"

"Partly, if not largely."

"I suppose you want us to leave?"

"No. It's as much Will's home as it is mine. But from now on the gun cupboard will stay locked, and I'll have the only key."

After Sue flounced out, Marty got out of his chair and closed the door. He remained standing. "It isn't finished, amigo. Because Will isn't the man we want. He is not the man who shot at you in the trees. Didn't you tell me he didn't leave the ranch that morning? He isn't the man who killed Kelly Garcia. And he wasn't even here last fall when Walter Borden was killed."

"All right," Tom said. "And you've eliminated Clyde, because his buckskin's tracks are not the horse tracks in the trees."

"And when Kelly Garcia was killed, Farley Wells was in Santa Fe, presence verified."

"Who's left?"

"I am going to reach far out on a hunch," Marty said. "What you thought you saw on the ground there in the trees. Describe it."

"I can't. I've told you. I had the idea that it was metallic and round and that's all."

"A coin?"

Tom shook his head. "I don't think so."

"What about a metal washer?"

Again the strained attempt to recall. Tom said at last, "I guess that could be. It's closer than a coin."

Marty said casually, "How about a spur rowel? Could that have been it?"

"It wasn't a spur. That I would have recognized."

"I said a rowel, a loose rowel, not the whole spur."

"It could be, I suppose. What about it?"

"Because," Marty said, "I saw a loose rowel recently and the spur it came from." He stood up. "As I said, a very far-out guess. But worth thinking about."

FARLEY Wells picked up the note at the hotel desk telling him to call a Houston number, and went to his room to return the call. "Farley here, J.R."

The quiet voice said, "There will not be much publicity, Farley, so I wanted you to have the word. Environmental guidelines are being relaxed in Washington because of the energy problem. That is now official. Stack emission standards have been lowered. I assume that you see what that means, Farley?"

"Yes, sir." It was obvious. "The high-sulfur-content coal comes into its own."

"Exactly. How is your project progressing, Farley?"

"Very well. The bill has already passed the House, and it looks very good for passage by the Senate."

"Can the governor be—persuaded, Farley? I told you that you had a free hand."

Which means free access to the purse, Farley thought before he answered, "I haven't seen him yet, sir, but when the bill comes out of the Senate, I will."

There was a pause. Then, "Very well, Farley. I leave it to you."

Farley said quickly, "One thing. Joe Harlow was up there last fall, calling on Tito Abeyta, the sheriff of Jicarilla County. Harlow said he was on a hunting trip." It was as close as he dared go to the actual question.

The quiet voice said merely, "Perhaps he was hunting, Farley." The telephone clicked dead.

Farley hung up slowly. He walked to the windows to stand staring again at the cathedral towers. Strength, he thought, power; they were what was important, weren't they? Then why this sudden feeling of distaste?

544

THE WEEK KELLY GARCIA was shot, the Las Grutas *Bugle* came out a day late. Consuelo brought Tom's copy to the office. On the front page a small box edged in black announced Kelly's death. Another small box announced the death of Carlita Vasquez, age eleven, after an illness of some duration.

Tom stared at the second item, thought about it, and then went out to the big hall. To Consuelo he said, "I'm going to Las Grutas." He walked out to one of the ranch jeeps.

He drove slowly on the winding road that climbed to the village. On his way he passed a small ornate cross set by the roadside, marking a *descanso*, a rest stop for pallbearers carrying a heavy coffin from church to grave.

Here in these mountains established customs died hard. But change was inevitable. Electricity had come, and the telephone, indoor plumbing and radio, bottled gas to cook by, even the miracle of television. These new things no longer met resistance, but the mystery of the atom was beyond comprehension.

Tom drove straight to the church. The priest met him in the doorway of his adobe house and ushered him inside. Piñon logs burned in the fireplace. "I hoped you would come," Father Enrique said. "You have heard, of course, of Carlita's death?"

"I am sorry about it, Padre. But the reactor had nothing to do with it. There has never been any radioactive material on the site. You must believe that."

"But there have been dead sheep and dead fish."

"From other causes."

"Who starts the bad rumors then?"

Remembering the thought Farley Wells had planted, Tom said, "What about the people of the commune in Jicarilla County?"

"Some of them are educated people," the priest said slowly. "Would they spread rumors deliberately?"

"Listen to me, Padre," Tom said. "There are people who truly believe that atomic reactors are too dangerous to be allowed. To them any means of stopping the building of a reactor is justified."

"Carlita will be buried tomorrow," the priest said. "I will say a mass for her soul. The village will mourn for her." He spread his hands. "If her illness was not caused by radiation, then the village must be told. I wonder if they will believe."

Tom parked the jeep off the road near the commune. Joe, two girls, and another man were working in the vegetable garden. Joe came to the gate of the garden fence.

"Hey, man. Slumming again?"

"This time," Tom said, "it's more than curiosity." He held out the paper and pointed to the notice of Carlita's death.

Joe read it quickly. "So? I didn't know the chick."

"The little girl with leukemia."

Nothing changed in Joe's face. "Too bad. But that's the chance you take when you play with fissionable material."

"You're talking about the atomic reactor in Long Valley?"

"What else, man?"

"There is no fissionable material there."

Joe's dark glasses were impenetrable. "Tell that to the girl's people."

"I'm telling you," Tom said.

"Okay, so you've told me. Why bother?" Joe gestured toward the vegetable garden. "Look, man, we grow our own food. Organic, you know? No fertilizers, no insecticides; we don't need them. And we don't need an atomic reactor lousing up the ecology either."

"And you've made your feelings known?"

"It's a free country, man. With free speech."

"Which doesn't include the right to shout 'Fire!' in a crowded theater, and that's what you've done with your rumors."

"Man, man." Joe was shaking his head slowly. "All we've said is the truth. The AEC says reactors are safe. They said those Central City mine tailings were safe too. And what about those dead sheep in Nevada? By-products of fission reaction are lethal!"

"And how do you feel about coal-fired generators?" Tom asked.

"They mess up the atmosphere, the air we have to breathe." Joe paused. "If you're going to ask what my solution is, it's this." His gesture took in the entire commune—buildings, garden, and open fields. "We have all we need, and all we want is to be left alone."

"If it's live and let live you want, then remember that it goes both ways. Stop scaring people who don't have your education and probably not your brains."

Joe hesitated. "Is that a warning, man?"

"You're a smart fellow," Tom said. "I shouldn't have to explain that when you scare people, you don't know what their reaction is going to be. The girl is dead. These people don't know what leukemia is. But they know what death is, and after they've buried her tomorrow some of them will start looking around to see who's responsible—for the rumors, for the lies."

TITO Abeyta leaned back in his chair, the telephone at his ear. For a long time he listened in silence. Then, "That's okay with me, Mr. Harlow," he said, "but not for a while yet. Things are a little tight around here." He listened again, and his good-natured expression changed. "You'll just have to take my word for it," he said. "Until things quiet down, I won't play."

Through the window he saw Marty Romero's pickup pull to the side of the road. "And I'll call you, Mr. Harlow," Tito said into the phone. "It's better if you don't call me."

When Marty walked through the doorway Tito was smiling again. "What's on your mind?"

"Kelly Garcia for one." Marty held up one hand, fingers spread. He touched the fingers as he talked. "This year's rustling for another. The dead man in the meadow for a third. And last year's rustling for a fourth." He was silent.

"You're going to put them all in one package?"

"I might. And I might throw in the shot somebody took at Tom Granger." Not Will's shot, he thought; we know about that.

Tito shrugged. "What's it got to do with me?"

"Have you ever had any trouble with the ranch?"

"No more than you'd expect. Drunks in town, that kind of thing." Tito's voice was concerned. "Why?"

"Just a thought."

"You thinking I might have some kind of grudge against the ranch, the Grangers?" Tito said. "Forget it."

Marty said, "Okay. For now. How about Kelly Garcia? Did he come to see you recently?"

"No, he didn't. Look—"

"I'm almost through," Marty said. "Do you remember the date of the first big snow last fall?"

Tito shook his head. "I don't know the date, but it was the day after the rustling. People weren't talking about anything else."

"And did you ever see that fellow Borden?"

Again the headshake. "Far as I know, never."

Marty stood ready to leave. "Thanks."

"For what?"

"For clearing away a little of the underbrush." Marty smiled, giving Tito the impression that a relentless and silent hunter had detected tracks; then he left.

Marty's face was thoughtful as he drove away from Tito's office. First a hunch out of nowhere, he thought; then a little sign here and a little sign there, and the hunch began to grow like an amanita, that deadly red and white toadstool.

He pulled suddenly over to the curb as he saw the parked state police car. He could see Benny Baca perched on a stool in the diner, and he went in to join him. Benny fitted into the community like a foot in an old boot. He would know many of its secrets.

"Have some coffee," Benny said. "At least, that's what they call it." The counterman drew a heavy white mug of steaming coffee and set it in front of Marty.

"When we leave here, let's ride around a little," Marty said.

They took the pickup. Marty drove. "Where does Tito Abeyta live?" he asked Benny.

"He's got a place out of town," Benny said.

"I want to see it," said Marty.

It was not much, an adobe house and an unpainted barn in a clearing in the trees. A barbed-wire fence marched off to a small meadow where three horses raised their heads and stared curiously. Near the house was a small corral. Marty headed straight for it, opened the gate, and walked inside. Benny started to follow.

"Just stay where you are," Marty said, and hunkered down to

study the dirt. Benny stared at the ground too and saw nothing but bare dirt and horse droppings.

"You want for me to bring in the horses?" Benny asked.

"No need." Marty stood up and had one last look around. "There are twelve different hoofprints in here. But only four of them are important. And I'm certain enough to be willing to bet they belong to that big sorrel with the blaze." He walked through the gate. "Let's have a look at the barn."

A horse trailer was backed inside. Against one wall were stacked bales of hay; their odor filled the air. Three bridles hung from nails, and a stock saddle rested on a wooden frame. "He lives alone?" Marty asked as he led the way outside.

"Always has."

They walked to the pickup. "What about friends? Girls?"

"He's the sheriff. He wouldn't mess around with any local chicks. What he does, he takes off for a few days maybe two, three times a year, usually up to Colorado."

Marty started up the truck. "Where does he go in Colorado? Denver?"

"I think Durango. It's closer." Benny hesitated. "I don't know what you're thinking, but—"

"Let's keep it that way," Marty said.

TOM sat waiting in the ranch station wagon outside the church, while inside the padre's voice rose and fell between chorused responses. Tom was not sure that he would be welcome at Carlita's graveside. But it was something that you did, as Matt had done before him, and certainly Tully too in his day. Loyalty up, loyalty down. That was a funny way to put it, and yet it was apt. He wished Tish were with him. She would understand.

The priest's voice was silent inside the church, and the sounds of foot-shuffling indicated that the service was over. Tom got out of the car as the small coffin appeared, carried by four men in worn, shiny dark suits. One by one they looked at Tom as they walked past toward the cemetery.

The graveside ceremony was loud with open mourning. When

the coffin had been lowered into the grave and the first shovelful of dirt thrown down, the mother, herself only in her twenties, had to be restrained from throwing herself into the grave. She was led away. By twos and threes the other mourners left the graveside. Tom, the priest, and an older woman remained. "This," the priest said, "is the grandmother."

The woman looked at Tom in silence. He spoke softly in Spanish. "I am sorry, *señora*. It is all there is to say."

The dark eyes searched Tom's face. Slowly the woman nodded. "Thank you, *patrón*."

Father Enrique walked with Tom back to the station wagon. "I have explained," the priest said, "that Carlita's death could not have been caused by radiation, that it was simply God's will that she should contract her rare disease. Whether my words will convince everyone, I do not know."

They had reached the car. "Not everyone, Padre. Look." The antenna was broken off. It lay across the hood.

The priest stared at it, and then looked up at Tom. "Who would do such a vicious thing?"

Tom picked up the antenna and tossed it into the car. "It is all right, Padre. Maybe it made somebody feel better."

9

WAYNE Carter waited for Tish in the lobby of La Fonda. He was here on impulse, although he was not usually an impulsive man, and he would have been hard pressed to explain why, except that it had something to do with Tom Granger.

At last Tish walked into the lobby. "I'm sorry I wasn't here." She hesitated. "Was there something—in particular?"

He smiled. "I just wanted to see you. It is as simple as that."

"I'm flattered." Jimmy Thomas, now this one—it had been a long time, if ever, since she had attracted this much male attention. And in just these few days her attitude had changed. Perhaps her new feeling of confidence was due to Tom, who had trusted her to be his eyes and ears and judgment in Santa Fe.

"I could buy you a drink," Wayne said, "or we could take a walk, or a drive. Whatever you'd like."

Tish was smiling. "I'd love a walk. Just give me time to change."

They parked in a picnic area and walked at a steady pace back into the mountains.

"I hear that the girl with leukemia died," Wayne said.

A red-tailed hawk effortlessly rode the updraft around the flank of the mountain. Tish watched it, envying its freedom. "The people in Las Grutas don't begin to understand what you are doing," she said. "They are afraid of you."

"Are you?" His voice was gentle.

"Not as a person," Tish said. "But people who know far more than I do say atomic reactors are not safe. Others who know just as much say they are. I don't know what to believe."

"Look," Wayne said, "what do I say? I don't have guilt feelings because I work in the same field that produced the Hiroshima bomb. My business is knowledge. How some may use what knowledge I produce is something else again. I hope it can be used beneficially, but if it isn't, I refuse the blame. Is that ignoble?"

"Please," Tish said. "I didn't mean to hurt you."

"Look." The words would not be stopped. "Are you in love with Tom Granger?"

Tish stopped walking. Wayne stopped too, and looked at her. The world was still.

"I don't think I am," Tish said slowly. "I—like him. Sometimes, that is. Sometimes I could—kick him."

"You do what he says."

"I earn my keep. I was raised as part of the family, but I have no claim on the ranch. It belongs to Tom and Will." Suddenly she smiled easily. "Let's go on."

It was an uphill walk to the last bend in the road. There, at something over eleven thousand feet, they could look out over mesaland and mountains rising clear against the limitless sky. A brownish haze marked the course of the Rio Grande. Wayne followed it with his finger. "That's the competition," he said. "Fossil-fuel generators. Here the pollution is only a minor annoyance. In cities it can be lethal. One day there may be a temperature inversion in Los Angeles that will turn their smog into a killer. In London a few years back smog killed about six thousand people. Los Angeles could be worse, much worse."

Tish had heard forecasts of catastrophe before. But now, as she looked at the brownish haze above the distant river, the concept of thousands of people choking to death was suddenly vivid and real. She turned and faced the evergreens and aspens standing cool and green. She caught Wayne's hand in hers. "Let's walk, and smell the trees, and look at birds. Look, there's another hawk."

WHEN they walked together into the lobby of La Fonda, Tom was at the desk. His face was grave. "We've been searching for you," he said to Wayne. "You've got trouble at the reactor. An explosion. One man dead. Quite a bit of damage."

Wayne said slowly, "You don't know how?"

Tom said, "Probably dynamite. You'd better go see for yourself."

Wayne hesitated, then nodded. "Sorry," he said to Tish.

Tish watched him go. "You didn't give him much warning." Her voice was quiet, but the accusation was plain.

"Explosions don't give much warning," Tom said. And then, "Is he the one you thought you were falling in love with?"

"No."

"Then who is it?"

Suddenly her lips were twitching with suppressed laughter. "What gives you the right to ask?"

Tom opened his mouth and closed it again carefully. Then, "Somebody has to keep an eye on you."

Tish was smiling openly now. "My love life is my own. Had you thought of that?" She turned and headed for the stairs.

TITO Abeyta said, "Two men were here?"

"*Sí.* One was the state policeman. The other I do not know. I had brought in wood for the fireplace. They did not see me. They were in the barn and—"

"Were they in the barn long?"

"No. They were longer in the corral. The man crouched. Like this." It was a fair imitation of Marty Romero studying the ground.

"Okay," Tito said. "Forget you saw them."

WILL's face was a mess. Both eyes were black and blue and swollen to slits when he reached the ranch.

"It was an accident, of course," Sue said. "You weren't really shooting at Tom, were you?"

"I've told you and told you." Will's voice was rising. "It was an accident."

"Lover," she said solemnly, "just between us, you swung and you missed. And there won't be another chance." There. It was out. She felt a sense of relief. "That Lieutenant Romero—"

"Lieutenant Romero," Will said, "would cut out your gizzard and not even blink. Or mine. Especially mine."

"Exactly. So I think we'd better leave. If anybody takes another shot at Tom, you'd better be far away."

The same idea had been in Will's mind. On the other hand . . . "Looking like this," he said, "go where?"

"You aren't very pretty, darling, but it won't last." She smiled suddenly. "Painful, but not fatal."

"It isn't funny."

"Now, don't be stuffy. If it had happened to somebody else, you'd break up. Particularly if it had happened to Tom."

"Things like this don't happen to Tom."

"Darling, you're trying to make me think I married the wrong brother. Every time you try to tear him down, you build him up."

Will said, "Okay, he's a regular John Wayne. But you talked me into trying to kill him—"

"And all you got was a broken nose and two black eyes." There was scorn in her voice now. "You aren't half the man he is, and you never were. In fact I'm not sure that you're any kind of man at all. Just a bundle of charm and a big smile."

"You never complained before."

"No, I didn't. As long as we stayed in our own world we got

along fine. But out here you begin thinking you're a he-man, and every day you just get smaller and smaller—"

"Damn it, shut up!"

Sue's expression changed. She said quietly, "All right, lover, I'll be quiet. I'll listen. What do you want to say?"

There was the trouble: he couldn't think of anything to say. Will heaved himself out of the chair and stalked out of the room, down the broad stairs, and out of the big house. A ranch station wagon was parked nearby. He got into it, started the engine with a roar, and sprayed gravel as he started off down the drive.

FROM the outside the reactor building looked untouched. But when Wayne Carter walked through the doorway he saw a great crater in dirt floor, twisted beams, shattered scaffolding, and blackened walls except in one area, where there was a curious stain. It took him some time to realize that the stain was blood.

Marty Romero walked over. "The dead man," he said, "is your guard, Pete Baca." He nodded toward the state policeman who stood staring at the stained wall. "That's his brother, Benny," he said. "Apparently work was finished for the day, and nobody else was here." He paused. "You had dynamite on the site?"

Wayne nodded. "There is solid rock here. We've had to blast."

Benny Baca walked over to Marty. "You want me anymore?"

"I'm afraid so," he said. Then to Wayne, "Let's go over to your office. We can talk there." He led the way to the trailer.

They sat on folding chairs. "A couple of possibilities," Marty said. "Pete Baca did it. Or he came to see what was going on and walked into it. If he did it, we want to know why. If he walked into it, we've got a murder investigation." Marty looked at Benny Baca. "He was your brother. What's your guess?"

Benny was sitting very straight. "What reason would Pete have to do it? He had a job. Jobs aren't that easy to find."

Marty looked at Wayne. "Will this set you back much?"

"I can't say," Wayne said. "We'll have to replace some of that damaged steel. We'll have to reschedule the work."

"But," Marty said, "the work won't stop? You'll still go on?" He answered his own question. "So if somebody was trying to stop you, that wasn't the way to do it?"

Wayne said, "Later on when the reactor is in place, an explosion like this would be terribly damaging. Now it is—"

"Just a nuisance?"

"You could say that. Only a madman would think of it."

Benny Baca sat staring, unseeing, at the far wall.

"Madman," Marty said, and nodded. He spoke to Benny. "What was Pete like? I didn't really know him."

Benny roused himself with effort. "Pete wasn't—loco. He was like me, like anybody. He helped his daughter, her husband, and their poor kid."

"He had other jobs before?"

"Sure. He drove truck. He pumped gas. He was in the army." Benny shrugged. "Same like everybody."

Marty said, "Had he ever handled explosives?"

"In the army. But—" Benny began.

Marty raised his hand for silence. "The padre told you that there was no radioactive material here on the site? That there had never been? Did you believe him?"

"If he say so, okay." Benny paused. "But what about the fish? The sheep? What about Carlita?"

Marty said quietly, "And Pete? What did he think? You said he helped his daughter, her husband, and their poor kid." He paused. "Was their poor kid Carlita?"

Benny frowned. "I forget you come in from outside. Pete was Carlita's *abuelo*—her grandfather. Me, I'm, how you say, great-uncle." He studied Marty's face. "You think that's what happened? Carlita dead, Pete he come up here and try to blow this place up? Maybe so other little kids won't get sick and die?"

Marty said gently, "What do you think, Benny?"

The trailer was still. Benny drew a deep breath, let it out slowly. He said at last, "Maybe. I don't know. Pete—" He shook his head.

"I don't think we need you anymore, Benny," Marty said. "Better go to your family." He watched Benny rise slowly from his chair. "Tell them," Marty said in a different, stronger voice, "that

555

what the padre says is so; there has never been any radioactive material here. Tell them that fish can be dynamited and sheep can be poisoned—"

Benny's head came up. "Who would do this?"

"Who starts rumors?"

Benny was thoughtful. He said at last, "Okay," and walked out.

Tom sat in Seth Porter's office. Jimmy Thomas was there too. "Jimmy," Seth said, "has been following Sam Waldo's bill pretty closely. And keeping Tish up-to-date."

Tom acknowledged Jimmy's efforts with a small nod. "Thanks," he said. And then, "Where do we stand?"

So this was Tom Granger, Jimmy thought, big as the side of a barn and so sure of himself that practically nothing could touch him. "Well, sir," Jimmy said, "it goes to a vote in the Senate today. It's close, but it ought to pass. Then it's up to the governor."

Tom said, "And what is our position if he signs it, Seth?"

Seth leaned back in his chair. "If you want to sell," he said, "you can. We can get a fair price." He paused. "Even after taxes, you and Will will be wealthy men by any standards."

"And if we don't want to sell?"

"There will be pressure," Seth said. "Not on you, but on the state to exercise its right of eminent domain, condemn the property, and buy it whether you want to sell or not."

Tom nodded slowly. "In that case we'll fight."

Seth took his time. "You've made up your mind? You're staying?"

"For a while." Automatic response. But, he told himself, it was no longer good enough. "Correction. I'm staying, period. Nobody, Will included, is going to run me off."

Seth's eyebrows rose in question. "Will? What's Will done?"

Tom hesitated. "He tried to kill me and make it look like a hunting accident." He told how it was. He added, "Just the two of us. No proof." He shrugged. "He won't try it again."

"Sure of that, son?"

The question was unanswerable.

WHEN MARTY ROMERO LEFT Long Valley he drove for a time on the Las Grutas road, then turned off on a dirt Forest Service road, and began a steep swinging climb around the shoulder of the mountain. Soon the ponderosa forest thinned out and the aspens disappeared. He came into the area of alpine tundra—patches of grass and hardy flowering plants clinging to what soil they could find. Still he climbed until he came at last to the abandoned lookout tower. There he stopped the truck and got out.

Looking down, he could see three roads winding among the brown foothills. And there was the crenellated ranch house. In the clear air Marty could see three of the Valdes kids romping by the gatehouse. He saw Will Granger come out of the main house, get into the station wagon, and drive off as if the devil himself were after him. Marty wondered idly where he was going.

He squatted on one heel, picked a blade of grass, and began to nibble on it while he brought his thoughts into focus.

The reactor explosion he thought he understood. He doubted if it could ever be proved that Pete Baca, in a paroxysm of grief and rage, had tried to destroy the building. But the implication was there, strong enough to satisfy most doubts.

But where lay the real blame? Not with an unbalanced Pete Baca, Marty thought, but with those who had spread the rumors and perhaps helped them along by poisoning a few sheep and maybe dynamiting fish in a stream. Enter the beautiful people of the commune? Quite probably, Marty said to himself, and tucked that conclusion away for further consideration.

And what about Señor Grande, Mister Big, Tito Abeyta. The horse tracks in the forest were those of the sorrel in Tito's pasture. So Tito had been there on his horse. No, it was pure guesswork that Tito was the rider. No guesswork at this stage. Slow down, Martín Romero.

What about the presence of a spur rowel, with the spur it had come from, on Tito's desk then? That rowel could have been what Tom saw at the scene of the shooting. *If* it was, then a very strong connection was indicated between the big man and the shot fired at Tom Granger the day after the rustling.

557

Was the rifle that had killed Walter Borden the same weapon that had killed Kelly Garcia? No possible way of knowing, since no bullet or cartridge case had ever been found. Borden had been shot from the trees, at two hundred yards or so, but Kelly Garcia had been shot from fifteen feet, and—wait a minute, wait a minute!

Since Borden had been shot from the trees, then rifle it was, beyond a doubt. And a rifle had turned up at the reactor site; but it was now in Pepe Martinez's hands and had been so at the time Kelly Garcia was killed. So that weapon could not have been used to kill Kelly Garcia.

Two rifles, then? Not necessarily. What about that .357 magnum Tito wears on his hip? It will shoot through a man just as well as any rifle, and is a more likely weapon to be carrying in daylight, when someone might happen to see, no? It fit. Marty felt a sense of triumph, quickly stifled.

Horse tracks. A loose spur rowel. A handgun capable of shooting through a man. Small signs *maybe* pointing in a single direction: toward Tito Abeyta.

Tito was sheriff of Jicarilla County, a big man among his people. Would he jeopardize that position for the rustling of a few head of cattle? Once again, slow down, Martín!

Was the rustling the real basis for two murders and one attempt? Take a long hard look at that premise.

Well, for one thing, the dates apparently were right; the first big snow of the fall came the day after the first rustling. Assume then, as Tom had guessed, that Borden had camped for the night near the forest area where the cattle had been gathered to be loaded into trucks after dark. Might he not have seen what went on? Or if he had not, might his mere presence when discovered have persuaded somebody that he had indeed been a witness?

In daylight, then, Borden, a potential if not a real danger, had been followed and gunned down in the meadow. And that day the snow came, covering Borden, tracks, and everything.

A rustling, followed quickly by a shooting. That was precisely what had happened again when Tom investigated the scene of the recent rustling. But this time the shot had missed.

The killer had not missed Walter Borden from two hundred yards. But from only seventy-five, with a target as large as Tom Granger, he had not drawn blood. Of course! The first time he was using a rifle. Suppose that the second time he had only his hand-gun? *Claro!* It was only in TV Westerns that shots fired from a handgun at over fifty yards went precisely where intended.

The pattern emerged: one rustling followed by a murder; a second rustling followed by an attempted murder. Then what about Kelly Garcia?

The answer remained the same. Garcia was a potential danger, as Borden and Tom Granger had been. He also had been nosing around, asking questions, maybe too many of the right questions. Then eliminate Kelly Garcia, this time from a distance of fifteen feet, where not even a handgun could very well miss.

So the rustlings were the probable root cause of Borden's and Kelly Garcia's deaths and Tom's near miss. All by the same hand? Likely, was it not? And only one man came to mind—Tito Abeyta.

What was it Benny Baca had said about Pete? That he had pumped gas, driven a truck, gone into the army—*like everybody else?* Like *almost* everybody else. But not at all like Tito Abeyta.

Tito had gone off to the cities of the football league, living in hotels and eating thick steaks and traveling by jet. There would have been girls, and wealthy men interested in meeting a big pro footballer. No gas pumping or truck driving for Tito Abeyta.

He had had six years of living it up; then the knee injury, the operation, and oblivion.

Marty rose and stretched himself. Idly he glanced down into the nearest valley and saw the dust plume that marked the station wagon Will Granger was still driving like a bat out of hell. So okay; he, Marty, was not a speed cop. He turned his thoughts back to Tito Abeyta, and, of course, to the ranch, because wherever you looked, it was there. El Rancho del Norte dominated villages like Dos Piedras and Las Grutas as thoroughly as those hilltop castles in the south of France had dominated their surrounding countrysides. To those who grew up in Dos Piedras and Las Grutas and stayed there, it was a normal and natural state of affairs.

Who grew up *and stayed there:* there was the operative phrase. Tito was the rare exception who had left, lived for a brief time in the Anglo world, and then come back. What would he feel?

Marty knew. The burning in your belly and the red rage in your mind. The futile attempts to cover yourself with your own culture, whatever that meant, after all those years of Anglo put-down.

Were these frustrations and hostilities enough to drive a man like Tito to lash out at that symbol, El Rancho del Norte, by organizing rustling strikes? All by himself? The rustlings had gone off like clockwork. That argued careful planning, and somehow Marty did not think that careful planning was Tito's style. He was more like a grizzly, inclined to charge his objective and overwhelm it.

So, who then? Or was it all tied together? Heckle the ranch by rustling? Threaten it with Sam Waldo's bill in Santa Fe? Spread rumors to discredit the reactor? Was it all one plan, with Tito merely a part of the plan? As Sam Waldo was? It all added up, did it not? So now what do we do about it?

We go back down like Moses from the mountaintop, Marty told himself, and we sit down with Tom Granger, because he is *el patrón* and these are his people, as they were Matt's before him.

THE station wagon Will drove was no sports car. But there was power under the hood and he used it savagely.

That damn Sue. Will had known that she could maneuver him, but as long as it wasn't obvious, his male pride had suffered little. Now Sue had allowed her scorn to show in that vicious comparison of himself with Tom.

A curve ahead. He stood on the brake, released it, and went into the turn accelerating. The rear wheels of the station wagon went into a swinging skid, scattering dirt and gravel into the canyon below. And then they were into the straight again, and Will could even smile faintly in minor triumph, before movement on the hillside caught his eye. He stared a moment in helpless fascination.

Three deer were coming down the slope in great bounds, heading for the stream. They saw the station wagon, and one stopped, but the other two came on. They reached the road, began to cross, and then hesitated, ears up, nostrils flared, as they faced the automobile that was hurtling toward them.

Will stood on the brake. The wagon swerved, straightened, and then, wheels locked, swerved again. There was no room for maneuver as Will fought the wheel, trying to come out of the skid.

The wagon struck the first deer broadside, and the force of the impact accentuated the skid. The wagon went over the side of the road and turned end over end as it dropped into the canyon. When it struck the rocks and burst into flames Will was already dead.

10

THE word of Will's death reached Tom in Santa Fe via a blue police cruiser. "All I know, sir," said the cop who had pulled Tom's car over to the curb, "is that your brother is dead. An auto accident. The state police alerted us."

Tom said an automatic, "Thank you." He started up the engine and pulled away from the curb. At a gas station he stopped to call Seth Porter. "The police tell me Will has been killed in an auto accident," he said. "I'm driving up."

"Do you want company?"

"No, thanks. Just see that Tish gets the word." He hung up and walked to the car.

Afterward he did not remember the drive to the ranch, only some of his thoughts. Will was dead, but where was grief? I didn't like him, but he was my brother. I wonder what might have been, if I had behaved differently toward him? There was no answer. Will was Will. The only power to change lay within himself.

Marty was waiting for him in the office. "I thought you'd like to know what happened, amigo." He had two shot glasses of bourbon poured. "I finally figured out how to get into that thing." He pointed at the tantalus.

"Thanks." Tom dropped into the desk chair and picked up the whiskey, but did not taste it. "Was anybody else hurt?"

"A deer had to be shot." Marty told of seeing the station wagon from the top of the mountain. "I didn't see him crash, but when I heard about it, I wasn't too surprised." He sipped his whiskey and waited.

"Does Sue know?"

Marty nodded. "This is a bad time, amigo, but there are things we have to talk about. Because if what I am thinking is right, you are still walking around with a gun pointed at your head. And that would leave no Grangers at all. This"—his gesture included the entire office, trophies, pictures, and memorabilia—"wasn't put together over all this time just to be thrown away."

In Seth's office Tom had made his decision to stay, but that decision was made in anger. This time it was something else. I belong here, he thought. Tully and Matt put the ranch together and passed it along to me. It is my responsibility, whether I like it or not. "Wait here," he said. "We'll talk after I've seen Sue."

He went up the broad stairs and down the hall to knock on the door of the suite Will and Sue had shared. Sue opened the door almost immediately. She was simply dressed in black pants and a creamy white blouse. They sat together on the small sofa. "I'm sorry," Tom said. "I don't know what else to say."

"I know." She was calm, composed. "We shouldn't have come here. I told him that. Will was—out of his league here. He was up against you, and there was no contest."

Tom got up and walked to the window. After a while he said, "That wasn't very kind."

"It doesn't matter. He's gone now. He tried to kill you. Now he's killed himself." She shook her head slowly. "We didn't work, because we had—all this." She drew a deep, unsteady breath. "But we didn't harm anybody until we came here!"

"Easy," Tom said. "Easy."

She smiled faintly. "Go away now, please. I may cry, and when I cry I'm a mess."

Tom walked down to the office. This time he tasted the whiskey. "All right," he said, "who's holding a loaded gun at my head?"

"Tito Abeyta."

Tom set down the whiskey glass. "You're putting me on."

"No." Marty's voice was grave. "Hear me out."

Will's death was for the moment forgotten. Tom concentrated on what Marty said. The pattern was right. Hoofprints, a spur rowel, and a .357 magnum, each a signpost pointing the way.

Tom's anger now was like nothing he had felt before. He had the eerie feeling that both Tully and Matt were watching to see how he would meet this challenge. What had been old Tully's response to the army colonel who had complained about his handling of some rustlers? "I held this ranch against Apaches. Do you think I'm going to take punishment from a flock of cattle thieves?"

"Tito," Tom said in a new, colder tone, "is your business. Mine is with the people behind him who had men shot and who spread fear. I want to settle with the ones who pull the strings."

Seth Porter called Tish at the hotel to tell her of Will's death. "I'm going back to the ranch," she said. "I don't know what good I can do, but I'll feel better just being there."

"I kind of thought you would, honey."

Tish hung up, and then she called Jimmy Thomas. "I'm sorry," she said, "but I have to go back to the ranch. Will Granger's been killed in an auto accident."

"I see." There was a pause. "I had big ideas for tonight. My roommates are clearing out for the evening."

"And you were planning to show me your etchings?"

"Something like that."

"Jimmy, I'm sorry."

There was a silence. Then, "I met your leader. Quite a fellow."

"Yes."

"Well," Jimmy said, "tonight probably wouldn't have worked anyway." He paused. "Would it?"

"I don't know, Jimmy, but I have to go now. I'm sorry." She hung up, and began to pack.

The scenery fled past. She saw it without looking, her eyes fixed on the road, from time to time checking the gauges. As somebody had taught her. Matt? No. It was Tom who had taught her some of the finer points of driving. And riding. And shooting. And walking

563

free in the meadows and forests and mountains of the ranch. They had once spent a night together miles from the ranch house, sitting against a low overhanging cliff, with a small fire warming them, watching the slow progress of the moon across the sky.

Old Matt had been furious. "Damn it, boy, you don't take a girl out and freeze her to death. You hear me?"

And Tom had said merely, "Yes, sir. My fault."

"It was mine," Tish had said. "I wanted to sit up all night and watch the moon."

"Your fault, boy," Matt said. "I agree with you. Females get ideas, but it's up to you to be responsible for them. Is that clear?"

"Yes, sir."

Responsible: there was the word. Some there were, like Tom, like Seth Porter, like Matt, who accepted the burden of command, and they were the ones you could lean on; they were the ones who could be trusted with power. Why had that word *power* come to mind? Was it because of Wayne Carter's trouble at the atomic power plant? Or because of Farley Wells and the power of money he wielded over Sam Waldo? Or the power of persuasion Seth Porter could exert on the governor of a state? Or was she thinking of the ranch and the power, both active and latent, within its enormous confines?

When Tish arrived at the ranch Joe Valdes held the gate for her with his dignified bow. At the house she put down her bag and knocked on the office door. There was no response, so she went in to find the room empty. Idly she wondered where Tom had gone. She closed the door and sat down at the desk to call Seth Porter in Santa Fe. When he answered she said, "Seth, Tom isn't here."

"No, honey. He's on his way down here." Seth paused. "I called him. Sam Waldo's bill passed the Senate an hour ago."

Tish closed her eyes. "What does that mean?" she said.

"It is possible," Seth said slowly, "that we are in for a fight."

"Have Tom call me, please," Tish said, and hung up.

How long she sat at the big desk, she never knew. She roused herself at a knock on the door. It was Sue, strangely quiet, almost subdued. "May I come in, please? I'm—afraid to be alone."

I don't like the woman, Tish thought, but I am sorry for her. "Of course," she said gently. "Tom has gone to Santa Fe." In the silence the phone rang. Tish picked it up as if it were a live thing.

"You wanted me to call." It was Tom.

He was angry, that was plain. "Seth told me about Will. I am sorry." She paused. "What about the arrangements?"

His voice was suddenly softer, easier. "Please take care of everything as you always do." There was even a hint of a smile in his voice now. "Do you remember Matt turning over that ring of keys to you in front of Will and me?"

"I remember." She was close to tears. "I'll look after things," she said. She hesitated. "And you look after yourself, do you hear?"

"I hear."

Tish hung up. Sue was watching her. "You've been in love with him for a long time, haven't you?" Sue said. There was a wistful quality in the words. "I don't blame you."

TURNING the other cheek was all very well as a Biblical injunction, Tom thought, but there was only one answer when you were attacked, and that was to fight. "I'll meet you at the governor's mansion," he told Seth Porter. "You set the time."

Seth punched a button on his desk and said to the switchboard girl, "I want to speak with the governor, honey." He hung up the phone and leaned back in his chair. "Tito Abeyta," he said. His voice was sad.

"Marty doesn't think he organized the rustling and neither do I," Tom said. "I don't see him pushing rumors about the reactor either. Just as Farley Wells is behind Sam Waldo, somebody is behind Tito, and he's the one we want."

Seth said mildly, "Do you know who's behind Farley Wells, son? Fellow named J. R. Benson. That mean anything to you?"

It did, of course, but nothing showed in Tom's face. "It just means that he's a bigger SOB than most. Because he has a few hundred million dollars, does that mean he can reach into a mountain valley and turn everybody's lives upside down? Does it mean he can buy a state legislature? Or run me off my own land?"

The phone rang and Seth picked it up, his eyes still on Tom's face. Into the phone he said, "Hello, Governor. I know you're a busy fellow, but this is a matter of some importance. Tom Granger and I would like to come see you this evening." He nodded then. "Six thirty. We'll be there." Seth hung up, and Tom walked out.

WHEN you hunted a grizzly bear, Marty thought, you came up-wind to him, and if possible on his blind side. Unfair, maybe, but also a tribute to the beast's strength, vitality, and cunning.

To Benny Baca, doing his job again, trying to bury his grief in familiar routine, Marty said, "Tell Tito Abeyta I want to see him at the Jicarilla DA's office, pronto."

Tito Abeyta, large and solid in his chair, scowled up at Benny Baca. "He wants me at the DA's office, why?"

"He didn't say. He just tell me to come tell you."

"I hear you were out at my place the other day," Tito said. "What did you want?"

Benny shrugged. "Marty, he just want to look around."

"And what did you find?"

"Just hoofprints. Marty say some of them belong to that big sorrel in the pasture." It still meant nothing to Benny.

Tito's voice altered almost to a growl. "I don't like people poking around without my permission." He pushed back his chair and stood up. "Okay," he said, easing his pistol holster into a comfortable position. "Go tell Romero I'm coming. Soon as I shut up here." He watched Benny drive off. "Damned if I'll meet him at the DA's office," Tito said softly. Then he walked out to his car.

Tito had no way of knowing how much Marty Romero knew or had figured out. But he had tied hoofprints to Tito's sorrel, and that was all Tito needed. It was time to collect a few clothes, pick up his stash of ready money, and get lost in Colorado.

Driving out of the village, Tito told himself that he had been a damn fool. No match at all for that smooth-talking Joe Harlow. Sure, Harlow had J. R. Benson behind him, and when you took on little chores for him, you tended to think you were walking around with a security blanket. But where was Harlow now?

He turned the car into the drive of his house, and got out. Marty was standing fifty yards away, his rifle at his shoulder. "I wouldn't try anything, Tito. Classic form of Western suicide, a handgun against a rifle. Just take it out slow and easy and drop it." He watched Tito drop the handgun; then he gestured with the rifle for the big man to step aside.

"Sneaky bastard, aren't you?" Tito said.

"I just put myself in your place. I was pretty sure you wouldn't want to see the DA and me together."

"WE'RE going to have a heart-to-heart talk," Tom told Sam Waldo, and watched the fat man's face lose some of its color. They were sitting in Sam's shabby hotel room.

"Your bill passed the Senate today," Tom said. "Now we're going to talk about it, who thought it up, who paid you to sponsor it and push it along—"

"Now you look here." Sam sat up straight. "You come in here and start throwing your weight around, and I'm not going to stand for it! I've got friends—"

"They aren't going to do you a bit of good, Sam." Tom's voice was quiet, even. "Pipsqueaks in Santa Fe have been trying to mess with Granger property for a hundred years. Do you know what happened to some of them?" He started to rise from his chair.

"Don't!" Sam's voice was a loud hoarse whisper. "Don't you lay a hand on me!" He was sweating.

Tom looked at his watch. "We have about an hour," he said. "I'm going to ask questions, and you're going to answer them. No witnesses, no tape recorder, just the two of us, Sam. Did you know my grandfather?"

Sam nodded violently.

"And his father?"

Sam swallowed hard. "I heard about him."

"They did what they had to do," Tom said. "And that was the way I was raised too. If you think I'm not prepared to do whatever I have to do to protect my property"—Tom paused for long emphasis—"then you'd better think again, Sam. Long and hard."

AT PRECISELY SIX THIRTY Seth Porter rang the bell at the white-columned governor's mansion, smiled at the maid, and followed her into the study. "Evening, Governor."

"Seth." The governor looked around. "Where's Granger?"

"He said he'd be here. I think he will."

They heard the doorbell ring again, and Tom's voice said, "My name is Granger. I believe I am expected." He came into the study, urging a reluctant Sam Waldo ahead of him. "I thought I would bring *this* along," he said. "Sit down, Sam. And listen."

The governor looked at Seth Porter. Seth said, "It's his play. I knew nothing about it."

So here it was, Tom thought, right up to him. "We Grangers are easy to get along with," he said. "Most times that is. I think that's been said before to somebody who sat in your chair, Governor."

The governor acknowledged the comment with a tight little smile. The story was well known.

"But," Tom said, "when they start coming at us from all sides, we tend to get a little riled. This is a tale, Governor, of fake rumors that have produced beatings, a senseless explosion, and a death at the reactor site; of organized cattle rustling which caused two murders and one attempted murder. And all of it to create support for the bill this little pipsqueak was hired to sponsor. And that bill has only one purpose: to stop the development of nuclear power in Long Valley so a selfish old man in Houston can sell his low-grade Four Corners coal. Does that sound incredible?"

Slowly the governor nodded. "In a word, yes."

Tom's face was cold. He looked at Sam Waldo. "You were paid to sponsor the bill, weren't you, Sam?"

"A campaign contribution. There's no law against that."

Tom nodded. "But you also spread some money around, didn't you, Sam? You see, when the lid blows off and your bill is tied to two murders and a few assorted felonies, I don't think a lot of your friends are going to know you any longer." The doorbell sounded a third time. "Here is one of them now." He looked at the governor. "I took the liberty of leaving a message for Farley Wells, saying you wanted to see him. He is Sam's—benefactor."

Farley Wells paused at the door to look around the room. "I don't believe I have had the pleasure, Governor. But I got your message and hurried right over."

"My message," Tom said. "Tito Abeyta is either already under arrest for rustling and murder, or he soon will be. You went to see him. Any connection?"

Surprise showed in Farley's face. "We talked of several things, but murder was not among them." Farley sat down. It was that damned fool, Joe Harlow, he thought. "I dislike being cross-examined," he added, "about matters I know nothing about."

"Then," Tom said, "let's take a matter you know a great deal about, Sam Waldo's bill." He paused. "As a matter of principle, Governor," he said, "I assume the state resents carpetbaggers coming in and pushing local people into sponsoring legislation?"

The governor nodded. "As a matter of principle, yes, we resent interference in our affairs."

Tom turned to Waldo. "Who thought up your bill, Sam?"

Sam squirmed. He looked at Farley. He looked at the governor. He looked at the floor. He found no comfort.

"Farley Wells will go back to Houston, Sam," Tom said. "You'll still be here. So will I."

Sam took a deep breath. He pointed to Farley. "He told me about the idea and it—sounded good to me. I mean, if the Grangers wanted to sell, all that land for people to fish and hunt in—"

The governor said, "We've heard the propaganda, Sam. Now let's hear about the—campaign contribution."

Sam swallowed hard. "Well," he said, "when a man goes to a lot of trouble and spends a lot of time—"

"And," Seth said, "maybe has to bribe a lot of people?"

Farley said, "If I were a defense attorney, Mr. Porter, I would object to your putting words in the witness's mouth."

Seth was smiling. "But this is not a court of law. It is an informal talk." He looked at Tom. "Go on, son."

Tom said, "I'm not a lawyer, but I doubt if there is anything actually illegal in what either Sam or Farley Wells did. I've heard of money changing hands in the legislature before."

"Then may I ask," Farley said, "what is the purpose of all this melodrama?" There was scorn in his voice.

Tom nodded. "You may. The purpose is to nail your hide to the barn door, and to do the same to the man whose interests you're serving, that SOB sitting in Houston."

Farley said, "You are quite free with your epithets."

"There'll be more," Tom said. "When I talk to him I'm going to tell him what I think of him." He saw the beginning of a smile on Farley's face. "Oh, yes," Tom said, "I will be able to talk to him. Because I got the number of the private line in Houston you called twice through La Fonda's switchboard." Then, addressing the governor, Tom said, "If I may use the phone?"

The governor hesitated and then nodded. Tom walked to the phone, picked it up, and began to dial. Seth watched Tom's face, which wore that Granger let's-step-right-up-and-see expression he had seen Matt wear so often. They were all alike, he thought. Oh, Will was a bad lemon, but from Tully to Matt to Tom the strain bred true, and he had a hunch that if Tom ever married and had kids, the line would continue.

Tom said into the phone, "J. R. Benson? My name is Granger, Tom Granger, and I'm standing here looking at one of your flunkies named Wells and the pipsqueak he hired in the legislature who goes by the name of Sam Waldo. Does that interest you?"

There was a pause. The quiet, uninflected voice said, "Go on, Mr. Granger."

"Your boys have blown it," Tom said. "All around. I've heard you don't like publicity. This time you're going to get it. You're going to be tied into two murders, a dynamiting death, cattle rustling, and a legislative bill that is against the public interest."

"I doubt it, Mr. Granger, I doubt it very much. There are libel laws, you know."

"I own a newspaper. It will print this story, and I will see that copies go across the country."

"Then I will sue, Mr. Granger."

"Will you? Because that is exactly what I want, everything out in the open, in a court of law where everybody can see how easy it is for a billionaire to turn an entire mountain village into a mad-house just by sending out orders that no atomic reactor is to get in the way of your low-grade coal. Sue, and be damned. We've held our land against Apaches. Do you think I'm going to roll over and play dead for you?"

Seth Porter was listening carefully, but his eyes were on Farley Wells. Farley was staring at Tom in actual fright.

The voice on the phone, still quiet, uninflected, said, "You are bluffing, of course."

Tom smiled. "Then call my bluff. Because the next edition of my paper will carry the entire story. The Las Grutas *Bugle* isn't a big paper, but it isn't a paper you can buy or intimidate."

There was a long pause. Then, "Let me speak to Farley Wells."

Tom held out the phone. Farley took it with a hand that was not quite steady. "Farley here, J.R." He listened. He glanced at Tom. "I'm afraid he means what he says, J.R.," he said. "That is the Granger reputation around here. I'm—sorry." He held out the phone to Tom, sat back, and closed his eyes.

Tom said, "Yes?"

"What is it you want from me, young man?"

"I want the name of a man, the man who ruined a perfectly decent sheriff, who created the rumors that drove mountain people out of their minds, and who was behind the cattle rustling on my ranch." Tom paused. "The name of your other flunky, the man you sent out here to do those things. That's the first thing I want."

"And the second?"

"Is for you to stay out of this part of the world. For good. Come in once again, and I'll spread the story across this whole country."

There was a long pause. Then slowly, reluctantly, "You have a deal, Mr. Granger. Farley will give you the name you want. Tell him I said to. And tell him to come back to Houston." The telephone went dead.

Tom hung up. He said to Farley, "You're to give me a name."

Farley opened his eyes and stood up. "The man's name is Joe Harlow. Tito knows him."

"And you're to go back to Houston."

Farley's smile was wan and weary. "Obviously." In silence he walked out of the room.

The governor said slowly, speaking to Tom, "I think your grandfather would approve." He paused. "I will veto the bill." He stood up. To Seth he said, "Thanks for an interesting evening."

THE road back to the ranch seemed longer than usual, but the moon was up, and Tom could see the great mountains. This was his country, he thought; he could never be content anywhere else. Content? That was the wrong word, because contentment implied satisfaction with things just as they were, static, unchanging. In his world, his life, there was always going to be change—new problems to face, decisions to make, struggles that could not be avoided—until at last they put him in a box and lowered him into the ground near old Matt.

He stopped the car and blinked the lights, and Joe Valdes came out of the small house to open the gate and hold it wide.

Tish and Sue were in the office, empty coffee cups at their sides. Tom sat down in the big desk chair and stretched out his legs.

"Two phone calls," Tish said. "Marty Romero called to say that the bear was in a cage."

I am sorry about Tito, Tom thought, but there was no other way.

"The other call," Tish said, "was Seth Porter. He told me what happened at the mansion." There was pride in her voice.

Tom shook his head. "No big thing," he said. "I just bullied an old man over the telephone." He looked at Sue. "What now for you?" His voice was gentle. "Do you want to stay here? It is your home for as long as you want it to be."

"It is not for me. As it was not for Will. But I thank you, anyway." She stood up from her chair. "You two belong here." She smiled at them both and walked out, closing the door behind her.

"She is right," Tish said. "You will carry on where Matt left off." She started to rise.

"Sit down," Tom said, and he waited until she was back in her chair. "I'll try," he said, "but I can't do it alone." It was clear to him now, at last, and he wondered that he had not seen it long before. "I need someone to hold my hand. Someone to help me up when I fall on my face. Somebody to listen to me and talk to me and tell me when I'm wrong." He smiled suddenly and spread his hands. "Somebody to share—everything."

Tish sat quiet, unbelieving.

"It has to be somebody I've come to know well," Tom said. "Somebody I can trust."

"What about love?" Her voice surprised her.

"That too." He shook his head. "No. That first of all." He paused. "I learn slowly." He paused again. "Would you be available for the—position?"

The room was still. Tish took her time. Then, "I will stay," she said. "I will help you."

THEY stood again in the family burial ground. Father Enrique, Seth Porter, Sue, Tish, Tom, and the ranch people, while the words were said and the coffin was lowered into the grave. Tom's eyes strayed around the fenced plot. There was Tully's tombstone and his wife's; there was Matt's and those of his two wives; there the stones of Tom's own parents. Will's would join them, and one day his own, and Tish's. Who would carry on then? A question yet to be answered, but the solution would come. He caught Tish's eye, smiled faintly, and watched her answering nod.

Sue by her own choice walked alone to the big house. Together Tish and Tom walked with Father Enrique to his pickup truck. "It is done," the priest said.

Tom shook his head. "Wrong, Padre." He looked around, at the grave site, at the mountains, at the limitless sky. Then he looked down at Tish. "It is just begun," Tom said.

"*Power* is fiction, of course," says Richard Martin Stern, "but it's drawn from actuality." Since 1965, Stern and his wife, Dorothy, have lived in Santa Fe, New Mexico. Thus he has seen firsthand the smoke that wafts down the Rio Grande from the mammoth coal-fired generators at Four Corners. Although Stern is not "a last-ditch conservationist," as he puts it, he has a deep regard for the environment.

Richard Martin Stern

In this, his seventeenth novel, he investigates an alternative to the pollution from fossil fuels: atomic power. During his research he talked with physicists at the Los Alamos Scientific Laboratory, where a breeder reactor is being developed. "Ultimately, we will turn to solar power. Until then," Stern warns, quoting one Los Alamos scientist, "we'll be living off principal—depleting the world's resources." Other themes in the book—the conflict between hippies and Chicanos, for example—reflect current concerns in New Mexico.

Before becoming a writer in 1945, Stern attended Harvard and worked as an advertising man, radio announcer, and manufacturing engineer. He has written more than a hundred short stories and serials for mass-circulation magazines. In 1959 he won an Edgar for his first mystery novel, and later served as president of the Mystery Writers Association of America. Currently Stern is working on a new novel, concerning a California banking family and a contested will.

ACKNOWLEDGMENTS

Page 3: *Mount Equinox, Winter,* an oil painting by Rockwell Kent, is used by courtesy of The Art Institute of Chicago.

Page 173, lines 12-13, 21, 28-32: Drake Activities Corp., Al Hoffman Songs, Inc., Hallmark Music Co., Inc., and Miller Music Co.: for eight lines of lyrics from "Mairzy Doats" by Milton Drake, Al Hoffman, and Jimmy Livingston. Copyright 1943 Miller Music Corp. Renewed 1971. All rights reserved. Used by permission.

Page 174, lines 7-9: from "Chattanooga Choo Choo" by Mack Gordon and Harry Warren. Copyright © 1941, renewed 1969 by Twentieth Century Music Corporation. All rights controlled by Leo Feist Inc. Used by permission.

Page 174, lines 25-28; page 286, lines 8-9: from "Don't Fence Me In" by Cole Porter. © 1944 Harms, Inc. Copyright renewed. All rights reserved. Used by permission of Warner Bros. Music.

Page 187, lines 27-29, 33-36: from "Beer Barrel Polka" ("Roll Out The Barrel," "Skoda Lasky") by Lew Brown, Wladimir A. Timm, Vasek Zeman, and Jaromir Vejvoda. "Skoda Lasky" copyright 1934 by Jana Hoffmanna, vva. Assigned to Shapiro, Bernstein & Co. Inc. Renewed. Copyright 1939 by Shapiro, Bernstein & Co. Inc. Renewed. International copyright secured. All rights reserved.

Page 189, lines 8-10: from "Saturday Night Is the Loneliest Night of the Week" by Sammy Cahn and Jule Styne. Used by permission of Jule Styne and Edward Traubner.